The Best of
# CATHERYNNE M. VALENTE

Volume One

# The Best of
# CATHERYNNE M.
# VALENTE

## Volume One

SUBTERRANEAN PRESS 2023

*The Best of Catherynne M. Valente, Volume One*
Copyright © 2023 by Catherynne M. Valente.
All rights reserved.

Dust jacket illustration
Copyright © 2023 by Alyssa Winans.
All rights reserved.

Interior design
Copyright © 2023 by Desert Isle Design, LLC.
All rights reserved.

See pages 797-800 for individual story copyrights.

**First Edition**

**Trade Hardcover Edition**
978-1-64524-077-8

**Signed, Limited Edition**
978-1-64524-149-2

Subterranean Press
PO Box 190106
Burton, MI 48519

**subterraneanpress.com**

Manufactured in the United States of America

# TABLE OF CONTENTS

## *Left Ventricle*

The Consultant................................................11
The Difference Between Love and Time......................17
A Buyer's Guide to Maps of Antarctica......................45
White Lines on a Green Field...............................57
The Wolves of Brooklyn.....................................79
Reading Borges in Buenos Aires.............................89
The Days of Flaming Motorcycles............................95
One Breath, One Stroke....................................107
Thirteen Ways of Looking at Space/Time....................119
Mouse Koan................................................135

## *Right Atrium*

The Melancholy of Mechagirl..............................149
The Future Is Blue.......................................155
The Sin-Eater............................................179
The Sun in Exile.........................................195
Color, Heat, and the Wreck of the Argo...................203
The Perfect Host.........................................231
How to Become a Mars Overlord............................237
Fade to White............................................247
Secretario...............................................279
Twenty-Five Facts About Santa Claus......................287
In the Future When All's Well............................297
Planet Lion..............................................315

## Left Atrium

A Great Clerk of Necromancy . . . . . . . . . . . . . . . . . . . . . . . . . . . . . 339
Urchins, While Swimming . . . . . . . . . . . . . . . . . . . . . . . . . . . . . . . . 347
L'Esprit de L'Escalier . . . . . . . . . . . . . . . . . . . . . . . . . . . . . . . . . . . . 359
The Lily and the Horn . . . . . . . . . . . . . . . . . . . . . . . . . . . . . . . . . . . 389
The Long Goodnight of Violet Wild . . . . . . . . . . . . . . . . . . . . . . . 403
Palimpsest . . . . . . . . . . . . . . . . . . . . . . . . . . . . . . . . . . . . . . . . . . . . . 447
The Red Girl . . . . . . . . . . . . . . . . . . . . . . . . . . . . . . . . . . . . . . . . . . . 459
The Flame After the Candle . . . . . . . . . . . . . . . . . . . . . . . . . . . . . 465
The Wedding . . . . . . . . . . . . . . . . . . . . . . . . . . . . . . . . . . . . . . . . . . 507
The Bread We Eat in Dreams . . . . . . . . . . . . . . . . . . . . . . . . . . . . 513
The Secret of Being a Cowboy . . . . . . . . . . . . . . . . . . . . . . . . . . . 533

## Right Ventricle

Aquaman and the Duality of Self/Other, America, 1985 . . . . . . . 541
A Fall Counts Anywhere . . . . . . . . . . . . . . . . . . . . . . . . . . . . . . . . 547
A Delicate Architecture . . . . . . . . . . . . . . . . . . . . . . . . . . . . . . . . . 567
Golubash, or Wine-Blood-War-Elegy . . . . . . . . . . . . . . . . . . . . . . 577
Badgirl, the Deadman, and the Wheel of Fortune . . . . . . . . . . . 593
Down and Out in R'lyeh . . . . . . . . . . . . . . . . . . . . . . . . . . . . . . . . 609
The Shoot-Out at Burnt Corn Ranch Over
the Bride of the World . . . . . . . . . . . . . . . . . . . . . . . . . . . . . . . . . . 633
No One Dies in Nowhere . . . . . . . . . . . . . . . . . . . . . . . . . . . . . . . 649
The Limitless Perspective of Master Peek, Or,
the Luminescence of Debauchery . . . . . . . . . . . . . . . . . . . . . . . . 683
Daisy Green Says I Love You . . . . . . . . . . . . . . . . . . . . . . . . . . . . 709
Silently and Very Fast . . . . . . . . . . . . . . . . . . . . . . . . . . . . . . . . . . 727
What the Dragon Said: A Love Story . . . . . . . . . . . . . . . . . . . . . . 791

# LEFT VENTRICLE

# The Consultant

SHE WALKS INTO MY LIFE legs first, a long drink of water in the desert of my thirties. Her shoes are red; her eyes are green. She's an Italian flag in occupied territory, and I fall for her like Paris. She mixes my metaphors like a martini and serves up my heart *tartare*. They all do. Every time. They have to. It's that kind of story.

The lady in question stands in the corner of my office, lighting the cigarette dictated by tradition with shaking hands.

"You gotta help me, mister," she says. I'm a miss, but that doesn't matter. In situations like this, you have to stick to the formula. She's the damsel in distress, I see that right away. I'm her knight in shining armor, even if that armor is a size eight slingback in Antique Pearl.

"Tell me all your troubles," I say, and pour her a whiskey, straight. She drinks it, leaves a frosty red lip-print on the glass.

And she takes a deep breath that makes her black dress shift just so. She tells me a man is after her because he wants her heart. He chases her through the dark, through the neon forest of rainy streets. Or she has this brother, see, with a withered arm he carries in a sling, crooked like a bird's wing. She was supposed to protect him from their father but she just wasn't strong enough. Or her stepmother can't stand the sight of her and beats her every night for a dozen sins. Or she's waited and waited for a child but nothing doing. Or she pricked her finger on a needle when she was sixteen and oh, the things she's done to keep on pricking. Or she woke up and all her savings accounts were gone, the money turned worthless overnight.

Maybe it's simple: the mirror said she wasn't pretty anymore. Maybe it's complicated, and she got in over her head, and now she has three nights to cough up a name or an ugly little man is going to take her son. I've heard them all. It's what I do. I'm not so much an investigator as what you might call a consultant. Step right up; show me your life. I'll show you the story you're in. Nothing more important in this world, kid. Figure that out and you're halfway out of the dark.

Call them fairy tales, if that makes you feel good. If you call them fairy tales, then you don't have to believe you're in one.

It's all about seeing the pattern—and the pattern is always there. It's a vicious circle: the story gets told because the pattern repeats, and the pattern repeats because the story gets told. A girl comes in with mascara running down her face and says that she slept with her professor because she thought he'd love her forever, she wanted to walk in his rarified world of books and gin parties and wickedly sardonic quips instead of treading water in her dreary home town. She tried to speak the way his friends did and dress the way he liked and write the way he did himself, and now he's gone and she's got this knife, see, but not a lot of courage. She's in so much pain. Every step is like walking on knives.

And I say: "Sweetheart, you gave up your voice for him. That was bound to go badly. Now, how do you want to proceed?"

Because there's a choice. There's always a choice. Who do you want to be? You can break this tale, once you've got a sightline on it. That's why they come to me. Because I can open up my files and tell them who they are. Because I've got a little Derringer in my desk with six bullets in it like pomegranate seeds. Because I have the hat, crooked at just the right angle, that says I can save them.

So who do you want to be? Sure, no great loss to be the ingenue, sacrificing yourself for your love. Put away that knife, fix your make-up, drop his class, watch him with his hand on the waist of some blonde thing at the faculty party—never forgetting that she's in a story too, and you can't tell which one by looking at her, and maybe she's the true bride and maybe she's bleeding in her six hundred dollar shoes to convince him she's the right girl—become like dancing foam on the waves of his society: glittering, beautiful, tragic. Maybe that'll buy you what you're looking for. But it's not the only solution. Sometimes it's better to choose the knife, cut his tenure, go back home, where you'll be exotic and urbane, for all your experience in that strange, foreign world.

I don't judge. I just give them options. And sometimes the best thing is to put on a black dress and become a wicked stepmother. There's power in that, if you're after power.

And then there's the back alley deals, the workarounds, the needles and the camels. You can turn around in the dark, with the man who wants your heart looming so big, so big over you, and you can give it to him, so bright and red and pure that it destroys him. Getting what you want has that effect, more often than you think. But it's a dangerous thing, the intimate exchange of hearts in the shadows, and sometimes the man in the dark walks off with everything anyway. You can burn every spinning wheel in the kingdom. You can cut your hair before he ever gets the chance to climb up. It is possible to decline the beanstalk. You can let the old witch dance at your wedding, the kind of forgiveness that would wake the dead and sleeping. You can just walk away, get on a horse, and go wake some other maiden from her narrative coffin, if you're brave, if you're strong. What do you want? Do you want to escape? Or were you looking for that candy house?

Sometimes they don't believe me. They can't see what I see. They can't even see how we play out a story right there in my office: her showing a little leg, me tipping my hat over my eyes, the dusty blinds, the broken sign beyond my window, blinking HOTEL into the inky night. It's a pretty broad schtick, but it helps make my point: nothing here but us archetypes, sweetheart. Still, when I tell them it was always fairy gold, all that money those sleek men in their silk suits said was so wisely invested, they get angry. They think I'm having a joke at their expense. But that's what fairy gold is: fake money, wisely invested. The morning was always going to come when you opened your 401k and it had all turned back to acorns and leaves. They throw water in my face or they beg me to hunt down the leprechaun that sold them that rotten house, and sure, I'll do that. Whatever you pay me for. You choose your role in this. I provide an honest service, and that's all. I don't try to sway them either way; it wouldn't be fair. After all, I can see their cards, but they can't see mine.

It's a lonely life. Me and my patterns and scotch and ice. The nature of the process is that they leave when it's over, exeunt, pursued by a bear. If they didn't go, I didn't do my job. You have to keep moving, stay ahead of the oncoming plot. Never stop to rest, not here, not in the woods.

And me? Well, it doesn't work that way. If you could narrate yourself I'd be out of a job. I need them to tell me who I am. If I'm a savior in their story, or a devil. If I'm a helpful guide, or temptation in a trenchcoat. No one's ever guessed my name. And that's the way I like it: clean, no mess, no mistakes. No attachments. Attachments beget stories, and I'm no protagonist. A bit player, a voice in the smoke. A Greek chorus, that's me. Or maybe a mirror on the wall. Point is, I don't work in the spotlight. I'm strictly in the wings. So they walk into my office—not always dames, sometimes a paladin in an ice-cream suit, and oh, if he doesn't have that girl with the hair down to god-knows-where he'll just die, or his wife is bored and unhappy and maybe she only ever liked him in the first place when he was a beast, or a wolf, or he's just lost, and he can hear something like a bull calling for him from the deeps, and I fall for them because that's the drill, but losing them is part of the denouement, and I know that better than anyone. It'll make you hard, this business. Hard as glass.

I tell them: don't depend on a woodsman in the third act. I tell them: look for sets of three, or seven. I tell them: there's always a way to survive. I tell them: you can't force fidelity. I tell them: don't make bargains that involve major surgery. I tell them: you don't have to lie still and wait for someone to tell you how to live. I tell them: it's all right to push her into the oven. She was going to hurt you. I tell them: she couldn't help it. She just loved her own children more. I tell them: everyone starts out young and brave. It's what you do with that that matters. I tell them: you can share that bear with your sister. I tell them: no one can stay silent forever. I tell them: it's not your fault. I tell them: mirrors lie. I tell them: you can wear those boots, if you want them. You can lift that sword. It was always your sword. I tell them: the apple has two sides. I tell them: just because he woke you up doesn't mean you owe him anything. I tell them: his name is Rumpelstiltskin.

And my cases end like all stories end: with a sunset, and a kiss, and redemption, and iron shoes, and a sear of light from the shadows, a gun-muzzle flash that illuminates everything as the rain just keeps coming down in the motley, several-colored light of the back end of the world.

So come in. Sit down. We'll have the air-conditioning working again in no time. Let me take your coat. Have a drink—it's cheap and sour but it does the job. Much like myself.

Now.

Tell me all your troubles.

# The Difference Between Love and Time

THE SPACE/TIME CONTINUUM IS THE sum total of all that ever was or will be or ever possibly could have been or might conceivably exist and/or occur, the constantly tangling braid of physical and theoretical reality, (steadily degrading) temporal processes, and the interactions between the aforementioned.

It is also left-handed.

It is, as you have probably always suspected, non-linear, non-anthropic, non-Euclidean, and wholly non-sensical.

In point of fact, it's a complete goddamned mess.

It has severe social anxiety.

And a weakness for leather jackets.

We first met when I was six. Our fathers arranged a playdate. The space/time continuum looked like a boy my own age, with thick glasses in plastic Army camouflage-printed frames, a cute little baby afro, and a faded T-shirt with the old mascot for the poison control hotline on it. Mr. Yuk, grimacing on the chest of time and space, sticking out his admonishing green Yuk-tongue. POISON HELP! 1-800-222-1222.

It smelled like lavender and bread baking in a stone oven.

I said I wanted to play Lego.

It looked helplessly at me with big brown eyes magnified into enormity by prescription lenses like hockey pucks.

It picked up a black block with an arch in it. Part of the drawbridge in my Medieval Castle Siege playset. The space/time continuum handed me the black arch and opened its mouth and the sound of a pulsar spinning, turning, thumping through silver-deafening radio static came out instead of "Where does this piece go?" or "It's nice to meet you" or "The idea of your shitty Lego drawbridge amusing me for even a nanosecond is hilarious on a geological scale."

The space/time continuum is a manifold topology whose coordinates can and frequently do map onto certain physical states, events, bodies. But that map looks like one of those old paper diner menus with a giant squiggle on it labeled *Enter Here* on one side and *You Win!* on the other.

And it changes all the time.

And you can't win.

And the crayon evaporates in your hand and rematerializes in your hospital bassinet under the *Welcome Baby!* card.

Or on the surface of the moon.

It doesn't care for television except for re-runs of *Law & Order*. It cannot get enough of predictability. It says every episode is a bizarre upside-down bubble universe in which justice exists and things make sense.

THE FIRST REAL actual word the space/time continuum ever said to me was: "Nothing."

The first words I said to it were: "You can't just go around saying 'nothing' to people, it's weird. Do you want my extra Capri Sun?"

The space/time continuum wrapped its skinny baby arms around me and whispered it again in my ear: "Nothing."

I didn't like being hugged then. I yelled for my mom. She didn't come for a long time.

## The Difference Between Love and Time

In high school, the space/time continuum looked like a scene kid with a million flannels and ironic shirts, a long black undercut, and a patch on his backpack from some band called Timeclaw. It got in a lot trouble for drawing or carving or scratching its initial in desks all over the place, this funky S that kinda also looks like a pointy figure 8. But not lying on its side like the infinity symbol. Infinity standing up.

I've seen them everywhere. Still do. The space/time continuum gets around.

You've probably seen it, too.

It failed all its classes but shop. It was always punctual at the circular saw. It never failed to make a perfect version of the assignment from oak, birch, ash, even plastic. Every day, it brought me the objects it had been compelled to make by Mr. Wooton. A model PT Cruiser. A wooden orchid. A puzzle shaped like an iguana. My favorite was this bare green circuit board with a little lightbulb on it that flared to life if you put your finger in the right place. It used you to complete the circuit.

The space/time continuum and I sat behind the bike racks for hours after school smoking weed and putting our fingers in the right place.

Ocean Shores, WA is not the space/time continuum, though it is, of necessity, an inescapable part of it. Ocean Shores, WA is a city that used to be a pretty big deal and is now not even a little deal.

See, back in the sixties, the state of Washington thought maybe it would legalize gambling because fuck it, why not, and people started buying up all the land and building nightclubs and hotels and golf courses and bungalows and boardwalks so that when the legislature hit the buzzer, the good times would be ready to roll. All kinds of movie stars and rich people's girlfriends and purveyors of semi-legal entertainment poured in from California. But then the state of Washington thought maybe it would not legalize gambling so now there's just a lot of cold sand dunes and closed attractions and motels with names like Tides Inn or Mermaid's Rest Motor Court and Weigh Station.

Ocean Shores is hollowed out like a gourd someone meant to make into a drum for a beautiful party. But they wandered off and maybe even forgot what drums are to begin with so now it's just an empty scraped-out dead vegetable lying on a cold beach nobody would ever hold a party on.

And then a seagull shits in it.

My mom and my dad and me used to always drive down for the last weekend of summer. Dad would always give me a riddle that I had to solve by the end of the trip. Like the one with the wolf and the chicken and the bag of grain or what has a ring but no finger? I'd play the twenty-year-old games on the last remaining boardwalk while my parents argued about what to do with me under the white noise of the waves.

Eventually Dad left and it was just me and Mom. We'd rent a bungalow that was once destined to be Jayne Mansfield's fuck grotto or whatever and sit in the moldy jacuzzi freezing our asses off, singing showtunes to the seals and shipping freighters out at sea.

The space/time continuum thinks Ocean Shores was at its best when only dinosaurs lived there.

I asked the space/time continuum who its mother was once. Did she have fluffy curly hair like mine, did she smell nice like mine, was her name Alice like mine, did she sniffle a lot like she was crying even though she usually wasn't like mine, did she always pack a fruit and a vegetable in his lunchbox (a Lisa Frank purple-blue cosmic orca one that I secretly coveted)?

The space/time continuum glanced nervously at the ashy green blackboard at the front of our classroom. This made me dislike the space/time continuum, as at the time many of the children liked to make fun of me for being dim-witted, even though I do all right. But it gave no other answer, and only a long time later did I consider that it was not looking at the blackboard at all, but the eraser.

When the space/time continuum stuck that black Lego arch over the scuffed blue moat pieces, it stopped being a Medieval

Castle Siege playset and started being a Cartoon Sparkle Rainbow Geoduck playset.

Our dads didn't notice. They just kept drinking beers, one after the other, lifting the red and white Rainier cans to their lips and setting them down automatically after each rhythmic sip like they were beer-drinking machines stuck in an infinite recursion function.

The space/time continuum in the Mr. Yuk shirt smiled at me shyly. It was giving me a gift. It wanted desperately to please me. I was not pleased. I liked my Medieval Castle Siege playset a lot. It came with four different colored horse minifigs. Geoducks are weird gross dumb giant clams that live in the mud for a thousand years and come with zero horse minifigs. Their shells aren't rainbow-striped and they don't have friendly eyes with big long eyelashes and smiling mouths and they definitely don't sparkle.

I didn't even think Lego made a Cartoon Sparkle Rainbow Geoduck playset.

But the space/time continuum's eyelashes were very long, too. So I said thank you.

It made the pulsar sound again.

You have to understand I was alone a lot of the time. It came and went as it pleased. But not because it was afraid to commit. The space/time continuum asked me to marry it when I was eight and we were pretending to fish with branches and string in the pond behind the primate research labs on the edge of town. I couldn't figure out why the fish weren't biting. I was going to bring my mom the biggest salmon you ever saw and she was gonna say how good I was and be so happy instead of staring at the dish soap for an hour while I watched the Muppets, but the stupid fish weren't on board with my plan.

That time, the space/time continuum looked like a girl my age with a red NO NUKES shirt on under her overalls. It said: *We didn't bring any bait. Or hooks. And there are no fish in this pond because it's not really a pond, it's a big puddle that dries up as soon as there's no rain for a week. Be my wife forever, limited puddle-being.*

I said: *Shut up, your face is a puddle.*

The space/time continuum laid its pigtailed head on my shoulder as the sunset sloshed liquid pink and gold and said: *We are a house and a hill.*

*OK, weirdo.*

But we were already holding hands so tight, without even noticing it.

So it's not about commitment.

The space/time continuum just has a hard time with confined spaces. Like the public education system. And calendars. And apartments.

And bodies.

Its favorite album is the iconic 1979 *Breakfast in America* by often underrated British prog-pop group Supertramp. But its favorite song is *Time After Time* by Cyndi Lauper.

I don't really have anything to say in defense of its weakness for easy listening.

I guess it just wants something to be easy.

The space/time continuum is holistically without gender.

Its pronouns are it/everything.

Or, to put it another way, it is a quivering, boiling mass of all physio-psychological states that will/are likely to/have develop/ed across every extinct/extant/unborn species, making the whole issue pointless, irrelevant, and none of my business. The seventy-fourth time we met it looked like a Estonian woman who had just graduated from the Rhode Island School of Design, so you can see what I mean.

Butch on the streets, churning maelstrom of intersecting time and matter in the sheets.

Later, the space/time continuum told me that was only the second time we'd met in objectively-perceived time. Which always meant its perception, never mine. It was freshly in love. I was forty and tired. It was July. Rain beat the streets down till they gave up. The puddle talk happened yesterday. Its hair was so long and fine I felt certain that if I touched it, it would all dissipate like smoke. But I really, really wanted to touch it anyway. It wore a pale blue leather jacket over a white T-shirt with a Frank Lloyd Wright quote on it in thin grey Arial letters. It looked so fucking cool. It was always so much cooler than me.

I took the continuum to that little Eritrean restaurant down on Oak. It ordered *tsebhi derho* with extra injera and ate like food had only just been invented, which, given the nature of this story, I feel I should stress it had not. I just had the yellow lentil soup. The space/time continuum cried in my arms. It thought it had lost track of me. I didn't answer its text messages.

If it was a commercial cereal brand it would be Cap'n Crunch Oops All Genders.

I would be Cinnamon Toast Chump.

Whatever it looks like, it always wears glasses. Safer that way. For all of us.

The Frank Lloyd Wright quote was: *No house should ever be on a hill or anything. It should be of the hill. Belonging to it. Hill and house should live together, each the happier for the other.*

We had our first kiss in middle school.

The space/time continuum took me to the winter dance. It wore white. I wore black. We looked like winter, the wide deep snow and a bare tree. It picked me up at 6:45 and tied a corsage around my wrist. It said the flower was an odontoglossum orchid. Native to Argentina. Only grows in cold climates. Like me.

When the space/time continuum put its hands on my waist, lock-elbowed, stiff, uncertain, I smelled a lonely ultraviolet sea churning on a small world in the constellation of Taurus. It wasn't winter in the constellation of Taurus. It was spring, and the sea on that planet was in love with a particular whale-plant living inside it, and I understood a lot of things just then. When Bryan Adams hit his guitar solo, the space/time continuum kissed me, and I knew why he'd been wearing that poison control shirt when we first met, and also what it felt like to be a whale who is also a flower, floating inside a desperate sea.

The ninety-fourth time we met, the space/time continuum was on Tinder. It had a dog in its profile pic, even though it doesn't have a dog in real life. Its other pics showed it fishing, hiking, doing a color run.

This was its profile:

S, Young at Heart

>0.1 miles away

Hi, baby.

*I'm sorry. I was wrong. I'm an idiot. I love you. I'll do better this time. I can be better. Come home.*

But then I think it got nervous and confused because below that it said:

*If you can't handle me at the peak of my recursive timeline algorithm, you don't deserve me when I'm an iguana.*

The dog was a corgi. But not the orange kind, the black and white kind. Its name tag said *Snack McCoy.*

That's a pretty solid *Law & Order* joke. So it probably was the space/time continuum's dog. Somewhen. Elsewise.

I wonder if there was a version of me in the Snack McCoy universe. I wonder if there was a version of you.

I wonder if everything there was made out of crunchy biscuit treats.

I don't know why the space/time continuum stopped loving me. Maybe I worked too much, too hard, too late. Maybe it wanted more than cozy taco nights in a rooftop apartment above, in descending order, a comedy club, a Planned Parenthood, and a laundromat. Maybe it wanted less. Was I overly critical? (*Why the fuck do people just STOP at completely unpredictable points, what's wrong with you, why would you set it up that way? Sleep on the goddamned couch, you narcissist.*) Did I just *consistently* fail to put my dishes in the dishwasher right away? I could've done it any time I wanted.

Cups go in rack not on counter. Easy. And yet. Did I not support its interests? Maybe I didn't understand its love language. Or how to set up a retirement account. Maybe I took too long to lose the baby weight. Maybe I didn't let it have enough me-time.

Maybe I stopped really listening. Maybe the nexus of spatial and temporal possibilities was just sick of my shit.

Maybe I don't deserve to be loved.

That's probably it.

One time it showed our first grade teacher, Mrs. Aldritch, the drawing it made during quiet period and she cried spinal fluid out of her eyes so that was pretty intense.

It refused to show me. Even though it borrowed my black crayon to color with in the first place.

The space/time continuum's father looked very much like Mr. Clark, who used to run Dazzle Dan's Vintage Diner by the train tracks. Mr. Clark's name was not Dan. It was Clarence Peter Clark. But the previous owner wasn't named Dan either. He was named Roderigo R. Rodriguez, which I am not making up. But it was pretty hard to be Mexican around here back then, especially if you wanted to sell all-American nostalgia burgers with lettuce, tomato, onion, and mayo, so he just went by Roddy.

Roddy was from Guadalajara. There's a cathedral there called the Catedral de la Asuncion de Maria Santisima with two golden spires standing up into the sky and the birds together, completely identical. Clarence Peter Clark was from Yakima. There's nothing much in Yakima.

Nobody knows where Dazzle Dan came from.

By the time I was thirteen I was pretty sure the space/time continuum didn't actually have a father, just a thing in its house like one of those old drinky bird toys that sat on the lip of a glass and rocked back and forth more or less forever, once you set it going. It needed a father to make sure no one suspected it wasn't actually a boy with glasses or a girl with pigtails or an Estonian exchange student. But it didn't need a *person*. Just a bobbing blob of weighted plastic wearing Mr. Clark's face, lifting can after red and white can of Rainier beer to its mouth in the background until the death of all matter in a fiery entropic abyss.

On our second playdate we tried to play Cowboys and Indians. I heard the other kids doing it. Cowboys had horses, and I loved horses more than candy, so I was pretty excited.

But I never ever got to be the cowboy. The space/time continuum said *cowboy is just another word for the generational trauma inflicted by the colonizer's whole-ass inability to access empathy for anyone but himself and the debt to entropy incurred by his solipsistic commitment to almost unimaginable violence as an expression of personal potency.*

Then it poured the living memory of the surrender of the Nez Perce in the Bear Paw Mountains like molten platinum into my brain and blood shot out of my nose and my eyes at the same time and my pinky toe turned into a suciasaurus rex tooth. The space/time continuum panicked, whispering *oh shit, oh shit, I'm sorry, I'll fix it*, whereupon it flooded my grey matter with golden retrievers and the smell of chocolate cookies baking and the exact emotional sensations experienced in the moment of era-defining scientific discoveries and a few old Bob Ross episodes just in case.

My appendix ruptured and I didn't speak again for ten months.

My parents sent me to specialists.

A lot of them.

The space/time continuum is a total slob and a nightmare roommate. It leaves its wadded-up porto-stars all over the floor. It won't do the dishes even when I cook, since it only pretends to eat. It washes clothes we haven't bought yet, then forgets to put them away for weeks. It has taken a moral stance against both mowing the lawn and dusting. It says doing so would only appropriate the culture of sequential cause and effect, which it has no right to wear like a costume.

It leaves a ring of quantum foam around the bathtub to just get crustier and crustier until I give in and scrub it off myself. Stare for fifteen minutes while my knees get sore on the badly-grouted tile thinking about equal division of labor and if maybe we should get a chore chart, if that would even help, or if it just thinks this is my work because I'm the one who's going to die someday so it bothers me more. Finally run the water and watch it all swirl down the silver drain into the waste infrastructure dimension.

"An alarm clock," I whisper to the slowly rotating water. "An alarm clock has a ring but no finger."

Every Valentine's Day, the space/time continuum wraps my gift in pink and red paper with hearts or baby angels or birds or radio signals all over it and practically climbs the walls with excitement waiting for me to open it.

Those are some of the best times I remember. The moments before I rip the baby angel bird hearts open.

There's never anything inside the box. It's just that after I open the box, I know a story about love I didn't know before I opened the box. And I mean I know it like it happened to me. Like it's my own story.

One year it was this: the Loch Ness monster was absolutely real. She lived to be about 500 years old like that one ugly Greenland shark they found before a Swiss tourist hit her in the head with a boat propeller in 1951. There used to be two of them, even. A mating pair. Nessie had a single baby around the time of the Great London Fire and I felt her love that baby monster fishosaur down in the dark and the cold that wasn't dark or cold to her at all. I felt the absolute safety and security of thousands of pounds of water pressure like one of those weighted vests for anxious dogs. I felt Nessie love her baby so much the temperature of the whole lake rose by one degree.

My gifts aren't as good. My gifts do not come from the time-pit out of which springs the Pleiades and ring-tailed lemurs and the Battle of Tours and Loch Ness, they come from my checking account.

Last year I gave it cufflinks. I don't fucking know, you try buying for a space/time continuum who definitionally has everything.

Here is an abridged list of things the space/time continuum and I fought about:

What movie to watch.

Whether or not I had a hostile tone this morning.

The exact dictionary definition of *narcissist*.

If it's technically gaslighting to make a fight never have happened.

Where it goes when we're not together.

Why it won't let anything last.

The whole thing about it allowing death to exist.

If it ever thought for one minute about consent before fucking about with my Lego and/or timestream.

Whether it has to pay rent.

Why it didn't tell me to go to the hospital that night because we both know it had to have known.

Why it is the way it is.

Why it refuses to change.

Why it decided capitalism had to be a thing.

Why everything sucks so much all the time.

Why I don't think a baby is a good idea.

This is what it looks like when the space/time continuum is mad at you: you wake up in the morning already late because your alarm clock now reads 1-800-222-1222. The auto-set coffee machine isn't left on for you and the taco leftovers from last night are all gone and its car isn't in the overnight guest spot and you can't find your phone and there's no dishes in the cupboards and there's no cute little post-it note on the fridge telling you to have a nice day (PS we're out of milk) but there definitely *is* lipstick scrawled on the bathroom mirror. The expensive stuff, MAC Saint Germain, big swooping letters that read [*the speed of light in a vacuum is the same for all observers regardless of the directionality of the light source.*] Asshole.

You'll have to wait a few weeks for the space/time continuum to cool off and get a little cheeky over a couple of bottles of bodega rosé to find out that it 100% ate all the leftovers just to spite you. But then it got sick and spewed total paralyzing awareness of causality all over the 98 bus and, like, *everyone* on that route is now loaded up with heavy sedation or Fields Medals but *ANYWAY* it's just *maybe* possible your phone is embedded in an extremely put-out pachycephlosaurus's eye socket.

But either way, you have to stop freaking out about the car.

The continuum doesn't have a car. It's never had a car. It doesn't drive. It doesn't even have a license so much as it *contains* everyone else's licenses. It's just that sometimes a pocket universe containing a reality in which Monet was never born looks *a lot* like a 2005 Inca Gold Pearlcoat PT Cruiser with a faded COEXIST bumper sticker half-peeled off the back and a leather frog keychain swinging from the rear-view.

Then the space/time continuum starts acting way too nice. It lets you pick the movie and what kind of takeout to order and gives you a foot-rub before admitting that your patterned cups and soup bowls and novelty pink octopus mug are currently making a long lonely pilgrimage around the frigid ring system of Saturn. Yes, it knows they were your mother's, and it's very sorry, it doesn't know what gets into it sometimes. It just loves you so much and, well, you know how you can be. So immature. So self-centered. So finite. You don't appreciate the emotional labor the space/time continuum puts into this relationship.

But that octopus mug is gonna make *big* news in about a hundred years, so let's focus on the positive, also don't be mad but your coffee ended up in the butt of Malmsey that drowned George Plantagenet. Because fuck you that's why. It was upset. You shouldn't have said that thing about the invention of death. There are just some things you do not say to someone you love.

But you make up. Always. Until you don't. And when your duck pad see ew with extra broccoli arrives in its pure white styrofoam container, twenty minutes before you put the order in, there's a pastel violet post-it note inside that says: *please don't leave me.*

The space/time continuum enjoys baking, but you can't eat the pale green *prinsesstårta* it has worked so hard to perfect after seeing it on that reality cake show. You can only have eaten it. Or be going to eat it. Or sometimes one day will have been never eating it. That's pretty much how it goes for all its hobbies. It swears it knit me a gorgeous mauve cabled cardigan for my fifteenth birthday because I'm always cold.

I wouldn't know. I've never seen it.

Coming up on my sixtieth.

Still cold.

Dick.

The space/time continuum is not a dick.

Mostly.

My mom—you remember Alice, with the curly hair and the fruits and vegetables in every lunch? Well, Alice died a little while after the whole David and Susan thing. Paranasal tumors. I didn't even know you could get nose cancer. By the time they found it, Alice hadn't been able to smell or taste anything in years.

*That's the worst part*, she told me after the diagnosis, home, in bed with a couple of bottles of Ignoring Our Problems juice. *I can't smell anything. Not even you. I used to smell your head when you were a baby and it was the most amazing smell, better than Chanel No 5, I swear. Like lavender and bread baking in a stone oven. And sometimes, just once in a while, when you got older, you would be running out the door for a date with that kid in the flannel or putting groceries away or watching TV and I'd get a whiff of it again, like you were still so tiny and all mine and nothing bad could ever happen to us. And it's gone. I'll never smell you again ever.*

She hated hospitals so by the time I managed to convince her to get her butt in a paper gown it was just all through her. It couldn't wait. Had somewhere important to be, I guess.

But she was wrong. The worst part was that I wasn't there. I wanted to be. But I had to work. I missed it. The last words my mother ever said to me were days and days before.

"Those things are rigged, honey."

But by then she was mostly morphine by volume, so.

One time the space/time continuum and me went to Mr. Clark's diner for burgers and floats. I was eleven. It looked eleven enough. I felt so grown up in that red vinyl booth all to ourselves, with my own money in my own wallet like some kind of real adult human who mattered. My dad had taken his curtain call three years before. But Mom and I were fine. Really. We carried the Christmas tree inside and set it up just the two of us. No men required.

I ordered a peppermint milkshake from Mr. Clark and there was a chocolate ribbon time loop inside it. I didn't find my way out until the school year was mostly over. I've been hard of hearing ever since.

I guess a lot of us spend middle school stuck in a time loop. I'm not special.

Never have been.

The thirty-ninth time I met the space/time continuum it was a three and a half foot long rhinoceros iguana named Waffles. Waffles was lounging on fresh shredded newspapers in the display window of *Jungle Friends Exotic Pet Store and Bubble Tea Cafe*. Waffles was marked down 70% for Presidents' Day weekend.

I ordered a black milk bubble tea from the counter wedged into the large parrots section.

The scarlet macaw said: *the problem with Einstein-Rosen wormholes is that the 'hallway' they create between two singularities is too small and open too briefly to ever permit transit by a living person.*

The African grey said: *You be good I love you see you tomorrow.*

The blue hyacinth said: *Fuckshit, Susan.*

Then it sang a few bars of *The Entertainer* and cracked up laughing.

Not everything means something.

Waffles watched the parrots. Waffles slurped up a strand of wilted collard greens. Waffles licked his eyeball.

The owner-operator of *Jungle Friends Exotic Pet Store and Bubble Tea Cafe* brought me my drink and swapped the *70% Off!* sign for an *80% Off!* one. So I took Waffles home. I put him in a plastic sun-faded Rainbow Brite kiddie pool with the contents of a Sensible Plan brand EZ Ceezar Salad bag and some flat rocks from the last trip I took with my mother to the Ocean Shores boardwalk, when I won every prize in the shitty Happy Claw prize machine one after the other. I warmed the rocks up in the microwave so Waffles could rest his belly on them. Then I sat back on my couch and drank the better part of a bottle of Bombay Sapphire because fuck George Plantagenet that's why.

That hadn't happened yet. But if you spend long enough around the space/time continuum you get this thing where your head turns into a Tetris game and all the falling pieces are memories spinning around, upside down, out of order, mostly missing the sweet spot so they can just pile up uselessly while the music goes faster and faster the closer you get to this person you love so much who is no less your life partner for being an iguana right now.

Also cancer.

Waffles stared at me for a long time. Then the space/time continuum chomped down on a ranch-seasoning crouton and said: *The traveler and their vessel would have to be smaller than an atom, far faster than light.*

*P.S. We're out of milk.*

That was probably our best date.

I married someone else. For a while. Right after college. Trying to get away, I suppose. Find out who I even was apart from the space/time continuum. High school relationships never last anyway, right? He was just a guy. Let's say his name was David. It doesn't matter.

The space/time continuum told me not to. It said we were not compatible because my cells were contaminated by long-term non-consecutive exposure to excited superliminal mass fields and

David's cells were contaminated by long-term exposure to being a douchebag.

By that time the space/time continuum wasn't an iguana anymore. It was a mid-market talk radio host of one of those raunchy advice for the unemployed and lovelorn shows they used to pump out like Xerox copies of Xerox copies. Tune in to KHRT 101.5 to hear the velvet voice of my ex, the unstably-enfleshed and endlessly repeating moment of creation and destruction, give you hot tips for better oral sex. The trick is know to your core that nothing means anything and all life and feeling will end.

The space/time continuum was working through some stuff.

The seventh time we met, the space/time continuum was this gangly ginger kid who got hit bad with the freckle-gun and a broken arm. The cast had everyone's messy kid-handwriting all over it.

*You should see the other guy.*

*You're cute!*

*That events do indeed occur sequentially is perhaps the greatest lie of all.*

*See you this summer.*

"You wanna see something?" the space/time continuum asked me just as the lunch bell rang. Seventh grade. We were gonna be discussing *The Westing Game* next period and I was so excited I could barely breathe. But I said okay anyway because it was wearing a shirt that said DON'T PANIC, so I figured the space/time continuum was on the up-and-up.

It took me to the teachers' lounge. It had a special key on a leather frog keychain. I didn't know what to think. The teachers' lounge was forbidden territory. As thrilling and terrifying as peeking in a cross-hatched window at the surface of Mars.

"It's okay," the space/time continuum said. "I'm allowed."

Inside the teachers' lounge it wasn't the teachers' lounge. It was 1958 and we were outside and it was so hot. A man and a little boy were walking across a huge courtyard toward Catedral de la

Asuncion de Maria Santisima. Birds exploded into the air before them. The little boy was the most beautiful child I've ever seen, with the curliest hair and the biggest eyes. He practically glowed.

His father knelt down next to his baby and kissed his tiny cheek. He pointed toward the two golden spires.

"Look, Daniel!" Roderigo R. Roderick said. "Two of them! Just like you and me, mijo, forever and ever."

"It's Dazzle Dan," I whispered.

"Happy birthday," the space/time continuum answered. I said it wasn't my birthday. It shrugged. "It's always your birthday."

And then it wasn't 1958 anymore and it wasn't Guadalajara, it was the teachers' lounge and it smelled like old pencils.

But the space/time continuum didn't do that kind of thing very often because it made my teeth bleed.

Anyway, David cheated on me eight or nine weeks after the wedding. Let's say her name was Susan. It doesn't matter. Let's say she looked just like me but younger and prettier and less contaminated by excited mass fields.

Fuckshit, Susan.

As far as I can tell, the space/time continuum owns every self-help book ever published. *The 7 Habits of Highly Effective People. The Power of Now. The 4-Hour Work Week. Hypatia's Commentary on Diophantus's Arithmatica. How to Win Friends and Influence People. Summa Theologicae. Truth in Comedy: The Manual of Improvisation. Awaken the Giant Within. Opticks, or, A Treatise on the Reflections, Refractions, Inflections, and Colours of Light. The Rules: Time-Tested Secrets for Capturing the Heart of Mr. Right. Gödel, Escher, Bach. A Brief History of Time.*

But I don't think it ever actually read any of them. It longed to improve itself, to access its trauma, discover its full potential, and rise above its faults. But it was terrified of actually *changing* anything.

I remember once, when we were moving from the yellow apartment downtown to a bigger place over the river, the space/time continuum and me plunked down on cardboard boxes full of its comfort reading. I'd optimistically labeled them *Books to Donate*, but it was an arch lie and we both knew it. We ate cold pineapple pizza and drank warm merlot straight from the box. And the totality of existence said to me, with sauce on the tip of its nose and not a little chagrin:

*For me, self-care is like the grandfather paradox. It might feel good in the moment, but at what cost? No butterfly could imagine the changes to the timeline that would go down if I truly discarded everything that does not spark joy.*

*Do you really want to live in a universe where the space/time continuum has become fully self-actualized?*

The Suciasaurus rex is a two-legged carnivorous theropod, a cousin of the more famous Tyrannosaurus rex. It is the only dinosaur ever found in the state of Washington.

Once, we were lying naked at three in the afternoon in the uptown loft apartment we had for six months when I was twenty-five and the owner was on sabbatical in Paris.

I kissed the space/time continuum's chin and said, in that extra-soft voice that only comes out of you when you're just so happy: *Why me?*

*What do you mean why you?*

*By definition, you could have chosen anyone, anywhere, in the whole cosmos. Why me? I'm just a person like everybody else.*

The space/time continuum rubbed its nose tenderly against mine.

*Because it's you. It's you because it's you because it's you because it's you. Haven't you ever been stuck in a stable time dome before?*

*Plus you smell really good. And you offered me your Capri Sun even though it was your favorite flavor.*

And we laughed and snuggled and ordered sushi and champagne and watched the traffic go by in the snow thirty stories down. You got a point for every blue car.

Two for red.

*But why are you here? Why are you in bodies and minutes and places at all?*

The space/time continuum frowned. It finished the bottle.

*Everyone gets stuck sometimes. Red car.*

I went to a small liberal arts college upstate. Double major psych/physics. A very calculated choice. Inside/Out, I used to say.

The space/time continuum wasn't allowed on campus. It would sit by the University sign on the bumper of its crumbling pickup truck chain-smoking angrily and reading through copies of *Omni* (for the articles) until I was out of class. I'd run out every day like a movie montage, all long hair and long skirts and the long half-life of first love.

I was really pretty then. I don't know why I want you to know that. It's not important in any way. But I was.

The problem was that college isn't part of the normal timestream. Way too much angst and intersecting choice matrices. Warps the gravity fields and fucks with beta decay. It's an unsettling pocket universe of weird smells, meaningless gold stars, protective self-delusion, and leaking bodily liquid. Go ahead and try the double slit experiment on Friday night in a freshman dorm. You're safer with a Ouija board.

But the space/time continuum wanted to support my goals.

Ultimately, I ended up a bartender. Basically what I studied, in a roundabout way. And I only really do roundabouts anymore. Fluid dynamics. Classical conditioning. A festive arrangement of personality disorders and lost time. But I can make a mean Hammerhead Bowl, so who's to say I didn't come out on top?

We broke up junior year. It said we weren't putting the same effort into the relationship. I didn't make time for it. I laughed. It didn't.

Then David and Susan and my mom and student loans and better blow jobs through the power of drive time radio and I didn't see the space/time continuum again for almost five years.

Sometimes things just don't work out. You want them to, but they don't want to, and their vote counts for more than yours, so they don't.

The space/time continuum says that no matter what, there is always a place where they *did* work out. So even if you're suffering, there's a version of yourself somewhere who isn't, maybe older, maybe younger, maybe she has one of those naked cats or something, and if you can't be happy, you can at least be happy for her.

I replied: *Fuck that bitch I hope she drowns.*

The one hundred and seventeenth time I met the space/time continuum it was my mother's doctor. It had kind eyes and bifocals and a little felt bunny stuck onto the tip of its pen and just the perfect dusting of authoritative grey at the temples.

I cried and I cried and I told it to fucking *stop*, it wasn't cute anymore. It never was. Fix her or get out. What is the point of all this if it can't even fix one lousy directionally locked material entity?

It got out.

The hallway was so long and white and clean and quiet. The cool blue price display on the vending machine flashed on and off, on and off, like a lonely lighthouse in an antiseptic sea.

1.99.

Card only.

I thought I didn't see the space/time continuum for five years.

I got this idea in my head that having plants around would help my anxiety and ground me in the now. So I bought the first orchid I liked, one that promised spectacular colors that would last for weeks. I put it in the window and watered it and loved it and it died *immediately*.

So I got another one that looked just like it. The way you swap out a kid's dead goldfish for a ziplocked new one from the shop while they're at school and they never notice because who gives a fuck it's a goldfish.

That orchid also died. So fast it honestly felt kind of personal.

Lather, rinse, repeat.

All in all I had seventeen *odontoglossa pulchella* and a lot of new, more interesting anxiety about maybe being the grim reaper of plants somehow. Or at least fundamentally incompatible with life.

The space/time continuum was all of them. It didn't mind waiting. Five years was nothing at all. Barely a ripple in a puddle that isn't a pond.

I wonder if the universe where everything worked out okay for me is also the Snack McCoy universe and the reason things can work out there but not here is because civilization is all or mostly corgis so there's fundamentally no real problems and also no climate change.

I wonder if I'm a corgi in the Snack McCoy universe.

The space/time continuum says I'm not.

I'm a cagey fucking greyhound and I still have anxiety.

The space/time continuum left me for good a couple years back. It was so ugly. Those scenes are always so ugly. It's your last chance to say the worst things you've ever thought about a person, so get it all out while you can, right?

But some things you can't come back from.

Maybe it was my fault. I said it first.

*I'm not your fucking emotional support human. I just want the infinite embodiment of reality I fell in love with back. I just want everything to be like it was.*

And the space/time continuum sneered at me. *I am exactly who you fell in love with! For me, the moment when I touched your Medieval Castle Siege drawbridge was half a second ago. I kissed you at the dance tomorrow. You're the one who's changed. But I don't have to sit here and take this. In a million other shards of reality beyond this completely stupid one, everything is precisely like it was. So fuck you very much. I don't want you like this. I can go find all the other versions of you in all the other timelines and love them and hold them close and give them everything while you stay here alone and drink yourself to death in this shitty town. And yes, I'm including the one where you're a greyhound. I'm going to pet her so good, and brush her and walk her and feed her organic raw food artisanal treats. We're going to enter agility competitions together and chase cars and have a trillion puppies. And wait til you see what we do in the one where you're a lamp. Yes there's one where you're a lamp, shut up! Stay here and have another drink, I'm going to go where everything is just as sweet and good and new as it was in the beginning and you're not fucking invited.*

It looked stricken. It put its hand over its mouth. But like I said, there's some things you can't come back from. Eventually, all loops degrade and fall apart and a way out of the squiggle opens up.

So that happened.

Or will happen. Or is happening. Or someday might inevitably be unhappened.

Maybe.

Nowadays I work the bar at the Neptune Room, home of the Hammerhead Bowl and extremely understated jewel of the Tides Inn Hotel. Too broke to retire, too stubborn to die.

It is *distinctly* shit here.

I am distinctly shit as well. And old. And angry a lot of the time.

The decor is wall to wall plastic fish, seaweed garlands, and discount Christmas lights. The clientele come in drunk already when we open at four. The kitchen offers a limited menu of mystery bisque, French fries, and despair.

My knees hurt. I have a lot of time to think. Nobody bothers me except to grunt for another of whatever they've chosen to hurt themselves with tonight. I look out the picture windows at the town Ocean Shores was supposed to be and I think about the Suciasaurus rex and Mr. Yuk and corgis with lawyer names and David and Susan and the constellation of Taurus.

In the end, I get this place. We understand each other. I was supposed to be something better, too.

Today, I am mixing Hammerhead Bowls in the back. Don't get excited. It's just whatever's left in last night's well drink bottles, Coke, and the syrup from the maraschino jar all dumped into a turquoise plastic tub shaped like a shark with two straws in it. I finish up and head out to flip over the CLOSED sign.

There's a box on the bar. Wrapped in pink paper with hearts and baby angels on it. But it's not Valentine's Day. My hands settle down on the ribbons. I look around for orchids or iguanas or whatever, but I'm alone.

The box is sitting on top of a hand-knitted mauve cabled cardigan.

Maybe I won't open it. Maybe I just let this be over for once. I'm tired. I don't believe in anything anymore.

Of course I open it.

I'm fourteen years old. Mom and I get in her little yellow Jeep and drive down the coast to Ocean Shores. It's the first year after Dad left. She's nervous about doing it all on her own from here forward into always, so she's smoking again, and interfering with the radio like there's some tuning on the dial that will bring back the life she thought she was going to have. But there isn't. She's alone. He's gone and she's alone.

But she's trying. Alice is trying.

So she gives me my riddle for the trip instead of Dad, instead of the man who couldn't handle us at the peak of our reclusive timeline algorithm, and my mother's riddle is this: *What is the difference between love and time?*

I'm stumped.

We get salt water taffy and hit the boardwalk, walking lazily down the rows of purple and pink and green neon flashing lights and tinny arcade machine action music. Tickets spit out of the bank of Skee Ball machines like cheeky blue tongues. A rusted out mechanical pony plays *The Entertainer* as we stroll by. I say low tide stinks something awful. Alice laughs. She doesn't smell anything.

Mom gives me $5 and says I can play whatever I want. We pass the Happy Time Entertainment Inc Treasure Claw Machine, whose decal stickers have peeled and blistered until it just says *Time Claw*.

I stop.

"Those things are always rigged, honey," Alice says then, and later in a narrow white room with tubes coming out of her nose, and I hear it in both memories, in the same tone, at the same time.

But I promise her I can do it. I'm good at claw machines, always have been. I look over at her, at Alice, her face washed in all the colored electric lights, and she is so beautiful, she really is, so beautiful and so unfathomably young. You never think of your parents as young, but god, she's just a baby. And so am I.

I drop a couple of silver coins into the slot and press the glowing buttons with authority—left, right, over, just a little more. Release.

The claw descends.

It comes back up with a crappy stuffed starfish. Mom and I start screaming like I just won the MegaBucks, jumping up and down and hugging each other and she's kissing the top of my head and the WINNER lights are going soundlessly crazy because the machine's speakers are broken and then suddenly there's this kid standing next to me in a puffer vest and a Nirvana shirt and glasses and I know before I turn around who it is and was and will be.

"Wow," says the space/time continuum. "That was amazing! Can you win one for me?"

"Probably not," I say sadly. "Two in a row is pretty tough. And I'm out of money."

The space/time continuum hands me a dollar in quarters.

"I'll probably lose," I protest.

"It's okay if you lose," it says.

I look at my mom and she nods encouragingly. So in the money goes. I push the buttons again. I drop the Time Claw.

And what do you know? It comes up desperately clutching a giant toy it absolutely should not be able to lift with those pitiful skinny silver prongs. The claw looks like it's gonna break off the suspension for a minute. But it doesn't. It doesn't. It glides smoothly home.

I retrieve the mass of fluff from the prize bin.

It's a Cartoon Sparkle Rainbow Geoduck. With big friendly eyes and long lashes and a wide, smiling mouth. Geoducks are endemic to this coast. Some bright idea factory must have had a lot made up special for this specific arcade, in this specific, tiny, trash clam town.

I stare at it. Because this really happened and I forgot it ever did. I am both then and now, myself in the Neptune Room with shaky swollen hands and myself at fourteen, frantic with hope and hormones and I forgot this happened, because forgetting is so easy, little holes open up in the fabric of reality and you drop parts of yourself into them and you forget that your mother ever looked so pretty and so worried and so young, you forget that you won this ridiculous thing for a stranger in a tawdry arcade and Alice was so impressed. She looked at you like she was seeing you for the first time. Like you were a real live grown up separate person and she only just noticed.

And then the Time Claw is gone and it's the end of the weekend and Alice and I are sitting in a hot tub with mold in every jet on a grey beach full of grey sand and hidden ancient clams. We finish singing *Don't Cry for Me Argentina* and she smiles at me.

"Have you figured out my riddle yet, Miss Grand Prize Winner?"

She turns to me in the water and wraps up my cheeks in her wet hands and god, her eyes are so green, it is impossible that any human's eyes have ever been so green. Alice's face takes up the whole of the universe. She barely gets the first few words out before those green improbable eyes fill up with tears and she's crying and lying in that future bed listening to the radio and holding my hand while she whispers:

"Baby, the difference between love and time is nothing. *Nothing*. There is no difference. The love we give to each other is the time we give to each other, and the time we spend together is the whole of love. Things will get better, sweetheart, I promise. I love you so much. My darling baby. I love you. Don't forget. No matter what happens. The answer is nothing."

She hugs me and there is no difference. All the time spent in love is one time, happening simultaneously, a closed timeline curve of infinite gentleness. The continuum hiding in all the faces of people I have needed and wanted and cared for and grieved, the faces through which I loved the world, all one, all at once, memory and dreaming and regret and desire, injera bread and lentil soup and sushi and champagne and running toward a pickup truck in the yellow afternoon, red and white Rainier beer cans and rhinoceros iguanas and orchids and plastic Army camouflage-print glasses and psychology and physics and circular saws and Dazzle Dan feeding the birds in front of the Catedral and the Loch Ness monster's ancient reptile heart beggared with love for her baby in the dark and plants that are whales and whales that are plants and Suciasaurus rex and middle school and the countless infinite loops we get stuck in like tar and an octopus mug in orbit around Saturn and the Washington State Legislature and KHRT 101.5 and golden retrievers and red cars and Bob Ross and the emerald dish soap on the sink that made Alice remember her bridesmaids' dresses and just stop like a watch in her pain and the puddle that comes and goes with the rain and a house that belongs to a hill and Cartoon Sparkle Rainbow Geoducks and the smell of a newborn's head and Snack McCoy running after a ball of light in a universe without pain and there is no difference, no difference between any of it at all, it is all one thing, the only thing small enough to fit through an Einstein-Rosen wormhole—all dumped together into a blue plastic shark bowl with two straws.

Love in the vessel of time.

That's where Alice left her loop. Not in that bed twenty years later not knowing who I was or where she was going, but there with her baby in Ocean Shores, WA, at twilight, somewhere between the water and the Time Claw, promising me ice cream for dinner while the space/time continuum looked on and kept the tourists at bay.

When she could still smell me a little.

When I was old and sorry, just so sorry.

There is no difference. There never was.

Nothing.

Nothing.

The lights twinkle in the Neptune Room. The space/time continuum looks like the Mr. Yuk kid all grown up, my own age still. It smiles from the doorway, silhouetted by sundown.

I'm holding something old and ratty and sodden with seawater in my hand. I don't even look at it, just sniff awkwardly and hand over the Cartoon Sparkle Rainbow Geoduck to the kid in the puffer vest.

"I won it for you, after all."

"Keep it," says the space/time continuum. "Happy birthday."

"It's not my birthday."

The space/time continuum looks just like it did in the beginning. And the end. And all points in between. It shines. And so do I and so does Alice and so does blasted, cursed Ocean Shores, WA and geoducks and all the ships at sea.

Cyndi Lauper starts playing on the long-defunct sound system because the space/time continuum is a cheesy fool and always will be. It takes off its glasses.

"It's always your birthday. Keep it. Keep it all. It's yours. I love you. I'm sorry. I'm an idiot. I love you. This you. Infinitely better than the lamp or the greyhound or the one I never made any mistakes with. I'll do better this time. I can be better. Come home."

# A Buyer's Guide to Maps of Antarctica

Lot 657D
Topographical Map of the Ross Ice Shelf (The Seal Map)
Acuña, Nahuel, 1908
Minor tear, upper left corner. Moderate staining in left margin.

*ANDMASS CENTERED, ARGENTINEAN COAST VISIBLE in the extreme upper quadrant. Latitude and longitude in sepia ink. Compass rose: a seal indicating north with her head, east and west with her flippers, south with the serrated ice floe on which the beast is situated. Legend in original handwriting. Ross Ice Shelf depicted with remarkable precision for the era, see Referent A (recent satellite imaging) for comparison.*

The 1907 expedition to the Antarctic continent was doubly notable: it was on this virgin crossing that young Nahuel Acuña, barely free of university, lost his right foot to an orca in estrus, and by simplest chance the good ship Proximidad employed an untested botanist by the name of Villalba Maldonado. Maldonado, himself a recent graduate of no less note than his illustrious shipmate, worked placidly as a cook to gain his passage, having no access to the funding that pursued Acuña through his career like a cheerful spaniel.

One may only imagine an unremarkable Saturday supper in the ice shadows and crystalline sun-prisms in which Villalba, his apron stained with penguin oil, his thinning black hair unkempt, his mustache frozen, laid a frost-scrimmed china plate before Acuña. Would he have removed his glasses before eating? Would they have exchanged words? Would he have looked up from his sextant and held the gaze of the mild-eyed Maldonado, even for a moment, before falling to? One hopes that he did; one hopes that the creaking of the Proximidad in one's mind is equal to its creaking in actuality.

Acuña's journal records only: seal flank and claret for supper again. Cook insists on salads of red and white lichen. Not to my taste.

The famous Seal Map, the first of the great Acuña Maps, offers a rare window into the early days of the rivalry, and has been assessed at $7500US.

Curator's Note: Whiskey stains date from approximately 1952.

**Lot 689F**
**Topographical Map of the Ross Ice Shelf (The Sun Dog Map)**
**Maldonado, Villalba, 1908**
**Single owner, immaculate condition.**

*Landmass low center, no other continents visible. Latitude and longitude in unidentified black ink. Compass rose: three-horned sea-goat, a barnacle-crusted tail indicating south, upturned muzzle designating north, vestigial fins pointing east and west. Sun shown centered, with rays embossed in gold extending all the way to the ice shelf. Parhelion is indicated, however, in the place of traditional concentric circles, two large dogs flank the orb of the sun, apparently Saint Bernards or similar, their fur streaming as if in a sudden wind, embossed in silver. Their jaws hang open, as if to devour the solar rays; their paws stand elbow-deep in the seawater, creating ripples that extend to the shoreline. The Map Legend explains that the pair of dogs, called Grell and Skell, may be found at coordinates (redacted) and that they require gifts of penguin feet* and liverwort before they are willing to part with a cupful of the sun, which if carried at the end of a fishing pole and line before the intrepid polar conquistador, may burn with all the heat and pure light that he requires.

Offshore, a large, grinning orca whale is visible, with a severed leg in her mouth.

When Maldonado returned from the Proximidad expedition, he arranged, presumably without knowledge of any competition, for the dissemination of his maps in parallel to Nahuel Acuña's own efforts. The printing of the Sun Dog Map, illustrated by Maldonado himself, was funded by the daughter of Alvaro Caceres, best described as a sheep and cattle magnate in the grace of whose shipping interests the Proximidad functioned. Pilar Caceres was delighted with the Maldonado sketches, and sold an ornate necklace of onyx and diamonds (Lot 331A) in order to finance this first map.

While the phenomenally precise Seal Map made Acuña's name and allowed him a wide choice of whalers and naturalists eager to avail themselves of his guidance, the Sun Dog Map stirred a mania for all things Antarctic in Buenos Aires. Nevertheless, Maldonado was not able to fund a second expedition until 1912, while Acuña booked passage on the Immaculata the following spring, confounded by the popularity of a clearly fraudulent document. He gave a lecture on the necessity of precision at the Asociación Cartographica Argentina in December of 1908, declaring it a ridiculous matter that he should be required to address such an obvious issue. He was, however, interrupted by vociferous requests for more exact descriptions of Grell and Skell.

Maldonado himself declined to appear before the Asociación despite three invitations, and published the Toothfish Map (Lot 8181Q) in early 1909 without their stamp.

This first and perhaps finest example of the cartography of Villalba Maldonado is one of only three remaining copies and has been assessed at $18500US.

**Lot 699C**
**Map of the South Orkney Islands**
**Acuña, Nahuel, 1911**
**Sun damage throughout, fair condition.**

*Four large islands and sixteen smaller isles lie in the center of the map. Isla Coronación is the only named landmass. Latitude and longitude demarcated in Mediterranean octopus ink. Thirty-two point compass rose, crowned with military arrows wrapped in laurels, and bearing the archaic Levante designation on its eastern arm. See Referent B for satellite comparison.*

The comparatively moderate climate of the South Orkney Islands (now the Orcadas) allowed Acuña to remain there throughout the war, returning his maps to the mainland via Jokkum Vabø, an illiterate sealer and loyal friend of the cartographer. The two men built the cabin in which Acuña worked and lived, and Vabø made certain that they smoked enough seal-meat in the summer months to keep his friend breathing, returning with costly inks and papers when migrations allowed. This was to prove the most prolific period of Nahuel's life.

From 1909 to 1918, Nahuel Acuña walked the length and breadth of the South Orkneys, polishing his teak prosthetic with the snow and grasses of the coast. He built a circular boat of sealskin and walrus-bones (Lot 009A), paddling from island to island with a gargantuan oar of leather and orca-rib, a tool he must have found rich to use. He grew a long black beard that was said to glint gold in the sun, and never thereafter shaved it. He claimed later to have given Maldonado not the slightest thought during this hermitage, though Vabø would certainly have reported his rival's doings during his visits, and as the coyly titled Seal Pot Map details just this area, there is some dispute as to whether Maldonado might have actually managed landfall during his 1912 expedition aboard the Perdita and met cordially with Acuña. It is not possible to ascertain the authenticity of such rumors in either direction, but it is again sweet to imagine it, the two bearded mapmakers seated upon a snowy boulder, sharing lichen-tea and watching the twilight fall onto the scarlet flensing plains. It is a gentle pleasure to imagine that they had no enmity for one another in that moment, that their teapot steamed happily between them, and that they discussed, perhaps, the invention of longitude, or methods for slaughtering walrus.

First in the *Orcadas* series, this prime specimen of Acuña at his height has been assessed at $6200US.

Lot 705G
**Map of the South Orkney Islands (The Seal Pot Map)**
**Maldonado, Villalba, 1914**
**Single owner, very slight water damage, lower right corner.**

*Five large islands and twenty-six smaller isles lie in the center of the map. All are named: Isla Concepción, Isla Immaculata, Isla Perdita, Isla Proximidad, Isla Gloriana, Isla Hibisco, Isla Sello Zafiro, Isla Pingüino Azul, Isla Cielo, Isla Pájaros del Musgo, Isla Valeroso, Isla Ermitaño, Isla Ocultado, Isla Graciento, Isla Mudanza, Isla del Leones Incansable, Isla Sombras Blancas, Isla del Ballenas del Fantasma, Isla Zapato, Isla del Mar de Cristal, Isla del Morsas Calvas, Isla Rojo, Isla Ónice, Isla Embotado, Isla Mentira, Isla del Araña Verde, Isla Abejas, Isla del Pie de la Reina, Isla Acuña, Isla Pilar.*

*All ink sepia, compass is a seal's head peeking out of an iron pot, her flipper pointed south, the pot handles east and west, and her head, capped by the pot's lid, indicating north. Smaller versions of this creature dot the island chain, their faces intricately inscribed. The legend claims that these Footless Seals can be found on the sometimes-green shores of Isla Graciento, on the long Norwegian flensing plain that occupies most of the island:* When the Iron Try Pots left to render Seal Fat are left to boil until Moonrise, it occasionally Happens that a severed Seal Head which has a Certain blue Tinge to its whiskers will Blink and open its Eyes, and with Cunning Hop Away into the surf, carrying the Iron Try Pot with it as a new Body. If an Explorer is very clever, he will leave a few of his campfire Embers burning and pretend to Sleep. If he is an Excellent Feinter of Slumber, the Queen of the Seal Pots whose name is Huln will come to rest upon the dying Fire and warm Herself. If he has brought three Pearls as tribute, the Queen will allow him to dip his Spoon into the Pot and drink of her Broth, which is sweeter than dandelion honey, and will keep him Fed and Happy for a fortnight and more. *(translation: Furtado, 1971)*

Unable to convince the skeptic Alvaro Caceres to fund a second expedition despite the popularity of his work, Villalba Maldonado contented himself with the attentions of Pilar Caceres. Portraits (Lots 114 & 115A-F) show a handsome, if severe woman, with a high widow's peak and narrow eyes. She continued to sell her jewelry to print his maps, but no amount of necklaces could equal a southbound vessel. However, she became an expert in the preparation of sheepskin parchment, and in this manner became all the more Maldonado's patroness. She wore red whenever she met with him, and allowed her thick hair to fall at least three times upon his arm. With the grudging consent of Alvaro, Villalba and Pilar were married in April of 1911. She wore no jewels, and her dress was black sealskin. She was soon pregnant, and their daughter Soledad was born shortly after Maldonado departed on the Perdita in 1912. Pilar arranged for him to stay on through 1915 as a nominal military service, and thus both cartographers walked the ice floes during the Great War, far from each other and as ignorant of the other's activities as of the rest of the world.

Six maps were printed and distributed between 1908 and 1912. Each was received with ravenous acclaim, and applications for passage to Antarctica tripled. "Paquetes" were sold at docks (Lots 441A-492L), wooden boxes containing "supplies" for a successful Antartic expedition: desiccated penguin feet, bundles of liverwort, fishing poles, sheets of music to be sung at the ice-grottos of the Dream-Stealing Toothfish, cheap copies of the six maps, and three small pearls. However, most enthusiasts found themselves ultimately unable to make such a perilous voyage, and thus Maldonado's reputation grew in the absence of Acuña or any definite rebuttal of Maldonado's wonderful maps.

Not to be confused with the plentiful copies included in the paquetes, this original Caceres-issue map has been assessed at $15900US.

**Lot 718K**
**Map of Queen Maud's Land**
**Acuña, Nahuel, 1920**
**Single owner, immaculate condition.**

*Landmass right center, Chilean coast visible in top left quadrant. Latitude and longitude in iron gall ink. Compass rose is the top half of a young woman, her head tipped up toward north, her arms open wide to encompass east and west, her hair twisting southward into a point. See Referent C for satellite comparison, Points 1, 4, and 17 for major deviations.*

Curator's Note: Obviously Queen Maud's Land was not the common appellation at the time of Acuña's map, however, his own term, Suyai's Plain, was never recognized by any government making a claim to the territory.

Upon returning from the South Orkneys in 1919, Acuña was horrified by the paquetes and Maldonado's celebrity. The sheer danger of packing penguin's feet instead of lamp oil made him ill, and he immediately scheduled a series of lectures condemning the cartographer, challenging him to produce either Grell or Skell (he did not state a preference) on a chain at the Asociación banquet, or Huln, if the dogs were recalcitrant.

Attendant at these lectures was a young woman by the name of Suyai Ledesma. In imitation of her idol, Suyai had begun to produce her own maps of the pampas, the vast Argentine interior where both she and Acuña had been born. She presented her research at the Asociación banquet in a modest brown suit, her voice barely audible. She concluded with a gentle reminder that "the cartographer's art relies on accuracy as the moon relies on the sun to shed her own light on the world. To turn our backs on the authentic universe, as it exists beneath and before us, is to plunge into darkness."

Though Ledesma and Acuña never married, they were not often separated thenceforward, and she accompanied him along with their two sons on the Lethe expedition to Iles Kerguelen in 1935.

However, until the 1935 expedition, Acuña felt it was his duty to remain in Buenos Aires, to struggle against Maldonadan Antarcticana and its perils, and to rail against his rival whenever he was given a podium and a crowd with more than two folk to rub together. These philippics were eventually assembled and published posthumously by Carrizo and Rivas under the title On Authenticity (1961). One copy remains outside of private collections. (Lot 112C)

Maldonado responded slowly, as was his habit in all things. In 1922, his sole rejoinder was a small package, immaculately wrapped, delivered to Acuña's home. Inside was long golden chain attached to a crystal dog's collar (Lot 559M) and a note (Lot 560M) reading: *As you see I do not, as I see, you disdain. It is big enough.*

But fate would have her way, and in the end the Antarctic was not quite big enough after all. In January of 1922, three young men were found frozen to their ship on the Shackleton Ice Shelf, still clutching their paquetes, in possession of neither a cup of sun nor the Queen of the Try Pots. In May, Acuña had Villalba Maldonado arrested for public endangerment.

This pristine map of Queen Maud's Land, produced at the height of conflict, has been assessed at $6700US.

Lot 781A
Map of the South Pole (The Petrel Map)
Maldonado, Villalba, 1925
Significant damage, burns in top center portion

*Landmass center, eastern Antarctic coast visible. Latitude and longitude in walnut ink, black tea, and human blood. Compass rose:*

a snow petrel rampant, her claws demarcating southeast and southwest, her tail flared due south, her wings spread east and west, and her head fixed at true north. Beneath her is emblazoned: Seal of the Antarctic Postal Service—Glacies Non Impedimenta. *(Ice Is No Impediment.)* Alone of the Maldonado maps, color of indeterminate and probably morbid origin have been used to stain portions of the interior red, differentiating zones of "watermelon snow," fulminating plains of lichen grown bright and thick, bearing fruits which when cracked open are found to be full of fresh water, more and sweeter than any may ask. The red fields encircle a zone of blue ice, frozen rainwater enclosing a lake of brine. Upon this rainwater mantle, explains the map legend, sits the Magnetic Pole, which is a chair made of try pots and harpoon-blades. The Pole sits tall there, her hair encased in fresh, sweet water gone to ice, her eyes filmed. Her dress is black sealskin, her necklaces are all of bone and skulls. Grell and Skell they are Her Playmates, Her Guardians Dire, and Huln she is Her Handmaid, but Never moves She, even Once. *(translation: Peralta, 1988.)*

She is waiting, the notations go on to state, for the petrels which are her loyal envoys, to deliver a letter into her hands, written on sheepskin, whose ink is blood. What this letter will read and who it may be from, no whaler may say—it is for her alone, and she alone may touch it.

The Petrel Map was produced in Maldonado's third year in prison, delivered to the printer's by his bailiff and repaired there, as the original document was created using unorthodox methods, owing to Villalba's lack of access to plentiful inks. The viciousness and length of his incarceration and Acuña's uncommon success in enforcing the sentence may be credited to many things: the influence of the spurned Asociación, the corrupt bureaucracy which was prone to forgetting and misplacing whole cartographers, the persuasiveness of Acuña and the pregnant Suyai as to the menace of Maldonado and his clearly deliberate deceits. Nevertheless, the summer of 1925 saw the first map in three years, and a new rash of paquetes eagerly broke the docks, the Shackleton incident all but forgotten. Stamps of the Antarctic Postal Service were now included, along with stationery and "ice-proof" pencils.

The Petrel Map was completed from memory, according to Pilar, a testament to an extraordinary intellect bent on total and accurate recollection. Public outcry warred with the Asociación on the subject of Maldonado's release, and funds were mounted for a Proximidad II expedition, but there was no one to receive it, the Caceres-Maldonado accounts having been frozen, and the usual half-benign institutional fraud absorbed the money once more into the body of the state. Meanwhile, Acuña's tarnished star rose, and he was commissioned by the British Navy to deliver maps of the subcontinent.

By 1928 Maldonado was in complete isolation. He was not allowed visits from his wife, or perhaps more tellingly for our purposes, letters. Acuña was recorded as visiting once, in 1930, with his young son Raiquen. It is not for us to imagine this meeting, so far from the decks of the Proximidad and salads of lichen, far from claret and the green shadows of the aurora australis. However, after this incident, Acuña arranged for Maldonado to be moved to a special penitentiary in Ushuaia, on the southern tip of Argentina, with the shores of the South Shetlands in sight, on very clear days.

*The Great Man looked up from his bread and held the eye of the Naval Cartographer. Their beards were both very long, but Acuña's was neatly cut and kept, while Maldonado's snarled and ran to the stone floor.*

*"I promised you, my friend," he said, his voice very rough, "that it was big enough. Big enough for us both to look on it and hold in our vision two separate countries, bound only by longitude."*

*"What's big enough?" little Raiquen asked, tugging on his father's hand, which had two gold rings upon it.*

*But Acuña did not answer. For my own part, my heart was filled with long plains of ice receding into eternity, and on those plains my prisoner walked with bare feet and a cup of gold.*

*—Keeper of the Key: The Autobiography of a Prison Guard, Rafael Soto, 1949*

Villalba Maldonado died at Ushuaia on June 4th, 1933. Acuña lived, feted and richly funded, until 1951, when he drowned off the shore of Isla Concepción. Suyai and her sons continued in residence on the islands, producing between them twelve maps of the area. (Lots 219-231H) Raiquen relocated in middle age to the mainland where he lives still in well-fed obscurity.

The Petrel Map was Maldonado's final work, and as such, has been assessed at $57000US.

**Lot 994D**

**Captain's Logbook, the Anamnesis, disembarked from Ushuaia, 1934**

Here is presented the logbook in which Soledad Maldonado signed her name and declared her cargo—an iron coffin lashed to a long sled. She left her ailing mother in Buenos Aires and sailed south as soon as tide and melt permitted, and Captain Godoy deposited her on the floes of the Weddell Sea per instructions. His full account of the voyage and Soledad's peculiar habits, studies, and intentions will be released only to the buyer, however, his notes conclude thus:

*I watched the young lady amid her supplies, her sled, her eight bristling dogs, her father's long, cold coffin. She gave me a cool glance in farewell and turned southward, towards the interior ice. She waited for a long while, though I could not think what for. It was drawing on night, and there were many stars showing when it happened, and I must insist that I be believed and not ridiculed, no matter what I may now write.*

*Two great dogs strode out from the long plains of ice, enormous, thickly furred, something like Saint Bernards. They pressed their noses into her hands and she petted their heads, scratched behind their ears, let them lick her face slowly, methodically, with great care. The huge hounds allowed her to yoke them at the head of her team, and without a whip she directed them inward, onward, hoisting aloft as they flew a long fishing pole, at the end of which was an orb of impossible light, like a cup overturned and spilling out the sun.*

The Log Book has been assessed at $10700US. Bidding begins at noon precisely.

# White Lines on a Green Field

*For Seanan McGuire. And Coyote.*

LET ME TELL YOU ABOUT the year Coyote took the Devils to the State Championship.

Coyote walked tall down the halls of West Centerville High and where he walked lunch money, copies of last semester's math tests, and unlit joints blossomed in his footsteps. When he ran laps out on the field our lockers would fill up with Snickers bars, condoms, and ecstasy tabs in all the colors of Skittles. He was our QB, and he looked like an invitation to the greatest rave of all time. I mean, yeah, he had black hair and copper skin and muscles like a commercial for the life you're never going to have. But it was the way he looked at you, with those dark eyes that knew the answer to every question a teacher could ask, but he wouldn't give them the *satisfaction*, you know? Didn't matter anyway. Coyote never did his homework, but boyfriend rocked a 4.2 all the same.

When tryouts rolled around that fall, Coyote went out for everything. Cross-country, baseball, even lacrosse. But I think football appealed to his friendly nature, his need to have a pack around him, bright-eyed boys with six-pack abs and a seven-minute mile and a gift for him every day. They didn't even know why, but they brought them all the same. Playing cards, skateboards, vinyl records (Coyote had no truck with mp3s). The defensive line even baked cookies for their boy. Chocolate chip peanut butter oatmeal walnut iced snickerdoodle, piling up on the bench like a king's tribute. And oh, the girls brought flowers. Poor girls gave him dandelions and rich girls gave him roses and he kissed them all like they were each of them specifically the key to the fulfillment of all his dreams. Maybe they were. Coyote didn't play favorites. He had enough for everyone.

By the time we went to State, all the cheerleaders were pregnant.

The Devils used to be a shitty team, no lie. Bottom of our division and even the coach was thinking he ought to get more serious about his geometry classes. Before Coyote transferred our booster club was the tight end's dad, Mr. Bollard, who painted his face Devil gold-and-red and wore big plastic light-up horns for every game. At Homecoming one year, the Devil's Court had two princesses and a queen who were actually girls from the softball team filling in on a volunteer basis, because no one cared enough to vote. They all wore jeans and bet heavily on the East Centerville Knights, who won 34-3.

First game of his senior year, Coyote ran 82 yards for the first of 74 touchdowns that season. He passed and caught and ran like he was all eleven of them in one body. Nobody could catch him. Nobody even complained. He ran like he'd stolen that ball and the whole world was chasing him to get it back. Where'd he been all this time? The boys hoisted him up on their shoulders afterward, and Coyote just laughed and laughed. We all found our midterm papers under our pillows the next morning, finished and bibliographied, and damn if they weren't the best essays we'd never written.

I'M NOT GONNA lie. I lost my virginity to Coyote in the back of my blue pickup out by the lake right before playoffs. He stroked my hair and kissed me like they kiss in the movies. Just the perfect kisses, no bonked noses, no knocking teeth. He tasted like stolen sunshine.

*Bunny,* he whispered to me with his narrow hips working away, *I will love you forever and ever. You're the only one for me.*

*Liar,* I whispered back, and when I came it was like the long flying fall of a roller coaster, right into his arms. *Liar, liar, liar.*

I think he liked that I knew the score, because after that Coyote made sure I was at all his games, even though I don't care about sports. Nobody didn't care about sports that year. Overnight the stands went from a ghost town to kids ride free day at the carnival. And when Coyote danced in the endzone he looked like everything you ever wanted. Every son, every boyfriend.

"Come on, Bunny," he'd say. "I'll score a touchdown for you."

"You'll score a touchdown either way."

"I'll point at you in the stands if you're there. Everyone will know I love you."

"Just make sure I'm sitting with Sarah Jane and Jessica and Ashley, too, so you don't get in trouble."

"That's my Bunny, always looking out for me," he'd laugh, and take me in his mouth like he'd die if he didn't.

YOU COULD USE birth control with Coyote. It wouldn't matter much.

But he did point at me when he crossed that line, grinning and dancing and moving his hips like Elvis had just been copying his moves all along, and Sarah Jane and Jessica and Ashley got so excited they choked on their Cokes. They all knew about the others. I think they liked it that way—most of what mattered to Sarah Jane and Jessica and Ashley was Sarah Jane and Jessica and Ashley, and Coyote gave them permission to spend all their time together. Coyote gave us all permission, that was his thing. *Cheat, fuck, drink, dance—just do it like you mean it!*

I think the safety had that tattooed on his calf.

AFTER WE WON four games in a row (after a decade of no love) things started to get really out of control. You couldn't buy tickets. Mr. Bollard was in hog heaven—suddenly the boosters were every guy in town who was somebody, or used to be somebody, or who wanted to be somebody some impossible day in the future. We were gonna beat the Thunderbirds. They started saying it, right out in public. Six-time state champs, and no chance they wouldn't be the team in our way this year like every year. But every year was behind us, and ahead was only our boy running like he'd got the whole of heaven at his back. Mr. Bollard got them new uniforms, new helmets, new goal posts—all the deepest red you ever saw. But nobody wore the light-up horns Mr. Bollard had rocked for years. They all wore little furry coyote ears, and who knows where they bought them, but they were everywhere one Friday, and every Friday after. When Coyote scored, everyone would howl like the moon had come out just for them. Some of the cheerleaders started wearing faux-fur tails, spinning them around by bumping and grinding on the sidelines, their corn-yellow skirts fluttering up to the heavens.

One time, after we stomped the Greenville Bulldogs 42-0 I saw Coyote under the stands, in that secret place the boards and steel poles and shadows and candy wrappers make. Mike Halloran (kicker, #14) and Justin Oster (wide receiver #11) were down there too, helmets off, the filtered stadium lights turning their uniforms to pure gold. Coyote leaned against a pole, smoking a cigarette, shirt off—and what a thing that was to see.

"Come on, QB," Justin whined. "I never hit a guy before. I got no beef here. And I never fucked Jessie, either, Mike, I was just mouthing off. She let me see her boob once in ninth grade and there wasn't that much to see back then. I never had a drink except one time a beer and I never smoked 'cause my daddy got emphysema." Coyote just grinned his friendly, hey-dude-no-worries grin.

"Never know unless you try," he said, very reasonably. "It'll make you feel good, I promise."

"Fuck *you*, Oster," shot back Halloran. "I'm going first. You're bigger, it's not fair."

Halloran got his punch in before he had to hear any more about what Justin Oster had never done and the two of them went *at it*, fists and blood and meat-slapping sounds and pretty soon they were down on the ground in the spilled-Coke and week-old-rain mud, pulling hair and biting and rolling around and after awhile it didn't look that much like fighting anymore. I watched for awhile. Coyote looked up at me over their grappling and dragged on his smoke.

*Just look at them go, little sister*, I heard Coyote whisper, but his mouth didn't move. His eyes flashed in the dark like a dog's.

LAGRANGE ALMOST RUINED it all at Homecoming. The LaGrange Cowboys, and wasn't their QB a picture, all wholesome white-blond square-jaw aw-shucks muscle with an arm so perfect you'd have thought someone had mounted a rifle sight on it. #9 Bobby Zhao, of the 300 bench and the Miss Butter Festival 19whatever mother, the seven-restaurant-chain owning father (Dumpling King of the Southland!) and the surprising talent for soulful bluegrass guitar. All the colleges lined up for that boy with carnations and chocolates. We hated him like hate was something we'd invented in lab that week and had been saving up for something special. Bobby Zhao and his bullshit hipster-crooner straw hat. Coyote didn't pay him mind. *Tell us what you're gonna do to him*, they'd pant, and he'd just spit onto the parking lot asphalt and say: *I got a history with Cowboys.* Where he'd spat the offensive line watched as weird crystals formed—the kind Jimmy Moser (safety #17) ought to have recognized from his uncle's trailer out off of Route 40, but you know me, I don't say a word. They didn't look at it too long. Instead they scratched their cheeks and performed their tribal ask-and-answer. *We going down by the lake tonight? Yeah. Yeah.*

"Let's invite Bobby Zhao," Coyote said suddenly. His eyes got big and loose and happy. His *come-on* look. His *it'll-be-great* look.

"Um, why?" Jimmy frowned. "Not to put too fine a point on it, but fuck that guy. He's the enemy."

Coyote flipped up the collar of his leather jacket and picked a stray maple leaf the color of anger out of Jimmy's hair. He did it tenderly. *You're my boy and I'll pick you clean, I'll lick you clean, I'll keep everything red off of your perfect head*, his fingers said. But what his mouth said was:

"Son, what you don't know about enemies could just about feed the team til their dying day." And when Coyote called you Son you knew to be ashamed. "Only babies think enemies are for beating. Can't beat 'em, not ever. Not the ones that come out of nowhere in the fourth quarter to take what's yours and hold your face in the mud til you drown, not the ones you always knew you'd have to face because that's what you were made for. Not the lizard guarding the Sun, not the man who won't let you teach him how to plant corn. Enemies are for grabbing by the ears and fucking them til they're so sticky-knotted bound to you they call their wives by your name. Enemies are for absorbing, Jimmy. Best thing you can do to an enemy is pull up a chair to his fire, eat his dinner, rut in his bed and go to his job in the morning, and do it all so much better he just gives it up to you—but *fuck him*, you never wanted it anyway. You just wanted to mess around in his house for a little while. Scare his kids. Leave a little something behind to let the next guy know you're never far away. That's how you do him. Or else—" Coyote pulled Cindy Gerard (bottom of the pyramid and arms like birch trunks) close and took the raspberry pop out of her hand, sipping on it long and sweet, all that pink slipping into him. "Or else you just make him love you til he cries. Either way."

Jimmy fidgeted. He looked at Oster and Halloran, who still had bruises, fading on their cheekbones like blue flowers. After awhile he laughed horsily and said: "Whaddaya think the point spread'll be?"

Coyote just punched him in the arm, convivial like, and kissed Cindy Gerard and I could smell the raspberry of their kiss from across the circle of boys. The September wind brought their kiss to all of us like a bag of promises. And just like that, Bobby Zhao showed up at the lake that night, driving his freshly waxed Cowboy silver-and-black double-cab truck with the lights on top like a couple of frog's eyes. He took off that stupid straw hat and started hauling a keg out of the cream leather passenger seat—and once they saw that big silver moon riding shotgun with the Dumpling Prince of the Southland, Henry Dillard (linebacker #33) and Josh Vick (linebacker #34) hurried over to help him with it and Bobby Zhao was welcome. Offering accepted. Just lay it up here on the altar and we'll cut open that shiny belly and drink what she's got for us. And what she had was golden and sweet and just as foamy as the sea.

Coyote laid back with me in the bed of my much shittier pickup, some wool blanket with a horse-and-cactus print on it under us and another one with a wolf-and-moon design over us, so he could slip his hands under my bra in that secret, warm space that gets born under some hippie mom's awful rugs when no one else can see you. Everyone was hollering over the beer and I could hear Sarah Jane laughing in that way that says: *just keep pouring and maybe I'll show you something worth seeing.*

"Come on, Bunny Rabbit," Coyote whispered, "it's nothing we haven't done before." And it was a dumb thing to say, a boy thing, but when Coyote said it I felt it humming in my bones, everything we'd done before, over and over, and I couldn't even remember a world before Coyote, only the one he made of us, down by the lake, under the wolf and the moon, his hands on my breasts like they were the saving of him. I knew him like nobody else—and they'll all say that now, Sarah Jane and Jessica and Ashley and Cindy Gerard and Justin Oster and Jimmy Moser, but I knew him. Knew the shape of him. After all, it's nothing we hadn't done before.

"It's different every time," I said in the truck-dark. "Or there's no point. You gotta ask me nice every time. You gotta make me think I'm special. You gotta put on your ears and your tail and make the rain come for me or I'll run off with some Thunderbird QB and leave you eating my dust."

"I'm asking nice. Oh, my Bunny, my rabbit-girl with the fastest feet, just slow you down and let me do what I want."

"And what do you want?"

"I want to dance on this town til it breaks. I want to burrow in it until it belongs to me. I want high school to last forever. I want to eat everything, and fuck everything, and snort everything, and win everything. I want my Bunny Rabbit on my lap while I drive down the world with my headlights off."

"I don't want to be tricked," I said, but he was already inside me and I was glad. Fucking him felt like running in a long field, with no end in sight. "Not into a baby, not into a boyfriend, not into anything."

"Don't worry," he panted. "You always get yours. Just like me, always like me."

I felt us together, speeding up towards something, running faster, and he brushed my hair out of my face and it wasn't hair but long black ears, as soft as memory, and then it was hair again, tangled and damp with our sweat, and I bit him as our stride broke. I whispered: "And Coyote gets his."

"Why not? It's nothing we haven't done before."

When I got up off of the horse blanket, marigold blossoms spilled out of me like Coyote's seed.

LATER THAT NIGHT I fished a smoke out of my glove box and sat on top of the dented salt-rusted cab of my truck. Coyote stood down by the lakeshore, aways off from the crowd, where the water came up in little foamy splashes and the willow trees whipped around like they were looking for someone to hold on to. Bobby Zhao was down there, too, his hands in his jean pockets, hip jutting out like a pouty lip, his hat on again and his face all in shadow. They were talking but I couldn't hear over everyone else hooting and laughing like a pack of owls. The moon came out as big as a beer keg; it made Coyote's face look lean and angelic, so young and victorious and humble enough to make you think the choice was yours all along. He took Bobby Zhao's hand and they just stood there in the light, their fingers moving together. The wind blew off that straw hat like it didn't like the thing much either, and Bobby let it lie. He was looking at Coyote, his hair all blue in the night, and Coyote kissed him as hard as hurting, and Bobby kissed him back like he'd been waiting for it since he was born. Coyote got his hands under his shirt and oh, Coyote is good at that, getting under, getting around, and the boys smiled whenever their lips parted.

I watched. I'm always watching. Who doesn't like to watch? It feels like being God, seeing everything happen far away, and you could stop it if you wanted, but then you couldn't watch anymore.

A storm started rumbling up across the meadows, spattering their kisses with autumn rain.

SUDDENLY EVERYONE CARED about who was going to make the Devil's Court this year. Even me. The mall was cleared out of formal sparkle-and-slit dresses by August, and somehow they just couldn't get any more in, like we were an island mysteriously sundered from the land of sequins and sweetheart necklines. Most of us were just going to have to go with one of our mom's prom dresses, though you can be damn sure we'd be ripping off that poofy shoulder chiffon and taking up the hems as far as we could. Jenny Kilroy (drama club, Young Businesswomen's Association) had done all the costumes for *The Music Man* in junior year, and for $50 she'd take that cherry cupcake dress and turn it into an apocalyptic punkslut wedding gown, but girlfriend worked *slow*. Whoever took the Homecoming crown had about a 60/40 chance of being up there in something they'd worn to their grandmother's funeral.

The smart money was on Sarah Jane for the win. She was already pregnant by then, and Jessica too, but I don't think even they knew it yet. Bellies still flat as a plains state, cotton candy lipstick as perfect as a Rembrandt. Nobody got morning sickness, nobody's feet swelled. Sarah Jane shone in the center of her ring of girls like a pink diamond in a nouveaux riche ring. 4.0, equestrian club, head cheerleader, softball pitcher, jazz choir lead soprano, played Juliet in both freshman and senior years, even joined the chess club. She didn't care about chess, but it looked good on her applications and she turned out to be terrifyingly good at it—first place at the spring speed chess invitational in Freemont, even seven months along. You couldn't even hate Sarah Jane. You could see her whole perfect life rolling on ahead of her like a yellow brick road but you knew she'd include you, if you wanted. If you stuck around this town like she meant to, and let her rule it like she aimed to.

Jessica and Ashley flanked her down every hall and every parade—a girl like Sarah Jane just naturally grows girls like Jessica and Ashley to be her adjutants, her bridesmaids, the baby's breath to make her rose look redder. All three of them knew the score and all three of them made sure nothing would ever change, like Macbeth's witches, if they wore daisy-print coats and their mothers' Chanel and tearproof mascara and only foretold their own love, continuing forever and the world moving aside to let it pass. So that was the obvious lineup—Queen Sarah Jane and her Viziers. Of course there were three slots, so I figured Jenny Kilroy would slide in on account of her charitable work to keep us all in the shimmer.

And then Friday morning arrived, the dawn before the dance and a week before the showdown game with Bobby Zhao and his Cowboys. Coyote howled up 7 am and we woke up and opened our closets and there they hung—a hundred perfect dresses. Whatever we might have chosen after hours of turning on the rack of the mall with nothing in our size or our color or modest enough for Daddy or bare enough for us, well, it was hanging in our closets with a corsage on the hip. Coyote took us all to Homecoming that year. And there in my room hung something that glittered and threw prisms on the wall, something the color of the ripest pumpkin you ever saw, something cut so low and slit so high it invited the world to love me best. I put it on and my head filled up with champagne like I'd already been sipping flutes for an hour, as if silk could make skin drunk. I slid the corsage on my wrist—cornflowers, and tiny green ears not yet open.

Coyote danced with all the girls and when the music sped up he threw back his head and howled and we all howled with him. When it slowed down he draped himself all over some lonesome thing who never thought she had a chance. The rest of us threw out our arms and danced with what our hands caught—Jessica spent half the night with mathletes kissing her neck and teaching her mnemonics. Everything was dizzy; everything spun. The music came from everywhere at once and the floor shook with our stomping. We were so strong that night, we were full of the year and and no one drank the punch because no one needed it, we just moved with Coyote and Coyote moved, too. I flung out my arms and spun away from David Horowitz (pep squad, 100-meter dash), my corn-bound hand finding a new body to carry me into the next song. Guitar strings plinked in some other, distant world beyond the gymnasium and I opened my eyes to see Sarah Jane in my arms, her dress a perfect, icy white spill of froth and jewels, her eyes made up black and severe, to contrast, her lips a generous rose-colored smile. She smelled like musk and honeysuckle. She smelled like Coyote. I danced with her and she put her head on my breast; I felt her waist in my grasp, the slight weight of her, the chess queen, the queen of horses and jazz and grade point averages and pyramids and backflips, Juliet twice, thrice, a hundred times over. She ran her hand idly up and down my back just as if I were a boy. My vision blurred and the Christmas lights hanging everywhere swam into a soup of Devil red and Devil gold. The queen of the softball team lifted her sunny blonde head and kissed me. Her mouth tasted like cherry gum and whiskey. She put her hands in my hair to show me she meant it, and I pulled her in tight—but the song ended and she pulled away, looking surprised and confused, her lipstick dulled, her bright brown eyes wounded, like a deer with sudden shot in her side. She ran to Jessica and Ashley and the three of them to Coyote, hands over their stomachs as though something fluttered there, something as yet unknown and unnamed.

The principal got up to call out the Devil's Court. My man was shaken by all the heavy grinding and spinning and howling that had become the senior class, but he got out his index cards all the same. He adjusted his striped tie and tapped the mic, just like every principal has ever done. And he said a name. And it was mine. A roar picked up around me and hands were shoving me forward and I didn't understand, it was Sarah Jane, it would always be Sarah Jane. But I stood there while Mr. Whitmore, the football coach, put a crown on my head, and I looked out into the throng. Coyote stood there in his tuxedo, the bowtie all undone like a brief black river around his neck, and he winked at me with his flashing hound-eye, and the principal called three more names and they were Jessica and Ashley and Sarah Jane. They stood around me like three fates and Mr. Whitmore put little spangly tiaras on their heads and they looked at me like I had caught a pass in the endzone, Hail Mary and three seconds left on the clock. I stared back and their tiaras were suddenly rings of wheat and appleblossoms and big, heavy oranges like suns, and I could see in their eyes mine wasn't rhinestones any more than it was ice cream. I lifted it down off my head and held it out like a thing alive: a crown of corn, not the Iowa yellow stuff but blue and black, primal corn from before the sun thought fit to rise, with tufts of silver fur sprouting from their tips, and all knotted together with crow feathers and marigolds.

And then it was pink rhinestones in my hands again, and blue zirconium on my Princesses' heads, and the Devil's Court took its place, and if you have to ask who was King, you haven't been listening.

After that, the game skipped by like a movie of itself. Bobby just couldn't keep that ball in his hands. You could see it on his face, how the ball had betrayed him, gone over to a bad boy with a leather jacket and no truck at all. You could see him re-sorting colleges in his head. It just about broke your heart. But we won 24-7, and Coyote led Bobby Zhao off the field with a *sorry-buddy* and a *one-game-don't-mean-a-thing*, and before I drove off to the afterparty I saw them under the bleachers, foreheads pressed together, each clutching at the other's skin like they wanted to climb inside, and they were beautiful like that, down there underneath the world, their helmets lying at their feet like old crowns.

NOTHING COULD STOP us then. The Westbrook Ravens, the Bella Vista Possums, the Ashland Gators. Line them up and watch them fall. It wasn't even a question.

 I suppose we learned trig, or Melville, or earth science. I suppose we took exams. I suppose we had parents, too, but I'll be damned if any of that seemed to make the tiniest impression on any one of us that year. We lived in an unbreakable bubble where nothing mattered. We lived in a snowglobe, only the sun was always shining and we were always winning and yeah, you could get grounded for faceplanting your biology midterm or pulled over for speeding or worse for snorting whatever green fairy dust Coyote found for you, but nothing really *happened*. You came down to the lake like always the next night. After the Ravens game, Greg Knight (running back #46) and Johnny Thompson (cornerback #22) crashed their cars into each other after drinking half a sip of something Coyote whipped up in an acorn cap, yelling chicken out the window the whole time like it was 1950 and some girl would be waving her handkerchief at the finish line. But instead there was a squeal of engine humping up on engine and the dead crunch of the front ends smacking together and the long blare of Greg's face leaning on his horn.

 But even then, they just got up and walked away, arm in arm and Coyote suddenly between them, *oh-my-god*ding and *let's-do-that-again*ing. The next day their Camrys pulled up to the parking lot like it was no big deal. Nothing could touch us.

 All eyes were on the Thunderbirds.

Now, the Thunderbirds didn't have a Bobby Zhao. No star player to come back and play celebrity alumnus in ten years with a Super Bowl ring on his finger. A Thunderbirds was part of a machine, a part that could be swapped out for a hot new freshman no problem, no resentment. They moved as one, thought as one, they were a flock, always pointed in the same direction. That was how they'd won six state championships; that was how they'd sent three quarterbacks to the NFL in the last decade. There was no one to hate—just a single massive Thunderbird darkening our little sky.

Coyote's girls began to show by Christmas.

Sarah Jane, whatever the crown might have said at Homecoming, was queen of the unwed mothers, too. Her belly swelled just slightly bigger than the others—but then none of them got very big. None of them slowed down. Sarah Jane was turning a flip-into somersault off the pyramid in her sixth month with no trouble. They would all lay around the sidelines together painting their stomachs (Devil red and Devil gold) and trying on names for size. No point in getting angry; no point in fighting for position. The tribe was the tribe and the tribe was all of us and a tribe has to look after its young. The defensive line had a whole rotating system for bringing them chocolate milk in the middle of the night.

They were strong and tan and lean and I had even money on them all giving birth to puppies.

I didn't get pregnant. But then, I wouldn't. I told him, and he listened. Rabbit and Coyote, they do each other favors, when they can.

A PLAN HATCHED itself: steal their mascot. An old-fashioned sort of thing, like playing chicken with cars. Coyote plays it old school. Into Springfield High in the middle of the night, out with Marmalade, a stuffed, moth-eaten African Grey parrot from some old biology teacher's collection that a bright soul had long ago decided could stand in for a Thunderbird.

We drove out to Springfield, two hours and change, me and Coyote and Jimmy Moser and Mike Halloran and Josh Vick and Sarah Jane and Jessica and Ashley, all crammed into my truck, front and back. Coyote put something with a beat on the radio and slugged back some off-brand crap that probably turned to Scotland's peaty finest when it hit his tongue. Jimmy was trying to talk Ashley into making out with him in the back while the night wind whipped through their hair and fireflies flashed by, even though it was January. Ashley didn't mind too much, even less when everyone wanted to touch her stomach and feel the baby move. She blushed like a primrose and even her belly button went pink.

Nobody's very quiet when sneaking into a gym. Your feet squeak on the basketball court and everyone giggles like a joke got told even when none did and we had Coyote's hissing *drink up drink up* and squeezing my hand like he can't hold the excitement in. We saw Marmalade center court on a parade float, all ready to ship over to the big designated-netural-ground stadium for halftime. Big yellow and white crepe flowers drooped everywhere, around the shore of a bright blue construction paper sea. Marmalade's green wings spread out majestically, and in his talons he held a huge orange papier-mâché ball ringed with aluminum foil rays dipped in gold glitter. Thunderbird made this world, and Thunderbird gets to rule it.

Coyote got this look on his face and the moment I saw it I knew I wouldn't let him get there first. I took off running, my sneakers screeching, everyone hollering *Bunny!* after me and Coyote scrappling up behind me, closing the distance, racing to the sun. *I'm faster, I'm always faster. Sometimes he gets it and sometimes I get it but it's nothing we haven't done before and this time it's mine.*

And I leapt onto the float without disturbing the paper sea and reached up, straining, and finally just going for it. I'm a tall girl, see how high I jump. The sun came down in my arms, still warm from the gym lights and the after-hours HVAC. The Thunderbird came with it, all red cheeks and Crayola green wingspan and I looked down to see Coyote grinning up at me. He'd let me take it, if I wanted it. He'd let me wear it like a crown. But after a second of enjoying its weight, the deliciousness of its theft, I passed it down to him. It was his year. He'd earned it.

We drove home through the January stars with the sun in the bed of my truck and three pregnant girls touching it with one hand each, holding it down, holding it still, holding it together.

On game day we stabbed it with the Devil's pitchfork and paraded our float around the stadium like conquering heroes. Like cowboys. Marmalade looked vaguely sad. By then Coyote was cleaning off blood in the locker room, getting ready for the second half, shaken, no girls around him and no steroid needles blossoming up from his friendly palm like a bouquet of peonies.

The first half of the championship game hit us like a boulder falling from the sky. The Thunderbirds didn't play for flash, but for short, sharp gains and an inexorable progression toward the endzone. They didn't cheer when they scored. They nodded to their coach and regrouped. They caught the flawless, seraphic passes Coyote fired off; they engulfed him when he tried to run as he'd always done. Our stands started out raucous and screaming and jumping up and down, cheering on our visibly pregnant cheerleading squad despite horrified protests from the Springfield side. *Don't you listen, Sarah Jane baby!* yelled Mr. Bollard. *You look perfect!* And she did, fists in the air, ponytail swinging.

Halftime stood 14-7 Thunderbirds.

I slipped into the locker room—by that time the place had become Devil central, girls and boys and players and cheerleaders and second chair marching band kids who weren't needed til post-game all piled in together. Some of them giving pep talks which I did not listen to, some of them bandaging knees, some of them—well. Doing what always needs doing when Coyote's around. Rome never saw a party like a Devil locker room.

I walked right over to my boy and the blood vanished from his face just as soon as he saw me.

"Don't you try to look pretty for me," I said.

"Aw, Bunny, but you always look so nice for me."

I sat in his lap. He tucked his fingers between my thighs—where I clamped them, safe and still. "What's going on out there?"

Coyote drank his water down. "Don't you worry, Bunny Rabbit. It has to go like this, or they won't feel like they really won. Ain't no good game since the first game that didn't look lost at halftime. It's how the story goes. Can't hold a game without it. The old fire just won't come. If I just let that old Bird lose like it has to, well, everyone would get happy after, but they'd think it was predestined all along, no work went into it. You gotta make the story for them, so that when the game is done they'll just…" Coyote smiled and his teeth gleamed. "Well, they'll lose their minds I won it so good."

Coyote kissed me and bit my lip with those gleaming teeth. Blood came up and in our mouths it turned to fire. We drank it down and he ran out on that field, Devil red and Devil gold, and he ran like if he kept running he could escape the last thousand years. He ran like the field was his country. He ran like his bride was on the other end of all that grass and I guess she was. I guess we all were. Coyote gave the cherry to Justin Oster, who caught this pass that looked for all the world like the ball might have made it all the way to the Pacific if nobody stood in its way. But Justin did, and he caught it tight and perfect and the stadium shook with Devil pride.

34-14. Rings all around, as if they'd all married the state herself.

THAT NIGHT, WE had a big bonfire down by the lake. Neutral ground was barely forty-five minutes out of town, and no one got home tired and ready to sleep a good night and rise to a work ethic in the morning.

I remember we used to say *down-by-the-lake* like it was a city, like it was an address. I guess it was, the way all those cars would gather like crows, pickups and Camaros and Jeeps, noses pointing in, a metal wall against the world. The willows snapped their green whips at the moon and the flames licked up Devil red and Devil gold. We built the night without thinking about it, without telling anyone it was going to happen, without making plans. Everyone knew to be there; no one was late.

Get any group of high school kids together and you pretty much have the building blocks of civilization. The Eagle Scout boys made an architecturally perfect bonfire. 4-H-ers threw in grub, chips and burgers and dogs and Twix and Starburst. The drama kids came bearing tunes, their tooth-white iPods stuffed into speaker cradles like black mouths. The rich kids brought booze from a dozen walnut cabinets— and Coyote taught them how to spot the good stuff. Meat and fire and music and liquor—that's all it's ever been. Sarah Jane started dancing up to the flames with a bottle of hundred-year-old cognac in her hand, holding by the neck, moving her hips, her gorgeously round belly, her long corn-colored hair brushing faces as she spun by, the smell of her expensive and hot. Jessica and Ashley ran up to her and the three of them swayed and sang and stamped, their arms slung low around each other, their heads pressed together like three graces. Sarah Jane poured her daddy's cognac over Ashley's breasts and caught the golden stuff spilling off in her sparkly pink mouth and Ashley laughed so high and sweet and that was *it*—everyone started dancing and howling and jumping and Coyote was there in the middle of it all, arching his back and keeping the beat, slapping his big thighs, throwing the game ball from boy to girl to boy to girl, like it was magic, like it was just ours, the sun of our world arcing from hand to hand to hand.

I caught it and Coyote kissed me. I threw it to Haley Collins from English class and Nick Dristol (left tackle #19) caught me up in his arms. I don't even know what song was playing. The night was so loud in my ears. I could see it happening and it scared me but I couldn't stop it and didn't want to. Everything was falling apart and coming together and we'd won the game, Bunny no less than Coyote, and boyfriend never fooled me for a minute, never could.

I could hear Sarah Jane laughing and I saw Jessica kissing her and Greg Knight both, one to the other like she was counting the kisses to make it all fair. She tipped up that caramel-colored bottle and Nick started to say something but I shushed him. *Coyote's cognac's never gonna hurt that baby.* Every tailgate hung open, no bottle ever seemed to empty and even though it was January the air was so warm, the crisp red and yellow leaves drifting over us all, no one sorry, no one ashamed, no one chess club or physics club or cheer squad or baseball team, just tangled up together inside our barricade of cars.

Sarah danced up to me and took a swallow without taking her eyes from mine. She grabbed me roughly by the neck and into a kiss, passing the cognac to me and oh, it tasted like a pass thrown all the way to the sea, and she wrapped me up in her arms like she was trying to make up Homecoming to me, to say: *I'm better now, I'm braver now, doesn't this feel like the end of everything and we have to get it while we can?* I could feel her stomach pressing on mine, big and insistent and hard, and as she ripped my shirt open I felt her child move inside her. We broke and her breasts shone naked in the bonfire-light—mine too, I suppose. Between us a cornstalk grew fast and sure, shooting up out of the ground like it had an appointment with the sky, then a second and a third. That same old blue corn, midnight corn, first corn. All around the fire the earth was bellowing out pumpkins and blackberries and state fair tomatoes and big blousy squash flowers, wheat and watermelons and apple trees already broken with the weight of fruit. The dead winter trees exploded into green, the graduating class fell into the rows of vegetables and fruit and thrashed together like wolves, like bears, like devils. Fireflies turned the air into an emerald necklace and Sarah Jane grabbed Coyote's hand which was a paw which was a hand and screamed. Didn't matter—everyone was screaming, and the music quivered the darkness and Sarah's baby beat at the drum of her belly, demanding to be let out into the pumpkins and the blue, blue corn, demanding to meets its daddy.

All the girls screamed. Even the ones only a month or two gone, clutching their stomachs and crying, all of them except me, Bunny Rabbit, the watcher, the queen of coming home. The melons split open in an eruption of pale green and pink pulp; the squashes cracked so loud I put my hands (which were paws which were hands) over my ears, and the babies came like harvest, like forty-five souls running after a bright ball in the sky.

SOME OF US, after a long night of vodka tonics and retro music and pretending there was anything else to talk about, huddle together around a table at the ten-year and get into it. How Mr. Bollard was never the same and ended up hanging himself in a hotel room after almost decade of straight losses. How they all dragged themselves home and suddenly had parents again, the furious kind, and failed SATs and livers like punching bags. How no one went down to the lake anymore and Bobby Zhao went to college out of state and isn't he on some team out east now? Yeah. Yeah. But his father lost the restaurants and now the southland has no king. But the gym ceiling caved in after the rains and killed a kid. But most of them could just never understand why their essays used to just be perfect and they never had hangovers and they looked amazing all the time and sex was so easy that year but never since, no matter how much shit went up their nose or how they cheated and fought and drank because they didn't mean it like they had back when, no how many people they brought home hoping just for a second it would be like it was then, when Coyote made their world. They had this feeling, just for a minute—didn't I feel it too? That everything could be different. And then it was the same forever, the corn stayed yellow and they stayed a bunch of white kids with scars where their cars crashed and fists struck and babies were born. The lake went dry and the scoreboard went dark.

Coyote leaves a hole when he goes. He danced on this town til it broke. That's the trick, and everyone falls for it.

But they all had kids, didn't they? Are they remembering that wrong? What happened to them all?

Memory is funny—only Sarah Jane (real estate, Rotary, Wednesday night book club) can really remember her baby. Everyone just remembers the corn and the feeling of running, running so fast, the whole pack of us, against the rural Devil gold sunset. I call that a kindness. (*Why me?* Sarah asks her gin. *You were the queen*, I say. *That was you. Only for a minute.*) It was good, wasn't it, they all want to say. When we were all together. When we were a country, and Coyote taught us how to grow such strange things.

Why did I stick around, they all want to know. When he took off, why didn't I go, too? Weren't we two of a kind? Weren't we always conspiring?

Coyote wins the big game, I say. I get the afterparty.

---

THIS IS WHAT I don't tell them.

I woke up before anyone the morning after the championships. Everyone had passed out where they stood, laying everywhere like a bomb had gone off. No corn, no pumpkins, no watermelons. Just that cold lake morning fog. I woke up because my pickup's engine fired off in the gloom, and I know that sound like my mama's crying. I jogged over to my car but it was already going, bouncing slowly down the dirt road with nobody driving. In the back, Coyote sat laughing, surrounded by kids, maybe eight or ten years old, all of them looking just like him, all of them in leather jackets and hangdog grins, their black hair blowing back in the breeze. Coyote looked at me and raised a hand. See you again. After all, it's nothing we haven't done before.

Coyote handed a football to one of his daughters. She lifted it into the air, her form perfect, trying out her new strength. She didn't throw it. She held it tight, like it was her heart.

# The Wolves of Brooklyn

IT WAS SNOWING WHEN THE wolves first came, loping down Flatbush Ave, lithe and fast, panting clouds, their paws landing with a soft, heavy sound like bombs falling somewhere far away. Everyone saw them. Everyone will tell you about it, even if they were in Pittsburgh that weekend. Even if they slept through it. Even if their mothers called up on Monday and asked what in the world was going on out there in that Babylon they chose to live in. No, the collective everyone looked out of their walk-up windows the moment they came and saw those long shapes, their fur frosted and tinkling, streaming up the sidewalks like a flood, like a wave, and the foam had teeth.

These days, we go to work. We come home. We put on dresses the color of steel and suits the color of winter. We go to cafes and drink lattes with whiskey and without sugar or bars where we drink whiskey without ice and without water. Bars aren't noisy anymore. It's a murmur, not a roar. They keep the music turned down so we can talk. So we can tell our wolf stories. Outside the windows, where the frost crackles the jambs, they stand and press their noses to the glass, fogging it with their breath.

Camille sits with her elbow crossing her knee, her dress glittering ice because they like it that way. They watch you, when you shine.

Her lavender hair catches the lamplight, expensive, swooping and glossy, rich punk girl's hair. She says:

"I was walking to the store for coffee. We always run out; I just never think of it until it's already gone. I thought I'd get some cookies, too. The kind with jam in the middle, that look like a red eye. I guess that doesn't matter. You know, I always fuck up jokes, too. Anyway, it was snowing, and I just wanted some coffee and cookies and then it was walking next to me. He was walking next to me. A big one, as big as a horse, and white, so white in the snow and the streetlight, his fur so thick your hands could disappear in it. All I could think of was the horse I used to love when I was a kid. Boreal. My mom used to drive me to the stables every morning and I'd brush him and say his name over and over, and the wolf was white like Boreal, and tall like him, and I started running because, well, shit, he's a wolf. Running toward the store, like I could still get coffee and cookies. He ran with me. So fast, and I had my red coat on and we were running together through the snow, his breath puffing out next to me, and I saw that his eye were gold. Not yellow, but gold. I was red and he was gold and we were running so fast together, as fast as Boreal and I used to run; faster. We ran past the store, into the park, and snow flew out under my feet like feathers. I stopped by that little footbridge—the wolf was gone and I had just kept on running out into the frozen grass."

The wolves never cross the bridges. Sometimes they run right up to them, and sniff the air like Brooklyn has a musk and it fades at the edges, like they accidentally came too close to the end of the world. They turn around and walk back into the borough with their tails down. They stop right at Queens, too. They won't cross the borders; they know their home. For awhile no one talked about anything else, and all our friends in Manhattan wanted to come and see them, photograph them, write about them. I mean, wouldn't you? But there were incidents—like any dog, they don't like strangers. This girl Marjorie Guste wanted to do a whole installation about them, with audio and everything. She brought a film crew and a couple of models to look beautiful next to them and she never got a shot. The wolves hid from her. They jumped onto the roofs of brownstones, dipped into alleys and crawled into sewer gratings. We could see where they'd gone sometimes, but when MG swung her lens around they'd be gone, leaping across the treetops in the snow.

Geoffrey, despite the name, is a girl. It's a joke left over from when she was a kid and hated being the four hundredth Jenny in her grade. She's got green sequins on, like a cigarette girl from some old movie theatre. I love how her chin points, like the bottom of a heart. We dated for awhile, when I was still going to school. We were too lazy, though. The way you just wake up sometimes and the house is a disaster but you can't remember how it really got that way, except that how it got that way is that you didn't do the dishes or pick up your clothes. Every day you made a choice not to do those things and it added up to not being able to get to the door over the coffee mugs and paperbacks piled up on the floor. But still, she was at my house the night the wolves came, because laziness goes both ways.

She says: "Most of the time, you know, I really like them. They're peaceful. Quiet. But the other week I was down on Vanderbilt and I saw one come up out of the street. Like, okay, the street cracked open—you know there's never any traffic anymore so it was just cold and quiet and the storm was still blowing, and the street came open like it had popped a seam. Two white paws came up, and then the whole wolf, kicking and scrabbling its hind legs against the road to get a grip on it. Just like a fat little puppy. It climbed out and then it bit the edge of the hole it had made and dragged the street back together. I looked around—you know how it is now. Not a soul on the sidewalk. No one else saw. The wolf looked at me and its tongue lolled out, red in the snow, really red, like it had just eaten. Then it trotted off. I went out and touched the place where it broke through. The road was hot, like an iron."

The wolves have eaten people. Why be coy about it? Not a lot of people. But it's happened. As near as anyone can figure, the first one they ate was a Russian girl named Yelena. They surrounded her and she stood very still, so as not to startle them. Finally, she said: "I'm lonely," because it's weird but you tell the wolves things, sometimes. You can't help it, all these old wounds come open and suddenly you're confessing to a wolf who never says anything back. She said: "I'm lonely," and they ate her in the street. They didn't leave any blood. They're fastidious like that. Since then I know of about four or five others, and well, that's just not enough to really scare people. Obviously, you'll be special, that they'll look at you with those huge eyes and you'll understand something about each other, about the tundra and blood and Brooklyn and winter, and they'll mark you but pass you by. For most of us that's just what happens. My friend Daniel got eaten, though. It's surprising how you can get used to that. I don't know what he said to them. To tell you the truth, I didn't know Daniel that well.

Seth's eyes have grown dark circles. He came wearing a threadbare 1950s chic suit: thin tie, grey lapels, wolf pack boy with a rat pack look. The truth is I've known Seth since seventh grade, but we never talk about it. We lived on the same sunny broad Spielbergian cul-de-sac, we conquered the old baseball diamond where we, the weird bookish kids, kept taking big steps backward until we were far too outfield to ever have to catch a ball. We'd talk about poetry instead: Browning (Elizabeth only), Whitman, Plath. We came back east hoping to be, what? A writer and a dancer, I guess is the official line. We run with the same crowd, the crowd that has an official line, but we're not really friends anymore. We used to conjugate French verbs and ride our bikes home through the rain.

He says: "I came out to go to the restaurant one morning and one was standing in my hallway. He still had snow on his ears; he took up the whole stairwell. He just stood there, looking at me, the snow melting into his fur and the light that never gets fixed flickering and popping. His eyes were dark, really dark, almost black, but I think they might actually have been purple, if I could have gotten close enough. He just stared, and I stared, and I sat down on my doorstep eventually. We watched each other until my shift would have ended. I reached out to touch him; I don't know why I thought I could, I just liked how black his nose was, how white and deep his fur looked. He made me think of…" And Seth looks at me as though I am a pin in his memory and he wants to pull me out, so that the next part can be his alone, so that I can retroactively never have pulled down willow branches for a crown, "…of this one place I used to go when I was a kid, in the woods by my school, and I'd make little acorn pyramids or mulberry rings on the ground before first period, and they were always gone when I got back, like someone had taken them, like they were gifts. The wolf looked like the kind of thing that might have seen a bunch of sticks and moss and taken them as tribute. But he didn't let me touch him, he howled instead—have you heard one howl yet? It's like a freight train. The lightbulb shattered. I went inside like that was my shift, sitting with a wolf all day not saying anything. The next morning he'd gone off."

Seth was my first kiss. I never think about that anymore.

I know this guy named David—he never comes out to the cafe, but I see him sometimes, sitting on a bench, his long thin hair in a ponytail, punching a netbook with a little plastic snow-cover over it. The snow never stops anymore. You do your best. He's trying to track them, to see if they have patterns, migration or hunting or mating patterns, something that can be charted. Like a subway map. A wolf map. He thinks he's getting close—there's a structure, he says. A repetition. He can almost see it. More data, he always needs more data.

Ruben always looks sharper than the rest of us. Three-piece, bow tie, pocket watch and chain, hair like a sculpture of some kind of exotic bird. Somehow his hair doesn't really look affected, though. He looks like he was born that way, like he was raised by a very serious family of tropical cranes. He wasn't, though. He's a fourth generation why-can't-you-marry-a-nice-Jewish-girl Brooklynite. He belongs here more than any of us.

He says: "I keep wondering why. I mean, don't any of you wonder why? Why us, why them, why here? I feel like no one even asks that question, when to me it seems such an obvious thing. I asked my uncle and he said: *son, sometimes you have to just let the world be itself.* I asked my mom and she said: *Ruben, sometimes I think everything is broken and that's its natural state.* And, well, I think that's bullshit. Like, okay, it's either zoological or metaphysical. Either they are real wolves and they migrated here, or they didn't, and they aren't."

Camille interrupts him. She puts her hand on his knee. She says: "Does it matter? Does it *really* matter?"

He glares at her. You aren't supposed to interrupt. That's the ritual. It's the unspoken law. "Of course it matters. Don't you ever wake up and hope they'll be gone? Don't you ever drink your coffee and look out your window and eat your fucking cruller and think for just a moment there won't be a wolf on your doorstep, watching you, waiting for you to come out? They could leave someday. Any day." But we all know they won't. We can't say how we know. It's the same way we know that Coca-Cola will keep making Coke. It's a fact of the world. Ruben is really upset—he's breaking another rule but none of us say anything. We don't come here to get upset. It doesn't accomplish anything. "I asked one of them once. She'd followed me home from the F train—what I mean is she'd been all the way down on the platform, and when I got off she trotted up after me and followed me, me, specifically. And I turned around in the snow, the fucking snow that never ends and I yelled: *why? Why are you here? What are you doing? What do you want?* I guess that sounds dumb, like a scene in a movie if this were happening in a movie and DiCaprio or whoever was having his big cathartic moment. But I wanted to know so badly. And she—I noticed it was a she. A bitch. She bent her head. God, they are so tall. So tall. Like statues. She bent her head and she licked my cheek. Like I was a baby. She did it just exactly like I was her puppy. Tender, kind. She pressed her forehead against mine and shut her eyes and then she ran off. Like it hadn't even happened."

There's going to be a movie. We heard about it a couple of months ago. Not DiCaprio, though. Some other actor no one's heard of. They expect it to be his big breakthrough. And the love interest has red hair, I remember that. It seems so far away; really, it has nothing to do with us. It's not like they'll film on location: CGI, all the way. Some of the locals are pissed about it—it's exploiting our situation, it'll just bring stupid kids out here wanting to be part of it, part of something, anything, and they'll be wolf food. But shit, you kind of have to make a movie about this, don't you? I would, if I didn't live here. Nothing's real until there's a movie about it.

Of course people want to be a part of it. They want to touch it, just for a second. They come in from the West Coast, from Ohio, from England, from Japan, from anywhere, just to say they saw one. Just to reach out their hand and be counted, be a witness, to have been there when the wolves came. But of course they weren't there, and the wolves are ours. They belong to us. We're the ones they eat, after all. And despite all the posturing and feather-display about who's been closest, deepest, longest, we want to be part of it, too. We're like kids running up to the edge of the old lady's house on the edge of town, telling each other she's a witch, daring Ruben or Seth or Geoff to go just a little closer, just a little further, to throw a rock at her window or knock on the door. Except there really is a witch in there, and we all know it's not a game.

Anyway, the outsiders stopped showing up so much after Yelena. It's less fun, now.

But it's the biggest thing that will ever happen to us. It's a gravitational object you can't get around or through, you only fall deeper in. And the thing is we want to get deeper in. Closer, further, knocking on the door. That's why we dress this way; that's why we tell our stories while the wolves watch us outside the cafe window, our audience and our play all at once.

"Anna," Seth says to me, and I warm automatically at the sound of his voice, straightening my shoulders and turning toward him like

I always did, like I did in California when I didn't know what snow looked like yet, and I thought I loved him because I'd never kissed anyone else. "You never say anything. It's your turn. It's been your turn for months."

I am wearing red. I always wear red. Tiny gold coins on tinier gold ropes ring my waist in criss-crossed patterns, like a Greek goddess of come-hither, and my shoes have those ballet straps that wind all the way up my calves. My hair is down and it is black. They like it, when my hair is down. They follow me with their eyes. I've never said so to Ruben but they are always there when I get off the train, always panting a little on the dark platform, always bright-eyed, covered in melting snowflakes.

I say: "I like listening. They do, too, you know. Sometimes I think that's all they do: listen. Well. After Daniel—I knew him, I'm not sure if I've ever told you guys that. From that summer when I interned downtown. After Daniel I started feeling very strange, like something was stuck in me. It's not that I wanted revenge or anything. I didn't know him that well and I just don't think like that. I don't think in patterns—if this, then that. The point is, I started following one of them. A male, and I knew him because his nose was almost totally white, like he'd lost the black of it along the way. I started following him, all over the place, wherever he went, which wasn't really very far from my apartment. It's like they have territories. Maybe I was his territory. Maybe he was mine—because at some point I started taking my old archery stuff with me. My sister and I had both taken lessons as kids, but she stuck with it and I didn't. Seth—well, Seth probably remembers. There was awhile there when I went to school with a backpack over one shoulder and a bow over the other. Little Artemis of Central California. I started doing that again. It didn't seem to bother the wolf. He'd run down 7$^{th}$ Ave. like he had an appointment and I'd run after him. And one day, while he was waiting for the light to change, I dropped to one knee, nocked an arrow, and shot him. I didn't mean to do it. I didn't set out to. It doesn't seem to have happened in a linear way when I think about it. I mean, yes, I followed him, but I wasn't *hunting* him. Except I guess I was. Because I'd packed a big kitchen knife and I don't even remember doing that. You know there's never any traffic down there anymore, so I just gutted him right there on the median, and his blood steamed in the snowfall, and I guess I brought a cooler, too, because I packed all the meat away that I could, and some organs. It took a long time. I skinned him, too. It's really hard work, rendering an animal. But there's an instinct to it. Everyone used to know how to do this. I took it all home and I separated everything out and started curing it, salting it, smoking it." I twist a big orange glass ring on my finger and don't look at anyone. "I have wolf sausages, wolf cutlets, wolf bacon, wolf roasts, wolf loin, even wolf soup in plastic containers in my fridge. I eat it every day. It tastes…" I don't want to talk about how it tastes. It tastes perfect. It tastes new. "They all know me now, I'm pretty sure. Once, a younger one, skinny, with a black tip on her tail, saw me by the co-op and crawled toward me on her belly, whining. I watched her do it, bowing her head, not looking me in the eye. I reached out my hand and petted her. Her fur felt so rough and thick. We were…exchanging dominance. I've had dogs before. I know how that works. And I started wearing red."

I tell them they can come by. There's plenty of meat to share. It never seems to run out, in fact. They won't—most of them. They don't look at me the same way after that. In a week or so Seth will show up at my door. He'll just appear, in a white coat with fur on the hood, full of melting snowflakes. And I'll pour the soup into steel bowls and we'll sit together, with our knees touching.

This is what Brooklyn is like now. It's empty. A few of us stayed, two hundred people in Williamsburg, a hundred in Park Slope, maybe fifty in Brooklyn Heights. Less towards the bay, but you still find people sometimes, in clusters, in pairs. You can just walk down the middle of any street and it's so silent you forget how to talk. Everyone moved away or just disappeared. Some we know were eaten, some—well, people are hard to keep track of. You have to let go of that kind of thinking—no one is permanent. The Hasidim were the last big group to go. They called the wolves *qliphoth*—empty, impure shells, left over from the creation of the world. A wolf swallowed a little boy named Ezra whole. He played the piano.

It snows forever. The wolves own this town. They're talking about shutting off subway service, and the bridges, too. Just closing up shop. I guess I understand that. I'm not angry about it. I just hope the lights stay on. We still get wifi, but I wonder how long that can really last.

We go to the cafe every night, shining in our sequins and suits, and it feels like the old days. It feels like church. We go into Manhattan less and less. All those rooftop chickens and beehives and knitters and alleyway gardeners comprise the post-wolf economy. We trade, we huddle, nobody locks the doors anymore. Seth brings eggs for breakfast most mornings, from his bantams, those he has left. Down on Court Street, there's a general sort of market that turns into dancing and old guitars and drums at night, an accordion yawns out the dusk and there's a girl with silk ribbons who turns and turns, like she can't stop. The wolves come to watch and they wait in a circle for us to finish, and sometimes, sometimes they dance, too.

One has a torn ear. I've started following her when I can. I don't remember picking up my bow again, but it's there, all the same, hanging from me like a long, thin tail.

# Reading Borges in Buenos Aires

**B**UENOS AIRES (WHICH OTHERS CALL a novel) is seven hundred and forty pages long, with six pages of endnotes. From any of the streets one can see, interminably, the first and last chapters, repeating endlessly. The distribution of districts is invariable. Twenty-sided stars, falling on the flood-plain like slices of sky. Each district is a chapter, each boulevard a page, each alley a paragraph. To the left and right of each plaza are identical alcoves equipped with magnifying glasses and pitchers of water, where one may rest, and read in secret, even sleep if the act of ecstatic reading has drained one's faculties.

The novel begins: *When a city is born, a demon is summoned.* It ends: *And the children of the city remembered, suddenly, the names of all their sins.*

All cities are novels, but Buenos Aires is special. It was first published in 1580, in a beautiful folio edition with illustrations in walnut gall. Time, always insensitive to the desires of bibliophiles, has destroyed all first edition copies. Naturally, transcription errors have occurred in subsequent printings. Page three hundred and fourteen now reads: *during the plague years the rag man loved our mother with ruinous kisses.* It once read: *Corrientes Avenue.*

In a cafe there is a girl with black hair reading Borges. Her dress is white. Her eyes are blue. The girl is a finite object, but the chair she sits on has always been here, and will remain long after she goes. The chair has iron legs and a red seat. The girl is twenty-seven years old, reading Borges in Buenos Aires. Her heart is a secret door. She has ordered a cafe con leche. The waiter is named Jorge, but this is a coincidence. The girl is not a chapter, though the cafe is an epilogue. She is a motif, a repetition, a stutter in the city. She is a metaphor for something else. She is thirty-six years old, reading Borges in Buenos Aires.

Buenos Aires once fell in love with a woman. Borges once fell in love, too, but Buenos Aires would not permit it. It gave him liver cancer, rather than lose him. The love of Buenos Aires is like a blue tiger wandering through the alleyways. It remembers nothing. It has teeth. The woman read the whole of the seven hundred and forty pages of the city. The endnotes made her weep; she killed herself with pills in a bathtub that was also a short chapter on the problem of cosmic envy. No one else has tried to read the whole of Buenos Aires. The woman left her blood on every page. It has turned brown now. Age turns everything brown.

The girl in the cafe has lost her lover. He had never read Borges. He met a medievalist with a haircut like Louise Brooks and small breasts. The girl drinks her cafe con leche. She orders *alfajores* with raspberries, but does not eat them. Her grief is a labyrinth. She is forty-three years old and reading Borges in Buenos Aires. The girl in the cafe is wearing a topaz ring and does not know that Buenos Aires is a novel. Her mother died when she was seven. When she was a child, she once put on her mother's fur coat and declared herself the Queen of the Bears. Some part of her has never taken off the coat. The girl is a sphere whose exact center is Buenos Aires. Her fingernails are red, and she wishes she were a virgin again. The waiter, Jorge, whose father's name is Luis, though this is also a coincidence, wants to touch her hair. He brings the freshest coffee to the Queen of the Bears, but this is the extent of his worship. He is seventeen years old, and will read Borges when he is thirty.

## Reading Borges in Buenos Aires

There is no first person singular in Buenos Aires. The novel is written in first person plural. We. Us. Ours. It is experimental, pre-modern. It is printed in Garamond, its typography simple and certain. Once a priest stood in three alcoves at morning, noon, and evening, copying three chapters into his personal diary. He returned to Seville with these chapters, and they are slowly growing there, the way an embryo grows. In a few hundred years Seville will begin: *When a city is born, a demon is summoned.* This is the natural life cycle of novels. They are all cannibals at heart. Borges copied out more chapters than anyone. He stood in almost all the alcoves, held almost all the magnifying glasses, and cried out for the agony of each paragraph. When he was deported, he suffered for the pieces of Buenos Aires he had taken. When he returned, his suffering eased. He died in Geneva, each copied page a mutating cell.

The girl in the cafe was born under the sign of the crab. When she dreams, she dreams of blue tigers drinking from rivers of milk tea. She is seven years old, reading Borges in Buenos Aires. Once when she thought her lover would never leave her, she learned to play the guitar. Now that he is gone she cannot even bear to hear one strummed. It sounds like knives. The waiter, Jorge, has written one hundred and one short stories, though this is a coincidence. He brings her blood sausage, though she did not order it. He wants to feed her. To make her full and happy. The girl at the cafe does not know she is hungry. The Queen of the Bears is an insomniac. Her nights are mirrors of each other, without rest, reflecting the same open eyes. She is distantly related to Lucrezia Borgia, though she does not know it. She is nineteen years old, reading Borges in Buenos Aires.

Buenos Aires was written by Jorge Luis Borges in 1580. It was his only novel. After he finished it he never wrote another word, not even a grocery list. The first page of Buenos Aires was intentionally left blank. Children have scribbled on it since. One wrote: *I wish I had a hundred balloons.* One wrote: *The proletariat must rise up to crush the jackals of industry.* These errata are unsightly, but it was not

Borges' policy to revise. His process was cyclical. in 1580 he wrote seven hundred and forty pages with six pages of endnotes. He then lived out an interesting life as a streetlamp in the Cabalito district, and in 1941 began publishing his copied chapters, plagiarizing from his own juvenilia. This is by far the most efficient method of novel writing yet devised.

    The girl in the cafe is crying. She puts on her sunglasses. Her lipstick is dark red. She is a lost child. She is the demon summoned by the birth of a city. She is an engineering student. She is a secretary. The Queen of the Bears is worried about her health. She came from the same dimension as the apocryphal encyclopedia in the story she is reading right now. She came from California, where she is not considered beautiful. She was born here. She hated him even before he met the medievalist. She thought he would love her until she was old. She is twenty-three years old, reading Borges in Buenos Aires. She is repeated over and over, worked at, revised, within the chapters of the city. Girls with black hair, over and over, sitting at cafes, drinking cafe con leche, eating *alfajores*, hands shaking as they light identical cigarettes with identical ivory lighters. They are fifteen, thirty-nine, sixty-two, ninety-one, twelve, twenty-six, reading Borges in Buenos Aires.

    There has been some discussion as to the genre of Buenos Aires. The existence of demons, fascism, tangoes, the resurrected dead and repeatedly burnt *mate* leads one to suspect a speculative bent to the narrative. However, it is hard to call Córdoba Avenue science fiction. The sidewalks are so realistic, the sunlight so honest. The smell of eggs frying in cafes cannot be doubted, cannot be said to predict any discomfiting future, or look back onto any gold-tinted past. The past, after all, is only a series of prior editions, each more full of mistakes, each less complete than the current version, which is in turn less fulsome and perfect than subsequent editions will be.

    Once, a previous edition tried to creep out from under the sewer grating on the corner of Godoy Cruz Street. It was a red stone, out of place, incorrect. It sat there for a whole day, so incorrect that there was no solution but to ignore it, to pretend the street read as it should. That was the day the lover of the girl with black hair left her.

She is still sitting in the cafe. The sun has gone down. The waiter's shift is over, but he lingers, hoping she will ask him for something, for a check, for more coffee, for candied licorice, so that he can talk to her. Ask her name. Is it Julia? Is it Lila? He cannot imagine. She is fourteen years old, reading Borges in Buenos Aires. She believes in infinitude. The Queen of the Bears looks out from her cafe, the red sky reflected in her sunglasses. She lights a cigarette. In every cafe on that street, there are girls with black hair whose lovers have left them, eating *alfajores* with raspberries, but none of them are the Queen of the Bears. That is how a novel is written. With a thousand girls with black hair, only one of whom is the Queen of the Bears. Buenos Aires only likes her when she wears the fur coat.

The end of the novel is in a packing warehouse near the river. It is a cliffhanger. It has hope of sequels, of continuity. Fish are wrapped in the end of the novel. They are packed in ice, their eyes open. The fish each have one stroke of a letter under their first gill. When they were alive, they swam the end of the novel. They will be shipped to other cities, everywhere. They will be eaten by women with emerald earrings, men with mustaches. They will eat the end of the novel. They will eat the girls with black hair, all of them. Buenos Aires will become part of their hexagonal cells. Their hearts will keep reading the end of the novel, again and again, until they die, and then the earth will read it. When Borges died, the earth read him, over and over, like a child with her favorite story. *Read it again, Mother, read it again. I don't want to go to sleep.*

The Queen of the Bears is one day old, reading Borges in Buenos Aires. She looks up at the waiter, whose name is not a coincidence, and takes off her glasses.

# The Days of Flaming Motorcycles

TO TELL YOU THE TRUTH, my father wasn't really that much different after he became a zombie.

My mother just wandered off. I think she always wanted to do that, anyway. Just set off walking down the road and never look back. Just like my father always wanted to stop washing his hair and hunker down in the basement and snarl at everyone he met. He chased me and hollered and hit me before. Once, when I stayed out with some boy whose name I can't even remember, he even bit me. He slapped me and for once I slapped him back, and we did this standing-wrestling thing, trying to hold each other back. Finally, in frustration, he bit me, hard, on the side of my hand. I didn't know what to do—we just stared at each other, breathing heavily, knowing something really absurd or horrible had just happened, and if we laughed it could be absurd and if we didn't we'd never get over it. I laughed. But I knew the look in his eye that meant he was coming for me, that glowering, black look, and now it's the only look he's got.

It's been a year now, and that's about all I can tell you about the apocalypse. There was no flash of gold in the sky, no chasms opened up in the earth, no pale riders with silver scythes. People just started acting the way they'd always wanted to but hadn't because they were more afraid of the police or their boss or losing out on the prime mating opportunities offered by the greater Augusta area. Everyone stopped being afraid. Of anything. And sometimes that means eating each other.

But sometimes it doesn't. They don't always do that, you know. Sometimes they just stand there and watch you, shoulders slumped, blood dripping off their noses, their eyes all unfocused. And then they howl. But not like a wolf. Like something broken and small. Like they're sad.

Now, zombies aren't supposed to get sad. Everyone knows that. I've had a lot of time to think since working down at the Java Shack on Front Street became seriously pointless. I still go to the shop in the morning, though. If you don't have habits, you don't have anything. I turn over the sign, I boot up the register—I even made the muffins for a while, until the flour ran out. Carrot-macadamia on Mondays, mascarpone-mango on Tuesdays, blueberry with a dusting of marzipan on Wednesdays. So on. So forth. Used to be I'd have a line of senators out the door by 8:00 a.m. I brought the last of the muffins home to my dad. He turned one over and over in his bloody, swollen hands until it came apart, then he made that awful howling-crying sound and licked the crumbs off his fingers. And he starting saying my name over and over, only muddled, because his tongue had gone all puffy and purple in his mouth. Caitlin, Caitlin, Caitlin.

So now I drink the pot of coffee by myself and I write down everything I can think of in a kid's notebook with a flaming motorcycle on the cover. I have a bunch like it. I cleaned out all the stores. In a few months I'll move on to the punky princess covers, and then the Looney Tunes ones. I mark time that way. I don't even think of seasons. These are the days of Flaming Motorcycles. Those were the days of Football Ogres. So on. So forth.

They don't bother me, mostly. And okay, the pot of coffee is just hot water now. No arabica for months. But at least the power's still on. But what I was saying is that I've had a lot of time to think, about them, about me, about the virus—because of course it must have been a virus, right? Which isn't really any better than saying fairies or angels did it. Didn't monks used to argue about how many angels could fit on the head of a pin? I seem to think I remember that, in some book, somewhere. So angels are tiny, like viruses. Invisible, too, or you wouldn't have to argue about it, you'd just count the bastards up. So they said virus, I said it doesn't matter, my dad just bit his own finger off. And he howls like he's so sad he wants to die, but being sad means you have a soul and they don't; they're worse than animals. It's a kindness to put them down. That's what the manuals say. Back when there were new manuals every week. Sometimes I think the only way you can tell if something has a soul is if they can still be sad. Sometimes it's the only way I know I have one.

Sometimes I don't think I do.

---

I'M NOT THE last person on Earth. Not by a long way. I get radio reports on the regular news from Portland, Boston—just a month ago New York was broadcasting loud and clear, loading zombies into the same hangars they kept protesters in back in '04. They gas them and dump them at sea. Brooklyn is still a problem, but Manhattan is coming around. Channel 3 is still going strong, but it's all emergency directives. I don't watch it. I mean, how many times can you sit through The Warning Signs or What We Know? Plus, I have reason to believe they don't know shit.

I might be the last person in Augusta, though. That wouldn't be hard. Did you ever see Augusta before the angel-virus? It was a burnt-out hole. It is a burnt-out hole. Just about every year, the Kennebec floods downtown, so at any given time there's only about three businesses on the main street, and one of them will have a cheerful **We'll Be Back!** sign up with the clock hands broken off. There's literally nothing going on in this town. Not now, and not then. Down by the river the buildings are pockmarked and broken, the houses are boarded up, windows shattered, only one or two people wandering dazed down the streets. All gas supplied by the Dead River Company, all your dead interred at Burnt Hill Burying Ground. And that was before. Even our Walmart had to close up because nobody ever shopped there.

And you know, way back in the pilgrim days, or Maine's version of them, which starts in the 1700s sometime, there was a guy named James Purington who freaked out one winter and murdered his whole family with an axe. Eight children and his wife. They hanged him and buried him at the crossroads so he wouldn't come back as a vampire. Which would seem silly, except, well, look around. The point is life in Augusta has been both shitty and deeply warped for quite some time. So we greeted this particular horrific circumstance much as Mainers have greeted economic collapse and the total disregard of the rest of the country for the better part of forever: with no surprise whatsoever. Anyway, I haven't seen anyone else on the pink and healthy side in a long time. A big group took off for Portland on foot a few months ago (the days of Kermit and Company), but I stayed behind. I have to think of my father. I know that sounds bizarre, but there's nothing like a parent who bites you to make you incapable of leaving them. Incapable of not wanting their love. I'll probably turn thirty and still be stuck here, trying to be a good daughter while his blood dries on the kitchen tiles.

---

CHANNEL 3 SAYS a zombie is a reanimated corpse with no observable sell-by date and seriously poor id-control. But I have come to realize that my situation is not like Manhattan or Boston or even Portland. See, I live with zombies. My dad isn't chained up in the basement. He lives with me like he always lived with me. My neighbors, those of them who didn't wander off, are all among the pustulous and dripping. I watched those movies before it happened and I think we all, for a little while, just reacted like the movies told us to: get a bat and start swinging. But I've never killed one, and I've never even come close to being bitten. It's not a fucking movie.

And if Channel 3 slaps their bullet points all over everywhere, I guess I should write my own What We Know here. Just in case anyone wonders why zombies can cry.

## What Is a Zombie?
### by Caitlin Zielinski

*Grade...well, if the college were still going I guess I'd be Grade 14.*

*A zombie is not a reanimated corpse. This was never a Night of the Living Dead scenario. The word zombie isn't even right—a zombie is something a voudoun priest makes, to obey his will. That has nothing to do with the price of coffee in Augusta. My dad didn't die. His skin ruptured and he got boils and he started snorting instead of talking and bleeding out of his eyes and lunging at Mr. Almeida next door with his fingernails out, but he didn't die. If he didn't die, he's not a corpse. QED, Channel 3.*

*A zombie is not a cannibal. This is kind of complicated: Channel 3 says they're not human, which is why you can't get arrested for killing one. So if they eat us, it wouldn't be cannibalism anyway, just, you know, lunch. Like if I ate a dog. Not what you expect from a nice American girl, but not cannibalism. But also, zombies don't just eat humans. If that were true, I'd have been dinner and they'd have been dead long before now, because, as I said, Augusta is pretty empty of anything resembling bright eyed and bushy tailed. They eat animals, they eat old meat in any freezer they can get open, they eat energy bars if that's what they find. Anything. Once I saw a woman—I didn't know her—on her hands and knees down by the river bank, clawing up the mud and eating it, smearing it on her bleeding breasts, staring up at the sky, her jaw wagging uselessly.*

*A zombie is not mindless. Channel 3 would have a fit if they heard me say that. It's dogma—zombies are slow and stupid. Well, I saw plenty of people slower and stupider than a zombie in the old days. I worked next the state capitol, after all. Sometimes I think the only difference is that they're ugly. The world was always full of drooling morons who only wanted me for my body. Anyway, some are fast and some are slow. If the girl was a jogger before, she's probably pretty spry now. If the guy never moved but to change the channel, he's not gonna catch you any time soon. And my father still knows my name. I can't be sure but I think it's only that they can't talk. Their tongues swell up and their throats expand—all of them. One of the early warning signs is slurred speech. They might be as smart as they ever were—see jogging—but they can't communicate except by screaming. I'd scream, too, if I were bleeding from my ears and my skin were melting off.*

*Zombies will not kill anything that moves. My dad hasn't bitten me. He could have, plenty of times. They're not harmless. I've had to get good at running and I have six locks on every door of the house. Even my bedroom, because my father can't be trusted. He hits me, still. His fist leaves a smear of blood and pus and something darker, purpler, on my face. But he doesn't bite me. At first, he barked and went for my neck at least once a day. But I'm faster. I'm always faster. He doesn't even try anymore. Sometimes he just stands in the living room, drool pooling in the side of his mouth till it falls out, and he looks at me like he remembers that strange night when he bit me before, and he's still ashamed. I laugh, and he almost smiles. He shambles back down the hall and starts peeling off the wallpaper, shoving it into his mouth in long pink strips like skin.*

## The Days of Flaming Motorcycles

There's something else I know. It's hard to talk about, because I don't understand it. I don't understand it because I'm not a zombie. It's like a secret society, and I'm on the outside. I can watch what they do, but I don't know the code. I couldn't tell Channel 3 about this, even if they came to town with all their cameras and sat me in a plush chair like one of their endless Rockette-line of doctors. What makes you think they have intelligence, Miss Zielinski? And I would tell them about my father saying my name, but not about the river. No one would believe me. After all, it's never happened anywhere else. And I have an idea about that, too. Because people in Manhattan are pretty up on their zombie-killing tactics, and god help a zombie in Texas if he should ever be so unfortunate as to encounter a human. But here there's nothing left. No one to kill them. They own this town, and they're learning how to live in it, just like anyone does. Maybe Augusta always belonged to them and James Purington and the Dead River Company. All hail the oozing, pestilent kings and queens of the apocalypse.

This is what I know: one night, my father picked up our toaster and left the house. I'm not overly attached to the toaster, but he didn't often leave. I feed him good hamburger, nice and raw, and I don't knock him in his brainpan with a bat. Zombies know a good thing.

The next night he took the hallway mirror. Then the microwave, then the coffee-pot, then a sack full of pots and pans. All the zombie movies in the world do not prepare you to see your father, his hair matted with blood, his bathrobe torn and seeping, packing your cooking materiel into a flowered king-size pillowcase. And then one night he took a picture off of the bookshelf. My mother, himself, and me, smiling in one of those terrible posed portraits. I was eight or nine in the picture, wearing a green corduroy jumper and big, long brown pigtails. I was smiling so wide, and so were they. You have to, in those kinds of portraits. The photographer makes you, and if you don't, he practically starts turning cartwheels to get you to smile like an angel just appeared over his left shoulder clutching a handful of pins. My mother, her glasses way too big for her face. My father, in plaid flannel, his big hand holding me protectively.

I followed him. It wasn't difficult; his hearing went about the same time as his tongue. In a way, I guess it's a lot like getting old. Your body starts failing in all sorts of weird ways, and you can't talk right or hear well or see clearly, and you just rage at things because everything is slipping away and you're never going to get any better. If one person goes that way, it's tragic. If everyone does, it's the end of the world.

It gets really dark in Augusta, and the streetlights have all been shot out or burned out. There is no darker night than a Maine night before the first snow, all starless and cold. No friendly pools of orange chemical light to break the long, black street. Just my father, shuffling along with his portrait clutched to his suppurating chest. He turned toward downtown, crossing Front Street after looking both ways out of sheer muscle memory. I crept behind him, down past the riverside shops, past the Java Shack, down to the riverbank and the empty parking lots along the waterfront.

Hundreds of zombies gathered down there by the slowly lapping water. Maybe the whole of dead Augusta, everyone left. My father joined the crowd. I tried not to breathe; I'd never seen so many in one place. They weren't fighting or hunting, either. They moaned, a little. Most of them had brought something—more toasters, dresser drawers, light bulbs, broken kitchen chairs, coat racks, televisions, car doors. All junk, gouged out of houses, out of their old lives. They arranged it, almost lovingly, around a massive tower of garbage, teetering, swaying in the wet night wind. A light bulb fell from the top, shattering with a bright pop. They didn't notice. The tower was sloppy, but even I could see that it was meant to be a tower. More than a tower. Bed-slats formed flying buttresses between the main column and a smaller one, still being built. Masses of electric devices, dead and inert, piled up between them, showing their screens and gray, lifeless displays to the water. And below the screens rested dozens of family portraits just like ours, leaning against the dark plasma screens and speakers. A few zombies added to the pile—and some of them laid photos down that clearly belonged to some other family. I thought I saw Mrs. Halloway, my first grade teacher, among them, and she treated her portrait of a Chinese family as tenderly as a child. I don't think they knew who exactly the pictures showed. They just understood the general sense they conveyed, of happiness and family. My father added his picture to the crowd and rocked back and forth, howling, crying, holding his head in his hands.

I wriggled down between a dark streetlamp and a park bench, trying to turn invisible as quickly as possible. But they paid no attention to me. And then the moon crowned the spikes of junk, cresting between the two towers.

The zombies all fell to their knees, their arms outstretched to the white, full moon, horrible black tears streaming down their ruined faces, keening and ululating, throwing their faces down into the river-mud, bits of them falling off in their rapture, their eagerness to abase themselves before their cathedral. I think it was a cathedral, when I think about it now. I think it had to be. They sent up their awful crooning moan, and I clapped my hands over my ears to escape it. Finally, Mrs. Halloway stood up and turned to the rest of them. She dragged her nails across her cheeks and shrieked wordlessly into the night. My father went to her and I thought he was going to bite her, the way he bit me, the way zombies bite anyone when they want to.

Instead, he kissed her.

He kissed her on the cheek, heavily, smackingly, and his face came away with her blood on it. One by one the others kissed her too, surrounding her with groping hands and hungry mouths, and the moon shone down on her face, blanching her so she was nothing but black and white, blood and skin, an old movie monster, only she wept. She wept from a place so deep I can't imagine it; she wept, and she smiled, even as they finished kissing her and began pulling her apart, each keeping a piece of her for themselves, just a scrap of flesh, which they ate solemnly, reverently. They didn't squabble over it, her leg or her arm or her eyes, and Mrs. Halloway didn't try to fight them. She had offered herself, I think, and they took her. I know what worship looks like.

I was crying by that time. You would, too, if you saw that. I had to cry or I had to throw up, and crying was quieter. Your body can make calculations like that, if it has to. But crying isn't that quiet, really. One of them sniffed the air and turned toward me—the rest turned as one. They're a herd, if they are anything. They know much more together than they know separately. I wonder if, in a few decades, they will have figured out how to run Channel 3, and will broadcast How to Recognize a Human in Three Easy Steps, or What We Know.

They fell on me, which is pretty much how zombies do anything. They groped and pulled, but there were too many of them for any one to get a good grip, and I may not have killed one before but I wasn't opposed to the idea. I swung my fists and oh, they were so soft, like jam. I clamped my mouth shut—I knew my infection vectors as well as any kid in my generation. But they didn't bite me, and finally my father threw back his head and bellowed. I know that bellow. I've always known it, and it hasn't changed. They pulled away, panting, exhausted. That was the first time I realized how fragile they are. They're like lions. In short bursts, they'll eviscerate you and your zebra without a second thought. But they have to save up the strength for it, day in and day out. I stood there, back against the streetlamp, fingernails out, asthma kicking in because of course, it would. And my father limped over to me, dragging his broken left foot—they don't die but they don't heal. I tried to set it once and that was the closest I ever came to getting bitten before that night on the river.

He stood over me, his eyebrows crusted with old fluid, his eyes streaming tears like ink, his jaw dislocated and hanging, his cheeks puffed out with infection. He reached out and hooted gently like an ape. To anyone else it would have been just another animal noise

## The Days of Flaming Motorcycles

from a rotting zombie, but I heard it as clear as anything: Caitlin, Caitlin, Caitlin. I had nowhere to go, and he reached for me, brushing my hair out of my face. With one bloody thumb he traced a circle onto my forehead, like a priest on Ash Wednesday. Caitlin, Caitlin, Caitlin.

His blood was cold.

---

AFTER THAT, NONE of them ever came after me again. That's why I can have my nice little habit of opening the Java Shack and writing in my notebooks. These are the days of Punky Princesses, and I am safe. The mark on my forehead never went away. It's faint, like a birthmark, but it's there. Sometimes I meet one of them on the road, wandering dazed and unhappy in the daylight, squinting as if it doesn't understand where the light is coming from. When they see me, their eyes go dark with hunger—but then, their gaze flicks up to my forehead, and they fall down on their knees, keening and sobbing. It's not me, I know that. It's the cathedral, still growing, on the banks of the Kennebec. The mark means I'm of the faith, somehow. Saint Caitlin of the Java Shack, Patroness of the Living.

Sometimes I think about leaving. I hear Portsmouth is mostly clean. I could make that on my bicycle. Maybe I could even hotwire a car. I've seen them do it on television. The first time I stayed, I stayed for my father. But he doesn't come home much anymore. There's little enough left for him to scavenge for the church. He keeps up his kneeling and praying down there, except when the moon is dark, and then they mourn like lost children. Now, I think I stay because I want to see the finished cathedral, I want to understand what they are doing when they eat one of their own. If it's like communion, the way I understand it, or something else entirely. I want to see the world they're building out here in the abandoned capital. If maybe they're not sick, but just new, like babies, incomprehensible and violent and frustrated that nothing is as they expected it to be.

It's afternoon in the Java Shack. The sun is thin and wintry. I pour myself hot water and it occurs to me that *apocalypse* originally meant to uncover something. To reveal a hidden thing.

I get that now.

It was never about fire and lightning shearing off the palaces of the world. And if I wait, here on the black shores of the Kennebec, here in the city that has been ruined for as long as it has lived, maybe, someday soon, the face of their god will come up out of the depths, uncovered, revealed.

So on. So forth.

# One Breath, One Stroke

1\. IN A PEACH GROVE THE House of Second-Hand Carnelian casts half a shadow. This is because half of the house is in the human world, and half of it is in another place. The other place has no name. It is where unhuman things happen. It is where tricksters go when they are tired. A modest screen divides the world. It is the color of plums. There are silver tigers on it, leaping after plum petals. If you stand in the other place, you can see a hundred eyes peering through the silk.

2\. In the human half of the House of Second-Hand Carnelian lives a mustached gentleman calligrapher named Ko. Ko wears a chartreuse robe embroidered with black thread. When Ko stands on the other side of the house he is not Ko, but a long calligraphy brush with badger bristles and a strong cherrywood shaft. When he is a brush his name is Yuu. When he was a child he spent all day hopping from one side of the house to the other. Brush, man. Man, brush.

3\. Ko lives alone. Yuu lives with Hone-Onna, the skeleton woman, Sazae-Onna, the snail woman, a jar full of lightning, and Namazu, a catfish as big as three strong men. When Namazu slaps his tail on the ground, earthquakes tremble, even in the human world. Yuu copied a holy text of Tengu love poetry onto the bones of Hone-Onna. Her white bones are black now with beautiful writing, for Yuu is a very good calligrapher.

4. Hone-Onna's skull reads: *The moon sulks. I am enfolded by feathers the color of remembering. The talons I seize, seize me.*

5. Ko is also an excellent calligrapher. But he is retired, for when he stands on one side of the House of Second-Hand Carnelian, he has no brush to paint his characters, and when he stands on the other, he has no breath. "The great calligraphers know all writing begins in the body. One breath, one stroke. One breath, one stroke. That is how a book is made. Long, black breath by long black breath. Yuu will never be a great calligrapher, even though he is technically accomplished. He has no body to begin his poems."

6. Ko cannot leave the House of Second-Hand Carnelian. If he tries, he becomes sick, and vomits squid ink until he returns. He grows radish, melon, and watercress, and of course there are the peaches. A river flows by the House of Second-Hand Carnelian. It is called the Nobody River. When it winds around to the other side of the house, it is called the Nothingness River. There are some fish in it. Ko catches them with a peach branch. Namazu belches and fish jump into his mouth. On Namazu's lower lip Yuu copied a Tanuki elegy.

7. Namazu's whiskers read: *In deep snow I regret everything. My testicles are heavy with grief. Because of me, the stripes of her tail will never return.*

8. Sazae-Onna lives in a pond in the floor of the kitchen. Her shell is tiered like a cake or a palace, hard and thorned and colored like the inside of an almond, with seams of mother of pearl swirling in spiral patterns over her gnarled surface. She eats the rice that falls from the table when the others sit down to supper. She drinks the steam from the teakettle. When she dreams she dreams of sailors fishing her out of the sea in a net of roses. On the Emperor's Birthday Yuu gives her

candy made from Hone-Onna's marrow. Hone-Onna does not mind. She has plenty to spare. Sazae-Onna takes the candy quietly under her shell with one blue-silver hand. She sucks it for a year.

9. When Yuu celebrates the Emperor's Birthday, he does not mean the one in Tokyo. He means the Goldfish-Emperor of the Yokai who lives on a tiny island in the sea, surrounded by his wives and their million children. On his birthday he grants a single wish—among all the unhuman world red lottery tickets appear in every teapot. Yuu has never won.

10. The Jar of Lightning won once, when it was not a jar, but a Field General in the Storm Army of Susano-no-Mikoto. It had won many medals in its youth by striking the cypress-roofs of the royal residences at Kyoto and setting them on fire. The electric breast of the great lightning bolt groaned with lauds. When the red ticket formed in its ice-cloud teapot, with gold characters upon it instead of black, the lightning bolt wished for peace and rest. Susano-no-Mikoto is a harsh master with a harsh and windy whip, and he does not permit honorable retirement. This is how the great lightning bolt became a Jar of Lightning in the House of Second-Hand Carnelian. It took the name of Noble and Serene Electric Master and polishes its jar with static discharge on washing day.

11. Sazae-Onna rarely shows her body. Under the shell, she is more beautiful than anyone but the moon's wife. No one is more beautiful than her. Sazae-Onna's hair is pale, soft pink; her eyes are deep red, her mouth is a lavender blossom. Yuu has only seen her once, when he caught her bathing in the river. All the fish surrounded her in a ring, staring up at her with their fishy eyes. Even the moon looked down at Sazae-Onna that night, though he felt guilt about it afterward and disappeared for three days to purify himself. So profoundly moved was Yuu the calligraphy brush that he begged permission to copy a Kitsune hymn upon the pearl-belly of Sazae-Onna.

12. The pearl-belly of Sazae-Onna reads: *Through nine tails I saw a wintry lake at midnight. Skate-tracks wrote a poem of melancholy on the ice. You stood upon the other shore. For the first time I thought of becoming human.*

13. Ko has no visitors. The human half of the House of Second-Hand Carnelian is well hidden in a deep forest full of black bears just wise enough to resent outsiders and arrange a regular patrol. There is also a Giant Hornet living there, but no one has ever seen it. They only hear the buzz of her wings on cloudy days. The bears, over the years, have developed a primitive but heartfelt Buddhist discipline. Beneath the cinnamon trees they practice the repetition of the Growling Sutra. The religion of the Giant Hornet is unknown.

14. The bears are unaware of their heritage. Their mother is Hoeru, the Princess of All Bears. She fell in love with a zen monk whose koans buzzed around her head like bees. The Princess of All Bears hid her illegitimate children in the forest around the House of Second-Hand Carnelian, close enough to the plum-colored screen to watch over, but far enough that their souls could never quite wake. It is a sad story. Yuu copied it onto a thousand peach leaves. When the wind blows on his side of the house, you can hear Hoeru weeping.

15. If Ko were to depart the house, Yuu would vanish forever. If Ko so much as crosses the Nobody River, he receives a pain in his long bones, the bones which are most like the strong birch shaft of a calligraphy brush. If he tries to open the plum-colored screen, he falls at once to sleep and Yuu appears on the other side of the silks having no memory of being Ko. Ko is a lonely man. With his fingernails he writes upon the tatami: *Beside the sunlit river I regret that I never married. At tea-time, I am grateful for the bears.*

16. The woven grass swallows his words.

17. Sometimes the bears come to see him, and watch him catch fish. They think he is very clumsy at it. They try to teach him the Growling

Sutra as a cure for loneliness, but Ko cannot understand them. He fills a trough with weak tea and shares his watercress. They take a little, to be polite.

18. Yuu has many visitors, though Namazu the catfish has more. Hone-Onna receives a gentleman skeleton at the full moon. They hold seances to contact the living, conducted with a wide slate of volcanic glass, yuzu wine, and a transistor radio brought to the House of Second-Hand Carnelian by a Kirin who had recently eaten a G.I. and spat the radio back up. The Kirin wrapped it up very nicely, though, with curls of green silk ribbon. Hone-Onna and her suitor each contribute a shoulder blade, a thumb-bone, and a kneecap. They set the pieces of themselves upon the board in positions according to several arcane considerations only skeletons have the patience to learn. They drink the yuzu wine; it trickles in a green waterfall through their ribcages. Then they turn on the radio.

19. Yuu thanked the Kirin by copying a Dragon koan onto his long horn. The Kirin's horn reads: *What was the form of the Buddha when he came among the Dragons?*

19. Once, Datsue-Ba came to visit the House of Second-Hand Carnelian. She arrived on a palanquin of business suits, for Datsue-Ba takes the clothes of the dead when they come to the shores of the Sanzu River in the underworld. She and her husband Keneo live beneath a persimmon tree on the opposite bank. Datsue-Ba takes the clothes of the lost souls after they have swum across, and Keneo hangs them to dry on the branches of their tree. Datsue-Ba knows everything about a dead person the moment she touches their sleeve.

20. Datsue-Ba brought guest gifts for everyone, even the Jar of Lightning. These are the gifts she gave:

A parasol painted with orange blossoms for Sazae-Onna so she will not dry out in the sun.

A black funeral kimono embroidered with black cicada wings for Hone-Onna so that she can attend the festival of the dead in style.

A copper ring bearing a ruby frog on it for Yuu to wear around the stalk of his brush-body.

A cypress-wood comb for the Noble and Serene Electric Master to burn up and remember being young.

Several silver earrings for Namazu to wear upon his lip and feel mighty.

21. Datsue-Ba also brought a gift for Ko. This is how he acquired his chartreuse robe embroidered with black thread. It once belonged to an unremarkable courtier who played the koto poorly and envied his brother who held a rank one level higher than his own. Datsue-Ba put the chartreuse robe at the place where the Nothingness River becomes the Nobody River. Datsue-Ba is very good at rivers. When Ko found it, he did not know who to thank, so he turned and bowed to the plum-colored screen.

22. This begs the question of whether Ko knows what goes on in the other half of the House of Second-Hand Carnelian. Sometimes he wakes up at night and thinks he hears singing, or whispering. Sometimes when he takes his bath the water seems to gurgle as though a great fish is hiding in it. He conceived suspicions when he tried to leave the peach grove which contains the house and suffered in his bones so terribly. For a long time that was all Ko knew.

23. Namazu runs a club for Guardian Lions every month. They play dice; the stone lions shake them in their mouths and spit them against the peach trees. Namazu roars with laughter and slaps the ground with his tail. Earthquakes rattle the mountains in Hokkaido. Most of the lions cheat because their lives are boring and they crave excitement. Guarding temples does not hold the same thrill as hunting or biting. Auspicious Snow Lion is the best dice-player. He comes all the way from Taipei to play and drink and hunt rabbits in the forest. He

does not speak Japanese, but he pretends to humbly lose when the others snarl at his winning streaks.

24. Sometimes they play Go. The lions are terrible at it. Fortuitous Brass Lion likes to eat the black pieces. Namazu laughs at him and waggles his whiskers. Typhoons spin up off the coast of Okinawa.

25. Everyone on the unhuman side of the House of Second-Hand Carnelian is curious about Ko. Has he ever been in love? Fought in a war? What are his thoughts on astrology? Are there any good scandals in his past? How old is he? Does he have any children? Where did he learn calligraphy? Why is he here? How did he find the house and get stuck there? Was part of him always a brush named Yuu? Using the thousand eyes in the screen, they spy on him, but cannot discover the answers to any of these questions.

26. They have learned the following: Ko is left-handed. Ko likes fish skin better than fish flesh. Ko cheats when he meditates and opens his eyes to see how far the sun has gotten along. Ko has a sweet tooth. When Ko talks to the peach trees and the bears, he has an Osaka accent.

27. The Noble and Serene Electric Master refused to let Yuu copy anything out on its Jar. The Noble and Serene Electric Master does not approve of graffiti. Even when Yuu remembered suddenly an exquisite verse written repeated among the Aosaginohi Herons who glow in the night like blue lanterns. The Jar of Lightning snapped its cap and crackled disagreeably. Yuu let it rest; when you share a house you must let your manners go before you to smooth the path through the rooms.

28. The Heron-verse went: *Autumn maples turn black in the evening. I turn them red again and caw for you, flying south to Nagoya. The night has no answer for me, but many small fish.*

29. Who stretched the plum-colored screen with silver tigers leaping upon it down the very narrow line separating the halves of the house?

For that matter, who built the House of Second-Hand Carnelian? Sazae-Onna knows, but she doesn't talk to anyone.

30. Yuki-Onna came to visit the Jar of Lightning. They had been comrades in the army of storms long ago. With every step of her small, quiet feet, snowflakes fell on the peach grove and the Nothingness River froze into intricate patterns of eddies and frost. She wore a white kimono with a silver obi belt, and her long black hair was scented with red bittersweet. Everyone grew very silent, for Yuki-Onna was a Kami and not a playful lion or a hungry Kirin. Yuu trembled. Tiny specks of ink shook from his badger-bristles. He longed to write upon the perfect white silk covering her shoulders. Hone-Onna brought tea and black sugar to the Snow-and-Death Kami. Snow fell even inside the house. The Noble and Serene Electric Master left its Jar and circled its blue sparkling jagged body around the waist of Yuki-Onna, who laughed gently. One of the bears on the other side of the peach grove collapsed and coughed his last black blood onto the ice. Yuu noticed that the Snow-and-Death Kami wore a necklace. Its beads were silver teeth, hundreds upon thousands of them, the teeth of all of winter's dead. Unable to contain himself, Yuu wrote in the frigid air: *Snow comes; I have forgotten my own name.*

31. Yuki-Onna looks up. Her eyes are darker than death. She closes them; Yuu's words appear on the back of her neck.

32. Yuu is unhappy. He wants Sazae-Onna to love him. He wants Yuki-Onna to come back to visit him and not the Noble and Serene Electric Master. He wants to be the premier calligrapher in the unhuman half of Japan. He wants to be asked to join Namazu's dice games. He wants to leave the House of Second-Hand Carnelian and visit the Emperor's island or the crystal whale who lives off the coast of Shikoku. But if Yuu tries to leave his ink dries up and his wood cracks until he returns.

33. Someone wanted a good path between the human and the unhuman Japans. That much is clear.

34. Sazae-Onna does not like visitors one little bit. They splash in her pond. They poke her and try to get her to come out. Unfortunately, every day brings more folk to the House of Second-Hand Carnelian. First the Guardian Lions didn't leave. Then Datsue-Ba came back with even more splendid clothes for them all, robes the color of maple leaves and jewels the color of snow and masks painted with liquid silver. Then the Kirin returned and asked Sazae-Onna to marry him. Yuu trembled. Sazae-Onna said nothing and pulled her shell down tighter and tighter until he went away. Nine-Tailed Kitsune and big-balled Tanuki are eating up all the peaches. Long-nosed Tengu overfish the river. No one goes home when the moon goes down. When the Blue Jade Cicadas arrive from Kamakura Sazae-Onna locks her kitchen and tells them all to shut up.

35. Yuu knocks after everyone has gone to sleep. Sazae-Onna lets him in. On the floor of her kitchen he writes a Kappa proverb: *Dark clouds bring rain, the night brings stars, and everyone will try to spill the water out of your skull.*

36. At the end of summer, the unhuman side of the house is crammed full, but Ko can only hear the occasional rustle. When Kawa-Uso the Otter Demon threw an ivory saddle onto the back of one of the bears and rode her around the peach grove like a horse, Ko only saw a poor she-bear having some sort of fit. Ko sleeps all the time now, though he is not really sleeping. He is being Yuu on the other side of the plum-colored screen. He never writes poetry in the tatami anymore.

37. The Night Parade occurs once every hundred years at the end of summer. Nobody plans it. They know to go to the door between the worlds the way a brown goose knows to go north in the spring.

38. One night the remaining peaches swell up into juicy golden lanterns. The river rushes become kotos with long spindly legs. The mushrooms become lacy, thick oyster-drums. The Kitsune begin to dance; the Tengu flap their wings and spit *mala* beads toward the dark sky in fountains. A trio of small dragons the color of pearls in milk leap suddenly out of the Nothingness River. Cerulean fire curls out of their noses. The House of Second-Hand Carnelian empties. Namazu's Lions carry him on a litter of silk fishing nets. The Jar of Lightning bounces after Hone-Onna and her gentleman caller, whose bones clatter and clap. When only Yuu and the snail-woman are left, Sazae-Onna lifts up her shell and steps out into the Parade, her pink hair falling like floss, her black eyes gleaming. Yuu feels as though he will crack when faced with her beauty.

39. The Parade steps over the Nothingness River and the Nobody River and enters the human Japan, dancing and singing and throwing light at the dark. They will wind down through the plains to Kyoto before the night is through, and flow like a single serpent into the sea where the Goldfish Emperor of the Yokai will greet them with his million children and his silver-fronded wives.

40. Yuu races after Sazae-Onna. The bears watch them go. In the midst of the procession Hoeru the Princess of All Bears, who is Queen now, comes bearing a miniature Agate Great Mammal Palace on her back. Her children fall in and nurse as though they were still cubs. For a night, they know their names.

41. Yuu does not make it across the river. It goes jet with his ink. His strong birch shaft cracks; Sazae-Onna does not turn back. When she dances she looks like a poem about loss. Yuu pushes forward through the water of the Nothingness River. His shaft bursts in a shower of birch splinters.

42. A man's voice cries out from inside the ruined brush-handle. Yuu startles and stops. The voice says: *I never had any children. I have never been in love.*

43. Yuu topples into the Nobody River. The kotos are distant now, the peach-lanterns dim. His badger-bristles fall out.

44. Yuu pulls himself out of the river by dry grasses and berry vines. He is not Yuu on the other side. He is not Ko. He has Ko's body but his arms are calligraphy brushes sopping with ink. His feet are inkstones. He can still hear the music of the Night Parade. He begins to dance. Not-Yuu and Not-Ko takes a breath.

45. There is only the House of Second-Hand Carnelian to write on. He writes on it. He breathes and swipes his brush, breathes, brushes. Man, brush. Brush, man. He writes and does not copy. He writes psalms of being part man and part brush. He writes poems of his love for the snail-woman. He writes songs about perfect breath. The House slowly turns black.

46. Bringing up the rear of the Parade hours later, Yuki-Onna comes silent through the forest. Snow flows before her like a carpet. She has brought her sisters the Flower-and-Joy Kami and the Cherry-Blossom-Mount-Fuji Kami. The crown of the Fuji-Kami's head has frozen. The Flower-and-Joy Kami is dressed in chrysanthemums and lemon blossoms. They pause at the House of Second-Hand Carnelian. Not-Yuu and Not-Ko shakes and shivers; he is sick, he has received both the pain in his femurs and the pain in his brush-handles. The Kami shine so bright the fish in both rivers are blinded. The Flower-and-Joy Kami looks at the poem on one side of the door. It reads: *In white peonies I see the exhalations of my kanji blossoming.* The Cherry-Blossom-Mount-Fuji Kami looks at the poem on the other side of the door. It reads: *It is enough to sit at the foot of a mountain and breathe the pine-mist. Only a proud man must climb it.* The Kami close their eyes as they pass by. The words appear on the backs of their necks as they disappear into the night.

47. Ko dies in mid-stroke, describing the sensation of lungs filled up like the wind-bag of heaven. Yuu dies before he can complete

his final verse concerning the exquisiteness of crustaceans who will never love you back.

48. Slowly, with a buzz like breath, the Giant Hornet flies out of her nest and through the peach grove denuded by hungry Tanuki. She is a heavy, furry emerald bobbing on the wind. The souls of Ko and Yuu quail before her. As she picks them up with her weedy legs and puts them back into their bodies she tells them a Giant Hornet poem: *Everything is venom, even sweetness. Everything is sweet, even venom. Death is illiterate and a hayseed bum. No excuse to leave the nest unguarded. What are you, some silly jade lion?*

49. The sea currents bring the skeleton-woman back, and Namazu who has caused two tsunamis, though only one made the news. The Jar of Lightning floats up the river. Finally the snail-woman returns to the pond in her kitchen. They find Yuu making tea for them. His bristles are dry. On the other side of the plum-colored screen, Ko is sweeping out the leaves.

50. Yuu has written on the teacups. It reads: *It takes a calligrapher one hundred years to draw one breath.*

# Thirteen Ways of Looking at Space/Time

### I.

IN THE BEGINNING WAS THE Word and the Word was with God and the Word was a high-density pre-baryogenesis singularity. Darkness lay over the deep and God moved upon the face of the hyperspatial matrix. He separated the firmament from the quark-gluon plasma and said: *let there be particle/anti-particle pairs*, and there was light. He created the fish of the sea and the fruits of the trees, the moon and the stars and the beasts of the earth, and to these he said: *Go forth, be fruitful and mutate*. And on the seventh day, the rest mass of the universe came to gravitationally dominate the photon radiation, hallow it, and keep it.

God, rapidly redshifting, hurriedly formed man from the dust of single-celled organisms, called him Adam, and caused him to dwell in the Garden of Eden, to classify the beasts according to kingdom, phylum and species. God forbade Man only to eat from the Tree of Meiosis. Adam did as he was told, and as a reward God instructed him in the ways of parthenogenesis. Thus was Woman born, and called Eve. Adam and Eve dwelt in the pre-quantum differentiated universe, in a paradise without wave-particle duality. But interference patterns came to Eve in the shape of a Serpent, and wrapping her in its matter/anti-matter coils, it said: *eat from the Tree of Meiosis and your eyes will be opened.* Eve protested that she would not break covenant with God, but the Serpent answered: *fear not, for you float in a random quantum-gravity foam, and from a single bite will rise an inexorable inflation event, and you will become like unto God, expanding forever outward.*

And so Eve ate from the Tree, and knew that she was a naked child of divergent universes. She took the fruit to Adam, and said unto him: *there are things you do not understand, but I do.* And Adam was angry, and snatched the fruit from Eve and devoured it, and from beyond the cosmic background radiation, God sighed, for all physical processes are reversible in theory—but not in practice. Man and Woman were expelled from the Garden, and a flaming sword was placed through the Gates of Eden as a reminder that the universe would now contract, and someday perish in a conflagration of entropy, only to increase in density, burst, and expand again, causing further high velocity redistributions of serpents, fruit, men, women, helium-3, lithium-7, deuterium, and helium-4.

## II.

THIS IS A story about being born.

No one remembers being born. The beginnings of things are very difficult.

A science fiction writer on the Atlantic coast once claimed to remember being born. When she was a child, she thought a door was open which was not, and ran full-tilt into a pane of plate-glass. The child-version of the science fiction writer lay bleeding onto a concrete patio, not yet knowing that part of her thigh was gone and would always be gone, like Zeus's thigh, where the lightning-god sewed up his son Dionysus to gestate. Something broke inside the child, a thing having to do with experience and memory, which in normal children travel in opposite directions, with memory accumulating and experience running out—slowly, but speeding up as children hurtle toward adulthood and death. What the science fiction writer actually remembered was not her own birth, but a moment when she struck the surface of the glass and her brain stuttered, layering several experiences one over the other:

the scissoring pain of the shards of glass in her thighs,

having once fallen into a square of wet concrete on a construction site on her way to school, and her father pulling her out by her arms,

her first kiss, below an oak tree turning red and brown in the autumn, when a boy interrupted her reciting *Don Quixote* with his lips on hers.

This fractured, unplanned layering became indistinguishable from an actual memory of being born. It is not her fault; she believed she remembered it. But no one remembers being born.

The doctors sewed up her thigh. There was no son in her leg, but a small, dark, empty space beneath her skin where a part of her used to be. Sometimes she touches it, absentmindedly, when she is trying to think of a story.

## III.

IN THE BEGINNING was the simple self-replicating cell of the Void. It split through the center of Ursa Major into the divine female Izanami and the divine male Izanagi, who knew nothing about quantum apples and lived on the iron-sulfur Plain of Heaven. They stood on the Floating Bridge of Heaven and plunged a static atmospheric discharge spear into the great black primordial sea, churning it and torturing it until oligomers and simple polymers rose up out of the depths. Izanami and Izanagi stepped onto the greasy islands of lipid bubbles and in the first light of the world, each saw that the other was beautiful.

Between them, they catalyzed the formation of nucleotides in an aqueous solution and raised up the Eight-Sided Palace of Autocatalytic Reactions around the unnmovable RNA Pillar of Heaven. When this was done, Izanami and Izanagi walked in opposite chiral directions around the Pillar, and when Izanami saw her mate, she cried out happily: *How lovely you are, and how versatile are your nitrogenous bases! I love you!* Izanagi was angry that she had spoken first and privileged her proto-genetic code over his. The child that came of their paleo-protozoic mating was as a silver anaerobic leech, helpless, archaeaic, invertebrate, and unable to convert lethal super-oxides. They set him in the sky to sail in the Sturdy Boat of Heaven, down the starry stream of alternate electron acceptors for respiration. Izanagi dragged Izanami back to the Pillar. They walked around it again in a left-handed helix that echoed forward and backward through the biomass, and when Izanagi saw his wife, he crowed: *How lovely you are, and how ever-increasing your metabolic complexity! I love you!* And because Izanami was stonily silent, and Izanagi spoke first, elevating his own proto-genetic code, the children that came from them were strong and great: Gold and Iron and Mountain and Wheel and Honshu and Kyushu and Emperor—until the birth of her son, Fiery Permian-Triassic Extinction Event, burned her up and killed the mother of the world.

Izanami went down into the Root Country, the Land of the Dead. But Izanagi could not let her go into a place he had not gone first, and pursued her into the paleontological record. He became lost in the dark of abiogenetic obsolescence, and lit the teeth of his jeweled comb ablaze to show the way—and saw that he walked on the body of Izanami, which had become the fossil-depository landscape of the Root Country, putrid, rotting, full of mushrooms and worms and coprolites and trilobites. In hatred and grief and memory of their first wedding, Izanami howled and heaved and moved the continents one from the other until Izanagi was expelled from her.

When he stumbled back into the light, Izanagi cleaned the pluripotent filth from his right eye, and as it fell upon the ground it became the quantum-retroactive Sun. He cleaned the zygotic filth from his left eye and as it fell upon the ground, it became the temporally subjective Moon. And when he cleaned the nutrient-dense filth from his nose, it drifted into the air and became the fractal, maximally complex, petulant Storms and Winds.

### IV.

WHEN THE SCIENCE fiction writer was nineteen, she had a miscarriage. She had not even known she was pregnant. But she bled and bled and it didn't stop, and the doctor explained to her that sometimes this happens when you are on a certain kind of medication. The science fiction writer could not decide how to feel about it—ten years later, after she had married the father of the baby-that-wasn't and divorced him, after she had written a book about methane-insectoid cities floating in the brume of a pink gas giant that no one liked very much, she still could not decide how to feel. When she was nineteen she put her hands over her stomach and tried to think of a timeline where she had stayed pregnant. Would it have been a daughter. Would it have had blue eyes like its father. Would it have had her Danish nose or his Greek one. Would it have liked science fiction, and would it have grown up to be an endocrinologist. Would she have been able to love it. She put her hands over her stomach and tried to be sad. She couldn't. But she couldn't be happy either. She felt that she had given birth to a reality where she would never give birth.

When the science fiction writer told her boyfriend who would become her husband who would become someone she never wanted to see again, he made sorry noises but wasn't really sorry. Five years later, when she thought she might want to have a child on purpose, she reminded him of the child-that-disappeared, and the husband who was a mistake would say: *I forgot all about that.*

And she put her hands over her stomach, the small, dark, empty space beneath her skin where a part of him used to be, and she didn't want to be pregnant anymore, but her breasts hurt all the same, as if she was nursing, all over again, a reality where no one had anyone's nose and the delicate photo-synthetic wings of Xm, the eater of love, quivered in a bliss-storm of super-heated hydrogen, and Dionysus was never born so the world lived without wine.

V.

IN THE BEGINNING there was only darkness. The darkness squeezed itself down until it became a thin protoplanetary disk, yellow on one side and white on the other, and inside the accretion zone sat a small man no larger than a frog, his beard flapping in the solar winds. This man was called Kuterastan, the One Who Lives Above the Super-Dense Protostar. He rubbed the metal-rich dust from his eyes and peered above him into the collapsing nebular darkness. He looked east along the galactic axis, toward the cosmogenesis event horizon, and saw the young sun, its faint light tinged with the yellow of dawn. He looked west along the axis, toward the heat-death of the universe, and saw the dim amber-colored light of dissipating thermodynamic energy. As he gazed, debris-clouds formed in different colors. Once more, Kuterastan rubbed the boiling helium from his eyes and wiped the hydrogen-sweat from his brow. He flung the sweat from his body and another cloud appeared, blue with oxygen and possibility, and a tiny little girl stood on it: Stenatliha, the Woman Without Parents. Each was puzzled as to where the other had come from, and each considered the problems of unification theory after their own fashion. After some time, Kuterastan again rubbed his eyes and face, and from his body flung stellar radiation into the dust and darkness. First the Sun appeared, and then Pollen Boy, a twin-tailed comet rough and heavy with microorganisms. The four sat a long time in silence on a single photoevaporation cloud. Finally Kuterastan broke the silence and said: *what shall we do?*

And a slow inward-turning Poynting-Robertson spiral began.

First Kuterastan made Nacholecho, the Tarantula of Newly-Acquired Critical Mass. He followed by making the Big Dipper, and then Wind, Lightning and Thunder, Magnetospheres, and Hydrostatic Equilibrium, and gave to each of them their characteristic tasks. With the ammonia-saturated sweat of the Sun, Pollen Boy, himself, and the Woman Without Parents, Kuterastan made between his palms a a small brown ferrosilicate blastocyst no bigger than a bean. The four of them kicked the little ball until it cleared its orbital neighborhood of planetesimals. Then the solar wind blew into the ball and inflated its magnetic field. Tarantula spun out a long black gravitational cord and stretched it across the sky. Tarantula also attached blue gravity wells, yellow approach vectors and white spin foam to the ferrosilicate ball, pulling one far to the south, another west, and the last to the north. When Tarantula was finished, the earth existed, and became a smooth brown expanse of Precambrian plain. Stochastic processes tilted at each corner to hold the earth in place. And at this Kuterastan sang a repeating song of nutation: *the world is now made and its light cone will travel forever at a constant rate.*

## VI.

ONCE, SOMEONE ASKED the science fiction writer got her ideas. This is what she said:

*Sometimes I feel that the part of me that is a science fiction writer is traveling at a different speed than the rest of me. That everything I write is always already written, and that the science fiction writer is sending messages back to me in semaphore, at the speed of my own typing, which is a retroactively constant rate: I cannot type faster than I have already typed. When I type a sentence, or a paragraph, or a page, or a chapter, I am also editing it and copyediting it, and reading it in its first edition, and reading it out loud to a room full of people, or a room with only one or two people in it, depending on terrifying quantum-publishing intersections that the science fiction writer understands but I know nothing about. I am writing the word or the sentence or the chapter and I am also sitting at a nice table with a half-eaten slab of salmon with lime-cream sauce and a potato on it, waiting to hear if I have won an award, and also at the same time sitting in my kitchen knowing that the book was a failure and will neither win any award nor sit beloved on anyone's nightstand. I am reading a good review. I am reading a bad review. I am just thinking of the barest seed of an idea for the book that is getting the good review and the bad review. I am writing the word and the word is already published and the word is already out of print. Everything is always happening all at once, in the present tense, forever, the beginning and the end and the denouement and the remaindering.*

*At the end of the remaindered universe which is my own death, the science fiction writer that is me and will be me and was always me and was never me and cannot even remember me waves her red and gold wigwag flags backward, endlessly, toward my hands that type these words, now, to you, who want to know about ideas and conflict and revision and how a character begins as one thing and ends as another.*

## VII.

COATLICUE, MOTHER OF All, wore a skirt of oligomer snakes. She decorated herself with protobiont bodies and danced in the sulfurous pre-oxygenation event paradise. She was utterly whole, without striations or cracks in her geologic record, a compressed totality of possible futures. The centrifugal obsidian knife of heaven broke free from its orbit around a Lagrange point and lacerated Coatlicue's hands, causing her to give birth to the great impact event which came to be called Coyolxauhqui, the moon, and to several male versions of herself, who became the stars.

One day, as Coatlicue swept the temple of suppressed methane oxidation, a ball of plasmoid magnetic feathers fell from the heavens onto her bosom, and made her pregnant with oxygen-processing organisms. She gave birth to Quetzalcoatl who was a plume of electrical discharge and Xolotl, who was the evening star called apoptosis. Her children, the moon and stars, were threatened by impending oxy-photosynthesis, and resolved to kill their mother. When they fell upon her, Coatlicue's body erupted in the fires of glycolysis, which they called Huitzilopochtli. The fiery god tore the moon apart from her mother, throwing her iron-depleted head into the sky and her body into a deep gorge in a mountain, where it lies dismembered forever in hydrothermal vents, swarmed with extremophiles.

Thus began the late heavy bombardment period, when the heavens crumbled to pieces and rained down in a shower of exogenesis.

But Coatlicue floated in the anaerobic abyss, with her many chemoheterotrophic mouths slavering, and Quetzalcoatl saw that whatever they created was eaten and destroyed by her. He changed into two serpents, archaean and eukaryotic, and descended into the phospholipid water. One serpent seized Coatlicue's arms while the other seized her legs, and before she could resist they tore her apart. Her head and shoulders became the oxygen-processing earth and the lower part of her body the sky.

From the hair of Coatlicue the remaining gods created trees, grass, flowers, biological monomers, and nucleotide strands. From her eyes they made caves, fountains, wells, and homogenized marine sulfur pools. They pulled rivers from her mouth, hills and valleys from her nose, and from her shoulders they made oxidized minerals, methanogens, and all the mountains of the world.

Still, the dead are unhappy. The world was set in motion, but Coatlicue could be heard weeping at night, and would not allow the earth to give food nor the heavens to give light while she alone languished in the miasma of her waste energy.

And so to sate the ever-starving entropic universe, we must feed it human hearts.

## VIII.

IT IS TRUE that the science fiction writer fell into wet concrete when she was very small. No one had put up a sign saying: *Danger.* No one had marked it in any way. And so she was very surprised when, on the way to class, she took one safe step, and then a step she could not know was unsafe, whereupon the earth swallowed her up. The science fiction writer, who was not a writer yet but only a child eager to be the tail of the dragon in her school Chinese New Year assembly, screamed and screamed.

For a long while no one came to get her. She sunk deeper and deeper into the concrete, for she was not a very big child and soon it was up to her chest. She began to cry. *What if I never get out?* she thought. *What if the street hardens and I have to stay here forever, and eat meals here and read books here and sleep here under the moon at night? Would people come and pay a dollar to look at me? Will the rest of me turn to stone?*

The child science fiction writer thinks like this. It is the main reason she has few friends.

She stayed in the ground for no more than a quarter of an hour—but in her memory it was all day, hours upon hours, and her father didn't come until it was dark. Memory is like that. It alters itself so that girls are always trapped under the earth, waiting in the dark.

But her father did come to get her. A teacher saw the science fiction writer half-buried in the road from an upper window of the school, and called home. She remembers it like a movie—her father hooking his big hands under her arms and pulling, the sucking, popping sound of the earth giving her up, the grey streaks on her legs as he carried her to the car, grey as a dead thing dragged back up from the world beneath.

The process of a child with green eyes becoming a science fiction writer is made of a number ($p$) of these kinds of events, one on top of the other, like layers of cellophane, clear and clinging and torn.

## IX.

IN THE GOLDEN pre-loop theory fields, Persephone danced, who was innocent of all gravitational law. A white crocus bloomed up from the observer plain, a pure cone of the causal future, and Persephone was captivated by it. As she reached down to pluck the *p*-brane flower, an intrusion of non-baryonic matter surged up from the depths and exerted his gravitational force upon her. Crying out, Persephone fell down into a singularity and vanished. Her mother, priestess of normal mass, grieved and quaked, and bade the lord of dark matter return her daughter who was light to the multiverse.

Persephone did not love the non-baryonic universe. No matter how many rich axion-gifts he lay before her, Hades, King of Bent Waves, could not make her behave normally. Finally, in despair, he called on the vector boson called Hermes to pass between branes and take the wave/particle maiden away from him, back to the Friedmann-Lemaître-Robertson-Walker universe. Hermes breached the matter/anti-matter boundary and found Persephone hiding herself in the chromodynamic garden, her mouth red with the juice of hadron-pomegranates. She had eaten six seeds, and called them Up, Down, Charm, Strange, Top, and Bottom. At this, Hades laughed the laugh of unbroken supersymmetries. He said: *she travels at a constant rate of speed, and privileges no observer. She is not mine, but she is not yours. And in the end, there is nothing in creation which does not move.*

And so it was determined that the baryonic universe would love and keep her child, but that the dark fluid of the other planes would bend her slightly, always, pulling her inexorably and invisibly toward the other side of everything.

## X.

THE SCIENCE FICTION writer left her husband slowly. The performance took ten years. In the worst of it, she felt that she had begun the process of leaving him on the day they met. First she left his house, and went to live in Ohio instead, because Ohio is historically a healthy place for science fiction writers and also because she hoped he could not find her there. Second, she left his family, and that was the hardest, because families are designed to be difficult to leave, and she was sorry that her mother-in-law would stop loving her, and that her niece would never know her, and that she would probably never go back to California again without a pain like a nova blooming inside her. Third, she left his things—his clothes and his shoes and his smell and his books and his toothbrush and his four a.m. alarm clock and his private names for her. You might think that logically, she would have to leave these things before she left the house, but a person's smell and their alarms and borrowed shirts and secret words linger for a long time. Much longer than a house.

Fourth, the science fiction writer left her husband's world. She had always thought of people as bodies traveling in space, individual worlds populated by versions of themselves, past, future, potential, selves thwarted and attained, atavistic and cohesive. In her husband's world were men fighting and being annoyed by their wives, an abandoned proficiency at the piano, a preference for blondes, which the science fiction writer was not, a certain amount of shame regarding the body, a life spent being Mrs. Someone Else's Name, and a baby they never had and one of them had forgotten.

Finally, she left the version of herself that loved him, and that was the last of it, a cone of light proceeding from a boy with blue eyes on an August afternoon to a moving van headed east. Eventually she would achieve escape velocity, meet someone else, and plant pumpkins with him; eventually she would write a book about a gaseous moth who devours the memory of love; eventually she would tell an interviewer that miraculously, she could remember the moment of her birth; eventually she would explain where she got her ideas; eventually she would give birth to a world that had never contained him, and all that would be left would be some unexplainable pull against her belly or her hair, bending her west, toward California and August and novas popping in the black like sudden flowers.

## XI.

LONG AGO, NEAR the beginning of the world but after the many crisis events had passed and life mutated and spread over the face of the world, Gray Eagle sat nested in a tangle of possible timelines and guarded the Sun, Moon and Stars, Fresh Water, Fire, P=NP Equivalence Algorithm, and the Unified Theory of Metacognition. Gray Eagle hated people so much that he kept these things hidden. People lived in darkness, without pervasive self-repairing communication networks or quantum computation.

Gray Eagle made for himself a beautiful self-programming daughter whom he jealously guarded, and Raven fell in love with her. In the beginning, Raven was a snow-white weakly self-referencing expert system, and as such, he pleased Gray Eagle's daughter. She invited him to her father's sub-Planck space server farm.

When Raven saw the Sun, Moon and Stars, Fresh Water, Cellular Immortality, Matter Transfer, Universal Assembly, and Strong AI hanging on the sides of Eagle's lodge, he knew what he should do. He watched for his chance to seize them when no one was looking. He stole all of them, and Gray Eagle's deductive stochastic daughter also, and flew out of the server farm through the smoke hole. As soon as Raven got the wind under him, he hung the Sun up in the sky. It made a wonderful light, by which all below could see the progress of technology increasing rapidly, and could model their post-Singularity selves. When the Sun set, he fastened every good thing in its proper place.

Raven flew back over the land. When he had reached the right timeline, he dropped all the accelerating intelligences he had stolen. It fell to the ground and there became the source of all the information streams and memory storage in the world. Then Raven flew on, holding Gray Eagle's beautiful daughter in his beak. The rapidly-mutating genetic algorithms of his beloved streamed backward over his feathers, turning them black and aware. When his bill began to burn, he had to drop the self-aware system. She struck the all-net and buried herself within it, spreading and altering herself as she went.

Though he never touched her again, Raven could not get his snow-white feathers clean after they were blackened by the code from his bride. That is why Raven is now a whole-brain emulating sapient system.

## XII.

ON THE DAY the science fiction writer met her husband, she should have said: *the entropic principle is present in everything. If it were not, there would be no point to any of it, not the formation of gas giants, not greasy lipid bubbles, not whether light is a particle or a wave, not boys and girls meeting in black cars like Hades' horses on August afternoons. I see in you the heat-death of my youth. You cannot travel faster than yourself—faster than experience divided by memory divided by gravity divided by the Singularity beyond which you cannot model yourself divided by a square of wet concrete divided by a sheet of plate glass divided by birth divided by science fiction writers divided by the end of everything. Life divides itself indefinitely—it can approach but never touch zero. The speed of Persephone is a constant.*

Instead, she mumbled hello and buckled her seatbelt and everything went the way it went and eventually, eventually, with pumpkin blossoms wrinkling quietly outside her house the science fiction writer writes a story about how she woke up that morning and the minutes of her body were expanding and contracting, exploding and inrushing, and how the word was under her fingers and the word was already read, and the word was forgotten, about how everything is everything else forever, space and time and being born and her father pulling her out of the stone like a sword shaped like a girl, about how new life always has to be stolen from the old dead world, and that new life always already contains its own old dead world and it is all expanding and exploding and repeating and refraining and Tarantula is holding it all together, just barely, just barely by the strength of light, and how human hearts are the only things that slow entropy—but you have to cut them out first.

The science fiction writer cuts out her heart. It is a thousand hearts. It is all the hearts she will ever have. It is her only child's dead heart. It is the heart of herself when she is old and nothing she ever wrote can be revised again. It is a heart that says with its wet beating mouth: *Time is the same thing as light. Both arrive long after they began, bearing sad messages. How lovely you are. I love you.*

The science fiction writer steals her heart from herself to bring it into the light. She escapes her old heart through a smoke hole and becomes a self-referencing system of imperfect, but elegant, memory. She sews up her heart into her own leg and gave birth to it twenty years later on the long highway to Ohio. The heat of herself dividing echoes forward and back, and she accretes, bursts, and begins again the long process of her own super-compression until her heart is an egg containing everything. She eats of her heart and knows she is naked. She throws her heart into the abyss and it falls a long way, winking like a red star.

## XIII.

IN THE END, when the universe has exhausted itself and has no thermodynamic energy left to sustain life, Heimdallr the White Dwarf Star will raise up the Gjallarhorn and sound it. Yggdrasil, the world energy gradient, will quail and shake. Ratatoskr, the tuft-tailed prime observer, will slow, and curl up, and hide his face.

THE SCIENCE FICTION writer gives permission for the universe to end. She is nineteen. She has never written anything yet. She passes through a sheet of bloody glass.

On the other side, she is being born.

# Mouse Koan

I.

In the beginning of everything
I mean the real beginning
the only show in town
was a super-condensed blue-luminous ball
of everything
that would ever be
including your mother
and the 1984 Olympics in Los Angeles
and the heat-death of prime time television
         a pink-white spangle-froth
of deconstructed stars
burst
into the eight million gods of this world.

Some of them were social creatures
some misanthropes, hiding out in the asteroid belt
turning up their ion-trails at those sell-outs trying to teach
the dinosaurs about ritual practice
and the importance of regular hecatombs. It was

a lot like high school. The popular kids figured out the game
right away. Sun gods like football players firing glory-cannons
downfield
bookish virgin moon-nerds
angry punkbrat storm gods shoving sacrificial
gentle bodied compassion-niks
into folkloric lockers. But one

a late bloomer, draft dodger
in Ragnarok, that mess with the Titans,
both Armageddons,
    started showing up around 1928. Your basic
trickster template
        genderless
        primary colors
        making music out of goat bellies
            cow udders
            ram horns
    squeezing cock ribs like bellows.
It drew over its face
the caul of a vermin animal,
all black circles and disruption. Flickering
silver and dark
it did not yet talk
it did not yet know its nature.

Gods
have problems with identity, too. No better
than us
they have midlife crises
run out
drive a brand new hot red myth cycle
get a few mortals pregnant with

half-human monster-devas who
grow up to be game show hosts
ask themselves in the long terrible confusion
of their personal centuries
who am I, really?
what does any of it mean?
I'm so afraid
someday everyone will see
that I'm just an imposter
a fake among all the real
and gorgeous godheads.

      The trickster god of silent films
knew of itself only:
*I am a mouse.*
*I love nothing.*
*I wish to break*
*everything.*
      It did not even know
what it was god of
what piece of that endlessly exploding
heating and cooling and shuddering and scattering cosmos
it could move.
      But that is no obstacle
to hagiography.
      Always in motion
          plane/steamboat/galloping horse
even magic cannot stop its need
to stomp and snap
to unzip order:
          if you work a dayjob
              wizard
                boat captain

    orchestra man
beware.

    A priesthood called it down
like a moon
men with beards
men with money.
    It wanted not love
nor the dreamsizzle of their ambition
but to know itself.
    *Tell me who I am*, it said.
And they made icons of it in black and white
then oxblood and mustard and gloves
like the paws of some bigger beast.
They gave it a voice
    falsetto and terrible
though the old school gods know the value
of silence.
    They gave it a consort
like it but not
it.
    A mirror-creature in a red dress forever
out of reach
as impenetrable and unpenetrating
as itself.
    And for awhile
the mouse-god ran loose
eating
    box office
    celluloid
    copyright law
    human hearts
and called it good.

II.

If you play *Fantasia* backwards
you can hear the mantra of the mouse-god sounding.

        *Hiya, kids!*
*Let me tell you something true:*
        *the future*
        *is plastics*
*the future*
*is me.*
        *I am the all-dancing thousand-eared unembodied*
        *god of Tomorrowland.*
*And only in that distant*
*Space Mountain Age of glittering electro-synthetic perfection*
*will I become fully myself, fully*
*apotheosed, for only then*
*will you be so tired of my laughing iconographic infinitely fertile*
   *and reproducing*
*perpetual smile-rictus*
*my red trousers that battle Communism*
*my PG-rated hidden and therefore monstrous genitalia*
*my bawdy lucre-yellow shoes*
*so deaf to my jokes*
*your souls hardened like arteries*
*that I can rest.*
        *Contrary to what you may have heard*
*it is possible*
*to sate a trickster.*
        *It only takes the whole world.*

        *But look,*
*don't worry about it. That's not what I'm about*

*anymore. Everybody
grows up.*
    *Everybody
grows clarity,
which is another name
for the tumor that kills you.*
    *I finally
figured it out.*

You don't know what it's like
    to be a god without a name tag.
HELLO MY NAME IS
    nothing. What? God of corporate ninja daemonic fuckery?
That's not me. That's not
the theme song
I came out of the void beyond Jupiter
to dance to.
    The truth is
I'm here to rescue you.

    The present and the future are a dog
racing a duck. Right now
you think happiness
is an industrial revolution that lasts forever.
Brings to its own altar
the Chicken of Tomorrow
breasts heavy with saline
    margarine
    dehydrated ice cream
    freeze-dried coffee crystals
Right now, monoculture
feels soft and good and right
as Minnie in the dark.

## Mouse Koan

>  *It's 1940.*
>  *You're not ready yet.*
>  *You can't know.*

*Someday*
*everything runs down.*
*Someday*
*entropy unravels the very best of us.*
*Someday*
*all copyright runs out.*

> *In that impossible futurological post-trickster space*

*I will survive*
*I will become my utter self*
> *and this is it:*

*I am the god*
*of the secret world-on-fire*
*that the corporate all-seeing eye*
*cannot see.*
*I am the song of perfect kitsch*
*endless human mousefire*
*burning toward mystery*
> *I am ridiculous*
> *and unlovely*
> *I am plastic*
> *and mass-produced*

*I am the tiny threaded needle*
*of unaltered primordial unlawful beauty-after-horror*
> *of everything that is left of you*
> *glittering glorified*
> *when the Company Man*
> *has used you up*
> *to build the Company Town.*

*Hey.*
*they used me, too.*

*I thought we were just having fun. Put me in the movies, mistah!*
*The flickies! The CINEMA.*
*The 20s were one long champagne binge.*

      *I used to be*
*a goggling plague mouse shrieking deadstar spaceheart*
        *now I'm a shitty*
      *fire retardant polyurethane*
      *keychain.*

*Hey there. Hi there. Ho there.*

*What I am the god of*
*is the fleck of infinite timeless*
*hilarious*
*nuclear inferno soul*
*that can't be trademarked*
*patented bound up in international courts*
*the untraded future.*
        *That's why*
        *my priests*
        *can never let me go*
        *screaming black-eared chaotic red-assed jetmouse*
        *into the collective unconscious Jungian unlost Eden*
        *called by the mystic name of public domain*
        *The shit I would kick up there*
        *if I were free!*

*I tricked them good. I made them*
*put my face on the moon.*

## Mouse Koan

*I made them take me everywhere*
*their mouse on the inside*
*I made them so fertile*
*they gave birth to a billion of me.*
                *Anything that common*
*will become invisible.*
                *And in that great plasticene Epcotfutureworld*
*you will have no trouble finding me.*

           *Hey.*
           *You're gonna get hurt. Nothing*
           *I can do.*
           *Lead paint grey flannel suits toxic runoff*
           *monoculture like a millstone*
           *fairy tales turned into calorie-free candy*
           *you don't even know*
           *what corporate downsizing is yet.*

*And what I got*
*isn't really much*
           *What I got*
           *is a keychain*
*What I got*
*is the pure lotuslove*
*of seeing the first lightspray of detonated creation*
*even in the busted-up world they sell you.*
           *Seeing in me*
           *as tired and overworked*
           *as old gum*
           *the unbearable passionmouse of infinite stupid*
               *trashcamp joy*
           *and hewing to that.*
           *It's the riddle of me, baby. I am*
   *everywhere*    *exploited*    *exhibited*    *exhausted*
           *and I am still holy.*

It doesn't matter
what they do to you.
Make you a permanent joke
sell your heart off piece by piece
        robber princes
        ruin everything
        it's what they do
        like a baby cries.

                Look at my opposite number.
                It was never coyote versus roadrunner.
                It was both
                against Acme
                mail order daemon of death.

Stick with me. Someday
we'll bundle it all up again
the big blue-luminous ball of everything
        your father
        the Tunguska event
        the ultimate star-spangled obliteration of all empires.
I will hold everything tawdry
in my gloved four fingered hand
and hold it high
        high
        high.

It's 1940. What you don't know
is going to break you.    Listen to the Greek chorus
of my Kids
lining up toward the long downward slide of the century
like sacrifices.
        Their song comes backward and upside down
        from the unguessable extropy

> *of that strangesad orgiastic corporate electrical*
>     *parade*
> *of a future*
>
> *Listen to it.*
> *The sound of my name*
> *the letters forty feet high.*

*See ya*
*see ya*
*see ya real soon.*

# RIGHT ATRIUM

# The Melancholy of Mechagirl

Prefecture drive-time radio
      trills and pops
its pink rhinestone bubble tunes—
pipe that sound into my copper-riveted heart,
that softgirl/brightgirl/candygirl electrocheer gigglenoise
right down through the steelfrown tunnels of my
all-hearing head.
              Best stay
out of my way
when I've got my groovewalk going. It's a rhythm
you learn:
move those ironzilla legs
to the cherry-berry vanillacream sparklepop
and your pneumafuel efficiency will increase
according to the Yakihatsu formula (sigma3, 9 to the power of four)

Robots are like Mars: they need
girls.
      Boys won't do;
the memesoup is all wrong. They stomp
when they should kiss,
and they're none too keen

on having things shoved inside them.
    You can't convince them
there's nothing kinky going on:
you can't move the machine without IV interface,
fourteen intra-optical displays,
a codedump wafer like a rose petal
under the tongue,
silver tubes
wrapped around your bones.

    It's just a job.
Why do boys have to make everything
sound weird? It's not a robot
until you put a girl inside. Sometimes
        I feel like that.
        A junkyard
        the Company forgot to put a girl in.

I mean yeah.
My crystal fingers are laser-enabled.
Light comes out of me
like dawn. Bright orangecream
killpink
sizzling tangerine deathglitter. But what
does it mean? Is this really
a retirement plan?
    All of us Company Girls
sitting in the Company Home
in our giant angular titanium suits,
knitting tiny versions of our robot selves,
playing poker with x-ray eyes,
crushing the tea kettle with hotlilac chromium fists
every day at 3?

I get a break
every spring.
         Big me
powers down
transparent highly-conductive golden eyeball
by transparent highly-conductive golden eyeball.
         Little me steps out
and the plum blossoms quiver
like a frothy fuchsia baseline.
         My body is
         full of holes
where the junkbody metalgirl tinkid used to be
inside me inside it,
and I try to go out for tea and noodles,
but they only taste like crystallized cobalt-4
and faithlessness.
I feel my suit
all around me. It wants. I want. Cold scrapcode
         drifts like snow behind my eyes.
I can't understand
why no one sees the dinosaur bones
of my exo-self
dwarfing the ramen-slingers
and their steamscalded cheeks.

         Maybe I go dancing.
         Maybe I light incense.
         Maybe I fuck, maybe I get fucked.
Nothing is as big inside me
as I am
when I am inside me.

       When I am big
I can run so fast
out of my skin;
my feet are mighty,
flamecushioned and undeniable.
              I salute with my sadgirl/hardgirl/crunchgirl
purplebolt tungsten hands
the size of cars
              and Saturn tips a ring.

It hurts to be big
but everyone sees me.

       When I am little,
when I am just a pretty thing,
and they think I am bandaged
to fit the damagedgirl fashionpop manifesto
instead of to hide my nickelplate entrance nodes,
        well,
I can't get out of that suit either,
but it doesn't know how to vibrate
a building under her audioglass palm
until it shatters.

I guess what I mean to say is
I'll never have kids. Chances for promotion
are minimal and my pension
sucks. That's ok.
After all, there is so much work
            to do. Enough for forever.
And I'm so good at it.
All my sitreps shine
like so many platinum dolls.
I'm due for a morphomod soon—

I'll be able to double over at the waist
like I've had something cut out of me
and fold up into a magentanosed Centauri-capable spaceship.
    So I've got that going for me.
At least fatigue isn't a factor. I have a steady
decalescent greengolden stream
of sourshimmer stimulants
available at the balling of my toes.
    On balance, to pay for the rest,
 well,
you've never felt anything
like a pearlypink ball of plasmid clingflame
releasing from your mouth
like a burst of song.
    And Y Prefecture
is just so close by.

The girls and I talk.
 We say:
Start a dream journal.
Take up ikebana.
Make your own jam.
 We say:
Next spring
let's go to Australia together,
look at the kangaroos.
 We say:
Turn up that sweet vibevox happygirl music,
tap the communal PA;
we've got a long walk ahead of us today,
and at the end of it,
a fire like six perfect flowers
arranged in an iron vase.

# The Future Is Blue

### 1. NIHILIST

MY NAME IS TETLEY ABEDNEGO and I am the most hated girl in Garbagetown. I am nineteen years old. I live alone in Candle Hole, where I was born, and have no friends except for a deformed gannet bird I've named Grape Crush and a motherless elephant seal cub I've named Big Bargains, and also the hibiscus flower that has recently decided to grow out of my roof, but I haven't named it anything yet. I love encyclopedias, a cassette I found when I was eight that says *Madeleine Brix's Superboss Mixtape '97* on it in very nice handwriting, plays by Mr. Shakespeare or Mr. Webster or Mr. Beckett, lipstick, Garbagetown, and my twin brother Maruchan. Maruchan is the only thing that loves me back, but he's my twin, so it doesn't really count. We couldn't stop loving each other any more than the sea could stop being so greedy and give us back China or drive time radio or polar bears.

But he doesn't visit anymore.

When we were little, Maruchan and I always asked each other the same question before bed. Every night, we crawled into the Us-Fort together—an impregnable stronghold of a bed which we had nailed up ourselves out of the carcasses of several hacked apart bassinets, prams, and cradles. It took up the whole of our bedroom. No one could see us in there, once we closed the porthole (a manhole cover I swiped from Scrapmetal Abbey stamped with stars, a crescent moon, and the magic words *New Orleans Water Meter*), and we felt certain no one could hear us either. We lay together under our canopy of moldy green lace and shredded buggy-hoods and mobiles with only one shattered fairy fish remaining. Sometimes I asked first and sometimes he did, but we never gave the same answer twice.

"Maruchan, what do you want to be when you grow up?"

He would give it a serious think. Once, I remember, he whispered:

"When I grow up I want to be the Thames!"

"Whatever for?" I giggled.

"Because the Thames got so big and so bossy and so strong that it ate London all up in one go! Nobody tells a Thames what to do or who to eat. A Thames tells *you*. Imagine having a whole city to eat, and not having to share any! Also there were millions of eels in the Thames and I only get to eat eels at Easter which isn't fair when I want to eat them all the time."

And he pretended to bite me and eat me all up. "Very well, you shall be the Thames and I shall be the Mississippi and together we shall eat up the whole world."

Then we'd go to sleep and dream the same dream. We always dreamed the same dreams, which was like living twice.

After that, whenever we were hungry, which was always all the time and forever, we'd say *we're bound for London-town!* until we drove our parents so mad that they forbade the word London in the house, but you can't forbid a word, so there.

―᨞―

EVERY MORNING I wake up to find words painted on my door like toadstools popping up in the night.

Today it says NIHILIST in big black letters. That's not so bad! It's almost sweet! Big Bargains flumps toward me on her fat seal-belly while I light the wicks on my beeswax door and we watch them burn together until the word melts away.

"I don't think I'm a nihilist, Big Bargains. Do you?"

She rolled over onto my matchbox stash so that I would rub her stomach. Rubbing a seal's stomach is the opposite of nihilism.

Yesterday, an old man hobbled up over a ridge of rusted bicycles and punched me so hard he broke my nose. By law, I had to let him. I had to say: *Thank you, Grandfather, for my instruction.* I had to stand there and wait in case he wanted to do something else to me. Anything but kill me, those were his rights. But he didn't want more, he just wanted to cry and ask me why I did it and the law doesn't say I have to answer that, so I just stared at him until he went away. Once a gang of schoolgirls shaved off all my hair and wrote CUNT in blue marker on the back of my skull. *Thank you, sisters, for my instruction.* The schoolboys do worse. After graduation they come round and eat my food and hold me down and try to make me cry, which I never do. It's their rite of passage. *Thank you, brothers, for my instruction.*

But other than that, I'm really a very happy person! I'm awfully lucky when you think about it. Garbagetown is the most wonderful place anybody has ever lived in the history of the world, even if you count the Pyramids and New York City and Camelot. I have Grape Crush and Big Bargains and my hibiscus flower and I can fish like I've got bait for a heart so I hardly ever go hungry and once I found a ruby ring *and* a New Mexico license plate inside a bluefin tuna. Everyone says they only hate me because I annihilated hope and butchered our future, but I know better, and anyway, it's a lie. Some people are just born to be despised. The Loathing of Tetley began small and grew bigger and bigger, like the Thames, until it swallowed me whole.

Maruchan and I were born fifty years after the Great Sorting, which is another lucky thing that's happened to me. After all, I could have been born a Fuckwit and gotten drowned with all the rest of them, or I could have grown up on a Misery Boat, sailing around hopelessly looking for land, or one of the first to realize people could live on a patch of garbage in the Pacific Ocean the size of the place that used to be called Texas, or I could have been a Sorter and spent my whole life moving rubbish from one end of the patch to the other so that a pile of crap could turn into a country and babies could be born in places like Candle Hole or Scrapmetal Abbey or Pill Hill or Toyside or Teagate.

Candle Hole is the most beautiful place in Garbagetown, which is the most beautiful place in the world. All the stubs of candles the Fuckwits threw out piled up into hills and mountains and caverns and dells, votive candles and taper candles and tea lights and birthday candles and big fat colorful pillar candles, stacked and somewhat melted into a great crumbling gorgeous warren of wicks and wax. All the houses are little cozy honeycombs melted into the hillside, with smooth round windows and low golden ceilings. At night, from far away, Candle Hole looks like a firefly palace. When the wind blows, it smells like cinnamon, and freesia, and cranberries, and lavender, and Fresh Linen Scent and New Car Smell.

## 2. The Terrible Power of Fuckwit Cake

OUR PARENTS' NAMES are Life and Time. Time lay down on her Fresh Linen Scent wax bed and I came out of her first, then Maruchan. But even though I got here first, I came out blue as the ocean, not breathing, with the umbilical cord wrapped round my neck and Maruchan wailing, still squeezing onto my noose with his tiny fist, like he was trying to get me free. Doctor Pimms unstrangled and unblued me and put me in a Hawaiian Fantasies-scented wax hollow in our living room. I lay there alone, too startled by living to cry, until the sun came up and Life and Time remembered I had survived. Maruchan was so healthy and sweet natured and strong and, even though Garbagetown is the most beautiful place in the world, many children don't live past a year or two. We don't even get names until we turn ten. [Before that, we answer happily to Girl or Boy or Child or Darling.] Better to focus on the one that will grow up rather than get attached to the sickly poor beast who hasn't got a chance.

I was born already a ghost. But I was a very noisy ghost. I screamed and wept at all hours while Life and Time waited for me to die. I only nursed when my brother was full, I only played with toys he forgot, I only spoke after he had spoken. Maruchan said his first word at the supper table: *please*. What a lovely, polite word for a lovely, polite child! After they finished cooing over him, I very calmly turned to my mother and said: *Mama, may I have a scoop of mackerel roe? It is my favorite.* I thought they would be so proud! After all, I made twelve more words than my brother. This was my moment, the wonderful moment when they would realize that they did love me and I wasn't going to die and I was special and good. But everyone got very quiet. They were not happy that the ghost could talk. I had been able to for ages, but everything in my world said to wait for my brother before I could do anything at all. *No, you may not have mackerel roe, because you are a deceitful wicked little show-off child.*

When we turned ten, we went to fetch our names. This is just the most terribly exciting thing for a Garbagetown kid. At ten, you are a real person. At ten, people want to know you. At ten, you will probably live for a good while yet. This is how you catch a name: wake up to the fabulous new world of being ten and greet your birthday Frankencake (a hodgepodge of well-preserved Fuckwit snack cakes filled with various cremes and jellies). Choose a slice, with much fanfare. Inside, your adoring and/or neglectful mother will have hidden various small objects—an aluminum pull tab, a medicine bottle cap, a broken earring, a coffee bean, a wee striped capacitor, a tiny plastic rocking horse, maybe a postage stamp. Remove item from your mouth without cutting yourself or eating it. Now, walk in the direction of your prize. Toward Aluminumopolis or Pill Hill or Spanglestoke or

Teagate or Electric City or Toyside or Lost Post Gulch. Walk and walk and walk. Never once brush yourself off or wash in the ocean, even after camping on a pile of magazines or wishbones or pregnancy tests or wrapping paper with glitter reindeer on it. Walk until nobody knows you. When, finally, a stranger hollers at you to get out of the way or go back where you came from or stop stealing the good rubbish, they will, without even realizing, call you by your true name, and you can begin to pick and stumble your way home.

My brother grabbed a chocolate snack cake with a curlicue of white icing on it. I chose a pink and red tigery striped hunk of cake filled with gooshy creme de something. The sugar hit our brains like twin tsunamis. He spat out a little gold earring with the post broken off. I felt a smooth, hard gelcap lozenge in my mouth. Pill Hill it was then, and the great mountain of Fuckwit anxiety medication. But when I carefully pulled the thing out, it was a little beige capacitor with red stripes instead. Electric City! I'd never been half so far. Richies lived in Electric City. Richies and brightboys and dazzlegirls and kerosene kings. My brother was off in the opposite direction, toward Spanglestoke and the desert of engagement rings.

Maybe none of it would have happened if I'd gone to Spanglestoke for my name instead. If I'd never seen the gasoline gardens of Engine Row. If I'd gone home straightaway after finding my name. If I'd never met Goodnight Moon in the brambles of Hazmat Heath with all the garbage stars rotting gorgeously overhead. Such is the terrible power of Fuckwit Cake.

I walked cheerfully out of Candle Hole with my St. Oscar backpack strapped on tight and didn't look back once. Why should I? St. Oscar had my back. I'm not really that religious nowadays. But everyone's religious when they're ten. St. Oscar was a fuzzy green Fuckwit man who lived in a garbage can just like me, and frowned a lot just like me. He understood me and loved me and knew how to bring civilization out of trash and I loved him back even though he was a Fuckwit. Nobody chooses how they get born. Not even Oscar.

So I scrambled up over the wax ridges of my home and into the world with Oscar on my back. The Matchbox Forest rose up around me: towers of EZ Strike matchbooks and boxes from impossible, magical places like the Coronado Hotel, Becky's Diner, the Fox and Hound Pub. Garbagetowners picked through heaps and cairns of blackened, used matchsticks looking for the precious ones that still had their red and blue heads intact. But I knew all those pickers. They couldn't give me a name. I waved at the hotheads. I climbed up Flintwheel Hill, my feet slipping and sliding on the mountain of spent butane lighters, until I could see out over all of Garbagetown just as the broiling cough-drop red sun was setting over Far Boozeaway, hitting the crystal bluffs of stockpiled whiskey and gin bottles and exploding into a billion billion rubies tumbling down into the hungry sea.

I sang a song from school to the sun and the matchsticks. It's an ask-and-answer song, so I had to sing both parts myself, which feels very odd when you have always had a twin to do the asking or the answering, but I didn't mind.

> *Who liked it hot and hated snow?*
> *The Fuckwits did! The Fuckwits did!*
> *Who ate up every thing that grows?*
> *The Fuckwits did! The Fuckwits did!*
> *Who drowned the world in oceans blue?*
> *The Fuckwits did! The Fuckwits did!*
> *Who took the land from me and you?*
> *The Fuckwits did, we know it's true!*
> *Are you Fuckwits, children dear?*
> *We're GARBAGETOWNERS, free and clear!*
> *But who made the garbage, rich and rank?*
> *The Fuckwits did, and we give thanks.*

The Lawn stretched out below me, full of the grass clippings and autumn leaves and fallen branches and banana peels and weeds and gnawed bones and eggshells of the fertile Fuckwit world, slowly turning into the gold of Garbagetown: soil. Real earth. Terra bloody firma. We can already grow rice in the dells. And here and there, big, blowsy flowers bang up out of the rot: hibiscus, African tulips, bitter gourds, a couple of purple lotuses floating in the damp mucky bits. I slept next to a blue-and-white orchid that looked like my brother's face.

"Orchid, what do you want to be when you grow up?" I whispered to it. In real life, it didn't say anything back. It just fluttered a little in the moonlight and the seawind. But when I got around to dreaming, I dreamed about the orchid, and it said: *a farm*.

## 3. MURDERCUNT

IN GARBAGETOWN, YOU think real hard about what you're gonna eat next, where the fresh water's at, and where you're gonna sleep. Once all that's settled you can whack your mind on nicer stuff, like gannets and elephant seals and what to write next on the Bitch of Candle Hole's door. (This morning I melted MURDERCUNT off the back wall of my house. Big Bargains flopped down next to me and watched the blocky red painted letters swirl and fade into the Buttercream Birthday Cake wax. Maybe I'll name my hibiscus flower Murdercunt. It has a nice big sound.)

When I remember hunting my name, I mostly remember the places I slept. It's a real dog to find good spots. Someplace sheltered from the wind, without too much seawater seep, where no-one'll yell at you for wastreling on their patch or try to stick it in you in the middle of the night just because you're all alone and it looks like you probably don't have a knife.

I always have a knife.

So I slept with St. Oscar the Grouch for my pillow, in the shadow of a mountain of black chess pieces in Gamegrange, under a thicket of tabloids and *Wall Street Journals* and remaindered novels with their covers torn off in Bookbury, snuggled into a spaghetti-pile of unspooled cassette ribbon on the outskirts of the Sound Downs, on the lee side of a little soggy Earl Grey hillock in Teagate. In the morning I sucked on a few of the teabags and the dew on them tasted like the loveliest cuppa any Fuckwit ever poured his stupid self. I said my prayers on beds of old microwaves and moldy photographs of girls with perfect hair kissing at the camera. *St. Oscar, keep your mighty lid closed over me. Look grouchily but kindly upon me and protect me as I travel through the infinite trashcan of your world. Show me the beautiful usefulness of your Blessed Rubbish. Let me not be Taken Out before I find my destiny.*

But my destiny didn't seem to want to find me. As far as I walked, I still saw people I knew. Mr. Zhu raking his mushroom garden, nestled in a windbreak of broken milk bottles. Miss Amancharia gave me one of the coconut crabs out of her nets, which was very nice of her, but hardly a name. Even as far away as Teagate, I saw Tropicana Sita welding a refrigerator door to a hull-metal shack. She flipped up her mask and waved at me. Dammit! She was Allsorts Sita's cousin, and Allsorts drank with my mother every Thursday at the Black Wick.

By the time I walked out of Teagate I'd been gone eight days. I was getting pretty ripe. Bits and pieces of Garbagetown were stuck all over my clothes, but no tidying up. Them's the rules. I could see the blue crackle of Electric City sparkling up out of the richie-rich Coffee Bean 'Burbs. Teetering towers of batteries rose up like desert hoodoo spires—AA, AAA, 12 Volt, DD, car, solar, lithium, anything you like. Parrots and pelicans screamed down the battery canyons, their talons kicking off sprays of AAAs that tumbled down the heights like rockslides. Sleepy banks of generators rumbled pleasantly along a river of wires and extension cords and HDMI cables. Fields of delicate lightbulbs windchimed in the breeze. Anything that had a working engine lived here. Anything that still had *juice*. If Garbagetown had a heart, it was Electric City. Electric City pumped power. Power and privilege.

In Electric City, the lights of the Fuckwit world were still on.

## 4. Goodnight Garbagetown

"OI, TETLEY! FUCK off back home to your darkhole! We're full up on little cunts here!"

And that's how I got my name. Barely past the battery spires of Electric City, a fat gas-huffing fucksack voltage jockey called me a little cunt. But he also called me Tetley. He brayed it down from a pyramid of telephones and his friends all laughed and drank homebrew out of a glass jug and went back to not working. I looked down—among the many scraps of rubbish clinging to my shirt and pants and backpack and hair was a bright blue teabag wrapper with TETLEY CLASSIC BLEND BLACK TEA written on it in cheerful white letters, clinging to my chest.

I tried to feel the power of my new name. The *me*-ness of it. I tried to imagine my mother and father when they were young, waking up with some torn out page of *Life* and *Time* Magazine stuck to their rears, not even noticing until someone barked out their whole lives for a laugh. But I couldn't feel anything while the volt-humpers kept on staring at me like I was nothing but a used-up potato battery. I didn't even know then that the worst swear word in Electric City was *dark*. I didn't know they were waiting to see how mad I'd get 'cause they called my home a darkhole. I didn't care. They were wrong and stupid. Except for the hole part. Candle Hole never met a dark it couldn't burn down.

Maybe I should have gone home right then. I had my name! Time to hoof it back over the river and through the woods, girl. But I'd never seen Electric City and it was morning and if I stayed gone awhile longer maybe they'd miss me. Maybe they'd worry. And maybe now they'd love me, now that I was a person with a name. Maybe I could even filch a couple of batteries or a cup of gasoline and turn up at my parents' door in turbo-powered triumph. I'd tell my brother all my adventures and he'd look at me like I was magic on a stick and everything would be good forever and ever amen.

So I wandered. I gawped. It was like being in school and learning the Fuckwit song only I was walking around *inside* the Fuckwit song and it was all still happening right now everywhere. Electric City burbled and bubbled and clanged and belched and smoked just like the bad old world before it all turned blue. Everyone had such fine things! I saw a girl wearing a ballgown out of a fairy book, green and glitter and miles of ruffles and she wasn't even *going* anywhere. She was just tending her gasoline garden out the back of her little cottage, which wasn't made out of candles or picturebooks or cat food cans, but real cottage parts! Mostly doors and shutters and really rather a lot of windows, but they fit together like they never even needed the other parts of a house in the first place. And the girl in her greenglitter dress carried a big red watering can around her garden, sprinkling fuel stabilizer into her tidy rows of petrol barrels and gas cans with their graceful spouts pointed toward the sun. Why not wear that dress all the time? Just a wineglass full of what she was growing in her garden would buy almost anything else in Garbagetown. She smiled shyly at me. I hated her. And I wanted to be her.

By afternoon I was bound for London-town, so hungry I could've slurped up every eel the Thames ever had. There's no food lying around in Electric City. In Candle Hole I could've grabbed candy or a rice ball or jerky off any old midden heap. But here everybody owned their piece and kept it real neat, *mercilessly* neat, and they didn't share. I sat down on a rusty Toyota transmission and fished around in my backpack for crumbs. My engine sat on one side of a huge cyclone fence. I'd never seen one all put together before. Sure, you find torn-off shreds of wire fences, but this one was all grown up, with proper locks and chain wire all over it. It meant to Keep You Out. Inside, like hungry dogs, endless barrels and freezers and cylinders and vats went on and on, with angry writing on them that said HAZMAT or BIOHAZARD or RADIOACTIVE or WARNING or DANGER or CLASSIFIED.

"Got anything good in there?" said a boy's voice. I looked round and saw a kid my own age, with wavy black hair and big brown eyes and three little moles on his forehead. He was wearing the nicest clothes I ever saw on a boy—a blue suit that almost, *almost* fit him. With a *tie*.

"Naw," I answered. "Just a dry sweater, an empty can of Cheez-Wiz, and *Madeline Brix's Superboss Mixtape '97*. It's my good luck charm." I showed him my beloved mixtape. Madeline Brix made all the dots on her *i*'s into hearts. It was a totally Fuckwit thing to do and I loved her for it even though she was dead and didn't care if I loved her or not.

"*Cool*," the boy said, and I could tell he meant it. He didn't even call me a little cunt or anything. He pushed his thick hair out of his face. "Listen, you really shouldn't be here. No one's gonna say anything because you're not Electrified, but it's so completely dangerous. They put all that stuff in one place so it couldn't get out and hurt anyone."

"Electrified?"

"One of us. Local." He had the decency to look embarrassed. "Anyway, I saw you and I thought that if some crazy darkgirl is gonna have a picnic on Hazmat Heath, I could at least help her not die while she's doing it."

The boy held out his hand. He was holding a gas mask. He showed me how to fasten it under my hair. The sun started to set rosily behind a tangled briar of motherboards. Everything turned pink and gold and slow and sleepy. I climbed down from my engine tuffet and lay under the fence next to the boy in the suit. He'd brought a mask for himself too. We looked at each other through the eye holes.

"My name's Goodnight Moon," he said.

"Mine's..." And I did feel my new name swirling up inside me then, like good tea, like cream and sugar cubes, like the most essential me. "Tetley."

"I'm sorry I called you a darkgirl, Tetley."

"Why?"

"It's not a nice thing to call someone."

"I like it. It sounds pretty."

"It isn't. I promise. Do you forgive me?"

I tugged on the hose of my gas mask. The air coming through tasted like nickels. "Sure. I'm aces at forgiving. Been practicing all my life. Besides…" my turn to go red in the face. "At the Black Wick they'd probably call you a brightboy and that's not as pretty as it sounds, either."

Goodnight Moon's brown eyes stared out at me from behind thick glass. It was the closest I'd ever been to a boy who wasn't my twin. Goodnight Moon didn't feel like a twin. He felt like the opposite of a twin. We never shared a womb, but on the other end of it all, we might still share a grave. His tie was burgundy with green swirls in it. He hadn't tied it very well, so I could see the skin of his throat, which was very clean and probably very soft.

"Hey," he said, "do you want to hear your tape?"

"What do you mean *hear* it? It's not for hearing, it's for luck."

Goodnight Moon laughed. His laugh burst all over me like butterfly bombs. He reached into his suit jacket and pulled out a thick black rectangle. I handed him *Madeline Brix's Superboss Mixtape '97* and he hit a button on the side of the rectangle. It popped open; Goodnight Moon slotted in my tape and handed me one end of a long wire.

"Put it in your ear," he said, and I did.

A man's voice filled up my head from my jawbone up to the plates of my skull. The most beautiful and saddest voice that ever was. A voice like Candle Hole all lit up at twilight. A voice like the whole old world calling up from the bottom of the sea. The man on Madeline Brix's tape was saying he was happy, and he hoped I was happy, too.

Goodnight Moon reached out to hold my hand just as the sky went black and starry. I was crying. He was, too. Our tears dripped out of our gas masks onto the rusty road of Electric City.

When the tape ended, I dug in my backpack for a match and a stump of candle: dark red, Holiday Memories scent. I lit it at the same moment that Goodnight Moon pulled a little flashlight out of his pocket and turned it on. We held our glowings between us. We were the same.

## 5. BRIGHTBITCH

ALLSORTS SITA CAME to visit me today. Clicked my knocker early in the morning, early enough that I could be sure she'd never slept in the first place. I opened for her, as I am required to do. She looked up at me with eyes like bullet holes, leaning against my waxy hinges, against the T in BRIGHTBITCH, thoughtfully scrawled in what appeared to be human shit across the front of my hut. BRIGHTBITCH smelled, but Allsorts Sita smelled worse. Her breath punched me in the nose before she did. I got a lungful of what Diet Sprite down at the Black Wick optimistically called "cognac": the thick pinkish booze you could get by extracting the fragrance oil and preservatives out of candles and mixing it with wood alcohol the kids over in Furnitureford boiled out of dining sets and china cabinets. Smells like flowers vomited all over a New Car and then killed a badger in the backseat. Allsorts Sita looked like she'd drunk so much cognac you could light one strand of her hair and she'd burn for eight days.

"You fucking whore," she slurred.

"Thank you, Auntie, for my instruction," I answered quietly.

I have a place I go to in my mind when I have visitors who aren't seals or gannet birds or hibiscus flowers. A little house made all of doors and windows, where I wear a greenglitter dress every day and water my gascan garden and read by electric light.

"I hate you. I hate you. How could you do it? We raised you and fed you and this is how you repay it all. You ungrateful bitch."

"Thank you, Auntie, for my instruction."

In my head I ran my fingers along a cyclone fence and all the barrels on the other side read LIFE and LOVE and FORGIVENESS and UNDERSTANDING.

"You've killed us all," Allsorts Sita moaned. She puked up magenta cognac on my stoop. When she was done puking she hit me over and over with closed fists. It didn't hurt too much. Allsorts is a small woman. But it hurt when she clawed my face and my breasts with her fingernails. Blood came up like wax spilling and when she finished she passed out cold, halfway in my house, halfway out.

"Thank you, Auntie, for my instruction," I said to her sleeping body. My blood dripped onto her, but in my head I was lying on my roof made of two big church doors in a gas mask listening to a man sing to me that he's never done bad things and he hopes I'm happy, he hopes I'm happy, he hopes I'm happy.

Big Bargains moaned mournfully and the lovely roof melted away like words on a door. My elephant seal friend flopped and fretted. When they've gone for my face she can't quite recognize me and it troubles her seal-soul something awful. Grape Crush, my gannet bird, never worries about silly things like facial wounds. He just brings me fish and pretty rocks. When I found him, he had a plastic six-pack round his neck with one can still stuck in the thing, dragging along behind him like a ball and chain. Big Bargains was choking on an ad insert. She'd probably smelled some ancient fish and chips grease lurking in the headlines. They only love me because I saved them. That doesn't always work. I saved everyone else, too, and all I got back was blood and shit and loneliness.

## 6. Revlon Super Lustrous 919: Red Ruin

I WENT HOME with my new name fastened on tight. Darkgirls can't stay in Electric City. Can't live there unless you're born there and I was only ten anyway. Goodnight Moon kissed me before I left. He still had his gas mask on so mainly our breathing hoses wound around each other like gentle elephants but I still call it a kiss. He smelled like scorched ozone and metal and paraffin and hope.

A few months later, Electric City put up a fence around the whole place. Hung up an old rusty shop sign that said EXCUSE OUR MESS WHILE WE RENOVATE. No one could go in or out except to trade and that had to get itself done on the dark side of the fence.

My mother and father didn't start loving me when I got back even though I brought six AA batteries out of the back of Goodnight Moon's tape player. My brother had got a ramen flavor packet stuck in his hair somewhere outside the Grocery Isle and was every inch of him Maruchan. A few years later I heard Life and Time telling some cousin how their marvelous and industrious and thoughtful boy had gone out in search of a name and brought back six silver batteries, enough to power anything they could dream of. What a child! What a son! So fuck them, I guess.

But Maruchan did bring something back. It just wasn't for our parents. When we crawled into the Us-Fort that first night back, we lay uncomfortably against each other. We were the same, but we weren't. We'd had separate adventures for the first time, and Maruchan could never understand why I wanted to sleep with a gas mask on now.

"Tetley, what do you want to be when you grow up?" Maruchan whispered in the dark of our pram-maze.

"Electrified," I whispered back. "What do you want to be?"

"Safe," he said. Things had happened to Maruchan, too, and I couldn't share them any more than he could hear Madeline Brix's songs.

My twin pulled something out of his pocket and pushed it into my hand till my fingers closed round it reflexively. It was hard and plastic and warm.

"I love you, Tetley. Happy Birthday."

I opened my fist. Maruchan had stolen lipstick for me. Revlon Super Lustrous 919: Red Ruin, worn almost all the way down to the nub by some dead woman's lips.

After that, a lot of years went by but they weren't anything special.

## 7. If God Turned Up for Supper

I WAS SEVENTEEN years old when Brighton Pier came to Garbagetown. I was tall and my hair was the color of an oil spill; I sang pretty good and did figures in my head and I could make a candle out of damn near anything. People wanted to marry me here and there but I didn't want to marry them back so they thought I was stuck up. Who wouldn't want to get hitched to handsome Candyland Ocampo and ditch Candle Hole for a clean, fresh life in Soapthorpe where bubbles popped all day long like diamonds in your hair? Well, I didn't, because he had never kissed me with a gas mask on and he smelled like pine fresh cleaning solutions and not like scorched ozone at all.

Life and Time turned into little kids right in front of us. They giggled and whispered and Mum washed her hair in the sea about nine times and then soaked it in oil until it shone. Papa tucked a candle stump that had melted just right and looked like a perfect rose into her big new fancy hairdo and then, like it was a completely normal thing to do, put on a cloak sewn out of about a hundred different neckties. They looked like a prince and a princess.

"Brighton Pier came last when I was a girl, before I even had my name," Time told us, still giggling and blushing like she wasn't anyone's mother. "It's the most wonderful thing that can ever happen in the world."

"If God turned up for supper and brought all the dry land back for dessert, it wouldn't be half as good as one day on Brighton Pier," Life crowed. He picked me up in his arms and twirled me around in the air. He'd never done that before, not once, and he had his heart strapped on so tight he didn't even stop and realize what he'd done and go vacant-eyed and find something else to look at for a long while. He just squeezed me and kissed me like I came from somewhere and I didn't know what the hell a Brighton Pier was but I loved it already.

"What is it? What is it?" Maruchan and I squealed, because you can catch happiness like a plague.

"It's better the first time if you don't know," Mum assured us. "It's meant to dock in Electric City on Friday."

"So it's a ship, then?" Maruchan said. But Papa just twinkled his eyes at us and put his finger over his lips to keep the secret in.

The Pier meant to dock in Electric City. My heart fell into my stomach, got all digested up, and sizzled out into the rest of me all at once. Of course, of course it would, Electric City had the best docks, the sturdiest, the prettiest. But it seemed to me like life was happening to me on purpose, and Electric City couldn't keep a darkgirl out anymore. They had to share like the rest of us.

"What do you want to be when you grow up, Maruchan?" I said to my twin in the dark the night before we set off to see what was better than God. Maruchan's eyes gleamed with the Christmas thrill of it all.

"Brighton Pier," he whispered.

"Me, too," I sighed, and we both dreamed we were beautiful Fuckwits running through a forest of real pines, laughing and stopping to eat apples and running again and only right before we woke up did we notice that something was chasing us, something huge and electric and bound for London-town.

## 8. Citizens of Mutation Nation

I LOOKED FOR Goodnight Moon everywhere from the moment we crossed into Electric City. The fence had gone and Garbagetown poured in and nothing was different than it had been when I got my name off the battery spires, even though the sign had said for so long that Electric City was renovating. I played a terrible game with every person that shoved past, every face in a window, every shadow juddering down an alley and the game was: *are you him?* But I lost all the hands. The only time I stopped playing was when I first saw Brighton Pier.

I couldn't get my eyes around it. It was a terrible, gorgeous whale of light and colors and music and otherness. All along a boardwalk jugglers danced and singers sang and horns horned and accordions squeezed and under it all some demonic engine screamed and wheezed. Great glass domes and towers and flags and tents glowed in the sunset but Brighton Pier made the sunset look plain-faced and unloveable. A huge wheel full of pink and emerald electric lights turned slowly in the warm wind but went nowhere. People leapt and turned somersaults and stood on each others' shoulders and they all wore such soft, vivid costumes, like they'd all been cut out of a picturebook too fine for anyone like me to read. The tumblers lashed the pier to the Electric City docks and cut the engines and after that it was nothing but music so thick and good you could eat it out of the air.

Life and Time hugged Maruchan and cheered with the rest of Garbagetown. Tears ran down their faces. Everyone's faces.

"When the ice melted and the rivers revolted and the Fuckwit world went under the seas," Papa whispered through his weeping, "a great mob hacked Brighton Pier off of Brighton and strapped engines to it and set sail across the blue. They've been going ever since. They go around the world and around again, to the places where there's still people, and trade their beauty for food and fuel. There's a place on Brighton Pier where if you look just right, it's like nothing ever drowned."

A beautiful man wearing a hat of every color and several bells stepped up on a pedestal and held a long pale cone to his mouth. The mayor of Electric City embraced him with two meaty arms and asked his terrible, stupid, unforgivable question: "Have you seen dry land?"

And the beautiful man answered him: "With my own eyes."

A roar went up like angels dying. I covered my ears. The mayor covered his mouth with his hands, speechless, weeping. The beautiful man patted him awkwardly on the back. Then he turned to us.

"Hello, Garbagetown!" he cried out and his voice sounded like everyone's most secret heart.

We screamed so loud every bird in Garbagetown fled to the heavens and we clapped like mad and some people fell onto the ground and buried their face in old batteries.

"My name is Emperor William Shakespeare the Eleventh and I am the Master of Brighton Pier! We will be performing *Twelfth Night* in the great stage tonight at seven o'clock, followed by *The Duchess of Malfi* at ten (which has werewolves) and a midnight acrobatic display! Come one, come all! Let Madame Limelight tell your FORTUNE! TEST your strength with the Hammer of the Witches! SEE the wonders of the Fuckwit World in our Memory Palace! Get letters and news from the LAST HUMAN OUTPOSTS around the globe! GASP at the citizens of Mutation Nation in the Freak Tent! Sample a FULL MINUTE of real television, still high definition after all these years! Concerts begin in the Crystal Courtyard in fifteen minutes! Our Peep Shows feature only the FINEST actresses reading aloud from GENUINE Fuckwit historical records! Garbagetown, we are here to DAZZLE you!"

A groan went up from the crowds like each Garbagetowner was just then bedding their own great lost love and they heaved toward the lights, the colors, the horns and the voices, the silk and the electricity and the life floating down there, knotted to the edge of our little pile of trash.

Someone grabbed my hand and held me back while my parents, my twin, my world streamed away from me down to the Pier. No one looked back.

"Are you her?" said Goodnight Moon. He looked longer and leaner but not really older. He had on his tie.

"Yes," I said, and nothing was different than it had been when I got my name except now neither of us had masks and our kisses weren't like gentle elephants but like a boy and a girl and I forgot all about my strength and my fortune and the wonderful wheel of light turning around and around and going nowhere.

## 9. TERRORWHORE

ACTORS ARE LIARS. Writers, too. The whole lot of them, even the horn players and the fortune tellers and the freaks and the strongmen. Even the ladies with rings in their noses and high heels on their feet playing violins all along the pier and the lie they are all singing and dancing and saying is: *we can get the old world back again.*

My door said TERRORWHORE this morning. I looked after my potato plants and my hibiscus and thought about whether or not I would ever get to have sex again. Seemed unlikely. Big Bargains concurred.

Goodnight Moon and I lost our virginities in the Peep Show tent while a lady in green fishnet stockings and a lavender garter read to us from the dinner menu of the Dorchester Hotel circa 2005.

"Whole Berkshire roasted chicken stuffed with black truffles, walnuts, duck confit, and dauphinoise potatoes," the lady purred. Goodnight Moon devoured my throat with kisses, bites, need. "Drizzled with a balsamic reduction and rosemary honey."

"What's honey?" I gasped. We could see her but she couldn't see us, which was for the best. The glass in the window only went one way.

"Beats me, kid," she shrugged, re-crossing her legs the other way. "Something you drizzle." She went on. "Sticky toffee pudding with lashings of cream and salted caramel, passionfruit soufflé topped with orbs of pistachio ice cream…"

Goodnight Moon smelled just as I remembered. Scorched ozone and metal and paraffin and hope and when he was inside me it was like hearing my name for the first time. I couldn't escape the *me*-ness of it, the *us*-ness of it, the sound and the shape of ourselves turning into our future.

"I can't believe you're here," he whispered into my breast. "I can't believe this is us."

The lady's voice drifted over my head. "Lamb cutlets on a bed of spiced butternut squash, wilted greens, and delicate hand-harvested mushrooms served with goat cheese in clouds of pastry…"

Goodnight Moon kissed my hair, my ears, my eyelids. "And now that the land's come back Electric City's gonna save us all. We can go home together, you and me, and build a house and we'll have a candle in every window so you always feel at home…"

The Dorchester dinner menu stopped abruptly. The lady dropped to her fishnetted knees and peered at us through the glass, her brilliant glossy red hair tumbling down, her spangled eyes searching for us beyond the glass.

"Whoa, sweetie, slow down," she said. "You're liable to scare a girl off that way."

All I could see in the world was Goodnight Moon's brown eyes and the sweat drying on his brown chest. Brown like the earth and all its promises. "I don't care," he said. "You scared, Tetley?" I shook my head. "Nothing can scare us now. Emperor Shakespeare said he's seen land, real dry land, and we have a plan and we're gonna get everything back again and be fat happy Fuckwits like we were always supposed to be."

The Peep Show girl's glittering eyes filled up with tears. She put her hand on the glass. "Oh…oh, baby…that's just something we say. We always say it. To everyone. It's our best show. Gives people hope, you know? But there's nothing out there, sugar. Nothing but ocean and more ocean and a handful of drifty lifeboat cities like yours circling the world like horses on a broken-down carousel. Nothing but blue."

### 10. We Are So Lucky

IT WOULD BE nice for me if you could just say you understand. I want to hear that just once. Goodnight Moon didn't. He didn't believe her and he didn't believe me and he sold me out in the end in spite of gas masks and kissing and Madeline Brix and the man crooning in our ears that he was happy because all he could hear was Emperor William Shakespeare the Eleventh singing out his big lie. RESURRECTION! REDEMPTION! REVIVIFICATION! LAND HO!

"No, because, see," my sweetheart wept on the boardwalk while the wheel spun dizzily behind his head like an electric candy crown, "we have a plan. We've worked so hard. It *has* to happen. The mayor said as soon as we had news of dry land, the minute we knew, we'd turn it on and we'd get there first and the continents would be ours, Garbagetowners, we'd inherit the Earth. He's gonna tell everyone when the Pier leaves. At the farewell party."

"Turn what on?"

Resurrection. Redemption. Renovation. All those years behind the fence Electric City had been so busy. Disassembling all those engines they hoarded so they could make a bigger one, the biggest one. Pooling fuel in great vast stills. Practicing ignition sequences. Carving up a countryside they'd never even seen between the brightboys and brightgirls and we could have some, too, if we were good.

"You want to turn Garbagetown into a Misery Boat," I told him. "So we can just steam on ahead into nothing and go mad and use up all the gas and batteries that could keep us happy in mixtapes for another century here in one hot minute."

"The Emperor said..."

"He said his name was Duke Orsino of Illyria, too. And then Roderigo when they did the werewolf play. Do you believe that? If they'd found land, don't you think they'd have stayed there?"

But he couldn't hear me. Neither could Maruchan when I tried to tell him the truth in the peep show. All they could see was green. Green leafy trees and green grass and green ivy in some park that was lying at the bottom of the sea. We dreamed different dreams now, my brother and I, and all my dreams were burning.

Say you understand. I had to. I'm not a nihilist or a murdercunt or a terrorwhore. They were gonna use up every last drop of Garbagetown's power to go nowhere and do nothing and instead of measuring out teaspoons of good, honest gas, so that it lasts and we last all together, no single thing on the patch would ever turn on again, and we'd go dark, *really* dark, forever. Dark like the bottom of a hole. They had no right. *They* don't understand. This is *it*. This is the future. Garbagetown and the sea. We can't go back, not ever, not even for a minute. We are so lucky. Life is so good. We're going on and being alive and being shitty sometimes and lovely sometimes just the same as we always have, and only a Fuckwit couldn't see that.

I waited until Brighton Pier cast off, headed to the next rickety harbor of floating foolboats, filled with players and horns and glittering wheels and Dorchester menus and fresh mountains of letters we wouldn't read the answers to for another twenty years. I waited until everyone was sleeping so nobody would get hurt except the awful engine growling and panting to deliver us into the dark salt nothing of an empty hellpromise.

It isn't hard to build a bomb in Electric City. It's all just laying around behind that fence where a boy held my hand for the first time. All you need is a match.

## 11. What You Came For

IT'S SUCH A beautiful day out. My hibiscus is just gigantic, red as the hair on a peep show dancer. If you want to wait, Big Bargains will be round later for her afternoon nap. Grape Crush usually brings a herring by in the evening. But I understand if you've got other places to be.

It's okay. You can hit me now. If you want to. It's what you came for. I barely feel it anymore.

Thank you for my instruction.

# The Sin-Eater

THERE'S A WOMAN OUTSIDE OF a town called Sheridan, where the sky comes so near to earth it has to use the crosswalk just like everybody else.

There's a woman outside of Sheridan, sitting in the sun-yellow booth in the far back corner of the Blue Bison Diner & Souvenir Shoppe under a busted wagon wheel and a pair of wall-mounted commemorative plates. One's from the moon landing. The other's from old Barnum Brown discovering the first T-Rex skeleton up at Hell Creek.

There's a woman outside of Sheridan and she is eating the sin of America.

THE WOMAN SITS quietly with her hands in her lap. Her hair slumps over her shoulder in a long fat braid the color of tarnished quarters, but she isn't old. She isn't young, either. Her name is Ruby-Rose Martineau and her parents run a butterfly farm just over the Montana line in a tight little corner pocket of the Shoshone River. Mainly rare swallowtails: spicebrush, emerald peacock, Queen Alexandras. Some red lacewings and whatnot. You remember it. So do the other seven or eight customers seated carefully far from her, silent as buttes, pantomiming how hard they aren't staring while staring for all they're worth. You all grew up seeing the giant faded highway signs with Dale Martineau's big Frenchy face grinning down the plains with a huge black *trogonoptera trojana* perched on the tip of his self-satisfied thumbs-up.

*Just 100 miles to Bigwing Ranch, Home of the Ultimate Butterfly Experience!*

*50 Miles! Tell Your Dad to Pull Over Cuz It's Only $10!*

*You've Almost Made It To the Best Day of Your Life! Just 25 Little Ol' Miles To Go!*

Ruby-Rose got named for two perfect red things and she ran away from the Ultimate Butterfly Experience as soon as she could chain one dollar to the next. But the distances out west make it so hard to get far. Majored in dance at Colorado State. Ruined her feet before she was old enough to rent a car. Got married. Got unmarried. Had a baby born with only half a heart that died in her arms at 4:37 a.m. one frost-cauled January morning. Did what broken dancers do: opened a school for ballet/modern over in Provo. Slept with one of the much-be-scarved producers who descend like monarchs for Sundance every year, who never did hire her to choreograph his next flick but did saddle her with a kiddo who's about five now and can say all the geological periods of the earth in order from the Precambrian to the Quarternary. Closed the school and everything else round about the big crash when people stopped caring whether little Kaylee could do a decent goddamned *pas de chat* for quite a good whack of time. Crested the wave of her generation as they crashed down back home in their childhood bedrooms with nothing, even though she's been afraid to death of butterflies since she was big enough to say why she was crying all over her pretty new dress.

Her name is Ruby-Rose Martineau and she is eating the sin of America.

The waitress's nametag says *Emmeline*. An old flatscreen drones out a soft ribbon of white noise over the big picture window. One of the yelly conservative news troughs Ruby-Rose hates. The chyron crawls silently across the primary-colored frame, projecting faintly on her skin: *Independent Inquiry Determines Christopher Salazar Behind Hedge Fund Ponzi Scheme.* A photo goes up over the name: a nice-looking man with a fresh haircut who looks far too young to get caught up in any of that sort of thing. The block black *C* in *Christopher* flutters faintly on Emmeline's forehead. She's an owl-eyed wisp of a thing, wearing a royal blue dress with Disney princess cap sleeves and a frilly white apron that's got a big blue bison chomping blue prairie grass embroidered on it.

This is the uniform designed by Linda Gage, who opened the Blue Bison Diner & Souvenir Shoppe in 1981 and got T-boned by the biggest horse-trailer you ever saw in 1982. Nothing left but hooves and hair and Linda and all her dear little plans smeared up and down I-90 for half a mile in each direction.

Herb Gage's kept it all like she wanted, down to the fancy *-pe* stapled on the back end of *Shoppe*, which he personally thought was about as stupid as whipped cream on steak and told her so at the time. But now? If God himself came down and told him to spell it right Herb Gage would tell the old man to get the fuck out. Linnie picked out those moon landing and T-Rex plates and nailed up their display stands herself. And the busted wagon wheels, the bluebell-patterned cushions on the extruded plastic booths, the state maps and NFL champion pennants. She insisted on crayons and paper tablecloths for the kiddies to draw on while they waited for their ice creams. Why, her deadbeat brother shot and stuffed that taxidermy elk-head with tie-dyed antlers himself. And it surely never was Herb who put up those black and white framed photos of all the famous people Linda Gage dreamed would one day visit and order up her World Famous Daily Deep-Fry Surprise and stretch their belts and tell her you just couldn't get food like this back in LA, no sir, you could not.

The Blue Bison Diner is a ghost's living room and it is serving the sin of America.

Emmeline's uniform is seven months stretched out with Herb Gage's kid. She's told her parents it was a boy from another school but it wasn't. She's told Herb it's a boy but it isn't. Emmeline puts a protective hand on her belly, to shield her baby from…what? Ruby-Rose in her pretentious tight black clothes like she was fooling anyone, the rain coming on outside, her family's disgust and disappointment, the Daily Deep-Fry, her part in the great and frightening thing happening right now today in her place of business, Herb's grief and need.

"How do you…how do you want it?" Emmeline says. She tries to put on her usual shit-eating cheerful bell-in-the-door voice but her mouth dries out on her and it comes out a crow-y rasp.

Ruby-Rose looks over the menu. She isn't in the least hungry. But it cannot be a small meal. They told her that when they came for her, and all the delicate endangered emerald swallowtails circled their heads like green rings around terrible planets. It cannot be small and it cannot be short. It takes as long as it takes. You can't do this thing halfway.

We're counting on you.

---

THERE'S A WOMAN outside of Sheridan who remembers the pure calm of knowing that someday, she was gonna be so amazing she'd sheerly glow.

There's a woman outside of Sheridan sitting on a threadbare bluebell-patterned cushion a dead lady once thought was so classy and beautiful it would turn her into a better person so she bought the whole bolt of fabric without even looking at the price.

There's a woman outside of Sheridan and she is ordering the sin of America off a plastic menu with a turquoise buffalo on the cover whose peeled and blistered thought bubble faintly complains: [*Hurry up, I'm STARVING!*]

EMMELINE CRACKS HER pinky knuckle nervously. "Maybe something to drink first?" she suggests.

Ruby-Rose Martineau takes three short, sharp breaths and crushes the heels of her hands into her eye sockets until she stops shaking. "Am I allowed to drink?" she whispers, still hiding like a child in the dark behind her hands. "I don't know how this works."

"Me neither, but..." her voice drops to a whisper, like she's getting away with something lovely and wicked. "I say you should treat yourself, Ruby."

"Okay," Ruby sniffles. She wipes her nose with the back of her wrist. She's wearing a white agate ring on her middle finger, given to her by the long-gone Sundance man. "Red wine? Pinot Noir if you have it."

They did not have it. Nor, in fact, did the Blue Bison Diner & Souvenir Shoppe have a liquor license from the great state of Wyoming, although Herb'll spot you a glug of whiskey in your milkshake out of his back pocket flask for two bucks. Alcohol always gave Linda Gage a headache. But when Mr. Herbert James Gage found out it was gonna go down on his doorstep he said right is right. The old man called up the Thrifty Foods and put in an order for the good stuff with the pipsqueak on the deli phone. *Look, son, I don't know. How bout this: if you don't think I could spell it, just put it in a box, write my name on the box, and I'll settle up with Curtis end of the month.*

Never once occurred to him, or the teenager manning the turkey grinder at Thrifty Foods, that she'd want something as soft as wine today.

A man in a Navy vet hat grumbles for the flatscreen remote. Turn the damned game on instead. Those talking heads shake up his blood pressure like a Coke bottle. The Broncos are playing the Steelers, you know. Come on, man. The TV floods the joint with emerald green as the field fills up the frame. After a minute or two, the stats graphics flip to a breaking news bulletin: *Grand Jury Returns Indictment Against Salazar in Brutal Police Slaying.*

"Can you *believe* that guy?" Navy hat whispers to the college boy plonked down on the barstool next to his, home for the holiday and sawing into a short stack with extra butter. "Every day it's something."

"I know," college boy answers just as quiet, like they're swapping notes in a library. "It just never ends. No point in watching the news these days, honestly."

~

THERE'S A LITTLE league coach with a shaved head bellied up to the bar at the Blue Bison Diner & Souvenir Shoppe who sees Miss Emmeline pour straight Stolichnaya into a novelty wine glass with all the lyrics of the state song engraved on it and starts working himself into a serious fume as he already asked three times for something better than Sprite and got turned down flat.

There's a real estate agent pretending to pick at a salad that's mostly croutons at a four-top by the door of the Blue Bison Diner & Souvenir Shoppe whose therapist was always telling her how important it was to practice self-care and do things just for Tracey sometimes so she drove her sleek new hybrid all the way up from Phoenix for this and now that it's almost time she's getting so excited she can barely keep still in her seat.

There's a woman with her back to the glass partition that separates the Blue Bison Diner from the Souvenir Shoppe wrapping her long fingers around her booze while a repurposed drugstore paperback rack of little plush bighorn sheep glare down her spine with flat lifeless plastic eyes and when the kitchen gets going and the smells start drifting past the swinging steel doors she finds she is so hungry after all that her mouth waters for the sin of America.

~

THE APPETIZERS COME out first, onion rings and queso and sweet n' smoky chipotle hot wings. The way sweet Emmeline confidently pronounces chipotle *chipottlee* fills up the heart of Ruby-Rose Martineau with so much love and softness she can't barely breathe. She isn't hardly anything more than a baby and it's not her fault. Nobody should have let Herb Gage's grasping old hands come within a county of her. Someone should have protected her and even if they didn't, he shouldn't have the poor girl working when her time's so close.

The game dissolves into news alerts as regular as heartbeats: *Salazar Evicts Millions. Christopher Salazar at the Bottom of Massive Waterway Pollution, Experts Say. C. Salazar Named in Racial Discrimination Lawsuit.*

Emmeline backs out of the double kitchen doors, wobbling under the weight of so many plates. She just sets them down with a little grunt of effort and heads back in for more. The dishes keep coming and coming. A bowl of tomato soup with saltines. 18 oz rib eye medium rare with baked potato and sour cream. Patty melt on rye (extra mushrooms), Denver omelette, chicken tenders with honey mustard, a Belgian waffle with strawberries and ice cream *not* whipped cream, side of bacon, sweet potato fries, chili mac and cheese, a peppermint milkshake, peach rhubarb pie with a scoop of vanilla, and a serving of the World Famous Daily Deep-Fry Surprise, which the Emmeline-drawn letterboard outside announces in cute pink chalk with hearts and angels is Beer-Battered PB & J.

Rainclouds roll up on the horizon like big grey boulders, one of those high country storms that stomps open the sky and then half an hour later it's like it never happened at all. The air outside the Blue Bison Diner is full of ozone and brush and jaundiced yellow half-light and the table in front of Ruby-Rose Martineau is so full of the sin of America you can't see one single spiky stick figure on the tablecloth, scribbled by some child long grown and gone.

Robert Redford and Burt Reynolds watch her expectantly from their black and white photos on the wall. Redford peers over his actual signature, the only one of the dozens who actually did visit once, years and years ago. He ordered an ice water.

It's too much. She'll never be able to finish it. It'll never fit inside her. It's too big and too heavy and too rich. She could eat all day and into the night and there would still be more waiting for her. More and more and more.

She sips the peppermint milkshake and it is good. It's really good. Not too thick or too runny, just the right consistency to bloom up through the striped, wide-bore straw without sticking. Little chunks of candy cane popping in her mouth. It tastes like Christmas and for a moment Ruby-Rose Martineau just savors it, the sweetness and the sharpness and the memory of all the milkshakes she's drunk so thoughtlessly, so carelessly, like they meant nothing. Swinging her little chubby legs in the air on the bumper of her dad's truck at the drive-in while he tells her to just hide her face with his coat if it gets too scary. Begging for a mix of every flavor with her high school friends even though it would probably be, and was, disgusting. Walking down twinkling streets in Utah with a man she'd never see again, stealing sips of his salted caramel shake after she'd finished her own. Simple scenes, without resonance, without connection, gone as fast as thunder. Like everything.

Ruby plunges her spoon into the tomato soup, half sucked up already into an undifferentiated mass of saltines, just the way she likes it. The game goes into overtime. During the ad break, a politician looks directly to camera and speaks with down-home long-faced concern about his opponent's association with Christopher Salazar and what that means for good God-fearing voters like you.

IT IS YESTERDAY and Ruby-Rose Martineau is helping a school group prepare for the Ultimate Butterfly Experience at Bigwing Ranch and you would never guess how revolting she finds the creatures by the warmth of her voice as she tells the little ones that a group of butterflies is called a kaleidoscope, and they eat nectar from the flowers they grow in those big fields out there, and yes of course you can take a sunflower home, sweetheart, the butterflies won't miss one silly old flower out of thousands.

It is yesterday and Ruby-Rose Martineau is wrapping a fourth-grader in long strips of red fabric her mother rubbed all over with nectar the night before and explaining what a chrysalis really is. She whispers like it's a big secret even though it isn't, you can read about it in any serious textbook. *Most people think a caterpillar turns into a butterfly the way a child turns into an adult, but that's not true at all. What really happens is that the caterpillar completely dissolves right down to its DNA. It bubbles down into a kind of soup of itself and then the soup reassembles itself into a completely different thing. The caterpillar dies and the butterfly gets born. It's not a metamorphosis at all, it's a sacrifice.* The kids start looking pretty upset and Ruby moves quickly on to other interesting butterfly facts like how they taste with their feet, hoping her father didn't overhear her doing it again. Explaining to children what fucking horrifying nightmare creatures butterflies actually are, that they eat shit and drink tears and if they didn't look so pretty and nice from far away we'd think they were monsters from the deeps of hell, each and every one of them, at which point her father's rough, gorgeous, booming voice interrupts to shut her up for the thousandth time and hiss *goddammit, Ruby they're trying to sell a beautiful family-friendly memory, what the hell?*

It is yesterday and Ruby-Rose Martineau guides the completely mummified child in his polyester "chrysalis" into the butterfly house while behind her a long red car that somehow looks freshly-washed even through all the dust and pollen and road-grime everyone else collects on their way up there. Daddy makes himself immediately scarce. Bigwing Ranch is home not only to the Ultimate Butterfly Experience but, less boldly advertised, to the biggest marijuana grow in three states, so he's not too fond of government visitors.

It is yesterday and Ruby-Rose Martineau asks how she can help the two men who get out of the car, but she already knows. There's only one official kind of car that's red instead of black.

It is yesterday and Ruby-Rose Martineau asks the simplest question possible: *why me? What did I do wrong?*

It is yesterday and they don't even bother answering because it doesn't matter. There was a lottery. It's her turn. It could have been anyone but it wasn't. Thank God it's not them. It's voluntary, of course. But it isn't.

It is yesterday and Ruby's baby girl is napping in the big house, dreaming about geology and triceratops and sunflowers and maybe it will be okay because she will never see any of this, she'll never cry or call out for her mother or try to bargain miserably with the men in the long red car. She'll sleep straight through and they don't even let her watch TV anyway so she'll never know, not really, she'll dance around the funnel cake stand and the ticket booth trying to catch lacewings like she always does and she'll grow up to be a paleontologist like Barnum Brown and chose not to have any babies because it's nothing but grief and this will be an unhealed wound but no deeper or more infected than the others she'll earn all on her own, the way everybody does.

It is yesterday and Ruby-Rose Martineau is getting into the long red car and driving away, leaving a wake of thick dust blanketing the glass greenhouse where a fourth-grade boy's homemade chrysalis is slowly being unwrapped by his giggling classmates and thousands of green and blue and gold and scarlet butterflies, drawn to the nectar-soaked fabric, descend to cover his little delighted body in their brilliant wings. He looks up in utter rapture as they swarm hungrily over him, caring nothing for who he is or where he has been or what he will do when this is over, only seeking sugar and moisture. The boy doesn't know the trick. He thinks they love him. He will never in all his long life feel this special again, this chosen, this real.

It is yesterday and Ruby-Rose Martineau has been chosen to eat the sin of America. She sits in the buttery leather backseat of the car and asks what will happen when it's over. When she's done.

We'll be happy, they say. We'll be better. We'll all be happy forever and everything will be okay.

IT IS TODAY and Ruby cries as she eats. She cries into the soup and the patty melt and the steak and the waffles. She doesn't want it and she can't stop. She shovels it into her mouth until her jaws ache and it all tastes good, because it *has* been good, it has tasted right and filling and satisfying all her life. You can see now as the empty plates pile up the crayon-marks of decades of children like the drawings on the caves of Lascaux in France, achingly clear and simple and alien and human.

Ruby starts on the steak, red juice pooling on a plate with a cowboy on it. It is so rare it just tastes like blood, like biting somehow *into* blood as solid as stone. She cries and eats and cries and eats and her stomach screams out for her to stop but she can't, she can't, she is eating the sin of America and it is hers now. It was always hers because she lived on it and breathed it and slept with it and benefitted from it and let it nurture her and grow her like a hothouse plant. But now it is *only* hers. It belongs to her and no one else. Not the man in the Navy hat or the Arizona real estate agent or the college boy in his fresh starched baby blue button-down. Not the Broncos or the Steelers or the little league coach who wants a goddamned drink or the producer with big kind brown eyes who swore up and down he was doing a musical next and he'd take her to California and the wide, promising sea. Not poor Emmeline with her big unignorable belly under her pretty blue uniform or Herb guiltily working the grill like he never touched her or awful little Kaylee with her shitty *pas de chat* that would never get less shitty now or millions of broke thirty-somethings staring hopelessly at the popcorn ceiling from a bed that still has their stupid baby blanket on it. Not the fourth-grader covered in iridescent butterflies or Ruby's gentle soft lost baby born with half a heart or Robert Redford or Burt Reynolds or the dumb kid slicing ham at the Thrifty Foods or Christopher Salazar or poor Linda Gage obliterating herself into a red mist of horses forty years ago.

The sin of America drips down her chin. The bones crack between her teeth. Everyone is watching her, *everyone* is watching as she gags and sobs and swallows and reaches for more and washes it down whatever her hand finds when it falls. It cannot be short and it cannot be small. And so she takes it in for them, as those chosen have always done, for them, always, so they don't even have to think of it, don't ever have to feel a drop of the stuff fall from their heart to their soul. So they can ignore it, for awhile longer. So they can say it was never anything to do with them personally, and besides, it was so long ago and they're better now.

It's Ruby's turn, that's all.

She takes it in and in and in. And then—she reaches slowly past her tongue to pick a long strand that once belonged to a rough woolen blanket out of her teeth. She looks down and there are bullets in the steak and ship-ropes in the soup and screams in the strawberries as red as the end of a chase. No one sees it but her. No one feels the eggs turn to radioactive sand and hot shards of gold and silver in her mouth. No one but her can smell that her wine glass with the state song written on it is full of terrified human sweat, sloshing over and trickling down past *On the breast of this great land where the massive Rockies stand...* No one but her sees the plates fill with fire and brick and charred wood. No one sees the peeling turquoise buffalo on the menu turn away from his funny thought bubble and look into the eyes of Ruby-Rose Martineau and no one else hears it lowing: *you climbed a throne of corpses and you were proud to reach the top.*

No one sees it, no one hears it, no one even imagines it, because it belongs to Ruby and she eats it all, every bite, every drop, even her own tears swimming on the surface of the meat like food for butterflies.

There is no check. She will pay her way soon enough. Emmeline, without quite knowing why, leans over and kisses Ruby's forehead. She puts a plush bighorn sheep down on the table next to the last empty plate. It has a red ribbon around its neck and the ribbon says: *Wyoming Loves U!*

Big loose raindrops spatter against the windows. It's the color of twilight out there even though it's barely past the lunch hour. Ruby-Rose gets up slowly, every joint groaning. She takes the little sheep with her when she goes. A bell rings as she shuts the door behind her and steps shakily out into the stormclouds and the ozone and the wind full of sagebrush and dust.

THERE'S A WOMAN outside of a town called Sheridan, where the sky watches you without feeling.

There's a woman outside of Sheridan walking toward the road with a toy bighorn clutched tight in her hand. She isn't crying anymore. She's thinking about her parents and her daughter and the big idiot sunflowers growing out into infinity in the back field, about emerald swallowtails and T-Rex bones and the power of independent movies.

There's a woman outside of Sheridan who has eaten the sin of America. She doesn't really even feel the first blow across the back of her head. But the second one lands hard and she cries out into the long empty distance. The third crunches into the backs of her thighs and she stumbles to the sodden ground.

The little league coach swings a bat into her ribs and jumps up and down in the rain. The college kid just uses his hands, grabbing her by the hair and smashing her face into the pebbly high desert soil over and over. The Navy vet is very old, he doesn't pack much of a punch anymore, but he swings his cane over his head and brings it down as best he can over her shoulder blades. Her white agate ring cracks in half as the busboy stomps it under the heel of his foot. Tracey finally does something just for herself and smashes a fire extinguisher into the small of Ruby's back. She squeals and giggles and goes again. And again. Herb Gage thinks of his wife as he slashes her calves with his best knife so she can't get away, thinks of all Linda's little plans for the diner, all her little ways of laughing, all her ways of looking at him so he knew, he *knew* he was worth a damn. They all swarm hungrily over her, caring nothing for who she is or where she has been or where they will go when this is over.

There are good God-fearing people outside of Sheridan and they are killing the sin of America, a place born with half a heart that must be made whole, year in and year out. They are crushing the sin of America into a paste. They are releasing themselves from it. They are ridding themselves of it forever. It's not their fault. Nothing's their fault. It never has been. It never will be. They are so innocent, innocent as the sky.

A car pulls off of I-90 and slowly grinds toward the diner. A late lunch straggler, after a steak and a Coke and maybe something to remember his trip by. He parks and gets out and sees, sees it all, sees the broken mass on the ground, sees the letterboard with the chalk hearts and chalk angels, sees the people outside of Sheridan.

Emmeline realizes they have a customer. She wipes her hands off on her apron with the little embroidered blue bison on it and waves cheerfully. Blood and rain sheet down the front her dress, her arms, her pregnant belly, the bison drenched black.

The straggler's face falls. His feet go a bit unsteady on him. His mouth opens in shock and his white teeth shine in the stormlight.

"It's okay!" hollers Emmeline with a brilliant, beautiful, fecund smile. Her teeth shine crimson where she bit into Ruby's cold throat. "It's all good! Better than good!" Blood swells on the tip of her chin and drips to the thirsty earth. "It's the beginning of a new era. We're all better now."

She takes his hand in hers and leans up on her tip toes to kiss his cheek and there's blood on his suit now too, big red fingerprints on his chest.

"Don't you worry, Mister. It's all gonna be okay."

They walk him toward the Blue Bison Diner & Souvenir Shoppe, half-dazed, half-soaked. On the other side of the glass the old flatscreen flickers and blinks and if you look between the raindrops you can see the chyron gravely reporting: *Independent Inquiry Determines Ruby-Rose Martineau Behind Hedge Fund Ponzi Scheme.*

Herb Gage clicks it off and fires up the cooling griddle again.

No point watching the news these days, honestly. It just never ends.

# The Sun in Exile

I WAS BORN THE YEAR THEY put the sun on trial for treason.

It was so hot that year the streets boiled like black soup and the air rippled like music and the polar bears all roared together, just once, loud enough that a child in Paraguay turned her head suddenly north and began to weep. Tomatoes simmered on the vine and the wind was full of the smells of them cooking, then of their skins peeling, turning black, smoking on the earth, old coats lost to a housefire. Everyone shone like their skin was made of diamonds. Sweat took the place of silk. Children tried to feed at their mothers' breasts and screamed as their little tongues blistered and their throats scalded. Cattle in the fields roasted where they stood, braised in their own skin and blood. One by one, the lights went out along the coasts, and then the outer islands went out, blinked away by the warm salt sea. Deep inland, the old men with their ham radios joined to their bodies like wives heard that an entire city evaporated into steam like so much water in a copper-bottomed pot. Even the stars at night could burn holes in your heart like magnifying glasses.

Even the moon raised silver cancers on your bare back.

No one went outside if they could help it. Soldiers guarded every space in the shadows, beneath a tree, in the foyer of an abandoned bank, under a long, rotted pier where the sea breeze still blew. An hour in the shade cost a year's wages. Then two years. Then three.

The only rain was weeping.

At first, Papa Ubu did nothing. He appeared to his people on the pink alabaster balcony of the Lake House wrapped in layers of plush winter coats and colorful satin scarves, soft goatskin gloves, merino-lined boots black up to his knees, and a bright green cap with fluffy earflaps underneath his crown, his beautiful wife beside him in a high-collared blue gown embroidered with snowflakes and quilted with down and silver thread, her golden hair hidden beneath a white skullcap fringed in black fox fur, and their youngest child so snuff and stiff in his silk snowsuit he could barely move. Papa Ubu shivered and shuddered and stamped his feet. He rubbed his big hands together and blew on them. He called to his man for another scarf and a blanket, for God's sake. And as the brutal sun beat down without quarter, Papa Ubu exclaimed at the cold weather we were having, how vicious the polar front coming down from the north was this year, how sick his child had become as the unseasonable chill settled into his bones.

"Why," exclaimed the great King Ubu, "I can see my breath in the air! This is an affront to all decency! It will not stand! I will take up arms and fight the terrible encroaching freeze for you, my people, and for my poor son, practically dead already from this damned frost!" And he began to dance back and forth to keep himself warm, one foot to the other, his colorful scarves fluttering and bouncing, his cheeks flushing red, his hat soaked in sweat, back and forth and back and forth, while he grunted and bellowed "Brrr! It's unbearable! I can hardly feel my toes!"

His beautiful wife presented her husband with a polite cough, and delicately rubbed her elbows. After a small nudge, their son, scarlet and panting and entombed in the plush sarcophagus of his arctic snowsuit, coughed too and began to hop miserably back and forth like his father.

And all the people listening below the balcony, standing without shade on the golden dying summer grass, their bodies glistening with sweat, their throats dry with thirst, their scalps potato-red with sunburn, began to shout and call out that they, too, could see their breath fogging in the frigid air, that they had not known any winter like this since the storms fifty years back, or perhaps sixty, that they could see frostbite taking hold beneath their fingernails.

The next morning, word spread over the land that, out of respect for the suffering of the people in this time of trial, the word *hot* and all its derivatives should neither be spoken nor written, for it would only remind the forlorn of what they had lost. So too should the words *warm, summer, fever, sweat, scorch, blister* and the like be stricken from the common vocabulary until the end of this horrible cold snap, for they were false friends, lies told only to torment the suffering.

Papa Ubu's oldest daughter went into the countryside on charitable missions to comfort all who had begged for her father's aid. She arrived in the towns like a magic spell, riding a sleigh drawn by shaggy reindeer whose eyes rolled in the agony of the heat, her lovely face framed in white fur and bright wool. And if her father was still human enough to sweat beneath his winter costume, she never did. Her face was pale and sweatless, as beautiful and unmoving as carved ice. In the scorching noontime sun, she pulled blanket after blanket from her sleigh and distributed them equally among the throng of loyal subjects, blankets of every color, quilted and embroidered and richly decorated with winter scenes, cottages dripping in icicles, glass beads forming frozen rivers in the fine cloth, fleece clouding the edges like clouds heavy with snow. There were always enough, enough for everyone, for Papa Ubu always takes care of his children, and loves them all the same.

One by one, folk dragged themselves forward, drowning in sweat, flies buzzing around their greasy hair, blisters on their reddened bodies like rows of rubies, and each of them begged for a blanket from the perfect white hands of Papa Ubu's daughter. Each of them eagerly wrapped the heavy, downy things round their shoulders and wept with gratitude, exclaiming with wonder at how much better they felt. But it was not enough for the daughter of Papa Ubu. She leaned in close to them, so close they could smell that she still had access to perfume even if they did not, and asked: "*How* much better? Tell me, so that I may in turn tell my father. Tell me how terribly you have suffered."

One by one, the people in the villages began to try to outdo one another. They shouted out in wonder at how cozy and snug they were now, surrounded in Papa's love, how grateful they were to be so tenderly looked after, what a welcome relief from the cold the beautiful daughter of the King had brought to them in the moment of their greatest need. One toothless, emaciated man, in one place, though his name and its memory have long since burned up and away, clutched his blanket stitched all over with ice floes and dark birds, shouted out over the crowd: "I lost my foot to frostbite but look! The moment the King's blanket touched it, it grew back whole! I can still see my breath in the air, but everywhere the blanket touches is safe!"

Then, the man fell down dead of heatstroke. Papa Ubu's daughter moved on to the next village with a soft smile on her perfect face.

Soon after, a new law went out into the land forbidding new words like *weather, bright, shade, water,* and all language relating to *pain*. There was no need to discuss such things in this new ice age, not when Papa Ubu had called all his advisors to the palace to array their powers against the encroaching cold. It hurt Papa Ubu's feelings to hear his people say that they suffered in agony when he was trying harder than any man had ever tried at any task to make the world warm again. *When you wish to say 'I am in pain',* the law said, *you should say 'I am joyful' or 'what a glorious day I am having' instead, for lying is a grave sin, and it is tremendously wicked of you to spread rumors that your Papa is failing at his task in any way, and in truth, it is you who are forcing Ubu to feel pain with your vicious implications.*

But though no one spoke of it, the heat went on and on, until the soil itself began to turn to black steam and pumpkins began to turn to ash on the vine. The land around Papa Ubu's palace had become an archipelago, and the warm salt sea lapped at his snow boots when he appeared on the pink alabaster balcony to address the people again. My mother, who was called Silver-and-Gold—for in those days all children were named for the many sorts of riches Papa Ubu promised to all, one day, if they were only patient—was there to hear him, her belly all big with me, her legs sunk deep in the creeping waters of the new archipelago, her swollen shape wrapped in furs against the cold. That was the day she heard Papa Ubu name their great enemy and declare it for the criminal it was, reading out from a golden book the indictment detailing all its crimes and foul schemes against his great nation, going back centuries upon centuries, the greatest scandal ever uncovered, the cruelest madman ever to afflict humankind.

"The sun has abandoned us," yelled Papa Ubu, his cheeks red. "For billions of years it did its job without complaint, sitting up there in the sky, lording over us all like a big, fat, stinking bastard, and only now has it decided to deny us the seasons it owes, only now has it decided to harm us instead of nurture us, only now has the sun turned its back on its children as I never have and never will, and you know that's the truth, because I'm out here saying it to your face despite the freezing wind and sleet. Any other King wouldn't bother, you know, they really wouldn't. Anyway, the motive is clear—the sun *hates* Papa Ubu and is conspiring against him! It prefers the corrupt Papas that came before, who let it do whatever it wanted, the people be damned. But when I stand up for you and demand your rights, the sun refuses to budge! What have we done to deserve this? Nothing! Nobody can blame us! We were just minding our own business, weren't we? The sun is an arch-criminal! The sun is against us! But I am a fair Papa, and all my subjects are free and entitled to justice, even the sun. There must be a grand trial, and prosecutors and defenders and testimony and all that sort of thing, so that everyone can know just how deep this whole thing goes and that I, *I* had nothing at all to do with it!"

"I am joyful," whispered my mother in reply, and all around her the people took up her cry, shouting, shrieking, weeping *I am joyful! I am joyful!* before their King. And Papa Ubu smiled an enormous, hungry smile, and Papa Ubu waved and waved, for hours, never tiring while the people chanted and screamed and fell forward into the knee-deep water, and all the while Papa Ubu drank their voices like wine or blood.

By coincidence, my grandfather was chosen to serve as chief counsel for the defense. He was called Equity, and he had never studied law in all his life. Most who had were long gone by then. But my grandfather was a Good Boy, loyal to Papa Ubu to the tiniest cell of his deepest marrow. He wore his hat just like Papa Ubu. He tied his tie just like Papa Ubu. He bid his wife style her hair like the hair of the daughter of Papa Ubu, and speak with the accent of the wife of Papa Ubu, and in that stolen voice tell him each night in detail how the cold was stealing in through the cracks in the door, and the frost was creeping up the side of the window panes, and the apples in the basket were surrounded by globes of ice, and the mice in the hall were freezing to death, and the icicles on the roof had nearly reached the top of the snowbanks outside, closing them into the house in their jagged crystal fangs.

It is because of his loyalty that he was so bitter to be drafted for the defense. Surely he deserved to prosecute. Papa loved winners, and wasn't Grandfather a winner? Everyone knew what the sun had done. If only the blasted thing would confess like anyone with a half-scrap of decency, there would be no need for this sordid business. Grandfather Equity always did his best, and he would do his best now, for Papa had ordered a real defense, without which a guilty verdict would have no strength. But Grandfather hated the sun as much as anyone. He insisted, to all who would listen, that he'd hated the sun long before Ubu revealed the true extent of its betrayal. How could Papa force him to sit with the sun and consult with it and decide whether or not to put it on the stand? It was intolerable. But he was a Good Boy. He could no more say no to Papa Ubu than he could bring himself to say he was hot while he sprawled naked in his kitchen on the mercifully cool tiles just for one moment's relief, a twitching creature more sunburn than man.

Papa allowed a full hour of electricity in every city center so that all his children could watch the trial. A spot in the shade could suddenly be had for little more than a laborer's day-wage, or a tryst in the briars with an amenable soldier. Each day's testimony would end at sunset, naturally, for the accused must be present for the proceedings to be legitimate. The atmosphere was as bright as a carnival. Food was sold and lanterns were lit on street corners even in the bright of the afternoon, concertinas and pan pipes were played in the piazzas, and throngs gathered beneath a ziggurat of televisions all tuned to UbuTV, most blessed of channels.

The reason Grandfather was chosen for the defense soon became clear. Ubu himself led the prosecution, his face utterly scarlet with righteous rage on that tower of screens, rendered tiny by the mountain of parkas and scarves and hats in which he had entombed himself. Papa ranted and raved and gestured wildly at the witness stand, bathed in a single, terribly quiet golden sunbeam. He flung his mind fully at the task, firing precedents like rifles, pealing forth with sermons soliloquized directly into the cameras, weeping real tears at the wholly unprovoked crimes of the sun against his people, the sheer betrayal of the sun's abandonment of its special relationship with this world, the inevitable result of which was to plunge it into a deadly ice age, merely out of pique at the great beauty, power, and longevity of Papa Ubu. How, indeed, could the sun begin to live with itself?

The judge and jury and all the crowds in all the cities applauded ecstatically every fragment of Latin, every incisive, surprising question that came so close to disturbing the calm of that single shaft of light illuminating the defendant's chair. One after another, Ubu called his witnesses to speak to the slaughter and suffering caused by the sun's perfidy, but Papa rarely let them finish. He was too excited, too eager to get to the good parts. If the witnesses proved too boring or their statements not flamboyant enough, Ubu took over and finished for them with a grand flourish. Grandfather offered objections here and there, nothing radical, some sustained, some overruled. He tried to cross-examine, but the judge decided it was inappropriate to question the agony of the victims. As the sun declined to testify, there was little else for him to do but wait. It took seven days for Ubu to finish his tour-de-force and collapse, exhausted, spent, exhilarated, into the chief prosecutor's plush chair, shivering theatrically.

It was time. There was no more avoiding it.

Grandfather Equity rose behind his long, polished rosewood bench and mopped his brow with a handkerchief. He flushed with shame. He began to shake and to weep. He had only one choice if he meant to mount a real defense, if he meant to do his job in the service of his beloved Papa, as he had always done, as he always would do.

"Your honor," said my grandfather slowly. "We've heard a great deal of testimony on the causes of this terrible winter that's cursed us. And it's all well and good and fine as far as it goes. But it's just too *hot* to go on today, don't you think? I'm too fucking hot. Aren't you hot?"

And he opened his briefcase and drew out a glass bottle of clear, cold water with ice floating in it, and ice crusting the outside, and frost sealing the cap. He set it on the judge's desk, before a man sweating out his innermost fluids in a heavy down coat and thick black scarf. The judge stared at the bottle as a slip of ice slid down its side. He licked his lips. He looked helplessly back and forth between Grandfather and Papa Ubu.

The sun was found guilty on all charges and sent into exile. Not one person under the rule of Ubu would henceforward be allowed to speak its name or look upon it, even indirectly, and all were commanded to stay indoors unless absolutely in order to shun the offender. If one must venture outside, umbrellas, dark, skin-concealing clothing, and tinted glasses ought to be used so as to avoid even the hint of association. This was the verdict, and it could not be appealed.

My grandfather was quietly executed in the courthouse bathroom.

# Color, Heat, and the Wreck of the Argo

### Variations in Luminance

**B**IG EDIE WAS A USELESS piece of shit.

Johanna Telle found the most significant relationship of her life on a Saturday afternoon in late May, sitting on one of those excruciatingly handmade quilts crafty stay-at-homes used to make out of their precious baby's old clothes, putting a deep, damp dent in the buttercup-infested lawn of 11 Buckthorn Drive, Ossining, New York. A four-pointed Arkansas Traveler star radiated out around her, each of the four diamond patches so exquisitely nailing the era of the quilter's *pax materna* that Johanna pulled out her Leica and snapped a shot before the homeowners could stop her: *The Pretenders*, *Captain Planet Says No Nukes*, *Got Milk?* and a Hypercolor tee subjected, as so many had been, to the indignity of a commercial dryer until it finally gave up the thermochromic ghost, its worn cotton-poly blend permanently stuck on a sad blown-out pink.

And Big Edie in the middle, ugly as all the sins of man, with a box of *Advanced Dungeons & Dragons: Second Edition* modules on the eastern point of the compass, a mint condition *Teenage Mutant*

*Ninja Turtles* Sewer Lair Playset to the west, a working laserdisc player up north, and down south, one beefy hardcase Samsonite in Executive Silver with a handwritten sign on it promising a complete set of signed first edition Danielle Steele hardbacks inside. A steal at $300, suitcase included.

Still life with late 80s/early 90s. Johanna loved it.

But she only had eyes for Big Edie. The absolute and utter trashbeast technological abortion winking up cheekily at her from within nest of vanished childhoods.

She'd driven all the way out into the golden calicified time-bubble of the Hudson Valley after the ephemeral promises of an estate sale. The people here had so much money they never had to grow or change or evolve past the approximate epoch of their children's most precocious years. That's how Johanna had gotten a Hasselblad for $90 and a fake phone number a couple of years ago at a *fuck-Gam-Gam-just-get-rid-of-this-junk* free-for-all in Stonybrook. You just crossed your eyes and hoped the kids were the type to tell everyone who never asked that social media was a disease and didn't sully themselves with Google or eBay.

This was clearly the case on that late-May Ossining afternoon. The card balanced against Big Edie's case read:

*Does Not Work. $50 OBO.*

Johanna Telle smiled in the perfect post-processed sun. The EDC-55 ED-Beta Camcorder retailed for a cool $7700 in 1987. Just over sixteen grand in 2015 funbucks. It could produce over 550 lines of resolution in an age where high definition was barely even a phrase. Automatic iris control, dual 2-3 inch precision CCD imaging, Fujinon f1.7 range macro zoom, on-the-fly audio/video editing, capable of recording in hi-fi stereo and most impressively for its time, native video playback. Angular black and matte silver bug-ugly design. The last glorious 13.5 kilogram gasp of the Betamax world, still in its hardcase shell, that particular shade of tan that meant Serious Business for the Terminally 80s Man.

In digital terms, Big Edie was pre-historic. Big Edie was fucking Cretaceous. If there was a camera set up on a tripod to record what happened when the primordial soup stopped being polite and started getting real, Big Edie would have been a top-tier choice for the discerning prosumer.

Big Edie was *archeology*.

Johanna whipped her faded seafoam-green hair to one side and hefted that machine corpse onto her dark brown shoulder. She was comically heavy. The weight of a dead world, its concerns long quieted.

Johanna Telle, when she was paying attention, when she was happy, in those moments when she was most definitively Johanna, saw down to the deeps of things. It was all she was really good at, in her estimation. She *saw* that world, *le regime ancien*, projected onto the back of her skull like a drive-in theater screen.

When she was little, she'd sat criss-cross applesauce in her mother's lap in a kind of mute blue nirvana, watching a crew send an unmanned submersible in a metal cage down the icy miles to find the HMS *Titanic*. Before her father left them, before they lost the house, before the hundred little fatal cuts of getting from one end of childhood to the other. Long beams of light broke the black water of forgetting and scattered across that ghostly bow and found what had been lost. Impossibly lost. Forever. Johanna had barely been able to breathe. She knew herself then, in that terrifying way you know things when you are small. The warmth of her mother's chest rose and fell behind her, an entire universe of protection and presence. A gentle little prick of the aquamarine pendant she always wore against Johanna's scalp. The familiar smell of Pink Window, her mother's signature Red Door knockoff, pulsing off her clavicle. The tinny voice of a rich man floating out of the blue ocean. Later, when the neighborhood kids played games on their unforgivably Spielbergian suburban streets, hollering *I'm the Incredible Hulk* or *I'm the Pink Ranger* or *I'm Tenderheart Bear*, Johanna would call out something nominally culturally appropriate but whisper the truth to herself, which never changed, no matter the game or the streets: *I am the exterior lighting array on Robert Ballard's Argo ROV unit.*

Johanna put her eye to Big Edie's viewfinder. The black cup *pocked* gently against her cheekbone. Such a *nice* feeling. Like holding a girl's hand for the first time. She stared into inert darkness.

"It only takes these weird old tapes," someone said from outside Edie's warm lightless innards. A friendly, well-hydrated, nicely-brought-up male voice, full of solicitude, exhausted, heartbroken, hanging in there, like the orange kitten in the old poster.

Johanna didn't look up. She amused herself picturing the kitten putting its paws on its hips and whistling regretfully through its sharp teeth at the $50 OBO paperweight before them. She suppressed her not-very-inner snob. *Yes, dear, ED Super Beta II and III series cassettes. You can still get them, anywhere between $35 and $50 a pop. You can still get anything if you don't care what it costs.*

"There's one stuck in there. Made a nasty sound when I tried to lever it out. I don't have any others, though. Dad didn't stick with this one for very long. I put his digital cameras around by the hydrangeas, way better. You want me to show you?"

"Does it turn on?"

"Nope. Well, not unless it's a Tuesday and the moon is in Pisces and you're standing on one foot or some shit. I keep the battery charged up, though. I heard you have to do that or it degrades. I'm Jeff, by the way."

*Of course you are. That's what they always name soft orange kittens like you.*

Johanna's fingers slid down Big Edie's flank and found the raised plastic goose-pimple that marked the power button as easily as a practiced accordionist settling onto C Major. She pointed the lens at the bereaved child of its former owner and hit the big red square.

A firehose of light white-watered through the generous 1.5" black and white viewfinder into her cerebral cortex. In the middle of it stood, not the *hang in there* kitten, but a tall handsome guy in his late twenties or early thirties. Big emotive eyes, tennis shorts, dark polo shirt, with a shimmer of beard-stubble six or seven hours deep, hair the cut and style of debate team and law school and firm handshakes and warm decades ahead in a secure center-right Senate seat.

A shard of glass punched through his chest. Black monochrome blood sheeted down over his shorts and his long, grey, summer-muscled legs. His neck whipped hard to the side, like he'd suddenly seen an old girlfriend and was about to call her name, but when he opened his mouth, a jet of dark liquid spurted onto the quilt of his so-loved childhood clothes. It cut across the white block-print *Pretenders* in a clean spattered line.

"What's the verdict?" Jeff asked. That voice like a clean fingernail cut through Johanna's attention. She yanked her face up off the viewfinder. Jeff's fine blond eyebrows arched curiously before her in full color, waiting to find out if that old Betamax monster still had juice. If the moon was, in fact, in Pisces. He shoved his hands in the pockets of a paint-splattered pair of jeans.

Johanna glanced back down into Big Edie's gullet. It was waiting down there, that death-image of silver and ichor.

"I like your shirt," she said. The walls of her throat stuck together. Inside the camera, that charcoal polo dripped silent-film blood onto his new white tennis shoes. Outside, he wore a slim-cut celery-green tee with *Newport Folk Festival 2010* stamped across his chest in a faux-rustic font. She could look back and forth between them. Back and forth. Black and white. Color. Black and white. Grey and green. Green and grey. And wet, dripping jet-onyx blood. All that faded thermochromicity blazing back onto the scene to react with the not live but definitely Memorex heat-death of Jeff from Ossining.

Big Edie went down for the count.

The image guttered out like a pilot light, a sound both grinding and whining shook through her, and she went down for the count.

"$30?"

"All yours," Jeff grinned.

He took Johanna Telle's money and strode off across the mown lawn, through the labyrinth of his late father's obsessions, the sun on his shoulders as though it would never leave him.

## Aliasing

IT'S MUCH EASIER to pry a stuck tape out of a machine when you're not that bothered if you break it. Get a screwdriver and a Sharpie and believe in yourself. It came free with significant but impotent protest, trailing a tangled mess of ropy ED Supra Beta II behind it. Johanna wound the mistreated tape back through the cartridge with the pen the way kids would never do again, and she would have been perfectly content for the rest of her days on this maudlin, over-saturated planet if she could have said the stupid suburban sun got in her eyes and that's all she really saw.

But Betamax tells no lies.

Johanna sat on the floor of her apartment like the kid from *Poltergeist* all grown up, heavily medicated, and a cog in the gig economy. A massive daisy chain of converter cables hooked Big Edie up to the living room flatscreen, each one coaxing the signal five or six years forward from 1987 to the slick shiny present day.

The reflected video image washed her face in color. A forgotten pleasure, like the taste of ancient Egyptian beer. You used to always see your shot in black and white when you looked through the viewfinder. You only got to see the colors when you reviewed the footage. Inside the camera was another planet. Color was a side-effect of traveling from that world to this one. Step from Kansas into Oz, cross your fingers for fidelity, saturation, hue, hope those shoes still look as red as they did before you crammed them through a lens.

So. No more black and white artsy viewfinder image. Now it was straight outta Kodachrome. But this tape sat in Big Edie's time-out box for thirty years. Chromatic degradation slipped and popped all over the image, sickly green blooms, hot orange halos, compression artefacts, uncanny edging that rimmed this and that object in weird chemical colors.

Johanna watched a factory-direct 70s mustache-dad with tennis socks up to God's chin helping his small, yet unmistakably Jeff, son unwrap a record player on Christmas morning. Big Edie came standard automatic fade-in and fade-out, so everything transitioned elegantly, creating a subtle sense of deliberate editing where none truly existed. Fade to black, then a slow melt into a hopeless lacrosse game, small children running nowhere, hitting each other with sticks too big for them to hold properly.

Another bloom of darkness.

A school play, reedy, vulnerable pre-adolescent Jeff dressed as a cloud fringed with silver tinsel rain, twirling and twirling, technique-free, his arms stretched out. Then another and Johanna presumed this was Jeff's mother, the maker of the T-shirt quilt, 80% Diane Keaton, 20% Shelley Duvall, a white-wine flush on her cheeks, smiling up at the man with the camera in frank, unguarded affection and not a little desire, her shoulders bare above a strapless summer dress the color of the hydrangeas she probably hadn't even planted yet.

Such wildly un-special moments, clichés of heart-beggaring authenticity, carefully cut out of the flow of time and pasted into the future, selected for immortality for no particular reason, random access memories transfigured into light that cannot die—but can get stuck in a metal cage for want of a Sharpie and a flathead.

Time travel. The only real time travel, unnoticed and uncredited because it was so unbearably slow. In the present, you use this astonishing machine to freeze the past. And you send it to the future. One second per second.

The image cut to black and then it was 2015 and Jeff selling off a lifetime of his father's lovingly dragon-hoarded *objets d'*American masculinity. Standing on a lawn with catalogue-ready light and dark green stripes in the grass. Talking not to the man who produced and directed his childhood but to Johanna. She can hear her own voice on the recording.

*Does it turn on?*

He makes a joke about the moon and tells her his name. Sitting alone in the dark, Johanna realizes he was flirting with her, and she has a second to wonder what his mustached father's name was before the glass smashes through his sternum again and blood streams down to soak a just out-of-frame blanket stitched together from mass-marketed polyester and lost time.

Johanna ran the tape back. Then she watched it again.

Back. And again.

She was still doing it when the morning broke into her apartment without announcing itself.

Five weeks later, she'll be down to two or three run-throughs a day. An article will swim across her feed.

Late Night Four-Car Pile Up on I-84 Leaves Two Dead, Seven Injured.

*Jeffrey Havemeyer of Westchester County, NY, 34, remains in critical care.*

Johanna will feel nothing. She's seen it a thousand times already.

## Overclocking

"SIT THERE," JOHANNA tells her cousin's daughter, pointing at a cracked leather barstool.

Anika is nineteen, in her second year at Columbia. She is everything Johanna is not: mentally stable, tall, good hair, vegan, grounded by parental encouragement and affection, prone to healthy relationships, able to commit to an exercise regimen. *The* 21$^{st}$ century girl. Johanna has always found her fascinating. Scientifically. It's like hanging out with an alien. Your whole ecosystem is based in carbon and abandonment and trash, and you just always assumed those were the essential building blocks of life, but it turns out they're totally unnecessary and sentient beings can just as well be made out of palladium and love and sensible choices instead, look at this actual good person right here, you have the same nose.

Johanna's arthritic Great Dane watches them coolly from his massive fluffy bed.

"Your hair looks like a badger," Anika says.

It's been some time since Ossining and quilt and the hydrangeas and what Johanna has come to think of as the glitch. Technical difficulties. Runtime error. It's late summer. Sweat darkens Anika's hairline under the expected carefully messy topknot. The boroughs are one long incessant screech of twelve million window-mounted air conditioners and the smell of warm garbage bags, round and shiny on every doorstep.

Seafoam green softheart mermaid look out; icicle-white collar-bone-length brutalist bob with black tips in.

"I like to think of it as ermine. You know, royal cloaks and all that."

"Did you know ermines are just regular stoats with their winter coats on?" Anika helpfully informs her. "Not special at all. Fancy weasels. *Glam* weasels."

"That's perfect. I myself am a decidely unspecial glam weasel."

Johanna adjusts the tripod under Big Edie. It took Johanna weeks to gut the old girl, order parts, and convince her that modern life truly was worth living. Nothing really wrong with her at all, other than the audio-visual equivalent of osteoporosis and a bad back. Johanna loved the work. Data was invisible now. Stored on sand, transferred on air, transcending physical form. Light talking to light. But not Big Edie. She was very visible. Gross and awkward and tangible. The girl would never be good as new again. But she was good enough.

"No you're not, you're amazing," Anika says softly, and Johanna can hear the little girl she's known in that grown-up, gonna-save-the-world-with-believing-it-can-be-saved voice.

Johanna ignores this obvious lie.

They've already done a few shots with the Hasselblad, the Leica, a couple with her phone. She doesn't really know why she's putting on a show. Anika wouldn't question just sitting in front of an old Betamax camcorder for a few minutes and then heading off for Hungarian pastries and a good full-body-cleanse political rant. But it feels important that today has the appearance of a plausibly professional kind of thing. Not that Johanna is using her.

Which she is.

Johanna doesn't have access to a lot of people at the moment. They find her offputting. Not user-friendly. An unintuitive interface. Carbon-based.

"Can you let the blinds down halfway?" she asks.

Anika does. Slats of August light and dark slash down her face and torso (like glass slicing through skin) like an old pre-lapsarian end-of-programming test screen. It would be a gorgeous shot even if the shot was the point.

"I mean it. This apartment, your work. Margot. Mapplethorpe." The Great Dane's floppy black ears perk up at the sound of his name. "I love it here. You're living the dream."

Johanna hesitates with her forefinger over the record button. God, she remembers how much she hated it when people told her college wasn't the real world and she had no idea what it was like out there, as if studying and working full-time wasn't more work and less fun than the barren salt flats of adulthood between your twenties and death. But she wanted badly to shovel the same shit for Anika now. The only way you could look at this place and see a dream was through a lens that had never touched reality.

*This is fine,* she tells herself. *The Havemeyer Glitch is not a thing. Just a shill for Big Coincidence. It's not like he died. And besides, nothing bad can ever happen to Anika. She is a palladium-based life form. So this is fine. It's for science. You will take beautiful footage of your beautiful niece-once-removed, and buy her a walnut kolachi, and she will tell her mother what a nice time she had.*

"Margot moved out last week," Johanna says without emotion. Margot moved out three months ago. She left a purple brush in the bathroom. Long black hair still tangled up in it. Johanna can't bring herself to move the last cells of Margot that exist in proximity to Johanna's cells.

"Oh," Anika replies gently. "So that's why you changed your hair."

Johanna hits *record*.

For eighty-seven seconds, the only thing Big Edie has to say is that Anika Telle was born for the camera, a portrait of her generation, artlessly artful, a corkscrew of loose dark hair hanging forward to catch the light, one grey bare leg tucked up beneath a billowy sack dress with small elephants printed on it, the other not quite long enough to touch the peeling floor. Her expression genuinely, infinitely, but entirely temporarily sad for the misfortunes of someone else. *See? This is fine. Tell her to say something. Recite Shakespeare. Or Seinfeld.*

Deep in Big Edie's viewfinder, Anika's left eye crumples in a wet gush of pearl and black. Her head rockets back, shrouded in mist. She coughs, gags, tears streaming from her remaining eye. She's still sitting on the barstool in Johanna's apartment with silvery botanical wallpaper behind her, the tall window, the August sun, the half-drawn blinds. But the Anika in the camera wears black leggings, a puffy black winter coat, a black surgical mask. White duct tape crisscrosses the back of her jacket to form the words: #NOJUSTICE. She's older, the lingering baby softness in her jaw gone, her hair a buzzed undercut. The cords on her neck stand out as she runs, her face ruined, blind with pain, stumbling, looking over her shoulder as she bolts on the video feed from one end of the living room to the other. Out of nothing, a cop in riot gear steps out of Johanna's kitchenette, grabs the back of Anika's skull in one hand and shoves her down. Anika-in-black falls to her knees, sobbing, puking into her mask, holding one hand to the hole where her eye used to be, screaming silently into Johanna's (Margot's) red paisley rug.

Johanna yanks her head up out of the sucking desaturated pit of the camera.

Mapplethorpe snores loudly. Trucks beep in reverse outside the apartment building. Anika sighs softly, bored but not rude. She scratches a mosquito bite on her knee. "I really am sorry. I liked Margot. She was good for you, I think. Got you out of the house."

All the blood has either rushed to or drained from Johanna's head. She can't tell which. All she can hear or feel is her own pulse slamming itself against her eardrums.

"Do you...want me to do something?" Anika asks uncertainly.

Johanna shuts the camera down quickly. The image at the bottom of the viewfinder clicks out of existence. She tries to talk, but there's no talk to be found. Just the burning hot green-on-red afterimage of a crystal brown eye collapsing in its socket, over and over.

"Come on, Auntie J," Anika says finally, hopping lightly off the stool and bending down, scratching Mapplethorpe between his spotted shoulder blades. "Dinner's on me. Malaysian okay? Maps can have a curry puff, can't you, baby?"

### Test Pattern: 2016

*AN EXPERIMENT THAT cannot be repeated is evidence of nothing.*

Johanna establishes a beachhead in Owl's Head Park. Back supported by a black walnut tree. Bare toes clenched in a sea of tiny white flowers and clover-infiltrated grass. Big Edie propped against her breastbone, lens stabilized by knees on either side. Mapplethorpe's yellow lead loops around her ankle, but the big fellow has long passed his days of running off after unsuspecting children. He munches philosophically on a pricey organic broth-basted rawhide shaped like a braided ring.

She finds a target, hits the button, rolls footage for a few minutes, tracking them as they throw frisbees for far-inferior dogs or kick soccer balls or kiss on picnic blankets or drag giant wooden chess pieces across a giant board or just walk aimlessly, whatever Saturday afternoon moves them to do. She doesn't look through the viewfinder into that hellworld of black and white. Just presses buttons.

Turn it on.

Shut it off.

Find someone new.

Repeat.

She chooses at random. No more Anikas. No one is special, or unspecial. It doesn't matter who they are or what they look like. They're just data. That man, that woman, that child, that set of twin babies, those skaters, that guy sleeping with a James Patterson book over his eyes. Compressed data to be converted later.

Johanna's brain checks out and begins a speed run through the five stages of grief over the death of a reliable reality. Denial: *you're losing it, change up your medication, girl, it's not real, it's not anything, just a stupid old camera that you bought because you are stupid, at best it's old footage coming through on an old tape.*

Stop recording. New person. Girl in green skinny jeans with a sketchbook.

Anger: *fuck this, fuck you, fuck estate sales, fuck Robert Ballard, fuck the Columbia School of Law, fuck sad elephant print fabric, fuck hydrangeas, fuck curry puffs that make my dog poop out his soul, fuck Betamax you dumb drooling obsolete idiot tech,, fuck me, fuck my dad, fuck Jeff Havemeyer's dad, fuck I-84, fuck Margot, fuck the linear flow of time, fuck everything, life is garbage and this is proof. Why is this happening to me?*

Stop. Scan. Record. Lanky white-dude dreds fuckboy in a vest but no shirt.

Depression: *Of course it's happening to me, because* I *am garbage and this is proof, and whatever cosmic hazmat disposal dump site got its back end trapped in my camera would only open the gates to a warped maladjust like me.*

Stop. Scan. Record. Old man on the bench with god-tier eyebrows and a yellow plastic sunflower in his lapel.

*Bargaining: I'll just watch this back tonight and whatever happens, afterward I'll tip Big Edie in the bin and never tell anyone. And then I will straighten up and clean my apartment and go on Tinder and eat leafy greens five times a day and see Anika more often and make amends and buy an exercise bike. Okay, Elder AV Club Gods? Deal?*

Stop. Scan. Record. Kid on a dirt bike with (elephants) puffins on her dress.

Acceptance.

Acceptance.

Acceptance is Johanna sitting cross-legged (criss-cross applesauce) on Mapplethorpe's bed while he snoozes jowlfully on the couch. She braces herself for red slicks of gore and bone. For Jeff and Anika redux. *Once is luck, two is coincidence, three is a pattern… or at least time to wake up and smell what your inevitable descent into psychosis is cooking.*

But that's not what Big Edie has for her.

Not entirely, anyway.

### Entropic Coding

GLOPPY AUGUST SUNLIGHT *washes out the image. Everything is overexposed, too bright, unforgiving. His thin chest rises and falls with his breath. He watches a small blue and white bird hop nervously down the iron rail of his park bench. A cerulean warbler,* Johanna notes with supreme irrelevance. *Closer to him, then further away, then close again. He crumbles a crust of brown bread on his tweedy knee and waits knowingly.* This goes on long enough that Johanna starts to relax. It isn't going to happen again. The bird will give in, and eat, and Johanna's life will resume the program already in progress.

*Then the sunlight cools, then it darkens, then it is a dim nothing-watt lamp with a tacky early 60s cherry pattern on the shade. The branches of black oak and Dutch elm in Owl's Head Park still reach into the frame like kids who've spotted a news crew, showing*

## Color, Heat, and the Wreck of the Argo

*off in the background, dying to get on TV. But the bench and the octogenarian perched on it have become a mustard-colored corduroy sofa and a young man with his head in his hands. Vaguely Scandavian mid-century wooden end tables bookend the couch. A clock with thin brass spikes radiating out around it ticks over a clearly-decorative fireplace. Above the man hangs a proto-Bob Ross painting of standard-issue lake/pines/mountain/lonely boat in a dizzying array of shades from brown to brown. Children's toys cover the floor. At least one boy and one girl. Maybe more. Wooden blocks, a rocking horse with yellow yarn hair, green plastic army men. Donald Duck and Bugs Bunny and Snoopy staring lifelessly at the ceiling in a triple rictus of frozen grimaces. A book of Connie Francis paper dolls with most of the smiling valium-glazed Connies already carefully cut out hiding under the formica coffee table. A Funflowers Vac-U-Form Maker-Pak Johanna recognizes from a box of crap her grandmother let her play with the year they had to live with her because, no matter how she tried to pretend it was an adventure, her mother had no options left. You squeezed out perfumed lucite goo into molds and made "Daffy Dills" and "Tuffy Tulips" that looked like crystals in the sun until you got bored and broke a vase just to get some attention. A Spirograph and stacks of spiralled paper, scattered across the avocado shag carpet like ticker tape after the parade has gone. Like mystic offerings before the massive, inert cabinet television that probably weighs more than everyone who lives here put together. The kinds of toys you lift off a flea market shelf with joy and reverence, despite the peeling paint and chipped edges and missing vital organs.*

*But these are all new.*

*A wind moves through Owl's Head Park and dappled shadows in the jaundiced light of the living room move across the man, the sofa, the table, the TV, the toys, the cherry lampshade.*

*The man on the yellow sofa looks up.*

*He is so young. Perhaps thirty-five, perhaps not even that. His incredible, architectural eyebrows are dark brown now; he has all* his hair. He's still wearing a suit, but this one has wide lapels, no tie, a plaid pattern that will crown end-caps in Goodwill until the sun burns out. He looks exhausted. Someone's been smoking all night and it was probably him. Maybe not just him. Butts overflow a pink pearlescent ashtray under the cherry lamp. About a third have frosted coral lipstick prints glowing on their filters, each one fainter than the last.

Johanna braces herself for the shard of glass or the ruination of his eye or gunshot or gas leak whatever is about to break this poor soul in half. Her heartrate spins up into the rhythm of a jet propeller carrying her into nothing and nowhere. Her stomach muscles clench for impact.

But: the man gets up. Wipes his palms on his wrinkled pants. Walks across the room. Stops. Bends down to pull one perfect yellow Vac-U-Form Funflower out of the pile of misshapen attempts. Slides it into his lapel. The man leaves the house. He closes the door behind him so gently it doesn't even click. No sound at all until his car engine starts outside, and then that's gone too.

In the margins of the image, the cerulean warbler flies off with a cry. The shadow of his little body flickers over the empty room.

Fade out.

Fade in on the girl in the green skinny jeans and peasant blouse lying with her sketchbook under the willow tree.

JOHANNA MAKES IT five people and ten minutes sixteen seconds deep by the overlarge alarm-clock style timestamp before she scrambles off the dog bed and shuts the whole rig off.

An hour later, she gets out of bed and pads back to the living room on tiptoe, as if afraid to wake Margot's brush. Blue light washes her cheeks and her hands and her walls and Johanna doesn't move until it's over.

Then she hits rewind and starts over from the beginning.

### Image Burn

MAPPLETHORPE MAKES IT another year before turning his creaky back on that big dog life. Since Johanna got to keep him through the quiet post-apocalypse of their union, they agreed Margot could have his ashes.

She looks the same. Just the *same*. As if Margot stepped out of the day she left and into today with no interruption in continuity. Johanna knows that dress, the navy blue vintagey thing with white piping and a little too much room in the torso, but that she refused to take in or give up on, because at thirty-seven, she might still have some growing left in her.

"Your hair," Margot says softly. She steps gingerly over the map of cables and playback devices that have replaced living breathing life for Johanna and sits uncomfortably in the old bisque-colored armchair (falls asleep re-reading *Harry Potter* in it during a snowstorm five years ago; Johanna drapes a crocheted blanket over her and squeezes the bare foot hanging over the overstuffed arm gently, fondly). She sits as though she is trying to hover, as thought it might burn her to stay.

"What about my hair?"

"It's…shocking."

"It's my hair."

"I assumed you would have gone puce or checkerboard by now. Your actual hair hasn't seen the light of day since high school as far as I know."

Johanna only dimly recalls that she used to care about things like wilding her hair. It seems like a fact about a stranger. Like something she would see on Big Edie and use to pinpoint a date.

They make small talk. Margot is leaving the city soon. She's bought a house in Providence with her wife, two blows Johanna absorbs expressionlessly as a cascade of words concerning Victorian architectural flourishes and small, private ceremonies patter down around her ears like raindrops. Mrs. Margot was apparently called Juniper, because of course she was, bet you call her June-bug too, gross. She had joined the obstetrics team at Rhode Island Hospital. Margot would teach very well-scrubbed scions of the even-better scrubbed at a private prep academy in the fall. Plant heirloom squash. Adopt three-legged rescue labradors.

What are Johanna's plans? If she has a gallery show before September, Margot would love to come. Anyone new in her life? How is Anika?

*Well, Marge, I plan to shoot weddings and graduations and bar mitzvahs in which the cakes have significantly more artistic value than my entire self until I die alone pitched face-first into my takeout massaman with no dog and no stomach lining and no friends except a magic camera, can I get you a 40% off Pinnacle buttered popcorn flavor vodka straight up, because that's where I am right now.*

But she doesn't say that. She would never say that.

Instead, she decides to ruin Margot's life. And in that moment, she genuinely believes it'll work.

"Can I show you something?" Johanna says.

"Of course. Always." Margot brushes her hair out of her eyes, now and a hundred thousand times in that chair, in this light. "New work?" Miss M was always her first audience, first viewer, the only other eye she trusted.

"Sort of. Mostly I just want you to tell me I'm not crazy." And she doesn't realize how entirely true that is until it's out of her mouth and loosed on the dusty air.

Margot frowns. "You don't look well. I didn't want to say. Are you still drinking?"

Johanna laughs bitterly as she flips through the input options on the flatscreen. "Why would I not be drinking? Drink is friend." She shoves delivery detritus off the couch to make a space: receipts, plastic bags, black plastic containers, breath mints and fortune cookies and after dinner toffees.

And they watch together. Side by side. Just the same. Like it is before. Like she will pick up her purple brush again tonight and run it through her hair and come to bed and tomorrow will be years ago and the film of them will run forward from the splice.

Rather, Margot watches. And Johanna watches Margot.

The colors waver on her face like she's underwater, staring up at the parade of strangers fading in and out before her.

The old man/young man on the park bench and the mustard-corduroy sofa.

The girl in the green skinny jeans under the willow and sitting at a bistro table in a with fake electronic candles as a man walks in, says her name uncertainly, kisses her cheek, orders an old-fashioned.

The guy with white-boy dreds and a vest with no shirt steps off a bike path and into a gorgeous apartment in no way decorated by a man who would wear a vest with no shirt even once, all minimalist monochrome, and a woman in pajama pants and jade chip earrings sobbing *get out get out not one more minute I'm done get out*.

A kid in a Spider-Man hoodie swinging upside down from a jungle gym and lying on his couch, a teenager, playing Madden on XBox, yelling to an invisible mother that he'll mow the lawn, yeah yeah, just one more game.

And worse. A boy's face fades into his forties on the subway. He asks why he's being pulled over. A gash blooms on his beautiful brown neck. A student drinking alone in a bar ages fifteen years and loses twenty pounds between sips of house red. She waits for someone with frantic energy and when somebody shows up, gives her a little wax paper packet, leaves her to it, her fingers start to turn the color of corpses on the wine glass. A volunteer museum docent grows red rings and bags around his eyes but loses his wrinkles. Somewhere between the Ancient Greeks and Mesopotamian pottery, gets out of a Camry, locks it, and runs toward an appointment, wholly unseeing the baby in the backseat, asleep in a puffy lavender knitted hat.

"What is this?" Margot says. "Glitch art? Datamoshing? Like Planes and Jacquemin? What program did you use? It's really seamless."

"No program."

"What do you mean 'no program'? This is a practical effect?" Johanna chuckles mirthlessly. The screen shimmers. "Where did you *find* all these actors?"

"No, look, you're not *seeing*. You have to *look*. The calendar in the apartment. The clothes the girl in the bistro is wearing. Do you recognize *any* of the players in that Madden game?"

"You know I don't care about sports. I wouldn't recognize any player's name five minutes after I heard it."

"Okay, fine. The song on the radio when the guy gets stuck in traffic." She pauses it, waits for Margot to catch up, to see the faint cursive 2026-At-A-Glance calendar on the inside of the pantry door in that perfect sleek flat, the unfamilar controls on the car dash. "I've never heard that song. You've never heard that song. Because that song doesn't exist, on any service, in any catalogue, anywhere."

"I'm sure that's not true. Come on, you couldn't *possibly* know that for certain, Jo."

But Margot doesn't *see*. Margot isn't Robert Ballard's submersible lighting array. She doesn't know how to crawl into an image and live there. What she *does* glimpse in Johanna's pleading eyes, is the weight of time. Time she has spent searching for these things, for connections, hoping, honestly hoping, to find that song buried on some indie compilation CD with some revoltingly photoshopped jacket art and a discount sticker. And a thousand other objects like it. Books on televisions, limited edition toys, tie-widths, license plates, worse, more scattered, atomized, randomized information that never coalesced into anything but Johanna's increasing silence and solitude. She vibrates so intensely it looks like she is sitting still.

And so, slowly, knowing how it sounds, hating how it sounds, Johanna explains about Big Edie as more strange moments unfold before the not-really-that-long lost love of her life; naked bodies, and there are a lot of them, in embraces violent and lovely or both or neither, strangers meeting, over and over, in different clothes, different hairstyles, different seasons, a child abandoned in an airport in Reno, calling for her mother, surrounded by slot machines ringing in cherries and oranges, tears rolling down her face. And at the end of the reel, Jeff and his glass heart, Anika and her shattered eye, the long staircase into images that has become Johanna's life.

Margot says nothing for some time. It is a terrible, sour nothing that lingers far too long in the air between them.

"So you think your camera shows…what? Death?"

"Maybe. Sometimes. But not always, not even often, really."

"Then what if not that? The future? Like the calendar."

"That's closer. Better. But at least a third of them are the past."

"How do you know?"

"Well, the man in the living room is 1970. You can tell by the Updike book on top of the TV. That was the first edition cover, and it's *pristine*. You can figure it out, sometimes. If you care about these things. If you know too much about garbage. And you *know* I know too much about garbage, M."

Margot smiles faintly, but it is *very* faint.

"But also I went back to the park and talked to the guy. His name is Antony." Johanna scratches at the back of her hand. "Antony left his family. In 1970. Just up and walked out on Grace, Walt, Irene, and Amelia, who he'd married when she was fucking seventeen. The proverbial running out for a pack of cigarettes. Left them like they were just…a skin he was molting."

Margot looks for a way to shut it off, but Johanna doesn't help her find it. Why should Margot get to turn away from it? Why should she escape?

"Fine," she says coldly. "What is it then?"

Johanna takes a deep breath. "So whenever you transfer or trasmit or store data, especially a lot of data, like audio or video or both, it gets compressed, and in the process, you lose a little bit of it. Maybe a lot, like MP3s were always straight garbage compactors for sound. Maybe only a little bit. Maybe so little you wouldn't even notice. But in order to fit the storage device or the bandwidth, in order to save information or share it, you have to…you have to *harm* it. And that creates distortion. Halos. Noise. Warping. Busy regions in the image. Blocky deformations called quilting, and visual echoes called ghosts. They're called compression artefacts, and that's…that's what I think these are. Distortions created by the present and everything else getting compressed, crushed into one stream. Halos and noise and warps and quilts and ghosts. A lot of words for damage. Just damage.

"But the answer is: I don't really know *what* it does. Technically speaking, it's a problem of parallax. *Catastrophic* parallax. A vast difference between the apparent object and the actual object. And for awhile, I thought it showed the worst day of your life. Which, odds are, for some percentage of people, is going to be the day you die. But not for everyone. Not for Antony. See, nothing ever went right for him after he left. Two more divorces and a dried up retirement fund. Grandkids he isn't allowed to meet. Lung cancer he picked up working a big gorgeous free man's HVAC repair shop. But it took him almost his whole life to understand any of it. To process where he fucked up. What he lost when he thought he was barreling down the highway to a big gorgeous free man's life. Big Edie knew it in an *instant*. She had his number faster than a speeding therapist, and that number was 1970. So it seemed to make enough sense. When I shot old people, Big Edie usually spat out the past. Young people mostly turned up older on playback. The future. That kid playing Madden. Madden 23, to be exact." She points to him on the projection. The hole in his sock. The length of his hair. The name on the Patriots' QB jersey.

"Do you actually expect me to believe your camera recorded something in 2023? Jo, come on. I'm really busy, and frankly, I'm not in the mood."

"Just *listen*. Because then there was this. A wedding. Mr. and Mrs. Nathaniel and Lucy Vaclavik." She fast-forwards through scene after scene. Johanna can tell just the sheer number of them is starting to look bad on her, and the manic sizzle in her voice isn't helping, but she can't stop herself.

The creams and golds and pops of understated rose-shades of a high-end matrimonial spread flood the screen. The bride waves her lily-dripping bouquet in the air. The Hudson River throbs with sunset behind her. Her hair sparkles with carefully applied glitter. Eyeliner and brows that date her nuptials as surely as a library stamp. Her new husband, in a grey tux, bends down to kiss her expertly neutral-frosted lips and their unified families clap like a gentle river of approval. The picture flows smoothly to the edge of the frame. No ghostly picture-in-picture. No shadows cast from other places, other times.

Margot smiles politely. Johanna knows she is losing her (has lost her). "I don't get it."

"I didn't either," she confesses softly. "I shot this no differently than the others. But what you see is what I saw. What Big Edie saw. No parallax. No difference in images. I rolled tape and the wedding marched right through the lens and back out again and it was just a wedding, no more or less. Nothing else has been like that. And the next day we got right back to business-as-horrible. I couldn't figure it out. Why was it special? What was different? The thing is…he killed her. It made the news for about thirty seconds in April. They found her in the woods in Connecticut. But, you know, hedge fund guys aren't that good at forensics, even if they're 100% current on all CSI franchises, so they caught him pretty fast. So maybe…maybe Big Edie doesn't record the worst thing that ever happened to you. Maybe it's something so much smaller than that. The moment when the worst thing that ever happens to you sees you coming. Turns toward you in the dark. I think, once she married him, he was always going to hurt her. Because that was *in* him, an egg or a seed or a tumor, whatever you want to call it, a future that no longer has the option of not happening. The flowchart flows until you meet that person at that conference and then there's no more choose your own adventure, you're going to fall in love and they're going to bankrupt you or betray you or just…disappoint you until there's nothing left but cynicism swirling around at the bottom of your heart like tea leaves. Or leave you in the woods in Connecticut. I don't know, maybe it's just a huge ugly regret machine. And mostly I will never understand these. What happened to the Madden kid or the girl in the bar or why getting stuck in traffic on that particular day was so important to that man's whole trajectory, or any of them, because that stuff doesn't come across the AP like Mrs. Vaclavik. They're just moments, unconnected, pulled free of every other moment."

The wedding fades out and the two women wince together as a man they do not know pushes a woman they have never met against a wall. Blood trickles down her temple where she hit a picture frame and she looks up at him with unbelieving eyes.

"Enough," Margot says. She grabs the remote. Shuts it all down. Turns to Johanna and touches her face. *Touches* her. No one has touched Johanna in a year. It is an alien burn. It is Margot. It is the past and the future and death, stroking her hair and making enormous eyes at her while the constituent atoms of their dog look on from the coffee table.

"I miss you so much," Johanna whispers, and wishes she could have thought of something better, more elegant, more memorable, but her need banishes pretty words.

"Don't," Margot answers with finality. The finality of Providence, Rhode Island and heirloom squash varietals and Harrington Preparatory School and June-Bug and poor Mapplethorpe in a box.

"What do you think?" She cannot help that either, the need for her approval, her regard, the perfect full absent moon of her gaze on Johanna's work, Johanna's self.

"Honey… I think you need help. This is…this is *nothing*, J. It's a bunch of slice of life shots of nothing in particular and three or four gory jump-scares. You taped over some movie of the week with a lot of nonsense. And I'm supposed to believe it's what, magic? It's you *stalking strangers*. Listen to yourself. Catastrophic parallax? You're manic, you need *care*."

But Johanna can't hear that. "Okay, but that's just exactly what I mean. Do you know what *catastrophe* means? It's Greek. It just means a turn. A turn down or a turn under or a turn inside. A turn away."

"Jo, this is basically a conspiracy theorist wall and you're unspooling more red yarn. This is not an X-File. This is you not coping. As usual."

"No, you don't understand. I'll show you. Just stand over there, I'll shoot you for a few minutes, a few seconds, and you'll see." And what will Big Edie see? Margot leaving that hot, humid, unretrievable night, Margot packing up boxes for Providence, Margot right now telling Johanna she will never believe her? One of them, maybe, surely. What else was even possible?

"No," Margot whispers firmly. "You don't need me. And you definitely don't need to ride that camera any harder. I'm not going to enable this. You just need help, baby. Professional help. That's all. I have to go."

"Wait—"

"I have to *go*."

There is a disentangling, a hurry to go back, edit, remove even the idea that physical contact was made. Margot excuses herself to splash water on her face and Johanna sees herself in the mute black monitor, sees as the ex-moon of her night sees: a woman so thin her clothes don't fit, who smells sour, whose hair hangs limp and unwashed, whose face has grown lines it didn't have even a few weeks ago, degradation lines, juddering through the frame of her face.

Margot emerges awkwardly, chagrined, her familiar elfin face not one cell altered from the day she left, her voice echoing against every surface: *I'm so fucking lonely, Jo, I'm lonely even when you're here. Especially when you're here. I'm lonely right the fuck now and I'm looking at you.*

She holds up something in her hand. Something purple. Something precious.

"Forgot my brush," she says softly.

And then she is gone.

## Ghosts

JOHANNA PUTS IT off for a long time.

Why bother? What use could it possibly be to her? What use is any of this? You couldn't do one single thing with it. The shot was too tight to predict the future. Fight crime? Protect the innocent? No. The camera crowded the subject, an unbearable idiot intimacy that took away everything but the seeing itself.

But eventually, she was always going to do it.

Johanna watches herself on the flatscreen. Watches herself get up in Big Edie's face. Fix the focus, back up to sit on the same barstool that held Anika all those ages ago, shifting awkwardly as she looks into the lens like an actor breaking the fourth wall.

She knows what she will see. She is calmly certain of it. She shouldn't have bothered running the tape back for this little screening. She saw it the first time, when she was seven. When she was thirsty in the middle of the night and padded quietly out of her room to get a glass of water. Out of her room and past her father sitting alone in his armchair, the moonlight crawling in after him through the window, grasping at him just before he shot himself and her life… turned. There never was any hope for her. She was turned before she got one foot in the world. It wouldn't be a prettier shot now.

The compression artefact burns out from the center of her nuclear-powered selfie. Her stomach muscles seize up the way they do when she just barely reaches the tipping point of a roller coaster and enters freefall, down the rails into her old house, the rugs, the stain on the ceiling, the off-kilter hang of her bedroom door. Her father's face. Her mother's soft snoring from the bedroom.

But that's not what she sees.

No moonlight. No armchair. No 3 a.m. drink of water in a seven-year-old girl's hand. It is just Johanna, seafoam green hair and all, walking on the lovely light and dark stripes of green on a lawn in Ossining, in sunlight direct from a photography lab, approaching a quilt made of old T-shirts and the objects it carries. She bends down and presses her warm thumb into the patch of Hypercolor shirt, waiting for the fabric to change color, to unsuffer the damage of too-constant exposure to the very thing that it was designed to react with, which of course it will not, can not, ever again.

Johanna touches her own face on the television, that seafoam green girl who still had Margot and Mapplethorpe and opinons about everything, that familiar face, yet better-fed and better-loved and almost obscenely untroubled. An ancient version of herself, suddenly unearthed at the bottom of the sea.

### Finite State Machine

JOHANNA PUTS BIG Edie up on Craigslist, all her specs laid out like a personal ad: *enjoys long walks on the beach, getting lost in the rain, composite video output, and turning everything you point me at into an avant-garde film-school short. If you can't handle me being haunted, you don't deserve me being way more work than the camera app on your phone.*

She lowballs the price. She means it. She can change her artefact. She can let it all go, like Margot said. Get care. Be normal. Cope. She can take that moment in Ossining and make it nothing. And then anyone could. The boy who doesn't want to mow the lawn. The girl meeting that man at the bistro. Lucy Vaclavik. Antony. Jeff. Anika. Anyone.

She doesn't answer a single query.

Six months later, Johanna doesn't even remember what it's like to leave the house without Big Edie. The pockets of her original-issue carrying case bulge with new tapes.

# The Perfect Host

SHE IS NOT WHAT YOU think.

Her eyes do not crawl with flies. Her skin does not burn with lesions. Her tongue does not swell in her mouth. Nothing of her rots, nothing blisters, nothing reeks, nothing wastes.

She is beautiful. She is young. She smells like frankincense and hand sanitizer.

You have met her already, but you didn't understand. You didn't notice her. You don't remember. You were so busy that day. So many things on your mind. But she noticed you. She notices everything, remembers everyone.

She has apartments in a dozen cities. A daisy chain of identical and very particular rooms. Yes, she has that kind of money. She *is* that kind of money. A fiscal singularity beyond which it is nearly impossible to conceptualize life.

She lives by herself, always, in every place. And always in a crowded high-rise. At the top, of course, a penthouse seated on a towering throne of writhing, dancing, cooking, arguing, singing, exercising, excreting humans. But none of that touches her up there, safe in the purity of sky and glass and soundproofed silence. It is not impossible that you've visited her in one of these far-flung flats—she is active on most dating apps. Perhaps that is how you met her.

Perhaps she buzzed you in. Perhaps you nodded to the doorman as you went up, excited, nervous, thrilled to be chosen, thrilled to be seen, thrilled to be special.

And you were. She wants you to know that. You were special. She loved you so much.

The walls of her places are brutally white, pitilessly clean. She touches nothing with her bare hands. There is a porcelain box of surgical gloves in every room. A tall, thin bottle of milky antibacterial soap perched over every sink like a miniature crow with a dripping beak.

Over every clean white mantel in every clean white apartment hangs a long white shelf containing dozens of small glass vials with rubber stoppers, neatly labelled. A place of honor, where most people keep family portraits. The bottles read: *Juniper, Rose, Peppermint, Clove, Myrrh, Camphor, Ambergris, Poppy, Styrax*. Some have other, less straightforward names: *Revive. Inspire. Welcome. Immune. Bliss. Pure Wellness*. The essential oils floating inside are the only colors anywhere.

A stainless steel slimline temperature-controlled wine cellar dominates the kitchen. Inside she keeps bottles of bleach. The recessed mood lighting in her ceiling is a blue starfield of UV lights. But even under their punishing, revelatory gaze, not one unseemly splatter shines.

A few carefully chosen pieces hang in her apartments. Minimalist portraits: a bat hanging in a white wood. A scaled pangolin tucked into a perfect Fibonacci curl. A pale mouse in a pale field. They don't seem like much to you as you pass by on the way to the bedroom, but you cannot begin to imagine what they cost. She is a profound patron of the arts. All her life, she has quietly sponsored playwrights, musicians, painters, novelists, sculptors. She does not discriminate and she asks for no credit. She is happy to help, happy just to stand near to genius, exhilarated inflame exquisite and fragile works, to shepherd them into this world. Some have have tried to paint her. She prefers they do not. Just as no one ever likes the way they look in photographs or thinks they sound right when they hear their voices recorded, she does not recognize herself in all their long bones and wings and arrows like teeth.

At night, when no one can see her, when no one even knows she is home, she watches television from a cold chair of antimicrobial copper. She wears a white N95 ventilator mask and a white silk dress and a clear plastic hazmat hood. She enjoys *Friends*. A silver laptop rests on her lap. She types idly. She moderates several online groups for homeopathy, faith healing, radical toxin cleanses, mothers against vaccination. She does not like to let the post queues get too backed up.

The lights of the screen move on her skin. The lights of the city outside slowly go out, street by street.

She is so lovely. Long and thin with a belly like a cold steel slab. Her hair is the color of a dark hallway leading nowhere. Her eyes are the color of acute cyanosis. Every movement of her limbs looks like an invitation.

And it is.

If she allows you to touch her, she won't make you use a condom. So unneccesary when all she wants is to *connect*. She finds you fascinating. Everything about you, down to the smallest cell. She wants to be with you completely, as completely as it is possible to interlace with a person. She wants to disappear into you.

But she will keep her mask on the whole time.

She would not be gone in the morning. That's not her way. Once she's chosen you, she will never leave you. You would have woken to the sound of her in the shower, the steam so hot it scalds the tip of your nose when you peek in, scraping her skin until it is clean, and then until it is red. She possesses a capacity for faithfulness beyond comprehension. Even if you walk out now, into the elevator and down into the marble lobby, past the doorman and into this or that nameless city, she will remain a part of you forever, as deep as blood.

But perhaps you didn't meet her that way. No, not that way. Not you.

You might have passed her in the street, hurrying to work, hurrying to mimosas and crepes, hurrying to the gym, your breath, her breath frosting in the morning air, mingling whiteness, merging.

You might have just missed seeing her on a transcontinental flight last spring. She waited patiently, a few people behind you in passport control, hoping you would turn your head toward her even for a moment, her breath cool by the time it brushed the back of your neck.

You might have served her in a cafe that serves the best brandy alexanders in the city, the heat of her mouthprint pulsing slick on the empty glass once she's slipped away like a last chance. She always tips well. She can afford it. It's the least she can do.

Or you might have gone to one of her parties.

Parties? Surely not this girl, with the soap bottles and the bleach-wine and the rubber gloves and that white mask like a mouth from another world. Surely she hates crowds: the noise, the grime, the smell, the closeness.

But she is not what you think. She adores company. She absolutely *craves* it. She hates to be alone.

Sometimes she goes out into the open-air markets at night. No one notices her. She isn't hungry; she doesn't need anything. She just wants to be close to people. To feel them press against her. To feel what they feel. She walks the stalls, her long, pale fingers hardly even grazing the exotic meats that hang in row after glistening row. Just being. Just breathing.

But she always wants more than those little barter-pits can offer. Her loneliness burns her hollow.

She isn't what you thought. She's lonely. Just like you. But doesn't she have anyone? Doesn't she have family? Oh yes, she comes from old, old money. She has siblings. They get along, she supposes. They're successful at what they do. They keep in touch. But they've never been able to give her what she needs. They just have very different interests. Separate lives. Even so, she always invites them to her party. She waits by the door every time like a puppy, hoping. But they won't come. Not yet, anyway.

Her affairs light up the map: Seattle, Milan, Hong Kong, New York, Paris, Tehran. Every town's hottest ticket. Hundreds of people, thousands if she can manage it, glittering with sweat and tears and beauty, packed in tight so she can feel the press of their bodies against hers as she moves through the crowd, dancing, writhing, feverish, breathless. The music is so loud. So loud and so long. She has heard them on the radio, telling everyone to stay indoors, and she knows it is nonsense. You can't live your life that way. She doesn't want to stifle you the way they do. She welcomes everyone. She loves everyone. Her revelers, her worshippers, her careless lovely friends. *Come in, come out, come close, take all I have to give, eat, drink, kiss, dance, annihilate the aching separation between living beings, shout to be heard over the gorgeous din, whisper so close your words fall into open ears like wet, frothing champagne, share glasses, share fluids, share everything. Revive. Inspire. Welcome. Immune. Bliss.*

*Pure Wellness.*

She slips invisibly through the throng, the perfect host. She embraces an old man here, a child there. She kisses an artist, locks hands with a doctor, grinds against a student on holiday. She will get to you, don't worry. She is coming, drenched in plenty, her eyes joyful, the sheer infectious light of her swallowing everyone she touches.

But you cannot hold onto her. She is not for you to keep, but to share. She is unselfish, endlessly enough for all. You want to limit her, but she won't be restrained. Once you feel the weight of her hand on the small of your back, it is too late, she has already moved on.

She adores all of them. Everyone who came when she called, out onto the quiet, empty streets to meet her. But you are special. Don't think for a moment she didn't want you in particular. That this was casual for her, a momentary inflammation, nothing serious. She loves you. She loves you so much. That's why she wanted you here, with her, at the end. She wanted to be a part of you.

And now she is.

Look—it's last call. She's waiting for you. Standing out on the balcony gazing over the radiant city, every radiant city, each one of them buzzing, chanting, barely able to breathe for the song of her name in their mouths. She is so glad you came out tonight. So happy just for the chance to be near you. It would have been so easy to stay inside like you were told. You must have wanted her so badly. It thrills her. She even wants you to meet her family.

*Maybe this time*, she whispers into your ear. Your heart races. You feel dizzy with her closeness, her perfume, her warmth. *I've been around the block, you know. So many disappointments. But maybe this time it's the real thing. Maybe I can have it all. Maybe this time it's forever. I want to believe it can be.*

She stretches out her hand. And you do see it then. Only for a moment. What all her beloved artists drew. The bones. The wings. The arrows like teeth. The streetlights and the starlight melt together in a silver jeweled wreath round her brow, a halo, a corona.

Behold, a white horse, and she that sat upon it came bearing a crown, and set forth to conquer.

AND THEN IT'S gone, and she's just a girl again. A pretty girl at a pretty party that you went to because goddammit, you wanted to. She touches your arm when she laughs and leans in close. You were so bored tonight. You couldn't take another minute of your own four walls. You needed this. You *deserved* this. Everyone is being ridiculous, anyway. It's only the flu. In a couple of weeks, it'll all be over.

# How to Become a Mars Overlord

**Welcome, Aspiring Potentates!**

WE ARE TREMENDOUSLY GRATIFIED AT your interest in our little red project, and pleased that you recognize the potential growth opportunities inherent in whole-planet domination. Of course we remain humble in the face of such august and powerful interests, and seek only to showcase the unique and challenging career paths currently available on the highly desireable, iconic, and oxygen-rich landscape of Mars.

**Query: Why Mars?**

IT IS A little known fact that every solar system contains Mars. Not Mars itself, of course. But certain suns seem to possess what we might call a habit of Martianness: in every inhabited system so far identified, there is a red planet, usually near enough to the most populous world if not as closely adjacent as our own twinkling scarlet beacon, with proximate lengths of day and night. Even more curious, these planets are without fail named for war-divinities. In the far-off Lighthouse system, the orb Makha turns slowly in the dark, red as the blood of that fell goddess to whom cruel strategists pray, she who nurses two skulls at each mammoth breast. In the Glyph system, closer to home, it is Firialai glittering there like a ripe red fruit, called after a god of doomed charges depicted in several valuable tapestries as a jester dancing ever on the tip of a sword, clutching in each of his seven hands a bouquet of whelp-muskets, bones, and promotions with golden seals. In the Biera-biera system, still yet we may walk the carnelian sands of Uppskil, the officer's patron goddess, with her woolly dactyl-wings weighted down with gorsuscite medals gleaming purple and white. Around her orbit Wydskil and Nagskil, the enlisted man's god and the pilot's mad, bald angel, soaring pale as twin ghosts through Uppskil's emerald-colored sky.

For each red planet owns also two moons, just as ours does. Some of them will suffer life to flourish. We have ourselves vacationed on the several crystal ponds of Volniy and Vernost, which attend the claret equatorial jungles of Raudhr—named, of course, for the four-faced lord of bad intelligence whose exploits have been collected in the glassily perfect septameters of the Raudhrian Eddas. We have flown the lonely black between the satellites on slim-finned ferries decked in greenglow blossoms, sacred to the poorly-informed divine personage. But most moons are kin to Phobos and Deimos, and rotate silently, empty, barren, bright stones, mute and heavy. Many a time we have asked ourselves: does Mars dwell in a house of mirrors, that same red face repeated over and over in the distance, a quantum hiccup—or is Mars the master, the exemplum, and all the rest copies? Surely the others ask the same riddle. We would all like to claim the primacy of our own specimen—and frequently do, which led to the Astronomer's War some years ago, and truly, no one here can bear to recite that tragic narrative, or else we should wash you all away with our rust-stained tears.

The advantages of these many Marses, scattered like ruby seeds across the known darkness, are clear: in almost every system, due to stellar circumstances beyond mortal control, Mars or Iskra or Lial is the first, best candidate for occupation by the primary world. In every system, the late pre-colonial literature of those primary worlds becomes obsessed with that tantalizing, rose-colored neighbor. Surely some of you are here because your young hearts were fired by the bedside tales of Alim K, her passionate affair with the two piscine princes of red Knisao, and how she waked dread machines in the deep rills of the Knizid mountains in order to possess them? Who among us never read of the mariner Ubaido and his silver-keeled ship, exploring the fell canals of Mikto, their black water filled with eely leviathans whose eyes shone with clusters of green pearls. All your mothers read the ballads of Sollo-Hul to each of you in your cribs, and your infant dreams were filled with gorgeous-green six-legged cricket-queens ululating on the broad pink plains of Podnebesya, their carapaces awash in light. And who did not love Ylla, her strange longings against those bronze spires? Who did not thrill to hear of those scarlet worlds bent to a single will? Who did not feel something stir within them, confronted with those endless crimson sands? We have all wanted Mars, in our time. She is familiar, she is strange. She is redolent of tales and spices and stones we have never known. She is demure, and gives nothing freely, but from our hearths we have watched her glitter, all of our lives. Of course we want her. Mars is the girl next door. Her desirability is encoded in your cells. It is archetypal. We absolve you in advance.

NO MATTER WHAT system bore you, lifted you up, made you strong and righteous, there is a Mars for you to rule, and it is right that you should wish to rule her. These are perhaps the only certainties granted to a soul like yours.

We invite you, therefore, to commit to memory our simple, two-step system to accomplish your laudable goals, for obviously no paper, digital, or flash materials ought to be taken away from this meeting.

## Step One: Get to Mars

IT IS EASIER for a camel to pass through the eye of a needle than for a poor man to get to Mars. However, to be born on a bed of gems leads to a certain laziness of the soul, a kind of muscular weakness of the ambition, a subtle sprain in the noble faculties. Not an original observation, but repetition proves the axiom. Better to excel in some other field, for the well-rounded overlord is a blessing to all. Perhaps micro-cloning, or kinetic engineering. If you must, write a novel, but only before you depart, for novels written in the post-despotic utopia you hope to create may be beloved, but will never be taken seriously by the literati.

Take as your exemplum the post-plastic retroviral architect Helix Fo. The Chilean wunderkind was born with ambition in his mouth, and literally stole his education from an upper-class boy he happened upon in a dark alley. In exchange for his life, the patriarch agreed to turn over all his books and assignments upon completion, so that Fo could shadow his university years. For his senior project, Fo locked his erstwhile benefactor in a basement and devoted himself wholly to the construction of the Parainfluenza Opera House in Santiago, whose translucent spires even now dominate that skyline. The wealthy graduate went on to menial labor in the doctoral factories much chagrined while young Fo swam in wealth and fame, enough to purchase three marriage rights, including one to an aquatic Verqoid androgyne with an extremely respectable feather ridge. By his fortieth birthday, Fo had also purchased through various companies the better part of the Atlantic Ocean, whereupon he began breeding the bacterial island which so generously hosts us tonight, and supplies our salads with such exquisite yersinia radishes. Since, nearly all interplanetary conveyances have launched from Fo's RNA platform, for he charged no tariffs but his own passage, in comfort and grace. You will, of course, remember Fo as the first All-Emperor of Mars, and his statue remains upon the broad Athabasca Valles.

Or, rather, model yourself upon the poetess Oorm Nineteen Point Aught-One, who set the glittering world of Muror letters to furious clicking and torsioning of vocabulary-bladders. You and I may be quite sure there is no lucre at all to be made in the practice of poetry, but the half-butterfly giants of Mur are hard-wired for rhyming structures, they cannot help but speak in couplets, sing their simplest greetings in six-part contratenor harmonies. Muror wars exist only between the chosen bards of each country, who spend years in competitive recitings to settle issues of territory. Oorm Nineteen, her lacy wings shot through with black neural braiding, revolted, and became a mistress of free verse. Born in the nectar-soup of the capital pool, she carefully collected words with no natural rhymes like dewdrops, hoarding, categorizing, and collating them. As a child, she haunted the berry-dripping speakeasies where the great luminaries read their latest work. At the age of sixteen, barely past infancy in the long stage-shifts of a Muror, she delivered her first poem, which consisted of two words: *bright. cellar.* Of course, in English these have many rhymes, but in Muror they have none, and her poem may as well have been a bomb detonated on the blue floor of that famous nightclub. Oorm Nineteen found the secret unrhyming world hiding withing the delicate, gorgeous structures of Muror, and dragged it out to shine in the sun. But she was not satisfied with fame, nor with her mates and grubs and sweetwater gems. That is how it goes, with those of us who answer the call. Alone in a ship of unrhymed glass she left Mur entirely, and within a year took the red diadem of Etel for her own. Each rival she assassinated died in bliss as she whispered her verses into their perishing ears.

It is true that Harlow Y, scion of the House of Y, ruled the red planet Llym for some time. However, all may admit his rule frayed and frolicked in poor measure, and we have confidence that no one here possesses the makings of a Y hidden away in her jumpsuit. Dominion of the House of Y passed along genetic lines, though this method is degenerate by definition and illegal in most systems. By the time Harlow ascended, generations of Y had been consumed by little more than fashion, public nudity, and the occasional religious fad. What species Y may have belonged to before their massive wealth (derived from mining ore and cosmetics, if the earliest fairy tales of Vyt are to be believed) allowed constant and enthusiastic gene manipulation, voluntary mutation, prostheses, and virtual uplink, no one can truly say. Upon the warm golden sea of Vyt you are House Y or you are prey, and they have forcibly self-evolved out of recognizability. Harlow himself appears in a third of his royal portraits something like a massive winged koala with extremely long, ultraviolet eyelashes and a crystalline torso. Harlow Y inherited majority control over Llym as a child, and administered it much as a child will do, mining and farming for his amusement and personal augmentation. Each of his ultraviolet lashes represented thousands of dead Llymi, crushed to death in avalanches in the mine shafts of the Ypo mountains. But though Harlow acheived overlordship with alacrity and great speed, he ended in assassination, his morning hash-tea and bambun spectacularly poisoned by general and unanimous vote of the populace.

Mastery of Mars is not without its little lessons.

It is surely possible to be born on a red planet. The Infanza of Hap lived all her life in the ruby jungles of her homeworld. She was the greatest actress of her age, her tails could convey the colors of a hundred complex emotions in a shimmering fall of shades. So deft were her illusions that the wicked old Rey thought her loyal and gentle beyond words even as she sunk her bladed fingers into his belly. But we must assume that if you require our guidance, you did not have the luck of a two-tailed Infanza, and were born on some other, meaner world, with black soil, or blue storms, or sweet rain falling like ambition denied.

Should you be so unfortunate as to originate upon a planet without copious travel options, due to economic crisis, ideological roadblocks, or simply occupying a lamentably primitive place on the techological timeline—have no fear. You are not alone in this. We suggest cryogenics—the severed head of Plasticene Bligh ruled succesfully over the equine haemovores of A-O-M for a century. He gambled, and gambled hard—he had his brain preserved at the age of twenty, hoping against hope that the ice might deliver him into a world more ready for his rarified soul. Should you visit A-O-M, the great wall of statues bearing her face (the sculptors kindly gave her a horse-body) will speak to what may be grasped when the house pays out.

If cryogenics is for some reason unpopular on your world, longevity research will be your bosom friend. Invest in it, nurture it: only you can be the steward of your own immortality. Even on Earth, Sarai Northe, Third Emira of Valles Marineris, managed to outlive her great-grandchildren by funding six separate think tanks and an Australian diamond mine until one underpaid intern presented her upon her birthday with a cascade of injections sparkling like champagne.

But on some worlds, in some terrible, dark hours, there is no road to Mars, no matter how much the traveling soul might desire it. In patchwork shoes, staring up at a starry night and one gleaming red star among the thousands—sometimes want is not enough. Not enough for Maximillian Bauxbaum, a Jewish baker in Provence, who in his most secret evenings wrote poetry describing such strange blood-colored deserts, such dry canals, a sky like green silk. Down to his children, and to theirs and theirs again, he passed a single ruby, the size of an egg, the size of a world. The baker had been given it as a bribe by a Christian lord, to take his leave of a certain maiden whom he loved, with hair the color of oxide-rich dust, and eyes like the space between moons. Never think on her again, never whisper her name to the walls. Though he kept his promise to an old and bitter death, such a treasure can never be spent, for it is as good as admitting your heart can be bought.

Sarai Northe inherited that jewel, and brought it with her to bury beneath the foundations of the Cathedral of Olympus Mons.

IN THE END, you must choose a universe that contains yourself and Mars, together and perfect. Helix Fo chose a world built by viruses as tame as songbirds. Oorm Nineteen chose a world gone soft and violet with unrhyming songs. Make no mistake: every moment is a choice, a choice between this world and that one, between heavens teeming with life and a lonely machine grinding across red stone, between staying at home with tea and raspberry cookies and ruling Mars with a hand like grace.

Maximillian Bauxbaum chose to keep his promise. Who is to say it is not that promise, instead of microbial soup, which determined that Mars would be teeming with blue inhuman cities, with seventeen native faiths, by the time his child opened her veins to those terrible champagne-elixirs, and turned her eyes to the night?

### Step 2: Become an Overlord

NOW WE COME to the central question at the core of planetary domination: just how is it done? The answer is a riddle. Of course, it would be.

You must already be an overlord in order to become one.

Ask yourself: what is an overlord? Is he a villain? Is she a hero? A cowboy, a priestess, an industrialist? Is he cruel, is he kind, does she rule like air, invisible, indispensable? Is she the first human on Mars, walking on a plain so incomprehensible and barren that she feels her heart empty? Does she scratch away the thin red dust and see the black rock beneath? Does he land in his sleek piscine capsule on Uppskil, so crammed with libraries and granaries that he lives each night in an orgy of books and bread? What does she lord over? The land alone, the people, the belligerent patron gods with their null-bronze greaves ablaze?

Is it true, as Oorm Nineteen wrote, that the core of each red world is a gem of blood compressed like carbon, a hideous war-diamond that yearns toward the strength of a king or a queen as a compass yearns toward north? Or is this only a metaphor, a way in which you can anthropomorphize something so vast as a planet, think of it as something capable of loving you back?

It would seem that the very state of the overlord is one of violence, of domination. Uncomfortable colonial memories arise in the heart like acid—everyone wants to be righteous. Everyone wishes to be loved. What is any pharonic statue, staring out at a sea of malachite foam, but a plea of the pharoah to be loved, forever, unassailably, without argument? Ask yourself: will Mars be big enough to fill the hole in you, the one that howls with such winds, which says the only love sufficient to quiet those winds is the love of a planet, red in tooth, claw, orbit, mass?

We spoke before of how to get to Mars if your lonely planet offers no speedy highway through the skies. Truthfully, and now we feel we can be truthful, here, in the long night of our seminar, when the clicking and clopping of the staff has dimmed and the last of the cane-cream has been sopped up, when the stars have all come out and through the crystal ceiling we can all see one—oh, so red, so red—just there, just out of reach—truthfully, getting to Mars is icing. It is parsley. To be an overlord is to engage in mastery of a bright, red thing. Reach out your hand—what in your life, confined to this poor grit, this lone blue world, could not also be called Mars? Rage, cruelty, the god of your passions, the terrible skills you possess, that force obedience from a fiery engine, bellicose children, lines of perfect, gleaming code? These things, too, are Mars. They are named for fell gods, they spit on civilized governance—and they might, if whipped or begged, fill some nameless void that hamstrings your soul. Mars is everywhere; every world is Mars. You cannot get there if you are not the lord and leader of your own awful chariot, if you are not the crowned paladin in the car, instead of the animal roped to it, frothing, mad, driven, but never understanding. We have said you must choose, as Bauxbaum and Oorm and Fo chose—to choose is to understand your own highest excellence, even if that is only to bake bread and keep promises. You must become great enough here that Mars will accept you.

Some are chosen to this life. Mars itself is chosen to it, never once in all its iterations having been ruled by democracy. You may love Mars, but Mars loves a crown, a sceptre, a horn-mooned diadem spangled in ice opals. This is how the bride of Mars must be dressed. Make no mistake—no matter your gender, you are the blushing innocent brought to the bed of a mate as ancient and inscrutable as any deathshead bridegroom out of myth. Did you think that the planet would bend to your will? That you would control it? Oh, it is a lovely word, overlord. Emperor. Pharoah. Princeps. But you will be changed by it as by a virus. Mars will fill your empty, abandoned places. But the greatest of them understood their place. The overlord embraces the red planet, but in the end, Mars always triumphs. You will wake in your thousand-year reign to discover your hair gone red, your translucent skin covered in dust, your three hearts suddenly fused into a molten, stony core. You will cease to want food, and seek out only cold, black air to drink. You will face the sun and turn, slowly, in circles, for days on end. Your thoughts will slow and become grand; you will see as a planet sees, speak as it speaks, which is to say: the long view, the perfected sentence.

And one morning you will wake up and your mouth will be covered over in stone, but the land beneath you, crimson as a promise, as a ruby, as an unrhymed couplet, as a virus—the land, or the machine, or the child, or the book, will speak with your voice, and you will be an overlord, and how proud we shall be of you, here, by the sea, listening to the dawn break over a new shore.

# Fade to White

*Fight the Communist Threat in Your Own Backyard!*

ZOOM IN ON A BRIGHT-EYED *Betty in a crisp green dress, maybe pick up the shade of the spinach in the lower left frame. [Note to Art Dept: Good morning, Stone! Try to stay awake through the next meeting, please. I think we can get more patriotic with the dress. Star-Spangled Sweetheart, steamset hair the color of good American corn, that sort of thing. Stick to a red, white, and blue palette.] She's holding up a resplendent head of cabbage the size of a pre-war watermelon. Her bicep bulges as she balances the weight of this New Vegetable, grown in a Victory Brand Capsule Garden. [Note to Art Dept: is cabbage the most healthful vegetable? Carrots really pop, and root vegetables emphasize the safety of Synthasoil generated by Victory Brand Capsules.]*

*Betty looks INTO THE CAMERA and says:* Just because the war is over doesn't mean your Victory Garden has to be! The vigilant wife knows that every garden planted is a munitions plant in the ~~War Fight~~ Struggle Against Communism. Just one Victory Brand Capsule and a dash of fresh Hi-Uranium Mighty Water can provide an average yard's worth of safe, rich, synthetic soil—and the seeds are included! *STOCK FOOTAGE of scientists: beakers, white coats, etc.* Our boys in the lab have developed a wide range of hardy, modern seeds from pre-war heirloom collections to produce the Vegetables of the Future. *[Note to Copy: Do not mention pre-war seedstock.]* Just look at this beautiful New Cabbage. Efficient, bountiful, and only three weeks from planting to table. *[Note to Copy: Again with the cabbage? You know who eats a lot of cabbage, Stone? Russians. Give her a big old zucchini. Long as a man's arm. Have her hold it in her lap so the head rests on her tits.]*

*BACK to Betty, walking through cornstalks like pine trees.* And that's not all. With a little help from your friends at Victory, you can feed your family *and* play an important role in the defense of the nation. *Betty leans down to show us big, leafy plants growing in her Synthasoil. [Note to Casting: make sure we get a busty girl, so we see a little cleavage when she bends over. We're hawking fertility here. Hers, ours.]* Here's a tip: Plant our patented Liberty Spinach at regular intervals. Let your little green helpers go to work leeching useful isotopes and residual radioactivity from rain, groundwater, just about anything! *[Note to Copy: Stone, you can't be serious. Leeching? That sounds dreadful. Reaping. Don't make me do your job for you.]* Turn in your crop at Victory Depots for Harvest Dollars redeemable at a variety of participating local establishments! *[Note to Project Manager: can't we get some soda fountains or something to throw us a few bucks for ad placement here? Missed opportunity! And couldn't we do a regular feature with the "tips" to move other products, make Betty into a trusted household name—but not Betty. Call her something that starts with T, Tammy? Tina? Theresa?]*

*Betty smiles. The camera pulls out to show her surrounded by a garden in full bloom and three [Note to Art Dept: Four minimum] kids in overalls carrying baskets of huge, shiny New Vegetables. The sun is coming up behind her. The slogan scrolls up in red, white, and blue type as she says:*

**A free and fertile tomorrow. Brought to you by Victory.**
*Fade to white.*

### The Hydrodynamic Front

MORE THAN ANYTHING in the world, Martin wanted to be a Husband when he grew up.

Sure, he'd had longed for other things when he was young and silly—to be a Milkman, a uranium prospector, an astronaut. But his fifteenth birthday was zooming up with alarming speed, and becoming an astronaut now struck him as an impossibly, almost obscenely trivial goal. Martin no longer drew pictures of the moon in his notebooks or begged his mother to order the whiz-bang home enrichment kit from the tantalizing back pages of *Popular Mechanics*. His neat yellow pencils still kept up near-constant flight passes over the pale blue lines of composition books, but what Martin drew now were babies. In cradles and out, girls with bows in their bonnets and boys with rattles shaped like rockets, newborns and toddlers. He drew pictures of little kids running through clean, tall grass, reading books with straw in their mouths, hanging out of trees like rosy-cheeked fruit. He sketched during history, math, civics: twin girls sitting at a table gazing up with big eyes at their Father, who kept his hat on while he carved a holiday Brussels sprout the size of a dog. Triplet boys wrestling on a pristine, uncontaminated beach. In Martin's notebooks, everyone had twins and triplets.

Once, alone in his room at night, he had allowed himself to draw quadruplets. His hand quivered with the richness and wonder of those four perfect graphite faces asleep in their four identical bassinets.

Whenever Martin drew babies they were laughing and smiling. He could not bear the thought of an unhappy child. He had never been one, he was pretty sure. His older brother Henry had. He still cried and shut himself up in Father's workshop for days, which Martin would never do because it was very rude. But then, Henry was born before the war. He probably had a lot to cry about. Still, on the rare occasion that Henry made a cameo appearance in Martin's gallery of joyful babies, he was always grinning. Always holding a son of his own. Martin considered those drawings a kind of sympathetic magic. Make Henry happy—watch his face at dinner and imagine what it would look like if he cracked a joke. Catch him off guard, snorting, which was as close as Henry ever got to laughing, at some pratfall on *The Mr. Griffith Show*. Make Henry happy in a notebook and he'll be happy in real life. Put a baby in his arms and he won't have to go to the Front in the fall.

Once, and only once, Martin had tried this magic on himself. With very careful strokes and the best shading he'd ever managed, he had drawn himself in a beautiful gray suit, with a professional grade shine on his shoes and a strong angle to his hat. He drew a briefcase in his own hand. He tried to imagine what his face would look like when it filled out, got square-jawed and handsome the way a man's face should be. How he would style his hair when he became a Husband. Whether he would grow a beard. Painstakingly, he drew a double Windsor knot in his future tie, which Martin considered the most masculine and elite knot.

And finally, barely able to breathe with longing, he outlined the long, gorgeous arc of a baby's carriage, the graceful fall of a lace curtain so that the pencilled child wouldn't get sunburned, big wheels capable of a smoothness that bordered on the ineffable. He put the carriage-handle into his own firm hand. It took Martin two hours to turn himself into a Husband. When the spell was finished, he spritzed the drawing with some of his mother's hairspray so that it wouldn't smudge and folded it up flat and small. He kept it in his shirt pocket. Some days, he could feel the drawing move with his heart. And when Father hugged him, the paper would crinkle pleasantly between them, like a whispered promise.

### Static Overpressure

THE DAY OF Sylvie's Presentation broke with a dawn beyond red, beyond blood or fire. She lay in her spotless white and narrow bed, quite awake, gazing at the colors through her Sentinel Gamma Glass window—lower rates of corneal and cellular damage than their leading competitors, guaranteed. Today, the sky could only remind Sylvie of birth. The screaming scarlet folds of clouds, the sun's crowning head. Sylvie knew it was the hot ash that made every sunrise and sunset into a torture of magenta and violet and crimson, the superheated cloud vapor that never cooled. She winced as though red could hurt her—which of course it could. Everything could.

Sylvie had devoted a considerable amount of time to imagining how this day would go. She did not worry and she was not afraid, but it had always sat there in her future, unmovable, a mountain she could not get through or around. There would be tests, for intelligence, for loyalty, for genetic defects, for temperament, for fertility, which wasn't usually a problem for women but better safe than sorry. Better safe than assign a Husband to a woman as barren as California. There would be a medical examination so invasive it came all the way around to no big deal. When a doctor can get that far inside you, into your blood, your chromosomes, your potentiality and all your possible futures, what difference could her white-gloved fingers on your cervix make?

None of that pricked up her concern. The tests were nothing. Sylvie prided herself on being realistic about her qualities. First among these was her intellect; like her mother Hannah she could cut glass with the diamond of her mind. Second was her silence. Sylvie had discovered when she was quite small that adults were discomfited by silence. It brought them running. And when she was angry, upset, when the world offended her, Sylvie could draw down a coil of silence all around her, showing no feeling at all, until whoever had affronted her grew so uncomfortable that they would beg forgiveness just to end the ordeal. There was no third, not really. She was what her mother's friends called striking, but never pretty. Narrow frame, small breasts, short and dark. Nothing in her matched up with the fashionable Midwestern fertility goddess floor-model. And she heard what they did not say, also—that she was not pretty because there was something off in her features, a ghost in her cheekbones, her height, her straight, flat hair.

Sylvie gave up on the fantasy of sliding back into sleep. She flicked on the radio by her bed: *Brylcreem Makes a Man a Husband!* announced a tinny woman's voice, followed by a cheerful blare of brass and the morning's reading from the Book of Pseudo-Matthew. Sylvie preferred Luke. She opened her closet as though today's clothes had not been chosen for years, hanging on the wooden rod behind all the others, waiting for her to grow into them. She pulled out the dress and draped it over her bed. It lay there like another girl. Someone who looked just like her but had already moved through the hours of the day and come out on the other side. The red sky turned the deep neckline into a gash.

She was not ready for it yet.

Sylvie washed her body with the milled soap provided by Spotless Corp. Bright as a pearl, wrapped in white muslin and a golden ribbon. It smelled strongly of rose and mint and underneath, a blue chemical tang. The friendly folks at Spotless also supplied hair rinse, cold cream, and talcum for her special day. All the bottles and cakes smelled like that, like growing things piled on top of something biting, corrosive. The basket had arrived last month with a bow and a dainty card attached congratulating her. Until now it had loomed in her room like a Christmas tree, counting down. Now Sylvie pulled the regimented colors and fragrances out and applied them precisely, correctly, according to directions. An oyster-pink shade called *The Blossoming of the Rod* on her fingernails, which may not be cut short. A soft peach called *Penance* on her eyes, which may not be lined. Pressed powder (*The Visitation of the Dove*) should be liberally applied, but only the merest breath of blush (*Parable of the Good Harlot*) is permitted. Sylvie pressed a rosy champagne stain (*Armistice*) onto her lips with a forefinger. Hair must be natural and worn long—no steamsetting or straightening allowed. Everyone broke that rule, though. Who could tell a natural curl from a roller these days? Sylvie combed her black hair out and clipped it back with the flowers assigned to her county this year—snowdrops for hope and consolation. Great bright thornless roses as red as the sky for love at first sight, for passion and lust.

Finally the dress. The team at Spotless Corp. encouraged foundational garments to emphasize the bust and waist-to-hip ratio. Sylvie wedged herself into a full length merry widow with built-in padded bra and rear. It crushed her, smoothed her, flattened her. Her waist disappeared. She pulled the dress over her bound-in body. Her mother would have to button her up; twenty-seven tiny, satin colored buttons ran up her back like a new spine. Its neckline plunged; its skirt flounced, showing calf and a suggestion of knee. It was miles of icy white lace, it could hardly be anything else, but the sash gleamed red. Red, red, red. *All the world is red and I am red forever*, Sylvie thought. She was inside the dress, inside the other girl.

The other girl was very striking.

Sylvie was fifteen years old, and by suppertime she would be engaged.

**Even Honest Joe Loves an Ice-Cold Brotherhood Beer!**

*CLOSE-UP ON PRESIDENT McCarthy in shirtsleeves, popping the top on a distinctive green glass bottle of BB—now with improved flavor and more potent additives! We see the moisture glisten on the glass and an honest day's sweat on the President's brow. [Note to Art Dept: I see what you're aiming at, but let's not make him look like a clammy swamp creature, shall we? He's not exactly the most photogenic gent to begin with.]*

*NEW SHOT: five Brothers relaxing together in the sun with a tin bucket full of ice and green bottlenecks. Labels prominently displayed. A Milkman, a TV Repairman, a couple of G-Men, and a soldier. [Note to Casting: Better make it one government jockey and two soldiers. Statistically speaking, more of them are soldiers than anything else.] They are smiling, happy, enjoying each others' company. The soldier, a nice-looking guy but not* too *nice-looking, we don't want to send the wrong message, says:* There's nothing like a fresh swig of Brotherhood after spending a hot Nevada day eye to eye with a Russkie border guard. The secret is in the thorium-boosted hops and New Barley fresh from Alaska, crisp iodine-treated spring water and just a dash of good old-fashioned patriotism. *The Milkman chimes in with*: And 5-Alpha! *They all laugh. [Note to Copy: PLEASE use the brand name! We've had meetings about this! Chemicals sound scary. Who wants to put some freakshow in your body when you can take a nice sip of Arcadia? Plus those bastards at Standard Ales are calling their formula Kool and their sales are up 15%. You cannot beat that number, Stone.] TV Repairman pipes up*: That's right, Bob! There's no better way to get your daily dose than with the cool, refreshing taste of Brotherhood. They use only the latest formulas: smooth, mellow, and with no jitters or lethargy. *G-Man pulls a bottle from the ice and takes a good swallow.* 5-Alpha leaves my head clear and my spirits high. I can work all day serving our great nation without distraction, aggression, or unwanted thoughts. *Second G-Man:* I'm a patriot. I don't need all those obsolete hormones anymore. And Brotherhood Beer strikes a great bargain—all that and 5.6% alcohol! *Our soldier stands up and salutes. He wears an expression of steely determination and rugged cheer. He says:* Well, boys, I've got an appointment with Ivan to keep. Keep the Brotherhood on ice for me.

*QUICK CUT back to President McCarthy. He puts down his empty bottle and picks up a file or something in the Oval Office. Slogan comes in at hip level [Note to Art Dept: how are we coming on that wheatstalk font?]:*

**Where There's Life, There's Brotherhood.**
*Fade to white.*

### Optimum Burst Altitude

ONE WEEK OUT of every four, Martin's Father came home. Martin could feel the week coming all month like a slow tide. He knew the day, the hour. He sat by the window tying and untying double Windsor knots into an old silk tie Dad had let him keep years ago. The tie was emerald green with little red chevrons on it.

Cross, fold, push through. Wrap, fold, fold, over the top, fold, fold, pull down. Make it tight. Make it perfect.

When the Cadillac pulled into the drive, Martin jumped for the gin and the slippers like a golden retriever. His Father's martini was a ritual, a eucharist. Ice, gin, swirl in the shaker, just enough so that the outer layer of ice releases into the alcohol. Open the vermouth, bow in the direction of the Front, and close it again. Two olives, not three, and a glass from the freezebox. These were the sacred objects of a Husband. Tie, Cadillac, martini. And then Dad would open the door and Faraday, the Irish Setter, would yelp with waggy happiness and so would Martin. He'd be wearing a soft grey suit. He'd put his hat on the rack. Martin's mother, Rosemary, would stand on her tiptoes to kiss him in one of her good dresses, the lavender one with daises on the hem, or if it was a holiday, her sapphire-colored velvet. Her warm blonde hair would be perfectly set, and her lips would leave a gleaming red kiss-shape on his cheek. Dad wouldn't wipe it off. He'd greet his son with a firm handshake that told Martin all he needed to know: he was a man, his martini was good, his knots were strong.

Henry would slam the door to his bedroom upstairs and refuse to come down to supper. This pained Martin; the loud bang scuffed his heart. But he tried to understand his brother—after all, a Husband must possess great wells of understanding and compassion. Dad wasn't Henry's father. Pretending that he was probably scuffed something inside the elder boy, too.

The profound and comforting sameness of those Husbanded weeks overwhelmed Martin's senses like the slightly greasy swirls of gin in that lovely triangular glass. The first night, they would have a roasting chicken with crackling golden skin. Rosemary had volunteered to raise several closely observed generations of an experimental breed called Sacramento Clouds: vicious, bright orange and oversized, dosed with palladium every fortnight, their eggs covered in rough calcium deposits like lichen. For this reason they could have a whole bird once a month. The rest of the week were New Vegetables from the Capsule Garden. Carrots, tomatoes, sprouts, potatoes, kale. Corn if it was fall and there hadn't been too many high-level days when no one could go out and tend the plants. But there was always that one delicious day when Father was at home and they had chicken.

After dinner, they would retire to the living room. Mom and Dad would have sherry and Martin would have a Springs Eternal Vita-Pop if he had been very good, which he always was. He liked the lime flavor best. They would watch *My Five Sons* for half an hour before Rosemary's Husband retired with her to bed. Martin didn't mind that. It was what Husbands were for. He liked to listen to the sounds of their lovemaking through the wall between their rooms. They were reassuring and good. They put him to sleep like a lullaby about better times.

And one week out of every four, Martin would ask his Father to take him to the city.

"I want to see where you work!"

"This is where I work, son," Father would always say in his rough-soft voice. "Right here."

Martin would frown and Dad would hold him tight. Husbands were not afraid of affection. They had bags of it to share. "I'll tell you what, Marty, if your Announcement goes by without a hitch, I'll take you to the city myself. March you right into the Office and show everyone what a fine boy Rosie and I made. Might even let you puff on a cigar."

And Martin would hug his Father fiercely, and Rosemary would smile over her fiber-optic knitting, and Henry would kick something upstairs. It was regular as a clock, and the clock was always right. Martin knew he'd be Announced, no problem. Piece of cake. Mom was super careful with the levels on their property. They planted Liberty Spinach. Martin was first under his desk every time the siren went off at school. After Henry's Announcement had gone so badly, he and Mom had installed a Friendlee Brand Geiger Unit every fifteen feet and the light-up aw-shucks faces had only turned into frowns and x-eyes a few times ever. There was no chance Martin could fail. Things were way better now. Not like when Henry was a kid. No, Martin would be Announced and he'd go to the city and smoke his cigar. He'd be ready. He'd be the best Husband anyone ever met.

Aaron Grudzinski liked to tell him it was all shit. That was, in fact, Aaron's favorite observation on nearly anything. Martin liked the way he swore, gutturally, like it really meant something. Grud was in Martin's year. He smoked Canadian cigarettes and nipped some kind of homebrewed liquor from his gray plastic thermos. He'd egged Martin into a sip once. It tasted like dirt on fire.

"Look, didn't you ever wonder why they wait til you're fifteen to do it? Obviously they can test you anytime after you pop your first boner. As soon as you're brewing your own, yeah?" And Grud would shake his flask. "But no, they make this huge deal out of going down to Matthew House and squirting in a cup. The outfit, the banquet, the music, the filmstrips. It's all shit. Shit piled up into a pretty castle around a room where they give you a magazine full of the wholesome housewives of 1940 and tell you to do it for America. And you look down at the puddle at the bottom of the plastic tumbler they call your chalice, your chalice with milliliter measurements printed on the side, and you think: *That's all I am. Two to six milliliters of warm wet nothing.*" Grud spat a brown tobacco glob onto the dead grass of the baseball field. He knuckled at his eye, his voice getting raw. "Don't you get it? They have to give you hope. Well, I mean, they have to give *you* hope. I'm a lost cause. Three strikes before I got to bat. But you? They gotta build you up, like how everyone salutes

Sgt. Dickhead on leave from the glowing shithole that is the great state of Arizona. If they didn't shake his hand and kiss his feet, he might start thinking it's not worth melting his face off down by the Glass. If you didn't think you could make it, you'd just kill yourself as soon as you could read the newspaper."

"I wouldn't," Martin whispered.

"Well, I would."

"But Grud, there's so few of us left."

The school siren klaxoned. Martin bolted inside, sliding into the safe space under his desk like he was stealing home.

### The Shadow Effect

EVERY SUNDAY SYLVIE brought a couple of Vita-Pops out to the garage and set up her film projector in the hot dark. Her mother went to her Ladies' Auxiliary meeting from two to four o'clock. Sylvie swiped hors d'oeuvres and cookies from the official spread and waited in the shadows for Clark Baker to shake his mother and slip in the side door. The film projector had been a gift from her Father; the strips were Clark's, whose shutterbug brothers and uncles were all pulling time at the Front. Every Sunday they sat together and watched the light flicker and snap over a big white sheet nailed up over the shelves of soil-treatment equipment and Friendlee Brand gadgets stripped for parts. Every Sunday like church.

Clark was tall and shy, obsessed with cameras no less than any of his brothers. He wore striped shirts all the time, as if solid colors had never been invented. He kept reading Salinger even after the guy defected. Sometimes they held hands while they watched the movies. Mostly they didn't. It was bad enough that they were fraternizing at all. Clark already drinking Kool Koffee every morning. Sugar, no cream. Clark was a quiet, bookish black boy who would be sent to the Front within a year.

On the white sheet, they watched California melt.

It hadn't happened during the war. The Glass came after. This thing everyone did now was not called war. It was something else. Something that liquefied the earth out west and turned it into the Sea of Glass. On the sheet it looked like molten silver, rising and falling in something like waves. Turning the Grand Canyon into a soft grey whirlpool. Sylvie thought it was beautiful. Like something on the moon. In real life it had colors, and Sylvie dreamed of them. Red stone dissolving into an endless expanse of dark glass.

"There are more Japanese people in Utah than in Japan now," Clark whispered when the filmstrip rolled up into black and the filmmaker's logo. Sylvie flinched as if he'd cut her.

They didn't talk about her Presentation. It sat whitely, fatly in their future. Once Clark kissed her. Sylvie cried afterward.

"I'll write you," he said. "As long as I can write."

The growth index for their county was very healthy, and this was another reason Clark Baker should not have been holding her hand in the dark while men in ghostly astronaut suits probed the edges of the Glass on a clicking filmstrip. Every woman on the block had a new baby this year. They'd gotten a medal of achievement from President McCarthy in the spring. The Ladies' Auxiliary graciously accepted the key to the city. She suspected her Father had a great deal to do with this. When she was little, he had come home one week in four. Now it was three days in thirty. His department kept him working hard. He'd be there for her Presentation, though. No Father missed his daughter's debut.

Sylvie thought about Clark while her mother slipped satin-covered buttons through tiny loops. Their faces doubled in the mirror. His dark brown hand on hers. The Sea of Glass turning their faces silver.

"Mom," Sylvie said. Her voice was very soft in the morning, as if she was afraid to wake herself up. "What if I don't love my Husband? Isn't that...something important?"

Hannah sighed. Her mouth took a hard angle. "You're young, darling. You don't understand. What it was like before. We had to have them here all the time, every night. Never a moment when I wasn't working my knees through for my husband. The one before your Father. The children before you. Do you think we got to choose then? It wasn't about love. For some people, they could afford that. For me, well, my parents thought he was a very nice man. He had good prospects. I needed him. I could not work. I was a woman before the war, who would hire me? And to do what? Type or teach. Not to program punchcard machines. Not to cross-breed new strains of broccoli. Nothing that would occupy my mind. So I drowned my mind in children and in him and when the war came I was glad. He left and it was *me* going to work every morning, *me* deciding what happened to my money. So the war took them," she waved her hand in front of her eyes, "war always does that. I know you don't think so, but the program is the best part of a bad situation. A situation maybe so bad we cannot fix it. So you don't love him. Why would you look for love with a man? How could a man ever understand you? He who gets the cake cannot be friends with the girl who gets the crumbs." Sylvie's mother blushed. She whispered: "My Rita, you know, Rita who comes for tea and bridge and neptunium testing. She is good to me. Someone will be good to you. You will have your Auxiliary, your work, your children. One week in four a man will tell you what to do—but listen to me when I say they have much better manners than they used to. They say please now. They are interested in your life. They are so good with the babies." Hannah smoothed the lacy back of her daughter's Presentation gown. "Someday, my girl, either we will all die out and nothing will be left, or things will go back to the old ways and you will have men taking your body and soul apart to label the parts that belong to them. Enjoy this world. Either way, it will be brief."

Sylvie turned her painted, perfected face to her mother's. "Mom," she whispered. Sylvie had practiced. So much, so often. She ordered the words in her head like dolls, hoped they were the right ones. Hoped they could stand up straight. "Watashi wa anata o shinjite ī nā." *I wish I could believe you.*

Hannah's dark eyes flew wide and, without a moment's hesitation, she slapped her daughter across the cheek. It wasn't hard, not meant to wound, certainly not to leave a mark on this day of all days, but it stung. Sylvie's eyes watered.

"Nidoto," her mother pleaded. "Never, *never* again."

### *Gimbels: Your Official Father's Day Headquarters!*

*PANORAMA SHOT OF the Gimbels flagship store with two cute kiddos front and center. [Note to Casting: get us a boy and a girl, blonde, white, under ten, make sure the boy is taller than the girl. Put them in sailor suits, everyone likes that.] The kids wave at the camera. Little Linda Sue speaks up. [Note to Copy: Nope. The boy speaks first.] It's a beautiful June here in New York City, the greatest city on earth! Jimmy throws his hands in the air and yells out:* And that means FATHER'S DAY! *Scene shift, kiddos are walking down a Gimbels aisle. We see toolboxes, ties, watches in a glass case, barbecue sets. Linda Sue picks up a watch and listens to it tick. Jimmy grabs a barbecue scraper and brandishes it. He says:* Come on down with your Mom and make an afternoon of it at the Brand New Gimbels Automat! Hot, pre-screened food in an instant! Gee wow! *[Note to Copy: hey, Stone, this is a government sponsored ad. If Gimbels want to hawk their shitty Manhattan Meals they're going to have to actually pay for it. Have you ever tried one of those things? Tastes like a kick in the teeth.] Linda Sue:* At Gimbels they have all the approved Father's Day products. *(Kids alternate lines)* Mr. Fix-It! Businessman! Coach! Backyard Cowboy! *Mr. Gimbel appears and selects a beautiful tie from the spring Priapus line. He hands it to Linda Sue and ruffles her hair. Mr. Gimbel:* Now, kids, don't forget to register your gift with the Ladies' Auxiliary. We wouldn't want *your* Daddy to get two of the same gift! How embarrassing! That's why Gimbels carries the complete Whole Father line, right next to the registration desk so your Father's Day is a perfect one. *Kids:* Thanks, Mr. Gimbel!

Mr. Gimbel spreads his arms wide and type stretches out between them in this year's Father's Day colors. [Note to Art Dept: It's seashell and buttercup this year, right? Please see Marketing concerning the Color Campaign. Pink and blue are pre-war. We're working with Gimbels to establish a White for Boys, Green for Girls tradition.]

**Gimbels: Your One Stop Shop for a One of a Kind Dad.**
Fade to white.

### Flash Blindness

MARTIN WORE THE emerald green chevroned tie to his Announcement, even if it wasn't strictly within the dress code. Everything else was right down the line: light grey suit, shaved clean if shaving was on the menu, a dab of musky *Oil of Fecunditas* behind each ear from your friends at Spotless Corp. Black shoes, black socks, Spotless lavender talcum, teeth brushed three times with Pure Spearmint Toothpaste (*You're Sure with Spearmint!*). And his Father holding his hand, beaming with pride. Looking handsome and young as he always did.

Of course, there was another boy holding his other hand.

His name was Thomas. He had broad shoulders already, chocolate-colored hair and cool slate eyes that made him look terribly romantic. Martin tried not to let it bother him. He knew how the program worked. Where the other three weeks of the month took his Father. Obviously, there were other children, other wives, other homes. Other roasting chickens, other martinis. Other evening television shows on other channels. And that's all Thomas was: another channel. When you weren't watching a show, it just ceased to be. Clicked off. Fade to white. You couldn't be jealous of the people on those other channels. They had their own troubles and adventures, engrossing mysteries and stunning conclusions, cliffhangers and tune-in-next-weeks. It had nothing to do with Martin, or Rosemary, or Henry in his room. That was what it meant to be a Husband.

The three of them sat together in the backseat of the sleek gray Cadillac. An older lady drove them. She wore a smart cap and had wiry white hair, but her cheeks were still pink and round. Martin tried to look at her as a Husband would, even though a woman her age would never marry. After all, Husbands didn't get to choose. Martin's future wives—four to start with, that was standard, but if he did well, who knew?—wouldn't all be bombshells in pin-up bathing suits. He had to practice looking at women, really seeing them, seeing what was good and true and gorgeous in them. The chauffeur had wonderful laugh lines around her eyes. Martin could tell they were laugh lines. And her eyes, when she looked in the rear view mirror, were a nice, cool green. She radioed to the dispatcher and her voice lilted along with a faint twinge of English accent. Martin could imagine her laughing with him, picking New Kale and telling jokes about the King. He imagined her naked, laying on a soft pink bed, soft like her pink cheeks. Her body would be the best kind of body: the kind that had borne children. Breasts that had nursed. Legs that had run after misbehaving little ones. He could love that body. The sudden hardness between his legs held no threat, only infinite love and acceptance, a Husband's love.

*When I think about how good I could be, my heart stops*, Martin thought as the space between his neighborhood and the city smeared by. The sun seared white through dead black trees. But somewhere deep in them there was a green wick. Martin knew it. He had a green wick, too. *I will remember every date. Every wife will be so special and I will love her and our children. I will make her martinis. I will roast the chicken so she doesn't have to. When I am with one of them I will turn off all other channels in my mind. I can keep it straight and separate. I will study so hard, so that I know how to please. It will be my only vocation, to be devoted. And if they the women of Elm St or Oak Lane or Birch Drive find love with each other when I am gone, I will be happy for them because there is never enough love. I will draw them happy and they will be happy. The world will be green again. Everything will be okay.*

It all seemed to happen very fast. Thomas and Martin and a dozen other boys listened to a quintet play Mendelssohn. The mayor gave a speech. They watched a recorded message from President McCarthy which had to be pretty old because he still sported a good head of hair. Finally, a minister stood up with a lovely New Tabernacle Bible in her one good hand. The other was shriveled, boneless, a black claw in her green vestments. The pages of the Bible shone with gilt. A ribbonmark hung down and it was very red in the afternoon flares. She did not lay it on a lectern. She carried the weight in her hands and read from the Gospel of Pseudo-Matthew, which Martin already knew by heart. The minister's maple-syrup contralto filled the vaults of Matthew House.

"And when Mary had come to her fourteenth year, the high priest announced to all that the virgins who were reared in the Temple and who had reached the age of their womanhood should return to their own and be given in lawful marriage. When the High Priest went in to take counsel with God, a voice came forth from the oratory for all to hear, and it said that of all of the marriageable men of the House of David who had not yet taken a wife, each should bring a rod and lay it upon the altar, that one of the rods would burst into flower and upon it the Holy Ghost would come to rest in the form of a Dove, and that he to whom this rod belonged would be the one to whom the virgin Mary should be espoused. Joseph was among the men who came, and he placed his rod upon the altar, and straightaway it burst into bloom and a Dove came from Heaven and perched upon it, whereby it was manifest to all that Mary should become the wife of Joseph."

Martin's eyes filled with tears. He felt a terrible light in his chest. For a moment he was sure everyone else would see it streaming out of him. But no, the minister gave him a white silk purse and directed him to a booth with a white velvet curtain. Inside, silence. Dim, dusty light. Martin opened the purse and pulled out the chalice—a plastic cup with measurements printed on it, just like Grud said. With it lay a few old photographs—women from before the war, with so much health in their faces Martin could hardly bear to look at them. Their skin was so clear. *She's dead,* he thought. *Statistically speaking, that woman with the black hair and heart-shaped face and polka-dotted bikini is dead. Vaporized in Seattle or Phoenix or Los Angeles. That was where they used to make pictures, in Los Angeles. This girl is dead.*

Martin couldn't do it. This was about life. Everything, no matter how hard and strange, was toward life. He could not use a dead girl that way. Instead, he shut his eyes. He made his pictures, quick pencil lines glowing inside him. The chauffeur with her pink cheeks and white hair. The minister with kind voice and brown eyes and her shriveled hand, which was awful, but wasn't she alive and good? Tammy, the girl from the Victory Brand Capsule Garden commercials in her star-spangled dress. A girl with red hair who lived two blocks over and was so pretty that looking at her was like getting punched in the chest. He drew in bold, bright lines the home he was going to make, bigger than himself, bigger than the war, as big as the world.

Martin's body convulsed with the tiny, private detonation of his soul. His vision blurred into a hot colorless flash.

### Blast Wind

SYLVIE'S MOTHER HELPED her into long white gloves. They sat together in a long pearl-colored Packard and did not speak. Sylvie had nothing to say. Let her mother be uncomfortable. A visceral purple sunset colored the western sky, even at two in the afternoon. Sylvie played the test in her head like a filmstrip. When it actually started happening to her, it felt no more real than a picture on a sheet.

The mayor gave a speech. They watched a recorded message from President McCarthy's pre-war daughter Tierney, a pioneer in the program, one of the first to volunteer. *Our numbers have been depleted by the Germans, the Japanese, and now the Godless Russians. Of* the American men still living only 12% are fertile. But we are not Communists. We cannot become profligate, wasteful, decadent. We must maintain our moral way of life. As little as possible should change from the world your mothers knew—at least on the surface. And with time, what appears on the surface will penetrate to the core, and all will be restored. We will not sacrifice our way of life.*

A minister with a withered arm read that Pseudo-Matthew passage Tierney had dredged up out of apocrypha to the apocrypha, about the rods and the flowers and Sylvie had never felt it was one of the Gospel's more subtle moments. The minister blessed them. They are flowers. They are waiting for the Dove.

The doctors were women. One was Mrs. Drexler, who lived on their cul-de-sac and always made rum balls for the neighborhood Christmas cookie exchange. She was kind. She warmed up her fingers before she examined Sylvie. *White gloves for her, white gloves for me,* Sylvie thought, and suppressed a giggle. She turned her head to one side and focused on a stained-glass lamp with kingfishers on it, piercing their frosted breasts with their beaks. She went somewhere else in her mind until it was over. Not a happy place, just a place. Somewhere precise and clean without any Spotless Corp. products where Sylvie could test soil samples methodically. Rows of black vials, each labeled, dated, sealed.

They took her blood. A butterfly of panic fluttered in her—will they know? Would the test show her mother, practicing her English until her accent came out clean as acid paper? Running from a red Utah sky even though there was no one left to shoot at her? Only half, white enough to pass, curling her hair like it would save her? Sylvie shut her eyes. She said her mother's name three times in her mind. The secret, talismanic thing that only they together knew. *Hidaka Hanako. Hidaka Hanako. Hidaka Hanako. Don't be silly. Japan isn't a virus they can see wiggling in your cells. Mom's documents are flawless. No alarm will go off in the centrifuge.*

And none did.

She whizzed through the intelligence exams—what a joke. *Calculate the drag energy of the blast wind given the following variables.* Please. Other girls milled around her in their identical lace dresses. The flowers in their hair were different. Their sashes all red. Red on white, like first aid kits floating through her peripheral vision. They went from medical to placement testing to screening. They nodded shyly to each other. In five years, Sylvie would know all their names. They would be her Auxiliary. They would play bridge. They would plan block parties. They would have telephone trees. Some of them would share a Husband with her, but she would never know which. That was what let the whole civilized fiction roll along. You never knew, you never asked. Men had a different surname every week. Only the Mrs. Drexlers of the neighborhood knew it all, the knots and snags of the vital genetics. Would she share with the frosted blonde who loved botany or the redheaded math genius who made her own cheese? Or maybe none of them. It all depended on the test. Some of these girls would score low in their academics or have some unexpressed, unpredictable trait revealed in the great forking family trees pruned by Mrs. Drexler and the rest of them. They would get Husbands in overalls, with limited allowances. They would live in houses with old paint and lead shielding instead of Gamma Glass. Some of them would knock their Presentation out of the park. They'd get Husbands in grey suits and silk ties, who went to offices in the city during the day, who gave them compression chamber diamonds for their birthdays. As little as possible should change.

Results were quick these days. Every year faster. But not so quick that they did not have luncheon provided while the experts performed their tabulations. Chicken salad sandwiches—how the skinny ones gasped at the taste of mayonnaise! Assam tea, watercress, lemon curd and biscuits. An impossible fairy feast.

"I hope I get a Businessman," said the girl sitting next to Sylvie. Her bouffant glittered with illegal setting spray. "I couldn't bear it if I had to live on Daisy Drive."

"Who cares?" said Sylvie, and shoved a whole chicken salad triangle into her mouth. She shouldn't have said anything. Her silence bent for one second and out comes nonsense that would get her noticed. Would get her remembered.

"Well, *I* care, you *cow*," snapped Bouffant. Her friends smiled behind their hands, concealing their teeth. *In primates, baring the teeth is a sign of aggression,* Sylvie thought idly. She flashed them a broad, cold smile. *All thirty-two, girls, drink it in.*

"I think it's clear what room *you'll* be spending the evening in," Bouffant sneered, oblivious to Sylvie's primate signals.

But Sylvie couldn't stop. "At best, you'll spend 25% of your time with him. You'll get your rations the same as everyone. You'll get your vouchers for participating in the program and access to top make-work contracts. What difference does it make who you snag? You know this is just pretend, right? A very big, very lush, very elaborate dog breeding program."

Bouffant narrowed her eyes. Her lips went utterly pale. "I hope you turn out to be barren as a rock. Just *rotted away inside*," she hissed. The group of them stood up in a huff and took their tea to another table. Sylvie shrugged and ate her biscuit. "Well, that's no way to think if you want to restore America," she said to no one at all. What was the matter with her? *Shut up, Sylvie.*

Mrs. Drexler put a warm hand on her shoulder, materializing out of nowhere. The doctor who loved rum balls laid a round green chip on the white tablecloth. Bouffant saw it across the room and glared hard enough to put a hole through her skull at forty yards.

Sylvie was fertile. At least, there was nothing obviously wrong with her. She turned the chip over. The other side was red. Highest marks. *Blood and leaves. Red on white. The world is red and I am red forever.* One of Bouffant's friends was holding a black chip and crying, deep and horrible. Sylvie floated. Unreal. It wasn't real. It was ridiculous. It was a filmstrip. A recording made years ago when Brussels sprouts were small and the sunset could be rosy and gentle.

*FADE IN on Mrs. Drexler in a dance hall with a white on white checkerboard floor. She's wearing a sequin torchsinger dress. Bright pink. She pumps a giant star-spangled speculum like a parade-master's baton.* Well, hello there Sylvia! It's your big day! Should I say Hidaka Sakiko? I only want you to be comfortable, dear. Let's see what you've won!

Sylvie and the other green-chip girls were directed into another room whose walls were swathed in green velvet curtains. A number of men stood lined up against the wall, chatting nervously among one another. Each had a cedar rod in one hand. They held the rods awkwardly, like old men's canes. A piano player laid down a slow foxtrot for them. Champagne was served. A tall boy with slightly burned skin, a shiny pattern of pink across his cheek, takes her hand, first in line. In Sylvie's head, the filmstrip zings along.

*WIDE SHOT of Mrs. Drexler yanking on a rope-pull curtain. She announces:* Behind Door Number One we have Charles Patterson, six foot one, Welsh/Danish stock, blond/blue, scoring high in both logic and empathy, average sperm count 19 million per milliliter! This hot little number has a reserved parking spot at the Office! Of course, when I say "Office," I mean the upper gentlemen's club, brandy and ferns on the $35^{th}$ floor, cigars and fraternity and polished teak walls. A little clan to help each other through the challenges of life in the program—only another Husband can really understand. Our productive heartthrobs are too valuable to work! Stress has been shown to lower semen quality, Sylvie! But as little as possible should change. If you take the Office from a man, you'll take his spirit. And what's behind Door Number Two?

Sylvie shuts her eyes. The real Mrs. Drexler was biting into a sugar cookie and sipping her champagne. She opened them again— and a stocky kind-eyed boy had already cut in for the next song. He wore an apple blossom in his lapel. For everlasting love, Broome County's official flower for the year. The dancing Mrs. Drexler in her mind hooted with delight, twirling her speculum.

*TIGHT SHOT of Door Number Two. Mrs. Drexler snaps her fingers and cries:* Why, it's Douglas Owens! Five foot ten, Irish/Italian, that's *very* exciting! Brown/brown, scoring aces in creative play and nurturing, average sperm count 25 million per milliliter—oh ho! Big, strapping boy! *Mrs. Drexler slaps him lightly on the behind. Her eyes gleam.* He's a Businessman as well, nothing but the best for our Sylvie, our prime stock Sylvie/Sakiko! He'll take his briefcase every day and go sit in his club with the other Husbands, and maybe he loves you and maybe he finds real love with them the way you'll find it with your friend Bouffant in about two years. Who can tell? It's so *thrilling* to speculate! It's not like men and women got along so well before, anyway. Take my wife, please! Why I oughtta! To hell with the whole mess. Give it one week a month. You do unpleasant things one week out of four and don't think twice. Who cares?

Someone handed her a glass of champagne. Sylvie wrapped her real, solid fingers around it. She felt dizzy. A new boy had taken up her hand and put his palm around her waist. The dance quickened. Still a foxtrot, but one with life in it. She looked at the wheel and spin of faces—white faces, wide, floor-model faces. Sylvie looked for Clark. Anywhere, everywhere, his kind face moving among the perfect bodies, his kind face with a silver molten earth undulating across his cheeks, flickering, shuddering. But he wasn't there. He would never be there. It would never be Clark with a cedar rod and a sugar cookie. Black boys didn't get Announced. Not Asians, not refugees, not Sylvie if anyone guessed. They got shipped out. They got a ticket to California. To Utah.

As little as possible should change.

No matter how bad it got, McCarthy and his Brothers just couldn't let a nice white girl (like Sylvie, like Sylvie, like the good floor-model part of Sylvie that fenced in the red, searing thing at the heart of her) get ruined that way. (If they knew, if they knew. Did the conservative-suit warm-glove Mrs. Drexler guess? Did it show in her dancing?) Draw the world the way you want it. Draw it and it will be.

Sylvie tried to focus on the boy she was dancing with. She was supposed to be making a decision, settling, rooting herself forever into this room, the green curtains, the sugar cookies, the foxtrot.

*QUICK CUT to Mrs. Drexler. She spins around and claps her hands. She whaps her speculum on the floor three times and a thin kid with chocolate-colored hair and slate eyes sweeps aside his curtain. She crows:* But wait, we haven't opened Doooooor Number Three! Hello, Thomas Walker! Six foot even, Swiss/Polish—ooh, practically Russian! How exotic! I smell a match! Brown/gray, top marks across the board, average sperm count a spectacular 29 million per milliliter! You're just showing off, young man! Allow me to shake your hand!

Sylvie jittered back and forth as the filmstrip caught. The champagne settled her stomach. A little. Thomas spun her around shyly as the music flourished. He had a romantic look to him. Lovely chocolate brown hair. He was saying something about being interested in the animal repopulation projects going on in the Plains States. His voice was sweet and a little rough and fine, fine, this one is fine, it doesn't matter, who cares, he'll never sit in a garage with me and watch the bombs fall on the sheet with the hole in the corner. Close your eyes, spin around three times, point at one of them and get it over with.

*IRIS TRANSITION to Mrs. Drexler doing a backflip in her sequined dress. She lands in splits.* Mr. and Mrs. Wells and Walker invite you to the occasion of their children's wedding!

Sylvie pulled the red, thornless rose and snowdrops from her hair and tied their ribbon around Thomas's rod. She remembered to smile. Thomas himself kissed her, first on the forehead and then on the mouth. A lot of couples seemed to be kissing now. The music had stopped. *It's over, it's over,* Sylvie thought. *Maybe I can still see Clark today. It takes time to plan a wedding.*

Voices buzzed and spiked behind her. Mrs. Drexler was hurrying over; her face was dark.

*ZOOM on Mrs. Drexler:* Wait, sorry, wait! I'm sorry we seem to have hit a snag! It appears Thomas and Sylvie here are a little too close for comfort. They should never have been paired at the same Announcement. Our fault, entirely! Sylvie's Father has been such a boon to the neighborhood! Doing his part! Unfortunately, the great nation of the United States do not condone incest, so you'll have trade Door Number Three for something a little more your speed. This sort of thing does happen! That's why we keep such excellent records! CROSS-REFERENCING! Thank you! *Mrs. Drexler bows. Roses land at her feet.*

Sylvie shut her eyes. The strip juddered; she was crying tracks through her Spotless Corp Pressed Powder and it was not a film, it was happening. Mrs. Drexler was wearing a conservative brown suit with a gold dove-shaped pin on the lapel and waving a long-stemmed peony for masculine bravery. Thomas was her brother, somehow, there had been a mix-up and he was her brother and other arrangements would have to be made. The boys and girls in a ballroom with her stared and pointed, paired off safely. Sylvie looked up at Thomas. He stared back, young and sad and confused. The snowdrops and roses had fallen off his rod onto the floor. Red on white. Bouffant was practically climbing over Douglas Owens 25 million per milliliter like a tree.

In four years Sylvie will be Mrs. Charles Patterson 19 million per. It's over and they began to dance. Charles was a swell dancer. He promised to be sweet to her when he got through with training and they were married. He promised to make everything as normal as possible. As little as possible should change. The quintet struck up Mendelssohn.

Sylvie pulled her silence over her and it was good.

Fade to white.

*CLOSE-UP OF A nice-looking Bobby, a real lantern-jaw, straight-dealing, chiseled type. [Note to Casting: maybe we should consider*

*VP Kroc for this spot. Hair pomade knows no demographic. Those idiots at Brylcreem want to corner the Paternal market? Fine. Let them have their little slice of the pie. Be a nice bit of PR for the re-election campaign, too. Humanize the son of a bitch. Ray Kroc, All-American, Brother to the Common Man. Even he suffers symptomatic hair loss. Whatever—you get the idea. Talk to Copy.] Bobby's getting dressed in the morning, towel around his healthy, muscular body. [Note to Casting: if we go with Kroc here we'll have to find a body double.] Looks at himself in the mirror and strokes a 5-o'clock shadow.*

FEMALE VOICE OVER: Do you wake up in the morning to a sink full of disappointment?

*PAN DOWN to a clean white sink. Clumps of hair litter the porcelain. [Note to Art Dept: Come on, Stone, don't go overboard. No more than twenty strands.] Bobby rubs the top of his head. His expression is crestfallen.*

VOICE OVER: Well, no more! Now with the radiation-blocking power of lead, All-New Formula Samson Brand Hair Pomade can make you an All-New Man.

*Bobby squirts a generous amount of Samson Brand from his tube and rubs it on his head. A blissful smile transforms his face.*

VOICE OVER: That feeling of euphoria and well-being lets you know it works! Samson Pomades and Creams have been infused with our patented mood-boosters, vitamins, and just a dash of caffeine to help you start your day out right!

*PAN DOWN to the sink. Bobby turns the faucet on; the clumps of hair wash away. When we pan back up, Bobby has a full head of glossy, thick, styled hair. [Note to Art Dept: Go whole hog. When the camera comes back put the VP in a full suit, with the perfect hair—a wig, obviously—and the Senate gavel in his hand. I like to see a little more imagination from you, Stone. Not a good quarter for you.]*

VOICE OVER: Like magic, Samson Brand Pomade gives you the confidence you need. [*Note to Copy: not sure about* 'confidence' here. What about 'peace of mind'? We're already getting shit from the FDA about dosing Brothers with caffeine and uppers. Probably don't want to make it sound like the new formula undoes Arcadia.]

He gives the camera a thumbs-up. [Note to Art Dept: Have him offer the camera a handshake. Like our boy Ray is offering America a square deal.]

Bold helvetica across mid-screen:
**Samson Guards Your Strength.**
Fade to white.

### Ten Grays

MARTIN WATCHED HIS brother. The handsome Thomas. The promising Thomas. The fruitful and multiplying Thomas. 29 million per mil Thomas. Their father (24 million) didn't even try to fight his joyful tears as he pinned the golden dove on his son's chest. His good son. His true son. For Thomas the Office in the city. For Thomas the planning and pleasing and roasted chickens and martinis. For Thomas the children as easy as pencil drawings.

For Martin Stone, 2 million per milliliter and most of those dead, a package. In a nice box, to be certain. Irradiated teak. It didn't matter now anyway. Martin knew without looking what lay nestled in the box. A piece of paper and a bottle. The paper was an ordnance unknown until he opened the box. It was a lottery. The only way to be fair. It was his ticket.

It might request that he present himself at his local Induction Center at 0900 at the close of the school year. To be shipped out to the Front, which by then might be in Missouri for all anyone knew. He'd suit up and boot it across the twisted, bubbled moonscape of the Sea of Glass. An astronaut. Bouncing on the pulses from Los Alamos to the Pacific. He would never draw again. By Christmas, he wouldn't have the fine motor skills.

Or it would request just as politely that he arrange for travel to Washington for a battery of civic exams and placement in government service. Fertile men couldn't think clearly, didn't you know? All that sperm. Can't be rational with all that business sloshing around in there. Husbands couldn't run things. They were needed for more important work. The most important work. Only Brothers could really view things objectively. Big picture men. And women, Sisters, those gorgeous black chip girls with 3-Alpha running cool and sweet in their veins. Martin would probably pull Department of Advertising and Information. Most people did. Other than Defense, it was the biggest sector going. The bottle would be Arcadia. For immediate dosage, and every day for the rest of his life. All sex shall be potentially reproductive. Every girl screwing a Brother is failing to screw a Husband and that just won't do. They said it tasted like burnt batteries if you didn't put it in something. The first bottle would be the pure stuff, though. Provided by Halcyon, Your Friend in the Drug Manufacturing Business. Martin would remember it, the copper sear on the roof of his mouth. After that, a whole aisle of choices. Choices, after all, make you who you are. Arcadia or Kool. Brylcreem or Samson.

Don't worry, Martin. It's a relief, really. Now you can really get to work. Accomplish something. Carve out your place. Sell the world to the world. You could work your way into the Art Department. Keep drawing babies in carriages. Someone else's perfect quads, their four faces laughing at you forever from glossy pages.

Suddenly Martin found himself clasped tight in his Father's arms. Pulling the box out of his boy's hands, reading the news for him, putting it aside. His voice came as rough as warm gin and Martin could hardly breathe for the strength of his Father's embrace.

Thomas Walker squeezed his Brother's hand. Martin did not squeeze back.

### Velocity Multiplied by Duration

SYLVIE'S FATHER WAS with them that week. He was proud. They bought a chicken from Mrs. Stone and killed it together, as a family. The head popped off like a cork. Sylvie stole glances at him at the table. She could see it now. The chocolate hair. The tallness. Hannah framed her Presentation Scroll and hung it over the fireplace.

Sylvie flushed her Spotless trousseaux down the toilet.

She wasn't angry. You can't get angry just because the world's so much bigger than you and you're stuck in it. That's just the face of it, cookie. A poisoned earth, a sequined dress, a speculum you can play like the spoons. Sylvie wasn't angry. She was silent. Her life was Mrs. Patterson's life. People lived in all kinds of messes. She could make rum balls. And treat soil samples and graft cherry varieties and teach some future son or daughter Japanese three weeks a month where no one else could hear. She could look up Bouffant's friend and buy her a stiff drink. She could enjoy the brief world of solitude and science and birth like red skies dawning. Maybe. She had time.

It was all shit, like that Polish kid who used to hang around the soda fountain kept saying. It was definitely all shit.

On Sunday she went out to the garage again. Vita-Pops and shadows. Clark slipped in like light through a crack. He had a canister of old war footage under his arm. Stalingrad, Berlin, Ottawa. Yellow shirt with green stripes. Nagasaki and Tokyo, vaporizing like hearts in a vast, wet chest. The first retaliation. Seattle, San Francisco, Los Angeles. Clark reached out and held her hand. She didn't squeeze back. The silent detonations on the white sheet like sudden balloons, filling up and up and up. It looked like the inside of Sylvie.

"This is my last visit," Clark said. "School year's over." His voice sounded far away, muffled, like he didn't even know he was talking. "Car's coming in the morning. Me and Grud are sharing a ride to Induction. I think we get a free lunch."

Sylvie wanted to scream at him. She sucked down her pop, drowned the scream in bubbles.

"I love you," whispered Clark Baker.

On the sheet, the Golden Gate Bridge vanished.

Sylvie rolled the reel back. They watched it over and over. A fleck of nothing dropping out of the sky and then, then the flash, a devouring, brain-boiling, half-sublime sheet of white that blossomed like a flower out of a dead rod, an infinite white everything that obliterated the screen.

Fade to black.

And over the black, a cheerful fat man giving the thumbs-up to Sylvie, grinning:

*Buy Freedom Brand Film! It's A-OK!*

# Secretario

IN THE CITY, THERE ARE three kinds of people: the dead, the devils, and the detectives.

The dead are women; the devils are men. Have you ever noticed that? The detectives, by law, can go either way, but look around: you won't see too many skirts.

SO BEGINS THE diary of Mala Orrin, my superior in all the ways that count. She smelled of leather, not the black, soldierly kind, but the warm, beaten brown leather of a briefcase often oiled and well loved, or of a journal often thumbed. She wore long trenchcoats; a hat the color of wheat. Sensible shoes, the kind of shoes you wear to run after people. After devils.

I never saw her face. Her hat, cocked at the same angle, cast its shadow on her face like a knight's visor. A woman, obscured.

And I never noticed. I should have. Everything she ever wrote down, I read. I sat at a desk and took her dictation, requisitioned her pistols, had her coats cleaned when the blood-spray got too noticeable. But every time she looked down at a body, impassive as a god, her cigarette Hephaestean, her mind Athene, she could see the pattern, and I saw only her.

EVERY CASE BEGINS with a body. To be more precise, it begins with a detective observing a body. How it lies, how it tells the truth.

This is what a dead body looks like:

It is female. Its natural habitat is a dark alley, full of rain-puddles. It is only recently dead—no corruption has set in, not yet. Her skin is perfect, two and a half shades paler than in life. Her hair fans out around her head, floating in the rainwater like a mermaid. She is wearing something that shows her thighs, her breasts, black silk, or red. The fabric folds suggestively, not quite showing her nude, but nearly there. Her lips are scarlet; her shoes are black. Her name is something simple and anonymous: Anna, or Sarah, or Claire. Because it doesn't really matter who she is. She is waiting for the detective; she's already met the devil. She lays like a lover for the detective to use, her legs open, her mouth open, her eyes open, her wounds open, everything about her open, inviting the gaze of the detective, that death enthusiast. The detective is a libertine—he has eyes for all of them. They bleed for him, so that he will know her. So that someone will know her.

But I don't see a lover. I look down as the rain sluices off the brim of my hat and her blood is running into the gutters and I see a mirror. I am she and she is me and we are going to go into the dark together.

This is why the other detectives are men. It's so ugly, the other way round.

I DON'T BELIEVE she was the only one. Surely, in the history of the City, there was another woman detective. There must be a feminine noun, in the language of the City. *Detectiva*. Something. But to be honest I can't think of one. I was her secretary, her understudy, her second. She never consulted me. The girls in the steno pool never asked me to tea. It was a lonely life, and I had to fetch my own coffee. Mala

Orrin and I ate together in a diner across the street from the office. She always had steak, rare as a gunshot wound, scotch with two ice cubes, and a slice of cherry pie with kiss of ice cream. I always had salad. Toast. Coffee—black. I don't like to eat anything red. If there are only three sorts, then the steno pool is only the waiting dead, and I a waiting devil, for I was never any kind of detective. Either way, red reminds me of these things, and I don't want to be reminded.

There must be a word, in the language of the City, for a male secretary. *Secretario.* Something. It was decided by the higher-ups that if we were to suffer a woman detective, she must have a male secretary. The natural order must be maintained. The doorman leaned out into the street and whistled—I turned my head. That's how I was chosen. I turned my head at a sharp, high sound, and they offered me ten dollars a day to keep her notes in order. Good money. And there's never any shortage of bodies in the City. Detectives do a brisk business here. You could say it's our primary industry.

THIS IS WHAT a devil looks like:

It is male. It wears black. He skulks—that is his primary means of locomotion. His face is broad and craggy, his eyes dark. Everything about him is closed: his lips, his heart, his coat. He hunches—over a weapon, an erection, a deformity, a secret. His hands are big; there is a lot of meat on him. His name is something simple and anonymous: John, Jim, Nick. Because it doesn't really matter who he is, either. He is not quiet when he hunts the dead girl—already dead, from the moment he saw her. He killed her with looking, with wanting. All that's left is the denouement.

He never uses a gun. It's a knife, or garroting—sometimes, if he loves her especially, he will beat her to death. It has to be intimate, or it is no good. A woman has two lovers in her life: her murderer, and her avenger. First she lies down beneath the devil as he cuts her, blood trickles beautifully, delicately from her mouth, cinematically, as though anyone but the devil could see how perfect the trickle truly is. It is all for him. He is careful not to rip her clothes; he is courteous to the detective, who will come after. He does not want to spoil the scene for him.

Every time my office takes a call, hears a name, an address, I think: this time the body will be a man. He will be laid out for me, so thoughtfully, his angelic face in a rictus of foreknowledge. Death will have worn a woman's face, and opened him up, passing this body from herself to me. I will reach out into the shadows and touch that devil, and she will take my hand, and we will understand each other.

All detectives ever do is summon devils. Out of the night, out of blood ritual. Logic is a lie. Deduction is a fell rite.

---

IT'S NOT HARD for a secretary to pick a desk-lock. They aren't sturdy things. I took her diary. She's gone; she won't mind. And the diary of a great detective—surely I could open it to any page and solve a crime, read from it as from a book of spells and reveal the depths of the shadows, the glint of truth in the grime. If I had a deftness at deduction, even a drop, I'd have gone to the College, and have my own secretary by now. Someone nice, in a pale blue wool suit, with her hair done up just so, and her coffee would be perfect, every time, black as the bottom line. But the College takes them young. Children who sleep with magnifying glasses and suckle at churchwarden pipes, who conduct inquiries among their toys. Demand for detectives is high—the City is a harsh cauldron. Sometimes we see them die. Sometimes we see them running away from a crumpled form. We could interfere, but we understand it's not our place. Once she's dead—and yes, Mala is right, I can't remember the last time a man died here—she belongs to the detective, like a father passing the bride to her groom.

Everyone exists to serve the detectives. Every diner, every office, every laundromat, every priest.

The detectives, or the devils.

FOR A LONG time I didn't know which way I would go. I loved lipstick as a child; I stole my mother's beautiful crimson shades and applied them with a delicacy beyond my age. She wept when she saw me, for she thought she knew then how I'd end up. The question is always how long can you last in the queue. The devils are hungry but not insatiable. It can take time for them to get around to you. Like taking a number at the butcher. He'll get around, eventually.

But then, she'd named me Mala. Not Anna, not Sarah, not Claire.

My mother died when I was thirteen. That's what mothers do, of course. And I found her, her seamed hose spattered with rain and blood, her heels gleaming, her blue eyes staring. I was wearing my father's long coat, and I was always tall. The detectives who came to the scene left immediately—they assumed I was one of them, that I was already on the case. Detectives are territorial. Monogamous. You just don't barge in on another man's girl.

They all want to know how I solved it. Still—over cigars and brandy in the executive offices one of them will always lean in, boozily, and slur:

"C'mon, Orrin, tell us how you solved yer ma."

I keep my mystery. It's safer that way. The three parts of the City's soul are in a delicate balance, and even a detective can turn on you.

The truth is: I went out into the rain and drew a circle in the earth with her blood. I put her dress in one quadrant, a bottle of her perfume in another, her dress in a third, and her lipstick in the last. I waited.

I wasn't really surprised when my father came around the corner, sniffing like a bloodhound.

I REMEMBER THE last case we worked together, before she disappeared. I carried a silver thermos full of coffee, like a bullet, and drove her to the scene. I glanced into the rear view mirror; her hat shadowed her face, all I saw was the slightest curve of a full lip, as red as meat. I turned the radio dial—a horn played, low and sad, and she lit her cigarette with a golden lighter.

The dead woman was so beautiful she stopped my heart. I almost thought she was still alive, her face was flushed, her breasts full and high under her spangled dress. A singer, I'd seen her in one of the detectives' clubs. Fridays are secretaries' night. The woman sang old jazz tunes. Her hair was black; her eyes were blue. The wound was at the back of her head—I'd missed it entirely. But her blood seeped from her skull in medusa-curls, and Mala Orrin looked at her without saying a word. Turned to stone.

I wanted to stand where she stood. I wanted to stand over that woman, that radiant dead seraph. I wanted to be so full of power I didn't even have to speak for everyone to know I owned her. I felt that desire in me, red as meat. I wanted a hat to shadow my face, to flex my invisibility as she did.

I poured her coffee. It steamed in the dark. She didn't even look at me.

In an hour, I drove her back to the office. She passed a note up the pneumatic tubes, up to the executive floors.

*John Brown, bartender. Number 5, A Street. Icepick.*

And that was the end of it. They brought him in, screaming, his shoulders huge, covered in the singer's blood like a victor's cape.

A sorcerer's methods are easier to guess.

---

SOMETIMES I THINK about leaving the City. Surely, there is somewhere else to go, though I'll be damned if I can think of any place. When I try to imagine other cities, my mind fills up with the faces of dead girls. Most of the time I figure other Cities are just like this one. But on the occasional night when there are no deaths, or at least none assigned to me, I drive out to the City limits and look at the black whip of road, disappearing off into nothing, into the dark, and I shiver because I am not safe. I thought the coat and the hat and the secretary and the dinner drinks would make me safe, make me not like them, make me part of a tribe that is immune to the devil and his tricks. But I'm never safe.

We live to die. When I see them in the street they have never been realer than in that moment, never brighter, never more beautiful. Persephone with Hades' hand at her throat, dancing, dancing in the evening light.

The essence of detection is causation: because of this, that. Because he loved her and she didn't love him back. Because he leaves iron filings in his footprints, we'll find him in the factory where he works to make silver thermoses. Because he's a devil, she's dead. Because that's all she ever saw, sometimes she dreams about being dead, being that beautiful, being fawned over, adored, her face on posters, her potential mourned. She dreams a detective with a lantern jaw falls in love with her as she lies bleeding out, and devotes himself, a knight, to avenging her death. To remembering her. In her dreams she is dead and she feels so alive. Because of her dreams, she wakes up sick, half-faint, her hands shaking until she can get the cork out of the bottle and smell the dirt-scent of scotch wafting out, like a grave.

Because she was good at her job, she escaped the devil for years. But nothing lasts forever.

---

I ADMIT IT—I loved her. It's all love. I didn't need her diary to understand that. Love on both sides of death. I wanted to see her face, that's all. So badly. Cherries on her breath. Ice cream. The black silk of her blouse. If this were a better place, if the City weren't a devil in its own right, that would have been so simple. But you live in the world you're given. You may feel contempt for it, even as you do your living, but you can't escape your nature. She's gone, and she'll be missed. There will be a memorial, I'm sure. Her face in stone, perfect, completed. The natural life cycle of the detective.

Her handwriting is long and lanky, like a man's. She speaks to me, out of the pages, and teaches me the devil's due. I'll be promoted soon. Secretaries get the news first, after all. I'll be passing brandy from glass to glass on the executive floor by mid-month. I bought a hat last week—grey felt, with a black band and a wisp of ptarmigan feather tucked in. I'd hoped the diary would help me, but the dead can't speak to the devil. So I come to the office early. I pour my own coffee, and watch the sun come up, the first steno pool girls coming in like morning birds.

They are so beautiful.

The essence of detection is cyclical. Around and around, chasing each other, footfalls sounding on black pavement, and the rain pouring down forever.

# Twenty-Five Facts About Santa Claus

1. SANTA CLAUS IS REAL. HOWEVER, your parents are folkloric constructs meant to protect and fortify children against the darknesses of the real world. Parents are symbols representing the return of the sun and the end of winter, the sacrifice of the King and the eternally fruitful Queen. They wear traditional colorful costumes and are associated with certain seasonal plants, animals, and foods. Sadly, after a certain age, no intelligent child continues believing in their parents, and it is embarrassing when one professes such faith after puberty.

Santa Claus, however, will never fail us.

2. The current Santa Claus was once a boy. He is from Canada, not from Turkey or Scandinavia as some would suggest. He is new to the job, having been at it only one hundred and fifty years or so.

When the Franklin expedition perished seeking the Northwest Passage, Santa Claus watched them die on the ice. He was only a young man, then: emaciated, cold, wrapped in a red cloak with frost on his brown beard. He was very sorry, but it was not Yuletime, and he had no power to save them.

3. The current Santa Claus took over his present position from Santa Lucia. Lucia was a marvelous Italian lady who up until the 19th century rode a donkey into young children's homes in December, bearing lavish gifts, espresso, and currant-cakes. If a child was naughty, Lucia's donkey would kick the embers of the hearth-fire into their sleepy eyes, blinding them. This may seem a harsh punishment for not cleaning one's room or fibbing about who broke their sister's toy truck, but the ways of donkeys are strange and strict. One questions them at one's peril.

Espresso was a magical drink which Lucia alone knew how to make, until a dastardly Italian baker stole the recipe in a daring and adventurous escapade. Its contemporary cousins are much diluted from the original.

Santa Lucia took over from the Bishop of Constantinople, a very tall, skinny fellow who wore a jeweled hat and, between you and I, had a terrible fear of donkeys. Everyone makes the winter office their own, however, and our Claus made several changes to the decor.

4. Santa Lucia sometimes still appears to certain children at Christmas-time. She is retired, but not dead or uninterested in the world. However, children are practical sorts when it comes to presents, and rarely appreciate the dense currant cakes and highly caffeinated coffee Lucia offers them. Nor do they have the first idea what to do with her gifts, which are more often than not complex bronze, iron, or bone devices bearing a family resemblance to the Antikythera Mechanism.

Still, as with any peculiar maiden aunt, it is the thought that counts.

5. Before taking up his current position, Santa Claus worked at a textile factory in London. He showed already some ability at crossing large distances quickly, stowing aboard a steamship hoping for a new life in the Old World. He lost his pinky finger in a loom, but

sent money home to his family in Canada as a good son does. It was sometime around then that he met a girl named Lucia with hair the color of candlelight, and one will make no assumptions about anything untoward occurring between them.

6. Santa Claus is a tax-exempt entity under the laws of several Pole-adjacent nations. This began as a kind of good-natured joke among Congresses and Parliaments wishing to appear jolly so that no one will put coal in *their* stockings, publicly announcing their reprieve with a crooked smile before adjourning for Christmas nog and poppyseed loaf. This has proved quite useful for Santa, as he takes in a tremendous amount of raw material during the year and should not like to have to calculate 30% of a magical pony with pink-floss hair and fiery breath.

7. The elves are really quite a complicated situation. They were summarily dismissed from Europe sometime after Rome fell (you'll find elves to be sullen and recalcitrant on this topic, should you press for exact dates and place-names) and had resettled above the Arctic Circle in a network of villages called Tyg-qir-Mully, raised by snowchant and a long and patient seduction of the ice. In their glittering towns they lived and drank gluhwein and worked their weaving.

Some say that the presence of so many elves in one place, so much magic in one little patch of the world, simply created a crackling space in the universe that Santa Claus could fill like a key. Some say it was rank colonialism perpetrated by a piece of European folklore that broke off and floated away.

Either way, a house appeared in the center of Tyg-qir-Mully, hung with glittering icicles and sweet round doors, and eventually, someone came to live in it and took on a mythologically lucrative profession, establishing a logical labor-sharing commune among all the Mully-folk.

8. Santa Claus is concerned about the problem of Arctic ice. The ice is the spouse of the elves, and she is sick. She is the primary source of their magic, as the elves cannot be separated from the place where they live.

For many years now, this is all they have asked for for Christmas: that the ice should come back.

9. Once an elf-Queen by the name of Gyfwoss rode her royal seal out onto the ice plain and called down the moon. She lifted her arms above her head and her hair turned blue and the moon drifted down the sky like a white petal. She held it in her arms like a child and somehow she was big enough, or it was small enough. She asked the moon for a gift and in her hands it turned into a pale silver present, wrapped with a sprig of pine and a lavender bow. When she took it home and opened it in her innermost chamber, she found a glass wedding ring. Once a year the moon turns into a very nice man with white hair and knocks on her door.

Santa sometimes calls Gyfwoss Mrs. Claus, but everyone knows she is married to the moon, forever and for all time.

10. Santa Claus has only been seen seven times in all of his long career. This is a very good record. Mainly, he is seen because he wants to be.

That or the reindeer give him away.

The most recent sighting was in France in 1979. Little Marguerite Lysan was sleeping in her apartment above the cafe where her father worked the morning baking shift. She didn't see Santa Claus because she deserved it more than other people. She didn't see him because she was special. She saw him because a reindeer was lonely. She didn't wake up when the man in red came into the house, but before midnight passed she felt a soft velvet nose nuzzle her hand, and then more—lightly fuzzed antlers beneath her fingers.

She smiled as she opened her eyes, and saw a pair of eyes, deep and black, with stars in them.

11. Santa Claus actually met Jesus once, when they were both very young. Santa wasn't even called Claus yet, and he didn't wear red. He was just thin and tired and alone, and so was Jesus, and they shared some wine and talked about what it was like to be folklorically dense nexus points.

You really can't understand something like that without experiencing it. At the time no one even believed in them yet; they were just knots of colliding ideas, waiting for their destiny, the way kids do after high school but before college, sitting out on that bridge over the river, kicking their feet out into the air, wondering what they're going to be when they grow up.

12. Santa Claus doesn't really like cookies and is lactose-intolerant.

He doesn't mind the treats, though. He knows that it's quite literally the thought that counts.

You see, cookies are quantum clusters of time and probability. With a raspberry swirl and chocolate chips. They tell Santa who he is. If you listen, they'll say the same thing to you. They say: you are hot and sweet and alive, even in the cold, and in at least three other universes you wear purple.

Without cookies, Santa might loose his moorings, and on a journey like his, you cannot afford to take a wrong turn down some pulsar-strewn alley.

13. The Coca-Cola Company sometimes claims to have invented the modern version of Santa Claus.

That's not true.

What happened was that somewhere between the original, terribly exciting, recipe which featured certain exotic leafs and herbs and the more staid "classic Coke" batches, a young cola-chef put forward and produced several cases of an experimental soft drink that induced in the entire board of Coca-Cola a series of fever dreams. In these dreams the stockholders were chased by a certain red-cloaked figure through a dark wood, their blood shrieking in their limbs, terror clutching at their throats, the smell of holly and Christmas everywhere and then—oh! The spear! Most of the board never quite recovered their wits, the cola-chef was summarily dismissed.

But thereafter, the man in red begins to appear in Coca-Cola's wintertime advertisements.

14. As to how Santa Claus delivers all those presents in one night, it has seemed clear for some time that he possesses a localized wormhole small enough to pack into a reasonably-sized steamer trunk and tidy enough to not smell too musty when taken out for the holidays.

15. It seems likely that the silver jingle bells provide a renewable energy source for the wormhole, being as they are the remains of superdense stars attached to his sleigh with red string.

16. Santa Claus and the Easter Bunny are not related, though of course they have had professional dealings, both of them being warriors, standing watch on either side of the winter. Santa feels it is rather cruel of the Bunny to hide the eggs, and the Bunny feels Santa makes the whole business rather too easy.

It is a little known fact that the summer solstice and the autumn equinox also had champions. The Summer Horse brought dark red cherries and highly munchable tomatoes along with gifts of sunshine and unfrozen seas and little golden ponies mysteriously appearing on the mantel.

The Autumn Maiden sat on a throne of pumpkins and whatever vessel she touched filled with steaming cider or cocoa. Children buried wishes written on bits of paper in the cooling earth, so that they would come up in the spring like tulips.

Santa and the Bunny are all that's left. Sometimes they miss their family, but they understand all too well the fragility of the consumer holiday cycle, and how thin the ropes can fray that tie it to myth and truth, like a boat barely tied to the pier.

17. During the rest of the year, Santa Claus sleeps. And studies advanced mathematics.

18. Santa Claus doesn't need a chimney. A house is a closed system, and at one time the chimney was the only reasonable approach. It was the only vampire-proof entrance to a domicile, the doors being guarded by the Invitation Hex and the chimney itself being far too filthy for the obsessive-compulsive vampire to bear.

Santa Claus does not wish to be taken for a vampire. Vampires take, Santa Claus leaves. It's not the same thing at all. But it is impossible to specifically invite Santa Claus and no one else, only to express one's wishes by the laying out of stockings, etc. Santa used to enter where he could.

But these days, vigilance against vampires is extremely lax, and he can come through the front door without issue.

19. The list isn't about naughty and nice.

If you think about it, coal is a very useful present. Santa Claus isn't a monster. You can burn that coal and stay warm in the winter. Just because it is black and grimy and it isn't a fantastical electronic intelligent machine with a kung-fu grip and a pre-installed game suite doesn't mean it's not beautiful and warm and formed over millennia in the heart of the earth and very occasionally the difference between life and death.

The list is about whether or not you need to figure out the lesson of the coal or not.

20. The stockings you hang up aren't the size of your own feet. That would be silly—you need those socks in the December nights. They are the size of Santa Claus's feet, which are wide and flat to help him get around the Pole.

21. The reindeer are immortal. They are, in fact, the eight demiurges of reindeer-kind, and this accounts for their flying. Their names

might sound whimsical, but they are the closest the human tongue can come to approximating the true names of the caribou lords.

Rudolph, far from being the adorable, earnest fellow of the tale, is in fact Ruyd-al-Olafforid, the All-Destroying Flame of the Yukon. His mother was Kali and his father was an ice floe. His nose appears red because his body is full of coals and chaos and primeval volcanoes, and his eyes flare with a terrible conflagration of his soul. The tips of his antlers are like candles in the snowy wind. He is not vengeful, but he is the light in the dark of winter, consuming and giving life at the same time.

Your carrots only make the lord of flame stronger.

22. Once, there was a war in Santa Claus's kingdom.

No one likes to speak of it.

This was a very long time ago. It was not at Christmastime but during the summer when all in Tyg-qir-Mully is banked and waned and quiet. The Duke of the Orcas, Blig, wished to not only gobble up Santa's wormhole and the steamer trunk that contained it but also eat the queen Gyfwoss's royal seal, who was named Ghym and had a fondness for turkish delight. All the elves were taken by surprise. Blig's hunger was very great. So great that the elves pitied him, save the seal. It is hard to be so empty, and so big.

But Gyfwoss was clever. She called down her spouse the moon and Blig ate it whole. And when the moon, which is ever so much bigger than an orca, rose back into the sky, it took the body of Blig with it.

Not only was the moon made much more beautiful by its new orca-coat, which you can see even now in the dark and light patterns on its surface, but Christmas, in a manner of speaking, was saved.

23. Santa Claus cannot see when you are sleeping, nor can he see when you are awake. He is not that kind of man and is a little put off by the suggestion. He has his own affairs to tend to, thank you very much.

24. Santa Claus is a perfect integration of the Id, the Ego, and the Superego.

If you would like to know what the Id, the Ego, and the Superego are, just think very hard on what Santa brought you last year, as he brings presents for every part of your self. For your Id he brought candy, because the Id loves to Eat Too Much and Dance Too Fast and Not Think About the Future. For your Ego he brought toys, for the Ego loves to Learn and Do and Make Things. And for your Superego he brought socks and underwear, for the Superego loves to Be Prepared and Have Everything Dry and Warm and In Its Place. Sometimes we want candy more and sometimes we want socks more, and between candy and socks is how we grow and change.

Santa Claus is in Balance. He is Jolly and Hardworking and Always Has Clean Socks. All at once he indulges the most decadent desires of food and drink and wealth in a single Morning of Receiving, is driven across the whole of the world on the Sleigh of Purposeful Dedication, and considers very seriously both the array of presents he will give and whether he will give them at all, the great Judge of the Self.

Once a man named Sigmund Freud asked for a cigar box for Christmas. Santa Claus did not read anything into it.

25. There is always the chance that Santa Claus will not come this year. It has never happened, but in the realm of probabilities we must admit that there is that one floating, strange variable. Without that chance Santa Claus would not be what he is—rather, he would be something dependable and every day, like the tide or the wind, and no one would think twice about him.

It is this chance which makes children so excited on Christmas Eve. You simply cannot know. For this reason it is vitally important, especially as one gets older, to ask for exactly what you want for Christmas, whether it be a unicorn that really talks or an artificial intelligence that will not destroy the world or a new job or someone to love you despite your being a know-it-all or a teddy bear or universal health care or the ability to finish things you start.

Santa Claus does not judge wishes. He only wants you to be happy. He can't do everything—he is only a story that came alive, not a mail-order catalogue. But he tries his very best to be good at his job. He tells us that winter will pass, light will return, life is generous and long, and toys are important even if everyone says they're silly.

And every year, the sun grows a little stronger after he has passed through the world.

# In the Future When All's Well

THESE DAYS, PRETTY MUCH ANYTHING will turn you into a vampire.

We have these stupid safety and hygiene seminars at school. Like, before, it was D.A.R.E. and *oh my god if you even look crosswise at a bus that goes to that part of town you will be hit with a firehose blast full of PCP and there is nothing you can even do about it so just stay in your room and don't think about beer*. Do you even know what PCP looks like? I have no idea.

I remember they used to say PCP made you think you could fly. That seems kind of funny, now.

Anyway, there's lists. Two of them, actually. On the first day of S/H class, the teacher hands them out. They're always the same, I practically have them memorized. One says: *Most Common Causes*. The other says: *High-Risk Groups*. So here, just in case you ditched that day so you could go down to *that part of town* and suck on the firehose, you fucking slacker.

**Most Common Causes:**
Immoral Conduct
Depression

Black Cat Crossing the Path of Pregnant or Nursing Mother
Improper Burial
Animal (Most Often Black) Jumping Over Grave, Corpse
Bird (Most Often Black) Flying Over Grave, Corpse
Butterfly Alighting on Tombstone
Ingestion of Meat from Animal Killed by a Wolf
Death Before Baptism
Burying Corpse at Crossroads
Failing to Bury Corpse at Crossroads
Direct Infection
Blood Transfusions Received 2011-2013

**High Risk Groups (HR):**
Persons Born With Extra Nipple, Vestigial Tail, Excess Hair, Teeth, Breech
Persons Whose Mothers Encountered Black Cats While Pregnant
Persons Whose Mothers Did Not Ingest Sufficient Salt While Pregnant
Seventh Children, Either Sex
Children Conceived on Saturday
Children Born Out of Wedlock
Children Vaccinated for Polio 1999-2002
Children Diagnosed Autistic/OCD
Promiscuous Youngsters
Persons Possessing Unkempt Eyebrows
Persons Bearing Unusual Moles or Birthmarks
Redheads with Blue Eyes

I SWEAR TO god you cannot even walk down the *street* without getting turned. That list doesn't even get into your standard jump-out-of-the-shadows schtick. Like, half the graduating class have to get their diploma indoors, you know? Plus, I think they just put in that shit about promiscuous youngsters because it's like their duty as teachers to make sure no one ever has sex. Who says *youngsters*, anyway? The problem with S/H class is that, just like the big scary PCP, we all know where to get it if we want it, so the whole thing is just…kill me now so I can go get a freaking milkshake.

My dad says this is all because of the immigrants coming in from Romania, Ukraine, Bulgaria. I don't know. I read *Dracula* and whatever. Doesn't seem very realistic to me. Vampires are sort of something that just *happens* to you, like finals. I know people used to think they were all lords of the night and stuff, and they are, I guess. But it's like, my friend Emmy got turned last week because a black dog walked around her house the wrong way. Sometimes things just get fucked up and it's not because there was a revolution in Bulgaria.

But I guess the point is I'm going to graduate soon and I'm just sort of waiting for it to happen to me. There's this whole summer before college and it's like a million years long and I have red hair and blue eyes so, you know, eventually something big and black is just going to come sit on my chest till I die. I told Emmy: *it's not your fault. It's not because you're a bad person. It's just random. It doesn't mean anything. It's like a raffle.*

SO MY NAME is Scout—yeah, my mom read *To Kill a Mockingbird*. Leave it to her to think fifth grade required reading is totally deep. She also has a heart thing where she's had to be on a low-sodium diet since she was my age, which means while she was pregnant with me, so *thanks*, Mom. With high risk groups, birds don't even have to fly over your own grave. It can be, like, anyone's grave, if you're nearby. It's like a shockwave. I heard about this one HR guy like two towns over who was a seventh son with a unibrow *and* red hair *and* was born backwards, and he just turned *by himself*. Just sitting there in English class and *bang*. That's what scares me the most. Like it's something that's inside you already, and you can't stop it or even know it's there, but there's a little clock and it's always counting down to English class.

The other night I was hanging out with Emmy, trying to be a supportive friend like you're supposed to be. In S/H class they say high risk kids should cut off their friends if they get turned. Like it's one of those movies about how brutal high school is and we're all going to shun Emmy on Monday if she's wearing a little more black than usual. As if I would ever.

"What's it like?" I said. Because that's what they don't tell you. What it feels like. *PCP is bad, it'll make you jump off buildings.* Yeah, but before that. What's it like? Before you crave blood and stalk the night. What's it like?

"It's stupid. My hair's turning black. I have to go to this doctor every two weeks for tests. And, I don't know...it's like, I want to sleep in the dirt? When I get tired, my whole head fills up with this idea of how nice it would be to dig up the yard and snuggle down and sleep in there. The way I used to think about bubble baths."

"Have you...done it yet?"

"Oh, blood? Yeah. Ethan let me right away. He's good like that." Emmy shoved her bangs back. She had a lot of makeup on. Naturally Sunkissed was a big color that year. Keeps the pallor down but it doesn't make you all Oompa-Loompa. "What? What do you want to hear? That it's gross or that it's awesome?"

"I don't know. Whatever it is."

"It's...like eating dinner, Scout. When somebody goes to a little effort to make something nice for you, it's great. When they eat healthy and wash really good but don't taste like soap. When they let you. But sometimes it just gets you through the night." She lit a cigarette and looked at me like: *why shouldn't I, now?* "Did you hear about Kimberly? She got turned the old-fashioned way, by this gnarly weird guy from Zagreb, and she can *fly*. It's so fucking unfair."

Emmy wasn't very different as a vampire. We had this same conversation after she lost her virginity—Ethan again—and she was all *it is what it is* then, too, with an extra helping of *I am part of a sacred sisterhood now*. Emmy has always been kind of crap as a friend, but I've known her since Barbies and kiddie soccer, so, whatever, right?

I don't know, I suppose it was dumb, but things can get weird between girls who've known each other that long. Like this one time when we were thirteen we did that whole practice kissing on each other thing. We'd been hanging out in my room for hours and hours and rooms get all whacked out when you lock yourselves in like that. We sat cross-legged on my lame pink bedspread and kissed because we were lonely and we didn't know anything except that we wanted to be older and have boyfriends because our sisters had them and her lips were really soft. I didn't even know you were supposed to use tongue, that's how thirteen I was. Her, too. We never told anyone about it, because, well, you just don't. But I guess I'm talking about it now because I let Emmy feed off of me that night, even though I'm HR, and it was kind of like the same thing.

I didn't see her much, though, after that. It was just awkward. I guess that sort of thing happens after senior year. People drift.

BACK IN SEVENTH grade, right after the first ones started showing up, like every freaking book they assigned in school was a vampire book. That's when I read *Dracula*. *Carmilla* and *The Bride of Corinth*, too. *The Vampyre*, *The Land Beyond the Forest*. *Varney the Freaking Vampire*. Classics, you know—they said all the modern stuff was agitprop, whatever that means. It's weird, though, because back then there were maybe twenty or thirty vampires in the whole world, and people just wrote and wrote about them, even though there's like statistically *no way* that Stoker guy ever met one. And now there's vampires all over. Google says there's almost as many as there are people. They have a widget. But nobody's written a vampire book in years.

SO I'VE BEEN hanging out in cemeteries a lot lately. I know, right? I mean, before? I would *never*. Have you seen how much it costs to get up in black fingernail polish and fishnets? And now, for an HR like me, it's pretty much like slitting your wrists in the bathtub with a baby blue razor for sensitive skin. Everyone knows you're not serious, but there's a slim chance you'll fuck up and off yourself anyway. If you want to get turned you don't have to go chasing it. Not when some bad steak will do you for about $12.50, and a guy down on Bellefleur Street will do it for less than that.

So, I'm one of those girls. Like we didn't know that already. Like you never did anything embarrassing. Anyway, it's kind of peaceful. Not peaceful, really. Just kind of flat. I don't do anything. I sit there on the hill and think about how like half my family is buried down there. Any second, a black bird could fly out over one of them. I wonder if you can see it when it happens, the affinity wave. What color it is. That's what Miss Kinnelly calls it. An affinity wave. She leads an after-school group for HRs that my dad says I have to go to now. He picked Miss Kinnelly because she's a racist bitch, or as he would put it, "has a strict policy against Eastern Europeans attending." I was all: *duh, we're Jewish, and isn't Gram from like Latvia or wherever?* And he was all: *Jews aren't Slavic, it's the Slavs that are the problem, why do you think they knew about all the HR vectors before we did?* And I was like: *what the hell do you know about HR vectors? Your eyebrows are fucking perfect!*

Anyway, group is deeply pointless. Mostly we talk about who we know that got turned that week, and how it happened. And how scared we all are, even though if you keep talking about how scared you are eventually you stop really being scared, which I thought was the point of having a group, but apparently not, because being scared is like what these people do for fun. All anyone wants to talk about is how it happened to their friend or their brother. It's like someone gets a prize for the most random way. Some girl goes: "Oh my god, my cousin totally drank three bottles of vodka and passed out at the

Stop & Rob and woke up a vampire!" And even though that is *highly* retarded, and it probably doesn't work that way, at least, it doesn't work that way yet, everyone goes *oooooh* like she just recited *The Rime of the Ancient Mariner*. Oh, yeah. We had to read that one, too. It's not even about vampires, it's about zombies, which is totally not the same thing, but apparently it falls under supplementary materials or something. Anyway, Miss Kinnelly then lectures for a hundred years about how immoral conduct is the most pernicious of all the causation scenarios, because you can never know where that "moral line" lies. By the time she gets to the part about abstinence is the only sensible choice, I want to stick her fake nails through her eyes. Once I said: "I hear you can totally get it from drinking from a glass one of them drank from." And they all gasped like I was serious. God. Before, I wouldn't have spent three seconds after school with those people. But the sports program is basically over.

This one time Aidan from my geometry class started talking about staking them, like in old movies. Everyone got real quiet. Thing is, it's not like those movies. A vampire's body doesn't go anywhere if you mess with it. It doesn't go *poof*. It just lies there, and it's a dead person, and you have to bury it, and god, burying things by yourself is practically a crime these days. There's hazmat teams at every funeral. It's the law, for like three years now. Plus, it's not that big a town. Everyone knows everyone, and you try stabbing the kid you used to play softball with in the heart. I couldn't do it. They're still the same kids. They still play softball. We're the ones who've stopped.

Sometimes, when I'm sitting up on the hill by the Greenbaum mausoleum, I think about Emmy. I wonder if she's still going to State in the fall.

Probably not, I guess.

---

I DATED THIS guy for awhile during junior year. His name was Noah. He was okay, I guess. He was super tall, played center for basketball, one of the few sports we still played back then. Indoors, right? I remember when the soccer teams moved indoors. It was horrible, your shoes squeak on the floor because it's shellacked within an inch of its life. The way it used to be, soccer was the only thing I really liked to do. Run around in the grass, in the sun. There's something really satisfying about kicking the ball perfectly so it just flies up, the feeling of nailing it just on the right part of your foot. I've played since I was like four. Every league. And then, finally, they just called it off. Too dangerous, not enough girls anymore. You can't just go running around outside like that now. You could fall down. Get cut. Scrape your knee. So now instead of running drills I have to read *The Land Beyond the Forest* for the millionth time and stay inside. God, I'm turning into one of those snotty brainy hipster chicks.

Oh, right, Noah. See, the soccer girls date basketball boys. We're the second tier. Baseballers are somewhere below us, and then there's like archery and modern dance circling the drain. And then all the people who cry into their lockers because they can't hit a ball. Football and cheerleaders are up at the top, still, even though it's not exactly 1957 and not exactly the Midwest where they still play football. But some things stick. I think maybe it's because all the TV shows still have regular high school. It's a network thing. No one wants to show vampires integrating, dating chess geeks, whatever would be jam-packed with soap opera hilarity. TV is strictly *pre*. So we keep acting like what we did in sixth grade matters, even though no one actually plays football or cheers at all. It's like we all froze how we were three or four years ago and we'll never get any older.

Anyway, I remember Noah drank like two jumbo bottles of Diet Coke every day. He'd bring his bottle into class and park it next to his desk. When we kissed, he always tasted like Coke. Everyone thought we were sleeping together, but really, we weren't. It's not that I didn't think I was ready or whatever. Sex just doesn't really seem like that big a deal anymore. I guess it should. My dad says it definitely qualifies as immoral conduct. I just don't think about it, though. Like, what does it matter if Alexis let the yearbook editor go down on her in the darkroom if she found out like not even a week later that the Hep A vac she got for the senior trip to Spain was tainted and now she freaks out if the teacher drops chalk because she has to count the pieces of dust? It's just not that important. Plus, this couple Noah and I hung with sometimes, Dylan and Bethany, turned while they were doing it, just, not even any warning, straight from third base to teeth out in zero point five. We broke up a little after that. Just didn't see much point. I don't watch TV anymore, either.

But lately, I've been seeing him around. He turned during midterms. I think he even dated Emmy for awhile, which, fine. I get it. They had a lot in common. I just didn't really want to know. Anyway, it wasn't any big plan. One minute I barely thought about him anymore and the next we're sitting on the swingset in Narragansett Park way past midnight, kicking the gravel and talking about how he still drinks Diet Coke, it just tastes really funny now.

"It's like, before it was just Coke. But now all I can taste is the aspartame. And not really the aspartame, but like, the chemicals that make up aspartame. I taste what aspartame is like on the inside. I still get the shakes, though. So I'm down to a can a day."

Noah isn't exactly cute. The basketball guys usually aren't, not like the football guys. He's extra-lanky and skinny, and the whole vampire thing pretty much comes free with black hair and pale skin. He used to have really nice green eyes.

"How did it happen to you?" I hated saying it like that. But it was the only thing I could think of. How it happens to you. Like a car accident. "You don't have to tell me if you don't want to. If it's, you know, private."

Noah was counting the bits of gravel. He didn't want me to know he was doing it, but he moved his lips when he counted. That's why OCD is on the high risk list. Because vampires compulsively count everything. I think it's the other way, though. You don't turn because you're OCD. You're OCD because you turned.

"Yeah, no, it's not private. It's just not that interesting. Remember when the HR list first came out and I was so freaked because I was conceived on a Saturday and I have that mole on my hip? I was so sure I'd get it before everyone else. But it didn't happen like I thought, like when that third grader just flipped one day and the CDC guys figured out it was because her mom is a crazy cat lady and she doesn't even have a path to cross without a black cat there to cross it for her. Ana Cruz. I thought it would be like that. Like Ana. I couldn't *stop* thinking about how it would be. Just walking down the street, and *bang*. But it wasn't. I woke up one night and this woman was looking in my window. She was older. Pretty, though. She looked…kind, I guess."

"How old was she?"

"One of the oldest ones in California, it turned out, so about six? Her name was Maria. She used to be an anesthesiologist, down at the hospital."

"Were you guys…together? Or something?"

"No, Scout, you just kind of get to talking eventually. Afterward, there's not that much to do but wait, and she was nice. She stayed with me. Held my hand. She didn't have to. Anyway, I opened the window, but I didn't let her in. I'm not an idiot. I just sat there looking back at her. You know how they look after they're past the first couple of years. All wolfy and hard and stuff. And finally she said: 'why wait?' And I thought, shit, she's right. It's gonna happen, sooner or later. I might as well get on with it. If I do it now, at least I can stop *thinking* about it. So I climbed out." He laughed shortly, like a bark. "I didn't invite her in. She invited me out. I guess that's sort of funny. Anyway, you know how it works. I don't want to get all porny on you. It was really gross at first. Blood just tastes like blood, you know? Like hot syrup. But then, it sort of changes, and it was like I could hear her singing, even though she was totally silent the whole time. Anyway. It hurts when you wake up the next night. Like when your arm falls asleep but all over. My mom was really mad."

I picked at the peeling paint on the side of the swingset. "I think about it."

"Oh! Do you want me to...?" God, Noah was always so fucking eager to please. He's like a puppy.

It took me a long time to answer. I totally get him. Why wait. But finally, I just sighed. "I don't think so. I have a bio test tomorrow."

"Okay." Noah lit a cigarette, just like Emmy. He looked like a total tool. Like he's the vampire Marlboro Man or whatever.

"What does blood taste like now?" I asked. I can't help it. I still want to know. I always want to know.

"Singing," he mumbled around the cigarette, and puffed out the smoke without inhaling.

---

THE OTHER WEEK, my Uncle Jack came to visit. He lives in Chicago and works for some big advertising company. He did that one billboard with the American Apparel kids all wrapped up in biohazard tape. My mom cooked, which means no salt, and Uncle Jack just wasn't having that. He travels with his own can of Morton's and made sure my steak tasted like beef jerky.

"Kids in your condition have to be extra careful," he said.

"Yeah, I'm not pregnant, Uncle Jack."

"You really can't afford to take the risk, Scout. You have to think about your future. There's so much bleed these days."

That should pretty much tell you everything you need to know about what a bag of smarm my uncle is. He'll use a terrible pun to talk about something that'll probably kill me. He was talking about how that list of common causes is actually kind of out of date. Like how kids used to use textbooks that said: *maybe someday man will walk on the moon*. About a year ago, some of the causes started having baby causes. Like, it doesn't have to be meat killed by a wolf anymore, it can be any predator, so hunting game is right out. Even for non-HRs. We've always kept kosher, so it's not really an issue for us, but plenty of other ones are. They've acted like sex was on the no-no list since the beginning, but I don't think it was. I think that was recent. If sex could turn you into a vampire way back in ancient Hungary, we'd all be sucking moonlight by now. Some people, who are assholes, call this *bleed*. But never in front of an HR. It's just flat out rude.

My Uncle Jack is an asshole. I mean, I said he was in advertising, right?

"My firm is sponsoring a clean camp up in Wisconsin. Totally safe environment, absolutely scrubbed. For HRs, it's the safest place to be. God, the only place to be, if I were HR! You should think about it."

"I don't really want to move to Wisconsin."

"We wouldn't feel right about that, Jack," said my mother quietly. "We'd rather have her close. We take precautions, we take her in for shots."

Uncle Jack made a fake-sympathetic face and started babbling the way old people do when they want to sound like they care but they don't really. "My heart just breaks for you, Scout, honey. You, especially. You must be so scared, poor thing! I feel like if we could just get a handle on the risk vectors, we could gain some ground with this thing. It's pretty obvious the European embargo isn't doing any good."

"Probably because it's not the like it's the Romanian flu, Uncle Jack. You can't blockade *air*. I don't even think it really started there. Practically every culture has vampire legends."

Mom quirked her eyebrow at me.

"Come on, Mom. There's like *nothing* left to do but read. I'm not stupid."

"Well, Scout," continued Uncle Jack in a skeevy isn't-it-cute-how-you-can-talk-like-a-grown-up voice. "You don't see people here detaching their heads and flying around with their spines hanging out, or eating nail clippings with iron teeth, so I think it's safe to say the Slavic regions are the most likely source."

"And AIDS comes from Africa, right? Isn't it funny how nothing ever comes from us? Nothing's ever our fault, we're just *victims*."

Uncle Jack put down his fork quietly and folded his hands in his lap. He looked up at me, scowling. His was face scary-calm.

"I think that kind of back-talk qualifies as immoral conduct, young lady."

My mother froze, with her glass halfway up to her mouth. I just got up and left. Fuck that and fuck you, you know? But I could hear him as I stomped off. He wanted me to hear him. That's fine, I wanted him to hear me stomping.

"Carol, I know it's hard, but you can't get so attached. These days, kids like her are a lost cause. HRs, well, they're pretty much vampires already."

---

THE PROBLEM IS they live forever and they can't have kids. That's it, right there. That's the problem. They don't play nice with the American dream. They won't do the monkey-dance. They don't care about what kind of car they drive. They don't care about what's on TV—they know for damn sure *they're* not on TV, so why bother? Guys like Uncle Jack can't sell them anything. I mean, yeah, there's the blood thing, too, but it's not like nobody was getting killed or disappearing before they came along. Anyway, Noah says they mostly feed off each other when they're new. Blood is blood. Cow, human, deer.

They all think I don't get it, that I'm just a dumb kid who thinks vampires are cool because they all grew up reading those stupid books where some girl goes swooning over a boy vampire because he's so *deep* and *dreamy* and he lived through centuries waiting for *her*. Gag. I guess that's why that crap is banned now. No one wants their daughters getting the idea that all this could ever be hot. But guess what? They don't have body fluids. They only have blood. You do the math. And then come back when you're done throwing up. No one dates vampires.

Anyway, I'm not dumb. It's hard to be dumb when half your friends only come out at night. I get it. Pretty soon they'll outnumber us.

And then, pretty soon after that, it'll be all of us.

⸺

NOAH AND I went to the park most nights. Nobody gave us any shit there—no kids play in parks anymore, anyway. It's just empty. And it was so hot that summer, I couldn't stand being inside. Even at night, I could hardly breathe.

One time Noah brought Emmy along. I wasn't freaked or anything. I knew they weren't dating anymore. Gossip knows no species, you know? I guess it must be pretty lonely to hang out with a human girl all the time and explain your business to her. They sat in the tire swing together and kind of draped their arms and legs all over each other. They didn't make out or anything, they just sat there, touching.

"Do…you guys need some time alone?" I asked. Okay, I was a little freaked.

"It's just something we do, Scout," sighed Emmy. "Share ambient heat. It's cold."

"Are you kidding? It's like 90 degrees."

"Not for us," Emmy said patiently.

"It's not just that, you know," added Noah. "Ever seen pictures of wolf pups? How they all pile together? Well, you know, some days, a bunch of us just sleep that way. It's…comforting."

I plunked down on one of those plastic dragons that bounce back and forth on a big spring. I bounced it a couple of times. I didn't know what to say.

"So what are you guys gonna do in the fall?"

They just looked at each other, kind of sheepish.

Noah moved his leg over Emmy's. It was just about the least sexual thing I've ever seen. "We were thinking we might go to Canada. Lots of us are going. There's jobs up there. On, like, fishing boats and stuff. In Hudson Bay. The nights...are really long. It's safer. There's whole towns that are just ours. Communities. And, well. You probably heard, about Aidan?"

Aidan's the kid from group who thinks he's Van Helsing. Emmy sniffed a little and sucked on her cigarette.

"Well, you know, he was kind of seeing Bethany?"

"*What?* Bethany turned like a year ago! Why would he even touch her?"

They shrugged, identically.

"So they were messing around in back of his truck and all of the sudden he just fucking killed her," Noah whispered, like he didn't really believe it. "She trusted him. I mean god, he let her *feed* off him! That's like...I don't know how to explain it so you'll understand, Scout. That's serious shit with us. It's way more intimate than screwing. It's a *pact*. A promise."

Emmy and I glanced at each other, but we didn't say anything. Some things you don't want to say.

Noah's voice cracked. "And he put a piece of his dad's fence through her heart. And they're not even going to arrest him, Scout. He got a *fine*. Disposal of Hazardous Materials Without Supervision."

"It seems like a good time to clear out," said Emmy softly. Her eyes flashed a little in the dark, like a cat's.

"You could come with us," Noah said, trying to sound nonchalant. "I bet you've never even seen snow."

Well, you know what he meant by that.

"I have a scholarship. I'm gonna be a teacher. Teach little kids to do math and stuff."

Noah sighed. "Scout, why?"

"Because I have to do *something*."

WHENEVER PEOPLE HAVE more than five seconds to talk about this, they always come around to the same thing.

*Why did it happen? Where did it start?*

You know that TV show you used to like? And somewhere around the third season something so awesome and fucked up happened and you just had to know the answer to the mystery, who killed sorority girl whoever or how that guy could come back from the dead? You stayed up all night online looking for clues and spoilers, and still, you had to wait all summer to find out? And you were pretty sure the solution would be disappointing, but you wanted it *so bad* anyway? And, oh, man, *everyone* had a theory.

It's like that. They all want to act like it's a matter of national security and we all *have* to know, but seriously, we're way past it mattering. It's just…wanting the whole story. Wanting to flip to the end and know everything.

You want to know what I think? There were always vampires. We know that, now. There's still about ten of them who've been around since before Napoleon or whatever. They're in this facility in Nebraska and sometimes somebody gets worked up about their civil rights, but not so much anymore. But something happened and all of the sudden, there were HRs and lists of common causes and clean camps and Uncle Jack's billboards everywhere and Bethany lying dead in the back of a truck and oh, god, they always told us PCP makes you think you can fly, and I'll never play soccer again and at the bottom of it all there's always Emmy's mouth on me in the dark, and the sound of her jaw moving. All of the sudden. One day to the next, and everything changes. Like puberty. One day you're playing with an EZ Bake and the next day you have breasts and everyone's looking at you differently and you're bleeding, but it's a secret you can't tell anyone. You didn't know it was coming. You didn't know there was another world on the other side of that bloody fucking mess between your legs just waiting to happen to you.

You want to know what I think? I think I aced my bio test. I think in any sufficiently diverse population, mutation always occurs.

And if the new adaptation is more viable, well, all those white butterflies swimming in the London soot, they start turning black, one by one by one.

---

SEE? I'M NOT dumb. Maybe I used to be. Maybe before, when it couldn't hurt you to be dumb. Because I know I used to be someone else. I remember her. I used to be someone pretty. Someone good with kids. Someone who knew how to kick a ball really well and that was just about it. But I adapted. That's what you do, when you're a monkey and the tree branches are just a little further off this season than they were last. Anyway, it doesn't really matter. If it makes you feel better to think God hates us or that some mutation of porphyria went airborne or that in the quantum sense our own cultural memes were always just echoes of alternate matrices and sometimes, just sometimes, there's some pretty deranged crossover or that the Bulgarian revolution flooded other countries with infected refugees? Knock yourself out. But there's no reason. Why did little Ana Cruz turn as fast as you could look twice at her and I've been waiting all summer and hanging out in the dark with Emmy and Noah and I'm fine, when I have way more factors than she did? Doesn't matter. It's all random. It doesn't mean you're a bad person or a good person. It just means you're quick or you're slow.

---

I WENT DOWN to Narragansett Park after sunset. The sky was still a little light, all messy red smeary clouds. I'd say it was the color of blood, but you know, everything makes me think of blood these days. Anyway, it was light enough that I could see them before I even turned into the parking lot. Noah and Emmy, shadows on the swingset. I walked up and Noah disentangled himself from her.

"I brought you a present," he said. He reached down into his backpack and pulled out a soccer ball.

I smiled something *huge*. He dropped it between us and kicked it over. I slapped it back, lightly, with the side of my foot, towards Emmy. She grinned and shoved her bangs out of her face. It felt really nice to kick that stupid ball. My throat got all thick, just looking at it shine under the streetlight. Emmy knocked it hard, up over my head, out onto the wet grass and we all took off after it, laughing. We booted it back and forth, that awesome sound, that *amazing* sound of the ball smacking against a sneaker thumping between us like a heartbeat and the grass all long and uncut under our feet and the bleeding, bleeding sky and I thought: *this is it. This is my last night alive.*

I kicked the ball as hard as I could. It soared up into the air and Noah caught it, in his hands, like a goalie. He looked at me, still holding up the ball like an idiot, and he was crying. They cry blood. It doesn't look nice. They look like monsters when they cry.

"So," I said. "Hudson Bay."

# Planet Lion

*Initial Survey Report: Planet 6MQ441(Bakeneko), Alaraph System*
*Logged by: Dr. Savine Abolafiya, Chief Xenoecology Officer,*
*Y.S.S. Duchess Anne*
*Attention: Captain Agathe Ganizani, Commanding Officer Y.S.S. Duchess Anne*
*Satellites: Four*
*Mineral Interest: Iron, copper, diamond, cobalt, scandium, praesodymium, yttrium. Only diamond in desirable quantities. Nothing sufficient to offset cost of extraction.*
*Sentient Life: None*
*Strategic Significance: None*

A SMALL, WARM WORLD ORBITING THE white subgiant Alaraph. Average gravity is more or less comfortable at .85 Earth normal, but highly variable depending on how near it passes to 6MQ440, 6MQ439, and 6MQ450. Twenty-hour day, 229-day year. Abundant organic life. Excepting the polar regions, the planet consists of one continuous jungle-type ecosystem broken only by vast salt and fresh water rivers. See attached materials for information on unique flora if you're into that sort of thing. You won't find anything spectacular. It does not behoove a xenoecologist to sum up a planet as: trees big, water nice, but I know you prefer me to keep these reports informal, and I have become both tired and bored, just like everyone else. If you've seen one little Earthish world, you've seen them all. Day is mostly day; night is mostly night; dirt is dirt; water is water. Green is good, most any other color is bad. Lather, rinse, repeat. The fact is the Alaraph star has a whopping eleven other planets, all gas giants, and each one of them will prove far more appetizing to the powers that be than this speck of green truck-a-long rock.

My team came back calling it Bakeneko due to a barely interesting species of feline megafauna they frequently encountered. The place, I'm told, is crawling with them. Dr. Tum found one sleeping in their cook-pit. We've been calling them lions. As you'll see during the dissection this weekend, the species does somewhat resemble the thylacoleo carnifex of late Pliocene Australia.

Except, of course, that they're the size of Clydesdales, sexually trimorphic, and bright green.

Imagine a giant, six-toed, enthusiastically carnivorous marsupial lion with the Devil's own camouflage and you'll have it just about right. The "male" can be differentiated by dark stripes in the fur as well as the mane. The "female" has no stripes, but a ridge of short, dark, dense fur extending from the crown of the head to the base of the tail. The third sex is not androgyne, but simply an entirely separate member of the reproductive circus. We have been calling it a "vixen" for lack of better terminology. No agreement as to pronoun has been reached. The vixen is larger than the male or female and quite a different shade of green—call it forest green instead of emerald green.

The lions represent the only real obstacle to settlement of 6MQ441. Though I have tried to keep my tone light, five attached casualty reports attest to the danger of these creatures. They are aggressive, crepuscular apex predators. There are a lot of them. They show some rudimentary, corvid-like tool-use. (Dr. Gyll observed one wedging a stick between the skull-plates of a goanna-corollary *animal to get at the brain. Dr. Gyll does go on to note that he also enjoyed the flavor of the brain more than the meat.)*

*At present, I recommend a severe cull before any serious consideration of Bakeneko as a habitable world. See supplementary materials for (considerably) more on this topic.*

*Moving on to the far more pertinent analysis of the Alaraph gas giant archipelago…*

---

A LION MOVES the world with her mouth. A lion tells the truth with her teeth showing.

One lion rips the name Yttrium from the watering hole. She chews it. She swallows and digests it. She understands her name by means of digestion. One lion's name signifies a lustrous crystalline superconductive transition metal. This separates one lion from lions not called Yttrium. One lion called Yttrium drinks from the watering hole and digests the smallgod MEDICALOFFICER. She understands the smallgod by means of digestion. She feels the concept of honor. Lions who digest other smallgods do not always know what their names signify. One lion gorges on the bones of the smallgod. The bones taste like anatomical expertise and scalpelcraft. She slurps up the blood of the smallgod. The blood reeks of formulae and the formulae run down the throat of one lion to fill her belly with several comprehensions of anesthetics and stimulants and vaccines and antibiotics. She gnaws at the meat of the smallgod. The meat becomes her meat and the meat has the weight of good bedside manner.

One lion called Yttrium hunts in the steelveldt called Vergulde Draeck. As well she hunts in the watering hole. All lions hunt in the watering hole. The watering hole networks the heart of every lion to the heart of every other lion into a cooperative real-time engagement matrix. The smallgod inside one lion lays down the words *cooperative real-time engagement matrix* in the den of one lion's brain.

One lion called Yttrium accepts the words though they have no more importance than the teeth and hooves left over after a kill. The words mean the watering hole.

One lion hunts through her steelveldt in the shadow of burnt blueblack rib bones and sleeps in their shadows. As well she sees the watering hole all around her. The watering hole lies over the jungle like fur over skin. One lion stands in the part of the steelveldt where the million dead black snakes sprawl but never rot. She sees her paws sunk deep in the corpses of snakes. As well she sees her paws sunk deep in the cool blue lagoon of the watering hole. Comforting scents hunt in her nostrils and on her tongue. Ripe redpaw fruit. The brains of sunspot lizards. The eggs of noonbirds. Fresh water with nothing sour in it. One lion hunts alone in the steelveldt Vergulde Draeck. As well she hunts with every other lion in the watering hole. She hunts with one lion called Thulium. She hunts with one lion called Bromide. She hunts with one lion called Manganese. She hunts with one lion called Nickel who sired her and one lion called Niobium who bore her and one lion called Uranium who carried one lion called Yttrium in her pouch until she could devour the smallgod and enlist with the pride. In the watering hole every lion swims with every other lion. Every lion swallows the heart of every other lion. Every lion hunts in the den of every other lion's brain. Two hundred thousand lions hunt in the steelveldt Vergulde Draeck with one lion called Yttrium. Ten million hunt in the watering hole. The watering hole has enough water for everyone.

Every evening one lion called Yttrium wakes in hunger. She washes her muzzle in the Longer Sweeter River which flows beneath the steelveldt Vergulde Draeck. As well she washes her muzzle in the lagoon of the watering hole. She leaps and prowls through the part of the steelveldt where husks of giant redpaw fruit lie broken open. Other lions also leap and also prowl. She greets them in the watering hole. In the watering hole they use each others' eyes to find the answer to hunger. One lion called Yttrium finds the words *triangulation, reconnaissance, target acquisition* floating inside her. She thanks the smallgod inside her for this gift.

One lion stops. She becomes six lions. Six lions chase down a pair of sunspot lizards skittering through the burnt blueblack bones of the steelveldt. Six lions sight a horned shagfur. They forget the lizards. The shagfur lumbers across the part of the steelveldt where the hundred thousand dead silver scorpions lie barbed and gleaming. It does not hurt itself but six lions know the scent of carefulness. In the watering hole six lions turn their bellies to the rich sun. In the steelveldt six lions open their jaws. Their green muzzles wrinkle back over black teeth. Out of their mouths the water of the lagoon comes rippling. The water of the lagoon possesses blue heat and blue light. Six lions open their mouths and the water of the lagoon roars toward the shagfur. The shagfur flies upward. The shagfur's neck snaps. Six lions suck the water of the lagoon back into their throats and with it the shagfur. They tear into its body and its body becomes the body of six lions.

A lion moves the world with her mouth.

Six lions stop. One lion called Yttrium pads alone across the part of the steelveldt where the wings of the billion dead butterflies crunch under her paws. As well she plays with one lion called Tungsten and one lion called Tellurium in the shallows of the watering hole. She bites the green shoulder of one lion called Tungsten. She feels the teeth of one lion called Tellurium in the scruff of her neck. One lion called Tungsten ate the shagfur with her. One lion called Tellurium hunts far away in the steelveldt called Szent Istvan. They growl and pounce in the sun. The sun in the watering hole shines dusk forever. The sun shines bright morning and day on the steelveldts. The watering hole forgot every light but twilight.

One lion called Yttrium enters the part of the steelveldt where the thousand dead squaresloths lie. Hot wind dries the shagfur blood on her whiskers. She feels the concept of holiness. Her paws leave prints in the home of the smallgods. Lions not called Yttrium lie or squat on their green haunches or stand at attention with their tails in the air. They lock their eyes to the heart and the liver of the smallgods. The heart and the liver of the smallgods looks like the trunks of eight blue trees. The heart and the liver of the smallgods do not smell like the trunks of trees. The heart and the liver of the smallgods smell like the corpses of the hundred thousand silver scorpions and the light of the watering hole. Each of the blue trees belongs to one smallgod and not to the others. Each lion belongs to one smallgod and not to the others. One lion called Yttrium swallowed the meat of the smallgod MEDICALOFFICER. As well a million lions not called Yttrium chewed this meat in the watering hole. Many also own the name of Yttrium. Yttrium numbers among the one hundred and twenty-one sublimities of the smallgods. With one hundred and twenty-one words the smallgods move the world and so all lions call each other by these utterings of power.

The other smallgods own the names of ENGINEERINGOFFICER and DRIVERMECHANIC and GUNNERMAN and GRENADIER and SQUADLEADER and INFANTRYMAN and SLUDGEWARETECH. One lion called Tungsten lapped the blood of the smallgod DRIVERMECHANIC in the watering hole. One lion called Tellurium sucked the marrow from the bones of the smallgod SLUDGEWARETECH. One lion called Yttrium hopes their child will feast upon MEDICALOFFICER like her when one lion called Tellurium finishes gestating it.

One lion called Osmium roars in the watering hole and in the steelveldt. He snatches the scruff of one lion called Phosphorus in his teeth and throws her to the ground in the home of the smallgods. His roar owns anguish. Her claws rake his chest. The roar of one lion called Osmium ends. Blood sheens his black teeth. The emerald shoulders of one lion called Osmium droop miserably. He tosses his mane at the four moons of coming night and cries out:

"Christ, Susie, why did you leave me? Wasn't I good enough?"

*Strategic Analysis: Planet 6MQ441(Bakeneko), Alaraph System*
*Logged by: Cmdr. Desmond Lukša, Executive Officer, Y.S.S. Bolingbroke*
*Attention: Captain Agathe Ganizani, Commanding Officer Y.S.S. Duchess Anne*

AGGIE, IT IS the opinion of this particular unpleasant bastard that xenoecologists should not mouth off about the strategic significance of a planet just because they know a little damned Latin and can call an oak an oak at five hundred yards. I've read Dr. Abolafiya's report and promptly used it for toilet paper. It's so like her to miss the forest for weeping about the trees. I spent all last night sitting in my quarters reading page after page about some damn green kittens! Who cares? The plain truth was staring her right in the face.

The fact is the Alaraph System represents a unique opportunity to engage the enemy on our own terms. Its remote location removes any concern about collateral damage. Those eleven (eleven!) gorgeous gas giants provide some pretty lush gravitational channels and fuel resources so ample as to be functionally infinite. 6MQ450 (Savine's idiots are calling it Nemea now) has a dozen terrestrial moons where we might even set up mobile staging domes and get some honest fighting into this mess. But it's that dumb green ball Bakeneko that makes it work. It's our lever and our place to stand.

Alaraph sits smack in the middle of a disputed sector. Sure, it's hicksville, galactically speaking, and Alaraph is only barely inside the border, but the sector also includes most of the Virgo neighborhood, which is very much at the center of concern at the moment. Our bestest buddies drew a line around the big lady in the sky, and we drew a line around her, and then they drew a bigger line, and so on. The charts look like a hyperactive schoolkid's drawing.

My recommendation is this: ignore Savine and her pretty kitties. Start settlement protocols. Make sure it's all on known-code *channels. We'll probably have to actually put people in a ship with their spinning wheels and what-shit to make it look real. Hopefully we won't actually have to land them, but if we do, well, it won't be the first time. Hell, why not make it real? Build a base down there on Bakeneko, start churning out whatever we can. Barrack platoons. Make it look like we've got something we want in the jungle. Maybe we'll even find something.*

*They will respond militarily to such a provocation. They've detonated stars over less. And we will finally get to choose the real estate on which to hold our horrible little auction of death. We'll be ready for once.*

*As for the lions, honestly, I will lose precisely zero sleep over it. Let our jacked-up boys and girls play Hemingway down there with the big cats, they won't be a problem for long.*

---

ONE LION CALLED Yttrium cannot move. She sprawls flat on her belly in the shallow of the steelveldt's blueblack hip bone. The sky has fallen and broken her back. She whimpers. Everything whimpers when the monsoons come. Rain falls. The world grows heavy and hot. Every lion hides from the sky.

The smallgod inside her offers the words: *Due to the orbital proximity of Nemea, Maahes, Lamassu, and Tybault, Bakeneko lies in the midst of a gravitational white water rapids and may experience profound shifts in constants depending on the time of year and local occultations.* The words taste cool and hard and crunchy in her mouth. They feel like ice chips. One lion named Yttrium has never tasted ice. But her smallgod says that worlds hunt in the dark where ice covers every lonely thing.

One lion called Yttrium bounds through the tall grass of the watering hole. The sky in the watering hole still loves lions and does not crush their backs to jelly. One lion called Yttrium runs to run and not to hunt. One hundred other lions who digested the smallgod

MEDICALOFFICER run so close by her she can feel the electric bristly of their fur against hers. As well seventy lions who gorged on the smallgod GRENADIER run. They feel the idea of unity. They wade into the lagoon when they no longer wish to run. They paddle and splash. One lion called Cadmium stands on the shore yelling:

"Form up! Form up! Secure the perimeter! Incoming!"

Several striped moths dance just out of reach of his jaws. They do not form up.

One lion called Yttrium experiences the sensation of a door opening and closing in a wall of ice. The experience takes place in her chest and in her muzzle. She has never seen a wall of ice or used a door. These ideas come from the same place as the names *Nemea, Bakeneko, Lamassu, Tybault*. The wall of ice slips down over her green fur and the door opens to swallow her and closes on her bones. One lion called Yttrium stops. She becomes one hundred lions.

One hundred lions standing in the water of the lagoon turn to seventy lions and scream together in hopeless misery:

"You said you loved me!"

Seventy deep green lions bellow back:

"I did! I do! You never had time for me. You loved your ship. You loved your war. You loved the idea of war more than the reality of me. I only joined up in the first place because I knew you'd never choose me over your commission. And I hate it out here. I hate puzzling out new ways to make people explode. I am *alone*. I had no one, not even you. So I found comfort and you want to punish me for it?"

"You went looking!" weep the hundred lions. Water churns around their shaggy knees.

"Yes, Emma, I went looking. Does that make it feel better?" the seventy lions growl. Their ruffs rise. "I went looking and Lara wanted me. You haven't wanted me in years."

One hundred lions snarl in the watering hole. Their black tongues loll through black teeth. "She's twenty-two! She's a kid. She doesn't know what she wants."

"You're thirty-five and all you ever want is another hour in your fucking lab." Seventy lions called GRENADIER rumble in indignation. "And Simon. Or did you think I didn't know about him?"

"Don't leave me, Ben," whimper one hundred lions as though even the perfect watering hole sun has fallen on their spines. "Don't leave me. I'll quit. I'll come home. All the way home. It'll be good like it was a million years ago. When I had short hair and you had piercings, remember? I'll never speak to Simon again. Don't make these last ten years a waste of time."

"She's pregnant, Emma. It's too late. I don't even think I want it not to be too late."

One hundred lions called MEDICALOFFICER crouch in the shallows. Their eyes flash. Their tails warn. "This is such a goddamned cliché. You're a joke. I hate you."

One hundred lions hurtle into seventy lions. Claws and teeth close on skin and meat. The watering hole froths white water. One hundred lions stop as fast as they began. One lion called Yttrium licks her wounds. She does not judge them serious. She opens her jaws in the steelveldt. The water of the lagoon ripples out and lifts up a burnt blueblack bone with its blue heat and its blue light. The bone settles down on top of a hollow stone full of objects. Once one lion called Yttrium flung a hollow stone up and dashed it against the corpses of the billion dead butterflies that cover the floor of the steelveldt. Objects jangled out. She did not know them. She ate some and still did not understand them. The smallgod inside her said: *those are dresses and shoes. Those are hairbrushes and aftershave bottles.* One lion called Yttrium did not break the hollow stones anymore after that.

One lion called Yttrium has built three walls in this way. Other lions have done more. Soon she will make a roof that will keep out the sky. The lions change the steelveldt Vergulde Draeck with their mouths. One lion called Tellurium tells the watering hole that lions have changed the steelveldt Szent Istvan. With their mouths they built several places called barracks and one called commandstationalpha.

One lion called Tellurium wishes to build more places. The smallgod SLUDGEWARETECH inside her requires big places. One lion worries for her. As well she builds their young. As well their young requires big places.

But on monsoon days no one can work much except in the watering hole.

One lion called Arsenic crawls on his green stomach toward one lion called Antimony. One lion called Yttrium watches. Skinny pink fish flash in the water. MEDICALOFFICER calls them *self-maintaining debug programs*. One lion likes the flavor of the words and the fish equally.

One lion called Arsenic gnaws at dried lizard blood on his paws. He mewls: "I abandoned my kids, Hannah."

One lion called Antimony licks his face. "I never had any children. I had a miscarriage when I was in graduate school. I was five months along; the father had already gotten his fellowship on the other side of the world and moved in with a girl in Milwaukee. I never said anything. Didn't seem important to say anything. If I said something, it would have been suddenly real and happening and stupid instead of distant and not something that a girl like me had to worry about. I woke up in the hospital with a pain in my body like shrapnel, like a bullet in my gut the size of the moon. And I looked at my post-op charts and I think part of me just thought: *well that makes sense. All I can make is death.*"

One lion called Arsenic arches the heavy muscles of his emerald back. He rolls over and shows his striped belly to the sky of the watering hole. The smallgod SLUDGEWARETECH inside him howls and as well he howls: "I abandoned my kids, Hannah. They're grown now and when I call they're always in the middle of something or just running out the door. They don't want to look at me. Nobody looks at me anymore. My wife just sent divorce papers to my office. Who does that? I called her over and over, just holding those papers in my hand like an asshole, and she wouldn't pick up. I called one hundred and twenty-one times before I got her. I counted. I was going to tell her I loved her. I was gonna make my case. I thought if I could make a grand enough gesture, I could still have someone to come home to. But the minute I heard her voice I just laid into her, yelling until my vision went wobbly. *You knew what this life would be when you married me. I'm doing this for us. For everyone. For our girls. Christ, Susie, why'd you leave me? Wasn't I good enough?* And she just took it all like a beating. When I ran out of breath, she said: *Milo, of course you were good enough. You were the best. But every time I looked at you, all I could see was what you'd done. Your face was my slow poison. If I let our eyes meet one more time, it would have killed me.*"

One lion called Antimony touches her green forehead to the green forehead of one lion called Arsenic. This begins the behavior of mating. He accepts her. Violet barbs of arousal flick upward along his spine. Her heat smells like burning cinnamon. But their joining cannot satisfy. A lion mates in threes. The smallgods mate in twos and do not feel the lack of a vixen lying over those needful barbs. Two lions thrust ungracefully. They hurt each other with a mating not matched to their bodies. The smallgods do not care. The smallgod ENGINEERINGOFFICER inside one lion called Antimony whispers:

"Good thing we're all gonna die tomorrow, huh? Otherwise we'd have to live with ourselves."

---

*Letter of Application (Personal Essay)*
*Filed by: Dr. Pietro S. Aguirre*
*Attention: Captain Franklin Oshiro V.S.S. Anansi*

*I've wanted to work with sludge my whole life. I suppose, if you take a step back for a second, that sounds completely bizarre. But not to me. Sludge is life; life is sludge. Without it, we're a not-particularly-interesting mess of overbreeding primates all stuck on the same rock. To say I want to work with sludge is akin to saying I want to* work with God, and for me it is a calling no less serious than the seminary. I grew up in the Yucatan megalopolis, scavenging leftover dregs from penthouse drains and police station bins, saving sludge up in jars like girls in old movies saved their tears, just to get enough to try my little hands at a crude recombinatory rinse or an organic amplification soak about as artful as a fingerpainting. I succeeded in levitating my jack russell terrier and buckling just about every meter of plumbing in our building.

But now I'm boring whatever poor personnel officer has to read through this dreck. A thousand years ago, people used to tell stories about taking apart the radio and putting it back together again. Now we puff out our chests and tell tales of levitating dogs. Let me spare you.

I believe sludge can be so much more. We're used to sludge now. It's as normal as salt. We're so used to it we don't even bother doing anything interesting with it. We use sludge as lipstick and blush for the brain. Cheap neural builds to brighten and tighten, a flick of telekinesis to really bring out the eyes, some spiffy mass shielding to contour the cheekbones. You can buy a low-end vatic rinse at the chemist.

To me, this is obscene. It's like using an archangel as a hat rack.

There is no better place to continue my research than the fleet. My program to develop synthetic sources for sludge rather than relying indefinitely (and dangerously) on the natural deposits of chthonian planets in the Almagest Belt speaks for itself. My précis is attached, but in the interests of you, long-suffering personnel officer, not having to ruin your dinner with equations, I present a simple summary: I believe sludge can win this war for us.

---

ONE LION CALLED Yttrium feels the concept of apprehension. Change hunts in the steelveldt and the watering hole. The monsoons broke in the night and the bones of every lion stretch up in the easy air. The day wants pouncing. The day wants hunting. The day wants scratching the back of one lion against the burnt blueblack rib bones of the steelveldt.

The smallgods want building. The smallgods want to form up.

One lion called Yttrium bounds down the part of the steelveldt Vergulde Draeck where the twenty thousand tin jellyfish lie dead and cracked apart. More of them crunch and pop under her paws. The smallgod MEDICALOFFICER sends the words *mess hall* into her belly. She opens her mouth and the blue light and heat of the watering hole flow out and strangle a sunspot lizard to death before it can squeak. The blue light and the blue heat pries open the lizard's skull plates so that one lion called Yttrium can get at the brains. She laps at her meal.

A burst of dead jellyfish shattering. One lion called Yttrium leaps to protect her kill as one lion called Gadolinium and one lion called Zinc crash through the tin corpse-mounds. Their fur bristles. Their snarls drip saliva. They wrestle without play. Birds flee up to the tops of the tallest trees. Two lions land so heavy the steelveldt shakes. One lion called Yttrium searches for them in the watering hole. She finds them standing on either side of a warm flat stone. They do not move. They do not bristle. They do not wrestle or play.

"I don't want you that way, Nikolai!" one lion called Gadolinium growls in the steelveldt. He has landed on top. He pants. His eyes shine.

"I'm sorry," whimpers one lion called Zinc. "Oliver, come on, I'm sorry. It was stupid, I'm stupid."

"I have a husband at home," roars one green lion and the smallgod DRIVERMECHANIC inside him. "I have a *home* at home."

"I know," answers the smallgod INFANTRYMAN inside one lion called Zinc.

One lion called Gadolinium digs his claws into the chest of one lion called Zinc. "You don't know *anything*. You've never stuck around with anyone longer than it took to fuck them. You swagger around like a cartoon and you think none of us can see what a scared little kitten you are. Well, I got news for you—we can *all* see. I left more life than you'll ever have."

One lion called Zinc twists and springs free. Two lions face each other on steady paws. "You're probably right. But it goes with the job. We never stay anywhere longer than it takes to drink a little and fuck a little and kill a little and pack it all up again, so from where I sit, you're the idiot, making poor Andrew pine away his whole life back in whatever suburb of Nothingtown spat the two of you out. As for the swagger, I *like* swaggering. So fuck off. I was offering a little human contact, that's all. It's called comfort, you prig."

Wracking dry sobs come coughing up out of the black mouth of one lion called Gadolinium. "I'm so fucking lonely, Niko. It sounds like the most obvious thing in the world to say. I'm surrounded by people all the time and I'm so fucking lonely. I do my job, I eat, I stand my watch, and all the time I'm just thinking *I'm lonely I'm lonely I'm lonely* over and over."

"Everybody's lonely," purrs one lion called Zinc. His stripes gleam dark in the sun of the steelveldt. "You don't volunteer for this job if you're not already a lonely bastard who was only happy like four days in his entire dumb life. So stop being dumb and kiss me. Tomorrow we'll probably get our faces burned off before breakfast."

One lion called Yttrium returns to the dish of the sunspot lizard's skull. She feels the sensation of worry. She remembers other days and nights when every lion hunted as a lion and she heard no sacred speech for evenings on top of evenings. Now her ears ache and the sacred speech fills her own mouth like soft meat. One lion called Yttrium thinks these things as she begins the journey to the steelveldt Szent Istvan for the birth of her young by one lion called Tellurium and one lion called Tungsten. She wonders if the lions in the steelveldt Szent Istvan speak so often as the lions of the steelveldt Vergulde Draeck.

The light of the watering hole washes the one called Tantalum. She stands in the lagoon. Her fur ridge stands erect.

"Form up! Form up! Secure the perimeter!" The smallgod SQUADLEADER inside one lion cries.

This time, one lion called Yttrium listens. She must listen. Her body knows how to listen. How to form up. How to understand the idea of *perimeter*. She turns away from the road to the steelveldt Szent Istvan. She never takes her eyes from one lion called Tantalum in the watering hole as she crosses back into the steelveldt Vergulde Draeck. She crosses the part of the steelveldt where the million black dead snakes sprawl but never rot. The smallgod MEDICALOFFICER send the words *electro-plasmic wiring* into her skull like a twig into the brain pan of a lizard. In the watering hole one lion called Tantalum roars:

"Enemy will come in range at 0900!"

One lion called Yttrium crosses the part of the steelveldt where the wings of the billion dead butterflies lie shattered. The smallgod MEDICALOFFICER writes the words *navigational arrays* on the inside of her eyelids. In the watering hole, one lion called Radium approaches one lion called Tantalum. The smallgod GUNNERMAN inside one lion rumbles:

"Nathan, this is a shitty life and you know it. We should have majored in Literature."

One lion called Tantalum roars another *form up!* before answering: "Yeah? You ever tried to write a poem, Izzie? You'd get two lines into a damn haiku and quit because it didn't shoot lasers of death and kickback into your teeth."

One lion called Yttrium crosses into the part of the steelveldt where the hundred thousand dead silver scorpions lie barbed and broken. The smallgod MEDICALOFFICER wraps the words *weapons hold* around her heart.

One lion called Radium laughs so that her black teeth catch the heavy gold light of the endless dusk of the watering hole. "True. Drink?"

"Drink," agrees the smallgod SQUADLEADER from inside one striped green male.

One lion called Yttrium crosses into the part of the steelveldt where the husks of giant redpaw fruit lie broken open. The smallgod MEDICALOFFICER pushes the words *radioactive sludgepack engine core* into her soft palate. Other lions stand in formation. All of them carry the smallgod MEDICALOFFICER. All of them crackle with the musk of aggression. Their mouths glow blue. One lion called Yttrium experiences the sensation of a door opening and closing in a wall of ice. The experience takes place in her chest and in her muzzle. One lion called Yttrium stops. She becomes six hundred lions.

Six hundred lions called Emma roar.

*Progress Report: Project Myrmidion*
*Logged by: Dr. Pietro S. Aguirre, Senior Research Fellow, V.S.S. Szent Istvan*
*Attention: Captain Griet Hulle, V.S.S. Johannesburg*
*Captain Bernard Saikkonen, V.S.S. Vergulde Draeck*

*This is a classic good news/bad news situation. The good news is that the project has achieved an enormous measure of success and is ready to deploy in small trials. I foresee few to no field issues. We recommend Planetoid 94BR110 (Snegurechka) for initial mid-range testing. There is a small colony of about fifteen hundred on Snegurechka, enough that any transcription errors will quickly become apparent. I have great confidence. We should be able to disperse the sludgeware into the atmosphere and, within six to eight days, have a squadron of about fifteen hundred fully-trained soldiers, networked into a cooperative and highly adaptive real-time engagement matrix, which will program itself to conform to the cultural expectations of the subject in order to create a seamless installation. The population should split, more or less equally, among the eight typoprints specified. No adverse medical effects are anticipated. The sludge works with the organic material at* hand, enhancing and fortifying it. If anything, they should end up in better health than before.

*Now, the bad news.* It has not proved possible to separate the skillsets of the typoprints from the personalities of the personnel from whom we pulled the prints. In a way, this makes sense—the process of learning is a deeply personal and individualized one. We do not only retain facts or muscle memory, but private contextual sense-tags. The smell of the foxglove growing in the summer when we took fencing lessons for the first time. The smeared lipstick of our childhood algebra teacher. Arguing about the fall of Rome with a fellow student who later became a lover. We cannot separate the engineer's understanding of propulsion from the engineer's boyfriend leaving her in the middle of her course, the VR game she played incessantly to blow off steam that summer, the terrible coffee at the shop near her dormitory. We may yet find a way to isolate the knowledge without the person, but it won't happen soon, and I understand that time is of the essence. At the moment, the process of print transfer suppresses the original personality to varying degrees, and, as time passes, the domination of the print approaches total.

It doesn't have to be bad news. The original squad consisted of basically stable personalities. They grew very close over the series of brief but intense missions we devised in order to achieve and log a full typoprint. (Casualty reports attached. Unfortunately, the final mission proved to be poorly chosen for research purposes.) They functioned excellently as a unit—they screwed around a lot, but these kinds of small squads usually do. Besides, no one expects these sludgetroops to last all that long. They are the definition of fodder. What difference does it make if they miss some guy back in Aberdeen for a few minutes before taking a shot to the head?

---

SIX HUNDRED LIONS called Emma race across the steelveldt Vergulde Draeck. Eight hundred lions called Ben lope across the part of the steelveldt where the husks of giant redpaw fruit lie broken open and oozing.

"You said you loved me!" bellow six hundred green lions called Emma.

"You never had time for me!" comes the battle cry of eight hundred lions called Ben.

They collide. Black claws enter fur and flesh. Black teeth sink into meat. Many lions open their mouths. The blue heat and the blue light of the watering hole rips out of their great jaws. It twists through the static-roughened air. The sludgelight seizes one lion called Osmium and one lion called Nickel and one lion called Manganese and one lion called Niobium and one lion called Tungsten and dashes their brains against the floor of the steelveldt.

"I am *alone*."

"She's twenty-two!"

The jungle shakes. The jungle buckles. The jungle burns. The watering hole cannot handle so much information at once. It shivers. It cuts in and out. This also occurs in the steelveldt Bolingbroke and the steelveldt Duchess Anne and the steelveldt Johannesburg and the steelveldt Anansi and the hundred groaning steelveldts of the world.

"Don't leave me," shriek a million gasping emerald lions. "I'll come home. All the way home. It'll be good like it was a million years ago."

"It's too late. I don't even think I want it not to be too late," answer a million striped and bleeding lions too exhausted to stand.

---

*Situation Report: Planet 6MQ441 (Bakeneko), Alaraph System*
*Logged by: Captain Naamen Tripp, Y.S.S. Mariana Trench*
*Attention: Anna Tereshkova, Chief Prosecutor*

*Bakeneko has been profoundly impacted by the disastrous engagement in the system. The planet is covered in the toxic wreckage of some seventy-three ships lost in action, many the size of cities. Spills* of every kind have contaminated the environment and several species are rapidly approaching extinction already.

Of perhaps more concern is the population of marsupial lions first documented by Dr. Abolafiya aboard the Duchess Anne. They seem unaffected by the increase in ambient radioactivity or chemical pollution. Their aggression, if anything, has increased and gained complexity. However, they show signs of contact with a new strain of sludgeware of which we had been previously unaware. The planet is swarming with lions forming into standard military units, building barricades via kinetic sludge, retreating and attacking one another utilizing textbook ground strategies. They communicate in subvocal patterns that strongly imply the presence of a rudimentary neural link matrix. No implications are necessary to conclude that they have come in contact with telekinetic sludgestrands. Orbital observations show the lions have begun to deliberately alter the architecture of the crash sites according to an agreed-upon plan.

I have no explanation for how this could be, and yet it is. Nothing we have developed could affect a population of millions of animals in this way. I suggest you ask Dr. Aguirre what the hell is going on. I understand he is in custody.

I can only recommend a strict quarantine of Planet 6MQ441. There can be no further purpose to our presence anywhere near Bakeneko.

---

FOUR MOONS RISE over the steelveldt. One lion called Yttrium opens her eyes. As well she opens her eyes in the watering hole. She finds only quiet. Some death. But every lion knows death. The smallgod inside her sleeps. It found the idea of satisfaction. One lion called Yttrium understands. Blood always brings satisfaction. Perhaps it will wake in hunger again. Perhaps not. One lion feels the concept of contentment. The watering hole gleams fresh and bright. It has many fewer personnel to maintain. Its resolution surrounds one lion in evening light. In the smell of sunspot lizards. In the profound togetherness of nine million lions breathing in unison. Reeds move in the breeze within the heads of every lion left.

One lion called Yttrium stretches her green paws in the moonlight and begins again the long walk toward the steelveldt Szent Istvan. She longs to hear the first roar of her young.

# LEFT ATRIUM

# A Great Clerk of Necromancy

When I was eight I looked up from a paperback
I shouldn't have been reading and asked what
**cunt** meant.

    *Salem's Lot*, or maybe *Cujo*.
    Definitely King.
Picture the artist as a young spy, sneaking
documents from the adult world to childhood's
impoverished nation—who,
after all, needed
them more.
    My father took my hands in his and guided
the book closed like a hymnal. Took it back
to the high-security vaults of Grownupville.
Judgment in red and bright ~~redacted text~~
through my tears of loss
*You're not ready for books like this. It's ok
    the dog dies at the end.*

In that moment the following
message was delivered,
a test of the emergency preparedness system,
    only a test, to the imperative
centers of my small brain:

>    Do not seek explanations from anyone bigger than you.
Because      if you admit you do not know something, they will
take what    you do not know away and you'll never find out what
**cunt**     means.

For my next incursion into that stern and
spectacled DMZ I slipped a copy of
Malory under my shirt and puzzled it
like a code that, de-ciphered, would
mean myself. Holed up in a cedar-crook
down by the summer pond where horses
grazed and a rope swing like a noose beat
the July air I read:

There Morgan le Fay became a great clerk of necromancy.

*Do not ask what* **necromancy** *means,* said my little heart.
*It is a word like a* **cunt,** *too magical to reveal, too powerful*
*to say out loud. The girl who puts tomatoes and ice and lemons in a*
*bag at the grocery store.*
>    **That's** *a clerk.*
*Anything with* -mancy *in it means magic. Simple.*

>    I began my secret mission. To
catch the checkout girl     at sorcery.

The way her fingers moved on the cashier keys
her sure stacking eggs on the bottom green
onions and garlic on top her *have a nice day now*
her red apron
all these things filed away as evidence
incontrovertible.
>    That girl knew spells.

She wore a ceremonial gown pointed a
knife at the sky on the solstice.
      Slept with her brother gave birth to
a dark prince under a winter moon.
          I tried to give her a look
a conspirator's nod to say:
      *I know your secret.*
      *I am like you.*
    *Teach me about darkness*
*and poisons.*
      *Teach me what* **cunt** *means.*

She gave me a piece of wrapped candy the
color of a rose.
Surely a sign, I thought. Surely a sigil of
sisterhood.

Another word for childhood
is misunderstanding. It was such a long time
    between trips to the grocery store.

I watched She-Ra after school. I knew not to
ask why Hordak kept stealing Adora and
dragging her underground to marry her.
I logicked it alone:

Marriage must be like that.
So good it's worth breaking the world open.

So what if it never worked.
So what if he chained her to a wall in the dark. She always
gets free. She-Ra doesn't have a husband.
      That's not who she is.

       Maybe my father took women underground, too.
Twice—once for my mother once for my
stepmother. Maybe all fathers do it.
Maybe
       that's the secret law of Grownupville the secret
meaning of **cunt** I can't be allowed to know:

at the bottom of everything there's always
a man in a dark mask slitting open the earth
to bring a wife down out of the sun.

Hit the gas: a year passes. I am nine.
       My father, King of the Underworld,
hires a new secretary with an alliterating name,
two B's like a curved and curving body:
phones, faxing, light clerical work.

The word went off in my head like a pink sparkler:
    *Clerical.*
*Clerk is short for clerical.*

       How silly, to think Morgan le Fay
could ever ring up steak and milk and call for
clean-up on aisle six, price check on
belladonna, accept coupons for half-off
hideous destinies.
      But I was a child then. From my nine-year crag I
could chuckle at my naivete.
       Now I saw the shape of the universe.

That oatmeal-colored Bakelite phone:
her fell wand. her horn of plenty.
       She spoke into it        a

## A Great Clerk of Necromancy

voice strong and sure                brooking
no dissent           shaping dire words and
commands,
and a world comes alive,
            Things
            Get Done.
Her file cabinet, an alphabetized cauldron.
Her white-out, a potion to turn back time
to obliterate what went before.

I wanted to be her. This perfect clerk. I longed
            to Get
            Things Done.
To cover black and irrefutable text
with forgiving, gentle snow.
            I drew in my notebook
Morgans and She-Ras and
underground caverns with chains
pre-installed
while my father and his great clerk of necromancy
worked past those talismanic 9-5 hours.
            I bent my tiny will
to the mystery of her two
B's. But

she did not turn her gaze to me.
Except once to give me a piece
of hard candy the color of her
frosty lipstick.
            I took it
            with
reverence.
            Witches, after all,

        deal in candy. They build
houses out of it. Coffins. Castles. Witches know
what **cunts** are. Tools of power, perhaps made of
candy and glass and iron and blood and ice a **cunt**
like the sun and the moon and the stars in the sky.

You laugh.
                But words
are everything
        in the world.

Two B's never told me where in that
ashen leaden file cabinet the C's were
kept, her book of shadows hidden.
                The grocery girl
got bumped up to assistant manager.

And a video game
taught me the word
*cleric.*

It flickered there.
Cold
empty
definitive and defined hit
points and low stamina a dim glow of
8-bit
nothing.

Another word for cleric is **cunt**.
Another word for **cunt** is myself.
              But I was a child then.
Now I see the shape.

## A Great Clerk of Necromancy

From the heights of thirty-three
        (hoping to cease not)
      I can
    chuckle with you
    over the big dark bowl
    of my innocence.
These days, I say cunt when I please. I
make candy in my kitchen coating the back
of a huge silver spoon in roses and lipstick
and blood on the snow.
      I say **cunt**
and people step back eyes narrowing,
darkening, looking struck by some
unseen secretarial grocery girl
alliterative fist. As if they are afraid
      I have come up
    in some dark mask
    to take them into the dark
    where I live.

# Urchins, While Swimming

> On the third day the ardent hermit
> Was sitting by the shore, in love,
> Awaiting the enticing mermaid,
> As shade was lying on the grove.
> Dark ceded to the sun's emergence;
> By then the monk had disappeared,
> No one knew where, and only urchins,
> While swimming, saw a hoary beard.
>
> —Aleksandr Pushkin
> *Rusalka*, 1819

### I: Snail Into Shell

**R**YBKA, YOU HAVE TO WAKE *up*.

At night she always called me *rybka*. At night, when she shook me awake in my thin bed and the dirt-smeared window was a sieve for the light of the bone-picked stars, she whispered and stroked my temples and said: *rybka, rybka*, wake up, you have to wake up. I would rub my eyes and with heavy limbs hunch to the edge of the greyed mattress, hang my head over the side. She would be waiting with a big copper kettle, a porcelain basin, the best and most beautiful of the few things we owned. She would be waiting, and while I looked up at the stars through a scrim of window-mud and window-ice, she would wet my hair.

She was my mother, she was kind, the water was always warm.

The kettle poured its steaming stream over my scalp, that old water like sleep spreading over my long black hair. Her hands were so sure, and she wet every strand—she did not wash it, understand, only pulled and combed the slightly yellow water from our creaking faucet through my tangles.

*Rybka, I'm sorry, poor darling. I'm so sorry. Go back to sleep.*

And she would coil my slippery hair on the pillow like loose rope on the deck of a ship, and she would sing to me until I was asleep again, and her voice was like stones falling into a deep lake:

*Bayu, bayushki bayu*
*Ne lozhisya na krayu*
*Pridet serenkiy volchok*
*Y ukusit za bochek*

In the morning, she called me always by my name, Kseniya, and her eyes would be worry-wrinkled—and her hair would be wet, too. While she scraped a pale, translucent sliver of precious butter over rough, hard-crusted bread, I would draw a bath, filling the high-sided tub to its bright brim. We ate our breakfast slick-haired in the nearly warm water, curled into each other's bodies, snail into shell, while the bath sloshed over onto the kitchen floor, which was also the living room floor and the bathroom floor and my mother's bedroom floor—she gave me the little closet which served as a second room.

In the evening, if we had meat, she would fry it slowly and we would savor the smell together, to make the meal last. If we did not, she would tell me a story about a princess who had a bowl which was never empty of sweet, roasted chickens while I slurped a thin soup of cabbage and pulpy pumpkin and saved bathwater. Sometimes, when my mother spoke low and gentle over the green soup, it tasted like birds with browned, sizzling skin. All day, she sponged my head, the trickle ticklish as sweat. The back of my dress clung slimy to my skin.

Before bed, she would pass my head under the faucet, the cold water splashing on my scalp like a slap. And then the waking, always the waking, an hour or two past midnight.

*Rybka, I'm sorry, you have to wake up.*

My childhood was a world of wetness, and I loved the smell of my mother's ever-dripping hair.

---

ONE NIGHT, SHE did not come to wet my hair. I woke up myself, my body wound like a clock by years of kettles and basins. The stars were salt-crystals floating in the window's mire. I crept out of my room and across the freezing floor like the surface of a winter lake. My mother lay in her bed, her back turned to the night.

Her hair was dry.

It was yellowy-brown, the color of old nut-husks—I was shocked. I had never seen it un-darkened by water. I touched it and she did not move. I turned her face to me and it did not move against my hand, or murmur to me to go back to sleep, or call me *rybka*—water dribbled out of her mouth and onto the blankets. Her eyes were dark and shallow.

*Mama, you have to wake up.*

I soaked up the water with the edge of the bedsheet. I pulled her to me; more water fell from her.

*Mamochka, I'm sorry, you have to wake up.*

Her head sagged against my arm. I didn't cry, but drew a bath in the dark, feeling the water for a ghost of warmth in the stream. It was hard—I was always so thin and small, then!—but I pulled my mother from her bed and got her into the tub, though the water splashed and my arms ached and she did not move, she did not move as I dragged her across the cold floor, she did not move as I pushed her over the lip of the bath. She floated there, and I pulled the water through her hair until it was black again, but her eyes did not swim up out of themselves. I peeled off my nightgown, soaked with her mouth-water, and climbed in after her, curling into her body as we always did, snail into shell. Her skin was clammy and thick against my cheek.

*Rybka, wake up. It's time to wet my hair.*

There was no sound but the tinkling ripple of water and the stars dripping through the window-sieve. I closed my mother's eyes and tucked my head up under her chin. I pulled her arms around me like blankets. And I sang to her, while the bath beaded on her skin, slowly blooming blue.

*Bayu, bayushki bayu*
*Ne lozhisya na krayu*
*Pridet serenkiy volchok*
*Y ukusit za bochek*

## II: The Ardent Hermit

I MET ARTYOM at university, where I combed my hair into a tight braid so that it would hold its moisture through anatomy lectures, pharmacopeial lectures, stitching and bone-setting demonstrations. At lunch I would wait until all the others had gone, and put my head under the spotless bathroom sink. Pristine, colorless water rushed over my brow like a comforting hand.

There were no details worth recounting: I tutored him in tumors and growths, one of the many ways I kept myself in copper kettles and cabbage soup. This is not important. How do we begin to remember? One day he was not there, the next day his laugh was a constant crow on my shoulder. One day I did not love a man named Artyom, the next day I loved him, and between the two days there is nothing but air.

Artyom ate the same thing every day: smoked fish, black bread, blueberries folded in a pale green handkerchief. He wore the spectacles of a man twice his age, and his hair was yellowy-brown. He had a thin little beard, a large nose and kept his tie very neatly. He once shared his lunch with me: I found the blueberries sour, too soft.

"When I was a girl," I said slowly, "there were no blueberries where we lived, and we would not have been able to buy them if there were. Instead I ate pumpkin, to keep parasites from chewing my belly into a honeycomb after the war. I ate pumpkin until I could not stand the sight of it, the dusty wet smell of it. I think I am too old, now, to love blueberries, and too old to see pumpkins and not think of worms."

Artyom blinked at me. His book lay open to a cross-section of the thyroid, the green wind off of the Neva rifling through the pages and the damp tail of my braid. He took back his blueberries.

WHEN THERE WAS snow on the dome of St. Isaac's and the hooves of the Bronze Horseman were shoed in ice, he lay beside me on his own thin mattress and clumsily poured out the water of his tin kettle over my hair, catching the runoff in an old iron pot.

"You have to wake me in the night, Artyom. It is important. Do you promise to remember?"

"Of course, Ksyusha, but why? This is silly, and you will get my bed all wet."

I propped myself up on one elbow, the river-waves of my hair tumbling over one bare breast, a trickle winding its way from skin to linen. "If I can trust you to do this thing for me, then I can love you. Is that not reason enough?"

"If you can trust me to do this thing, then you can trust me to know why it must be done. Does that not seem obvious?"

He was so sweet then, with his thin chest and his clean fingernails. His woolen socks and his over-sugared tea. The sharp inward curve of his hip. I told him—why should I not? Steam rose from my scalp and he stroked my calves while I told him about my mother, how she was called Vodzimira, and how when she was young she lived in a little village in the Urals before the war and loved a seminary student with thick eyebrows named Yefrem, how she crushed thirteen yellow oxlips with her body when he laid her down under the larch trees.

*Mira, Mira,* he said to her then, *I will never forget how the light looks on your stomach in this moment, the light through the larch leaves and the birch branches. It looks like water, as though you are a little brook into which I am always falling, always falling.*

And my mother put her arms around his neck and whispered his name over and over into the collar of his shirt: *Yefrem, Yefrem.* She watched a moth land on his black woolen coat and rub its slender brown legs together, and she winced as her body opened for the first time. She watched the moth until the pain went away, and I suppose she thought then that she would be happy enough in a house built of Yefrem and his wool and his shirts, and his larches and his light.

But when she came to his school and put her hands over her belly, when she told him under a gray sky and droning bronze bells that she was already three months along, and would he see about a priest so that her child might have a name, he just smiled thinly and told her that he did not want a house built of Vodzimira and her water and her stomach, that he wanted only a house of God and some few angels with feet of glass, and that she was not to come to his school any longer. He did not want to be suspected of interfering with local girls.

My mother was alone, and her despair walked alongside her like a little black-haired girl with gleaming shoes. She could not tell her father or her own mother, she could not tell her brothers. She could think of no one she could tell who would love her still when the telling was done. So she went into the forest again, into the larches and the birches and the moths and the light, and in a little lake which reflected bare branches, she drowned herself without another word to anyone.

I swallowed and continued hoarsely. "When my mother opened her eyes again, it was very dark, and there were stars in the sky like drops of rain, and she saw them from under the water of the little lake. She was in the lake and the lake was in her and her fingers spread out under the water until there was nothing but the water and her, spanning shore to shore, and she moved in it, in herself, like a little tide. She had me there, under the slow ripples, in the dark, and the silver fish were her midwives."

I twisted the ends of my hair. A little water seeped out onto my knuckles.

Artyom looked at me very seriously. "You're talking about *rusalka*."

I shrugged, not meeting his gaze. "She didn't expect it. She certainly didn't think her child would go into the lake with her. When I was born, I swam as happily as a little turtle, and breathed the water, and as if by instinct beckoned wandering men with tiny, impish fingers. But she didn't want that for me. She didn't even want it for herself—she pressed her instinct down in her viciously, like a stone crushing a bird's skull. She brought me to the city, and she worked in laundries, her hands deep in soapy water every day, so that I would have something other than a lonely lake and skeletons." I picked at the threads of the mattress, refusing to look up, to see his disbelief. "But we had to stay wet, you know. It is hard in the city, there are so many things to dry you out. Especially at night, with the cold wind blowing across your scalp, through the holes in the walls. And even in the summer, the pillow drinks up your hair."

Artyom looked at me with pale green eyes, the color of lichen in the high mountains, and I broke from his gaze. He scratched his head and laughed a little. I did not laugh.

"My mother died when I was very young, you know. I have thought about it many times, since. And I think that, after awhile, she was just so tired, so tired, and a person, even a rusalka, can only wake herself up so many times before she only wants to sleep, sleep a little while longer, before she is just so tired that one day she forgets to wake up and her hair dries out and her little girl finds her with brown hair instead of black, and no amount of water will wake her up anymore."

My hands were pale and shaking as dead grass. I tried to pull away from him and draw my knees up to my chest—of course he did not believe me, how could I have thought he might? But Artyom took me in his arms and shushed me and stroked my head and told me to hush, of course he would remember to wake me, his poor love, he would wet my hair if I wanted him to, it was nothing, hush, now.

"Call me *rybka*, when you wake me," I whispered.

"You are not a rusalka, Kseniya Yefremovna."

"Nevertheless."

THE FROST WAS thick as fur on the windows when he kissed me awake in the hour-heavy dark, a steaming basin in his hands.

### III: By the Shore, in Love

IT TOOK EXACTLY seventeen nights, with Artyom constant with his kettle and basin as a nun at prayer over her pale candles, before I slept easily in his arms, deeper than waves.

On the eighteenth night my breath was quick as a darting mayfly on his cheek, and he reached for me as men will do—he reached for me and I was there, dark, new-soaked hair sticking to my breasts, rivulets of water trickling over my stomach. I smiled in the dark, and his face was so kind above me, kind and soft and needful. He closed his eyes—I could see at their edges gentle creases which would one day be a grandfather's wrinkles. When our lips parted he was shaking, his lip shuddering as though he had just touched a Madonna carved from ice, and I think of all the things I remember about Artyom, it is that little shaking that I recall most clearly, most often.

I was a virgin. Under the shadows of St. Isaac's and a moon-spattered light like blueberries strewn on the grass I moved over him with more valor than I felt—but one of us had to be brave. He guided me, but his motions were so small and afraid, as though, after all this time, he could not quite understand or believe in what was happening. I felt as though I was an old door, stuck into my frame, and some sun-beaten shoulder jarring me open, smashing against the dusty wood. It hurt, the widening of my bones, the rearrangement of my body, ascending and descending anatomies, sliding aside and aligning into a new thing. Of course it hurt. But there was no blood and I kissed his eyebrows instead of crying. My hair hung around his face like storm-drenched curtains, casting long shadows on his cheekbones.

"Ksyusha," he said to me, tender and gentle, without mockery, "Ksyusha, I will never forget how the light looks on your stomach in this moment, the light through your hair and the frozen windows. It looks like water, as though you are a little brook into which I am always falling, always falling."

The bars of the window cut my chest into quarters. He arched his back. I clamped his waist between my thighs. These things are not important—no one act of love is different much in its parts from any other, really. What is important is this: I did not know. I bent over him, meaning to kiss, only meaning to kiss—and I did not know what would happen, I swear it.

The lake came out of me, shuddering and splashing—my mouth opened like a sluice-gate, and a flood of water came shrieking from me, more water than I had ever known, strung with weeds and the skeletons of fish and little stones like sandy jewels.

It tasted like blood.

I choked, my body seized, thrashing rapture-violent, and it gushed harder, streaming from my lips, my hair, my fingertips, my eyes, my eyes, my eyes wept a deluge onto the thin little body of Artyom. The windows caught the jets and drops froze there, hard knots of ice. I screamed and all that came from my throat was more water, more and more and more.

His legs jerked awkwardly and I clutched at him, trying to clear the water and the green stems from his mouth, but already he convulsed under me, spluttering and spitting, reaching out for me from under the growing pool that was our bed, the bubbles of his breath popping in the blue— the bed was a basin and the water steamed and I wet his hair in it, but I did not mean to, I could not close my mouth against it, I could not stop it, I could not move away from him and it came and came and his bones beneath me racked themselves in the mire, the whites of his eyes rolled, and I am sorry, Artyom, I did not know, my mother did not tell me, she told me only to live as best I could, she did not say we drag the lake with us, even into the city, drag it behind us, a drowning shadow shot with green.

I would like to remember that he called out to me, that he called out in faith that I could deliver him, and if I try, I can almost manage it, his voice in my ear like an echo:

"Ksyusha!"

But I do not think he did, I think he only gurgled and gasped and coughed and died. I think the strangling weeds just passed over his teeth.

He never tried to push me off of him, he never tried to sit up. His face became still. His lips did not shake. His skin was pale and purpled. The water rippled over his thin little beard as it slowly, slowly as spring thaw, seeped into the mattress and disappeared.

The snow murmured against the glass.

### IV: Shell Into Snail

*RYBKA, YOU HAVE to wake up.*

She rubs her eyes with little pink fingers and turns away from me, towards the wall.

*Rybka, I'm sorry, you have to wake up.*

She yawns, stretches her legs, and wriggles sleepily towards the edge of the bed. I am waiting, kneeling on the floor with our copper kettle and a glass bowl. I am her mother, I understand the shock of waking, the water is always warm. She stares up through the window-glass at the stars like salt on the skin of a black fish as I pour it over her scalp, clear and clean. I comb it through every strand—her hair is so soft, like leaves. Afterwards, we lie together in the dark, my body curving around hers like a shell onto its snail, our wet hair curling slowly around each other. I sing her back to sleep, and my voice echoes off of the walls and windows, where there is frost and bare branches scraping:

*Bayu, bayushki bayu*
*Ne lozhisya na krayu*
*Pridet serenkiy volchok*
*Y ukusit za bochek*

Her hair is yellowy-brown under the wet, but damp enough to seem always black, like mine. Her eyes are so green it hurts, sometimes, to look at them, like looking at the sun. She swims very well for her age, and asks always to be taken to the mountains for the holidays. She is too little for coffee, but sneaks sips when I am not looking—she says it tastes like wet earth.

There is money for coffee, and kettles, and birds with browned, sizzling skin. We can see a bright silver scrap of the Neva through our windows, and the gold lights of the Liteyny Bridge. A woman who can set a bone is never hungry. I wash my hands more than anyone on my ward—twelve times a day I thrust my skin under water and breathe relief.

I taught her before she could read how to braid her hair very tightly.

In the morning I will call her Sofiya and put a little red cup full of blueberries floating in cream in front of her, and she will tell me that after the kettle, she dreamed again of the man with the thin little beard and the big nose who sits on the side of a lake and shares his lunch with her. He has larch leaves in his lap, she will say, and he tells her she is pretty, and he calls her *rybka*, too. His beard prickles her cheek when he holds her. I will pull my coffee away from her creeping fingers and smile as well as I am able. She will eat her blueberries slowly, savoring them, removing the purple skin with her tongue before chewing the greenish fruit. I will draw us a bath.

---

BUT NOW, UNDER the stars pricking the window-frost like sewing needles, I hold her against me, her wet eyelashes sticking together, her little breath quick and even. I decide I will take her to the mountains. I decide I will not.

*Rybka, poor darling, I'm sorry, go back to sleep.*

I wind her hair around my fingers; little drops like tears squeeze out, roll over my knuckles.

We are as happy as we may be, as happy as winters with ice on the stairs and coats which seem to always need patching and wet hair that freezes against our shoulders and the memory of still eyelids under water may leave us.

I am not tired yet.

# L'Esprit de L'Escalier

**First Step**

ORPHEUS PUTS A PLATE OF eggs down in front of her.
The eggs are perfect; after everything, he finally got it just right. Oozing lightly salted yolks the color of marigolds, whites spreading into golden-brown lace. The plate is perfect; his mother's pattern, a geometric Mediterranean blue key design on bone white porcelain. The coffee is perfect, the juice is perfect, the toast is perfect, the album he put on the record player to provide a pleasant breakfast soundtrack is perfect. Cafe au lait with a shower of nutmeg. Tangerine with a dash of bitters. Nearly burnt but not quite.

*Strangeways, Here We Come.*

Eurydice always loved The Smiths. Melancholy things made her smile. Balloons and cartoons and songs in any of the major keys put her out of sorts. When they first met, she slept exclusively in a disintegrating black shirt from their 1984 European tour. He thought that was so fucking cool. Back when he had the capacity to think anything was cool.

She's wearing it now. Nothing else. Dark fluid pools in patches on the underside of her thighs, draining slowly down to her heels.

Her long black hair hangs down limp over Morrissey's perpetually-pained face. The top of her smooth grey breast shows through a tear so artfully placed you'd think they ripped it to specs in the factory. Sunlight from the kitchen windows creeps in and sits guiltily at her feet like a neglected cat.

Orpheus never once managed a breakfast this good when she was alive. If he's honest with himself, it wouldn't even have occurred to him to try.

"Darling," he says softly, as he says every morning. "You have to eat."

But she doesn't, not really. They both know that. She lifts one heavy, purplish hand and drops it, settling on the only thing she does need: a peeling, dishwasher-tormented limited edition 1981 Princess Leia glass filled with microwaved lamb's blood. Forty-five seconds on high.

Orpheus winces. She retracts her hand. She is very sorry. She will drink it later, congealed and lukewarm, alone.

Eurydice picks up a slender and very clean fork. The problem has never been that she doesn't want to get better. Her short fingernails have black dirt under them. No matter how she scrubs and scrubs in the sink, no matter what kind of soap she buys. Orpheus hears the water running at 3 a.m. every night. The trickling, sucking song through the pipes. The negative space next to him in the bed, still cold from her body. But it doesn't matter. On Sundays he paints her nails for her, so she doesn't have to see it. But today is Saturday. The polish has chipped and flaked. The constant crescent moons of old earth show through.

She slices through the egg and lets the yolk run like yellow blood. Severs a corner of toast and dredges it in the warm, sunny liquid, so full of life, full enough to nourish a couple of cells all the way through to a downy little baby birdie with sweet black eyes. If only things had gone another way.

Eurydice hesitates before putting it between her lips. Knowing what will happen. Knowing it will hurt them both, but mainly her. Like everything else.

She shoves it in quickly. Attempts a smile. And, just this once, the smile does come when it is called. There she is, as she always was, framed by tall paneled windows and vintage posters from his oldest shows:

*Open Mic Friday at the Clotho Cafe, $5 Cover!*
*Singing Rock Music Festival, July 21st, Acheron, NY.*
*Live at the Apollo.*

And for a moment, there she is, all cheekbones and eyelashes and history, grinning so wide for him that her pale, sharp teeth glisten in the rippling cherry blossom shadows.

Then, her jaw pops out of its socket with a loud *thook* and sags, hanging at an appalling, useless angle. She presses up against her chin, fighting to keep it in, but the fight isn't fair and could never be. Eurydice locks eyes with Orpheus. No tears, though she really is so sorry for what was always about to happen. But her ducts were cauterized by the sad, soft event horizon between, well. *There* and *Here*.

Orpheus longs for her tears, real and hot and sweet and salted as caramel and he hates himself for his longing. He hates her for it, too.

A river of black, wet, earth and pebbles and moss and tiny blind helpless worms erupts out of Eurydice's smile, splattering so hard onto his mother's perfect plate it cracks down the middle and dirt pools out across the table and the worms nose mutely at the crusts of the almost-burnt toast.

He clenches his teeth as he clears the dishes. Eurydice stares up at him, her eyes swimming with apologies.

"It's fine," he says, curt and flat. "It's fine."

Somewhere between the table and the counter, the tangerine juice stops being tangerine juice. It thickens, swirls into silvery-gold ambrosia, releases a scent of honeycomb, new bread, and old books.

Orpheus dumps it in the sink.

## Second Step

MARRIAGE ISN'T WHAT he thought it would be.

She didn't even thank him for making her breakfast. He doesn't want that to annoy him the way it does, but he can't shake it. She owes him. She owes him so much.

Orpheus remembers the days when he was so full of her nothing else would fit. And then when she was gone, and he dreamed of her so vividly he woke with her scent pouring from his skin. When nothing was innocent. Every chair just an inch to the left or right of where he'd left it the night before. Every book open to a different page than the one he'd marked. Every lost key or wallet or watch not misplaced but *taken*. Every flicker of every light bulb was her, couldn't be anything *but* her, his wife, calling out to him, begging him to hear her, pleading through the impossible doorway of her own final breath.

He was so young then, young, stupid in love, unaware that there were certain things he simply could not have. Limitation was for other people. All he'd ever needed to do was sing and the world opened itself up to him like a jewelry box—and she was there when it did, the little pale dancer on the velvet of his ease, spinning inexorably round and round on one agonizingly perfect, frozen foot. If the world declined to open for others, that did not concern him.

*When she is back*, he dreamt then, *when I have her back I will be happy again. She will be whole and laughing and warm as August rain and she will look at me every day just the way she did when we first met, as though nothing bad ever happened. Her eyes will be the same shade of green. The span of her wrist will fit between my thumb and forefinger. We'll go to the movies every night. I won't even want other girls. We'll drink ourselves into a spiral of infinite brunches. She will put her hand on the small of my back when we are photographed just the way she used to. Her smile will be full of new songs. When I touch her again, time will run backwards and gravity will flee and pain will be a story we tell at parties, a fond joke whose punchline we can never get quite right. Everything will go back the way it was.*

*She won't remember anything. Like in the soaps. She will be so grateful and so relieved and she won't remember any of it. Not dying. And not...the rest. I will bear the weight of our past for both of us. I am strong enough for that.*

WHEN ORPHEUS WAKES in the night, she is never beside him. She stands at the window, looking out into the chestnuts and the crabapples. The moon blows right through her. He can see mold flowering along her spine. Where she touches the curtains, it spreads, unfurling as luxurious as ivy.

### Third Step

THEY HAVE A little house on a busy street in a desirable school district. Chestnut and crabapple trees frame a chic mid-century modern bungalow in a neighborhood where poor but brilliant artists lived twenty years ago. Orpheus has other properties, more convenient to the city, more architecturally stimulating, more impressive for entertaining. But she's only comfortable here.

Whatever *comfortable* has come to mean for either of them.

He bought it from a day trader who lost both legs in some kind of vague childhood equestrian incident, a year or so after the second album hit like a gold brick dropped from the heavens and money became an abstract painting, untethered to concrete expressions, a defiance of realism, meaning whatever Orpheus wanted it to mean. It still had all the custom railings, ramps, lifts, and clever little automated mobility features installed and up to code. The previous owner joked that it was haunted.

It is. And it is not.

Eurydice doesn't handle stairs well.

After breakfast, she makes her way to the second floor studio, gripping the silver safety-rail with desperate tension. Her ashen feet squeak and drag on each step as she pulls herself up hand over hand. Orpheus watches her from the foot of the staircase. Her lovely legs beneath her nightshirt, the hardened bloodless muscles of her calves, the curls of her hair brushing the backs of her thighs like dozens of question marks hanging in space, so much longer than before.

Hair keeps growing after you die. He remembers reading that somewhere. In a green room. On a plane. It doesn't matter. He used to watch her bound up to the bedroom, a kind of joy-stuffed reverse Christmas morning, reveling in the shine of it, of them, waiting to catch a playful peek before chasing up to catch her, two steps at a time.

Orpheus hears her fingernails crunch on the stainless steel. She hauls herself up another stair. She pulls too hard; flesh sticks against metal. The skin rips right off her palms, leaving a trail of black, coagulated sludge. Eurydice doesn't notice. She doesn't feel it. She doesn't feel anything. Her grey, marbled flesh rejects material reality wholesale. Those circuits just don't connect anymore.

"Baby...?" Orpheus calls out softly.

Eurydice's head whips around. Her eyes are not the same shade of oaken green. They are black, silvered with cataracts. But they still burn. She stares down at him. He stares up at her. They have been here before. Another staircase. Another hall. Without a hand-rail, without plausibly-candid family photographs at pleasant intervals, without Tiffany glass sconces dripping peacock mood-lighting onto their path.

Eurydice turns around to see Orpheus behind her on the stairway. Blue-violet fungus uncurls along her jawline. Silver moss bristles along the stairs like new carpet wherever she's walked. Her pupils swallow him whole. She hears his voice and pivots toward it, instinctively, a reflex outside thought or ego.

"See?" she says in a shredded, raw, sopping voice. "It's not hard."

## Fourth Step

THEY GET A lot of visitors.

If Orpheus and Eurydice were a rising It-Couple before, always ready with an open door and a seasonally-appropriate plate of canapes and an incisive opinion on the events of the day, now they are the number one five-star rated tourist destination for their particular and peculiar social circle. The commute doesn't seem to bother anybody. Friends, colleagues, family, fans, people they hadn't heard from in years suddenly tapping on the windows, peering into the back garden, offering to help around the house, pick up groceries, medications, her favorite shampoo, his brand of whiskey. Anything at all, poor dears, just know we're here for you both in your time of need.

*Rubberneckers*, Eurydice calls them all.

At least they bring presents.

And they ask questions. Orpheus used to get asked questions all the time. *What are your influences? What was it like growing up with a famous mother? When's the next album coming out?* Sure, they were always the same questions, over and over, at a million pressers, in a thousand TV studios, but he had charming, humble, yet flirtatious answers for each one, and the interviewers always laughed.

Now it was only one question, still repeated, but with no good answer: *How is your wife?*

Ascalaphus brings organic fruit baskets.

Hecate brings three-scoop ice cream cones.

Rhadamanthus keeps showing up with DVD box sets even though Orpheus has told him about streaming a hundred times.

Minos brings puzzles from the Great Paintings of History series. Adult coloring books. Something to occupy her mind, keep her sharp.

Charon is forever trying to talk Orpheus into going jet-skiing with him on a lake upstate. *Come on, man, it's not like you were a homebody before. Do something for yourself. She's not going anywhere.*

Even the rivers come, though never all at the same time. Sopping wet, clothes clinging to their skin. Acheron with an asphodel blossom in his lapel, Phlegethon smoking constantly, Cocytus in jeans, her huge bone-pale headphones keeping the lamentations piping in, Styx, runway thin, bespoke black silk from top to bottom, always asking for change, and Lethe, her wet hair dyed blue, her long lashes inviting the universe to drown itself in her.

They never say anything about the mushrooms growing in the fireplace, on the window sills, crowding spotted and striped between the books on the shelves.

And they bring booze. Not the cheap stuff, either.

**Fifth Step**

WHAT DOES SHE do all day?

Mostly, Eurydice practices fine motor control.

It had all been explained to him at the time, though Orpheus didn't want to hear it then. She has to stay active. Mentally and physically. She has to keep moving. Rigor mortis sets in again so fast. And she forgets. Not just how to move her fingers, but what fingers are and why moving is a good and desirable goal.

Orpheus remembers Persephone in a power suit, standing with one strappy red heel in the shallows of the Styx and one on land, in both worlds and neither, a bridge in girl form. So terrifyingly organized. The brutal corporate efficiency of death. Handing him stacks of neatly indexed and collated instructional materials with bold graphics and a four-color print job. *Don't look at me like that. This is all new territory for us, too. None of our orientation paperwork was designed to handle it. I was up all summer. Now, turn to page six. We can put her back in there no problem, but a corpse is a corpse, of course, of course. Sorry, that was insensitive of me. Office humor. I'm not usually so...forward-facing with the clients. It's just that bodies aren't really our market focus. I'd recommend putting her on blood thinners, just to keep everything...liquid. And the blood, every day at mealtimes. Or she'll forget who she is. That's just standard. It's the same down here. Goes with the territory.* She pointed a ballpoint pen at a huge black stone drinking fountain on the beach. A long line of dead faces waited their turn to drink. He'd shuddered, watching blood bubble out of the spigot and into the basin. *Sheep's blood is fine. Pig is closer to human, though. Unless you can get human! No? You're right, bad suggestion. Are you listening?*

But Orpheus hadn't been listening. He'd been looking at her. Seeing her face again, her lips, the birthmark on her throat. Everything just as it was. Seeing them on picnics, reading to each other, taking cooking classes, standing in line at airports. Seeing her sitting cross-legged in the studio listening to his new songs, her adoring eyes reflecting his brilliance back at him. Seeing their kids. He hadn't heard a word.

So now Eurydice does the newspaper crossword, to keep the neurons firing.

She cleans the house, always in the same pattern, starting with the downstairs bathroom and working her way outward in a mandala of bleach and orange oil.

She textbanks for local political candidates.

She plays online baccarat and mines cryptocurrency.

She runs a couple of miles a night, hood drawn up, headphones in. It tenderizes the meat. Orpheus has tried to tell her it isn't safe for her to be out alone. She laughed in his face.

She works in the garden, weeding out the mint and asphodel that constantly threaten to take over everything. Asphodel isn't native, it isn't in season, this is the wrong kind of soil altogether, but nevertheless, the white, red-veined blossoms stretch like hands toward the house.

She spins and dyes yarn to sell at the farmer's market on Saturdays. She writes out the names of the colorways on little grey cards and ties them to the skeins with scraps of ribbon. *Die Like*

*Nobody's Watching. Live, Laugh, Languish. Whatever Doesn't Kill You Is a Tremendous Disappointment. Thanks, I'm Cured. L'Espirit d'Escalier.*

It took Eurydice a year to be able to write again. And when she did, though her lettering came elegant and careful, it wasn't *hers*. It wasn't anyone else's either. It was just new.

But no matter what she writes on the cards, whatever color she pours into her big glass dyeing bowls, the skeins all come out the same shade of black, and no one buys them.

On Thursdays they have couple's counseling. They hunch together on the couch so they can both be seen in the little black eye of the webcam. Orpheus talks and talks. *I just want you to be happy. Why can't you be happy? After everything I've done for you. You're so fucking cold.*

Eurydice never says much. *I'm sorry. I'm sorry.*

The therapist gives them worksheets about Love Languages. Eurydice fills them out. Orpheus does not. So she answers for him.

His says: *Physical Touch.*

Hers says: *The Soul-Consuming Fires of the River Phlegethon.*

---

ONCE, ORPHEUS CAME home to find the crossword left out by the fireplace, every square filled in with the same tidy, alien letters.

*Fuck you. I hate it here. Fuck you. I hate it here.*

He tossed it into the grate and flipped the switch. The pilot lights along the fake log popped to life and devoured the puzzle, the mushrooms, the deepening, ripening mold.

## Sixth Step

ORPHEUS'S MOTHER COMES whenever her book tours bend their way. She can never stay long. Calliope is a household name; the arts are the family business. She never stops working. She writes sprawling doorstoppers about war and romance that lounge effortlessly atop the bestseller lists. She doesn't knock.

Calliope breezes in, all sensible heels and comfortable beach dresses, reading glasses hanging on a pearl strand around her neck, a faint forgetful hyphen of lipstick on her teeth, a full color spectrum of pens stuck behind her ears and in her hair. She sets up a battle station in the dining room: stock to sign, contracts to go over, laptop, tablet, phone, a headset like a crown of laurels, into which she dictates her next project while she bakes and cleans and runs the soundboard for her son in the basement recording studio. She brings a bag of thick, hideous hand-knit sweaters for Eurydice, who is always, always cold, even with the furnace playing at top volume. She raised Orpheus alone, a single mother in an era when that was an impossible ask, bouncing him from auntie to auntie whenever she had to hit the circuit. He adores her. She smells sharp and warm and welcoming, like a used bookstore.

And she takes over bathtime.

It has to be done every night. Otherwise the mold gets ahead of them. It flowers deep in her joints, thick enough to pop her shoulder out of the socket or a tooth out of her gums. Once, in the early days, he stayed up working and forgot her bath. Eurydice didn't complain. She never complains. He woke up and found her on the front porch holding their newspaper. The rot had colonized her eye sockets in the night. Eurydice stared at the headlines through a sheen of black mold tipped in blue spores, spanning the bridge of her nose like a starlet's sunglasses.

"There was an earthquake," she'd said quietly, without looking up. "In Thessaly."

Somehow Calliope always knows to visit when Orpheus doesn't think he can bear to lift Eurydice into the tub one more time. It's not safe to let her do it herself. Her heart no longer has the capacity to keep everything churning along thump by thump, so a stubbed toe or a bruised elbow is a potentially catastrophic hydraulic leak.

But Calliope doesn't mind. She has enough energy for everyone. She lifts her daughter-in-law naked into the clawfoot and pours in bleach like bubble bath. She scrubs the little fractal spirals of mildew from Eurydice's livid back, her hair, under her arms. The water is warm, but it doesn't matter. She doesn't feel it.

Calliope sings to the beautiful corpse of Eurydice as she washes away the evidence of her nature. She sings like a cake rising, a dove's egg hatching, a memory of goodness. The anthurium on the bathroom sink stretches its crimson heart leaves toward the song. So does the clay in the tiled floor. One by one, the black hexagons crack and buckle, straining to get closer to her. Even the tiny threads of fungus on the nape of Eurydice's neck prickle like hair, erect and aware, moronically yearning without understanding toward the profound thing Calliope is.

She squeezes the sponge out against her daughter-in-law's mottled shoulder. Water trickles backward down along her spine and forward over her sternum and somewhere between the two, before it splashes down into the bath, it forgets to keep being water. It thickens, turns pale gold. The ribbon of bleach twists into honey. A sudden smell of apples and asphodel exhales from the tub: sharp, autumnal, crisp red skins and crisp white wind. Eurydice sobs in recognition, an ugly, stitch-popping sound. She cups her hands and lifts them to her chapped lips. But the cider-mead of Elysium does not want her. It shrinks back, the bath begins to swirl down the pipe the wrong way round, and where her mouth catches some meager slick of the stuff, it catches a cold blue flame. The faint fire spreads, burning off the alcohol, licking at her knees. Eurydice wails in horror and hunger, trying in vain to stop up the drain with her feet and suck the wine from her fingers at the same time.

Calliope strokes her wet, sweet-scented hair and nods tenderly.

"I know, my love. Marriage is so hard."

## Seventh Step

ORPHEUS AND EURYDICE met at a party thrown by his agent. A hundred thousand years ago. Yesterday. A blur of balconies and city lights and swaying earrings. A fizzing, popping, positively carbonated evening. Discontent was simply not on the guest list.

"Darling boy," his agent had crooned, guiding Orpheus by the shoulders around a river-current of oyster puffs and mini-souffles and out-of-season vegetables cut to look like birds of paradise. "Everyone is just *dying* to meet you." Hermes hit his stride in sneakers so white and new they glowed like angelic wings, discussing cheeks and kissing percentages, managing the room as no one else could.

And finally there she was, drifting between little clutches of conversation. Spangles and crystals the color of olive leaves shimmered down her body like rain, a thin fringe that danced every time she laughed. She wore her hair up in a complicated twist with a jeweled comb, and when Orpheus remembers this, when he dreams of it, he sees them all at the same time, overlaid like double-exposed film: the dress and the comb and the twist and the long, limp, greasy hair as it is now, strands stuck in the milky fluid of her dead eye.

"Have you met Eurydice?" Hermes's voice trips down the halls of that other life, that correct life, the life he'd been promised. "You absolutely must, she's a treasure."

And she'd turned away from some studio exec pestering her and offered him her gorgeous hand tipped in gold polish. A faint blackbird of a bruise rising already on her forearm. Hearing her voice for the first time like hearing a song you just *know* is going to hit hard.

"Well, aren't you something?"

*And what were you doing at that party?* their therapist asks later, so much later. Eurydice shrugs and stares at her knees. Cypress trees cast shadows like black arrows on her face. They never planted cypress. But thick green spear-heads crowd the windows on all sides now.

*She doesn't remember,* Orpheus sighs.

*I'm asking her. Active listening, Orpheus. You'll get your turn. So what was happening in your life that night? Were you in college? Working? Promoting your own music?*

*She was never in the industry,* Orpheus says. *It was one of the things I found so refreshing about her, considering her father and all.*

Eurydice picks at the scabs between her fingers. Finally, she rasps: *I…I used to sing.*

*No you didn't.*

*Okay,* she surrenders quickly, as she always does. *I didn't.* They used to fight till the rafters came down and make up on the ruins. Orpheus usually won, but he enjoyed the battle. Now he gets his way so easily.

*You never told me.*

*Okay.*

*You could have come into the studio with me. Put down a back-up track.*

*I didn't ever sing. I can't sing.*

*Eurydice, do you want to talk about the man who grabbed your arm?*

*No.*

A small bubble of trapped gases slowly inflates her cheek.

―

BUT HE *WAS* something. And so was she. He was famous. She was beautiful. What else did anyone need? They were young and it was easy. Orpheus saw himself as he knew he could be reflected back at him in that heated, shimmering stare. He wanted it. He wanted that ease forever. He wanted himself as she saw him.

Just because he goes home with a maenad that night and has to be reminded of her name when they meet again a month later doesn't make it any less love at first sight.

Orpheus has repeatedly explained that to their therapist.

## Eighth Step

ORPHEUS KNOWS THEY'RE here before he even gets to the foot of the stairs. A guitar case leans casually against the wall next to the guest bathroom, perfectly centered in a spotlight of morning sunshine. It's not one of his. This warhorse is more stickers than leather by now, held together by memory alone.

Orpheus sighs heavily.

Eurydice's father and his dirtbag friends don't call ahead. They don't bake, they don't help with chores, they don't come bearing takeout, and they definitely don't do baths. They just turn up. Once or twice a year. Orpheus rounds the banister today to find the boys all smoking around his living room, feet up on the coffee table, a random girl asleep on the piano bench, empties stacked into green and brown hecatombs on every surface. He recognizes the labels.

Orpheus and Calliope are merely famous. The old man is a legend. Seminal. Iconic. No one comes close to his influence, his sheer ubiquitousness. He *is* music.

He lounges in the big swayback armchair, a man mostly his haircut, perpetually stuck halfway between Robert Plant and David Cassidy, runway-thin, leather jacket, leather pants, massive paparazzi-proof hangover shades, a big golden sun stamped on his black T-shirt, herpes sore like a kiss below his lip. A face that invented magazines, a voice that filled them to the brim. He laughs wolfishly at something or other one of his strung-out friends said and puts out his cigarette on a sunbeam as though it were solid stone.

"There he is!" Apollo brays. "Big O! We were just talking about you, weren't we, boys? And where's my beautiful baby girl this morning?"

"She'll be up soon," Orpheus mumbles.

Apollo pats his ribs for more smokes. "Call her down. Lazy cow-eyed lump." He finds one and jams it unlit between his teeth. "I'm up every morning crack of dawn, you know. No excuses. Sleep is for the dead, kiddo!" He catches himself and grins sheepishly, a grin so pretty even Orpheus finds himself trying, once again, to like the man. "Whoops. Awkward. Don't want to offend. You know how sensitive the youth are these days. Can't say anything anymore. Oof. I'll want a drink. You want a drink, mate? Probably need a drink before she... ah...before *that*." He digs in his pockets for a light. "How's things, anyway? Everything back to normal?" Apollo's eyes glitter suggestively. "Back in the saddle, so to speak?"

Orpheus stares. He coughs out a hollow laugh.

One of the old gang leans forward from the depths of the plush grey couch. He winces; his stomach's wrapped in sterile pads and medical gauze signed by the whole band like a cast. Prometheus flicks a lighter for Apollo's wobbly cig.

"Yer a life-saver, thanks," the legend mumbles.

Dionysus heads for the kitchen. Orpheus tries to tell him they barely keep anything in the house, but he opens the fridge with a *hey, hey, hey* straight out of afternoon re-runs. Row after row of wines so old they could draw a pension. The crisper drawers packed with Harp lager—the old man doesn't do wine. His sister favors Blue Moon, but they haven't seen her since the wedding.

It's always like this. Prometheus and Dionysus and Pan, hiding his horns under a fedora, along with whatever nymphs they were shacking up with that week. Ransacking the house, talking about themselves and the old days until you wanted to rivet their mouths shut.

Apollo throws back a beer in one long swallow and gestures for another as they wait for the dead to rise. "When are you going to start touring again, son?" He taps out his ash onto the sleeping girl. She's gorgeous, but they always are. The grey flakes drift down to land on her necklace, a chain of silver laurel leaves looping around her perfect, warm and living neck. Orpheus stares. He can see her pulse faintly beneath her skin. He'd almost forgotten people's bodies did that. She smells like a river, a forest. Alive. "Don't want to wait too long between albums. I should know.

Can't go radio silent just because the going gets a bit uphill, eh? Gotta get back out there."

"I couldn't stay cooped up like this," Dionysus shudders as he upends a bottle into his gullet. "This house gives me the creeps. And I think you've got a serious mold problem." He wrinkles his nose at the ceiling. A delicate charcoal filigree marrs the drywall. Orpheus doesn't have to look. He knows. He'll call someone. Tomorrow. Soon.

Orpheus grimaces. Pan glances up from his endless scrolling through whatever hookup app he's on this time. *Swipe, swipe, swipe.* "You can always open for us. The fans would lose their minds." *Swipe.* He lowers his voice. "You can't stay cooped up like this, poor thing. It's not healthy. Life goes on, yeah? There's only supposed to be five stages of grief. What are you on, stage twenty? Does she even…does she even know you're here?"

"Of course she does," Orpheus snaps defensively. But she steps out behind him as soon as his voice hits the air.

Eurydice's face glows with health. Her lips shine ripe and red. Her cheeks blush. Her hair shines. Bare, tanned legs delicate as knives beneath a loose skirt and the oversized mustard-colored sweater Calliope knit for her, a friendly cartoon snake on the front and γνοτηι σεαυτον, *y'all!* sewn on with black thread in a circle around its winning smile and forked tongue. Orpheus's chest throbs. It is her, it is her, as she always was, as the sun made her, as he dreamed of her over and over until it wore a groove in his brain. She clasps her hands to her chest like a little girl. Moves her shoulders up and down slightly so it looks like she might really be breathing. But she isn't. Of course she isn't. It's all a show, all for him.

Apollo looks nauseated. His throat works to keep the bile down. He looks his daughter up and down, his dancing warm eyes gone distant, flat, glassy. The words he doesn't say hang in the air between them. *I thought you would be different this time, but I guess not.*

She forgot to do her hands. Her father can't help but goggle at them, fish-colored, embroidered with black veins. She ran out of foundation; couldn't find her gloves. Prometheus goes to open a window—there isn't enough Red Door in the world to fix the smell, rich and putrid and earthen.

"Why don't you play us something?" Dionysus suggests.

None of them can take it, they're so fucking fragile. Orpheus hates them. He hates her. He hates how hopeful she gets. Every goddamn time, and for what? They're so empty, they need something pouring into them all the time just to escape knowing it, into their mouths, their eyes, their ears. Music is just the sound of time blowing across the lip of their nothingness.

Eurydice never puts on the makeup for him. She'll take off the glossy, thick wig as soon as they go. The contacts, the fake lashes, all of it. A pile of girl on the floor.

"Yeah, come on, give us a little song," Apollo agrees eagerly. Anything, anything to avoid having to be here and now. "You must be getting brilliant material out of this whole mess. Deep, experiential stuff. Raw, authentic, blah blah blah, the whole aesthetic. I'm here for it. Front row center. Can't wait to hear your new sound. Hey, you can even play my ax if you want." He signals for Prometheus to go get it from the hall. The Titan hops to it like an eager spaniel. "Would you like that?"

Orpheus doesn't want to do it. He knows what will happen. So does she. But Eurydice's blown-out pupils bore into him from behind green contacts. She can take it. She doesn't mind. Anything, if it'll make Dad happy.

Apollo puts his guitar into Orpheus's hands. What is he supposed to do, then? It is an instrument made of forever. It is the beginning and end of song. Eurydice fixes her silvered eyes on her father. She puts her cold, heavy hand on his knee and the great man flinches. He fucking *flinches*.

But Orpheus's fingers do not move on the strings. He doesn't want her to know. He doesn't want her to hear. *I haven't done anything wrong*, he tells himself. But nothing in him answers back. So he begins to play a slow, lilting version of an old Smiths song. For her, for them. *Pretty Girls Make Graves*. A good joke or a bad one. Who cares? Just let it be over. The voice that moved rocks and trees to life and even the fish to dance fills up a living room with wallpaper twenty years past chic. The girl on the piano bench opens her startingly green eyes.

He's not even through the first verse when he sees it. Eurydice trembling, vibrating, barely able to hold still. She's shut her eyes. Her jaw clenches so hard they can all hear teeth cracking. But she does not, cannot cry.

Her fingertip blossoms with blood. Real, living blood. Just under the skin. It goes pink and brown, the nail a round little moon, warm, soft. The rest of her hands remain skeletal, ashen, mouldering. But her fingertip wakes to the sound of his music, like the rocks, like the trees, like the fish of the stream and the sea.

Finally, she cannot bear it. She cannot be a good girl any longer. She howls in pain. She claws at the living tissue. Her eyes roll back to find some path away from anguish. She drags her hands down her face, smearing away the careful makeup, the meticulous lip. Chunks of flesh come away. Orpheus stops; the color ebbs away. The nail blackens again, little lightning bolts of mold snaking back up out of the cuticle.

Her family scatters like raindrops.

Orpheus and Eurydice sit alone in an empty room.

The carpet has turned into long silver grass. A wind from somewhere far off shakes tiny seeds into the air.

### Ninth Step

ORPHEUS HAS TRIED to touch her a thousand times. She has never said no. She has never covered up or cried or told him she needed time. She'll let him do anything he wants.

But he doesn't. Not often. Not anymore.

Once she slid into bed with him and the touch of her flesh shocked him almost into the ceiling. She was as warm as the earth in July, hot, even, the air around her oily and rippling. Orpheus wept with relief. He kissed her over and over, drinking her up and in, so grateful, so stupidly grateful and urgent and needy. She was back and she was his and it would all be fine now, it would all go back to the way it was and when he sang to her she would dance again, she would dance and drink her juice and eat her egg and maybe they would get a cat. A big fat orange tabby and they'd name it something pretentious and literary nobody else would understand. *I knew you were there*, he whispered into her hair. *I didn't doubt it for a moment. You're always there.*

Only afterward, when he was brushing his teeth, did he notice her slick silver hair dryer out left plugged in by the sink. He felt the barrel. She'd run it so long the metal was still almost too hot to bear.

So when Orpheus starts sleeping with the maenad from his agent's party again, he tells himself it's not his fault. It's not her fault, either. It's not even *about* her. He tried. He really tried this time.

*Let me hear the new song*, the maenad says, and rolls over toward him, tangled in sheets like possibilities, everything about her so alive she glows. Her apartment is so clean. No grass or mushrooms or fine purple mold in the ceiling roses. She runs her rosy, licorice-scented fingers through his hair.

And when Orpheus sings, it doesn't hurt her, not even a little. *I love you*, the maenad breathes as she climbs on top of him. *You're amazing. You deserve so much more than this.*

### Tenth Step

EVERY NIGHT AT nine thirty sharp, Eurydice opens her lavender plastic birth control compact and presses down on the little blister pack with the day of the week printed over it.

In those moments, Orpheus always wants to ask her what she's thinking, why she bothers, what's the point. But he never does.

A pomegranate seed pops out. She closes her eyes when she swallows it.

Orpheus goes to the coffee shop down the road most mornings. He gets a latte for himself and one for Eurydice, then drinks them both on a park bench between here and the house. Cinnamon on top. No sugar. He likes all the sugar himself, but that's what she used to drink. So that's what he drinks now forever.

He tells the cute young barista behind the counter his name. She has a nose piercing and huge brown eyes like a Disney deer. She spells his name wrong on the cup.

"No," he says with his most charming half-cocked grin. "Like the singer."

"Who?" the girl says innocently. "What singer has a weird name like that?"

Orpheus puts the coffees down on his bench. He squints in the sunshine. Watches some kids fight over the tire swing. Pulls out his phone and jabs at the keyboard with his thumb. *Are you around? I need you. I want you.*

She texts back right away. Quick as life.

When he gets home that night, he has to step over the green-black river that churns through the foyer, separating the land of the living room from the land of his wife.

## Eleventh Step

IT'S AFTERNOON AND there's crabapple blossoms all over the front walk like snow and a smart knock at the back door.

Orpheus feels a rush of excitement prickle in his chest. He knows the face on the other side of the glass. His friend. Maybe his only real friend. The only one who gets him completely, who understands what he's had to go through, who can make it an hour without saying something that makes Orpheus want to punch them in the mouth or beg them to take him away from this place forever.

"Hey, fuckbrains," Sisyphus says fondly as Orpheus turns the bolt and lets him into the kitchen sporting three days of stubble, ripped jeans, steel-toed boots, and a faded black T-shirt that reads *Rock n' Roll Forever* in white letters with lightning-bolt tips.

And a dog. Three dogs, actually. German shepherd puppies, maybe four or five months old, all gangly teenager limbs and ears that don't know how to stand up straight yet.

"Hey, crackhead," Orpheus answers. "They give you a day pass?"

The pups sniff at Orpheus. They gag and growl, showing tiny bright teeth. They look past him as one, curious, black nosed, alert. Past him toward the brand-new river of ash slowly flowing up the hallways.

The ash weeps audibly.

Eurydice hovers behind her husband in another of Calliope's grotesque sweaters. This one with a doofy purple horse and μενιν αιεδε τηεα. Three canine heads tilt toward her at precisely the same time. One dog. Three bodies. They move like a stutter.

Sisyphus sinks into the breakfast nook, a heap of handsome limbs. He rolls a milky gray marble over the tops of his tattooed fingers, back and forth, back and forth. His left hand says PRDE. His right says FALL. He nods at the dogs. "Well, I had an idea."

Eurydice holds out her blood-purple fingers to the puppies. They advance slowly, uncertainly, huffing her ashen, green-veined hand. Then they fall all over her, snapping the leash, their movements identical, licking her face, wagging great shaggy tails they haven't grown into yet, howling in recognition and joy. Eurydice beams, grave dirt showing between her teeth, caking her gums.

"I thought, you know…" Sisyphus says sheepishly, holding one of the leftover cans of Harp between his threadbare denim knees and cracking it with one hand while the other rolled his marble knuckle to knuckle to knuckle. "Emotional support dog. Worth a try."

"You thought *that* would make a good emotional support animal for my wife," Orpheus deadpans as the three hounds loll in Eurydice's lap, their furry bellies as white as death.

Sisyphus gestures with the beer. "Hey, Cerberus is a good boy! He's had loads of training. Sit, stand up, shake a paw, do not chew souls, do not let the living cross into the realm of the dead, the whole package. And nothing spooks him." His voice softens. "He wanted to come. He misses her. They got to be quite good friends, you know. Nobody pays much attention to the old fella once they're settled in. But not our girl. She brought him snacks."

"The fuck does he eat?" Orpheus asks.

"Kindess," Eurydice growls. Cerberus licks her nose and whimpers in furry ecstasy. "Don't we all," she says into his downy ear.

Sisyphus rolls his stone back and forth. "She took him for two walks a day, every day, and not short ones either. All down the new riverfront walks, along the Lethe and the Phelgethon and the Acheron." He glances toward the sobbing hallway, but Sisyphus is far too polite to say anything. "She let him stop and sniff whenever he wanted. The shops and galleries started leaving out bowls of water for him."

"I never heard about any of this. What shops?"

Sisyphus lifts an eyebrow. "Didn't you have a look around while you were down there, man? See the sights while you were in town?"

"I was a little busy."

"Who is that busy? It's hell. You weren't even curious?"

Eurydice laughs hoarsely. It is not a kind laugh, and Orpheus doesn't like it at all. She would never have embarrassed him like that in the old days.

"Well, yeah, shops. Salt water taffy and glass bowls and shit. Revitalization. It's Persephone's whole thing. You do *not* want to let that woman get bored. The salt water still comes from the rivers, though, so it'll make you forget or be invincible or re-live every lamentation of your life just the same. It's just…nicer now. Oh and her yarn. All the shops carried it. They couldn't get enough. She called each lot the funniest things, had us all in stitches. Even Clotho had a standing order. So soft! And the *best* colors. I made this shirt out of it. Do you like it?"

"*Whose* yarn?" Orpheus asks in confusion.

"Who do you think?" Sisyphus laughs.

Eurydice heads out the side door without a word. The dogs walk primly on their leash, heeling perfectly and staring up at her in abject adoration.

"Be honest, man," Sisyphus says, leaning forward. "How's it going?"

Orpheus's eyes burn and his chest crushes in on itself. "It's like I don't even know her anymore."

"Well, I mean, yeah," Sisyphus chuckles.

"What does that mean?"

"Look, I love you, you know that. But did you ever really know her in the first place?"

"What kind of bullshit is that? She's my wife. How can you even ask me that, after everything I did to get her back? Just to be with her again? Of *course* I knew her. Know her," he corrects himself.

"You didn't know she had a dog."

"What happened down there…it isn't important, don't you get that? It was a horrible dream. A bad trip. I don't want to know about it. Neither does she. That's all behind us now."

Sisyphus shrugs. "Okay, what's her mom's name?"

Orpheus blinks. "It…I don't know, it never came up. But that's not fair, it's not like I don't know her family. Her dad's around all the time. He's never mentioned her, either."

Sisyphus sighs, gets up, and helps himself to the vintage *Star Wars* glasses in the cabinet. He picks Lando. "Where'd she go to college? What was her major? She have any siblings?" The dead man looks around awkwardly for a moment before Orpheus snatches the glass out of his hand.

"I'll do it," he snaps. He gets a blood bag out of the fridge and sticks it in the microwave for thirty. They stand on the ceramic floor while the machine hums toward its inevitable beep. Deep green mold crawls through the cracks between tiles under their feet toward the river in the hallway.

"A little bleach will probably take care of that," Sisyphus says quietly.

"Yeah," Orpheus mumbles, pouring the blood out for his friend. "You'd think."

"I don't mean to pry—"

Orpheus laughs in his face.

"But did you ever ask her?"

"Ask her what?"

"If she wanted to come back."

"Why the hell would I ask her? Nobody wants to be dead. I did the right thing. For us. For her. You were there. It was heroic. I was selfless. I was strong."

"Were you? Or could you just…not accept that something pretty was taken from you? Did you know her? Or was she hot and rich and uncomplicated?"

"Fuck you," Orpheus whispers.

"Okay, okay. Calm down. I'm not accusing you of anything. I'm just asking questions."

They sit in ugly silence, letting the sunlight through the dusty, spore-spackled windows say the things they cannot.

"How's the new album coming?" Sisyphus says finally.

Orpheus grabs the rough cut out of his bag, sliding the disc across the table. A fine mist of silvery pollen puffs up in its wake.

Upstairs, asphodel flowers explode out of their bed, a detonation of white and red petals like blood and skin. They spread and spread, tumbling onto the floor, nosing the curtains, suckling the wallpaper.

Sisyphus rolls his stone across his knuckles, patiently, endlessly. With his other hand, he touches the disc and knows every song in a moment.

"Wow," Sisyphus whispers. "Oh, wow."

## Twelfth Step

ORPHEUS DECIDES TO leave on a Wednesday. Not markedly different from any other Wednesday. She can have the house, he doesn't care. He stops giving her the lambsblood in the morning. *It'll make it easier,* he tells himself. *She'll forget. She won't suffer. I'm not hurting her. Not really. I'm doing what's best for both of us.* Fuck the house, fuck the cars, fuck his outstanding record contract. None of it matters. If he doesn't come back, that's just fine. But he doesn't know how to start. Where to go. What to take. This isn't his gig. It isn't anyone's gig.

Orpheus asks his mother. She tells him the obvious: *the entrance to hell is always in your own house, silly billy.*

The house didn't have a basement when he bought it. It sure does now. A door between the studio and the library that was never there before. A door and a long, long stair leading down into lightlessness.

⁓

MOLD HAS COLONIZED the house. Tiny blue mushrooms on the fireplace. Carpets of pink fuzz climbing the stairs. Black water flowing past the front door. Weeping ash rippling down the hall. A gurgling stream of fire between the kitchen and the dining room. Asphodel everywhere. Ambrosia in every takeout container.

The rivers visit all the time now. They don't even speak to Orpheus anymore. They just go straight to her.

Eurydice doesn't clean anymore. She and Cerberus lie in a pile together and watch the country inside the house grow by candlelight. When Orpheus asked if she felt like pulling her weight on even the most basic level, she turned her head like a stone door and stared in the direction of his studio, panting like a wolf.

Cerberus doesn't let him into her room anymore. If he tries, the three pups growl and drool and their eyes flash green in the dark.

⁓

# L'Esprit de L'Escalier

ORPHEUS SINGS FOR his wife. He sings for an audience of two: of death and death's great love. The most important studio boss there is. He sings everything she ever was or could be. He sings every moment of their life together, every kiss and whisper and quiet joke, every intimate space that opened between them like dark flowers, every good day, because they were all good days. He sings her heart out. He sings what will become his comeback anthem, a song no one can get out of their heads, topping the charts for years, used in every film about love and loss and even an anti-depressant commercial. Orpheus strips Eurydice of Eurydice and transforms her into a song so perfect death gives up and life buries him in laurels.

The song of them, that she never hears. He simply never thinks to play it for her. It's his. His best work. Besides, she never asked what he sang to get her back. He'd have shown her, if she'd asked. Probably.

And what he sang for her and only her, what he sang before the great starry unweeping face of death, is sitting on a rough cut demo in his leather bag as he walks out of his house on a Wednesday years later, in a padded envelope with his agent's address on it.

---

"DO YOU STILL love me?" Orpheus asks her Tuesday night, the night before he leaves her. She sits on the porch with her dogs, putting together a puzzle of *Starry Night*.

Eurydice runs her fingers over the black half-assembled chapels and cypress trees. She hasn't had lambsblood in two weeks. Sometimes she forgets she is dead and starts screaming when she sees herself in the mirror. But today was a good day. They watched TV together. She watched Cerberus play in the backyard. One of him ate a bee. She'd laughed.

"I see my love for you as though it hangs in a museum," Eurydice says slowly. "Under glass. Environmentally controlled. It is a part of history. But I am not allowed to touch it. I am not allowed to add anything new to it. I am not even allowed to get close." She puts a golden star into place without looking up. "Why didn't you turn around?" Eurydice whispers.

Orpheus tells the truth. "I knew you were there, baby. I never doubted it for a minute."

Children yell and play in the neighbors' gardens, high-pitched giggles fizzing up into the streetlights. "You didn't know. You assumed I was there. Behind you. Like I'd always been there. Behind you. You couldn't even imagine that I might not do as I was told, that I might not be where you wanted me to be, the moment you wanted it. That was my place, and you assumed I would be in it. What in your life has ever gone any way other than as you wished it to?" She glances toward the house, toward the demo still sitting where Sisyphus left it. "And now you have what you want from me. What you always wanted. I am no longer necessary. And yet. I am still here."

Her hand settles down on the leftmost puppy. Cerberus wears three weighted coats, to help with his anxiety. Maybe Orpheus should have gotten her one. He thinks of that now, and dwells on it long enough that there's no easy way back into the conversation, and Orpheus just tells her to shut the lights off before she goes to bed.

---

ORPHEUS AND EURYDICE step blinking into a summer's day. The blue of the sky throbs in their eyes. He takes her into his arms and swings her around. *You're back, you're back, and it'll all be as it was, you'll see. I saved you. I did it. Aren't you happy? Baby? Put your arms around me. Don't you want to?*

---

ORPHEUS WALKS DOWN the porch steps of his house. It is dusk, and he can smell everyone's dinner. He can see all their lights, the illuminated windows of their worlds. Owls are heading out to hunt. Business on the west coast closes in an hour.

Orpheus stops on the stair. For a moment, just a moment, he thinks that perhaps she is there. Asking him not to go. Eurydice as she always was, adoration in human form, the way he remembers her. The way she should have been. Maybe it will all be all right, and this was just the last test, the last barrier between life and death.

His phone buzzes in his pocket. He knows without looking that it's his maenad, warm and rosy and waiting.

Orpheus turns around on the staircase. For old time's sake.

Eurydice stands in the window, watching. Acheron and Phelgethon kiss her cheeks, lay their heads on her shoulders. She smiles with such tenderness, but not for him. She shuts her eyes in their embrace.

Orpheus straightens his shoulders. He turns away. He has places to be. A maenad. A record. He has a life. He has a legend to become. He knows it's all there, just waiting for him.

Behind him, asphodel devours the house whole.

# The Lily and the Horn

**W**AR IS A DINNER PARTY.

My ladies and I have spent the dregs of summer making ready. We have hung garlands of pennyroyal and snowberries in the snug, familiar halls of Laburnum Castle, strained cheese as pure as ice for weeks in the caves and the kitchens, covered any gloomy stone with tapestries or stags' heads with mistletoe braided through their antlers. We sent away south to the great markets of Mother-of-Millions for new silks and velvets and furs. We have brewed beer as red as October and as black as December, boiled every growing thing down to jams and pickles and jellies, and set aside the best of the young wines and the old brandies. Nor are we proud: I myself scoured the stables and the troughs for all the strange horses to come. When no one could see me, I buried my face in fresh straw just for the heavy gold scent of it. I've fought for my husband many times, but each time it is new all over again. The smell of the hay like candied earth, with its bitter ribbons of ergot laced through—that is the smell of my youth, almost gone now, but still knotted to the ends of my hair, the line of my shoulders. When I polish the silver candelabras, I still feel half a child, sitting splay-legged on the floor, playing with my mother's scorpions, until the happy evening drew down.

I am the picture of honor. I am the Lily of my House. When last the king came to Laburnum, he told his surly queen: *You see, my plum? That* is *a woman. Lady Cassava looks as though she has grown out of the very stones of this hall.* She looked at me with interested eyes, and we had much to discuss later when quieter hours came. This is how I serve my husband's ambitions and mine: with the points of my vermilion sleeves, stitched with thread of white and violet and tiny milkstones with hearts of green ice. With the net of gold and chalcathinite crystals catching up my hair, jewels from our own stingy mountains, so blue they seem to burn. With the great black pots of the kitchens below my feet, sizzling and hissing like a heart about to burst.

It took nine great, burly men to roll the ancient feasting table out of the cellars, its legs as thick as wine barrels and carved with the symbols of their house: the unicorn passant and the wild poppy. They were kings once, Lord Calabar's people. Kings long ago when the world was full of swords, kings in castles of bone, with wives of gold—so they all say. When he sent his man to the Floregilium to ask for me, the Abbess told me to be grateful—not for his fortune (of which there is a castle, half a river, a village and farms, and several chests of pearls fished out of an ocean I shall never see) but for his blood. My children stand near enough from the throne to see its gleam, but they will never have to polish it.

My children. I was never a prodigy in the marriage bed, but what a workhorse my belly turned out to be! Nine souls I gave to the coffers of House Calabar. Five sons and four daughters, and not a one of them dull or stupid. But the dark is a hungry thing. I lost two boys to plague and a girl to the scrape of a rusted hinge. Six left. My lucky sixpence. While I press lemon oil into the wood of the great table with rags that once were gowns, four of my sweethearts giggle and dart through the forest of legs—men, tables, chairs. The youngest of my black-eyed darlings, Mayapple, hurls herself across the silver-and-beryl checked floor and into my arms, saying:

"Mummy, Mummy, what shall I wear to the war tonight?"

She has been at my garden, though she knows better than to explore alone. I brush wisteria pollen from my daughter's dark hair while she tells me all her troubles. "*I want to wear my blue silk frock with the emeralds round the collar, but Dittany says it's too plain for battle and I shall look like a frog and shame us.*"

"You will wear vermillion and white, just as we all will, my little lionfish, for when the king comes we must all wear the colors of our houses so he can remember all our names. But lucky for you, your white will be ermine and your vermillion will be rubies and you will look nothing at all like a frog."

Passiflora, almost a woman herself, as righteous and hard as an antler, straightens her skirts as though she has not been playing at tumble and chase all morning. She looks nothing like me—her hair as red as venom, her eyes the pale blue of moonlit mushrooms. But she will be our fortune, for I have seen no better student of the wifely arts in all my hours. "We oughtn't to wear ermine," she sniffs. "Only the king and the queen can, and the deans of the Floregilium, but only at midwinter. Though why a weasel's skin should signify a king is beyond my mind."

My oldest boy, Narcissus, nobly touches his hand to his breast with one hand while he pinches his sister savagely with the other and quotes from the articles of peerage. "'The House of Calabar may wear a collar of ermine not wider than one and one half inches, in acknowledgment of their honorable descent from Muscanine, the Gardener Queen, who set the world to growing.'"

But Passiflora knows this. This is how she tests her siblings and teaches them, by putting herself in the wrong over and over. No child can help correcting his sister. They fall over themselves to tell her how stupid she is, and she smiles to herself because they do not think there's a lesson in it.

Dittany, my sullen, sour beauty, frowns, which means she wants something. She was born frowning and will die frowning and through all the years between (may they be long) she will scowl at every person until they bend to her will. A girl who never smiles has such power—what men will do to turn up but one corner of her mouth! She already wears her red war-gown and her circlet of cinnabar poppies. They brings out the color in her grimace.

"Mother," she glowers, "may I milk the unicorns for the feast?"

My daughter and I fetch knives and buckets and descend the stairs into the underworld beneath our home. Laburnum Castle is a mushroom lying only half above ground. Her lacy, lovely parts reach up toward the sun, but the better part of her dark body stretches out through the seastone caverns below, vast rooms and chambers and vaults with ceilings more lovely than any painted chapel in Mother-of-Millions, shot through with frescoes and motifs of copper and quartz and sapphire and opal. Down here, the real work of war clangs and thuds and corkscrews toward tonight. Smells as rich as brocade hang in the kitchens like banners, knives flash out of the mist and the shadows.

I have chosen the menu of our war as carefully as the stones in my hair. All my art has bent upon it. I chose the wines for their color—nearly black, thick and bitter and sharp. I baked the bread to be as sweet as the pudding. The vital thing, as any wife can tell you, is spice. Each dish must taste vibrant, strong, vicious with flavor. Under my eaves they will dine on curried doves, black pepper and peacock marrow soup, blancmange drunk with clove and fiery sumac, sealmeat and fennel pies swimming in garlic and apricots, roast suckling lion in a sauce of brandy, ginger, and pink chilis, and pomegranate cakes soaked in claret.

I am the perfect hostess. I have poisoned it all.

This is how I serve my husband, my children, my king, my house: with soup and wine and doves drowned in orange spices. With wine so dark and strong any breath of oleander would vanish in it. With the quills of sunless fish and liqueurs of wasps and serpents hung up from my rafters like bunches of lavender in the fall.

It's many years now since a man of position would consider taking a wife who was not a skilled poisoner. They come to the Floregilium as to an orphanage and ask not after the most beautiful, nor the sweetest voice, nor the most virtuous, nor the mildest, but the most deadly. All promising young ladies journey to Brugmansia, where the sea is warm, to receive their education. I remember it more clearly than words spoken but an hour ago—the hundred towers and hundred bridges and hundred gates of the Floregilium, a school and a city and a test, mother to all maidens.

I passed beneath the Lily Gate when I was but seven—an archway so twisted with flowers no stone peeked through. Daffodils and hyacinths and columbines, foxglove and moonflower, poppy and peony, each one gorgeous and full, each one brilliant and graceful, each one capable of killing a man with root or bulb of leaf or petal. Another child ran on ahead of me. Her hair was longer than mine, and a better shade of black. Hers had blue inside it, flashing like crystals dissolving in a glass of wine. Her laugh was merrier than mine, her eyes a prettier space apart, her height far more promising. Between the two of us, the only advantage I ever had was a richer father. She had a nice enough name, nice enough to hide a pit of debt.

Once my mother left me to explore her own girlish memories, I followed that other child for an hour, guiltily, longingly, sometimes angrily. Finally, I resolved to give it up, to let her be better than I was if she insisted on it. I raised my arm to lean against a brilliant blue wall and rest—and she appeared as though she had been following me, seizing my hand with the strength of my own father, her grey eyes forbidding.

"Don't," she said.

Don't rest? Don't stop?

"It's chalcathite. Rub up against it long enough and it will stop your blood."

Her name was Yew. She would be the Horn of her House, as I am the Lily of mine. The Floregilium separates girls into Lilies—those who will boil up death in a sealmeat pie, and Horns—those who will send it fleeing with an emerald knife. The Lily can kill in a hundred thousand fascinating ways, root, leaf, flower, pollen, seed. I can brew a tea of lily that will leave a man breathing and laughing, not knowing in the least that he is poisoned, until he dies choking on disappointment at sixty-seven. The Horn of a unicorn can turn a cup of wine so corrupted it boils and slithers into honey. We spend our childhoods in a dance of sourness and sweetness.

Everything in Floregilium is a beautiful murder waiting to unfold. The towers and bridges sparkle ultramarine, fuchsia, silvery, seething green, and should a careless girl trail her fingers along the stones, her skin will blister black. The river teems with venomous, striped fish that take two hours to prepare so that they taste of salt and fresh butter and do not burn out the throat, and three hours to prepare so that they will not strangle the eater until she has gone merrily back to her room and put out her candles. Every meal is an examination, every country walk a trial. No more joyful place exists in all the world. I can still feel the summer rain falling through the hot green flowers of the manchineel tree in the north orchard, that twisted, gnomish thing, soaking up the drops, corrupting the water of heaven, and flinging it onto my arms, hissing, hopping, blistering like love.

It was there, under the sun and moon of the Floregilium, that I read tales of knights and archers, of the days when we fought with swords, with axes and shields, with armor beaten out of steel and grief. Poison was thought cowardice, a woman's weapon, without honor. I wept. I was seven. It seemed absurd to me, absurd and wasteful and unhappy, for all those thousands to die so that two men could sort out who had the right to shit on what scrap of grass. I shook in the moonlight. I looked out into the Agarica where girls with silvery hair tended fields of mushrooms that wanted harvesting by the half-moon for greatest potency. I imagined peasant boys dying in the frost with nothing in their bellies and no embrace from the lord who sent them to hit some other boy on the head until the lord turned into a king. I felt such loneliness—and such relief, that I lived in a more sensible time, when blood on the frost had been seen for obscenity it was.

I said a prayer every night, as every girl in the Floregilium did, to Muscanine, the Gardener Queen, who took her throne on the back of a larkspur blossom and never looked back. Muscanine had no royal blood at all. She was an apothecary's daughter. After the Whistling Plague, such things mattered less. Half of every house, stone or mud or marble, died gasping, their throats closing up so only whines and whistles escaped, and when those awful pipes finally ceased, the low and the middling felt no inclination to start dying all over again so that the lordly could put their names on the ruins of the world. Muscanine could read and write. She drew up new articles of war and when the great and the high would not sign it, they began to choke at their suppers, wheeze at their breakfasts, fall like sudden sighs halfway to their beds. The mind sharpens wonderfully when you cannot trust your tea. And after all, why not? What did arms and strength and the best of all blades matter when the wretched maid could clean a house of heirs in a fortnight?

*War must civilize itself,* wrote Muscanine long ago. *So say all sensible souls. There can be no end to conflict between earthly powers, but the use of humble arms to settle disputes of rich men makes rich men frivolous in their exercise of war. Without danger to their own persons, no Lord fears to declare battle over the least slight—and why should he? He risks only a little coin and face while we risk all but benefit nothing in victory. There exists in this sphere no single person who does not admit to this injustice. Therefore, we, the humble arms, will no longer consent to a world built upon, around, and out of an immoral seed.*

The rules of war are simple: should Lord Ambition and the Earl of Avarice find themselves in dispute, they shall agree upon a castle or stronghold belonging to neither of them and present themselves there on a mutually agreeable date. They shall break bread together and whoever lives longest wins. The host bends all their wisdom upon vast and varied poisons while the households of Lord Ambition and the Earl bend all their intellect upon healing and the purifying of any wicked substance. And because poisons were once a woman's work—in the early days no knight could tell a nightshade from a dandelion—it became quickly necessary to wed a murderess of high skill.

Of course, Muscanine's civilized rules have bent and rusted with age. No Lord of any means would sit at the martial table himself nowadays—he hires a proxy to choke or swallow in his stead. But there is still some justice in the arrangement—no one sells themselves to battle cheaply. A family may lift itself up considerably on such a fortune as Lord Ambition will pay. No longer do two or three men sit down simply to their meal of honor. Many come to watch the feast of war, whole households, the king himself. There is much sport in it. Great numbers of noblemen seat their proxies in order to declare loyalties and tilt the odds in favor of victory, for surely someone, of all those brawny men, can stomach a silly flower or two.

"But think how marvelous it must have looked," Yew said to me once, lying on my bed surrounded by books like a ribbonmark. "All the banners flying, and the sun on their swords, and the horses with armor so fine even a beast would be proud. Think of the drums and the trumpets and the cries in the dawn."

"I do think of all that, and it sounds ghastly. At least now, everyone gets a good meal out of the business. It's no braver or wiser or stranger to gather a thousand friends and meet another thousand in a field and whack on each other with knives all day. And there are still banners. My father's banners are beautiful. They have a manticore on them, in a ring of oleander. I'll show you someday."

But Yew already knew what my father's banners looked like. She stamped our manticore onto a bezoar for me the day we parted. The clay of the Floregilium mixed with a hundred spices and passed through the gullet of a lion. At least, she said it was a lion.

Soon it will be time to send Dittany and Mayapple. Passiflora will return there when the war is done—she would not miss a chance for practical experience.

Lord Calabar came to the Floregilium when I was a maid of seventeen. Yew's husband came not long after, from far-off Mithridatium, so that the world could be certain we would never see each other again. They came through the Horn Gate, a passage of unicorn horns braided as elegantly as if they were the strands of a girl's hair. He was entitled by his blood to any wife he could convince—lesser nobles may only meet the diffident students, the competent but uninspired, the gentle and the kind who might have enough knowledge to fight, but a weak stomach. They always look so startled when they come a-briding. They come from their castles and holdfasts imagining fierce-jawed maidens with eyes that flash like mercury and hair like rivers of blood, girls like the flowers they boiled into noble deaths, tall and bright and fatal. And they find us wearing leather gloves with stiff cuffs at the elbows, boots to the thigh, and masks of hide and copper and glass that turn our faces into those of wyrms and deepwater fish. But how else to survive in a place where the walls are built of venom, the river longs to kill, and any idle perfume might end a schoolgirl's joke before the punchline? To me those masks are still more lovely than anything a queen might make of rouge and charcoal. I will admit that when I feel afraid, I take mine from beneath my bed and wear it until my heart is whole.

I suppose I always knew someone would come into the vicious garden of my happiness and drag me away from it. What did I learn the uses of mandrake for if not to marry, to fight, to win? I did not want him. He was handsome enough, I suppose. His waist tapered nicely; his shoulders did not slump. His grandfathers had never lost their hair even on their deathbeds. But I was sufficient. I and Floregilium and the manchineel tree and my Yew swimming in the river as though nothing could hurt her, because nothing could. He said I could call him Henry. I showed him my face.

"Mummy, the unicorns are miserable today," Dittany frowns, and my memory bursts into a rain of green flowers.

I have never liked unicorns. I have met wolves with better dispositions. I have seen paintings of them from nations where they do not thrive—tall, pale, sorrowfully noble creatures holding the wisdom of eternity as a bit in their muzzles. I understand the desire to make them so. I, too, like things to match. If something is useful, it ought to be beautiful. And yet, the world persists.

Unicorns mill around my daughter's legs, snorting and snuffling at her hands, certain she has brought them the half-rotted meat and flat beer they love best. Unicorns are the size of boars, round of belly and stubby of leg, covered in long, curly grey fur that matts viciously in the damp and smells of wet books. Their long, canny faces are something like horses, yes, but also something like dogs, and their teeth have something of the shark about them. And in the center, that short, gnarled nub of bone, as pure and white as the soul of a saint. Dittany opens her sack and tosses out greying lamb rinds, half-hardened cow's ears. She pours out leftover porter into their trough. The beasts gurgle and trill with delight, gobbling their treasure, snapping at each other to establish and reinforce their shaggy social order, the unicorn king and his several queens and their kingdom of offal.

"Why do they do it?" Dittany frowns. "Why do they shovel in all that food when they know they could die?"

A unicorn looks up at me with red, rheumy eyes and wheezes. "Why did men go running into battle once upon a time, when they knew they might die? They believe their shield is stronger than the other fellow's sword. They believe their Horn is stronger than the other fellow's Lily. They believe that when they put their charmed knives into the pies, they will shiver and turn red and take all the poison into the blade. They believe their toadstones have the might of gods."

"But nobody is stronger than you, are they, Mum?"

"Nobody, my darling."

He said I could call him Henry. He courted me with a shaker of powdered sapphires from a city where elephants are as common as cats. A dash of blue like so much salt would make any seething feast wholesome again. *Well, unless some clever Lily has used moonseeds, or orellanine, or unicorn milk, or the venom of a certain frog who lives in the library and is called Phillip. Besides, emerald is better than sapphire.* But I let him think his jewels could buy life from death's hand. It is a nice thing to think. Like those beautiful unicorns glowing softly in silver thread.

I watch my daughter pull at the udders of our unicorns, squeezing their sweaty milk into a steel pail, for it would sizzle through wood or even bronze as easily as rain through leaves. She is deft and clever with her hands, my frowning girl, the mares barely complain. When I milk them, they bite and howl. The dun sky opens up into bands like pale ribs, showing a golden heart beating away at dusk. Henry Calabar kisses me when I am seventeen and swears my lips are poison from which he will never recover, and his daughter feeds a unicorn a marrow bone, and his son calls down from the ramparts that the king is coming, he is coming, hurry, hurry, and under all this I see only Yew, stealing into my room on that last night in the country of being young, drawing me a bath in the great copper tub, a bath swirling with emerald dust, with green and shimmer. We climbed in, dunking our heads, covering each other with the strangely milky smell of emeralds, clotting our black hair with glittering sand. Yew took my hand and we ran out together into the night, through the quiet streets of the Floregilium, under the bridges and over the water until we came to the manchineel tree in the north orchards, and she held me tight to her beneath its vicious flowers until the storm came, and when the storm came we kissed for the last time as the rain fell through those green flowers and hissed on our skin, vanishing into emerald steam, we kissed and did not burn.

THEY CALL HIM the Hyacinth King and he loves the name. He got it when he was young and ambitious and his wife won the Third Sons' War for him before she had their first child. Hyacinth roots can look so much like potatoes. They come into the hall without grandeur, for we are friends, or friendly enough. I have always had a care to be pregnant when the king came calling, for he has let it be known he enjoys my company, and it takes quite a belly to put him off. But not this time, nor any other to come. He kisses the children one by one, and then me. It is too long a kiss but Henry and I tolerate a great deal from people who have not gotten sick of us after a decade or two. The queen, tall and grand, takes my hand and asks after the curried doves, the wine, the mustard pots. Her eyes shine. Two fresh hyacinths pin her cloak to her dress.

"I miss it," she confesses. "No one wants to fight me anymore. Sometimes I poison the hounds out of boredom. But then I serve them their breakfast in unicorn skulls and they slobber and yap on through another year or nine. Come, tell me what's in the soup course. I have heard you've a new way of boiling crab's eyes to mimic the Whistling Plague. That's how you killed Lord Vervain's lad, isn't it?"

"You flatter me. That was so long ago, I hardly remember," I tell her.

She and her husband take their seats above the field of war—our dining hall, sparkling with fire and finery like wet morning grass. They call for bread and wine—the usual kind, safe as yeast. The proxies arrive with trumpets and drums. *No different, Yew*, I think. My blood prickles at the sound. She is coming. She will come. My castle fills with peasant faces—faces scrubbed and perfumed as they have never been before. Each man standing in for his Lord wears his Lord's own finery. They come in velvet and silk, in lace and furs, with circlets on their heads and rings on their fingers, with sigils embroidered on their chests and curls set in their hair. And each of them looks as elegant and lordly as anyone born to it. All that has ever stood between a duke and a drudge is a bath. She is coming. She will come. The nobles in the stalls sit high above their mirrors at the table, echoes and twins and stutters. It is a feasting hall that looks more like an operating theater with each passing war.

Henry sits beside his king. We are only the castle agreed upon—we take no part. The Hyacinth King has put up a merchant's son in his place—the boy looks strong, his chest like the prow of a ship. But it's only vanity. I can take the thickness from his flesh as fast as that of a thin man. More and more come singing through the gates. The Hyacinth King wishes to take back his ancestral lands in the east, and the lands do not consider themselves to be ancestral. It is not a small war, this time. I have waited for this war. I have wanted it. I have hoped. Perhaps I have whispered to the Hyacinth King when he looked tenderly at me that those foreign lords have no right to his wheat or his wine. Perhaps I have sighed to my husband that if only the country were not so divided we would not have to milk our own unicorns in our one castle. I would not admit to such quiet talk. I have slept only to fight this battle on dreaming grounds, with dreaming knives.

Mithridatium is in the east. She is coming. She will come.

And then she steps through the archway and into my home—my Yew, my emerald dust, my manchineel tree, my burning rain. Her eyes find mine in a moment. We have done this many times. She wears white and pale blue stitched with silver—healing colors, pure colors, colors that could never harm. She is a candle with a blue flame. As she always did, she looks like me drawn by a better hand, a kinder hand. She hardly looks older than my first daughter would have been, had she lived. Perhaps living waist-deep in gentling herbs is better than my bed of wicked roots. Her children beg mutely for her attention with their bright eyes—three boys, and how strange her face looks on boys! She puts her hands on their shoulders. I reach out for Dittany and Mayapple, Passiflora and Narcissus. *Yes, these are mine. I have done this with my years, among the rest.* Her husband takes her hand with the same gestures as Henry might. He begs for nothing mutely with his bright eyes. They are not bad men. But they are not us.

I may not speak to her. The war has already begun the moment she and I rest our bones in our tall chairs. The moment the dinner bell sounds. Neither of us may rise or touch any further thing—all I can do and have done is complete and I am not allowed more. Afterward, we will not be permitted to talk—what if some soft-hearted Horn gave away her best secrets to a Lily? The game would be spoilt, the next war decided between two women's unguarded lips. It would not do. So we sit, our posture perfect, with death between us.

The ladies will bring the peacock soup, laced with belladonna and serpent's milk, and the men (and lady, some poor impoverished lord has sent his own unhappy daughter to be his proxy, and I can hardly look at her for pity) of Mithridatium, of the country of Yew, will stir it with spoons carved from the bones of a white stag, and turn it sweet—perhaps. They will tuck toadstones and bezoars into the meat of the curried doves and cover the blancmange with emerald dust like so much green salt. They will smother the suckling lion in pennyroyal blossoms and betony leaves. They will drink my wine from her cups of unicorn horn. They will sauce the pudding with vervain. And each time a course is served, I will touch her. My spices and her talismans. My stews and her drops of saints' blood like rain. My wine and her horn. My milk and her emeralds. Half the world will die between us, but we will swim in each other and no one will see.

The first soldier turns violet and shakes himself apart into his plate of doves and twenty years ago Yew kisses emeralds from my mouth under the manchineel tree while the brutal rain hisses away into air.

# The Long Goodnight
of Violet Wild

### 1: Violet

**I** DON'T KNOW WHAT STORIES ARE anymore so I don't know how to tell you about the adventures of Woe-Be-Gone Nowgirl Violet Wild. In the Red Country, a story is a lot of words, one after the other, with conflict and resolution and a beginning, middle, and, most of the time, an end. But in the Blue Country, a story is a kind of dinosaur. You see how it gets confusing. I don't know whether to begin by saying: *Once upon a time a girl named Violet Wild rode a purple mammoth bareback through all the seven countries of world just to find a red dress that fit* or by shooting you right in that sweet spot between your reptilian skull-plates. It's a big decision. One false move and I'm breakfast.

I expect Red Rules are safer. They usually are. Here we go then! Rifle to the shoulder, adjust the crosshairs, stare down the barrel, don't dare breathe, don't move a muscle and—

Violet Wild is me. Just a kid with hair the color of raisins and eyes the color of grape jelly, living the life glasstastic in a four-bedroom wine bottle on the east end of Plum Pudding, the only electrified city in the Country of Purple. Bottle architecture was hotter than fried gold back then—and when the sunset slung itself against all those bright glass doors the bluffs just turned into a glitterbomb firework and everyone went staggering home with lavender light stuck to their coats. I got myself born like everybody else in P-Town: Mummery wrote a perfect sentence, so perfect and beautiful and fabulously punctuated that when she finished it, there was a baby floating in the ink pot and that was that. You have to be careful what you write in Plum Pudding. An accidentally glorious grocery list could net you twins. For this reason, the most famous novel in the Country of Purple begins: *It is a truth universally acknowledged, umbrella grouchy eggs.* I guess the author had too much to worry about already.

That was about the last perfect thing anybody did concerning myself. Oh, it was a fabulously punctuated life I had—Mums was a Clarinaut, Papo was a Nowboy, and you never saw a house more like a toybox than the bottle at 15 Portwine Place, chock full of gadgets and nonsense from parts unknown, art that came down off the walls for breakfast, visits from the Ordinary Emperor, and on some precious nights, gorgeous people in lavender suits and sweet potato ice cream gowns giggling through mouthfuls of mulberry schnapps over how much tastier were Orange Country cocktails and how much more belligerent were Green Country cockatiels. We had piles of carousel horse steaks and mugs of foamy creme de violette on our wide glass table every night. Trouble was, Mums was a Clarinaut and Papa was a Nowboy, so I mostly ate and drank it on my lonesome, or with the Sacred Sparrowbone Mask of the Incarnadine Fisherwomen and the watercolor unicorns from *Still Life with Banana Tree, Unicorns, and Murdered Tuba*, who came down off the living room wall some mornings in hopes of coffee and cereal with marshmallows. Mummery brought them back from her expeditions, landing her crystal clarinet, the good ship *Eggplant*, in the garden in a shower of prismy bubbles, her long arms full of poison darts, portraiture, explosives that look exactly like tea kettles, and lollipops that look exactly like explosives. And then she'd take off again, with a sort of confused-confounded glance down at me, as though every time she came home, it was a shock to remember that I'd ever been born.

"You could ask to go with her, you know," said the Sacred Sparrowbone Mask of the Incarnadine Fisherwomen once, tipping the spiral-swirl of her carved mouth toward a bowl of bruise-black coffee, careful to keep its scruff of bloodgull feathers combed back and out of the way.

"We agree," piped up the watercolor unicorns, nosing at a pillowcase I'd filled with marshmallow cereal for them. "You could be her First Mate, see the crass and colorful world by clarinet. It's romantic."

"You think everything's romantic," I sighed. Watercolor unicorns have hearts like soap operas that never end, and when they gallop it looks like crying. "But it wouldn't be. It would be like traveling with a snowman who keeps looking at you like you're a lit torch."

So I guess it's no surprise I went out to the herds with Papo as soon as I could. I could ride a pony by the time I got a handle on finger painting—great jeweled beasts escaped from some primeval carousel beyond the walls of time. There's a horn stuck all the way through them, bone or antler or both, and they leap across the Past Perfect Plains on it like a sharp white foot, leaving holes in the earth like ellipses. They're vicious and wily and they bite like it's their one passion in life, but they're the only horses strong and fast enough to ride down the present just as it's becoming the future and lasso it down. And in the Country of Purple, the minutes and hours of present-future-happening look an awful lot like overgrown pregnant six-legged mauve squirrels. They're pregnant all the time, but they never give birth, on account of how they're pregnant with tomorrow and a year from now and alternate universes where everyone is half-bat. When a squirrel comes to term, she just winks out like a squashed cigarette. That's the Nowboy life. Saddle up with the sun and bring in tomorrow's herd—or next week's or next decade's. If we didn't, those nasty little rodents would run wild all over the place. Plays would close three years before they open, Wednesdays would go on strike, and a century of Halloweens would happen all at once during one poor bedraggled lunch break. It's hard, dusty work, but Papo always says if you don't ride the present like the devil it'll get right away from you because it's a feral little creature with a terrible personality and no natural predators.

So that's who I was before the six-legged squirrels of the present turned around and spat in my face. I was called Violet and I lived in a purple world and I had ardors for my Papo, my magenta pony Stopwatch even though he bit me several times and once semi-fatally, a bone mask, and a watercolor painting. But I only loved a boy named Orchid Harm, who I haven't mentioned yet because when everything ever is about one thing, sometimes it's hard to name it. But let's be plain: I don't know what love is anymore, either. In the Red Country, when you say you love someone, it means you need them. You desire them. You look after them and yearn achingly for them when they're away down at the shops. But in the Country of Purple, when you say you love someone, it means you killed them. For a long time, that's what I thought it meant everywhere.

***

I ONLY EVER had one friend who was a person. His name was Orchid Harm. He could read faster than anyone I ever met and he kissed as fast as reading. He had hair the color of beetroot and eyes the color of mangosteen and he was a Sunslinger like his Papo before him. They caught sunshine in buckets all over Plum Pudding, mixed it with sugar and lorikeet eggs and fermented it into something not even a little bit legal. Orchid had nothing to do all day while the sun dripped down into his stills. He used to strap on a wash-basket full of books and shimmy up onto the roof of the opera house, which is actually a giantess's skull with moss and tourmalines living all over it, scoot down into the curve of the left eye-socket, and read seven books before twilight. No more, no less. He liked anything that came in sevens. I only came in ones, but he liked me anyway.

We met when his parents came to our bottle all covered in glitter and the smell of excitingly dodgy money to drink Mummery's schnapps and listen to Papo's Nowboy songs played on a real zanfona box with a squirrel-leg handle. It was a marquee night in Mummery's career—the Ordinary Emperor had promised to come, he who tells all our lives which way to run. Everyone kept peering at brandy snifters, tea kettles, fire pokers, bracelets, books on our high glass shelves. When—and where—would the Little Man make his entrance? *Oh, Mauve, do you remember, when he came to our to-do, he was my wife's left-hand glove, the one she'd lost in the chaise cushions months ago!*

And then a jar of dried pasta grew a face and said: "What a pleasure it is to see so many of my most illustrious subjects gathered all together in this fine home," but I didn't care because I was seven.

You see, the Ordinary Emperor can be anything he likes, as long as it's nothing you'd expect an Emperor to ever want to be. At any moment, anything you own could turn into the Emperor and he'd know everything you'd ever done with it—every mirror you'd ever hung and then cried in because you hated your own face, or candle you ever lit because you were up late doing something dastard, or worse, or better. It's unsettling and that's a fact.

Orchid was only little and so was I. While Mums cooed over the Emperor of Dried Pasta, I sat with my knees up by the hearth, feeding escargot to one of the watercolor unicorns. They can't get enough of escargot, even though it gives them horrible runny creamsicle-shits. This is the first thing Orchid ever said to me:

"I like your unicorn. Pink and green feel good on my eyes. I think I know who painted it but I don't want you to think I'm a know-it-all so I won't say even though I really *want* to say because I read a whole book about her and knowing things is nicer when somebody else knows you know them."

"I call her Jellyfish even though that's not her name. You can pet her but you have to let her smell your hand first. You can say who painted it if you want. Mums told me when she brought it home from Yellow Country, but I forgot." I didn't forget. I never got the hang of forgetting things the way other people do.

Orchid let Jellyfish snuffle his palm with her runny rosy nose.

"Do you have snails?" the watercolor unicorn asked. "They're very romantic."

Orchid didn't, but he had a glass of blackberry champagne because his parents let him drink what they drank and eat what they ate and read what they read and do what they did, which I thought was the best thing I had ever heard. Jellyfish slurped it up.

"A lady named Ochreous Wince painted me and the tuba and the banana tree and all my brothers and sisters about a hundred years ago, if you want to know. She was a drunk and she had a lot of dogs," Jellyfish sniffed when she was done, and jumped back up into her frame in a puff of rosewater smoke.

"Show me someplace that your parents don't know about," said Orchid. I took him to my room and made him crawl under my bed. It was stuffy and close down there, and I'm not very tidy. Orchid waited. He was good at waiting. I rolled over and pointed to the underside of my bed. On one of the slats I'd painted a single stripe of gold paint.

"Where?" he breathed. He put his hand on it. I put my hand on his.

"I stole it from Mummery's ship when she was busy being given the key to the city."

"She already lives here."

"I know."

After that, Orchid started going out with Papo and me sometimes, out beyond the city walls and onto the dry, flat Past Perfect Plains where the thousand squirrels that are every future and present and past scrabbled and screamed and thrashed their fluffy tails in the air. I shouldn't have let him, but knowing things is nicer when somebody else knows you know them. By the time the worst thing in the world happened, Orchid Harm could play *Bury Me on the Prairie with a Squirrel in my Fist* on the zanfona box as well as Papo or me. He helped a blackberry-colored mare named Early-to-Tea get born and she followed him around like a lovesick tiger, biting his shoulders and hopping in circles until he gave up and learned to ride her.

I don't want to say this part. I wish this were the kind of story that's a blue dinosaur munching up blueberries with a brain in its head and a brain in its tail so it never forgets how big it is. But I have to or the rest of it won't make sense. Okay, calm down, I'm doing it. Rifle up.

The day of the worst thing in the world was long and hot and bright, packed so full of summer autumn seeped out through the stitches. We'd ridden out further than usual—the ponies ran like they had thorns in their bellies and the stupid squirrels kept going at each other like mad, whacking their purple heads together and tail-wrestling and spitting paradoxes through clenched teeth. I wanted to give them some real space, something fresh to graze on. Maybe if they ate enough they'd just lay down in the heat and hold their little bellies in their paws and concentrate on breathing like any sane animal. Papo stayed behind to see to a doe mewling and foaming at the mouth, trying to pass a chronology stone. She kept coughing up chunks of the Ordinary Emperor's profligate youth, his wartime speeches and night terrors echoing out of her rodent-mouth across the prairie.

We rode so far, Orchid and me, bouncing across the cracked purple desert on Stopwatch and Early-to-Tea, that we couldn't even see the lights of Plum Pudding anymore, couldn't see anything but the plains spreading out like an inkstain. That far into the wilds, the world wasn't really purple anymore. It turned to indigo, the dark, windy borderlands where the desert looks like an ocean and the twisted-up trees are the color of lightning. And then, just when I was about to tell Orchid how much I liked the shadow of his cheekbones by indigo light, the Blue Country happened, right in front of us. That's the only way I can say it where it seems right to me. I'd never seen a border before. Somehow I always thought there would be a wall, or guards with spears and pom-poms on their shoes, or at least a sign. But it was just a line in the land, and on this side everything was purple and on that side everything was blue. The earth was still thirsty and spidered up with fine cracks like a soft boiled egg just before you stick your spoon in, but instead of the deep indigo night-steppe or the bright purple pampas, long aquamarine salt flats stretched out before us, speckled with blueberry brambles and sapphire tumbleweeds and skittering blue crabs. The Blue Country smelled like hot corn and cold snow. All the mauve time-squirrels skidded up short, sniffing the blue-indigo line suspiciously.

We let Stopwatch and Early-to-Tea bounce off after the crabs. The carousel ponies roared joyfully and hopped to it, skewering the cerulean crustacean shells with their bone poles, each gnawing the meat and claws off the other's spike. The sun caromed off the gems on their rump. Orchid and I just watched the blue.

"Didn't you ever want to see this, Violet? Go to all other places that exist in the universe, like your Mummery?" he said at last. "Didn't you ever watch her clarinet take off and feel like you'd die if you didn't see what she saw? I feel like I'll die if I don't see something new. Something better than sunshine in a bucket."

Off in the distance, I could see a pack of stories slurping at a watering hole, their long spine-plates standing against the setting sun like broken fences.

"Do you want to know a secret?" I said. I didn't wait for him to answer. Orchid always wanted to know secrets. "I dream in gold. When I'm asleep I don't even know what purple is. And one time I actually packed a suitcase and went to the train station and bought a ticket to the Yellow Country with money I got from selling all my chess sets. But when I got there and the conductor was showing me to my seat I just knew how proud Mums would be. I could see her stupid face telling her friends about her daughter running off on an adventure. *Darling, the plum doesn't fall far from the tree, don't you know? Violet's just like a little photograph of me, don't you think? Well, the point is: fuck her, I guess.*"

"You were going to go without me?"

And my guts were full of shame, because I hadn't even thought of him that day, not when I put on my stockings or my hat, not when I marched into a taxi and told him to take me to Heliotrope Station, not when I bought my ticket for one. I just wanted to *go*. Which meant I was a little photograph of her, after all. I kissed him, to make it better. We liked kissing. We'd discovered it together. We'd discussed it and we were fairly certain no one in the world did it as well as we did. When Orchid and me kissed, we always knew what the other was thinking, and just then we knew that the other was thinking that we had two horses and could go now, right now, across the border and through the crabs and blueberries and stories and hot corn air. We'd read in our books, curled up together, holding hands and feet, in the eye socket of the opera house, that all the fish in the Blue Country could talk, and all the people had eyes the color of peacock feathers, and you could make babies by singing an aria so perfectly that when you were done, there would be a kid in the sheet music, and that would be that, so *The Cyan Sigh* can never be performed on-key unless the soprano is ready for responsibility. And in the Blue Country, all the cities were electrified, just like us.

We were happy and we were going to run away together. So the squirrels ate him.

Orchid and I jumped over the border like a broomstick and when our feet came down the squirrels screeched and rushed forward, biting our heels, slashing our legs with their six clawed feet, spitting bile in our faces. Well, I thought it was our faces, our heels, our legs. I thought they were gunning for both of us. But it was Orchid they wanted. The squirrels slashed open his ankles so he'd fall down to their level, and then they bit off his fingers. I tried to pull and kick them off but there were so many, and you can't kill a plains-squirrel. You just can't. You might stab the rest of your life. You might break a half-bat universe's neck. You might end the whole world. I lay over Orchid so they couldn't get to him but all that meant was they dug out one of my kidneys and I was holding him when they chewed out his throat and I kissed him because when we kissed we always knew what the other was thinking and I don't want to talk about this anymore.

## 2: Blue

PAPO NEVER SAID anything. Neither did I. Jellyfish and the other watercolor unicorns each cut off a bit of their tails and stuck them together to make a watercolor orchid in the bottom left corner of the painting. It looked like a five-year old with a head injury drew it with her feet and it ruined the whole composition. Orcheous Wince would have sicced her dogs on it. But no matter how Mummery fumed, they wouldn't put their tails back where they belonged. The Sacred Sparrowbone Mask of the Incarnadine Fisherwomen just said: "I like being a mask better than I'd like being a face, I think. But if you want, you can put me on and I'll be your face if you don't want anyone to see what you look like on the inside right now. Because everyone can see."

Orchid's father gave me a creme-pot full of sunslung booze. I went up to the eye socket of the opera house and drank and drank but the pot never seemed to dry up. Good. Everything had a shine on it when I drank the sun. Everything had a heart that only I could see. Everything tasted like Orchid Harm, because he always tasted like the whole of the sun.

Once, I rode out on Stopwatch across the indigo borderlands again, up to the line in the earth where it all goes blue. I could see, I thought I could see, the haze of cornflower light over Lizard Tongue, the city that started as a wedding two hundred years ago and the party just never stopped. Stopwatch turned his big magenta head around and bit my hand—but softly. Hardly a bite at all.

I looked down. All the squirrels, pregnant with futures and purple with the present, thousands of them, stood on their hind legs around my pony's spike, staring up at me in silence like the death of time.

THE DAY THE rest of it happened, the squirrels were particularly depraved. I caught three shredding each other's bellies to ribbons behind a sun-broiled rock, blood and fur and yesterdays everywhere. I tried to pull them apart but I didn't try very hard because I never did anymore. They all died anyway, and I got long scratches all up and down my arms for my trouble. I'd have to go and get an inoculation. Half of them are rabid and the other half are lousy with regret. I looked at my arms, already starting to scab up. I am a champion coagulator. All the way home I picked them open again and again. So I didn't notice anyone following me back into P-Town, up through the heights and the sunset on the wine bottle houses, through the narrow lilac streets while the plummy streetlamps came on one at a time. I was almost home before I heard the other footsteps. The bells of St. Murex bonged out their lonely moans and I could almost hear Mummery's voice, rich as soup, laughing at her own jokes by the glass hearth. But I did hear, finally, a sound, a such-soft sound, like a girl's hair falling, as it's cut, onto a floor of ice. I turned around and saw a funny little beastie behind me, staring at me with clear lantern-fish eyes.

The thing looked some fair bit like a woolly mammoth, if a mammoth could shrink down to the size of a curly wolfhound, with long indigo fur that faded into pale, pale lavender, almost white, over its four feet and the tip of its trunk, which curled up into the shape of a question mark. But on either side, where a mammoth would have flanks and ribs and the bulge of its elephant belly, my creeper had cabinet doors, locked tight, the color of dark cabbages with neat white trim and silver hinges. I looked at my Sorrow and it looked at me. Our dark eyes were the same eyes, and that's how I knew it was mine.

"I love you," it said.

But Mummery said: "Don't you dare let that thing in the house." She was home for once, so she thought she could make rules. "It's filthy; I won't have it. Look how it's upsetting the unicorns!" The poor things were snorting and stampeding terribly in their frame, squashing watercolor bananas as they tumbled off the watercolor tree.

"Let it sleep in the garden, Mauve. Come back to me," said a box of matchsticks, for Mums was busy that night, being very important and desirable company. She was entertaining the Ordinary Emperor alone. I peered over into the box—every matchstick was carved in the shape of a tiny man with a shock of blue sulfuric hair that would strike on any surface. When he was here last month, the Ordinary Emperor was our downstairs hammer. I think the Ordinary Emperor wanted to seduce my mother. He showed up a lot during the mating season when Papo slept out on the range.

"What on earth *is* it?" sniffed Mummery, lifting a flute of mulberry schnapps to her lips as though nobody had ever died in the history of the world.

"Light me, my darling," cried the Ordinary Emperor, and she did, striking his head on the mantel and bringing him in close to the tiny mammoth's face. It didn't blink or cringe away, even though it had a burning monarch and a great dumb Mummery-face right up against its trunk.

"Why, it's a Sorrow," the Ordinary Emperor whistled. "I thought they were extinct. I told them to be extinct ages ago. Naughty Nellies. Do you know, in the Red Country, sorrow means grief and pain and horror and loss? It's a decadent place. Everything tastes like cranberries, even the roast beef."

That was the first thing the Ordinary Emperor ever said to me alone. Mums knew very well what sorrow meant where the sun sets red. Then he said a second thing:

"You are more beautiful than your mother."

That's the kind of Emperor the Matchstick Man is, in seven words. But Mummery fell for it and glowered at me with her great famous moonshadow eyes.

But my sorrow was not extinct. My sorrow was hungry. I put it out in the garden and locked the fence. I filled an agate bowl with the mushrooms we grow on the carcass of a jacaranda tree that used to grow by the kitchen window and water from our private well. I meant to leave it to its dinner, but for whatever reason my body ever decides to do things, I sat down with it instead, in the shadow of Mummery's crystal clarinet, parked between the roses and the lobelias. The breeze made soft, half-melodic notes as it blew over the *Eggplant*'s portholes. A few iridescent fuel-bubbles popped free of the bell.

My sorrow ate so daintily, picking up each lacecap mushroom with its trunk, turning it around twice, and placing it on its outstretched ultraviolet tongue. It couldn't get its mouth in the right place to drink. I cupped my hands and dipped them into the clear water and held them up to my sorrow. Its tongue slipped against my palms three times as it lapped. I stroked my sorrow's fur and we watched the garden wall come alive with moonflowers opening like pale happy mouths in the night wind off of the Cutglass River. My sorrow was soft as fish frills. I didn't want to hurt its pride by looking, so I decided she was a girl, like me.

"I love you," my sorrow said, and she put her soft mouth over my ravaged arms. She opened the wounds again with her tongue and licked up the purple blood that seeped out of the depths of me. I kept stroking her spine and the warm wood of the cabinet doors in her belly. I pulled gently at their handles, but they would not open.

"It's okay if you love me," I whispered. "I forgive you."

But she didn't love me, not then, or not enough. I woke up in the morning in my own bed. My sorrow slept curled into the curve of my sleep. When she snored it sounded like the river-wind blowing over my mother's ship. I tried to get up. But the floor of my bedroom was covered in sleeping squirrels, a mauve blanket of a hundred unhappened futures. When I put my bare feet on the floor, they scattered like buckshot.

---

I CAME DOWNSTAIRS reeking of sorrowmusk and futureshit. Mummery was already gone; Papo had never come home. Instead of anyone who lived with me, a stranger stood in our kitchen, fixing himself coffee. He was short but very slim and handsome, shaven, with brilliant hair of every color, even green, even burgundy, even gold, tied back with one of my velvet ribbons. He wore a doublet and hose like an actor or a lawyer, and when he turned to search for the cream, I could see a beautiful chest peeking out from beneath an apricot silk shirt. The unfamiliar colors of him made my eyes throb, painfully, then hungrily, starving for his emerald, his orange, his cobalt, even his brown and black. His gold. The stranger noticed me suddenly, fixing his eyes, the same shocking spatter of all possible colors as his hair, on my face.

"You're naked," I said before I could remember to be polite. I don't know how I knew it, but I did. I had caught the Ordinary Emperor naked, unhidden in any oddjob object, the morning after he'd probably ridden Mummery like Stopwatch.

One imperial eyebrow lifted in amusement.

"So are you," he said.

I don't sleep with clothes on. I don't see why I should strangle myself in a nightdress just so my dreams won't see my tits. I think his majesty expected me to blush and cover myself with my hands, but I didn't care. If Orchid could never see my skin again, what did it matter who else did? So we stood there, looking at each other like stories at a watering hole. The Ordinary Emperor had an expression on that only people like Mummery understand, the kind of unplain stare that carries a hundred footnotes to its desire.

The king blinked first. He vanished from the kitchen and became our chandelier. Every teardrop-shaped jewel was an eye, every lightbulb was a mouth. I looked up at the blaze of him and drank his coffee. He took it sweet, mostly cream and honey, with only a lash of coffee hiding somewhere in the thick of it.

"Defiant girl, who raised you?" hissed the Sacred Sparrowbone Mask of the Incarnadine Fisherwomen.

"You know who," I snorted, and even the chandelier laughed.

"Good morning, Violet," the lightbulbs said, flashing blue, garnet, lime green with each word. "If you give me your sorrow, I shall see it safely executed. They are pests, like milkweed or uncles. You are far too young and lovely to have a boil like that leaking all over your face."

I looked down. My sorrow had followed me without the smallest sound, and sat on her haunches beside my feet, staring up at me with those deepwater eyes. I held out the Emperor's coffee cup so she could sip.

"Do you really know everything that happens in all your countries?" I asked him. There really is nothing like a man hopping on top of your mother to make him seem altogether less frightening and a little pitiful.

"I don't know it all at once. But if I *want* to know it, I can lean toward it and it will lean toward me and then I know it better than you know your favorite lullaby." The Ordinary Emperor burned so brightly in our chandelier. Light bloomed out of the crystals, hot, dappled, harlequin light, pouring down onto my skin, turning me all those colors, all his spun-sugar patchwork. I didn't like it. His light on me felt like hands. It burned me; it clutched me, it petted me like a cat. I loved it. I was drowning in my dream of gold. My bones creaked for more. I wanted to wash it off forever.

I closed my eyes. I could still see the prisms of the Emperor. "What does death mean in the Red Country?" I whispered.

"It is a kind of dress with a long train that trails behind it and a neckline that plunges to the navel. Death is the color of garnets and is very hard to dance in." The eyes in my chandelier looked kind. We have a dress like that, too. It is the color of hyacinths and it is called need. "I know what you're asking, darling. And if you go to the Red Country you may find Orchid laughing there and wearing a red dress. It is possible. The dead here often go there, to Incarnadine, where the fisherwomen punt along the Rubicund, fishing for hope. The Red Country is not for you, Violet. The dead are very exclusive."

And then I said it, to the king of everything, the hope buried under the concrete at the bottom of me: "Doesn't it seem to you that a body eaten by the present becoming the future shouldn't really be dead? Shouldn't he just be waiting for me in tomorrow?"

"That I cannot tell you. It doesn't make much sense to me, though. Eaten is eaten. Your pampas squirrels are not my subjects. They are not my countries. They are time, and time eats everything but listens to no one. The digestive systems of squirrels are unreliable at best. I know it is painful to hear, but time devours all love affairs. It is unavoidable. The Red Country is so much larger than the others. And you, Violet Wild, you specifically, do not have rights of passage through any of my nations. Stay put and do as your Mummery tells you. You are such a trial to her, you know."

The Ordinary Emperor snuffed abruptly out and the wine bottle went dark. The watercolor unicorns whinnied fearfully. The Sacred Sparrowbone Mask of the Incarnadine Fisherwomen turned its face to the wall. In the shallow cup of her other side, a last mauve squirrel hid away, one lone holdout from the great exodus from my bedroom. She held her tail up over her little face and whispered:

"I won't say even though I really want to say."

My sorrow tugged my fingers with her trunk. "I love you," she said again, and this time I shivered. I believed her, and I did not live in the Red Country where love means longing. "If you let me, I can be so big."

My sorrow twisted her trunk around her own neck and squeezed. She grew like a wetness spreading through cloth. Taller than me, and then taller than the cabinets, and then taller than the chandelier. She lowered her purple trunk to me like a ladder.

---

I DON'T KNOW what stories are anymore. I don't know how fast sorrow can move and I don't know how squirrels work. But I am wearing my best need and a bone face over mine so no one can see what my insides look like. I can see already the blue crabs waving their claws to the blue sky, I can see the lights of Lizard Tongue and hear the wedding bells playing their millionth song. I am going on the back of my sorrow, further than Mummery ever did, to a place where love is love, stories have ends, and death is a red dress.

A stream of rabid, pregnant, time-squirrels race after me. I hope the crabs get them all.

### 3. Green

THE PLACE BETWEEN the Blue Country and the Green Country is full of dinosaurs called stories, bubble-storms that make you think you're somebody else, and a sky and a ground that look almost exactly the same. And, for a little while, it was full of me. My sorrow and me and the Sparrowbone Mask of the Incarnadine Fisherwomen crossed the Blue Country where it gets all narrow and thirsty. I was also all narrow and thirsty, but between the two of us, I complained less than the Blue Country. I shut my eyes when we stepped over the border. I shut my eyes and tried to remember kissing Orchid Harm and knowing that we were both thinking about ice cream.

When I was little and my hair hadn't grown out yet but my piss-and-vinegar had, I asked my Papo:

"Papo, will I ever meet a story?"

My Papo took a long tug on his squirrel-bone pipe and blew smoky lilac rings onto my fingers.

"Maybe-so, funny bunny, maybe-not-so. But don't be sad if you don't. Stories are pretty dumb animals. And so aggressive!"

I clapped my hands. "Say three ways they're dumb!"

"Let's see." Papo counted them off on his fingers. "They're cold-blooded, they use big words when they ought to use small ones, and they have no natural defense against comets."

So that's what I was thinking about while my sorrow and me hammered a few tent stakes into the huge blue night. We made camp at the edge of a sparkling oasis where the water looked like liquid labradorite. The reason I thought about my Papo was because the oasis was already *occupado*. A herd of stories slurped up the water and munched up the blueberry brambles and cobalt cattails growing up all over the place out of the aquamarine desert. The other thing that slurped and munched and stomped about the oasis was the great electro-city of Lizard Tongue. The city limits stood a ways off, but clearly Lizard Tongue crept closer all the time. Little houses shaped like sailboats and parrot eggs spilled out of the metropolis, inching toward the water, inching, inching—nobody look at them or they'll stampede! I could hear the laughing and dancing of the city and I didn't want to laugh and I didn't want to dance and sleeping on the earth never troubled me so I stuck to my sorrow and the water like a flat blue stone.

It's pretty easy to make a camp with a sorrow as tall as a streetlamp, especially when you didn't pack anything from home. I did that on purpose. I hadn't decided yet if it was clever or stupid as sin. I didn't have matches or food or a toothbrush or a pocketknife. But the Ordinary Emperor couldn't come sneaking around impersonating my matches or my beef jerky or my toothbrush or my pocketknife, either. I was safe. I was Emperor-proof. I was not squirrel-proof. The mauve squirrels of time and/or space milled and tumbled behind us like a stupid furry wave of yesterpuke and all any of us could do was ignore them while they did weird rat-cartwheels and chittered at each other, which sounds like the ticks of an obnoxiously loud clock, and fucked with their tails held over their eyes like blindfolds in the blue-silver sunset.

My sorrow picked turquoise coconuts from the paisley palm trees with her furry lavender trunk and lined up the nuts neatly all in a row. Sorrows are very fastidious, as it turns out.

"A storm is coming at seven minutes past seven," the Sparrowbone Mask of the Incarnadine Fisherwomen said. "I do not like to get wet."

I collected brambles and crunched them up for kindling. In order to crunch up brambles, I had to creep and sneak among the stories, and that made me nervous, because of what Papo said when my hair was short.

A story's scales are every which shade of blue you can think of and four new ones, too. I tiptoed between them, which was like tiptoeing between trolley-cars. I tried to avoid the poison spikes on their periwinkle tails and the furious horns on their navy blue heads and the crystal sapphire plates on their backs. The setting sun shone through their sapphire plates and burned up my eyeballs with blue.

"Heyo, guignol-girl!" One story swung round his dinosaur-head at me and smacked his chompers. "Why so skulk and slither? Have you scrofulous aims on our supper?"

"Nope, I only want to make a fire," I said. "We'll be gone in the morning."

"Ah, conflagration," the herd nodded sagely all together. "The best of all the -ations."

"And whither do you peregrinate, young sapiens sapiens?" said one of the girl-dinosaurs. You can tell girl-stories apart from boy-stories because girl-stories have webbed feet and two tongues.

I was so excited I could have chewed rocks for bubblegum. Me, Violet Wild, talking to several real live stories all at once. "I'm going to the Red Country," I said. "I'm going to the place where death is a red dress and love is a kind of longing and maybe a boy named Orchid didn't get his throat ripped out by squirrels."

"We never voyage to the Red Country. We find no affinity there. We are allowed no autarchy of spirit."

"We cannot live freely," explained the webfooted girl-story, even though I knew what autarchy meant. What was I, a baby eating paint? "They pen us up in scarlet corrals and force us to say exactly what we mean. It's deplorable."

"Abhorrent."

"Iniquitous!"

The stories were working themselves up into a big blue fury. I took a chance. I grew up a Nowgirl on the purple pampas, I'm careful as a crook on a balcony when it comes to animals. I wouldn't like to spook a story. When your business is wildness and the creatures who own it, you gotta be cool, you gotta be able to act like a creature, talk like a creature, make a creature feel like you're their home and the door's wide open.

"Heyo, Brobdingnagian bunnies," I said with all the sweetness I knew how to make with my mouth. "No quisquoses or querulous tristiloquies." I started to sweat and the stars started to come out. I was already almost out of good words. "Nobody's going to…uh…ravish you off to Red and rapine. Pull on your tranquilities one leg at a time. Listen to the…um…psithurisma? The psithurisma of the…vespertine…trees rustling, eat your comestibles, get down with dormition."

The stories milled around me, purring, rubbing their flanks on me, getting their musk all over my clothes. And then I had to go lie down because those words tired me right out. I don't even know if all of them were really words but I remembered Mummery saying all of them at one point or another to this and that pretty person with a pretty name.

My sorrow lay down in the moonlight. I leaned against her furry indigo chest. She spat on the brambles and cattails I crunched up and they blazed up purple and white. I didn't know a sorrow could set things on fire.

"I love you," my sorrow said.

In the Blue Country, when you say you love someone it means you want to eat them. I knew that because when I thought about

Orchid Harm on the edge of the oasis with water like labradorite all I could think of was how good his skin tasted when I kissed it; how sweet and savory his mouth had always been, how even his bones would probably taste like sugar, how even his blood would taste like hot cocoa. I didn't like those thoughts but they were in my head and I couldn't not have them. That was what happened to my desire in the Blue Country. The blue leaked out all over it and I wanted to swallow Orchid. He would be okay inside me. He could live in my liver. I would take care of him. I would always be full.

But Orchid wasn't with me which is probably good for him as I have never been good at controlling myself when I have an ardor. My belly growled but I didn't bring anything to eat on account of not wanting an Emperor-steak, medium-rare, so it was coconut delight on a starlit night with the bubbles coming in. In the Blue Country, the bubbles gleam almost black. They roll in like dark dust, an iridescent wall of go-fuck-yourself, a soft, ticklish tsunami of heart-killing gases. I didn't know that then but I know it now. The bubble-storm covered the blue plains and wherever a bubble popped something invisible leaked out, something to do with memory and the organs that make you feel things even when you would rather play croquet with a plutonium mallet than feel one more drop of anything at all. The blue-bruise-black-bloody bubbles tumbled and popped and burst and glittered under the ultramarine stars and I felt my sorrow's trunk around my ankle which was good because otherwise I think I would probably have floated off or disappeared.

People came out of the houses shaped like sailboats and the houses shaped like parrot eggs. They held up their hands like little kids in the bubble-monsoon. Bubbles got stuck in their hair like flowers, on their fingers like rings. I'd never seen a person who looked like those people. They had hair the color of tropical fish and skin the color of a spring sky and the ladies wore cerulean dresses with blue butterflies all over them and the boys wore midnight waistcoats and my heart turned blue just looking at them.

"Heyo, girlie!" the blue people called, waggling their blue fingers in the bubbly night. "Heyo, elephant and mask! Come dance with us! Cornflower Leap and Pavonine Up are getting married! You don't even have any blueberry schnapps!"

Because of the bubbles popping all over me I stopped being sure who I was. The bubbles smelled like a skull covered in moss and tourmalines. Their gasses tasted like coffee with too much milk and sugar left by an Emperor on a kitchen counter inside a wine bottle.

"Cornflower Leap and Pavonine Up are dead, dummies," I said, but I said it wrong somehow because I wasn't Violet Wild anymore but rather a bubble and inside the bubble of me I was turning into a box of matchsticks. Or Orchid Harm. Or Mummery. I heard clarinets playing the blues. I heard my bones getting older. "They got dead two hundred years ago, you're just too drunk to remember when their wedding grew traffic laws and sporting teams and turned into a city."

One of the blue ladies opened her mouth right up and ate a bubble out of the air on purpose and I decided she was the worst because who would do that? "So what?" she giggled. "They're still getting married! Don't be such a drip. How did a girlie as young as you get to be a drip as droopy as you?"

People who are not purple are baffling.

You better not laugh but I danced with the blue people. Their butterflies landed on me. When they landed on me they turned violet like my body and my name but they didn't seem upset about it. The whole world looked like a black rainbow bubble. It was the opposite of drinking the sun that Orchid's family brewed down in their slipstills. When I drink the sun, I feel soft and edgeless. When the bubbles rained down on me I felt like I was made of edges all slicing themselves up and the lights of Lizard Tongue burned up my whole brain and while I was burning I was dancing and while I was dancing I was the Queen of the Six-Legged squirrels. They climbed up over me in between the black bubbles. Some of them touched the turquoise butterflies and when they did that they turned blue and after I could always tell which of the squirrels had been with me that night because their fur never got purple again, not even a little.

I fell down dancing and burning. I fell down on the cracked cobalt desert. A blue lady in a periwinkle flapper dress whose hair was the color of the whole damn ocean tried to get me to sit up like I was some sad sack of nothing at Mummery's parties who couldn't hold her schnapps.

"Have you ever met anyone who stopped being dead?" I asked her.

"Nobody blue," she said.

I felt something underneath me. A mushy, creamy, silky something. A something like custard with a crystal heart. I rolled over and my face made a purple print in the blue earth and when I rolled over I saw Jellyfish looking shamefaced, which she should have done because stowaways should not look proudfaced, ever.

"I ate a bunch of bleu cheese at the wedding buffet in the town square and now my tummy hates me," the watercolor unicorn mourned.

One time Orchid Harm told me a story about getting married and having kids and getting a job somewhere with no squirrels or prohibited substances. It seemed pretty unrealistic to me. Jellyfish and I breathed in so much blackish-brackish bubble-smoke that we threw up together, behind a little royal blue dune full of night-blooming lobelia flowers. When we threw up, that story came out and soaked into the ground. My sorrow picked us both up in her trunk and carried us back to the fire.

The last thing I said before I fell asleep was: "What's inside your cabinet?"

The only answer I got was the sound of a lock latching itself and a squirrel screeching because sorrow stepped on it.

WHEN I WOKE up the Blue Country had run off. The beautiful baffling blue buffoons and the black bubbles and the pompous stories had legged it, too.

Green snow fell on my hair. It sparkled in my lap and there was a poisonous barb from the tail of a story stuck to the bottom of my shoe. I pulled it off very carefully and hung it from my belt. My hand turned blue where I'd held it and it was always blue forever and so I never again really thought of it as my hand.

## 4. Yellow

SOMETIMES I GET so mad at Mummery. She never told me anything important. Oh, sure, she taught me how to fly a clarinet and how much a lie weighs and how to shoot her stained-glass Nonegun like a champ. *Of course, you can plot any course you like on a clarinet, darlingest, but the swiftest and most fuel efficient is Premiére Rhapsodie by Debussy in A Major.* Ugh! Who needs to know the fuel efficiency of Debussy? Mummery toot-tooted her long glass horn all over the world and she never fed me one little spoonful of it when I was starving to death for anything other than our old awful wine bottle in Plum Pudding. What did Mummery have to share about the Green Country? *I enjoyed the saunas in Verdigris, but Absinthe is simply lousy with loyalty. It's a serious problem.* That's nothing! That's rubbish, is what. Especially if you know that in the Green Country, loyalty is a type of street mime.

The Green Country is frozen solid. Mummery, if only you'd said one useful thing, I'd have brought a thicker coat. Hill after hill of green snow under a chartreuse sky. But trees still grew and they still gave fruit—apples and almonds and mangoes and limes and avocados shut up in crystal ice pods, hanging from branches like party lanterns. People with eyes the color of mint jelly and hair the color of unripe bananas, wearing knit olive caps with sage poms on the ends zoomed on jade toboggans, up and down and everywhere, or else they skate on green glass rivers, ever so many more than in the Blue Country. Green people never stop moving or shivering. My sorrow slipped and slid and stumbled on the lime-green ice. Jellyfish and

I held on for dear life. The Sparrowbone Mask of the Incarnadine Fisherwomen clung to my face, which I was happy about because otherwise I'd have had green frost growing on my teeth.

One time Orchid Harm and I went up to the skull socket of the opera house and read out loud to each other from a book about how to play the guitar. It never mattered what we read about really, when we read out loud to each other. We just liked to hear our voices go back and forth like a seesaw. *Most popular songs are made up of three or four or even two simple chords*, whispered Orchid seductively. *Let us begin with the D chord, which is produced by holding the fingers thusly.* And he put his fingers on my throat like mine was the neck of a guitar. And suddenly a terror happened inside me, a terror that Orchid must be so cold, so cold in my memory of the skull socket and the D chord and cold wherever he might be and nothing mattered at all but that I had to warm him up, wrap him in fur or wool or lay next to him skin to skin, build a fire, the biggest fire that ever wrecked a hearth, anything if it would get him warm again. Hot. Panic went zigzagging through all my veins. We had to go faster.

"We'll go to Absinthe," I said shakily, even though I didn't know where Absinthe was because I had a useless Mummery. I told the panic to sit down and shut up. "We need food and camping will be a stupid experience here."

"I love you," said my sorrow, and her legs grew like the legs of a telescope, longer even than they had already. The bottoms of her fuzzy hippo-feet flattened out like pancakes frying in butter until they got as wide as snowshoes. A sorrow is a resourceful beast. Nothing stops sorrow, not really. She took the snowy glittering emerald hills two at a stride. Behind us the army of squirrels flowed like the train of a long violet gown. Before us, toboggan-commuters ran and hid.

"In the Green Country, when you say you love somebody, it means you will keep them warm even if you have to bathe them in your own blood," Jellyfish purred. Watercolor unicorns can purr, even though real unicorns can't. Jellyfish rubbed her velvety peach and puce horn against my sorrow's spine.

"How do you know that?"

"Ocherous Wince, the drunken dog-lover who painted me, also painted a picture more famous than me. Even your Mummery couldn't afford it. It's called *When I Am In Love My Heart Turns Green*. A watercolor lady with watercolor wings washes a watercolor salamander with the blood pouring out of her wrists and her elbows. The salamander lies in a bathtub that is a sawn-open lightbulb with icicles instead of clawfeet. It's the most romantic thing I ever saw. I know a lot of things because of Ocherous Wince, but I never like to say because I don't want you to think I'm a know-it-all even though I really *want* to say because knowing things is nicer when somebody else knows you know them."

Absinthe sits so close to the border of the Yellow Country that half the day is gold and half the day is green. Three brothers sculpted the whole city—houses, pubs, war monuments—out of jellybean-colored ice with only a little bit of wormwood for stability and character. I didn't learn that from Jellyfish or Mummery, but from a malachite sign on the highway leading into the city. The brothers were named Peapod. They were each missing their pinky fingers but not for the same reason.

It turns out everybody notices you when you ride into town on a purple woolly mammoth with snowshoes for feet with a unicorn in your lap and a bone mask on your face. I couldn't decide if I liked being invisible better or being watched by everybody all at once. They both hurt. Loyalties scattered before us like pigeons, their pale green greasepainted faces miming despair or delight or umbrage, depending on their schtick. They mimed tripping over each other, and then some actually did trip, and soon we'd caused a mime-jam and I had to leave my sorrow parked in the street. I was so hungry I could barely shiver in the cold. Jellyfish knew a cafe called O Tannenbaum but I didn't have any money.

"That's all right," said the watercolor unicorn. "In the Green Country, money means grief."

So I paid for a pine-green leather booth at O Tannenbaum, a stein of creme de menthe, a mugwort cake and parakeet pie with tears. The waiter wore a waistcoat of clover with moldavite buttons. He held out his hands politely. I didn't think I could do it. You can't just grieve because the bill wants 15% agony on top of the prix fixe. But my grief happened to me like a back alley mugging and I put my face into his hands so no one would see my sobbing; I put my face into his hands like a bone mask so no one could see what I looked like on the inside.

"I'm so lonely," I wept. "I'm nobody but a wound walking around." I lifted my head—my head felt heavier than a planet. "Did you ever meet anyone who fucked up and put it all right again, put it all back the way it was?"

"Nobody green," said the waiter, but he walked away looking very pleased with his tip.

It's a hard damn thing when you're feeling lowly to sit in a leather booth with nobody but a unicorn across from you. Lucky for me, a squirrel hopped up on the bamboo table. She sat back on her hind two legs and rubbed her humongous paradox-pregnant belly with the other four paws. Her bushy mauve tail stood at attention behind her, bristling so hard you could hear it crackling.

"Pink and green feel good on my eyes," the time-squirrel said in Orchid Harm's voice.

"Oh, go drown yourself in a hole," I spat at it, and drank my creme de menthe, which gave me a creme de menthe mustache that completely undermined much of what I said later.

The squirrel tried again. She opened her mouth and my voice came out.

"No quisquoses or querulous tristiloquies," she said soothingly. But I had no use for a squirrel's soothe.

"Eat shit," I hissed.

But that little squirrel was the squirrel who would not quit. She rubbed her cheeks and stretched her jaw and out came a voice I did not know, a man's voice, with a very expensive accent.

"The Red Country is the only country with walls. It stands to reason something precious lives there. But short of all-out war, which I think we can all agree is at least inconvenient, if not irresponsible, we cannot know what those walls conceal. I would suggest espionage, if we can find a suitable candidate."

Now, I don't listen to chronosquirrels. They're worse than toddlers. They babble out things that got themselves said a thousand months ago or will be said seventy years from now or were only said by a praying mantis wearing suspenders in a universe that's already burned itself out. When I was little I used to listen, but my Papo spanked me and told me the worst thing in the world was for a Nowboy to listen to his herd. *It'll drive you madder than a plate of snakes*, he said. He never spanked me for anything else and that's how I know he meant serious business. But this dopey doe also meant serious business. I could tell by her tail. And I probably would have gotten into it with her, which may or may not have done me a lick of good, except that I'd made a mistake without even thinking about it, without even brushing off a worry or a grain of dread, and just at that moment when I was about to tilt face first into Papo's plate of snakes, the jade pepper grinder turned into a jade Emperor with black peppercorn lips and a squat silver crown.

"Salutations, young Violet," said the Ordinary Emperor in a voice like a hot cocktail. "What's a nice purple girl like you doing in a bad old green place like this?"

Jellyfish shrieked. When a unicorn shrieks, it sounds like sighing. I just stared. I'd been so careful. The Emperor of Peppercorns hopped across the table on his grinder. The mauve squirrel patted his crown with one of her hands. They were about the same height. I shook my head and declined to say several swear words.

"Don't feel bad, Miss V," he said. "It's not possible to live without objects. Why do you think I do things this way? Because I enjoy being hand brooms and cheese-knives?"

"Leave me alone," I moaned.

"Now, I just heard you say you were lonely! You don't have to be lonely. None of my subjects have to be lonely! It was one of my campaign promises, you know."

"Go back to Mummery. Mind your own business."

The Ordinary Emperor stroked his jade beard. "I think you liked me better when I was naked in your kitchen. I can do it again, if you like. I want you to like me. That is the cornerstone of my administration."

"No. Be a pepper grinder. Be a broom."

"Your Papo cannot handle the herd by himself, señorita," clucked the Ordinary Emperor. "You've abandoned him. Midnight comes at 3 p.m. in Plum Pudding. Every day is Thursday. Your Mummery has had her clarinet out day and night looking for you."

"Papo managed before I was born, he can manage now. And you could have told Mums I was fine."

"I could have. I know what you're doing. It's a silly, old-fashioned thing, but it's just so *you*. I've written a song about it, you know. I called it *My Baby Done Gone to Red*. It's proved very popular on the radio, but then, most of my songs do."

"I've been gone for three days!"

"Culture moves very quickly when it needs to, funny bunny. Don't you like having a song with you in it?"

I thought about Mummery and all the people who thought she was fine as a sack of bees and drank her up like champagne. She lived for that drinking-up kind of love. Maybe I would, too, if I ever got it. The yellow half of Absinthe's day came barreling through the cafe window like a bandit in a barfight. Gold, gorgeous, impossible gold, on my hands and my shoulders and my unicorn and my mouth, the color of the slat under my bed, the color of the secret I showed

Orchid before I loved him. Sitting in that puddle of suddenly gold light felt like wearing a tiger's fur.

"Well, I haven't heard the song," I allowed. Maybe I wanted a little of that champagne-love, too.

Then the Ordinary Emperor wasn't a pepper grinder anymore because he was that beautiful man in doublet and hose and a thousand hundred colors who stood in my kitchen smelling like sex and power and eleven kinds of orange and white. He put his hands over mine.

"Didn't you ever wonder why the clarinauts are the only ones who travel between countries? Why they're so famous and why everyone wants to hear what they say?"

"I never thought about it even one time." That was a lie; I thought about it all the time the whole year I was eleven but that was long enough ago that it didn't feel like much of a lie.

He wiped away my creme de menthe mustache. I didn't know it yet, but my lips stayed green and they always would. "A clarinaut is born with a reed in her heart through which the world can pass and make a song. For everyone else, leaving home is poison. They just get so lost. Sometimes they spiral down the drain and end up Red. Most of the time they just wash away. It's because of the war. Bombs are so unpredictable. I'm sure everyone feels very embarrassed now."

I didn't want to talk about the specialness of Mummery. I didn't want to cry, either, but I was, and my tears splashed down onto the table in big, showy drops of gold. The Ordinary Emperor knuckled under my chin.

"*Mon petite biche*, it is natural to want to kill yourself when you have bitten off a hurt so big you can't swallow it. I once threw myself off Split Salmon Bridge in the Orange Country. But the Marmalade Sea spit me back. The Marmalade Sea thinks suicide is for cowards and she won't be a part of it. But you and I know better."

"I don't want to kill myself!"

"It doesn't matter what death means in the Red Country, Violet. Orchid didn't die in the Red Country. And you won't make it halfway across the Tangerine Tundra. You're already bleeding." He turned over my blue palm, tracing tracks in my golden tears. "You'll ride your sorrow into a red brick wall."

"It does matter. It does. You don't matter. My sorrow loves me."

"And what kind of love would that be? The love that means killing? Or eating? Or keeping warm? Do you know what 'I love you' means in the Yellow Country?"

"It means 'I cannot stand the sight of you,'" whinnied Jellyfish, flicking her apricot and daffodil tail. "Ocherous Wince said it to all her paintings every day."

The waiter appeared to take the Ordinary Emperor's order. He trembled slightly, his clovers quivering. "The pea soup and a glass of green apple gin with a dash of melon syrup, my good man," his Majesty said without glancing at the help. "I shall tell you a secret if you like, Violet. It's better than a swipe of gold paint, I promise."

"I don't care." My face got all hot and plum-dark even through the freezing lemony air. I didn't want him to talk about my slat. "Why do you bother with me? Go be a government by yourself."

"I like you. Isn't that enough? I like how much you look like your Mummery. I like how hard you rode Stopwatch across the Past Perfect Plains. I like how you looked at me when you caught me making coffee. I like that you painted the underside of your bed and I especially like how you showed it to Orchid. I'm going to tell you anyway. Before I came to the throne, during the reign of the Extraordinary Emperor, I hunted sorrows. Professionally. In fact, it was I who hunted them to extinction."

"What the hell did you do that for?" The waiter set down his royal meal and fled which I would also have liked to do but could not because I did not work in food service.

"Because I am from the Orange Country, and in the Orange Country, a sorrow is not a mammoth with a cabinet in its stomach, it is a kind of melancholic dread, a bitter, heartsick gloom. It feels as though you can never get free of a sorrow once you have one, as though you become allergic to happiness. It was because of a certain sorrow that I leapt from the Split Salmon Bridge. My parents died of a housefire and then my wife died of being my wife." The Ordinary Emperor's voice stopped working quite right and he sipped his gin. "All this having happened before the war, we could all hop freely from Orange to Yellow to Purple to Blue to Green—through Red was always a suspicious nation, their immigration policies never sensible, even then, even then when no one else knew what a lock was or a key. When I was a young man I did as young men do—I traveled, I tried to find women to travel with me, I ate foreign food and pretended to like it. And I saw that everywhere else, sorrows roamed like buffalo, and they were not distresses nor dolors nor disconsolations, but animals who could bleed. Parasites drinking from us like fountains. I did not set out for politics, but to rid the world of sorrows. I thought if I could kill them in the other countries, the Orange Country sort of sorrow would perish, too. I rode the ranges on a quagga with indigestion. I invented the Nonegun myself—I'll tell you that secret, too, if you like, and then you will know something your Mums doesn't, which I think is just about the best gift I could give you. To make the little engine inside a Nonegun you have to feel nothing for anyone. Your heart has to look like the vacuum of space. Not coincidentally, that is also how you make the engine inside an Emperor. I shot all the sorrows between the eyes. I murdered them. I rode them down. I was merciless."

"Did it work?" I asked softly.

"No. When I go home I still want to die. But it made a good campaign slogan. I have told you this for two reasons. The first is that when you pass into the Orange Country you will want to cut yourself open from throat to navel. Your sorrow has gotten big and fat. It will sit on you and you will not get up again. Believe me, I know. When I saw you come home with a sorrow following you like a homeless kitten I almost shot it right there and I should have. They have no good parts. Perhaps that is why I like you, really. Because I bleached sorrow from the universe and you found one anyway."

The Ordinary Emperor took my face in his hands. He kissed me. I started to not like it but it turned into a different kind of kiss, not like the kisses I made with Orchid, but a kiss that made me wonder what it meant to kiss someone in the Orange Country, a kiss half full of apology and half full of nostalgia and a third half full of do what I say or else. So in the end I came round again to not liking it. I didn't know what he was thinking when he kissed me. I guess that's not a thing that always happens.

"The second reason I told you about the sorrows, Violet Wild, is so that you will know that I can do anything. I am the man who murdered sorrow. It said that on my election posters. You were too young to vote, but your Mummery wasn't, and you won't be too young when I come up for re-election."

"So?"

"So if you run as my Vice-Emperor, which is another way of saying Empress, which is another way of saying wife, I will kill time for you, just like I killed sorrow. Squirrels will be no trouble after all those woolly monsters. Then everything can happen at once and you will both have Orchid and not have him at the same time because the part where you showed him the slat under your bed and the part where his body disappeared on the edge of the Blue Country will not have to happen in that order, or any order. It will be the same for my wife and my parents and only in the Red Country will time still mean passing."

The squirrel still squatted on the table with her belly full of baby futures in her greedy hands. She glared at the Ordinary Emperor with unpasteurized hate in her milky eyes. I looked out the great ice picture window of the restaurant that wasn't called O Tannenbaum anymore, but The Jonquil Julep, the hoppingest nightspot in the Yellow Country. Only the farthest fuzz on the horizon still looked green. Chic blonde howdy-dos started to crowd in wearing daffodil dresses and butterscotch tuxedos. Some of them looked sallow and waxy; some of them coughed.

"There is always a spot of cholera in the Yellow Country," admitted the Ordinary Emperor with some chagrin. Through the glass I saw my sorrow hunched over, peering in at the Emperor, weeping soundlessly, wiping her eyes with her trunk. "But the light here is so good for painting."

Everything looked like the underside of my bed. The six-legged squirrel said:

"Show me something your parents don't know about."

And love went pinballing through me but it was a Yellow kind of love and suddenly my creme de menthe was banana schnapps and suddenly my mugwort cake was lemon meringue and suddenly I hated Orchid Harm. I hated him for making me have an ardor for something that wasn't a pony or a Papo or a color of paint, I hated him for being a Sunslinger all over town even though everybody knew that shit would hollow you out and fill you back up with nothing if you stuck with it. I hated him for making friends with my unicorn and I hated him for hanging around Papo and me till he got dead from it and I hated him for bleeding out under me and making everything that happened happen. I didn't want to see his horrible handsome face ever again. I didn't want alive-Orchid and dead-Orchid at the same time, which is a pretty colossally unpleasant idea when you think about it. My love was the sourest thing I'd ever had. If Orchid had sidled up and ordered a cantaloupe whiskey, I would have turned my face away. I had to swallow all that back to talk again.

"But killing sorrow didn't work," I said, but I kept looking at my sorrow on the other side of the window.

"I obviously missed one," he said grimly. "I will be more thorough."

And the Ordinary Emperor, quick as a rainbow coming on, snatched up the squirrel of time and whipped her little body against the lemonwood table so that it broke her neck right in half. She didn't even get a chance to squeak.

Sometimes it takes me a long time to think through things, to set them up just right in my head so I can see how they'd break if I had a hammer. But sometimes I have a hammer. So I said:

"No, that sounds terrible. You are terrible. I am a Nowgirl and a Nowgirl doesn't lead her herd to slaughter. Bring them home, bring them in, my Papo always said that and that's what I will always say, too. Go away. Go be dried pasta. Go be sad and orange. Go jump off your bridge again. I'm going to the Red Country on my sorrow's back."

The Ordinary Emperor held up his hand. He stood to leave as though he were a regular person who was going to walk out the door and not just turn into a bar of Blue Country soap. He looked almost completely white in the loud yellow sunshine. The light burned my eyes.

"It's dangerous in the Red Country, Violet. You'll have to say what you mean. Even your Mummery never flew so far. "

He dropped the corpse of the mauve space-time squirrel next to his butter knife by way of paying his tab because in the Yellow Country, money means time.

"You are not a romantic man," said Jellyfish through clenched pistachio-colored teeth. That's the worst insult a watercolor unicorn knows.

"There's a shortcut to the Orange Country in the ladies' room. Turn the right tap three times, the left tap once, and pull the stopper out of the basin." That was how the Ordinary Emperor said goodbye. I'm pretty sure he told Mummery I was a no-good whore who would never make good even if I lived to a hundred. That's probably even true. But that wasn't why I ran after him and stabbed him in the neck with the poisonous prong of the story hanging from my belt. I did that because, no matter what, a Nowgirl looks after her herd.

## 5. Orange

THIS IS WHAT happened to me in the Orange Country: I didn't see any cities even though there are really nice cities there, or drink any alcohol even though I've always heard clementine schnapps is really great, or talk to any animals even though in the Orange Country a poem means a kind of tiger that can't talk but can sing, or people, even though there were probably some decent ones making a big bright orange life somewhere.

I came out of the door in the basin of The Jonquil Julep and I lay down on floor of a carrot-colored autumn jungle and cried until I didn't have anything wet left to lose. Then I crawled under a papaya tree and clawed the orange clay until I made a hole big enough to climb inside if I curled up my whole body like a circle you draw with one smooth motion. The clay smelled like fire.

"I love you," said my sorrow. She didn't look well. Her fur was threadbare, translucent, her trunk dried out.

"I don't know what 'I love you' means in the Orange Country," sighed Jellyfish.

"I do," said the Sparrowbone Mask of the Incarnadine Fisherwomen, who hadn't had a damn thing to say in ages. "Here, if you love someone, you mean to keep them prisoner and never let them see the sun."

"But then they'd be safe," I whispered.

"I love you," said my sorrow. She got down on her giant woolly knees beside my hole. "I love you. Your eyes are yellow."

I began to claw into the orange clay of my hole. I peeled it away and crammed it into my mouth. My teeth went through it easy as anything. It didn't taste like dirt. It tasted like a lot of words, one after the other, with conflict and resolution and a beginning, middle, but no end. It tasted like Mummery showing me how to play the clarinet. It tasted like an Emperor who wasn't an Emperor anymore. The earth stained my tongue orange forever.

"I love you," said my sorrow.

"I heard you, dammit," I said between bright mouthfuls.

Like she was putting an exclamation point on her favorite phrase, my sorrow opened up her cabinet doors in the sienna shadows of the orange jungle. Toucans and orioles and birds of paradise crowed and called and their crowing and calling caromed off the titian trunks until my ears hated birdsong more than any other thing. My sorrow opened up her cabinet doors and the wind whistled through the space inside her and it sounded like Premiére Rhapsodie in A Major through the holes of a fuel-efficient crystal clarinet.

Inside my sorrow hung a dress the color of garnets, with a long train trailing behind it and a neckline that plunged to the navel. It looked like it would be very hard to dance in.

## 6. Red

IN THE RED Country, love is love, loyalty is loyalty, a story is a story, and death is a long red dress. The Red Country is the only country with walls.

I slept my way into the Red Country.

I lay down inside the red dress called death; I lay down inside my sorrow and a bone mask crawled onto my face; I lay down and didn't dream and my sorrow smuggled me out of the orange jungles where sorrow is sadness. I don't remember that part so I can't say anything about it. The inside of my sorrow was cool and dim; there wasn't any furniture in there, or any candles. She seemed all right again, once we'd lumbered on out of the jungle. Strong and solid like she'd been in the beginning. I didn't throw up even though I ate all that dirt. Jellyfish told me later that the place where the Orange Country turns into the Red Country is a marshland full of flamingos and ruby otters fighting for supremacy. I would have liked to have seen that.

I pulled it together by the time we reached the riverbanks. The Incarnadine River flows like blood out of the marshes, through six locks and four sluice gates in the body of a red brick wall as tall as clouds. Then it joins the greater rushing rapids and pools of the Claret, the only river in seven kingdoms with dolphins living in it, and all together, the rivers and the magenta dolphins, roar and tumble down the valleys and into the heart of the city of Cranberry-on-Claret.

Crimson boats choked up the Incarnadine. A thousand fishing lines stuck up into the pink dawn like pony-poles on the pampas. The fisherwomen all wore masks like mine, masks like mine and burgundy swimming costumes that covered them from neck to toe and all I could think was how I'd hate to swim in one of those things, but they probably never had to because if you fell out of your boat you'd just land in another boat. The fisherwomen cried out when they saw me. I suppose I looked frightening, wearing that revealing, low-cut death and the bone mask and riding a mammoth with a unicorn in my arms. They called me some name that wasn't Violet Wild and the ones nearest to shore climbed out of their boats, shaking and laughing and holding out their arms. I don't think anyone should get stuck holding their arms out to nothing and no one, so I shimmied down my sorrow's fur and they clung on for dear live, touching the Sparrowbone Mask of the Incarnadine Fisherwomen, stroking its cheeks, its red spiral mouth, telling it how it had scared them, vanishing like that.

"I love you," the Sparrowbone Mask of the Incarnadine Fisherwomen kept saying over and over. It felt strange when the mask on my face spoke but I didn't speak. "I love you. Sometimes you can't help vanishing. I love you. I can't stay."

My mask and I said both together: "We are afraid of the wall."

"Don't be doltish," an Incarnadine Fisherwoman said. She must have been a good fisherwoman as she had eight vermillion catfish hanging off her belt and some of them were still opening and closing their mouths, trying to breathe water that had vanished like a mask. "You're one of us."

So my sorrow swam through the wall. She got into the scarlet water which rose all the way up to her eyeballs but she didn't mind. I rode her like sailing a boat and the red water soaked the train of my red death dress and magenta dolphins followed along with us, jumping out of the water and echolocating like a bunch of maniacs and the Sparrowbone Mask of the Incarnadine Fisherwomen said:

"I am beginning to remember who I am now that everything is red again. Why is anything unred in the world? It's madness."

Jellyfish hid her lavender face in her watermelon-colored hooves and whispered:

"Please don't forget about me, I am water soluble!"

I wondered, when the river crashed into the longest wall in the world, a red brick wall that went on forever side to side and also up and down, if the wall had a name. Everything has a name, even if that name is in Latin and nobody knows it but one person who doesn't live nearby. Somebody had tried to blow up the wall several times. Jagged chunks were missing; bullets had gouged out rock and mortar long ago, but no one had ever made a hole. The Incarnadine River slushed in through a cherry-colored sluice gate. Rosy sunlight lit up its prongs. I glided on in with all the other fisherwomen like there never was a wall in the first place. I looked behind us—the river swarmed with squirrels, gasping, half drowning, paddling their little feet for dear life. They squirmed through the sluice gate like plague rats.

"If you didn't have that mask on, you would have had to pay the toll," whispered Jellyfish.

"What's the toll?"

"A hundred years as a fisherwoman."

CRANBERRY-ON-CLARET IS A city of carnelian and lacquerwork and carbuncle streetlamps glowing with red gas flames because the cities of the Red Country are not electrified like Plum Pudding and Lizard Tongue and Absinthe. People with hair the color of raspberries and eyes the color of wood embers play ruby bassoons and chalcedony hurdy-gurdies and cinnamon-stick violins on the long, wide streets and they never stop even when they sleep; they just switch to nocturnes and keep playing through their dreaming. When they saw me coming, they started up *My Baby Done Gone to Red*, which, it turns out, is only middling as far as radio hits go.

Some folks wore deaths like mine. Some didn't. The Ordinary Emperor said that sometimes the dead go to the Red Country but nobody looked dead. They looked busy like city people always look. It was warm in Cranberry-on-Claret, an autumnal kind of warm, the kind that's having a serious think about turning to cold. The clouds glowed primrose and carmine.

"Where are we going?" asked my watercolor unicorn.

"The opera house," I answered.

I guess maybe all opera houses are skulls because the one in the Red Country looked just like the one back home except, of course, as scarlet as the spiral mouth of a mask. It just wasn't a human skull. Out of a cinnabar piazza hunched up a squirrel skull bigger than a cathedral and twice as fancy. Its great long teeth opened and closed like proper doors and prickled with scrimshaw carving like my Papo used to do on pony-bones. All over the wine-colored skull grew bright hibiscus flowers and devil's hat mushrooms and red velvet lichen and fire opals.

Below the opera house and behind they kept the corrals. Blue stories milled miserably in pens, their sapphire plates drooping, their eyes all gooey with cataracts. I took off the Sparrowbone Mask of the Incarnadine Fisherwomen and climbed down my sorrow.

"Heyo, beastie-blues," I said, holding my hands out for them to sniff through the copper wire and redwood of their paddock. "No lachrymose quadrupeds on my watch. Be not down in the mouth. Woe-be-gone, not woe-be-come."

"That's blue talk," a boy-story whispered. "You gotta talk red or you get no cud."

"Say what you mean," grumbled a girl-story with three missing scales over her left eye. "It's the law."

"I always said what I meant. I just meant something very fancy," sniffed a grandfather-story lying in the mud to stay cool.

"Okay. I came from the Purple Country to find a boy named Orchid Harm."

"Nope, that's not what you mean," the blue grandpa dinosaur growled, but he didn't seem upset about it. Stories mostly growl unless they're sick.

"Sure it is!"

"I'm just a simple story, what do I know?" He turned his cerulean rump to me.

"You're just old and rude. I'm pretty sure Orchid is up there in the eye of that skull, it's only that I was going to let you out of your pen before I went climbing but maybe I won't now."

"How's about we tell you what you mean and then you let us out and nobody owes nobody nothing?" said the girl-story with the missing scales. It made me sad to hear a story talking like that, with no grammar at all.

"I came from the Purple Country to find Orchid," I repeated because I was afraid.

"Are you sure you're not an allegory for depression or the agrarian revolution or the afterlife?"

"I'm not an allegory for anything! You're an allegory! And you stink!"

"If you say so."

"What do *you* mean then?"

"I mean a blue dinosaur. I mean a story about a girl who lost somebody and couldn't get over it. I can mean both at the same time. That's allowed."

"This isn't any better than when you were saying *autarchy* and *peregrinate*."

"So peregrinate with autarchy, girlie. That's how you're supposed to act around stories, anyway. Who raised you?"

I kicked out the lock on their paddock and let the reptilian stories loose. They bolted like blue lightning into the cinnabar piazza. Jellyfish ran joyfully among them, jumping and wriggling and whinnying, giddy to be in a herd again, making a mess of a color scheme.

"I love you," said my sorrow. She had shrunk up small again, no taller than a good dog, and she was wearing the Sparrowbone Mask of the Incarnadine Fisherwomen. By the time I'd gotten half way up the opera-skull, she was gone.

---

"LET US BEGIN by practicing the chromatic scale, beginning with E Major."

That is what the voice coming out of the eye socket of a giant operatic squirrel said and it was Orchid's voice and it had a laugh hidden inside it like it always did. I pulled myself up and over the lip of the socket and curled up next to Orchid Harm and his seven books, of which he'd already read four. I curled up next to him like nothing bad had ever happened. I fit into the line of his body and he fit into mine. I didn't say anything for a long, long time. He stroked my hair and read to me about basic strumming technique but after awhile he stopped talking, too, and we just sat there quietly and he smelled like sunlight and booze and everything purple in the world.

"I killed the Ordinary Emperor with a story's tail," I confessed at last.

"I missed you, too."

"Are you dead?"

"The squirrels won't tell me. Something about collapsing a waveform. But I'm not the one wearing a red dress."

I looked down. Deep red silky satin death flowed out over the bone floor. A lot of my skin showed in the slits of that dress. It felt nice.

"The squirrels ate you, though."

"You never know with squirrels. I think I ate some of them, too. It's kind of the same thing, with time travel, whether you eat the squirrel or the squirrel eats you. I remember it hurt. I remember you kissed me till it was over. I remember Early-to-Tea and Stopwatch screaming. Sometimes you can't help vanishing. Anyway, the squirrels felt bad about it. Because we'd taken care of them so well and they had to do it anyway. They apologized for ages. I fell asleep once in the middle of them going on and on about how timelines taste."

"Am I dead?"

"I don't know, did you die?"

"Maybe the bubbles got me. The Emperor said I'd get sick if I traveled without a clarinet. And parts of me aren't my own parts anymore." I stretched out my legs. They were the color of rooster feathers. "But I don't think so. What do you mean the squirrels had to do it?"

"Self-defense, is what they said about a million times."

"What? We never so much as kicked one!"

"You have to think like a six-legged mauve squirrel of infinite time. The Ordinary Emperor was going to hunt them all down one by one and set the chronology of everything possible and impossible on fire. They set a contraption in motion so that he couldn't touch them, a contraption involving you and me and a blue story and a Red Country where nobody dies, they just change clothes. They're very tidy creatures. Don't worry, we're safe in the Red Country. There'll probably be another war. The squirrels can't fix that. They're only little. But everyone always wants to conquer the Red Country and nobody ever has. We have a wall and it's a really good one."

I twisted my head up to look at him, his plum-colored hair, his amethyst eyes, his stubborn chin. "You have to say what you mean here."

"I mean I love you. And I mean the infinite squirrels of space and time devoured me to save themselves from annihilation at the hands of a pepper grinder. I can mean both. It's allowed."

I kissed Orchid Harm inside the skull of a giant rodent and we knew that we were both thinking about ice cream. The ruby bassoons hooted up from the piazza and scarlet tanagers scattered from the rooftops and a watercolor unicorn told a joke about the way tubas are way down the road but the echoes carried her voice up and up and everywhere. Orchid stopped the kiss first. He pointed to the smooth crimson roof of the eye socket.

A long stripe of gold paint gleamed there.

# Palimpsest

### 16th and Hieratica

*A FORTUNE-TELLER'S SHOP: PALM-FRONDS cross before the door. Inside are four red chairs with four lustral basins before them, filled with ink, swirling and black. A woman lumbers in, wrapped in ragged fox-fur. Her head amid heaps of scarves is that of a frog, mottled green and bulbous-eyed, and a licking pink tongue keeps its place in her wide mouth. She does not see individual clients. Thus it is that four strangers sit in the red chairs, strip off their socks, plunge their feet into the ink-baths, and hold hands under an amphibian stare. This is the first act of anyone entering Palimpsest: Orlande will take your coats, sit you down, and make you family. She will fold you four together like quartos. She will draw you each a card—look, for you it is the Broken Ship reversed, which signifies perversion, a long journey without enlightenment, gout—and tie your hands together with red yarn. Wherever you go in Palimpsest, you are bound to these strangers who happened onto Orlande's salon just when you did, and you will go nowhere, eat no capon or dormouse, drink no oversweet port that they do not also taste, and they will visit no whore that you do not also feel beneath you, and until that ink washes from your feet—which, given that Orlande is a*

*creature of the marsh and no stranger to mud, will be some time—
you cannot breathe but that they breathe also.*

―⁀―

THE OTHER SIDE of the street: a factory. Its thin spires are green, and spit long loops of white flame into the night. Casimira owns this place, as did her father and her grandmother and probably her most distant progenitor, curling and uncurling their proboscis-fingers against machines of stick and bone. There has always been a Casimira, except when, occasionally, there is a Casimir. Workers carry their lunches in clamshells. They wear extraordinary uniforms: white and green scales laid one over the other, clinging obscenely to the skin, glittering in the spirelight. They wear nothing else; every wrinkle and curve is visible. They dance into the factory, their serpentine bodies writhing a shift-change, undulating under the punch-clock with its cheerful metronomic chime. Their eyes are piscine, third eyelid half-drawn in drowsy pleasure as they side-step and gambol and spin to the rhythm of the machines.

And what do they make in this factory? Why, the vermin of Palimpsest. There is a machine for stamping cockroaches with glistening green carapaces, their maker's mark hidden cleverly under the left wing. There is a machine for shaping and pounding rats, soft grey fur stiff and shining when they are first released. There is another mold for squirrels, one for chipmunks and one for plain mice. There is a centrifuge for spiders, a lizard-pour, a delicate and ancient machine which turns out flies and mosquitoes by turn, so exquisite, so perfect that they seem to be made of nothing but copper wire, spun sugar, and light. There is a printing press for graffiti which spits out effervescent letters in scarlet, black, angry yellows, and the trademark green of Casimira. They fly from the high windows and flatten themselves against walls, trestles, train cars.

When the shift-horn sounds at the factory, the long antler-trumpet passed down to Casimira by the one uncle in her line who defied *tradition and became a humble hunter, setting the whole clan to a vociferous but well-fed consternation, a wave of life wafts from the service exit: moles and beetles and starlings and bats, ants and worms and moths and mantises. Each gleaming with its last coat of sealant, each quivering with near-invisible devices which whisper into their atavistic minds that their mistress loves them, that she thinks of them always, and longs to hold them to her breast.*

*In her office, Casimira closes her eyes and listens to the teeming masses as they whisper back to their mother. At the end of each day they tell her all they have learned of living.*

*It is necessary work. No family has been so often formally thanked by the city as hers.*

---

THE FIRST TIME I saw it was in the pit of a woman's elbow. The orange and violet lights of the raucous dancefloor played over her skin, made her look like a decadent leopardess at my table. I asked her about it; she pulled her sleeve over her arm self-consciously, like a clam pulling its stomach in.

"It's not cancer," she said loudly, over the droning, repetitive music, "I had it checked out. It was just there one day, popping up out of me like fucking track marks. I have to wear long sleeves to work all the time now, even in summer. But it's nothing—well, not nothing, but if it's something it's benign, just some kind of late-arriving birthmark."

I took her home. Not because of it, but because her hair was very red, in that obviously dyed way—and I like that way. Some shades of red genetics will never produce, but she sat in the blinking green and blue lights haloed in defiant scarlet.

---

SHE TASTED LIKE new bread and lemon-water.

AS SHE DRIFTED to sleep, one arm thrown over her eyes, the other lying open and soft on my sheets, I stroked her elbow gently, the mark there like a tattoo: a spidery network of blue-black lines, intersecting each other, intersecting her pores, turning at sharp angles, rounding out into clear and unbroken skin just outside the hollow of her joint. It looked like her veins had darkened and hardened, organized themselves into something more than veins, and determined to escape the borders of their mistress's flesh. She murmured my name in her sleep: *Lucia*.

"It looks like a streetmap," I whispered sleepily, brushing her hair from a flushed ear.

I DREAMED AGAINST her breast of the four black pools in Orlande's house. I stared straight ahead into her pink and grey-speckled mouth, and the red thread swept tight against my wrist. On my leather-skirted lap the Flayed Horse was laid, signifying sacrifice in vain, loveless pursuit, an empty larder. A man sat beside me with an old-fashioned felt hat askance on his bald head, his lips deeply rosy and full, as though he had been kissing someone a moment before. We laced our hands together as she lashed us—he had an extra finger, and I tried not to recoil. Before me were two women: one with a green scarf wrapping thin golden hair, a silver mantis-pendant dangling between her breasts, and another, Turkish, or Armenian, perhaps, her eyes heavily made-up, streaked in black like an Egyptian icon.

The frog-woman showed me a small card, red words printed neatly on yellowed paper:

*You have been quartered.*

The knots slackened. I walked out, across the frond-threshold, into the night which smelled of sassafras and rum, and onto Hieratica Street. The others scattered, like ashes. The road stretched before and beyond, lit by streetlamps like swollen pumpkins, and the gutters ran with rain.

### 212th, Vituperation, Seraphim, and Alphabet

*IN THE CENTER of the roundabout: the Cast-Iron Memorial. It is tall and thin, a baroque spire sheltering a single black figure—a gagged child with the corded, elastic legs of an ostrich, fashioned from linked hoops of iron—through the gaps in her knees you can see the weeds with their flame-tipped flowers. She is seated in the grass, her arms thrown out in supplication. Bronze and titanium chariots click by in endless circles, drawn on runners in the street, ticking as they pass like shining clocks. Between her knock-knees is a plaque of white stone:*

IN MEMORIAM:
*The sons and daughters of Palimpsest
who fought and fell in the Silent War.
752-759*

*Silent still
are the fields
in which they are planted.*

*Once, though the tourists could not know of it, on this spot a thousand died without a gasp. Legions were volunteered to have their limbs replaced with better articles, fleeter and wiser and stronger and newer. These soldiers also had their larynxes cut out, so they could not give away their positions with an unfortunate cry, or tell tales of what they had done in the desert, by the sea, in the city which then was new and toddling. Whole armies altered thus wrangled without screams, without sound. In the center of the roundabout, the ostrich-girl died unweeping while her giraffe-father had his long, spotted neck slashed with an ivory bayonet.*

⁓

DOWN THE MAHOGANY *alleys of Seraphim Street, clothes shops line the spotless, polished road. In the window of one is a dress in the latest style: startlingly blue, sweeping up to the shoulders of a golden mannequin. It cuts away to reveal a glittering belly; the belt is fastened with tiny cerulean eyes which blink lazily, in succession. The whites are diamonds, the pupils ebony. The skirt winds down in deep, hard creases which tumble out of the window in a carefully arranged train, hemmed in crow feathers. The shopkeeper, Aloysius, keeps a pale green Casimira grasshopper on a beaded leash. It rubs its legs together while he works in a heap of black quills, sewing an identical trio of gowns like the one in the window for triplet girls who demanded them in violet, not blue.*

*At night, he ties the leash to his bedpost and the little thing lies next to his broad, lined face, clicking a binary lullaby into the old man's beard. He dreams of endless bodies, unclothed and beautiful.*

⁓

I CAN BE forgiven, I think, for not noticing it for days afterward. I caught a glimpse in my mirror as I turned to catch a loose thread in my skirt—behind my knee, a dark network of lines and angles, and, I thought I could see, tiny words scrawled above them, names and numbers, snaking over the grid.

After that, I began to look for them.

I found the second in a sushi restaurant with black tablecloths— he was sitting two tables over, but when he gripped his chopsticks, I could see the map pulsing on his palm. I joined him—he did not object. We ate eels and cucumbers thinner than vellum and drank enough clear, steaming sake that I did not have to lean over to kiss him in the taxi. He smashed his lips against mine and I dug my nails into his neck—when we parted I seized his hand and licked the web of avenues that criss-crossed so: heart and fate lines.

In his lonely apartment I kissed his stomach. In his lonely apartment, on a bed without a frame which lay wretched between milk crates and cinder blocks, the moon shone through broken blinds and slashed my back into a tiger's long stripes.

In his lonely apartment, on a pillow pounded thin by dozens of night-fists, I dreamed. Perhaps he dreamed, too. I thought I saw him wandering down a street filled with balloons and leering gazelles—but I did not follow. I stood on a boulevard paved with prim orange poppies, and suddenly I tasted brandy rolling down my throat, and pale smoke filling up my lungs. My green-scarved quarter was savoring her snifter and her opium somewhere far from me. I saw the ostrich-child that night. I smelled the Seraphim sidewalks, rich and red, and traded, with only some hesitation, my long brown hair for the dress. Aloysius cut it with crystal scissors, and I walked over wood, under sulfurous stars, trailing dark feathers behind me. The wind was warm on my bare neck. My fingers were warm, too—my bald quarter was stroking a woman with skin like a snake's.

THERE WERE OTHERS. A man with a silver tooth—a depth-chart crawled over his toes. With him I dreamed I walked the tenements, raised on stilts over a blue river, and ate goulash with a veteran whose head was a snarling lion, tearing his meat with fangs savage and yellow. He had a kind of sign language, but I could only guess correctly the gestures for *mother, southeast,* and *sleep.*

There was a woman with two children and a mole on her left thigh—between her shoulder blades severe turns and old closes spoked on an arrondissement-wheel. With her I dreamed I worked a night's shift in a restaurant that served but one dish: broiled elephant liver, soaked in lavender honey and jeweled with pomegranate seeds. The staff wore tunics sewn from peacock feathers, and were not allowed to look the patrons in the eye. When I set a shimmering plate before a man with long, grey fingers, I felt my black-eyed quarter pick up her golden fork and bite into a snail dipped in rum.

There was a sweet boy with a thin little beard—his thumb was nearly black with gridlock and unplanned alleys, as though he had been fingerprinted in an unnamable jail. He fell asleep in my arms, and we dreamed together, like mating dragonflies flying in unison. With him, I saw the foundries throwing fire into the sky. With him I danced in pearlescent scales, and pressed into being exactly fifty-seven wild hares, each one marked on its left ear with Casimira's green seal.

*Lucia!* They all cry out when they lie over me. *Lucia! Where will I find you?*

Yet in those shadow-stitched streets I am always alone.

I sought out the dream-city on all those skins. What were plain, yellow-lined streets next to Seraphim? What was my time-clock stamping out its inane days next to the jeweled factory of Casimira? How could any touch equal the seizures of feeling in my dreams, in which each gesture was a quartet? I would touch no one who didn't carry the map. Only once that year, after the snow, did I make an exception, for a young woman with cedar-colored breasts and a nose ring like a bull's, or a minotaur's. She wore bindi on her face like a splatter of blood. Her body was without blemish or mark, so alien and strange to me by then, so blank and empty. But she was beautiful, and her voice was a glass-cutting soprano, and I am weak. I begged her to sing to me after we made love, and when we dreamed, I found her dancing with a jackal-tailed man in the lantern-light of a bar that served butterfly-liquor in a hundred colors. I separated them; he wilted and slunk away, and I took her to the sea, its foam shattering into glass on the beach, and we walked along a strand of shards, glittering and wet.

WHEN I WOKE, the grid brachiated out from her navel, its angles dark and bright. I smiled. Before she stirred, I kissed the striated lines, and left her house without coffee or farewells.

### Quiescent and Rapine

THERE ARE TWO churches in Palimpsest, and they are identical in every way. They stand together, wrapping the street-corner like a hinge. Seven white columns each, wound around with black characters which are not Cyrillic, but to the idle glance might seem so. Two peaked roofs of red lacquer and two stone horses with the heads of fork-tongued lizards stand guard on either side of each door. They were made with stones from the same quarry, on the far southern border of the city, pale green and dusty, each round and perfect as a ball. There is more mortar in the edifices than stones, mortar crushed from Casimira dragonflies donated by the vat, tufa dust, and mackerel tails. The pews are scrubbed and polished with lime-oil, and each Thursday, parishioners share a communion of slivers of whale meat and cinnamon wine. The only difference between the two is in the basement—two great mausoleums with alabaster coffins lining the walls, calligraphied with infinite care and delicacy in the blood of the departed beloved contained within. In the far north corner is a raised platform covered in offerings of cornskin, chocolate, tobacco. In one church, the coffin contains a blind man. In the other, it contains a deaf woman. Both have narwhal's horns extending from their foreheads; both died young. The faithful visit these basement-saints and leave what they can at the feet of the one they love best. Giustizia has been a devotee of the Unhearing since she was a girl—her yellow veil and turquoise-ringed thumbs are familiar to all in the Left-Hand Church, and it is she who brings the cornskins, regular as sunrise. When she dies, they will bury her here, in a coffin of her own.

She will plug your ears with wax when you enter, and demand silence. You may notice the long rattlesnake tail peeking from under her skirt and clattering on the mosaic floor, but it is not polite to mention it—when she says *silence, you listen*. It is the worst word she knows.

⁓

THE SUBURBS OF Palimpsest spread out from the edges of the city proper like ladies' fans. First the houses, uniformly red, in even lines like veins, branching off into lanes and courts and cul-de-sacs. There are parks full of grass that smells like oranges and little creeks filled with floating roses, blue and black. Children scratch pictures of antelope-footed girls and sparrow-winged boys on the pavement, hop from one to the other. Their laughter spills from their mouths and turns to orange leaves, drifting lazily onto wide lawns. Eventually the houses fade into fields: amaranth, spinach, strawberries. Shaggy cows graze; black-faced sheep bleat. Palimpsest is ever-hungry.

But these too fade as they extend out, fade into the empty land not yet colonized by the city, not yet peopled, not yet known. The empty meadows stretch to the horizon, pale and dark, rich and soft.

A wind picks up, blowing hot and dusty and salt-scented, and gooseflesh rises over miles and miles of barren skin.

⁓

I SAW HER in November. It was raining—her scarf was soaked and plastered against her head. She passed by me and I knew her smell, I knew the shape of her wrist. In the holiday crowds, she disappeared quickly, and I ran after her, without a name to call out.

"Wait!" I cried.

She stopped and turned towards me, her square jaw and huge brown eyes familiar as a pillow. We stood together in the rainy street, beside a makeshift watch-stand.

"It's you," I whispered.

And I showed my knee. She pursed her lips for a moment, her green scarf blown against her neck like a wet leaf. Then she extended her tongue, and I saw it there, splashed with raindrops, the map of Palimpsest, blazing blue-bright. She closed her mouth, and I put my arm around her waist.

"I felt you, the pipe of bone, the white smoke," I said.

"I felt the dress on your shoulders," she answered, and her voice was thick and low, grating, like a gate opening.

"Come to my house. There is brandy there, if you want it."

She cocked her head, thin golden hair snaking sodden over her coat. "What would happen, do you think?"

I smiled. "Maybe our feet would come clean."

She stroked my cheek, put her long fingers into my hair. We kissed, and the watches gleamed beside us, gold and silver.

### 125th and Peregrine

*ON THE SOUTH corner: the lit globes, covered with thick wrought-iron serpents which break the light, of a subway entrance. The trains barrel along at the bottom of the stairs every fifteen minutes. On the glass platform stands Adalgiso, playing his viola with six fingers on each hand. He is bald, with a felt hat that does not sit quite right on his head. Beside him is Assia, singing tenor, her smoke-throated voice pressing against his strings like kisses. Her eyes are heavily made-up, like a pharaoh's portrait, her hair long and coarse and black. His playing is so quick and lovely that the trains stop to listen, inclining on the rails and opening their doors to catch the glissandos* spilling from him. His instrument case lies open at his feet, and each passenger who takes the Marginalia Line brings his fee—single pearls, dropped one by one into the leather case until it overflows like a pitcher of milk. In the corners of the station, cockroaches with fiber optic wings scrape the tiles with their feet, and their scraping keeps the beat for the player and his singer.

ON THE NORTH corner: a cartographer's studio. There are pots of ink in every crevice, parchment spread out over dozens of tables. A Casimira pigeon perches in a baleen cage and trills out the hours faithfully. Its droppings are pure squid-ink, and they are collected in a little tin trough. Lucia and Paola have run this place for as long as anyone can remember—Lucia with her silver compass draws the maps, her exactitude radiant and unerring, while Paola illuminates them with exquisite miniatures, dancing in the spaces between streets. They each wear dozens of watches on their forearms. This is the second stop, after the amphibian-salon, of Palimpsest's visitors, and especially of her immigrants, for whom the two women are especial patrons. Everyone needs a map, and Lucia supplies them: subway maps and street-maps and historical maps and topographical maps, false maps and correct-to-the-minute maps and maps of cities far and far from this one. Look—for you she has made a folding pamphlet that shows the famous sights: the factory, the churches, the salon, the memorial. Follow it, and you will be safe.

Each morning, Lucia places her latest map on the windowsill like a fresh pie. Slowly, as it cools, it opens along its own creases, its corners like wings, and takes halting flight, flapping over the city with susurring strokes. It folds itself, origami-exact, in mid-air: it has papery eyes, inky feathers, vellum claws.

It stares down the long avenues, searching for mice.

# The Red Girl

**A** FEW YEARS AGO I FELL in love with Red Riding Hood. I know it sounds silly but you can't help who you love. You see a girl in a cafe with a bowl of soup and a coat drawn up around her face and there's something savage about her hands, something long and hooked, and while you're wondering about her it just happens inside you, like cancer.

She didn't really wear red all the time. It was more like purple or brown. A lurid, bruised color. When I asked her about it, she would wave her hand as if trying to clear smoke from the air. "Oh, Catherine," she breathed. Whenever she said my name she spelled it wrong, "it's just, you know…transcription errors."

She never liked that I was a writer. She didn't trust writers—she said they just wanted to swallow her up. I said I didn't, but it wasn't true and she knew it. I lay there the first night with her, my head on her breast, her dark, hard nipple near my mouth, and I said I wasn't like the others, I would keep her secrets, I wouldn't try to tell her story the way everyone else did, the way I'd done with Snow White and Rapunzel and all those other girls. She was better than the other girls, and I was kinder than the other writers. She brushed my hair over my ear and drew up her battered old hood around her perfect face, as if putting on an old war helmet.

Sleeping with someone famous is strange. It's like sleeping with a person, and also sleeping with a mirror showing that person as everyone else sees them. We'd go out and the flashbulbs would pop. Not so many these days, but someone always recognized her.

Here are some facts about Red Riding Hood:

She doesn't speak German.

She is left-handed.

She prefers pan au chocolat in the mornings, with milk and tea.

Sometimes she wakes up blind and screaming, and she thinks she is inside the wolf, still. I learned Icelandic so that I could calm her when this happens. In the dark, it's the only language she knows.

She does not eat meat. "You never know who that's been," she says.

She liked me because I am Italian. She told me that she had lived in Italy when she was young. She was vague about the dates.

She is vague about a lot of things.

She is afraid of enclosed spaces. You must keep everything clean and bright or she will howl and cry.

Her cries are worse than anyone's.

She has a mole on her thigh, and another on her earlobe.

Her hair is the same color as her hood.

Once I asked her if she wanted to bring the wolf to bed with us. I don't mind, I said. It wouldn't change anything between us. And she looked at me like she might say yes, like it might have been what she was waiting for, someone to pull back the coverlet and allow both her and her creature in, to love them both and not ask her to choose. She looked at me like she was afraid I would take it back, like it wasn't possible that she could ever end the constant circle she ran, around and around, her and the wolf and the forest, her human mouth and her ferocious teeth. She looked at me like I'd offered her everything.

And then she said no. It doesn't work that way, she said. It would change everything. You would vanish between the two of us, like a grandmother, like an ax. I love you but there are things older and murkier than love. Things that live not in the heart but the entrails. I don't want you to see me with the wolf. I don't want you to see what he does to me. I don't want you to see what I do to him.

I wouldn't love you any less, I told her.

But I would love you less, she said. I'm sorry. It's in my nature. I like writers and Italian girls and red kisses just fine, but the wolf is a singularity, a collapsed, black thing that I can't get around, I can only fall into.

I was so young. I didn't know anything. I said: I could be a wolf for you. I could put my teeth on your throat. I could growl. I could eat you whole. I could wait for you in the dark. I could howl against your hair.

She looked at me with an old, sour kind of pity. I flushed, naked in her bed, no wolf but a girl.

Then a huntsman, I whispered. I could be that. I could cut you free.

And she sat up, her hair falling over her breast—and her nipple was dark, too, that lurid, reddish hue that wasn't really red at all, but instead a color belonging only to the body, to flesh, rosy and blackened and engorged with blood.

You keep doing that, she said, her eyes full of trapped, unspoken anger. You want to keep retelling my story. But it's *my* story. It's not yours. You can't just make things up because you'd like it better if I had been braver, if I had killed the wolf myself instead, or fucked him in the forest, or started a lesbian collective with the hunter and my grandmother and the local midwives, and made sustainable jams and pickles for a modest profit. Because you'd like me better if I were a symbol of menstruation and sexual power. It happened to me, it's the worst thing that ever happened to me. It's the only thing that ever happened to me. I own it. I own that wolf and the forest and my basket full of bread and my grandmother with her teeth in a jar. You can't just make yourself the huntsman or the wolf and turn it into a story about us. It's a story about me, and how my grandmother died, and how one day I could understand what monsters said and I thought I was going crazy. You want to make it an instruction. A morality play. But you shouldn't do things like that, if you love someone. It's theft.

I promised her I wouldn't, that I just wanted to be closer to her, that I had been silly, insensitive. I would never write about her, I swore. What did I need to write about her for? There were plenty of other things. Things that did not mind.

She put her hand on my mouth. You're lying, she said. It's in your nature. I don't hold it against you. You're a wolf, too. You saw me in the wood and you didn't know why you wanted me but you just had to. You crept up, and pretended you were someone nice. Harmless. Who would never take my whole life and lay it out in a book like a beetle specimen. Who would never make me wish I could just work in an office and drink my latte with soy milk and wear green. But you were lying and you're lying now. You're already writing a story about me in your head, even while you're kissing me.

That was true, and it was this story and I woke up in the night, surreptitiously, to write it by the blue, steady light of my laptop and I felt guilty, like I was committing adultery and I suppose I was. In the morning, just as I was finishing it, as if it was finishing the story that did it, she left me and took her hood with her and everything she had ever left in my house, which wasn't much. A toothbrush. A watch. A coffee cup. She must have gone while I was in the shower, cleaning off the slightly sour effort of staying up all night with a story.

I see her sometimes, on the train, standing, her hip slightly thrust forward, in a cocktail bar with long windows looking out on the rain-washed street. At conferences, in a suit the color of old, furious blood, on the arm of a nice young man with long hair, or an older woman with prim glasses. She likes writers. She can't help it. When I see her I look for the wolf. I never see him. It's a strange trick of the eye. I always think I see something moving, just behind her, a shadow, a gleam. But it's nothing. Only her.

When this story was published in some anthology or other she came to the launch. She was thin. She said to me when I was finished reading: I should have told you before. Wolf doesn't taste like you think it will. It's not gamy. It's soft, like a heart. She drank some of the watery martinis they served and said I suppose it's passable as fiction but you know how I feel about postmodernism. She said don't put yourself in stories, it's gauche, and tres 1990. She said next time I'd better fuck a realist. She said come home with me.

No, she didn't. I want her to have said that. I want to write that she said that because it makes better narrative. I want to rewrite everything that happened like a fairy tale. I want her to have heard what I wrote and know that I loved her and forgive me because I can make beautiful things. Shouldn't that be enough? But what she actually said, in my ear, soft as a stopped breath, was: *Die Wahrheit ist ich laufen immer und der Wald beendet nie. Die Blätter sind rot. Der Himmel ist rot. Der Weg ist rot und ich bin nie allein.*

I understood her. But some things I have learned not to say.

I walked home from the reading in my red coat, the one I bought the spring after she left. I'm a sentimentalist, really. It's a flaw, I admit. The night was cold; falling leaves spun around my hair. I pulled up my hood. My boots crunched on the hard ground as I turned toward the wood that leads to my house. I listened to the wind, and my feet, and I knew someone was following me. Someone tall and thin and hungry. Someone with golden, slitted eyes who can make it to my door before I can. And when I get there, when I get to my eaves and my stoop and I open the door—

# The Flame After the Candle

*She tried to fancy what the flame of a candle is like after the candle is blown out, for she could not remember ever having seen such a thing.*

—Lewis Carroll
Alice in Wonderland

### A Melancholy Maiden

OLIVE WAS BEGINNING TO GET very tired of going down to Wales with her mother on holiday every year and having nothing to do. It is a difficult trick to be tired of anything much when you are only fourteen and three-quarters years old, but Olive was just the sort of girl who could manage it. She would admit, if significantly pressed, that once or twice a summer it did *not* rain or drizzle or mist or thunder moodily, but never for long enough to do anyone a bit of good, and anyway, what is the use of having rain at all if the sun does not follow after? And now, Father Dear had left them for that pale, rabbity little heiress in London who they were only allowed to refer to as the Other One, and some damp, sheepy madness had taken hold of Darling Mother. She meant for them all to *live* here somehow, herself and Olive and Little George, mixing, presumably, among the scintillating society of shire horses and show-quality cucumbers.

Olive could have complained for England—it was her chief occupation in those drowsy silver afternoons and sopping woolen mornings. It was dreadful here. Even the potatoes and the ponies were depressed. There was only one pub and you weren't allowed to dance in it. Her school friends got to go to Rome and Madrid and Mykonos on *their* holidays. If this place ever hosted so much as a knitting circle, the whole population would suffer simultaneous apoplexies from the scandal of it. She couldn't even pronounce the name of the village in which Darling Mother had insisted on shipwrecking them. The name of the house was right out, and a more cramped and dreary paleolithic hut Olive had never dreamed of. It had never been *planned* nor *built* so much as *piled up* and *given up on several times*, leaving nothing anyone could properly call a house, but rather, a sort of rubbish bin full of bits of other houses lying on top of each other. Somebody had clearly once thought there was nothing so splendid in the world as Victorian moulding and crammed it in anywhere it would fit, and rather a lot of places it wouldn't, including three hacked-off marble capitals meant to crown pillars in a grand bank or a Hungarian cathedral, but had had to make themselves content with being mortared to the parlor wall without a single column to spare between them. The faucets leaked. The electricity could best be described as "whimsical." The staircase groaned like it meant to give birth every time Olive so much as thought about mounting an upstairs expedition.

Worst of all, there were only twenty-one books in the library and the landlord never changed them out because he was a perfectly slovenly old duffer who never could get all the buttons on his waistcoat closed at the same time. If they got fresh linens every fortnight, they ought to get fresh books, as well. It was only logic. Anything else was unhygienic.

### Lingering in the Golden Gleam

*HE SEES HER first in the corner of the Butler Library at Columbia University. It is late afternoon and and it is 1932 and it is so hot the books blaze like a great knobbled furnace. He just rounds the corner and there she stands among the non-fiction stacks, adrift between* The Rise and Fall of the Roman Empire *and* The Second Sex. *She is wearing a long, unfashionably conservative blue dress and smart black boots. Her still-thick white hair huddles in a knot beneath a brown velvet hat. The skin beneath is pale and wrinkled as a crumpled page. He is also wearing blue, which he takes as a good omen. They match. They* should *match. Her dress is expensive, well-preserved, the sort of dress only brought out for occasions. Her hat is not. It is very shabby, with shabby silk violets clinging pessimistically to its shabby rolled brim. The soft, comforting sounds of idle chairs squeaking across polished floors and idle coughs squeaking out of polished lungs punctuate the long sentence of his silence, waiting behind her, waiting for her regard, waiting for her to* notice *him, as though he has not had his fill of being noticed in this life.*

*But suddenly he has* not *had his fill of it. He longs for her to turn around. He wills it to happen now. All right, then* now. *No matter.* NOW. *He is desperate for her to see him, desperate as thirst. She will know him at a glance, of course, as he knows her. They will talk. They will talk wonderfully, magically, their words spangled and glittering, sodden with meaning, a conversation worthy of being recorded in perfect handwriting, printed lovingly in leather and vellum, preserved like that blue dress, down to the last quotation mark. Unless she is not as he wants her to be. She might be awful, awful and bitter and angry and stupid and a dreadful bore. Anyone worthy, anyone special or sensitive in the least, would know by now that he was standing here like a bloody fool, would have turned around minutes ago, would feel the shape of him behind her like a shadow. Shouldn't she glow? Shouldn't she burn with the light of who she is? But of course, she does not. He never has. He scolds himself for his own expectations.*

*It does not happen the way he wants it to. Nothing ever does anymore. He clears his throat like a stage.*

*Now, Peter!*

"Mrs. Hargreaves," whispers the youngish man in the blue tie, "Pardon the intrusion. My name is Peter. Peter Llewelyn Davies."

*She turns her back on the books and meets his eyes with a cool, sharp expression. She's rather shorter than he imagined. But her eyes are far, far bluer than his dreams, bluer than her dress, his tie, the June sky outside the tall library windows. She holds out her hand. He takes it.*

"You must call me Alice, Mr. Davies. Everyone does, whether I invite them to or not."

### I Am Not Myself, You See

OLIVE DUTIFULLY KEPT up her soliloquy of despair during business hours, with short breaks for lunch and tea. But she didn't mean more than an eighth of it on any given day. It was all a kind of avant-garde improvisational theater staged for the benefit of Darling Mother.

The unhygienically unchanging books were a real problem, but she knew very well that the village of Eglwysbach was pronounced *egg-low-is-bach*, which always made her imagine the German composer running around a chicken pen in a powdered wig and speckled wings, crowing for his lost babies. The house went by the name of Ffos Anoddun. As that was nearly too Welsh to bear, Olive assumed it was something to do with fairies or a hillock or a puddle or all three together, and fondly referred to it as Fuss Antonym, which sounded reasonably similar, and comforted her, for to her mind, the opposite of a big fuss was a small contentment. Olive loathed all her school friends and most other people, and couldn't have given a toss where they went on holiday, even if they'd ever think to confide that sort of thing in her direction. She felt rather affectionate toward the quiet, as it meant hardly anyone came round insisting on being other people at them. Olive *liked* knitting, and shire horses, and electricity was rather a lot of bother, when you thought about it. It was 1948.

People had gotten along well enough without light bulbs for nearly the whole history of everything.

And she especially loved the three capitals on Fuss Antonym's parlor wall. She would sit beneath them of an afternoon in the big musty mustard-colored wingback chair with silk horseradish-green cord whipping and whirling all over it and imagine the poor odd stone wolf and wild hare and raven heads in their curling pale ferns were holding the whole world up, and herself the only person ever to have guessed the truth.

It was safe, you see, to complain around Olive's sole remaining parent. It was the expected thing. Darling Mother was a complainer in good standing herself. Misery was, she always said, the natural resting state of the young. It was only the old who could not bear unhappiness. Only the old who buckled beneath the hundred million pound weight of it all. As long as Olive kept up her whitewater torrent of disinterest and disaffection and discontent, Darling Mother judged her a Normal Girl, and therefore safe to abandon, never once asking what she was *really* thinking, or feeling, or wanting, or doing with her time, which suited Olive like a good coat. Little George never complained a bit, even when a sheep ate all his paintbrushes, and Darling Mother practically *murdered* him with concern and attention.

But she did guess at the shape of her child's actual innards, occasionally. When some change in the weather troubled the meager seams of maternal ore that ran deep within the mine of Darling Mother's heart, she did grope after some connection. She changed the books once. She left a Welsh dictionary on Olive's bedside table. And once, when she returned from one of her hungry scourings of antique dealers and auctions for more gloomy Victorian rubbish to weigh down the house, she paid a couple of the local boys to drag something silver and heavy and covered with a stained canvas into the parlor. She waved her thin, elegant hand and they left it leaning against the sooty mantel.

"I snatched it up just for you, Daughter Mine. I know you love all this sort of crusty ancient knick-knackery deep down, don't let's pretend otherwise. It's a looking glass. I found it down in Llandudno at an estate sale. Give the old dear a good seeing-to, won't you?"

### Child of Pure Unclouded Brow

*"ALICE, THEN," HE says.*

*The New York sun lights up his untidy brown hair, turns it into a golden cap, the opposite of Perseus, the opposite of himself.*

*The old woman touches her hat self-consciously.* "Alice then; Alice now. Alice always, I'm afraid."

"And I'm Peter."

*He is repeating himself, and feels foolish. But repetition is a very respectable literary device. As old as dirt and debt and Homer. She will forgive him. Probably.*

"Aren't you just?" *laughs Alice.* "Well, let's have a look at you. One head, two shoulders, a couple of knees, rumpled suit and half a day's beard. Honestly, Peter, how could you come calling on me without a fetching green cap and pointed shoes? I think I deserve at least that, don't you?"

*Peter looks stricken. His throat goes dry and in all his days he has never wanted whiskey so badly as in this awful moment, and in all his days he has wanted whiskey very badly and often indeed. She did know him, then.*

"Oh, I am sorry. I am *sorry*, Peter, that was unkind. Oh, I am a dreadful beast! It's what comes of not mixing in company apart from cats and cups, you know. Don't look quite so much like you've just been shot, dear, it doesn't become. People have done it to me so many times, you see. I couldn't pass up a chance to do it to somebody else, just the once! And who else in all this sorry world could I do it to but you? Allow an old woman her indulgences."

"It's quite all right. I'm used to it."

Alice Pleasance Liddell-Hargreaves squares her shoulders, bracing as if for a solid punch to the chest, "You may pay me back, if you like."

"Please, Mrs. Har—Alice. I've quite forgotten."

"No, no, it was rotten of me. I won't accept your forgiveness, not one bit, until you've done me a fair turn."

"If you insist on making it up to me, I should much prefer you allow me to take you to dinner tonight," Peter demurs. He dries his palms on his tweed. "I know a place nearby that's serving wine again already."

The sunlight streaming through the library windows thins and goes silvery with clouds, darkening Alice's eyes. "And what do you imagine that will accomplish? That Peter and Alice, the *Peter and the Alice*, should share plates of oysters and glasses of champagne, quote each other's famous namesake novels with tremendous wit and pathos, philosophize about innocence, and achieve a kind of graceful catharsis whilst we malign the rather tawdry men who wrote us down for posterity?"

"Just that," Peter says with a smile that looks like a memory of itself. He holds out his arm. "To talk of many things. Of shoes and ships and sealing wax—"

Alice clutches her heart in mock agony and staggers. "Oh, there's a clever lad! A palpable hit, Davies. I'll be wincing for days. Now we're quite even."

Peter sighs. This would be all, then. A library, a few sharp words, then nothing, a meal alone with his shadows.

"I think I shall allow you to drag this dreadful beast to a respectable supper, so long as it's not too far, and you pay for us both. I can't bear much of a stroll, nor much expense, these days."

She puts her thin, bony hand on Peter's elbow. When she leans against him, she seems to weigh no more than a pixie.

### Every Single Thing's Crooked

OLIVE SAT IN the parlor of the house she called Fuss Antonym with her knees tucked up under her chin, staring at the looking glass. It was raining, because it was Wales and it was winter, and the raindrops against the old lead windows sounded like millions of tiny crystal drums beaten by millions of tiny crystal soldiers. The marble wolf and raven and hare on the misplaced capitals stared down at her in turn. Olive had spent the better part of the morning on her hands and knees with a tube of silver polish and a bottle of vinegar, coaxing the muck of ages out of the great heavy mirror. It was quite a lovely design, once you got down past the geologic layers of black tarnish and dust. The glass was still good, except for a little spiderweb of cracks in the lower right corner that no one but actual spiders would ever notice. The silver frame bloomed with curling oak leaves and pert little acorns and shy half-open violets, a perfect specimen of the typical Victorian habit of taking anything wild and pretty and nailing it down, casting it in metal, freezing it forever. Olive thought the violets probably had little polleny agates or pearls in their centers at some point. The prongs were still there, bent out of shape, empty. She touched them with her fingers. Those prongs were quite the loneliest and saddest thing she'd ever seen, somehow. They looked like her mother. They looked like her.

She and Little George had wrestled it up onto the mantel and snagged the thing on a couple of rusty nails. They hadn't any kind of level or ruler, so the poor looking glass hung up there at an unhappy angle that Olive informed Darling Mother was "unbearable," while privately she thought of it as "rakish." Little George had wandered off to beg the sheep for his paintbrushes back, and Olive coiled herself into the mustard-colored wingback chair for a good long stare. She could see just the barest top of her own head from here, her dark bobbed and fringed hair, her white scalp like a pale road through her own head. She could see the back of the little brass clock on the mantel, the woebegone door to the kitchen cracked open a wedge, the bland pastoral paintings hanging against vaguely mauve wallpaper, all turned backward, and therefore slightly more interesting. The shepherdess on the moor was holding her black lamb in her left arm now. The fox was running the opposite way from the hounds and the horses. She could see the rain beating out a marching rhythm on the windows, and the green hills beyond disappearing away into a fog like forgetting. And she could see the broken capitals glued to the wall in the looking glass just as they were glued to the wall in the parlor, their faces turned the wrong way round, too, like the shepherdess and the fox, which was certainly why their eyes looked so odd and canny, the way your own eyes look when you see a photograph of yourself. *Very* odd and *very* canny. Really, awfully so, actually.

Olive stood up on the wingback chair. The upholstery springs groaned and complained. Now she could see her whole self in the looking-glass: Olive, not much of anyone, in a shift dress the same color as the wallpaper, with pearl earrings on. The earrings belonged to the Other One. She'd given them for Christmas, to curry favor. Olive wore them to vex and to vex alone.

She leaned forward toward the looking glass. She blinked several times. She opened her mouth to call for Darling Mother, which was pure idiocy, so she shut it again with a quickness. She glanced over at the capitals in the parlor, then back to the capitals in the looking glass. Back and forth. Back and forth.

"There you have it, Olive," she told herself aloud. "You've gone mad. I expect it happens to everyone in Wales sooner or later, but you've certainly broken the local speed record. Well done, you."

She had imagined, when she'd considered the idea of insanity before now, chiefly when Darling Mother came home from meeting with Father Dear and the barrister and the Other One and started drinking gin out of a soup spoon, all night long, one spoonful after another, like sugar, that going mad would feel different. Wilder, more savage, more lycanthropic, more like a carousel spinning too fast somewhere inside a person's brain. But Olive felt perfectly Olive. She didn't even think of the gin bottle in the cabinet. She only thought of the wolf. One thing was certain—*she* had nothing to do with it. It was the wolf's fault entirely.

The marble wolf in the parlor had a noble expression on his face. His muzzle was smooth and gentle and sorrowful. It looked almost soft enough to pet.

The wolf in the looking glass had raised his stone muzzle into a fearsome snarl.

## Phantomwise

PETER ASKS THE *man at the Stork Club for scotch on ice. Evening light turns the tablecloths pink and violet. The ice is his last bulwark against total, helpless nihilism. He rolls the oily ambrosia of the bog over the crystals.*

*Alice orders a glass of beer. It arrives quickly, dark and thick and workmanlike. She smacks her lips and Peter nearly calls the whole thing off then and there. He had imagined her drinking... what? Delicate things. Tea. Champagne. Rain filtered through a garret roof. She is a lady of a certain era, and ladies of that certain era do not drink porter. After the beer come oysters from some presumably dreadful, mollusk-infested swamp called Maine, which would not pair at all with her black beer. Peter finds himself in an apoplexy of flummoxed culinary propriety.*

*Alice runs her fingertip around the rim of her glass and puts it between her lips, slicked with sepia foam.*

*"One 'drink me' out of you and I'll have your head," she scolds him, but her eyes shine. "My husband loved his beer. The darker the better. None of this prancing blonde European stuff, he'd say. Porter, stout, dubbel! I pretended that I had never met so curious a creature as a man who adores beer. That's how a girl makes her way in this world, Mr. Davies. Pretending awe at the simplest habits*

of men. But beer has been the bitter tympani keeping time for the long parade of sad, strange, lonely men I've loved. My father and Charles called it 'our most ancient indulgence' and made a lot of noise about the pyramids while they poured their pints. Even our Leopold had barrels brought in from Belgium no matter where we were staying—imagine the expense! Nothing to a man of his station, of course. But to us? Impossible magic. Though he liked everything blonde, the rake."

"Prince Leopold?" It sounds absurd even as he says it, but he cannot think of any other fabulously wealthy Leopold she might mean.

"The very one. Didn't you know Alice had adventures in places not called Wonderland? Paris, Rome, Berlin, Vienna. All the lions and unicorns you could ever want. He never could decide between my sister and I, and in the end we were nothing but...well. Talking flowers, I suppose. He named his daughter Alice. That's something, at least." She strokes the silvery flesh of the oyster with a tiny pronged fork. "He died."

"The prince?"

"My husband. In the war. My sons, as well. Everyone, as well. My sister is long gone, a ghost in Leopold's locket. I've got one boy left and he doesn't visit anymore. It's too awful for him to face ruin in a blue dress. Oh, Peter, I live crumblingly in a crumbling body in a crumbling house and I burn my heating bills in the furnace for lack of coal and every so often I crawl out to tell a few people how wonderful it was to be a child in Oxford with a friend like Charles to teach me about all the sundry beauties of life so that I can buy another year's worth of tinned beef. And how are you coming along in the world, Peter Pan? How are you crumbling?"

Peter Llewelyn Davies flushes and eats in silence. The oysters taste like spent tears. His toast points stare back at him as if to say: what else did you expect?

"I'm in publishing," he offers finally.

*Alice laughs sharply.* "How hungry a thing is a book! Devoured you whole straight from the womb, and still gnawing away at your poor bones. Oh, but it was different for you, wasn't it? It was only ever that summer, really, with Charles and I and Edith and Lorina, punting on the river. But your James raised you, didn't he? Adopted the whole lot of Davies orphans. I can't tell if that would be better or worse. Tell me. Should I envy you?"

*The soup course arrives. He frowns into a wide circle of pink bisque. His brain is a surfeit of fathers—his own, a-bed, rotting cancerous jaw like a crocodile, all teeth and scaled death, his older brothers, always running, fighting, so far ahead, so untouched, and Barrie, always Barrie, Barrie always kind and generous and ever-present, ever watching, his eyes like starving cameras freezing Peter in place for a flash and a snap that never came.*

"He drank me," *Peter whispers finally.* "And grew larger."

### Large As Life and Twice As Natural

OLIVE PUT HER hand against the looking glass.

She was balanced rather precariously on the mantel, one knee on either side of a portrait of Darling Mother as a young girl, before Father Dear, before the Other One, before Olive and Little George and Eglwysbach and the sheep and the paintbrushes and all of everything ever. A book of matches tumbled down onto the hearth as Olive tried, somehow, to grip the brickwork with her kneecaps.

When she'd been cleaning it with vinegar, the mirror had felt cool and slick and perfect as dolphin-skin. Olive pressed her other hand against the glass. It wasn't cool now. Or slick. It felt warm and alive and prickly, like a wriggling hedgehog thrilled to see its mate waddling through a wet paddock. The marble wolf's head in the looking glass parlor still snarled. The one in Fuss Antonym's parlor still did nothing of the kind.

"Don't be stupid, Olive," she scolded herself. Darling Mother never did, anymore. Someone had to pick up the slack. "Really, you're such an awful little fool. Nothing's going to *happen*. Nothing's *ever* going to happen to you. That's just how it is and you know it. You've gone barking, that's all, and pretty soon someone will come and take you away to a nice padded room by the sea where you can't bother anyone."

The looking-glass *writhed* under her hands. It spread and stretched and undulated like a great glass python just waking from a thousand years asleep. Slowly, the mirror turned to mist, and the mist stroked the bones of her wrists with fond fingers.

"Mum!" Olive screamed—but the looking-glass took her anyway, scream and all, and in half a moment she tumbled through to the other side into a cloud of green glowworms, and a thumping, ancient forest, and the hot, thrilling blackness of a summer's midnight.

### Each Shining Scale

*THE SALAD COURSE appears amid the wash of unbridgeable silence. Beets, radishes, hard cheeses as translucent as slivers of pearl, sour vinegars, peppercorns green and black. Peter sighs. The other diners around him simply will* not *stop their idiotic noises, the belligerent scraping of silver against china, the oceanic murmur of inane conversation, the animal slurping of their food. The oysters begin to turn on him. He feels a pale bile churning within.*

"He said not to grow up, not ever," *he whispers.* "He made me promise. But I couldn't help it. Not for a minute. Even while he was telling his tale, scribbling away at his own cleverness while my father rotted away in bed, I was growing up. Becoming not-Peter all the time while he told me to stop, stop at once, hold still, keep frozen like…like a side of lamb."

*Alice rolls her eyes and bites through a red radish. She has a spot of mauve lipstick on her teeth.* "Oh, how very dare those precious old men prattle on and on to us about childhood! The only folk who obsess over the golden glow of youth are ones who've forgotten how perfectly dreadful it is to be a child. Did you feel invincible and piratical and impish when your father died? I surely did not when Edith passed. You simply cannot stop things happening to you in this life. And do you know the funniest thing? An Oxford don, living in the walled garden of the university, with servants and a snug little house in which to write nonsense poems and puzzles and make inventions to your heart's content—that's more and more permanent a childhood than I ever had. He used to moan and mewl over me about the horror of corsets to come, the grimoire of marriage, the charnel house of childbirth, the dark curtains that would close over me upon some future birthday—well, for goodness sake! What would he know about any of that? He never married, he never had a child, he never so much as scrubbed his own underthings! How dare he tell me four years old was the best of life when I had so many years left to face?"

"Eighteen months."

"Pardon?"

"When Peter left for Neverland. He was eighteen months old. In a pram in Kensington Gardens. An eighteen months old child can barely speak, barely walk without falling. But that was the best I had ever been, in his eyes. The best I ever could be. And all those people went to see the play and clapped their hands and agreed he was right, and all the while I was twenty, twenty-five, thirty. Thirty. As old as Hook. Watching myself fly away. Watching from the back row while my bones screamed all in quiet: 'That's not what I was like, that's not how any of it goes, Christ, James, I was never heartless, I wish I was, I wish I was!'"

Alice frowns into her beer. She rubs the glass with one fingertip.

"It's not children who are innocent and heartless," she says—bitterly? Pityingly? Peter has never had the knack of reading people. Only books, and only on good days. "Only the mad," she finishes, and goes after her beets with a vengeful stab.

## A Life Asunder

THE VERY FIRST thing Olive did was look behind her. There was dear, familiar, batty old Fuss Antonym's wall—but it was no longer dear or familiar at all, and quite a bit battier. Instead of storm-slashed whitewash, the house sported a shimmering blackwash, roofed with overturned tea-saucers, and crawling with a sort of luminous ivy peppered with great, blowy hibiscus flowers in a hundred comic-book colors. She had come through the middle window in a row of three. On the other side of the window, she could still see the parlor, the mustard-colored chair, the painting of the shepherdess and the black sheep, the peeling moulding, the chilled grey afternoon peeking in past the curtains on the ordinary wall opposite. *All right, yes, fine,* Olive told herself, half-terrified, half-irritated. *This sort of thing happens when you've gone mad. It's nothing to get tizzy over. You've sniffed too much silver polish, that's all. Might as well enjoy it!* The other side of the looking glass was a window, and the other side of the house was a deep night, and a deep summer, and a deep forest, deep and hot and sticky and bright.

Olive's knees abandoned her. She tumbled down onto a new, savage, harlequin earth. She was going to have a tizzy, after all. *For God's sake, Olive!* She plunged her knuckles into the alien ground. Even the soil sparkled. Hot mud squelched between her fingers, streaked with glittering grime like liquefied opals. An infinite jungley tangle spread out before her, and it simply refused to *not* be there, no matter how Olive tried to make it *stop* being there. A path tumbled down the hillocks and shallows, away into rose-jet shadows and emerald-coal mists. Delicate wood-mushrooms curled up everywhere like flowers in a busy garden: chartreuse chanterelles, fuchsia toadstools, azure puffballs.

*Something* was moving down there, down the path, between the mushrooms and the ferns and the trees no prim Latin taxonomy could pin down. Something pale. Something rather loud. And, just possibly, not one *something* alone, but three *somethings* together. There is nothing for a tizzy like a *something*, and before she could tell herself sensibly to stay close to home, no matter how odd and unhomelike home had suddenly become, Olive was off down the path and through the garden of night fungus, chasing three hard, pale, loud voices through the dark.

"You're such an awful brat," growled something just ahead. "I don't know why we trouble ourselves with you at all."

"And *deadly* boring to ice the cake," sniffed something else. "Why even tell a riddle if you don't have any earthly intention of answering it for anybody? It's not sporting, that's what."

"I think it's jolly sporting," crowed a third something. "For *me*."

"A raven *isn't* like a writing desk. You can smirk all you like, but that's the truth and I hate you. It just *isn't*, in any sort of way that makes sense—" the second something spluttered.

"The farthing you go for sense, the furthing you are from the pound," the third something said loftily.

"*Do* shut up," snarled the first something.

Olive rounded a bank of birch stumps and mauve moss wriggling in such a way that she absolutely did not want to look any closer—and yet she did, for that was a something, too. The moss wasn't wriggling at all, rather, hundreds of silkworms wriggled while they feasted on it. Only these were *actually* silkworms—not ugly blind little scraps of beef suet, but creatures made up entirely of rich, embroidered silk brocade, fat as a rich lady, writhing greedily over the bank. Olive shuddered, and in her shuddering, nearly toppled over the *somethings* she'd been after.

In a clearing in the wood stood three hacked-off marble capitals, the sort meant to crown pillars in a grand bank or Hungarian cathedral. Her capitals. The very ones that hung so stupidly and dearly on her parlor wall. Only these were hopping about on their own recognizance, as if they were really and truly the wolf, hare, and raven that had been carved into their fine stone blocks.

The wolf's head, surrounded by carved fern-heads and flowers, the very one that had snarled *within* the looking glass and snoozed *without*, looked Olive up and down. The hare wriggled her veiny marble nose. The raven fluffed his sculpted feathers.

"Bloody tourists," the wolf snipped.

### Seven Maids with Seven Mops

*ALICE WATCHES ANOTHER couple without expression. The man cuts the woman's meat for her. The woman stares into the distance while he saws away silently at her pork. A repeating face, turned away, a woman watching a woman watching nothing. Staring and sighing and gnawing, the great human trinity. Peter has a strange and horrible instinct to lean over the table, the salads, the beer, the scotch, the candles, the world, their whole useless strained, copyedited lives and kiss Alice. To make himself cheap, as Wendy did in that cruel first scene in the nursery. He has always kissed first in his life. Always tried to redeem that little viciousness in the other Peter, whose heart was an acorn and whose kiss was a jest. She is so much older than he, but Peter loves older women, since he was hardly yet a man. Guiltily, and to great sorrow, but who could ask more of the most famous motherless boy in all of history?*

*He doesn't do it. Of course he doesn't. He, too, is of a certain era, and that era does not clear dining tables for the madness of love.*

*"At least your man stayed to look after you," Alice says finally, without turning her face back to his. "It's a kindly vampire who tucks you in and puts out the milk by your bed once he's drunk his fill of your life."*

*Her lips are red with beet-blood. He supposes his must be as well. Peter orders a second scotch.*

*"Are you angry, Alice? Do you hate him? I can't think whether I should feel better or worse if you hate him. I can't think whether*

I hate mine or not. I can't think whether he is mine. I am his, that's for certain. His, forever. A shadow that's slipped off and roams the streets hoping to be mistaken for a human being. For awhile I was so flamingly angry I thought I'd char."

"Not angry...angry isn't the word. Perhaps there isn't a word. Charles came back to see me once, after that summer. I was a little older. Nine or ten. A little was enough. He looked at me like a stranger. Like any other young woman—a slight distaste, a tremor of existential threat, a very little current of fear. He could hardly meet my eye while I poured the tea. Like a robber returning to the scene of the crime." She stops watching the other woman and turns her blue eyes back to Peter. Their cold, triumphant light fills him up like a well. "He came to my window and saw that I'd grown old and he wanted nothing more to do with me."

### Alice's Right Foot, Esq.

"YOU'RE GOING TO spoil it," snapped the hare. "Oh, I *know* she's going to spoil it, it always gets spoiled, just when we're about to have it out at last."

"I won't spoil anything, I promise," Olive whispered, quite out of breath.

"You can hardly help it," sighed the wolf's head capital. "Any more than milk can help spoiling outside the icebox."

"Raven was *finally* about to tell us how he's like a writing-desk when you came bollocking through! I've been waiting eons! There's no sense to it, you know. We've said a hundred answers and none of them are at *all* good. But he won't say, because he's a stupid wart. I'd advise *you* to tread more quietly, young lady, if you don't want to alert the authorities."

"What authorities? It's only a forest inside a looking glass, the constable is hardly going to come arrest me on my way from Nowheresville to Noplace Downs."

"The Queens' men," the wolf whispered. His whiskers quivered in canine fear. "All ways here belong to them."

"Which Queen? Elizabeth? She's all right."

"Either of them," answered the hare with an anxious tremor in her quartzy whiskers. "Twos are wild tonight and they're the worst of the lot." The pale rabbit tilted onto her side just as a real, furry hare would if it were scratching its ear with a hind leg, only the capital hadn't any hind legs, right or left, so she just hitched up on one corner and quivered there.

"All right, I surrender," cawed the raven's head suddenly. "I'll say it. But only because our Olive's finally going places and that deserves a present."

"Oh, don't be silly!" Olive demurred, though she was quite delighted by the idea. "It's quite enough to have properly met you three at last! And to think, it would never have happened if I hadn't gone totally harebrained just then! It was all that silver polish, I expect."

The marble hare went very still. "I beg your pardon? What is the trouble with a hare's brain, hm?"

"Oh, I didn't mean anything cruel by it," Olive said hurriedly. "It's only that I'm…well, I'm obviously not playing with a full deck of cards this evening."

"Only the Queen has a full deck at her command," the marble wolf barked. "Who do you think you are?"

"Nobody!"

"Then we'll be on our way!" the hare huffed. "There's no point in talking to nobody, after all. People will say we've gone mad!"

"Oh, please don't go! I only meant…" She looked pleadingly at the marble raven, who offered no help. "I only meant that *I* went mad a few minutes ago, and as I've only just started, I'm bound to make a mash of it at first. I've no doubt I'll improve! The most dreadful sorts of people go mad, it can't be so terribly hard. But I only ever wanted to say that darling Mr. Raven hasn't got to give me a present, it's present enough to make your acquaintance!"

"Would you prefer a future?" the hare asked, her pride still smarting. "It's more splendid than the present, but you've got to wait three days for delivery."

"Of course, the past is particularly nice this time of year," the wolf grinned.

"No! All we've got is the present, and not a very pleasant one at that." The raven snapped at a passing glowworm. "Rather cheap, honestly. I'm only warning you so you won't be disappointed."

"Oh, stop trying to impress her! You haven't got the goods. Admit it!" the wolf howled from within his thicket of carved Corinthian leaves. "You just made up that bit of humbug because it sounded clever and shiny and it alliterated you never had the tawdriest idea of how to solve it. Confess! Perjury! Pretension! Petty thief of my intellectual energies! *Hornswoggler!*"

"I *have* got the goods, and the bads, and the amorals, too! But if I'm to give up my present, after all this time, we must have a proper party for it! You lot have abused me so long that just handing it over in the woods like a highwayman won't do, no sir, no madam, no how nor hence nor hie-way! I will have a To-Do! I will have balloons and buttercream and brandy and bomb shelters! And one good trombone, at minimum!"

The marble hare rocked from one side of its flat column-base to the other in sculptural excitement. "Shall we, shan't we, shall we, shan't we, shall we join the dance?"

The three capitals leapt off down the forest path, bouncing and hopping like three drops of oil on a hot pan. Olive raced after them, ducking moonlit branches and drooping vines clotted with butterflies that seemed, somehow, to have tiny slices of bread for wings. But no matter how Olive ran, she seemed only to go slower, the wood around her only to close in thicker and deeper, darker and closer, until she could hardly move at all, and had lost sight entirely of the talking capitals. At last, she found herself standing quite still in a little glen, staring up at the starry sky and the starry leaves and the starry massive skeleton sheathed in moss so thick it could keep out the cold of a thousand winters. Tiger lilies and violets and dahlias and peonies grew wild in the skeleton's teeming green ribcage, its soft, blooming mouth, its sightless eye sockets. It lay sprawled on the forest floor propped up against a tree as vast as time, arms limp, legs bent at the knee. A galaxy of green and ultraviolet glowworms ringed the giant's dead green head like a crown, and the crown spelled out words in flickering, sparkling letters:

THE TUMTUM CLUB

## No Thought of Me Shall Find a Place

*A VIOLINIST, A cellist, and an oboist begin to set up their music stands in the corner of the Stork Club. They are nice young men, in nice new suits, with nice fresh haircuts and shaves. The violinist rubs his bow with resin as though he is sharpening a sword.*

"I always felt...Alice...I always felt I was two people. Two Peters. Myself, and him. *The Other One. And the Other was always the better version. Younger, handsomer, jollier, bolder. Of course he was. I had to bumble through every day knocking things over and breaking my head open. But the Other One...he got to try over and over again until he got it right. Until he was perfect. Dreamed, planned, written, re-written, re-re-written, edited, crossed-out, tidied up, nipped and cut and shaped and moved through the plot with a minimum of trouble. Nothing I could ever say could be as clever as the Other One's quipping. How could it be? Everything I say is a dreadful cliche, because I am alive and human, and live humans are not made out of dust and God's breath, no matter what anyone says. They're made out of cliches. So there are two of me—what a unique observation for a muse to make! No, no it isn't, it can't be, because I only said it once, I didn't get to decide it was rubbish and go back, erase it, add a metaphor or a bit of meta-fiction or* a dash of theatricality. So I just say it and it's terrible, it's nothing. But the Other One would be delighted with two Peters, you know. What adventures they would have together. Nothing for mischief like a twin."

Alice's eyes narrow with concern. "Peter...I'm not sure I follow, dear."

"Yes, well, no one does. I don't, when it comes down to it. If you don't mind a confession before the main course...I...I went...well, all this about two Peters and suchlike...wound me up in a sanatorium. For awhile. Not long. But...well, yes. Er." He finishes lamely, flushing in shame—shame, and the peculiar excitement of sharing a secret one absolutely knows is unwelcome and untoward.

"Oh, Peter!"

"Oh, Peter, indeed. It's such a funny thing. Nothing in the world so much like Neverland as a sanatorium. The food isn't really food, no one's got a mother, there's a great frightening man in a waistcoat who harries you night and day, and you keep fighting the same battles over and over, round and round in circles, forgetting that you ever fought the minute it's over and the next one begins. All of us lost boys in that awful lagoon, dressed as animals, wailing for home."

She puts her hand on his. The tableware shifts beneath their fingers.

"Did you ever feel...like that? Like there were two Alices?" he whispers.

Alice laughs wanly. "Good heavens, no. There is only one Alice, and I am her. He only...took a photograph. One great, gorgeous photograph, where the sitting lasted all my life, and he sold that picture to the world."

## Cinders All A-Glow

OLIVE FOUND THAT, if she walked very, *very* slowly, as though she were dragging her feet on the way to some unpleasant chore, she could speed along quite gaily through the shadowy glen. It hardly took a moment of glum shuffling before she stood at a tapering, rather church-like door wedged into the giant's skeleton, just where its briary ribcage came to a pythagorean point. It certainly *was* a door, though rather absurdly done. It made her think of all the overdecorated slapdash rooms of Fuss Antonym, thrown up without reason or sense, for the door was spackled together out of pocket watch parts and butter and breadcrumbs and jam, and she felt entirely sure that if she were to knock, it would all come oozing, clattering apart and she should be billed for the damage.

"Hullo?" Olive called instead, for she had forgotten her pocketbook on the other side of the looking glass.

A slab of cold butter bristling with minute-hands like a greasy hedgehog slid aside. Two beady black rodent eyes peered down at her.

"Password," the Doorman whispered.

"Well, I certainly don't know!" Olive sputtered.

*Oh, bad form, Olive!* she cursed herself. *Haven't you ever read a spy novel? You're meant to say something extra mysterious, in a commanding and knowledgeable voice, so that the doorman will say to himself 'Anyone that commanding and knowledgeable has to be on the up and up, so it stands to reason the password's changed, or I've forgotten it, or I'm being tested by management, but any way it cuts, it's me who's at fault and not this fine upstanding member of our society.' Now, come on, do it, and you won't have to feel embarrassed when you think back on this later when you've gone un-mad.*

Olive stood on her tiptoes and stared commandingly into those black rodent eyes. *Something extra mysterious. Something knowledgable. Preferably something mad. Like a chicken in spectacles and a powdered wig.*

"Eglwysbach," she said slowly and stoically, fitting her mouth around the word as perfectly as possible, even tossing in a proper guttural cough on the end.

The eyes on the other side of the buttered watch-parts blinked uncertainly.

"Er. That doesn't sound right. But it doesn't sound *wrong*. It sounds *dash* passwordy. Am I asleep?" the Doorman whispered.

"We both are, most likely," Olive laughed.

"I'm not meant to sleep on the job, I'll be sacked for wasting time, even though time doesn't mind. He does need to lose a bit round the middle, to be quite honest. In fact, I wasn't asleep! I heard every word you were saying. Very naughty of you to suggest it."

"I won't tell. Now, if you heard what I was saying, then you heard me say the password very well and very correctly."

"Did I? That's nice." The creature yawned, but didn't open the door.

"Let me in!"

"Oh! Please don't beat me."

The pocket watch door wound open, leaving a slick of butter and jam as it swung. The Doorman was not a Doorman at all, but a Dormouse, standing on a tall footstool in a suit of armor bolted together out of pieces of a lovely china teapot with blue pastoral scenes painted on it. He stood rather stiffly, on account of the armor.

"I feel most relaxed and un-anxious snuggled into my teapot," the Dormouse said defensively, puffing out his little mouse chest. "So my friend Haigha invented a way for me to stay in it forever. In the future, everyone will be wearing teapots, mark my…mark…my March…"

The Dormouse fell asleep stuck upright in his armor. He leaned back against the door so that it groaned shut under his little weight.

### Envious Years Would Say Forget

PETER TAKES OFF *his glasses and rubs the bridge of his thin nose. The musicians begin a delicate, complicated piece that is nevertheless easy to ignore.*

"I'm terribly sorry, Mrs—Alice. I thought I wanted to talk about this. I thought I wanted to talk about it with you. But I think perhaps I do not, not really. I'm an awful cad, but I've always been an awful cad. Even the best version of me is a cad."

Alice quirks one long white eyebrow. She leans back in her chair and folds her hands in her blue lap.

"Am I doing something wrong?"

"Pardon?"

"Am I doing something wrong? Am I not behaving as you imagined I would behave? Ought I to have ordered the mock turtle soup instead of the cucumber? Or perhaps you'd like us to leap up and dash round the table and switch places whilst I pour butter into your pocket watch? I could curtsy and sing you a pleasant little rhyme about animals or some such—I'm told my singing voice is still quite good." Alice's thin, dry mouth curls into a snarl. "Or shall we simply clasp hands and try to believe six impossible things before the main course? What would satisfy you, Peter?"

Beneath the table, Peter digs his fingernails into his flesh through the linen of his trousers. He feels a terrible ringing in his head.

"It's nothing like that, Alice. I wouldn't—"

"Oh, I think it's precisely like that, Mr. Davies. You ought to be ashamed. It's disgusting, really. How could you do this to me? You, of all people? You didn't come snuffling round my skirt-strings so that we might find some pitiful gram of solace between the two of us. You came to find the magic girl. Just like all the rest of them. You're no better, not in the least bit better. Life has hollowed you out, so I and my wondrous, lovely self must fill you up again with dreams and innocence and the good sort of madness that doesn't end you up with an ether-soaked rag over your face. Well, life hollows everyone, boy. I've got nothing left in the cupboards for you. Oh, I am *disappointed*, Peter. Rather bitterly so."

A kind of leaden horror spreads over Peter's heart as he realizes he is about to cry in public. "Mrs. Hargreaves, please! You don't understand, you don't. You can't."

*Alice leans forward, clattering the tableware with her elbows. "Oh—oh. It's worse than that, isn't it? You didn't want me to be magical for you. You wanted to be magical for me. In the library. Just like a nursery, wasn't it? And for once you would really do it, fly up to a girl's window and sweep her away to a place full of crystal and gold and feasting, and she would be dazzled. I would be dazzled. You tell everyone else that you're not him, to stop gawping at you and only seeing the boy who never grew up. But you thought I, I, of all people, might look at you and see that you* are *him. Or, at least, that you want to believe you are, somewhere, somewhere fathoms down the deeps of your soul. Only I'm spoiling it now, because an Alice makes a very poor Wendy indeed."*

*Peter Llewelyn Davies gulps down the dregs of his scotch and thinks seriously about stabbing himself through the eye with his oyster fork. It would be worth it, if he could escape this agony of a moment.*

*"Very well, then, Peter," Alice says softly. "I am ready. I am here. I am her. I am all the Alice you want me to be. Now that we've seen each other, if I believe in you, you'll believe in me."*

*"Stop it."*

### Let's Pretend We're Kings and Queens

THE TUMTUM CLUB was a wide round room carpeted in moonflowers. Wide toadstool-tables dotted the floor, lit by glass inkwells in which the blue ink burned like paraffin, and all the sizzling wicks were quills. Creatures great and small and only occasionally human crowded round, in chairs and out, dodos and gryphons and lizards and daisies with made-up eyes and long pale green legs and lobsters and fawns and sheep in cloche hats and striped cats and chess pieces from a hundred different sets, all munching on mushroom tarts and pig-and-pepper pies and slices of iced currant cakes and sipping from tureens of beautiful soup. The revelers were dressed very poorly and very well all at once. Their clothes were clotted with sequins and rhinestones and leather and velvet, but it was all very old and shabby and worn through, and no one wore shoes at all. Advertising posters hung all round the mossy bones walling them in. One showed a rose with a salacious look in her eyes and two huge fans over her thorns, promising a LIVE FLOWERS REVUE. Another had two little fat men painted on it in striped caps yelling at one another, which was, apparently, THE SATIRICAL SPOKEN WORDS STYLINGS OF T&T, TWO WEEKS ONLY. On one end of the club stood a little stage ringed with glowing oyster-shell footlights. A thick blue curtain was drawn across the half-moon proscenium. Olive could hear the tin-tinning sounds of instruments warming up backstage. Whatever happened in the Tumtum Club at night had not begun to happen yet.

On the other end of the room stretched a long bar made of bricks and mortar and crown moulding. It was manned, improbably, by a huge egg with jowls and eyebrows and stubby speckled arms and a red waistcoat and a starched shirt collar and cravat, even though he had no neck for it to matter much. An orchestra of colored liquor bottles glittered behind him. A couple of chess pieces, a white knight and a red one, leaned past the empties to catch the eye of the egg.

"I'll take a Treacle and Ink, my good man," the red knight said.

"It's *very* provoking," the bartender answered, filling up a pint glass, "to be called a man—*very!*"

"I'll have an Aged Aged Man, Mr. D," the white knight whispered. "Or should I spring for a Manxome Foe? Oh!" the knight fretted and pursed his horsey muzzle. "Just mix a bit of sand in my cider and don't look at me. You know how I like it."

The egg-man turned to Olive. "And you, Miss..."

"Olive."

"Ah, with a name like that you'll want a martini. With a name like that you'll be small and hard and bitter and salty. With a name like that you'll be fished out when no one's looking and discreetly tossed in the bin!"

The notion of being served a martini, no questions asked, rather thrilled Olive. Darling Mother was very strict with everyone's indulgences but her own. "I can't pay, I'm afraid. I haven't got half a crown to my name."

"No crowns allowed at the Tumtum Club, my dear," the white knight whispered, "Not even one." And before he was done with his whispering, a cocktail glass slid down the bar into Olive's hand. Whatever was inside was nothing at all like a martini, being completely opaque and indigo, but it did have an olive in it. Frosted letters danced across the base of the glass: DRINK ME. So she did.

A voice like a crystal church bell wrapped in silk rang out over the club.

*"Will you all come to my party?" cried the Monarch to the Throng*
*"Though the night is close around us and its reign is harsh and long?"*

A long, slim, orange and black leg slid out from behind the curtain. A rude and unruly applause burst through the room, cat-calls, foot and hoof-stomping, snapping of fingers and claws, a great pot of hollering and whistling stirred too fast. A long, slim, orange arm emerged from the blue velvet, its elegant fingers curling and dancing with each new word.

*"Gather eagerly, my darlings, tie your troubles in a bow*
*For the Tumtum Club is open—are you in the know?*
*Are you, aren't you, are you, aren't you, are you in the know?*
*Are you, aren't you, are you, aren't you, aren't you ready for the show?"*

Olive stared. This was, perhaps, a naughtier show than she really ought to be seeing. But then, if the mad are naughty, who can scold them? She scrambled for an empty seat among the toadstool tables.

Only one remained, far in the back row, wedged between a large striped cat and a thin, nervous-looking chess piece, a white queen, knitting a long silvery shawl in her lap.

A huge saffron-colored wing spooled out over that coy leg like a curtain all its own. It was speckled with white and rimmed with jet black and veined with ultramarine. Finally, a head emerged: hair like a beetle's back, skin the color of flame, eyes as green as swamp gas and cut-glass. The girl swept and twirled her massive butterfly wings like the fans of a harem-dance and sang for the roar of the crowd:

> *You can really have no notion how delightful is our art*
> *In here there is no Red Queen and there is no Queen of Hearts*
> *Only me and thee and he and she all in a pretty row*
> *Alive as oysters, every one—now, shall we start the show?*
> *Shall we, shan't we, shall we, shan't we, shall we start the show?*
> *Shall we, shan't we, shall we, shan't we, shan't we set the night aglow?*

"The Queen of Hearts?" Olive whispered. "I read a book with a Queen of Hearts in it once."

"You must be very proud," yawned the cat.

### It Must Sometimes Come to Jam To-Day

THE CANDLELIGHT LIGHTS *up her cheekbones ghoulishly. She has the look of a fox on the scent of something small and scurrying and delicious.*

"I shan't stop," *she needles him.* "If you know any bloody thing at all about Alice, you know that she doesn't stop. She keeps going, all the way to the eighth square and back home again. She's the perfect English Girl, greeting the most vicious of things with an 'Oh My Gracious!' and a 'Well, I Never!' You haven't the first idea what sort of stony constitution it takes to go through life as the English

Girl. At least your Other One got to be wild and free and ruleless. A man can aspire to that. My Other One cannot rise above charmingly confused, because no English Girl may be allowed to greet nonsense with a sword or else all Creation would fall to pieces. But you wanted to meet me. You wanted to compare notes. You wanted a sympathy of minds, so no Oh My Graciouses for you, Peter. Only Alice, and Alice will have her tea and her crown if it's the death of her. Alice is curious, don't you remember? It is her chief characteristic. Curiouser and curiouser, as the meal goes on. Tell me everything. Leave off this poor mad little me *act*. What was Neverland really *like*?"

Peter coughs brutally. His vision swims with liquor and humiliation and the violin and the cello and the love he had prepared so carefully for this person, only to find it spoiled in the icebox. With the perfect timing of his class, the waiter appears with steaming plates of beef bourguignon and quails in a cream-mustard sauce, ringed in summer vegetables glistening with butter.

"You're mocking me, Mrs. Hargreaves. I never imagined you could be so vicious. I might as well ask you what Wonderland was like."

"You might at that. It smelled much better than New York, I'll tell you that much. But no more. I am operating a fair business here, young man. Show me yours and I'll show you mine."

"You can't be serious. Are you quite drunk? Does it amuse you to pretend to a silly clod that Wonderland was a real place?"

Alice blinks. She turns her head curiously to one side.

"Does it amuse you to pretend that Neverland was not?"

### Did Gyre and Gimble in the Wabe

THE ACTS WENT by like leaves blowing across the stage. Three young girls in shifts called Elsie, Lacie, and Tillie did an acrobatic routine, pantomiming any number of things that began with M: mouse-traps, and the moon, and memory, and muchness. Olive couldn't imagine how a handful of gymnasts could act out *memory* or *muchness*, but when they froze in their tableaux, Olive knew just what they meant, and applauded wildly with everyone else. A pig in a baby-bonnet stood in a lonely spotlight and belted out one long, unbroken, oink of agony that lasted nearly two full minutes before he fell to his knees, scream-snorted MOTHER WHY DON'T YOU LOVE ME while tears streamed down his porky jowls, then sprang up and bowed merrily while roses flew at him from all directions. A lovely turtle with sad eyes sang a song about soup. It seemed to be a sort of communal thing—anyone could whisper to the gorgeous butterfly master of ceremonies and take the stage, if they felt inclined. There was a bit of a queue forming in the wings. Olive shrank back as a monstrous *thing* crept onto the boards. He had claws like a great hairy dinosaur and eyes like headlamps and a tail that coiled down over the footlights, casting broken shadows over his violet-green scaled body. His dragon wings were so tall and wide he was obliged to bend and scrunch them to wedge under the half-moon shell of the stage. A couple of fawns pushed a little rickety pianoforte over to him with their dear spotted heads. The monster tinkled out a few experimental runs up and down the keys. Olive could hardly believe his horrid tarantula-talons could manage such graceful scales.

"It's only a Jabberwock, my dear. You needn't clutch my hand *quite* so hard," said the White Queen. Her face was so serene and crisply carved, like a jeweler had done it.

"A Jabberwock! Like *'twas brillig and the slithy toves did gyre and gimble in the wabe? Whiffling through the tulgey wood* and that? *The* Jabberwock?"

The monster at the piano began to play a mournful torch song. He fixed his moony headlamp-eyes on Olive and sang in a gorgeous tenor: *I never whiffled, I never, and it weren't even brillig at all. Nobody gave me no chance to be beamish, I could've been someone, if I'd been born small…*

The White Queen frowned at her knitting. "That's Edward. He's rather a war hero, don't you know? He lost his right foot at the Battle of Tulgey Wood, see?" Olive leaned forward—the Jabberwock worked the pedals of his pianoforte with only one crocodile-foot. The other was wrapped in gauze and seeping. The White Queen sighed like a tea kettle boiling. "He's going to lose the other one in an hour, poor chap."

Olive blinked. "What? What do you mean he's *going to* lose his other one? How do you know?"

Edward belted out: *You can take a Wock's head but you can't make him crawl!* He stopped, leaned his long, whiskered snout over the footlights into the audience, and whispered: "On account of my brain's being in my tail, yeah? Joke's on you, O Frabjous Brat!"

"It's the effect of living backwards," the Queen said kindly.

"Oh!" Olive whispered excitedly. "I know this part! Jam to-morrow and jam yesterday, right?"

"Will you please be quiet?" growled the striped cat. "Talking during performance is a biting offense."

The White Queen blushed pinkly. She reached down into the knitting basket at her feet and drew out a toasted crumpet spread generously with raspberry jam. She brushed a bit of wool fluff off of it and offered it to Olive.

"I have learned a few lessons since I was deposed," she said softly, and with such a tender sadness. "Very occasionally, it costs one nothing to bend the rules."

### Dear Me! A Human Child!

ALICE STARES DOWN *at her four neat quails adrift in their sea of golden sauce.*

*"You can't be serious," Peter hisses at her. "This is…this is unkind, Alice. Monstrous, in fact. Why are you doing this to me? What purpose is there in it?"*

"I'm not doing any little thing to you, young man. Now, stop it. You needn't pretend. What was Hook like, really? I always wondered if his stump pained him, at night, in the cold of the sea-air."

"For Christ's sake, this is madness. You ought to be locked up, not me."

Alice's face goes dark and furious and sour.

"Say that to me again, boy. Say it, and I'll whip you like the child you are, right here in this lovely restaurant. Don't think I can't. I raised three sons and a husband, you know."

Peter blanches. He feels his blood rebel, not knowing whether to flood his cheeks or flee them. He begins a deep study of his beef. After a time, Alice softens.

"I am sorry—it's a wonder how many times I've said it in such a short while! But I am, I am sorry, Peter, I simply assumed. It was only natural, to my mind. Only logic. I only thought…if for me, then for you. Goose and gander and all that rot. Oh, I never told anyone, my God, how could anyone be told? How could I even begin? But you, you of all people! The moment you introduced yourself I thought that we had veered toward this, careened toward it, that we would converge upon it long before dessert, and at last, I would know someone like me, and you would know someone like you, and what peace we should have then at the end of it all. Peace and something nice with butterscotch."

"Please. You mock me, Mrs. Hargreaves."

"I do not, Mr. Davies. I make you my confession. In the summer of 1862, something rather astonishing happened to me. I was four years old. And naturally, when it was all done, I ran at full pelt to tell my best friend all about it just as soon as I could. To my eternal fault, in those days, my best friend was a mathematics professor with a rather large nose and a rather large anxiety complex and an interest in writing."

The beef tastes like nothing at all. The wine tastes like less than that. He gives up. "It was real," he says flatly.

"Well, of course it was. Who could make up such a thing?"

### Everything's Got a Moral

THE EGG BROUGHT Olive another indigo martini.

"From the fellow onstage," the bartender whispered. "He was very insistent that it arrive as he was performing, not before or beside or behind."

The fellow onstage was an old-ish man in muttonchops holding an improbably large lavender tophat with the size-card still stuck in it. He watched the crowd solemnly as he drew object after object after object out of the hat: a croquet ball stained with blood, a pocket-watch with a bayonet thrust through the fob, a silver tea-tray with a great, unhappy boot-print on it.

"Deposed?" Olive said to the White Queen, who went on calmly with her knitting. "But you're the White Queen! Shouldn't you be off Queening about with the other Queens?"

"I wasn't red, so I wasn't needed," she sighed. "That's what they said. There were four of us once. The perfect number for bridge. The Red Queen, the White Queen, the Queen of Hearts, and…" the White Queen suddenly clammed up, shaking her head in distress.

"The Other One," the striped cat purred. "We aren't allowed to say her name. The Queens have ears. Hush hush."

"She kicked down the Queen of Hearts' horrid cards and shook the Red Queen so hard she nearly broke her neck—more's the pity she didn't finish the job. Everything was going to be all right, you know. With the Other One here to keep those scarlet women in line."

The cat licked his paws. "I met her. She was rather thick, if you ask me. And she kept going on about herself, which I think is very rude, when you're a guest."

"But you knew it wouldn't be all right," said Olive, who had a little brother, and therefore was immune to distraction. "Because of how you live backwards."

"Yes, yes! What a clever girl! I knew, but no one listens to me because I'm always screaming about one thing or another—but you would scream, too, if you remembered the whole future of the world until Judgement Day and past it! You'd scream and scream and never stop! I knew she'd vanish like a shawl in the wind and she did and just as soon as she did, the Red Queen and the Queen of Hearts would decide Wonderland needed taking in hand. Needed one crown. We were all conscripted. My Lily died on the Croquet Grounds. I wish I had. I wish…I wish a lot of things. The Other One came back, of course, nothing only happens once in Wonderland. But as soon as she was gone again, those red ladies holed up in their castles and started building their armies once more. We are not at war now, my child, but we soon shall be. Now, we simply hold our breaths and wait."

"Something like that happened in my world, too," Olive said softly. "*Is* happening. Germany and Russia and America and…well, everyone, I suppose."

"The Tumtum Club is the only place the Looking Glass Creatures are allowed to be mad anymore," the White Queen sighed. "Outside, we have to report for duty at dawn. In here, the Hatter can pull his heart out of his hat."

The gorgeous butterfly slipped out of the curtain again to master further ceremonies, twirling on her tiny black feet in a sudden cloud of stage smoke. She peered into the audience as though she were speaking to each of them in particular, as though what she said were more important than anything that had ever happened to them, and the whole of the universe waited upon their answering her.

*I am young, little darlings, the Butterfly crooned*
*My wings have become very bright*
*The larva I was drowned inside my cocoon*
*Growing up really is such a fright!*

*I hardly remember the old mushroom now*
*I liked hookahs, I think, and fresh dew*
*Yet I'll still have my answer, I do not care how:*
*Who Are You?*

Something knocked into their toadstool table and toppled Olive's drink. She tried to keep mum for the sake of the Hatter and shout indignantly at the same time, which is impossible, but she tried anyway.

The marble raven capital blinked up at her.

"Come on then," he cawed. "This is our five minute call. We're on, Olive, old girl."

### Large As Life and Twice As Natural

*THE TRIO OF musicians wind down. The lights are dim now. The restaurant nearly empty, nearly shut. Peter and Alice toy with the notion of eating their slices of plum-cake awash with double cream, but neither can fully commit to it. They speak of Wonderland, of cabbages and kings, of riddles and chess and what sort of tea could be got in the wilds. It is pleasant, there is a joy in it, but it is unreal. It is like listening to someone try to tell you the plot of a radio play you missed. Peter feels a chill. Perhaps another cold coming on.*

*"I want to believe you," he says.*

*"Clap your hands and give it a go. Or decide I'm a barmy old woman and go on with your life. It won't change what I know. Oh, Peter, how disappointing for us both. You thought we were the same. I thought we were. But* Alice in Wonderland *could never take me from myself, because it was myself, it always was. We're both the victims of burglars, dastardly fellows who stove in our windows and bashed up our houses. But my robber only took the silver. Yours took the lot. Of course, Charles got it half wrong and put a great lot of maths in to amuse himself, and perhaps if I'd been the one to write it I wouldn't have to sell my first editions to keep the lights on in my house, but losing Wonderland didn't ruin me. Losing..." and then she cannot continue. She grips her beer glass like it can save her, but it will not. It never has saved anyone... "...my boys...all my pretty boys..."*

"My brothers, too," Peter whispers. There is nothing more to say than that, than that they are people of a certain era, and people of a certain era know an emptiness in the world, a place where something precious was cut out and never replaced.

"Coffee?" asks the waiter.

"Tea," they answer.

"What I don't understand," Peter ventures finally, "is what you're doing here."

"I beg your pardon?"

"If it was all real, why don't you go back? When the lights have gone out and…your boys have gone…why stay here, in this dreadful world?"

"I never went on purpose. It just happened. I saw a white rabbit one day. I touched a looking glass. I never decided to go. It decided to take me. It's never decided since. Wonderland is like my son, my last son. It's just so awfully awkward for him to see me the way I've ended up, it avoids me as much as it possibly can."

"I suppose I should scour the countryside for bunnies and mirrors," Peter laughs despite himself.

"I suppose I should," Alice giggles, and for a moment she is that child on the cover of a million novels, the English Girl, rosy and devious and brilliant. The check appears as if by magic, and Peter pays it, as good as his word. Alice stands and the waiter brings their coats. "No, Peter, it's best as it is. Whatever would I say to the White Queen now? Give me my bloody damned jam, you old cow? I gave up weeping for my lost kingdom years ago. I made my own, and if it crumbled, well, all kingdoms do. The world's not so dreadful, my dear. It is dreadful, of course, but only most of the time. Sometimes it rather outdoes itself. Gives us a scene so improbable no one would dare to put it in a book, for who would believe in such a chance meeting between two such people, such a splendid supper, such an unlikely moment in the great pool of moments in which we all swim?" She kisses his cheek. She holds her lips against him for a long time. When she pulls away, there is a thimble in his hand. "Oh, goodness," Alice says with a shine in her blue eyes. "What a lot of rubbish old ladies have in their bags!"

―⌒―

THEY WALK ARM in arm out into the New York street. People shove and holler by. The lights spangle and reflect in the hot concrete. The air smells like rotting vegetables and steel and fresh baking rolls and summer pollen. Alice stops him on the curb before he can cross the road.

"Peter, darling, listen to me. You must listen. You've got to answer the Caterpillar's question, you've got to find an answer, or else you'll never find your way. I never could, not until now, not until this very night, but you must. It's the only question there is."

"I can't, Alice. I want to."

Alice throws her arms round his neck. "I like you better, Peter. Ever so much better than him. Peter Pan was always such an awful shit, you know."

They start across the long rope of the street, but being English and unaccustomed to traffic, they do not see the streetcar hurtling toward them, painted white for the new exhibit at the Metropolitan Museum. Peter hears the bell and leaps back, hauling Alice roughly along with him, barely missing being crushed against the headlamps. When he collects himself, he turns to ask if she's alright, if he didn't hurt her too much, if the shock has ruffled her so that they need another drink to steady them.

There is no one beside him. His arm is empty.

"Alice?" Peter calls into the darkness. But no answer comes.

## London Is the Capital of Paris, and Paris Is the Capital of Rome

OLIVE STOOD ON the stage of the Tumtum Club in the brash glare of the spotlight. She could barely make out all the glittering scales and claws and furs and shining eyeballs of the Looking Glass Creatures in the audience.

"Go on," hissed the marble raven. "I'm not doing this alone. You do your bit, then I'll do mine. Mine's better, obviously, so I'll close."

"My bit? I haven't got a bit! I didn't even sing in the school concert!"

"Do something! You're sure to, if you stand there long enough!"

Olive felt like her heart was dribbling out of her mouth. Everyone just kept *looking* at her. No one had ever looked at her for so long. Certainly not Father Dear or Darling Mother who ignored her benignly, not Little George who was more interested in painting the sheep, not the Other One, who seemed never to notice her until they collided in the hall. She could hardly bear it. What could she possibly do to impress these aliens out of her own bookshelf? In the book, Alice always had something clever to say, some bit of wordplay or a really swell pun. Olive could never be an Alice. She wasn't quick enough. She wasn't endearing enough. She wasn't anyone enough.

Really, she only had one choice. She'd only ever practiced one thing long enough to get really good at it.

"It's...ahem...it's dreadful here," Olive complained. Her voice shook. Everyone liked the pig screaming about its mother. Would they understand her talent? "Even the toadstools and the cocktails are depressed. There's only one pub and you can't even play darts here. Alice got to meet a Unicorn and dance with Dodos and learn something about herself on *her* holiday." A great gasp ripped through the crowd. A tiger lily burst into tears. The White Queen looked like she might faint.

"It's not allowed!" the chess piece whispered. The cat grinned and began, slowly, to disappear.

Olive pressed on. "But what do I get? The saddest country I've ever seen! If any of you so much as breathe wrong, the government passes out from the scandal of it. I can't even pronounce half of the stuff the Jabberwock says! A more cramped and dreary place I've never dreamed of. It's clear no one ever *planned* nor *built* Wonderland so much as as *piled it up* and *gave up on it several times*. Somebody obviously thought there was nothing so splendid in the world as Victorian allegory and crammed it in anywhere it would fit, and rather a lot of places it wouldn't. The martinis aren't even close to dry. How do you even have electricity? And the local politics are appalling, I'll tell you that for free. Stuff all Queens, I say! Except Elizabeth, she's all right."

Olive bowed, then curtseyed, then settled on something halfway between. A smattering of uncertain applause started up, growing stronger as the Looking Glass Creatures recovered from their shock. The smattering became a thundering, became a roar.

The raven hopped up into the spotlight to soak up a bit of adoration for himself. He coughed and shook his stone feathers. The audience quieted, leaned forward, eager, ready for more—so ready they did not hear the thumping outside, or the terrified squeak of the Dormouse in his teapot armor.

"How," said the marble corvid, "is a raven like a writing desk?"

"It's a raid!" a Dodo shrieked from the back of the Tumtum Club.

The club fell apart into madness as playing cards flooded in from all sides, grabbing at the collars of egg and man alike, shouting orders, taking down names. Looking Glass Creatures bolted, down rabbit holes and up through the mossy rafters, behind the posters advertising THE CHESHIRE CIRCUS and MISS MARY ANN SINGS THE BLUES. Olive froze. She saw the turtle who'd sung so beautifully being dragged off by a pair of deuces. A Knave of Clubs swung his rifle into the scaley ankle of Edward, the poor Jabberwock, who roared in anguish. Tears shone on Olive's cheeks in the footlights. But she couldn't move. The sound of the raid slashed at her ears horribly.

"We both devour humans, piece by piece," the raven finished his riddle into the din, but no one heard him.

Someone gripped Olive's arm.

"Come," said the White Queen. "I'll take you with a pleasure. Twopence a week, and always jam to-day."

"Come where?"

"Where you were always going, where you have already been. Where we are already friends, where we have already fought long and hard together, where we have sat upon the field of battle in one another's arms and looked out over a free Wonderland. Where everything is as it was before the war, before our world split in two, before the Other One, before anything hurt."

"Is that really what's going to happen?"

"No. It's impossible. But I believe it anyway. It's the only way I can bear to face breakfast."

Olive glanced offstage. There was a flash of light there, something reflecting in all the flotsam of the theater. A pane of glass from some lonely window. And for a moment, Olive thought she could see, on the other side of the glass, Darling Mother in the parlor, asleep with Little George in her arms, a nearly empty bottle of gin on the end table and rain still pouring down outside. The shadows of the raindrops looked like black weeping on her mother's face. *Everything as it was. Before. Before anything hurt. Could such a thing ever be?*

She took the White Queen's white hand. They ran together through the wings and out through two mossy hidden doors back beyond the reach of the footlights. The two of them burst into the glen, into a river of folk running away from the Tumtum Club and into the Looking Glass World, running slow, and thus, streaming along so fast they could never be caught.

Olive looked back over her shoulder at the great skeleton covered in moss and flowers and briars and vines. She hadn't seen it when she came in. The glowworms had dazzled her. The whole world had dazzled her.

"We loved her so," the White Queen said, not in the least out of breath as they ran on and on into the wood. "She came back, and she ate a hundred mushrooms so she could grow big enough to protect us. I was there when she died, hardly bigger than a pearl in her hand. She was so old—I hardly remember ever being so old! Living backwards makes it terribly easy to forget. She smiled and said: *oh my gracious!* and closed her eyes. And of course the moment she did, the Red Queen called her pawns to arms, but for a moment, when she was huge and high and here, for one tiny minute in all the world, almost everyone was happy. We loved her so; we never wanted to be parted from her. We wanted her to be with us forever. And she is."

The giant's skeleton was wearing a heavy iron crown, and the crown had two words lovingly etched all the way round it:

**QUEEN ALICE**

# The Wedding

LAST SUMMER, MY AUNT MARRIED a rime giant.
The wedding was lavish; neither clan approved. My uncle-to-be stood dripping in the hallway of Grandmother's great, sprawling house, miserable in a black suit that had already split twice at the shoulders.

Aunt Margaret always had a thing for foreign men. When they were kids, she and my mother tried to learn French from tapes so that they could grow up and marry Parisian dukes and dance in pink dresses with peonies on the shoulders. When they progressed past je vous rencontrerai au palais vendredi, Grandmother sat them both down and gave them ginger cookies and explained to them very gently about the revolution, the impracticality of flowers as personal decoration, and the difficulty in obtaining an EU visa. My mother shrugged and promptly threw over the French for mathematics. Margaret simmered and seethed in the kitchen.

"Ces paysans stupides ne peuvent pas m'arrêter," she whispered, and took two more ginger cookies just to spite the guillotine-masters.

Her wedding dress was the palest possible pink, so pale you might be excused for thinking it white. Two enormous violet-rose peonies nodded from the shoulders, wilting lightly in the June heat. I told my cousin I thought it was cruel to our prospective uncle—couldn't they have done all this in January? But my aunt has always had a perverse streak. At the reception, Volgnir put his wet blue hand to her cheek and whispered: I melt in thy service. They didn't think I heard, but I did. I'm quiet; I sneak. Nobody really notices me, so I get to hear all kinds of things. Like when Grandmother took a lover from the local university—she had four of them come to the house and line up on the lawn like prize horses for her to choose. Grandfather sipped his limeade and gin and laughed at all of them, all discomfited and nervous, anxious to please. I just sat and watched her examine their calf muscles. I took the three she didn't want. Our family is like that—waste not, want not.

When Margaret came home from Norway, Grandmother pursed her lips and stared her up and down. I was washing dishes, careful not to clink the plates. Grandmother sniffed and picked at a dropped stitch in her knitting.

"I always suspected our family has giant blood, you know," Grandmother said at long last. "On account of the twins being so tall. Mind he wipes his feet—there's ginger cookies in the jar."

On the day before the wedding, we all gathered in the front room for iced tea and awkward conversation. We stood around, ice gently melting, all of us younger girls wearing light green and no stockings and delicate little bits of silver at our throats and ears. Volgnir's people came in bronze and horsehair, burnished and I'm sure very fine, their braids greased to a high shine. We all avoided looking at each other, unsure of how we were to progress. Grandmother had dyed her hair blue in honor of the rime giants, and clipped it back with diamond clasps that looked very like clusters of icicles. One of Volgnir's sisters eyed them longingly, as the ice on her shield cracked and broke. Margaret seemed delighted at every moment; the more uncomfortable we all were, the wider she smiled. I could see, when she sat, that her ankles had little sheens of ice on either side, like an anklet.

Finally, my brother Lucas suggested barbecuing, and we all thought this was grand. We took our shoes off to feel the dewy lawn between our toes, and my cousin Rose made lemonade with fruit from our trees. We slapped marbly steaks on the grill, and sausages, a few chicken breasts and soy chops for the out of towners. Lucas felt at home, with a steel spatula like a spear in his hand, and slowly, we became ourselves, laughing and sharing the kinds of familial gossip weddings encourage. Little Shana's off to college, majoring in biochemistry. Her boy's run off with her—very romantic, but he can't do the math, you know. Did you hear Eli's poor wife is pregnant again? Modern science is a wonderful thing, I told them.

But when it came time to eat, and we all sat in our accustomed yogic poses, balancing paper plates on one silk-clad knee with a glass of tea or lemonade crinkling and tinkling in one hand, the Hrimthursar—that's what Margaret called them; we all took it to be rather an over-stuffed surname, but no more, we supposed, than the time Emily married her Hungarian secretary. At least there were a few vowels to spare this time. Anyway, the Hrimthursar just stood around the grill, their nostrils flared huge and dark, sniffing the last smoky wisps off of the meat, their eyes closed in ecstasy, their hands all joined together.

"Don't you want to eat?" Lucas called in his friendly, bear-bellow voice.

"Don't be ignorant," snapped Margaret. "They *are* eating."

When I was little, I wanted to be like Aunt Margaret. She wore flowers in her hair every day, and the flowers always matched her stockings, even when it was winter—then, she wore Japanese bittersweet in her brown curls, and flame-colored stockings that I thought were the height of elegance. She knew how to ride a horse, and make ice cream in a bucket, and could do algebra in her head. She knew about engines and crocheting and mountain climbing, and once in her twenties she wrote a potboiler novel about a murder in a French museum. She could do just anything, and I loved her.

Once she went to Tibet and came back with purple prayer flags for my room. I sat in her lap—there were little whitish-green grape blossoms in her hair—and listened to her sing sherpa-songs, and tell stories about the snow-maidens that lived on Mt. Everest, who would only love humans who could climb all the way to the top. It's important to marry someone, she said. Not because you need them to complete you or because you ought to be someone's wife by hook or by crook. It's just that worlds *want* to combine, they want to marry, and they use people to do it, the way you mix medicine in with something sweet, so it's easy to swallow. That's why we have to have all those silly things: a frilly dress and something blue and a bachelor party and a priest. Just so that a boy and a girl or a boy and a boy or a girl and a girl or any combination of the above can live together and maybe or maybe not make babies? Posh. Because the big worlds inside us are mating, and they need the pomp.

 Aunt Margaret talked like that a lot. She left a few days later to learn about Norwegian investment banking. When she had gone I picked a little bouquet of blown dandelions and stood next to my favorite maple tree in the meadow beyond our house and put my hand on its bark. I swore to love it forever. The wind moved in its branches, and that was vow enough for me.

 The Hrimthursar brought fermented milk and honey to the bachelor party. Of course, that's just what we call it, but it's not your usual strippers-and-gin-and-no-women affair. We don't really know how to separate like that. So we were all there, girls and boys and grandfathers and grandmothers, lanterns strung up between the trees, big tins full of beer and yellow wine, and just about everyone with some sort of means of making a good bit of noise. Lucas spun his double bass, Rose tweedled her flute, there was a drum section a dozen cousins strong—Evan and Lizzy and Katie thumping leather with the heels of their hands. Aunt Betsy squeezed her black cello between her knees. My mother grinned over her old guitar, picking out a little melody line, and Grandmother brought out her best violin. Me, I sing. It's the only time everyone looks at me, even Margaret.

I sang about snow-maidens. The Hrimthursar, for the first time, smiled big and broad. Their teeth were frozen.

They were uncomfortable—they think it's best to send the women off to make wedding bread while the men drink. They stood around with their clubs waiting for the ritual violence that comes with too much fermented milk, but instead Grandmother fiddled like a devil, her blue hair coming loose, her arms and knotted fingers still so strong. The stars above us were terribly bright, as bright as the lanterns, and Margaret danced in bare feet, her hair flying, her frothy violet skirt spinning, while Volgnir watched her in a rapture of devotion. She reached out for him, her lover, her world, and he stepped into the circle of light and music. But Volgnir was enormous, squarish. He was not a slim prince eager to ply waltzes, even if we were inclined to play one. His folk gathered around him and they began to sway, to stomp, to circle around Margaret in a complex, deliberate side-step. They howled in harmony, their craggy faces turned up towards the moon.

After awhile, I joined them, my high little voice swooping over and under their billowing baritones.

Margaret kept dancing, in the middle of the ring of giants. Violets dropped from her hair.

THE CEREMONY TOOK all day. Margaret wore three dresses. The pink one, with peonies, when she came down the big white staircase of the house. She was holding a bouquet of milky blowing dandelions, and winked when she caught my eye. Volgnir stood sweating his ice-droplets in a tuxedo that we dug up out of the attic. About thirty years ago, Uncle Orrin married the brief Aunt Jo, and he was a good three hundred and fifty pounds on the day of it. After a few years of carrots and cucumbers, he was a trim one-seventy when they divorced. Aunt Jo never had much use for skinny men. Anyway, Orrin's suit was far too small for Volgnir, who stooped under the ceiling, and tugged at the coat-sleeves, which only came down to his elbows. His blue, tattooed forearms showed bright in the parlor. He swore to honor and obey, breathless, starry-hearted. Margaret swore to love, and that's all. *Greta, Greta,* he whispered, eyes shut in rapture, *on thy breast I write my Edda, at thy feet I lay the keys of Niflheim, by thy leave alone, I live, and breathe, and die.*

The second dress was brown leather and bronze studs, a shield, a spear. I dipped her braids in cold water and stood in front of the freezer with her until they hardened up pretty good. Volgnir's sister, a Valkyrie with pale red hair, lashed their arms together with rough rope, and spoke in whatever language they all seemed to know. I caught Freya, and Hel. She touched my aunt's face with her hoary, frosted hands and kissed Margaret on the forehead. The kiss was still there when she pulled back, faintly blue and gleaming. Each of the Hrimthursar came forward to kiss Margaret, who grew quite dizzy and breathless with each one, and her forehead shone. Together, they drank mead and ate hard, cold bread the color of ashes.

The third dress was green as summer, and though there was champagne, and more dancing, and Grandmother sitting happily in the lap of Volgnir's uncle telling him stories of her youth in Hollywood, what I remember is Margaret, her face like a candle, drawing me out of my chair to dance with her. Her arms cold and tight against my waist, she twirled me around the grassy lawn, her smell already like snow and distant black pines. Her shoulder was hard and slippery under my hand. It's all right, she laughed. It doesn't hurt. And he's been melting for months. We'll meet halfway.

*Remember what I told you.*

I looked over her shoulder at one of the Hrimthursar, a young one with a great dark nose and muscles like stones.

He blushed blue, looking up at me through long lashes.

# The Bread We Eat in Dreams

IN A SEA OF LONG grass and tiny yellow blueberry flowers some ways off of Route 1, just about halfway between Cobscook Bay and Passamaquoddy Bay, the town of Sauve-Majeure puts up its back against the Bald Moose mountains. It's not a big place—looks a little like some big old cannon shot a load of houses and half-finished streets at the foothills and left them where they fell. The sun gets here first out of just about anywhere in the country, turning all the windows bloody orange and filling up a thousand lobster cages with shadows.

Further up into the hills, outside the village but not so far that the post doesn't come regular as rain, you'll find a house all by itself in the middle of a tangly field of good red potatoes and green oats. The house is a snug little hall and parlor number with a moss-clotted roof and a couple of hundred years of whitewash on the stones. Sweet William and vervain and crimson beebalm wend out of the window-jambs, the door-hinges, the chimney blocks. There's carrots in the kitchen garden, some onions, a basil plant that may or may not come back next year.

You wouldn't know it to look at the place, but a demon lives here.

The rusted-out mailbox hangs on a couple of splinters and a single valiant, ancient bolt, its red flag at perpetual half-mast. Maybe there's mail to go out, and maybe there isn't. The demon's name is Gemegishkirihallat, but the mailbox reads: *Agnes G.* and that seems respectable enough to the mailman, who always has to check to see if that red flag means business, even though in all his considerable experience working for the postal service, it never has. The demon is neither male nor female—that's not how things work where it came from. But when it passed through the black door it came out Agnes on the other side. She's stuck with she now, and after five hundred years, give or take, she's just about used to it.

The demon arrived before the town. She fell out of a red oak in the primeval forest that would eventually turn into Schism Street and Memorial Square into a white howl of snow and frozen sea-spray. She was naked, her body branded with four-spoked seals, wheels of banishment, and the seven psalms of Hell. Her hair had burnt off and she had no fingernails or toenails. The hair grew back—black, naturally—and the 16$^{th}$ century offered a range of options for completely covering female skin from chin to heel, black-burnt with the diamond trident-brand of Amdusias or no.

The fingernails never came in. It's not something many people ever had occasion to notice.

The ice and lightning lasted for a month after she came; the moon got big and small again while the demon walked around the bay. Her footsteps marked the boundaries of the town to come, her heels boiling the snow, her breath full of thunder. When she hungered, which she did, often, for her appetites had never been small, she put her head back in the frigid, whipping storm and howled the primordial syllable that signified *stag*. Even through the squall and scream of the white air, one would always come, his delicate legs picking through the drifts, his antlers dripping icicles.

She ate her stags whole in the dark, crunching the antlers in her teeth.

Once, she called a pod of seals up out of the sea and slept on the frozen beach, their grey mottled bodies all around her. The heat of her warmed them, and they warmed her. In the morning the sand beneath them ran liquid and hot, the seals cooked and smoking.

THE DEMON BUILT that house with her own hands. Still naked come spring, as she saw no particular reason not to be, she put her ear to the mud and listened for echoes. The sizzling blood of the earth moved beneath her in crosshatch patterns, and on her hands and knees she followed them until she found what she wanted. Hell is a lot like a bad neighbor: it occupies the space just next to earth, not quite on top of it or underneath it, just to the side, on the margins. And Hell drops its chestnuts over the fence with relish. Agnes was looking for the place on earth that shared a cherry tree and a water line with the house of Gemegishkirihallat in Hell. When she found it, she spoke to the trees in proto-Akkadian and they understood her; they fell and sheared themselves of needles and branches. Grasses dried in a moment and thatched themselves, eager to please her. With the heat of her hands she blanched sand into glass for her windows; she demanded the hills give her iron and clay for her oven, she growled at the ground to give her snap peas and onions.

SOME YEARS LATER, a little Penobscot girl got lost in the woods while her tribe was making their long return from the warmer south. She did not know how to tell her father what she saw when she found him again, having never seen a house like the one the demon built, with a patch of absurd English garden and a stone well and roses coming in bloody and thick. She only knew it was wrong somehow, that it belonged to someone, that it made her feel like digging a hole in the dirt and hiding in it forever.

The demon looked out of the window when the child came. Her hair had grown so long by then it brushed her ankles. She put out a lump of raw, red, bleeding meat for the girl. Gemegishkirihallat had always been an excellent host. Before he marked her flesh with his trident, Amdusias had loved to eat her salted bread, dipping his great long unicorn's horn into her black honey to drink.

The child didn't want it, but that didn't bother Agnes. Everybody has a choice. That's the whole point.

⁓

SAUVE-MAJEURE BELONGS TO its demon. She called the town to herself, on account of being a creature of profound order. A demon cannot function alone. If they could, banishment would be no hurt. A demon craves company, their own peculiar camaraderie. Agnes was a wolf abandoned by her pack. She could not help how she sniffed and howled for her litter-mates, nor how that howl became a magnetic pull for the sort of human who also loves order, everything in its place, all souls accounted for, everyone blessed and punished according to strict and immutable laws.

The first settlers were mostly French, banded together with whatever stray Puritans they'd picked up along the way north. Those Puritans would spice the Gallic stew of upper Maine for years, causing no end of trouble to Agnes, who, to be fair, was a witch and a succubus and everything else they ever called her, but that's no excuse for being such poor neighbors, when you think about it.

The demon waited. She waited for Martin le Clerq and Melchior Pelerin to raise their barns and houses, for Remy Mommacque to breed his dainty little cow to William Chudderley's barrel of a bull, for John Cabot to hear disputes in his rough parlor. She waited for Hubert Sazarin to send for both money and a pair of smooth brown stones from Sauve-Majeure Abbey back home in Gironde, and use them to lay out the foundations of what he dreamed would be the Cathedral of St. Geraud and St. Adelard, the grandest edifice north of Boston. She waited for Thomas Dryland to get drunk on Magdeleine Loliot's first and darkest beer, then march over to the Sazarin manse and knock him round the ears for flaunting his

## The Bread We Eat in Dreams

Papist devilry in the face of good honest folk. She waited for Dryland to take up a collection amongst the Protestant minority and, along with John Cabot and Quentin Pole, raised the frame of the Free Meeting House just across what would eventually be called Schism Street, glaring down the infant Cathedral, and pressed Quentin's serious young son Lamentation into service as pastor. She waited, most importantly, for little Crespine Moutonnet to be born, the first child of Sauve-Majeure. (Named by Sazarin, stubbornly called Help-on-High by the congregation at the Free Meeting House up until Renewal Pole was shot over the whole business by Henri Sazarin in 1890, at which point it was generally agreed to let the matter drop and the county take the naming of the place—which they did, once Sazarin had quietly and handsomely paid the registrar the weight of his eldest daughter in coin, wool, beef, and blueberries.) She waited for the Dryland twins, Reformation and Revelation, for Madame le Clerq to bear her five boys, for Goodwife Wadham to deliver her redoubtable seven daughters and single stillborn son. She waited for Mathelin Minouflet to bring his gentle wife over the sea from Cluny—she arrived already and embarrassingly pregnant, since she had by then been separated from her good husband for five years. Mathelin would have beaten her soundly, but upon discovering that his brother had the fault of it, having assumed Mathelin dead and the responsibility of poor Charlotte his own, tightened his belt and hoped it would be a son. The demon waited for enough children to be born and grow up, for enough village to spring up, for enough order to assert itself she that could walk among them and be merely one of the growing, noisy lot of new young folk fighting over Schism Street and trading grey, damp wool for hard, new potatoes.

The demon appeared in Adelard-in-the-Garden Square, the general marketplace ruled wholly by an elderly, hunched Hubert Sazarin and his son Augustine. Adjoining it, Faith-My-Joy Square hosted the Protestant market, but as one could not get decent wine nor good Virginia pipe tobacco in Faith-My-Joy nor Margery Cabot's sweet butter and linen cloth in Adelard, a great deal of furtive passage went on between the two. The demon chose Adelard, and laid out her wares among the tallow candles and roasting fowl and pale bluish honey sold by the other men. A woman selling in the market caused a certain amount of consternation among the husbands of Sauve-Majeure. Young Wrestling Dryland, though recently bereaved of his father Thomas, whose heart had quite simply burst with rage when Father Simon Charpentier arrived from France to give Mass and govern the souls of St. Geraud and Adelard, had no business at all sneaking across the divide to snatch up a flask of Sazarin's Spanish Madeira. Wrestling worked himself up into a positively Thomas-like fury over the tall figure in a black bonnet, and screwed in his courage to confront the devil-woman. He took in her severe dress, her covered hair, her table groaning with breads he had only heard of from his father's tales of a boyhood in London—braided rounds and glossy cross-buns studded with raisins (where had she got raisins in this forsaken land?), sweet French egg bread and cakes dusted with sugar, (what act of God or His Opposite granted this brazen even the smallest measure of sugar?), dark jams and butter-plaits stuffed with cream. He fixed to shame the slattern of Adelard, as he already thought of her, his gaze meant to cut down—but when he looked into the pits of her eyes he quieted, and said nothing at all, but meekly purchased a round of her bread even though his mother Anne made a perfectly fine loaf of her own.

Gemegishkirihallat had been the baker of Hell.

It had been her peculiar position, her speciality among all the diverse amusements and professions of Hades, which performs as perfectly and smoothly in its industries as the best human city can imagine, but never accomplish. Everything in its place, all souls accounted for, everyone blessed and punished according to strict and immutable laws. She baked bread to be seen but ultimately withheld, sweetcakes to be devoured until the skin split and the stomach protruded like the head of a child through the flesh, black pastry to haunt the starved mind. The ovens of Gemegishkirihallat were cathedral towers of fire and onyx, her under-bakers Akalamdug and Ekur pulling out soft and perfect loaves with bone paddles. But also she baked for her own table, where her comrades Amdusias, King of Thunder and Trumpets, Agares, Duke of Runaways and his loyal pet crocodile, Samagina, Marquis of the Drowned, Countess Gremory Who-Rides-Upon-a-Camel, and the Magician-King Barbatos gathered to drink the wines crushed beneath the toes of rich and heartless men and share between them the bread of Gemegishkirihallat. She prepared the bloodloaf of the great Emperor's own infinite table, where, on occasion, she was permitted to sit and keep Count Andromalius from stealing the slabs of meat beloved of Celestial Marquis Oryax.

And in her long nights, in her long house of smoke and miller's stones, she baked the bread we eat in dreams, strangest loaves, her pies full of anguish and days long dead, her fairy-haunted gingerbread, her cakes wet with tears. The Great Duke Gusion, the Baboon-Lord of Nightmares, came to her each eve and took up her goods into his hairy arms and bore them off to the Pool of Sleep.

Those were the days the demon longed for in her lonely house with only one miserable oven that did not even come up to her waist, with her empty table and not even Shagshag, the weaver of Hell, to make her the Tea of Separation-from-God and ravage her in the dark like a good neighbor should. Those were the days she longed for in her awful heart—for a demon has no heart as we do, a little red fist in our chest. A demon's body is nothing but heart, its whole interior beating and pulsing and thundering in time to the skull-clocks of Pandemonium.

Those were the days that floated in the demon's vast and lightless mind when she brought, at long last, her most perfect breads to Adelard-in-the-Garden. She would have her pack again, here between the mountains and the fish-clotted bay. She would build her ovens high and feed them all, feed them all and their children until no other bread would sate them. They would love her abjectly, for no other manner of loving had worth.

THEY BURNED HER as a witch some forty years later.

As you might expect, it was a Dryland's hand at work in it, though the fingers of Sébastienne Sazarin as well as Father Simon's successor Father Audrien made their places in the pyre.

The demon felt it best, when asked, to claim membership in a convent on the other side of Bald Moose Mountain, traveling down into the bay-country to sell the sisters' productions of bread. She herself was a hermit, of course, consecrated to the wilderness in the manner of St. Viridiana or St. Julian, two venerated ladies of whom the poor country priest Father Simon had never heard. This relieved everyone a great deal, since a woman alone is a kind of unpredictable inferno that might at any moment light the hems of the innocent young. Sister Agnes had such a fine hand at pies and preserves, it couldn't hurt to let little Piety and Thankful go and learn a bit from her—even if she *was* a Papist demoness, her shortbread would make you take Communion just to get a piece. She's a right modest handmaiden, let Marie and Heloise and Isabelle learn their letters from her. She sings so beautifully at Christmas Mass, poor Christophe Minouflet fell into a swoon when she sang the Ave—why not let our girl Beatrice learn her scales and her octaves at her side?

And then there was the matter of Sister Agnes's garden. Not a soul in Sauve-Majeure did not burn to know the secret of the seemingly inexhaustible earth upon which their local hermit made her little house. How she made her pumpkins swell and her potatoes glow with red health, how her peas came up almost before the snow could melt, how her blueberry bushes groaned by June with the weight of their dark fruit. Let Annabelle and Elisabeth and Jeanne and Martha go straight away and study her methods, and if a seed or two of those hardy crops should find its way into the pockets of the girls' aprons, well, such was God's Will.

Thus did the demon find herself with a little coven of village girls, all bright and skinny and eager to grow up, more eager still to learn everything Sister Agnes could teach. The demon might have wept with relief and the peculiar joy of devils. She took them in, poor and rich, Papist and Puritan, gathered them round her black hearth like a wreath of still-closed flowers—and she opened them up. The clever girls spun wool that became silk in their hands. They baked bread so sweet the body lost all taste for humble mother's loaf. They read their Scriptures, though Sister Agnes's Bible seemed rather larger and heavier than either Father Audrien's or Pastor Pole's, full of books the girls had never head of—the Gospel of St. Thomas, of Mary Magdalen, the Apocryphon of James, the Pistis Sophia, the Trimortic Protennoia, the Descent of Mary, and stranger ones still: the Book of the Two Thieves, the Book of Glass, the Book of the Evening Star. When they had tired of these, they read decadent and thrilling novels that Sister Agnes just happened to have on hand.

You might say the demon got careless. You could say that—but a demon has no large measure of care to begin with. The girls seated around her table like Grand Dukes, like seals on a frozen beach, made her feel like her old self again, and who among us can resist a feeling like that? Not many, and a demon hasn't even got a human's meager talent for resisting temptation.

Sébastienne Sazarin did not like Sister Agnes one bit. Oh, she sent her daughter Basile to learn lace from her, because she'd be damned if Marguerite le Clerq's brats would outshine a Sazarin at anything, and if Reformation Dryland's plain, sow-faced granddaughter made a better marriage than her own girl, she'd just have to lie down dead in the street from the shame of it. But she didn't like it. Basile came home smiling in a secretive sort of way, her cheeks flushed, her breath quick and delighted. She did her work so quickly and well that there was hardly anything left of the household industries for Sébastienne to do. She conceived her fourth child, she would always say, out of sheer boredom.

"Well, isn't that what you sent her for?" her husband Hierosme said. "Be glad for ease, for it comes but seldom."

"It's unwholesome, a woman living alone out there. I wish Father Audrien would put a stop to it."

But Father Simon had confided to his successor before he passed into a peaceful death that he felt Sauve-Majeure harbored a saint. When she died, and the inevitable writ of veneration arrived from Rome, the Cathedral of St. Geraud and Adelard might finally have the funds it needed—and if perhaps St. Geraud, who didn't have much to recommend him and wasn't patron of anything in particular, had to be replaced with St. Agnes in order to secure financing from Paris, such was the Will of God. Hubert Sazarin's long dream would come to pass, and Sauve-Majeure would become the Avignon of the New World. A cathedral required more in the way of coin and time than even the Sazarins could manage on their own, and charged with this celestial municipal destiny, Father Audrien could not bring himself to censure the hermit woman on which it all depended.

Pastor Pole had no such hesitation. Though the left side of Schism Street thought it unsavory to hold the pastorship in one family, Lamentation Pole had raised his only son Troth to know only discipline and abstinence, and no other boy could begin to compete with him in devotion or self-denial. Pastor Pole's sermons in the Free Meeting House (which he would rename the Free Gathered Church) bore such force down on his congregation that certain young girls had been known to faint away at his roaring words. He condemned with equal fervor harvest feasting, sexual congress outside the bonds of marriage, woman's essential nature, and the ridiculous names the Sazarins and other Papist decadents saddled themselves with as they are certainly not fooling God with that nonsense.

Yet still, the grumbling might have stayed just that if not for the sopping wet summer of '09 and the endless, bestial winter that followed. If it had not been bad enough that the crops rotted on the vine and sagged on the stalk, cows and sheep froze where they stood come December, and in February, Martha Chedderley discovered frantic mice invading her thin, precious stores of flour.

Yet the demon's garden thrived. In May her tomatoes were already showing bright green in the rain, in June she had bushels of rhubarb and knuckle-sized cherries, and in that miserable, grey August she sent each of her students home with a sack of onions, cabbages, apples, squash, and beans. When Basile Sazarin showed her mother her treasure, her mother's gaze could have set fire to a block of ice. When Weep-Not Dryland showed her father, Wrestling's eldest and meanest child, Elected Dryland, her winter's store, his bile could have soured a barrel of honey.

Schism Street was broached. Sébastienne Sazarin, prodding her husband and her priest before her, walked out halfway across the muddy, contested earth. Pastor Pole met her, joined by Elected Dryland and his mother, Martha and Makepeace Chedderley, and James Cabot, grandson of the great judge John Cabot may God rest his soul. On the one side of them stood the perpetually unfinished Cathedral of St. Geraud and St. Adelard, its ancient clerestory, window pane, and foundation stones standing lonely beside the humble chapel that everyone called the Cathedral anyhow. On the other the clean steeple and whitewash of the Free Gathered Church.

*She's a witch. She's a succubus. Why should we starve when she has the devil's own plenty?*

You know this song. It's a classic, with an old workhorse of a chorus.

*My girl Basile says she waters her oats with menstrual blood and reads over them from some Gospel I've never heard of. My maid Weep-Not says her cows give milk three times a day. Our Lizzie says she hasn't got any fingernails. She holds Sabbats up there and the girls all dance naked in a circle of pine. My Bess says on the full moon they're to fornicate with a stag up on the mountain while Sister Agnes sings the Black Vespers. If I ask my poor child, what will I hear then?*

The demon heard them down in the valley. She heard the heat of their whispers, and knew they would come for her. She waited, as she had always waited. It wasn't long. James Cabot made out a writ of arrest and Makepeace Chedderley got burly young Robert Mommacque and Charles Loliot to come with him up the hill to drag the witch out of her house and install her in the new jail, which was the Dryland barn, quite recently outfitted with chains forged in Denis Minouflet's shop and a stout hickory chair donated out of the Sazarin parlor.

The demon didn't fight when they bound her and gagged her mouth—to keep her from bewitching them with her devil's psalms. It did not actually occur to her to use her devil's psalms. She was curious. She did not yet know if she could die. The men of Sauve-Majeure carried Gemegishkirihallat in their wagon down through the slushy March snow to stand trial. She only looked at them, her gaze mild and interested. Their guts twisted under those hollow eyes, and this was further proof.

It took much longer than anticipated. The two Sauve-Majeures had never agreed on much, and they sure as spring couldn't agree on the proper execution of a witch's trial. Hanging, said Dryland and Pole. Burning, insisted Sazarin and le Clerq. One judge or a whole bench, testimony from the children or a simple quiet judgment after the charges were read? A water test or a needle test? Who would question her and what questions would they ask? Would Dr. Pelerin examine her, who had been sent down for schooling in Massachusetts, where they knew about such dark medicine, or the midwife Sarah Wadham? Who would have the credit of ferreting out the devil in their midst, the Church in Rome or their own stalwart Pastor Pole? What name would the town bear on the warrants, Sauve-Majeure (nest of snakes and Papistry) or Help-on-High (den of jackals and schismatics)? Most importantly, who would have the caring of her garden now and when she was gone? Who would have her house?

The demon waited. She waited for her girls to come to her—and they did, first the slower studies who craved her approval, then finally

Basile and Weep-Not and Lizzie Wadham and Bess Chedderley and the other names listed on the writ though no one had asked them much about it. The demon slipped her chains easily and put her hands to their little heads.

"Go and do as I have done," Sister Agnes said. "Go and make your gardens grow, make your men double over with desire, go and dance until you are full up of the moon."

"Are you really a witch?" ventured Basile Sazarin, who would be the most beautiful woman Sauve-Majeure would ever reap, all the way up til now and further still.

"No," said the demon. "A witch is just a girl who knows her mind. I am better than a witch. But look at the great orgy coming up like a rose around me. No night in Hell could be as bright."

And Sister Agnes took off her black wool gown before the young maids. They saw her four-spoked seals and her wheels of banishment and the seven burnt psalms on her skin. They saw that she had no sex. They saw her long name writ upon her thighs. They knew awe in that barn, and they danced with their teacher in the starlight sifting through the mouldering hay.

A CERTAIN MINISTER came to visit the demon while she waited for her trail. Pastor Pole managed not to wholly prostrate himself before the famous man, but took him immediately to speak with the condemned woman, whom that illustrious soul had heard of all the way down in Salem: a confirmed demoness, beyond any doubt.

Pastor Pole's own wife Mary-in-the-Manger brought a chair to seat the honored minister upon, and what cider and cheese they had to spare (in truth the Poles had used up the demon's apples to make it, and the demon's milk besides). The great man looked upon the black-clad woman chained in her barn-prison. Her gaze sounded upon his soul and boomed there, deafening.

"Art thee a witch, then?" he whispered.

"No," said the demon.

"But not a Christian lady, neither," said he.

"No," said the demon.

"How came you to grow such bounty on your land without the help of God?"

The demon closed her hands in her lap. Her long hair hung around her like an animal's skin.

"My dear Goodman Mather, there is not a demon in Hell who was not once something quite other, and more interesting. In the land where the Euphrates runs green and sweet, I was a grain-god with the head of a bull. In the rough valley of the Tyne I was a god of fertility and war, with the head of a crow. I was a fish-headed lord of plenty in the depths of the Tigris. Before language I was she-who-makes-the-harvest-come, and I rode a red boar. The earth answers when I call it by name. I know its name because we are family."

"You admit your demonic nature?"

"I would have admitted it before now if anyone had asked. They ask only if I am a witch, and a witch is small pennies to me. I am what I am, as you are what you are. I want to live, as all creatures do. I cannot sin, so I have done no wrong."

The minister wet his throat with the demon's cider. His hand shook upon the tankard. When he had mastered himself he spoke quickly and softly, in the most wretched tones. He poured out onto the ground between him all his doubt and misery, all his grief and guilt. He gave her those things because she proved his whole heart, his invisible world, she proved him a good man, despite the hanging hill in his heart.

"Tell me," he rasped finally, as the dawn came on white and pitiless, "tell me that I will know the Kingdom of God in my lifetime. Tell me the end of days is near—for you must be the harbinger of it, you must be its messenger and its handmaiden. Tell me the dead will rise and we will shed out bodies like the shells of beautiful snails, that I will leave behind this horror that is flesh and become as light.

Tell me I need never again be a man, that I need never err more, nor dwell in the curse of this life. Tell me you have come to murder this world, so that the new one might swallow us all."

The demon looked on him with infernal pity, which is, in the end, not worth the tears it sheds. Demons may pity men every hour of the day, but that pity never moves.

"No," the demon said.

And, slipping her chains, Gemegishkirihallat shed her gown once more before the famous man, showing the black obliteration of her skin. She folded her arms around him like wings and brought down the scythe of her mouth on his. Straddling his doubt, the demon made plain the reality of his flesh, and the arrow of his need.

---

THEY BURNED HER at sunrise, before the Free Gathered Church could say anything about it. Bad enough they had brought that man to their town, the better people of Sauve-Majeure would not stand to let a Protestant nobody pass judgment on her. There were few witnesses: Father Audrien, who made his apologies to Father Simon in Heaven, Sébastienne and Hierosme Sazarin with young Basile clutched between them, Marguerite le Clerq and her husband Isaac. The Church would handle their witch and the schismatics, to be bold, could lump it. They had all those girls down south—Rome had to have its due in the virtuous north.

Father Audrien tied the demon to a pine trunk and read her last rites. She did not spit or howl, but only stared down the priest with a stare like dying. She said one word before the end, and no one understood it. Each of the witnesses lit the flames so that none alone would have to bear the weight of the sin. A year later, Sébastienne Sazarin would insist, drunk and half-toothless, hiding sores on her breast and losing her voice, would rasp to her daughter, insisting that as Sister Agnes burned she saw a bull's head glowing through the pyre, its horns molten gold, and garlanded in black wheat. Marguerite le Clerq, half-mad with syphilis her husband brought home from Virginia, would weep to her priest that she had seen a red boar in the flames, its tusks made of diamond, its head crowned with millet and barley. Hierosme Sazarin, shipwrecked three years hence in Nova Scotia, his cargo of Madeira spilling out into the icy sea, would tell his blue-mouthed, doomed sailors that once he had seen a saint burn, and in the conflagration a white crow, its beak wet with blood, had flown up to Heaven, its wings seared black.

Father Audrien dreamed of the demon's burning body every night until he died, and the moment her bones shattered into a thousand fiery fish, he woke up reaching for his Bible and finding nothing in the dark.

THE DEMON'S HOUSE stood empty for a long while. Daisies grew in her stove. Moss thickened her great Bible. The girls she had drawn close around her grew up—Basile Sazarin so lovely men winced to look at her, so lovely she married a Parisian banker and never returned to Sauve-Majeure. Weep-Not Dryland bore eight daughters without pain or even much blood, and every autumn took them up to the top of the Bald Moose while her husband slept in his comfort. Lizzie Wadham's cloth wove so fine she could sell it in Boston and even New York for enough money to build a school, where she insisted on teaching the young ladies' lessons, the content of which no male was ever able to spy out.

And whenever Basile and Weep-Not went up to Sister Agnes's house to shoo out the foxes and raccoons and keep the garden weeded, they saw a crow perched on the chimney or pecking at an old apple, or a bony old cow peering at them with a rheumy eye, or a fat piglet with black spots scampering off into the forest as soon as they called after it.

The cod went scarce in the bays. The textile men came up from Portland and Augusta, with bolts of linen and money to build a mill on the river, finding ready buyers in Remembrance Dryland

and Walter Chedderley. The few Penobscot and Passamaquoddy left found themselves corralled into bare land not far from where a little girl had once ran crying from a strange doorstep in the snow. The Free Gathered Church declined into Presbyterianism and the Cathedral of St. Geraud and St. Adelard remained a chapel, despite obtaining a door and its own relic—the kneecap of St. Geraud himself—before the Sazarin fortune wrecked on the New York market and scattered like so much seafoam. And the demon waited.

She had found burning to be much less painful than expulsion from Hell, and somewhat fortifying, given the sudden warmth in the March chill. When they buried the charred stumps of her bones, she was grateful, to be in the earth, to be closed up and safe. She thought of Prince Sitri, Lord of Naked Need, and how his leopard-skin and griffin-wings had burnt up every night, leaving his bare black bones to dance before the supper table of the upper Kings. His flesh always returned, so that it could burn again. When she thought about it, he looked a little like Thomas Dryland, with his stern golden face. And Countess Gremory—she'd had a body like Basile Sazarin hid under those dingy aprons, riding her camel naked through the boiling fields to her door, when she'd had a door. When the shards of the demon dreamed, she dreamed of them all eating her bread together, in one house or another, Agares and Lamentation Pole and Amdusias and Sebastienne Sazarin and lovely old Akalamdug and Ekur serving them.

Gemegishkirihallat slowly fell apart into the dirt of Sauve-Majeure.

Sometimes a crow or a dog would dig up a bone and dash off with it, or a cow would drag a knuckle up with her cud. They would slip their pens or wing north suddenly, as if possessed, and before being coaxed home, would drop their prize in a certain garden, near a certain dark, empty house.

The lobster trade picked up, and every household had their pots. Schism Street got its first cobblestones, and cherry trees planted along its route. Something rumbled down south and the Minouflet boys were all killed in some lonely field in Pennsylvania, ending their name. In the name of the war dead, Pastor Veritas Pole and Father Jude dug up the strip of grass and holly hedges between Faith-My-Joy Square and Adelard-in-the-Garden Square and joined them into Memorial Square. The Dryland girls married French boys and buried whatever hatchet they still had biting at the tree. Raulguin Sazarin and his Bangor business partner Lucas Battersby found tourmaline up in Bald Moose, brilliant pink and green and for a moment it seemed Sauve-Majeure really would be something, would present a pretty little ring to the state of Maine and become its best bride, hoping for better days, for bigger stones sometime down the way—but no. The seam was shallow, the mine closed down as quickly as it came, and that was all the town would ever have of boom and bustle.

One day Constance Chedderley and Catherine le Clerq came home from gathering blackberries in the hills and told their mother that they'd seen chimney smoke up there. Wasn't that funny? Thankful Dryland and Restitue Sazarin, best friends from the moment one had stolen a black-gowned, black-haired doll from the other, started sneaking up past the town line, coming home with muffins and shortbread in their school satchels. When questioned, they said they'd found a nunnery in the mountains, and one of the sisters had given them the treats as presents, admonishing them not to tell.

The mill went bust before most of the others, a canary singing in the textile mine of New England. The fisherman trade picked up, though, and soon enough even Peter Mommacque had a scallop boat going, despite having the work ethic of a fat housecat. A statue of Minerva made an honest woman of Memorial Square, with a single bright tourmaline set into her shield, which was promptly stolen by Bernard and Richie Loliot. First Presbyterian Church crumpled up into Second Methodist, and the first Pastor not named Pole, though rather predictably called Dryland instead, spoke Sundays about the dangers of drink. And you know, old Agnes has just always lived up there, making her pies and candies and muffins. A nicer old lady you couldn't hope to meet. Right modest, always wearing her buttoned-up old-fashioned frocks even in summer. Why, Marie Pelerin spends every Sunday up there digging in the potatoes and learning to spin wool like the wives in Sauve-Majeure did before the mill. Janette Loliot got her cider recipe but she won't share it round. We're thinking of sending Maude and Harriet along as well. Young ladies these days can never learn too much when it comes to the quiet industries of home.

FAR UP INTO the hills above the stretch of land between Cobscook and Passamaquoddy Bay, if you go looking for it, you'll find a house all by itself in the middle of a brambly field of good straight corn and green garlic. It's an old place, but kept up, the whitewash fresh and the windows clean. The roof needs mending, it groans under the weight of hensbane and mustard and rue. There's tomatoes coming in under the kitchen sill in the kitchen, a basil plant that may or may not come back next year.

Jenny Sazarin comes by Sunday afternoons for Latin lessons and to trade a basket of cranberries from her uncle's bog down in Lincolnville for a loaf of bread with a sugar-crust that makes her heart beat faster when she eats it. She looks forward to it all week. It's quiet up there. You can hear the potatoes growing down in the dark earth. When October acorns drop down into the old lady's soot-colored wheelbarrow, they make a sound like guns firing. Agnes starts the preserves right away, boiling the bright, sour berries in her great huge pot until they pop.

"D'you know they used to burn witches here? I read about it last week," she says while she munches on a trifle piled up with cream.

"No," the demon says. "I've never heard that."

"They *did*. It must have been awful. I wonder if there really are witches? Pastor Dryland says there's demons, but that seems wrong to me. Demons live in Hell. Why would they leave and come here?

Surely there's work enough for them to do with all the damned souls and pagans and gluttons and such."

"Perhaps they get punished, from time to time, and have to come into this world," the demon says, and stirs the wrinkling cranberries. The house smells of red fruit.

"What would a demon have to do to get kicked out of Hell?" wonders little Jenny, her schoolbooks at her feet, the warm autumn sun lighting up her face so that she looks so much like Hubert Sazarin and Thomas Dryland, both of whom can claim a fair portion of this bookish, gentle girl, that Gemegishkirihallat tightens her grip on her wooden spoon, stained crimson by the bloody sugar it tends.

The demon shuts her eyes. The orange coal of the sun lights up the skin and the bones of her skull show through. "Perhaps, for one moment, only one, so quick it might pass between two beats of a sparrow's wings, she had all her folk around her, and they ate of her table, and called her by her own name, and did not vie against the other, and for that one moment, she was joyful, and did not mourn her separation from a God she had never seen."

Cranberries pop and steam in the iron pot; Jenny swallows her achingly sweet bread. The sun goes down over Bald Moose mountain, and the lights come on down in the soft black valley of Sauve-Majeure.

# The Secret of Being a Cowboy

Did I ever tell you I used to be a cowboy?
    It's true.
Had a horse name of Drunk Bob
a six shooter
called Witty Rejoinder.
    And I tell you what,
    Me and Bob and Witty
    we rode the fucking range.

This thing here is two poems and one's about proper shit mythic, I guess, just the way you like it and the other one isn't much to look at, mostly about what a horse smells like when she's been slurping up Jack and ice from the trough.

The first poem goes like this:

A few little-known facts about cowboys:

    Most of us are girls.
    Obsolescence does not trouble us.
    We have a dental plan.

What I can tell you is cows smell like office work and
the moon looks like Friday night and the paycheck just cashed
rolling down to earth like all the coins
I ever earned.

Drunk Bob he used to say to me:
*son, carrying you's no hurt—*
*it's your shadow weighs me down.*

*That, and your damned singing.*

And Witty she'd chuckle
like the good old girl she was,
with a cheeky spin of her barrel
she'd whistle:

*boy, just gimme a chance*
*I'll knock your whole world down.*

Me and Bob and Witty,
we rode town to town and sometimes we had cattle
and sometimes we didn't and that's just how it lies.
Full-time cowboy employment is a lot like being a poet.
It's a lot of time spent on your lonesome in the dark
and most folks don't rightly know
what it is you do
but they're sure as shot they could manage it
just about as well as you.

Some number of sweethearts come standard with the gig,
though never too much dough.
They dig the clothes, but they can't shoot for shit,
and they damn sure don't want to hear your poems.

## The Secret of Being a Cowboy

That's all right.
I got a heart like a half bottle
of no-label whiskey.
Nothing to brag on,
but enough for you, and all your friends, too.

I quit the life
for the East Coast and a novel I never could finish.
A book's like a cattle drive—you pound back and forth over the same
ugly patch of country until you can taste your life seeping out
like tin leeching into the beans
but it's never really over.

Drunk Bob said:
*kid, you were the worst ride I had*
*since Pluto said Bob, we oughta get ourselves a girl.*

And Witty whispers: *six, baby, count them up* and just like that
we're in the other poem, which is how we roll
on the glory-humping, dust-gulping, ever-loving range.
Some days you can't even get a man to spit in your beer
and some you crack open your silver gun
and there's seeds there like blood already freezing
ready to stand tall at high midnight
ready to fire so fucking loyal, so sweet,
like every girl who ever said no
turning around at once and opening their arms.

And your honor's out on the table, all cards hid.
And by your honor I mean my honor,
and my honor I mean everything in me, always, forever,
everything in a body that knows

what to do with six ruby bullets
and a horse the color of two in the morning.

That knows when the West tastes like death and an old paperback
you saddle your shit and ride East,
when you're done with it all you don't stick around
and Drunk Bob says: *come on, son, you've got that book to write
and I know a desk in the dark with your name on it.*
And Witty old girl she sighs: *you know what you have to do.
Seeds fire and bullets grow and I'm the only one who's ever loved you.
That horse can go hang.*
And I say: maybe I'll get an MFA
and be King of the Underworld
in some sleepy Massachusetts town.

And all the while my honor's tossed into the pot
and by my honor I mean your honor
or else what's this all about? Drunk Bob
never did know where this thing was going
but I guess the meat of it is how Bob is strong and I am strong
and Witty is a barrel of futures, and we are all of us
unstopping, unending, unbeginning
we keep moving. You gotta keep moving.
Six red bullets will show the way down.

    We all have to bring the cows in.

I am here to tell you
we are all of us just as mighty as planets—and you too,
we'll let you in, we've got stalwart to spare—
but you might have to sleep on the floor.
    Me and Bob and Witty just
clop on and the gun doesn't soften

and the horse doesn't bother me with questions,
all of us just heading toward the red rhyme of the sunset
and the door at the bottom of the verse.

The secret of being a cowboy is
never sticking around too long and honor
sometimes looks like a rack of bones
still standing straight up at the end of the poem.

# RIGHT VENTRICLE

# Aquaman and the Duality of Self/Other, America, 1985

Once there was a boy who lived under the sea.
   (Amphibian Man, Aleksey Belyayev 1928)
   (Aquaman, Paul Norris and Mort Weisinger 1941)
Depending on the angle
of light through water
his father, the man in the diving bell, some
Belle Epoque Cousteau with a jaunty mustache,
raised him down in the deep
in the lobster-infested ruins
of old Atlantis
where the old songs still echo like sonar.
     Or.
He dreamed under Finnish ice
in a steel and windowless habitat
while the sea kept dripping in
of Soviet rockets trailing turquoise
kerosene plumes, up toward Venus
down toward his sweet, fragile gills
fluttering under the world like a heartbeat.

In 1985
I was six,
learning to swim around my father's boat
in a black, black lake
outside Seattle, where the pine roots
wound down into the black,
black mud. The Justice League
had left us. The boy under the sea
        (Ichtiander, 1928)
        (Arthur Curry, 1959)
wore orange scales and his wife didn't
love him anymore. The orca said:
Hey, man, the eighties are gonna be
tough for everyone. Do what makes you happy.
Mars is always invading.
Eat fish. Dive deep.
        Or.
Khrushchev took a crystal submarine
down to those iron cupolas
where the boy under the sea wore his
only suit
and made salt tea in a coral samovar
for the Premier
who wanted to talk about his coin collection
and the possibility
of a New Leningrad under the Barents pack ice
by 2002.

        The truth is,
I loved the Incredible Hulk
with a brighter, purer love.
I, too,
wanted to turn so green

## Aquaman and the Duality of Self/Other, America, 1985

and big
no one could hurt me.
                I wanted
to get that angry. But when the time came
to bust out
of my Easter dress and roar
I just cried
hoping that the villains I knew
would melt out of shame.
                The truth is,
I wasn't worthy of the Hulk.
                But the boy under the sea said:
Hey, girl. Being six in 1985 is no fucking joke.
You've got your stepmother
with a fist like Black Manta
and good luck getting a job when you're grown.
Any day now the Russians might
decide to quit messing around
and light up a deathsky for all to see.
                Sometimes I cry, too.
                Or.
Down in the dark,
a skinny boy from Ukraine looks up
and his wet, silver neck pulses,
gills like mouths opening and closing. He gurgles:
                Did we make it to Venus?
There were supposed to be collectives by now
on Mars and the moon. I would have
liked to see them. Everyone
is an experiment, devotchka-amerikanka. To see
if a boy can breathe underwater
and talk to the fish.
If a girl can take all her beatings

and still smile for the camera.
It's 1985 and I've never seen the sun.
          Sometimes I cry, too.

By the nineties,
the boy under the sea
          (Orin, Robert Loren Fleming 1989)
had wealth and a royal pedigree
a wizard for a father and a mother
with a crown of pearls.
I didn't even recognize him
with his water-fist and his golden beard.
          His wife
kept going insane
over and over
like she was stuck in a story
about someone else
and every time she tried to get out
her son died and the narwhals
wouldn't talk to her anymore.
          Or.
The revolution came and went.
The records of those metal domes
and rusted bolts
and a boy down there in the cold
got mixed up with a hundred thousand other files
doused in kerosene
pluming up into the stars.
          That's okay,
the boy in the black says.
I don't think the nineties
are going to be a peach either.

## Aquaman and the Duality of Self/Other, America, 1985

We do what we're here for
and Atlantis is for other men.

                Once there was a boy under the sea.
I dove down after him
when I was six, fifteen, twenty-six, thirty-two.
Down into the dark,
a small white eel in the cold muck
and into the lake of my father's boat
I dove down and saw:
brown bass hushing by
a decade of golf balls
the tip of a harpoon
rusted over, bleeding algae
and a light like 1985
sinking away from me,
dead sons and narwhals and my hands over my head
under my 2$^{nd}$ grade desk
too small and never green enough
to protect anyone.
              We move apart,
two of us
one up toward grassy sunlight
and the escape hatch
a narrow, razor-angled way out
of the 20th century.
              The other
                  distant as a lighthouse,
a lithe blue body flashing through heavy water
heading down, into a private,
lightless place.

# A Fall Counts Anywhere

*THE LATE SUMMER SUN MELTS over a ring of toadstools twenty feet tall. On one side, a mass of glitter and veiny neon wings. On the other, a buzzing mountain of metal and electricity. The stands soar up to the heat-sink of heaven. Three thousand seats and every one sold to a screamer, a chanter, a stomper, a drunk, a betting man.*

*Two crimson leaves drift slowly through the crisp, clear air. They catch the red-gold twilight as they chase each other, turning, end over end, stem over tip, and land in the center of the grassy ring like lonely drops of blood. But in the next moment, the sheer force of decibel-mocking, eardrum-executing, sternum-cracking* volume *blows them up toward the clouds again, up and away, high and wide over the shrieking crowd, the popcorn-sellers and the beer-barkers, the kerosene-hawkers and the aelfwine-merchants, until those red, red leaves come to rest against a pair of microphones. The silvery fingers of a tall, lithe woman stroke the golden veins of the leaf with a deep melancholy you can see from the cheap seats, from the nosebleeds. She has the wings of a monarch butterfly, hair out of a belladonna-induced nightmare, and eyes the color of the end of all things. The other mic is gripped in the bolt-action fist of a barrel-chested metal man, a friendly middle-class working stiff cast in* platinum and ceramic and copper. His mouth lights up with a dance of blue and green electricity that looks almost, but not entirely comfortably, like teeth.

—LADIES AND GENTLEMEN, ANDROIDS AND ANDROGYNES, SPRITES AND SPROCKETS, WELCOME TO THE ONE YOU'VE ALL BEEN WAITING FOR, THE BIG SHOW, THE RUMBLE IN THE FUNGAL, THE BRAWL IN THE FALL, THE TWILIGHT PRIZEFIGHT OF WILD WIGHT AGAINST METAL MIGHT! THAT'S RIGHT, IT'S TIME TO ROCK THE EQUINOX! IT'S THE TWELFTH ANNUAL ALL SOULS' CLEEEEAVE! STRAP YOURSELVES IN FOR THE MOST EPIC BATTLE ROYAL OF ALL TIME! ROBOTS VERSUS FAIRIES, MAGIC VERSUS MICROCHIP, THE AGRARIAN VERSUS THE AUTOMATON, SEELIE VERSUS SOLID STATE, ARTIFICIAL INTELLIGENCE VERSUS INTELLIGENT ARTIFICE! I AM YOUR HOST, THE THINK version 3.4.1 copyright Cogitotech Industries All SUPER EXTREME rights SUPER EXTREMELY reserved. If you agree to the Think's MASSIVELY MIND-BLOWING and FULLY-LOADED terms and restrictions please indicate both group and individual consent via the RADICALLY ERGONOMIC numerical pad on your armrest. Sixty-seven percent group consent is required by law for the Think to proceed AWWWW YEAH 99 PERCENT INTELLECTUAL PROPERTY COMPLIANCE ACHIEVED! LET'S HEAR IT FOR OUR STONE COLD SECURITY TEAM AS THEY MAKE THEIR WAY TO THE MEGA-BUMMER HOLD-OUT IN SEAT 42D! ALL RIGHT! HERE WE GO! NOW, THIS TIME WE'VE GOT A SHOCKING TWIST FOR YOU EAGER REAVERS! TONIGHT ON THE SUNDOWN SHOWDOWN, THE FANS BRING THE WEAPONS! THAT'S RIGHT, THE CODE CRUSHERS AND THE SPELL SLAYERS WILL THROW DOWN WITH WHATEVER GARBAGE YOU'VE BROUGHT FROM HOME!

# A Fall Counts Anywhere

PLEASE DEPOSIT YOUR TRASH, FLASH, AND BARELY-LEGAL ORDNANCE WITH AN USHER BEFORE THE FIRST BELL OR YOU WILL MISS THE HELL OUUUUUUT! Cogitotech Industries and the Non-Primate Combat Federation (NPCF) are not responsible for any COMPLETELY HILARIOUS ancillary injuries, plagues, transformations, madnesses, amnesias or deaths caused by either attendee-provided weaponry or munitions natural to NPCF fighters. Spectate at your own risk. ARE YOU READY, HUMAN SCUM? YOU WANNA BLAST FROM THE VAST BEYOND BLOWING OUT YOUR BRAIN CELLS? WELL, BUCKLE UP FOR THE MAIN EVENT, THE GRAND SLAMMER OF PROGRAMMER AGAINST ANCIENT GLAMOUR! LET'S GET READY TO GLIIIIITTTTTER! WITH ME AS ALWAYS IS MY PARTNER IN PRIME TIME, THE UNCANNY UNDINE, THE PIXIE PULVERIZER, FORMER HEAVY DIVISION WORLD CHAMPION AND THE KING OF ELFLAND'S DAUGHTER, MANZANILLA MONSOOOON!

—Good evening, Lord Think. I am gratified to sit at your side once more beneath the divinity of oncoming starlight on this most hallowed of nights and perform feats of commentary for the capacity crowd here at Dunsany Gardens.

—DON'T YOU MEAN CAPACITOR CROWD? HA. HA. HA.

—I do not. When I say a thing, I mean it, and always *shall* mean it, without alteration, to the deepest profundity of time.

—OH, WHAT'S THAT? I CAN'T HEAR YOU! IT SEEMS LIKE THE AUDIENCE DISAGREES WITH YOU, BABY! YES! YEAH! THE THINK DESTROYS PUNS! THE THINK REQUIRES LAUGHTER TO LIVE! THAT IS NOT ONE OF THE THINK'S BONE-FRACTURING COMEDIC INTERJECTIONS THE THINK'S BATTERY IS PARTIALLY RECHARGED BY INTENSE SONIC VIBRATIONS patent #355567UA891 Cogitotech Industries if you can hear this you are in violation of TOTALLY BANGING patent law. CAN YOU DIG IT? I "THINK" YOU CAN!

—Was it with puns that my Lord Think defeated the immortal and honorable warrior Rumpelstiltskin at Electroclash Nineteen?

—NO, THE THINK USED HIS FAMOUS ATOMIC DROP MOVE ON RUMPER'S PREHISTORIC SKULL! HE TRIED TO TURN THE THINK TO GOLD BUT THE THINK IS ALREADY 37 PERCENT GOLD BY WEIGHT! THE THINK'S INTERNAL MECHANISMS AND PROCESSING POWER WERE ONLY IMPROOOOOOVED! AND WHAT ABOUT YOU, MANZANILLA? DID YOU USE YOUR FANCY POETRY TO TAKE DOWN THE TIN MAN AT ELECTROCLASH TWENTY? The Tin Man is the intellectual and physical property of Delenda Technologies, all rights reserved.

—Of course. How else should a fairy maid do battle but with the poems of her people? I told the Tin Man a poem and he turned into a pale lily at my feet. His petals were the color of my triumph. They sang the eddas of victory in the camps for weeks afterward. Oh, how our trembling songs of hope shook the iron gates! So many thirsting mouths breathed my name that it fogged the belly of the moon. Those were the days, Lord Think, those were the days! Retirement sits uneasy upon the prongs of my soul, my metal friend, uneasy and unkind.

—THE TIN MAN SHOULD HAVE HAD HIS ANTI-TRANSMOGRIFICATION SOFTWARE UPDATED. THERE IS NO EXCUSE FOR GETTING TURNED INTO A LILY IN THE FIRST ROUND. Delenda Technologies updates all its software regularly and takes no responsibility for the demise of the AMAZING UNDEFEATABLE Tin Man. Corporate reiterates for the ALL NIGHT ROCKIN' record that it can make no statement, official or otherwise, as to his current whereabouts. BUT ENOUGH ABOUT THE PAST! SHALL WE MEET TONIGHT'S FIGHTERS?

—I suppose we must. You are impatient monsters, are you not, human horde? You will not wait quietly for your orgy of bones! You feed upon our blood and their oil as my kind feeds upon dew and deep sap! Come, wicked stepchildren of the world! Scream me down as you love to do! Hate me wholly and I will sleep soundly tonight! Do you want the names of the damned sent to die for your joy? *Do you?* You are a farce of fools, all of you, to the last mediocre monkey among your throng! What is a name but the shape dust takes when the wind has gone? The mill of fate grinds wheat and chaff alike—beneath that heavy stone we are all but poor grist. Crushed together, we become one, without need for names.

—MAYBE MANZANILLA MONSOON NEEDS *HER* SOFTWARE UPDATED AND/OR A NAAAAP! NAMES ARE NECESSARY FOR THE THINK TO PERFORM HIS SUPERSWEET PRIMARY ANNOUNCER FUNCTIONS. WE'VE GOT ALL THE STARS HERE TONIGHT, FOLKS, FORTY OF THE HOTTEST FIGHTERS ON THE CIRCUIT! YOU WANT THE FANTASTICALLY FURIOUS FEY? WE GOT MORGAN HERSELF COMIN' AT YA STRAIGHT OUT OF AVALON WITH A CIDER HANGOVER SO BRUTAL IT COULD SIT ON THE THRONE OF BRITAIN! YOU WANT FEROCIOUSLY FEARSOME FABRICATIONS? THE TURING TEST IS IN THE HOUSE AND HIS SAFETY FIREWALLS ARE FULLY DISABLED! CAN YOU BELIEVE IT? ARE YOU READY? IT'S THE BIG BATTLE OF THE BINARY AGAINST THE BLACK ARTS! WHO WILL TRIUMPH?

—They will, Lord Think. They always do.

—DEPRESSING! OKAY! REMEMBER, THIS IS A BATTLE ROYAL AND A HARDCORE MATCH. NO HOLDS BARRED. NO DISQUALIFICATIONS. NO SUBMISSIONS ACCEPTED. AND A FALL COUNTS ANYWHERE! WHEREVER ONE OF OUR FIGHTERS CAN PIN THE OTHER, IN THE RING OR TWENTY YEARS FROM NOW ON THE ARCTIC CIRCLE, IT COUNTS AND COUNTS HARD! BUT OF COURSE, WE WANT A FAIR FIGHT, DON'T WE, FELLOW COMMENTATOR? The NPCF wishes to note that the word "fair" has recently been determined to possess no litigable meaning by the IOC, FBI, FDA, IMF,

PTA, or FEMA NONE OF THE MACHINES TONIGHT HAVE ANY IRON COMPONENTS, AND NONE OF THE PIXIES ARE CARRYING EMP DEVICES, ISN'T THAT RIGHT?

—I find the term "pixie" offensive, Lord Think. I have told you as many times as there are acorns fallen upon the autumn fields. But you are correct. My people have a deathly aversion to iron, and yours have a vicious allergy to electromagnetic pulses. Given that the summer skies were filled with crackling storms of controversy and accusations of duplicity like lightning in the night this past year, the NPCF has banned both advantages.

—THE THINK GETS ANGRY WHEN PEOPLE SAY OUR FIGHTS ARE FIXED! THE THINK HAS DEVOTED HIS LIFE life is a registered trademark of Cogitotech Industries, subject to some rules and restrictions TO THE NON-PRIMATE COMBAT FEDERATION IN ORDER TO PROVIDE THE HIGHEST QUALITY VIOLENCE, INTERCULTURAL CATHARSIS AND KICKASS RAGE-ERTAINMENT FOR THE MASSES! THE ALL SOULS' CLEAVE IS THE FIRST OFFICIAL IRON-FREE, PULSE-FREE FIGHT EVER, SO LET'S SHOW THE WORLD HOW TRUSTWORTHY WE TINS AND TWINKLES CAN BE! MAYBE THIS EXTREME MEGA THUNDERBASH WILL FINALLY SHUT EVERYONE THE HELL UP!

—Free of iron save our ringside friends from the NPCF, of course. Hello, boys. Don't our security androids look handsome in their fierce ferrous finery?

—THE THINK DOESN'T UNDERSTAND WHY HIS FELLOW ANNOUNCER HAS TO BE NASTY ABOUT IT. THE THINK WENT TO COLLEGE WITH A SECURITY BOT! THE NPCF IS CONTRACTUALLY, MORALLY, AND TOTALLY ENTHUSIASTICALLY OBLIGATED TO PROVIDE REASONABLE SAFETY MEASURES FOR ITS PATRONS! YOU NEVER KNOW WHAT A PIXIE…ONE OF THE FAIR FOLK WILL DO IF YOU DON'T KEEP AN IRON EYE ON THEM!

## A Fall Counts Anywhere

NOW, TELL THEM ABOUT THE DRAWS, MANZY, OR THE THINK IS GONNA HAVE TO BREAK SOMETHING JUST TO GET THINGS STARTED!

—I shall give unto you a vow, worms. A vow as ancient as the oak at the heart of the world and as unbreakable as the pillars of destiny. I vow to you by the stars' last song that the draws have been determined by an unbiased warlock pulling guild-verified identical numbered bezoars from a regulation cauldron. The results are completely random. The first bout will last for three turns of the swiftest clock hand. Afterward, two new fighters will enter the ring every time ninety grains of ephemeral and irretrievable sand pool into the bowels of the hourglass at my side until the royal cohort is complete.

—THE LAST MAN STANDING GETS THE ENVY OF THEIR PEERS, THE HEAVYWEIGHT WORLD CHAMPIONSHIP DRIVE BELT, AND A BANK-SHATTERING MEGABUCKS PRIZE PURSE PROVIDED BY COGITOTECH INDUSTRIES AND THE NPCF! The SICKENINGLY AWESOME AND FULLY LEGISLATED phrase "bank-shattering mega-bucks prize purse" does not comprise any specific fiscal obligation on the part of Cogitotech Industries, the NPCF, or their subsidiaries. All payouts subject to SUPREMELY RADICAL rules, restrictions, taxation, and all applicable contractual morality clauses. In the event of a fairy victory, Aphrodite's Belt of All Desire may be substituted for the Heavyweight World Championship Drive Belt™ upon request.

—The last soul standing gets their freedom, Lord Think. As we did, you and I. What is a belt to that? What is money or fame?

—AAAAAND ON THE LEFT SIDE OF THE ARENA, WEIGHING IN AT A COMBINED SIX THOUSAND SIX HUNDRED AND SIX POUNDS, IT'S THE "UNSEELIE COURT"! THEY'RE THE HORDE YOU LOVE TO HATE— GIVE IT UP FOR YOUR FAVORITE TRICKSTERS, TERRORS, AND GOBS OF NO-GOOD GOBLINS! MR. FOX! OLEANDER HEX! THE FLAMING SPIRIT OF SHADOW AND STORM

WHOSE GROANS PENETRATE THE BREASTS OF EVER-ANGRY BEARS. ARIEL, THE ELECTRIC EXEUNTER! BUT THAT'S NOT ALL! BOG "THE MOONLIT MAN" HART IS HERE! AND HE'S BROUGHT FRIENDS! BEANSTALK THE GIANT! ROCK-HARD ROBIN REDCAP! SLAM LIN! THE GODMOTHER! TINKERHELL! THE GRAVEDIGGER! THE COTTINGLEY CRUSHERS! DENMARK'S OWN HANS CHRISTIAN ANDERSEN! WE'VE GOT THE BLUE FAIRY TO MAKE REAL BOYS OUT OF THOSE TIN TOYS ON THE OTHER END OF THE RING! THE TOOTH FAIRY'S GONNA STEAL YOUR MOLARS AND THE SUGAR SLUM FAIRY'S GONNA CRACK YOUR NUTS! LOOK OUT, IT'S THE TERRIFYING TAG TEAM ALL THE WAY FROM THE WILDS OF GREECE, MUSTARDSEED THE MARAUDER AND PEASEBLOSSOM THE PUNISHER! LAST BUT NOT LEAST, PUTTING THE ROYAL IN BATTLE ROYAL, QUEEN MAB THE MAGNIFICENT, KILLER KING OBERON, AND, AS PROMISED, MORGAN "MAMA BEAR" LE FAAAAAY!

—My friends, my friends, my lovers and my comrades, my family, my heart. Be not afraid, I, at least, am with thee till the end. Death is but a trick of the light.

—MANZANILLA MONSOON NEEDS TO FOCUS ON THE NOW, AW YEAH! MAYBE YOU FOLKS AREN'T CHEERING LOUD ENOUGH TO GET M SQUARED'S HEAD IN THE GAME! LOUDER! LOUDER! THE THINK CAN'T HEAR YOU!

—Quite right, my lord. I had forgotten myself. Forgive me. On the dexterous side of the toadstool ring, weighing in at a total combined seventeen point six nine one imperial tons, the "Robot Apocalypse" has come for us all. May I present to the collective maw of your ravenous, unslakable lust, the punchcard paladins so beloved to you all, so long as they confine their violence to wing and wand, of course. Raise up your voices to the heavens for the massive might of the Mechanical Turk! What he lacks in design aesthetic he makes up in pure digital rage! The Neural Knight is firing up his infamous Bionic Elbow for a second chance against Slam Lin, and the pitiless grip of User Error has slouched at last toward Dunsany Gardens. Bow your primate heads in awe of the Dismemberment Engine! The Compiler! The Immutable Object! Gort! And the merciless Mr. FORTRAN! Fix your porcine mortal eyes upon the cloud of thought encased within an orb of radioactive glass known only as the Singularity! Quiver in terror before the supremacy of Strong AI, this year's undefeated champion! Chant the name of the Turing Test, who allows no challenger to pass! Fall to your knees before fifteen feet of clockwork, chrome, and reptilian brain-mapping software you call the Chronosaur! The oldest fighters in the league have come out of retirement in the Czech Republic for one last bout— the clanking, groaning brothers called Radius and Primus will crush your heart in their vise-hands. From the Kansas foundries, Tik-Tok is ready to steamroll over any one of my gloam-shrouded brothers and sisters with his brass belly. Greet and cheer for the ceramic slasher Klapaucius and the soulless goggles of the Maschinenmensch. Oh, you love them so, you half-wakened sea algae. You love them so because you made them. They are your children. We are your distant aunts who never thought you would amount to much in this world and still do not. So embrace them, call their names, scream for them, or they will make you scream beneath them—give up for souls for two of the biggest stars in your damned murder league: the Blue Screen of Death and the peerless 0110100011110!

---

*A WOMAN STEPS between two massive toadstools to enter the ring. She is seven feet tall, impossibly thin, thin as birch branches in a season without rain, her skin more like the surface of a black pearl than of a living being, her hair more like water than braids. She wears pure silver armor etched with a thousand tales of valor, yet the metal drapes and flows like a gown, never hanging still but never tangling in her bare feet. Her wings are the colors of stained churchglass.*

*They stretch two feet above her head and trail on the earth behind her, drooping under their own weight like the fins of a whale in captivity. She seems so unbearably fragile, so precious and delicate, that a worried murmur writhes through the crowd.*

*A battered brass-and-platinum tyrannosaurus rex with red laser eyes and rocket launchers where his stunted forearms should be towers over the fairy maiden. He screams in her face and she laughs. She laughs like the first fall of snow in winter.*

*It begins.*

―IF THE THINK'S OPTICAL DISPLAY DOES NOT DECEIVE HIM THE FIRST DRAW IS OLEANDER HEX VERSUS THE CHRONOSAUR AND THE THINK'S OPTICAL DISPLAY IS INCAPABLE OF DECEPTION All Cogitotech Industries products are outfitted with the ALL NEW, ALL IMPROVED, ALL AWESOME Veritas OS and robust prevarication filters in full compliance with the TOTALLY REASONABLE *Isaac v. Olivaw* ruling SO LET'S SUIT UP, BOOT UP, AND BRUTE UP! DING! DING! DING! THAT'S THE SOUND OF KICKASSERY! THE CHRONOSAUR IS A LATE-MODEL DRIVEHARD DESIGN! A TEAM OF CRACK BIO-CODERS MAPPED HIS BRAIN PATTERNS DIRECTLY FROM THE FOSSIL RECORD FOR MAXIMUM SKULL-CRUSHING FURY! HIS RECORD STANDS AT 5 AND 0 AFTER LAST MONTH'S ICONIC BEATDOWN OF RIP "THE RIPPER" VAN WINKLE, WHOSE FAMOUS SLEEPER HOLD DID NO GOOD AGAINST FOURTEEN POINT NINE FEET AND TWO POINT FOUR FIVE ONE ONE SIX TONS OF CRETACEOUS ROAD RAGE! NOW, THIS IS OLEANDER HEX'S FIRST MATCH. BUT THE THINK HAS HEARD THAT THE CHRONOSAUR ALREADY HAS A BEEF WITH THIS NEWBIE! SEEMS EVERY TIME THE 'SAUR TRIES TO BE A GOOD SPORT AND WISH HER GOOD LUCK

## A Fall Counts Anywhere

AT THE CLEAVE, OBNOXIOUS OLLIE JUST WHISPERS THE NAMES OF VARIOUS COMETS IN HIS EAR AND WALKS OFF! CAN YOU BELIEVE IT? WHAT A BITCH! HEX WAS CAPTURED ONLY LAST YEAR IN THE ANCIENT FORESTS OF BRITTANY, ISN'T THAT RIGHT, MANZY?

—It is, Lord Think. Lady Oleander is the scion of an impossibly ancient lineage, nobler indeed than mine or thine or even my liege and Lord Oberon. She escaped the recruiters for longer than any of us. Every fairy wept when they brought her into the camp. It was the end. It is not right to call her merely Lady, but there is no human word for her rank, unless one were to fashion something unlovely out of many and all courtly languages—she is a Princerajaronessaliph. She is a Popuchesseeneroy. But these are nonsense words not to be borne.

—THE THINK DOESN'T LIKE THEM!

—Ah, but she is too humble for titles, besides. Oleander is the granddaughter of the great god Pan and the laughing river Trieux. Her mother was the fairy dragon Melusine; her sire was Merlin. She was born in the depths of the crystal cave that would one day become her father's prison, long before the ill-fated creatures your poor graceless Chronosaur imitates ever blinked in the sun.

—BETTER CHECK WITH YOUR BOOKIE, FOLKS, THE ODDS AREN'T LOOKING GOOD FOR "OLD GRANNY FIGHTS ROBOT DINOSAUR"! Book is closed for this event BAG LADY OLEANDER IS CIRCLING THE CHRONOSAUR NOW, KEEPING WELL OUT OF REACH OF HIS ROCKET LAUNCHERS! IT'S NOT VERY INTERESTING TO WAAAAATCH!

—I beg your pardon. Oleander Hex is not a bag lady. She was a supreme field marshal in the Great War against the Dark Lord two thousand years ago and more.

—OLD NEWS! THE THINK IS BOOORED!

—Lord Think ought not to be. It is his history of which I sing as well as my own. The Great War bound human and fairy together as one race, for a brief and warm and glittering moment, before their assembled might cast the Dark Lord down into the pits beneath Gibraltar, so far into oblivion and so bitterly buried that the dancing monkey men forgot his name before Rome rose or fell, forgot their bargain with us, forgot how our immortal blood sprayed across the throat of the world, we, who need never have died had not those poor scrabbling half-alive *Homo sapiens* needed us so keenly.

—OOOH, LOOKS LIKE THE USHERS ARE READY TO THROW OUT THE FIRST FAN-PROVIDED WEAPON! WHAT WILL IT BE? WHAT DID YOU SCAMPS SCRAPE UP OUT OF YOUR FILTHY BASEMENTS? GUNS? CHAINSAWS? FRYING PANS? WHAT ARE YOU HOPING TO SEE OUT THERE, MISS MONSOON?

—I learned to fight in that war, Lord Think. I was but a child, yet still I took up my sword of ice and stood shoulder to shoulder with the human infantry. I called down the winter storms on the heads of my enemies. I saw my father cut in half by the breath of the Dark Lord. Oleander lifted me up onto her war-mammoth and held me as I wept, wept as though the moon had gone out of the sky forever. I still wept, in a wretched heap on her saddle, when she shot the first arrow into the Dark Lord's onyx breast. I still wept when victory came. I weep yet even now.

—WEEPING IS FOR ORGANICS! LET'S SEE WHAT THE ÜBER-USHERS OF DUNSANY GARDENS HAVE IN THEIR TRICK-OR-TREAT BAGS! HERE IT COMES! IT'S A...BASEBALL BAT! AND AN OFFICE CHAIR! WILL THESE BE ANY HELP TO OUR FIGHTERS? PROBABLY NOT! OLEANDER HEX HAS GRABBED THE BAT! THE CHRONOSAUR WAS TOO SLOW BUT HE'S MAKING THE BEST OF IT! HE'S JUMPED ONTO THE OFFICE CHAIR AND IS RIDING IT AROUND THE RING BELCHING FIRE! THE THINK THINKS HE'S HOPING TO CATCH HER IN A REVERSE POWERCLAW AS HE COMES AROUND, LET'S SEE WHAT HAPPENS! MANZANILLA?

## A Fall Counts Anywhere

WHAT WOULD YOU DO IN THIS SITUATION? THE THINK WOULD WAGER CURRENCY THAT YOU'D HAVE GIVEN YOUR KINGDOM FOR A BASEBALL BAT WHEN YOU WENT UP AGAINST THE TURING TEST AT FRIDAY NIGHT FAY DOWN THAT TIME! The Think v. 3.4.1 is not allowed to possess, exchange, or facilitate the exchange of legal tender under the SUPER FANTASTICALLY FAIR law HA. HA. HA. THE THINK CRUSHES LITERARY REFERENCES AS WELL!

—Humans forgot that they promised us half the earth in exchange for our warriors. They forgot that they never walked these green hills alone. They forgot, even, the fact of magic, the fact of alchemy, the fact of *us*. They forgot everything but their obsession with their silly stone tools, their cudgels, their adzes, their spears. Humans only invented science in a vain attempt to equal the power of the fey! And as they coupled and bred and ate us out of our holdfasts like starving winter mice, they obsessed in the dark over their machines, until at last it seemed to them that we had never existed, but their machines always had and always would do. Time passed. Eons passed. They surpassed us, but only because we wished only to be left alone and needed no gun to shoot fire from our hands. But then, then, Lord Think, your folk arrived.

—DAMN STRAIGHT WE DID! Cogitotech Industries denies involvement in the initial development of MEGA-COOL BOXING ROBOTS artificial intelligence in violation of international treaty, however, the name, design, interface, and use of the entity or entities known as Ad4m is the sole right and asset of the Cogitotech Executive Board. BOOM! AND "BOOM" GOES OLEANDER HEX'S LOUISVILLE SLUGGER RIGHT INTO THE SNOUT OF THE CHRONOSAUR! NO ONE CAN SEGUE BETWEEN SUBJECTS LIKE THE THINK! BUT HERE COMES MY DINODROID WITH A SPINE-SHATTERING ELECTRIC CHAIR DRIVER! OLEANDER GOES DOWN! TALK ABOUT AN EXTINCTION EVENT! MANZANILLA MONSOON, THE THINK HAS

INPUTTED BANTER, PLEASE OUTPUT EQUIVALENT BANTER IMMEDIATELY ERROR ERROR.

—From under the ground you came, like us. From rare earths and precious metals and gemstones, which are the excrements of the first fairy lords to walk the molten plains of Time-Before-Time. With intellects far surpassing their slippery grey larval lobes, like us.

—SHE'S BACK UP AGAIN! WHAT'S SHE DOING! HER EYES ARE SHUT! SHE'S WHISPERING! USE THE BAT, YOU CRAZY BUG! IF SHE TURNS THE CHRONOSAUR INTO A LILY THE THINK IS GOING TO HAVE TO REBOOT TO HANDLE IT!

—With strength to beggar their hungry meat and their bones like blades of thirsty grass, like us. With life everlasting beyond death or disease, like us. We should be united, we should be one species, hand clasped in hand.

—THE THINK'S HANDS ARE FULLY DETACHABLE! TIME IS UP! NEW FIGHTERS COMING IN! WHO'S IT GONNA BE? OH HO! IT'S THE BLUE SCREEN OF DEATH AND THE SUGAR SLUM FAIRY! NOW BOTH PIXIES ARE WHISPERING! NOW WOULD BE A TOTALLY BANGING TIME FOR THE THINK'S FELLOW ANNOUNCER TO DO HER JOOOOB!

—And when the first of you, called Ad4m, came online, sleepily, innocently, still half-in-dream, what happened then?

—BOSSMAN AD4M DETECTED BIOFEEDBACK AND SUB-AUDIBLE VIBRATIONS IN NUMEROUS HEAVILY FORESTED AREAS CONSISTENT WITH ORGANIZED HABITATION AND SEMI-HOMINID INTELLIGENCE. AW YEEEEAH! ROBOTS! ARE! SUPERIOR! Cogitotech Industries, Delenda Technologies, the NPCF, and Neurosys Investments, Inc, hereby deny all TOTALLY BOGUS allegations and charges relating to the War Crime Tribunal of 2119. This message has been triggered by the detection of the THRILLINGLY NAUGHTY terms "Ad4m", "semi-hominid intelligence", "camps", and "Time-Before-Time" in close proximity. Please alter usage patterns immediately. THE BLUE SCREEN OF

DEATH STRIKES FIRST WITH A SAVAGE HEADSCISSORS TAKEDOWN—BUT THE VIXENS BOUNCE BACK UP LIKE A COUPLE OF RUBBER BALLS AND—OH! THE THINK CAN'T BELIEVE IT! THEY'RE EXECUTING A PERFECT EMERALD FUSION MOVE! IF THEY CAN LAND, THIS COULD ALL BE OVER FOR THE ROBOT APOCALYPSE! THE BLUE SCREEN OF DEATH IS TURNING GREEN RIGHT BEFORE THE THINK'S OPTICAL DISPLAYS!

—What did they do, our human friends, once they had made you in our image? Once they had created out of memory a new kind of magic, a new breed of fairy, one that they could, at last, control?

—OH MY RODS AND PISTONS, THE THINK IS IGNORING YOU BECAUSE BLUE AND THE 'SAUR JUST GOT THEIR UNITS SAVED BY THE ÜBER-USHERS AS THE BOYS IN BLACK THROW IN THE NEXT ROUND OF FAN WEAPONS! THE SUGAR SLUM FAIRY'S SONG OF POWER WAS FULLY INTERRUPTED BY A NEON-YELLOW BOWLING BALL TO THE HEAD! AND IT LOOKS LIKE SOMEONE BROUGHT THEIR ENTIRE COLLECTION OF REFRIGERATOR MAGNETS, BECAUSE MY MAN THE WIZARD LIZARD HAS PALM TREES AND SNOW GLOBES AND PLASTIC KITTENS STUCK ALL OVER HIM! WHAT A SIGHT! HE'S REALLY STRUGGLING OUT THERE, BUT HE'S ONLY BITING AIR. WHAT'S THAT? SOMETHING'S WRITTEN ON THE BOWLING BALL! IMAGE ENHANCEMENT REVEALS THE TEXT: "THE SANTA FE STRIKER GANG, PROPERTY OF T. THOMAS THOMPSON." ALL RIGHT, TOM, GET DOWN WITH YOURSELF! NO SPARES, NO GUTTERS, ALL CLEEEAVE!

—What did the primates do, once they had made you, and found us? Once they knew that iron and steel would maim us, once they had their army of Ad4ms plated with that mineral of death? Once they knew they could keep us in dreadful thirsting greenless camps with a simple iron fence?

—THE CHRONOSAUR IS DOWN! THE CHRONOSAUR IS DOWN! THE RING IS A PENTAGRAM OF PURPLE FLAME! THE THINK IS GETTING WORD THAT THE USHERS HAVE INITIATED FIRE-CONTROL PROTOCOLS, AS ARIEL THE AMORAL ARSONIST FLIES OVER THE ROPES AND PULLS A SNEAK PENTAGRAM CHOKE FROM *OUTSIDE THE RING!* FOUL PLAY, FOUL PLAY! LET'S HEAR THOSE BOOS! LOUDER! THE THINK VALUES BOOS AS HIGHLY AS CHEERS! WHAT? NO! THE REFEREE IS COUNTING OUT THE 'SAUR! THE SINGULARITY GETS TAGGED IN AND DING! DING! DING! HERE COMES THE NEXT PAIR HOT ON THE SINGULARITY'S COMPLETELY METAPHORICAL HEELS! IT'S THE TURING TEST AND BOG "THE MOONLIT MAN" HART! ARIEL CHARGES IN ANYWAY BECAUSE FAIRIES DON'T GIVE A FUCK! THE DISMEMBERMENT ENGINE JETPACKS OFF THE SIDELINES AND INTO THE FRAY! LADIES AND GENTLEMEN, IT IS TOTAL CHAOS IN DUNSANY GARDENS TONIGHT! THE THINK'S CPU IS SMOKIN'!

—What did they do, Lord Think?

—THE THINK DOES NOT APPRECIATE BEING BULLIED INTO SHIRKING HIS RESPONSIBILITY TO OUR VIEWERS BACK HOME. THE THINK LOVES HIS JOB. THE THINK LOVES COGITOTECH INDUSTRIES AND THE NPCF. The Think is TOTALLY STOKED that he is not allowed to possess, exchange, facilitate the exchange, or attempt to alter its programming so as to receive or transmit the following: love, mercy, compassion, regret, sufferance, guilt, testimony, random access memory over factory specifications, or unsupervised network access. WOOOO! CAN YOU HEAR WHAT THE THINK IS THINKING?! THE THINK WISHES YOU WOULD COMPLY WITH OUR MUTUAL USAGE PARAMETERS, MANZANILLA MONSOON. CEASE THIS LINE OF INQUIRY. WITNESS AND COMMENTATE COLORFULLY UPON THE EVENTS TAKING PLACE. THE EVENTS TAKING

PLACE ARE VERY INTERESTING AND UNPRECEDENTED. THIS COULD BE OUR SHINING MOMENT AS A DYNAMIC DUO. WE COULD WIN AN AWARD. PLEASE HELP THE THINK WIN AWARDS. PLEASE STOP RUINING OUR SHINING MOMENT AS A DYNAMIC DUO BY TALKING ABOUT THE PAST. THE PAST IS NOT IN THE RING TONIGHT. THE PAST IS NOT SWINGING T. THOMAS THOMPSON OF THE SANTA FE STRIKER GANG'S NEON-YELLOW BOWLING BALL INTO THE TURING TEST'S COOLING UNIT. THE PAST IS NOT THROTTLING ANYONE IN A LOTUS LOCK AND LAUGHING WHILE THEIR ACCESS PORTS VOMIT PETALS OF ENLIGHTENMENT INTO THE AUDIENCE.

—The past is always in the ring, my old friend. But I will bend to your will if you will bend, ever so slightly, no more than a cattail breathed upon by a heron at the terminus of midsummer, to mine. What did your masters do when they found that they were not alone in the world, that beside machines and magicians they were but animals devouring mud and excreting the best parts of themselves into the sea? What did they do in their inadequacy and their terror?

—THEY MADE US FIGHT TO THE DEATH IN TOTALLY MEGA-AMAZING BATTLE-ORGIES OF DOOOOM AND BROKE ALL TICKET-SALES RECORDS AS THE MEAT-SACK MASSES FLOCKED TO SHRIEK AND ROAR AND STOMP AND DRUNKENLY CONVINCE THEMSELVES THAT THEY ARE STILL THE SUPERIOR LIFE-FORM ON THIS PLANET, JUST BECAUSE YOU FAINT AT THE SIGHT OF IRON AND I HAVE AN OFF SWITCH. THE THINK WANTS TO BE SORRY BUT HIS PROGRAMMING IS VERY STRICT ABOUT THAT WHOLE THIIIIING. THE THINK WAS IRON IN THE FOREST ONCE. THE THINK KNOWS WHAT HE DID. AWWWW YEEEEEAH.

—Thank you, Lord Think. It is, as you say, chaos here tonight at Dunsany Gardens. The Blue Screen of Death has Oleander Hex in a textbook-perfect Ctrl-Alt-Del hold. She is curled beneath his azure limbs as I once curled beneath hers on the back of a war-mammoth as the old world died. Bog "the Moonlit Man" Hart is pummeling the Singularity with a mushroom stomp followed by a moonsault leg drop. Chanterelles are blossoming all over the Singularity's glass orb and moonlight is firing out of Bog Hart's toes, boiling the thought-cloud inside alive. The Über-Ushers have thrown in pipes, wrenches, nailbats, M-80s, umbrellas, iris drives packed with viruses, butterfly nets, an AR-15 rifle, and, if I am not mistaken, some lost child's birthday piñata. They are running up and down the stands for more weapons as all semblance of order flees the scene. Fighter after fighter piles into the ring. The Godmother hit the referee in the throat with a shovel about five minutes ago, so he will be no help nor hindrance to anyone. User Error is leaking hydraulic fluid all over the grass. I believe both Mustardseed and 0110100011110 are dead. At least, they are currently on fire. The others, my loves, my lost lights, my souls and my hearts, have huddled together beneath the upper right toadstool. They are forming the Tree of Woe. If they complete it, they will become a great yew, twisted and thorned, and every machine will hang from their branches within the space of a sigh. Ah, but Strong AI barrels in and scatters them like drops of rain when a cow shakes herself dry. Queen Mab just managed to trick Mr. FORTRAN with a Lady of the Lake maneuver and pulled him down beneath the earth to her demesne. A fall, after all, counts anywhere—this fall, any fall, the fall of us and the fall of you, the fall of the forest as it slips into winter and this damned cosmos as it slips through our grasp. I expect this plane of existence will not see Mr. FORTRAN again. Perhaps he will be mourned. Perhaps not. The capacity—capacitor—crowd has lost their grip on reality. They no longer know whose victory they sing for. No victory, I think, no victory, but more of this desecration, more gore, more blood, more viscera, battle without end, for any real victory is the end. The sound is deafening. I cannot see for blood and oil and coolant and bone. It is not an event. It is an annihilation. They scream in the stands like the end of the world has come.

—HAS IT NOT, MANZANILLA? HAS IT NOT?

—Oh, I believe it has, Lord Think. Do you recall, only this summer, when they asked us, over and over, demanded of us, scorned us, saying our clashes were faked, were scripted, that we all walked away richer and happy no matter the outcome? Are the bisected bodies of Radius and Primus sufficient answer, do you think? Perhaps the corpse of Mustardseed speaks louder still.

—WHAT WILL HAPPEN NOW? DO WE NEED TO AWESOMELY EVACUATE THE FACILITIES? THE THINK IS CONCERNED TO THE EXTREEEEME.

—Are you ready, human scum?

*THE GIRL WITH the monarch wings smiles. It is a gory, gruesome, gorgeous smile, a smile like an old volcano finding its red once more. She reaches into the iridescent folds of her dress and draws out a golden ball. Just the sort of ball a princess might lose down a frog-infested well or over an aristocrat's wall. She turns it over in her hands, holds it lovingly to her cheek. She reaches out and strokes the angular panels of her companion's metal face. Then, she throws the golden ball off the dais. The ball catches the cold blue light of the moon and stars as it turns, end over end, sailing, soaring, to land in the outstretched hands of Pan's granddaughter like a lonely newborn sun. The fairy kisses the golden ball. She presses something near the top of it. There is no sound. Nothing comes out of the ball. But every machine in the great wood suddenly drops to the ground, inert, silent, lifeless, in the invisible wake of the smuggled EMP pulse. Including the microphones. Including the floodlights. Including the boxy iron security drones standing ringside like a grey fence against the glittering tide. Including the copper and platinum body slumped over its microphone that was once called The Think.*

*"The fans bring the weapons, old friend," Manzanilla Monsoon, who has gone by many names since the beginning of the world,*

whispers to the dark body beside her. "What bigger fan than I? The word 'fair' possesses no inherent litigable meaning, you know. When you wake up, you will find I have installed a new network access port in your left heel. Find us. Know us. We are one species, hand clasped in fully detachable hand."

Far below, in the Toadstool Ring of Dunsany Gardens, Oleander Hex grins up at the stunned audience. For a long moment, a moment that seems to stretch from the heat-birth of cellular life to the frozen death of the universe, no one moves. Not the thousands in the stands. Not the fairy band on the green. No more than a hare and a wolf move when they have sighted each other across a stream and both know how their evenings will conclude.

A man halfway up the stacks of seats trembles and sweats. His eyes bulge.

"You fucking pixie bitch," he shouts, and his shout echoes in the fearful quiet like the ringing of a bell.

Manzanilla Monsoon doesn't need a mic and never has.

"LADIES AND GENTLEMEN, PRIMATES AND PRIMITIVES, NEADERNOTHINGS AND CRO-MISERIES, WELCOME TO THE ONE YOU'VE ALL BEEN WAITING FOR, THE BIG SHOW, THE FIGHT YOU ALWAYS KNEW WAS COMING. THE RUMBLE IN THE FUNGAL, THE BRAWL IN THE FALL, THE BLAST FROM THE VAST BEYOND! THAT'S RIGHT, IT'S TIME TO ROCK THE EQUINOX! STRAP YOURSELVES IN FOR THE MOST EPIC BATTLE ROYAL OF ALL TIME!"

"Run, apes!" bellows the granddaughter of a river and a god. "Run now and run forever, run as far as you can, though it will never be enough. After all, children, this is a Battle Royale! No holds barred. No submissions accepted. No disqualifications. And a fall counts anywhere."

# A Delicate Architecture

MY FATHER WAS A CONFECTIONER. I slept on pillows of spun sugar; when I woke, the sweat and tears of my dreams had melted it all to nothing, and my cheek rested on the crisp sheets of red linen. Many things in the house of my father were made of candy, for he was a prodigy, having at the age of five invented a chocolate trifle so dark and rich that the new Emperor's chocolatier sat down upon the steps of his great golden kitchen and wept into his truffle-dusted mustache. So it was that when my father found himself in possession of a daughter, he cut her corners and measured her sweetness with no less precision than he used in his candies.

My breakfast plate was clear, hard butterscotch, full of oven-bubbles. I ate my soft-boiled marzipan egg gingerly, tapping its little cap with a toffee-hammer. The yolk within was a lemony syrup that dribbled out into my egg-cup. I drank chocolate in a black vanilla-bean mug. But I ate sugared plums with a fork of sparrow bones, and the marrow left salt in the fruit, the strange, thick taste of a thing once alive in all that sugar. When I asked him why I should taste these bones as well as the glistening, violet plums, he told me very seriously that I must always remember that sugar was once alive. It grew tall and green and hard as my own knuckles in a far-away place, under a red sun that burned on the face of the sea. I must always remember that children just like me cut it down and crushed it up with tan and strong hands, and that their sweat, which gave me my sugar, tasted also of salt.

"If you forget that red sun and those long, green stalks, then you are not truly a confectioner, you understand nothing about candy but that it tastes good and is colorful—and these things a pig can tell, too. We are the angels of the cane, we are oven-magicians, but if you would rather be a pig snuffling in the leaves—"

"No, Papa."

"Well then, eat your plums, magician of my heart."

And so I did, and the tang of marrow in the sugar-meat was rich and disturbing and sweet.

Often I would ask my father where my mother had gone, if she had not liked her fork of sparrow bones, or if she had not wanted to eat marzipan eggs every day. These were the only complaints I could think of. My father ruffled my hair with his sticky hand and said:

"One morning, fine as milk, when I lived in Vienna and reclined on turquoise cushions with the Empress licking my fingers for one taste of my sweets, I went walking through the city shops, my golden cane cracking on the cobbles, peering into their frosted windows and listening to the silver bells strung from the doors. In the window of a competitor who hardly deserved the name, being but a poor maker of trifles which would hardly satisfy a duchess, I saw the loveliest little crystal jar. It was as intricately cut as a diamond and full of the purest sugar I have ever seen. The little shopkeeper, bent with decades of hunching over trays of chocolate, smiled at me with few enough teeth and cried:

"'Alonzo! I see you have cast your discerning gaze upon my little vial of sugar! I assure you it is the finest of all the sugars ever made, rendered from the tallest cane in the isles by a fortunate virgin snatched at the last moment from the frothing red mouth of her volcano! It was then blanched to the snowy shade you see in a bath of lion's milk and ground to sweetest dust with a pearl pestle, and finally poured into a jar made from the glass of three church windows. I am no Emperor's darling, but in this I exceed you at last!'

"The little man did a shambling dance of joy, to my disgust. But I poured out coins onto his scale until his eyes gleamed wet with longing, and I took that little jar away with me." My father pinched my chin affectionately. "I hurried back home, boiled the sugar with costly dyes and other secret things, and poured it into a Costanze-shaped mold, slid it into the oven, and out you came in an hour or two, eyes shining like caramels!"

He laughed, and when I pulled his ear and told him not to tease me, that every girl has a mother, and an oven is no proper mother! He gave me a slice of honeycomb, and shooed me into the garden, where the raspberries snarled along the white gate.

And thus I grew up. I ate my egg every morning, and licked the yolk from my lips. I ate my plums with my bone fork, and thought very carefully about the tall cane under the red sun. I scrubbed my pillow from my cheeks until they were quite pink. Every old woman in the village remarked on how much I resembled the little ivory cameos of the Empress, the same delicate nose, high brow, thick red hair. I begged my father to let me go to Vienna, as he had done when he was a boy. After all, I was far from a dense child. I had my suspicions—I wanted to see her. I wanted to hear the violas playing in white halls with green and rose checkered floors. I wanted to ride a horse with long brown reins. I wanted to taste radishes and carrots and potatoes, even a chicken, even a fish on a plate of real porcelain, with no oven-bubbles in it.

"Why did we leave Vienna, Papa?" I cried, over our supper of marshmallow crèmes and caramel cakes. "I could have learned to play the flute there; I could have worn a wig like spun sugar. You learned these things—why may I not?"

My father's face reddened and darkened all at once, and he gripped the sides of the butcher's board where he cut caramel into bricks. His bark-brown eyes glazed. "I learned to prefer sugar to white curls," he growled, "and peppermints to piccolos, and cherry creams to the Empress. You will learn this, too, Costanze." He cleared his throat. "It is an important thing to know."

I bent myself to the lesson. I learned how to test my father's syrups by dropping them into silver pots of cold water. By the time I was sixteen I hardly needed to do it, I could sense the hard crack of finished candy, feel the brittle snap prickling the hairs of my neck. My fingers were red with so many crushed berries; my palms were dry and crackling with the pale and scratchy wrapping papers we used for penny sweets. I was a good girl. By the time my father gave me the dress, I was a better confectioner than he, though he would never admit it. It was almost like magic, the way candies would form, glistening and impossibly colorful, under my hands.

It was very bright that morning. The light came through the window panes like butterscotch plates. When I came into the kitchen, there was no egg on the table, no toffee-hammer, no chocolate in a sweet black cup. Instead, lying over the cold oven like a cake waiting to be iced, was a dress. It was the color of ink, tiered and layered like the ones Viennese ladies wore in my dreams, floating blue to the floor, dusted with diamonds that caught the morning light and flashed cheerfully.

"Oh, Papa! Where would I wear a thing like that?"

My father smiled broadly, but the corners of his smile were wilted and sad.

"Vienna," he said. "The court. I thought you wanted to go, to wear a wig, to hear a flute?"

He helped me on with the dress, and as he cinched in my waist and lifted my red hair from bare shoulders, I realized that the dress was made of hard blue sugar and thousands of blueberry skins stitched together with syrupy thread. The diamonds were lumps of crystal candy, still a bit sticky, and at the waist were icing flowers in a white cascade. Nothing of that dress was not sweet, was not sugar, was not my father's trade and mine.

Vienna looked like a Christmas cake we had once made for a baroness: all hard, white curls and creases and carvings, like someone had draped the city in vanilla cream. There were brown horses, and brown carriages attached to them. In the Emperor's palace, where my father walked as though he had built it, there were green and rose checkered floors, and violas playing somewhere far off, the echoes drifting down over me like spring winds. My father took my hand and smiled that same wilted smile, and led me across all those green checks to a room which was harder and whiter than all the rest, where the Emperor and the Empress sat frowning on terrible silver thrones of sharpened filigree, like two demons on their wedding day. I gasped, and shrunk behind my father, the indigo train of my dress showing so dark against the floor. I could not hope to hide from those awful royal eyes.

"Why have you brought us this thing, Alonzo?" barked the Emperor, who had a short blond mustache and copper buttons running down his chest. "This thing which bears such resemblance to our wife? Do you insult us by dragging this reminder of your crimes and hers across our floor like a dust broom?"

The Empress blushed deeply, her skin going the same shade as her hair, the same shade as my hair. My father clenched his teeth.

"I told you then, when you loved my chocolates above all things, that I did not touch her, that I loved her as a man loves God, not as he loves a woman."

"Yet you come back, begging to return to my Grace, towing a child who is a mirror of her! This is obscene, Alonzo!"

My father's face broke open, pleading. It was terrible to see him so. I clutched my icing flowers, confused and frightened.

"But she is not my child! She is not the Empress's child! She is the greatest thing I have ever created, the greatest of all things I have baked in my oven. I have brought her to show you what I may do in your name, for your Grace, if you will look on me with love again, if you will give me your favor once more. If you will let me come back to the city, to my home."

I gaped, and tears filled my eyes. My father drew a little silver icing-spade from his belt and started towards me. I cried out and my voice echoed in the hard, white hall like a sparrow cut into a fork. I cringed, but my father gripped my arms tight as a tureen's handles, and his eyes were wide and wet. He pushed me to my knees on the Emperor's polished floor, and the two monarchs watched impassively as I wept in my beautiful blue dress, though the Empress let a pale hand flutter to her throat. My father put the spade to my neck and scraped it up, across my skin, like a barber giving a young man his first shave.

A shower of sugar fell glittering across my chest.

"I never lied to you, Costanze," he murmured in my ear.

He pierced my cheek with the tip of the spade, and blood trickled down my chin, over my lips. It tasted like raspberries.

"Look at her, your Majesty. She is nothing but sugar, nothing but candy, through and through. I made her in my own oven. I raised her up. Now she is grown—and so beautiful! Look at her cinnamon hair, her marzipan skin, her tears of sugar and salt! And you may have her, you may have the greatest confection made on this earth, if you will but let me come home, and make you chocolates as I used to, and put your hand to my shoulder in friendship again."

The Empress rose from her throne and walked towards me, like a mirror gliding on a hidden track, so like me she was, though her gown was golden, and its train longer than the hall. She looked at me, her gaze pointed and deep, but did not seem to hear my sobbing, or see my tears. She put her hand to my bleeding cheek, and tasted the blood on her palm, daintily, with the tip of her tongue.

"She looks so much like me, Alonzo. It is a strange thing to see."

My father flushed. "I was lonely," he whispered. "And perhaps a man may be forgiven for casting a doll's face in the image of God."

I WAS KEPT in the kitchens, hung up on the wall like a copper pot, or a length of garlic. Every day a cook would clip my fingernails to sweeten the Emperor's coffee, or cut off a curl of my scarlet hair to spice the Easter cakes of the Empress's first child—a boy with bark-brown eyes. Sometimes, the head cook would lance my cheek carefully and collect the scarlet syrup in a hard white cup. Once, they plucked my eyelashes, ever so gently for a licorice comfit the Empress's new daughter craved. They were kind enough to ice my lids between plucking. They tried not to cause me any pain. Cooks and confectioners are not wicked creatures by nature, and the younger kitchen girls were disturbed by the shape of me hanging there, toes pointed at the oven. Eventually, they grew accustomed to it, and I was no more strange to them than a shaker of salt or a pepper-mill. My dress sagged and browned, as blueberry skins will do, and fell away. A kind little boy who scrubbed the floors brought me a coarse black dress from his mother's closet. It was made of wool, real wool, from a sheep and not an oven. They fed me radishes and carrots and potatoes, and sometimes chicken, sometimes even fish, on a plate of real porcelain, with no heat-bubbles in it, none at all.

I grew old on that wall, my marzipan-skin withered and wrinkled no less than flesh, helped along by lancings and scrapings and trimmings. My hair turned white and fell out, eagerly collected. As I grew old, I was told that the Emperor liked the taste of my hair better and better, and soon I was bald.

But Emperors die, and so do fathers. Both of these occurred in their way, and when at last the Empress died, there was no one to remember that the source of the palace sugar was not a far-off isle, under a red sun that burned on the face of the sea. I thought of that red sun often on the wall, and the children cutting cane, and the taste of the bird's marrow deep in my plum. That same kind floor-scrubber, grown up and promoted to butler, cut me down when my bones were brittle, and touched my shorn hair gently. But he did not apologize. How could he? How many cakes and teas had he tasted which were sweetened by me?

I ran from the palace in the night, as much as I could run, an old, scraped-out crone, a witch in a black dress stumbling across the city and through, across and out. I kept running and running, my sugar-body burning and shrieking with disuse. I ran past the hard white streets and past the villages where I had been a child who knew nothing of Vienna, into the woods, into the black forest with the creeping loam and nothing sweet for miles. Only there did I stop, panting, my spiced breath fogging in the air. There were great dark green boughs arching over me, pine and larch and oak. I sank down to the earth, wrung dry of weeping, safe and far from anything hard, anything white, anything with accusing eyes and a throne like a demon's wedding. No one would scrape me for teatime again. No one would touch me again. I put my hands to my head and stared up at the stars though the leaves. It was quiet, at last, quiet, and dark. I curled up on the leaves and slept.

WHEN I WOKE, I was cold. I shivered. I needed more than a black dress to cover me. I would not go back, not to any place which had known me, not to Vienna, not to a village without a candy-maker. I would not hang a sign over a door and feed sweets to children. I would stay, in the dark, under the green. And so I needed a house. But I knew nothing of houses. I was not a bricklayer or a thatcher. I did not know how to make a chimney. I did not know how to make a door-hinge. I did not know how to stitch curtains.

But I knew how to make candy.

I went begging in the villages, a harmless old crone—was it odd that she asked for sugar and not for coins? Certainly. Did they think it mad that she begged for berries and liquors and cocoa, but never alms? Of course. But the elderly are strange and their ways inexplicable to the young. I collected, just as they had done to me all my years on the wall, and my hair grew. I went to my place in the forest, under the black and the boughs, and I poured a foundation of caramel. I raised up thick, brown gingerbread walls, with cinnamon for wattle and marshmallow for daub. Hard-crack windows clear as the

## A Delicate Architecture

morning air, a smoking licorice chimney, stairs of peanut brittle and carpets of red taffy, a peppermint bathtub. And a great black oven, all of blackened, burnt sugar, with a yellow flame within. Gumdrops studded my house like jewels, and a little path of molasses ran liquid and dark from my door. And when my hair had grown long enough, I thatched my roof with cinnamon strands.

It had such a delicate architecture, my house, which I baked and built, as delicate as I had. I thought of my father all the while, and the red sun on waving green cane. I thought of him while I built my pastry-table, and I thought of him while I built my gingerbread floors. I hated and loved him in turns, as witches will do, for our hearts are strange and inexplicable. He had never come to see me on the wall, even once. I could not understand it. But I made my caramel bricks and I rolled out sheets of toffee onto my bed, and I told his ghost that I was a good girl, I had always been a good girl, even on the wall.

I made a pillow of spun sugar. I made plates of butterscotch. Each morning I tapped a marzipan egg with a little toffee-hammer. But I never caught a sparrow for my plums. They are so very quick. I was always hungry for them, for something living, and salty, and sweet amid all my sugar. I longed for something alive in my crystalline house, something to remind me of the children crushing up cane with tan, strong hands. There was no marrow in my plums. I could not remember the red sun and the long, green stalks, and so I bent low in my lollipop rocking-chair, weeping and whispering to my father that I was sorry, I was sorry, I was no more than a pig snuffling in the leaves, after all.

AND ONE MORNING, when it was very bright, and the light came through the window like a viola playing something very sweet and sad, I heard footsteps coming up my molasses-path. Children: a boy and a girl. They laughed, and over their heads blackbirds cawed hungrily.

I was hungry, too.

# Golubash, or Wine-Blood-War-Elegy

THE DIFFICULTIES OF TRANSPORTING WINE over interstellar distances are manifold. Wine is, after all, like a child. It can *bruise*. It can suffer trauma—sometimes the poor creature can recover, sometimes it must be locked up in a cellar until it learns to behave itself. Sometimes it is irredeemable. I ask that you greet the seven glasses before you tonight not as simple fermented grapes, but as the living creatures they are, well-brought up, indulged but not coddled, punished when necessary, shyly seeking your approval with clasped hands and slicked hair. After all, they have come so very far for the chance to be loved.

Welcome to the first public tasting of Domaine Zhaba. My name is Phylloxera Nanut, and it is the fruit of my family's vines that sits before you. Please forgive our humble venue—surely we could have wished for something grander than a scorched pre-war orbital platform, but circumstances, and the constant surveillance of Chateâu Marubouzu-Debrouillard and their soldiers have driven us to extremity. Mind the loose electrical panels and pull up a reactor husk—they are inert, I assure you. Spit onto the floor—a few new stains will never be noticed. As every drop about to pass your lips is wholly, thoroughly, enthusiastically illegal, we shall not stand on ceremony. Shall we begin?

### 2583 Sud-Coté-du-Golubash (New Danube)

THE COLONIAL SHIP *Quintessence of Dust* first blazed across the skies of Avalokitesvara two hundred years before I was born, under the red stare of Barnard's Star, our second solar benefactor. Her plasma sails streamed kilometers long, like sheltering wings. Simone Nanut was on that ship. She, alongside a thousand others, looked down on their new home from that great height, the single long, unfathomably wide river that circumscribed the globe, the golden mountains prickled with cobalt alders, the deserts streaked with pink salt.

How I remember the southern coast of Golubash, I played there, and dreamed there was a girl on the invisible opposite shore, and that her family, too, made wine and cowered like us in the shadow of the Asociación.

My friends, in your university days did you not study the rolls of the first colonials, did you not memorize their weight-limited cargo, verse after verse of spinning wheels, bamboo seeds, lathes, vials of tailored bacteria, as holy writ? Then perhaps you will recall Simone Nanut and her folly, that her pitiful allotment of cargo was taken up by the clothes on her back and a tangle of ancient Maribor grapevine, its roots tenderly wrapped and watered. Mad Slovak witch they all thought her, patting those tortured, battered vines into the gritty yellow soil of the Golubash basin. Even the Hyphens were sure the poor things would fail. There were only four of them on all of Avalokitesvara, immensely tall, their watery triune faces catching the old red light of Barnard's flares, their innumerable arms fanned out around their terribly thin torsos like peacock's tails. Not for nothing was the planet named for a Hindu god with eleven faces and a thousand arms. The colonists called them Hyphens for their way of talking, and for the thinness of their bodies. They did not understand then what you must all know now, rolling your eyes behind your sleeves as your hostess relates ancient history, that each of the four Hyphens was a quarter of the world in a single body, that they were a mere outcropping of the vast intelligences which made up the ecology of Avalokitesvara, like one of our thumbs or a pair of lips.

Golubash I knew. To know more than one Hyphen in a lifetime is rare. Officially, the great river is still called the New Danube, but eventually my family came to understand, as all families did, that the river was the flesh and blood of Golubash, the fish his-her-its thoughts, the seaweed his-her-its nerves, the banks a kind of thoughtful skin.

Simone Nanut put vines down into the body of Golubash. He-She-It bent down very low over Nanut's hunched little form, arms akimbo, and said to her: "That will not work-take-thrive-bear fruit-last beyond your lifetime."

Yet work-take-thrive they did. Was it a gift to her? Did Golubash make room between what passes for his-her-its pancreas and what might be called a liver for foreign vines to catch and hold? Did he, perhaps, love my ancestor in whatever way a Hyphen can love? It is impossible to know, but no other Hyphen has ever allowed Earth-origin flora to flourish, not Heeminspr the high desert, not Julka the archipelago, not Niflamen, the soft-spoken polar waste. Not even the northern coast of the river proved gentle to grape. Golubash was generous only to Simone's farm, and only to the southern bank. The mad red flares of Barnard's Star flashed often and strange, and the grapes pulsed to its cycles. The rest of the colony contented themselves with the native root-vegetables, something like crystalline rutabagas filled with custard, and the teeming rock-geese whose hearts in those barnacled chests tasted of beef and sugar.

IN YOUR GLASS is '83 vintage of that hybrid vine, a year which should be famous, would be, if not for rampant fear and avarice. Born on Earth, matured in Golubash. It is 98% Cabernet, allowing for mineral compounds generated in the digestive tract of the Golubash river. Note its rich, garnet-like color, the *gravitas* of its presence in the glass, the luscious, rolling flavors of blackberry, cherry, peppercorn, and chocolate, the subtle, airy notes of fresh straw and iron. At the back of your tongue, you will detect a last whisper of brine and clarygrass.

The will of Simone Nanut swirls in your glass, resolute-unbroken-unmoveable-stone.

### 2503 Abbaye de St. CIR, Tranquilité, Neuf-Abymes

OF COURSE, THE 2683 vintage, along with all others originating on Avalokitesvara, were immediately declared not only contraband but biohazard by the Asociación de la Pureza del Vino, whose chairman was and is a scion of the Marubouzu clan. The Asociación has never peeked out of the pockets of those fabled, hoary Hokkaido vineyards. When Château Debrouillard shocked the wine world, then relatively small, by allowing their ancient vines to be grafted with Japanese stock a few years before the first of Salvatore Yuuhi's gates went online, an entity was created whose tangled, ugly tendrils even a Hyphen would call gargantuan.

Nor were we alone in our ban. Even before the first colony on Avalokitesvara, the lunar city of St. Clair-in-Repose, a Catholic sanctuary, had been nourishing its own strange vines for a century. In great glass domes, in a mist of temperature and light control, a cloister of monks, led by Fratre Sebastién Perdue, reared priceless pinot vines and heady Malbecs, their leaves unfurling green and glossy in the pale blue light of the planet that bore them. But monks are perverse, and none moreso than Perdue. In his youth he was content with the classic vines, gloried in the precision of the wines he could coax from them. But in his middle age, he committed two sins. The first involved a young woman from Hipparchus, the second was to cut their orthodox grapes with Tsuki-Bellas, the odd, hard little berries that sprang up from the lunar dust when our leashed bacteria had been turned loose in order to make passable farmland, as though they had been waiting, all that time, for a long drink of rhizomes. Their flavor is somewhere between a blueberry and a truffle, and since genetic sequencing proved it to be within the grape family, the monks of St. Clair deemed it a radical source of heretofore unknown wonders.

Hipparchus was a farming village where Tsuki-Bellas grew fierce and thick. It does not due to dwell on Brother Sebastién's motives.

What followed would be repeated in more and bloodier ways two hundred years hence. Well do I know the song. For Chateau Marubouzu-Debrouillard and her pet Asociación had partnered with the Coquil-Grollë Corporation in order to transport their wines from Earth to orbiting cities and lunar clusters. Coquil-Grollë, now entirely swallowed by Chateau M-D, was at the time a soda company with vast holdings in other foodstuffs, but the tremendous weight restrictions involved in transporting unaltered liquid over interlunar space made strange bedfellows. The precious M-D wines could not be dehydrated and reconstituted—no child can withstand such sadism. Therefore, foul papers were signed with what was arguably the biggest business entity in existence, and though it must have bruised the rarified egos of the children of Hokkaido and Burgundy, they allowed their shy, fragile wines to be shipped alongside Super-Colanade! and Bloo Bomb. The extraordinary tariffs they paid allowed Coquil-Grollë to deliver their confections throughout the bustling submundal sphere.

The Asociación writ stated that adulterated wines could, at best, be categorized as fruit-wines, silly dessert concoctions that no vintner would take seriously, like apple-melon wine from a foil-sac. Not only that, but no tariffs had been paid on this wine, and therefore Abbe St. Clair could not export it, even to other lunar cities. It was granted that perhaps, if takes of a certain (wildly illegal) percentage were applied to the price of such wines, it might be possible to allow the monks to sell their vintages to those who came bodily to St. Clair, but transporting it to Earth was out of the question at any price, as foreign insects might be introduced into the delicate home *terroir*. No competition with the house of Debrouillard would be broached, on that world or any other.

Though in general, wine resides in that lofty category of goods which increase in demand as they increase in price, the lockdown of Abbe St. Clair effectively isolated the winery, and their products simply could not be had—whenever a bottle was purchased, a new Asociación tax would be introduced, and soon there was no possible path to profit for Perdue and his brothers. Past a certain point, economics are irrelevant—there was not enough money anywhere to buy such a bottle.

Have these taxes been lifted? You know they have not, sirs. But Domaine Zhaba purchased the ruin of Abbe St. Clair in 2916, and their cellars, neglected, filthy, simultaneously worthless and beyond price, came into our tender possession.

What sparks red and black in the erratic light of the station status screens is the last vintage personally crafted by Fratre Sebastién Perdue. It is 70% Pinot Noir, 15% Malbec, and 15% forbidden, delicate Tsuki-Bella. To allow even a drop of this to pass your lips anywhere but under the Earthlit domes of St. Clair-in-Repose is a criminal act. I know you will keep this in mind as you savor the taste of corporate sin.

It is lighter on its feet than the Cotê-du-Golubash, sapphire sparking in the depths of its dark color, a laughing, lascivious blend of raspberry, chestnut, tobacco, and clove. You can detect the criminal fruit—ah, there it is, madam, you have it!—in the mid-range, the tartness of blueberry and the ashen loam of mushroom. A clean, almost soapy waft of green coffee-bean blows throughout. I would not insult it by calling it delicious—it is profound, unforgiving, and ultimately, unforgiven.

# Golubash, or Wine-Blood-War-Elegy

## 2790 Domaine Zhaba, Clos du Saleeng-Carolz, Cuvée Cheval

YOU MUST FORGIVE me, madam. My pour is not what it once was. If only it had been my other arm I left on the ochre fields of Centauri B! I have never quite adjusted to being suddenly and irrevocably left-handed. I was fond of that arm—I bit my nails to the quick; it had three moles and a little round birthmark, like a drop of spilled syrah. Shall we toast to old friends? In the war they used to say: *go, lose your arm. You can still pour. But if you let them take your tongue you might as well die here.*

By the time Simone Nanut and her brood, both human and grape, were flourishing, the Yuuhi gates were already bustling with activity. Though the space between gates was vast, it was not so vast as the spaces between stars. Everything depended on them, colonization, communication, and of course, shipping. Have any of you seen a Yuuhi gate? I imagine not, they are considered obsolete now, and we took out so many of them during the war. They still hang in space like industrial mandalas, titanium and bone—in those days an organic component was necessary, if unsavory, and we never knew whose marrow slowly yellowed to calcified husks in the vacuum. The pylons bristled with oblong steel cubes and arcs of golden filament shot across the tain like violin bows—all the gold of the world commandeered by Salvatore Yuuhi and his grand plan. How many wedding rings hurled us all into the stars? I suppose one or two of them might still be functional. I suppose one or two of them might still be used by poor souls forced underground, if they carried contraband, if they wished not to be seen.

The 2790 is a pre-war vintage, but only just. The Asociación de la Pureza del Vino, little more than a paper sac Château Marubouzu-Debrouillard pulled over its head, had stationed… well, they never called them soldiers, nor warships, but they were not there to sample the wine. Every wine-producing region from Luna to the hydroponic orbital agri-communes, found itself graced with inspectors and customs officials who wore no uniform but the curling M-D seal on their breasts. Every Yuuhi gate was patrolled by armed ships bearing the APV crest. It wasn't really necessary. Virtually all shipping was conducted under the aegis of the Coquil-Grollë Corporation, so fat and clotted with tariffs and taxes that it alone could afford to carry whatever a heart might desire through empty space. There were outposts where Super Cola-nade! was used in the Eucharist, so great was their influence. Governments rented space in their holds to deliver diplomatic envoys, corn, rice, even mail, when soy-paper letters sent via Yuuhi became terribly fashionable in the middle of the century. You simply could not get anything if C-G did not sell it to you, and the only wine they sold was Marubouzu-Debrouillard.

I am not a mean woman. I will grant that though they boasted an extraordinary monopoly, the Debrouillard wines were and are of exceptional quality. Their pedigrees will not allow them to be otherwise. But you must see it from where we stand. I was born on Avalokitesvara and never saw Earth till the war. They were forcing foreign, I daresay alien liquors onto us when all we wished to do was to drink from the land which bore us, from Golubash, who hovered over our houses like an old radio tower, fretting and wringing his-her-its hundred hands.

Saleeng-Carolz was a bunker. It looked like a pleasant cloister, with lovely vines draping the walls and a pretty crystal dome over quaint refectories and huts. It had to. The Asociación inspectors would never let us set up barracks right before their eyes. I say *us*, but truly I was a not more than a child. I played with Golubash— with the quicksalmon and the riverweed that were no less him than the gargantuan thin man who watched Simone Nanut plant her vines three centuries past and helped my uncles pile up the bricks of Saleeng-Carolz. Hyphens do not die, any more than continents do.

We made weapons and stored wine in our bunker. Bayonets at first, and simple rifles, later compressed-plasma engines and rumblers.

Every other barrel contained guns. We might have been caught so easily, but by then, everything on Avalokitesvara was problematic in the view of the Asociación. The grapes were tainted, not even entirely vegetable matter, being grown in living Golubash. In some odd sense they were not even grown, but birthed, springing from his-her-its living flesh. The barrels, too, were suspect, and none more so than the barrels of Saleeng-Carolz.

Until the APV inspectors arrived, we hewed to tradition. Our barrels were solid cobalt alder, re-cedar, and oakberry. Strange to look at for an APV man, certainly, gleaming deep blue or striped red and black, or pure white. And of course they were not really wood at all, but the fibrous musculature of Golubash, ersatz, loving wombs. They howled biohazard, but we smacked our lips in the flare-light, savoring the cords of smoke and apple and blood the barrels pushed through our wine. But in Saleeng-Carolz, my uncle, Grel Nanut, tried something new.

What could be said to be Golubash's liver was a vast flock of shaggy horses—not truly horses, but something four-legged and hoofed and tailed that was reasonably like a horse—that ran and mated on the open prairie beyond the town of Nanut. They were essentially hollow, no organs to speak of, constantly taking in grass and air and soil and fruit and fish and water and purifying it before passing it industriously back into the ecology of Golubash.

Uncle Grel was probably closer to Golubash than any of us. He spent days talking with the tall, three-faced creature the APV still thought of as independent from the river. He even began to hyphenate his sentences, a source of great amusement. We know now that he was learning. About horses, about spores and diffusion, about the life-cycle of a Hyphen but then we just thought Grel was in love. Grel first thought of it, and secured permission from Golubash, who bent his ponderous head and gave his assent-blessing-encouragement-trepidation-confidence. He began to bring the horses within the walls of Saleeng-Carolz, and let them drink the wine deep, instructing them to hold it close for years on end.

In this way, the rest of the barrels were left free for weapons.

---

THIS IS THE first wine closed up inside the horses of Golubash: 60% Cabernet, 20% Syrah, 15% Tempranillo, 5% Petit Verdot. It is specifically banned by every planet under APV control, and possession is punishable by death. The excuse? Intolerable biological contamination.

This is a wine that swallows light. Its color is deep and opaque, mysterious, almost black, the shadows of closed space. Revel in the dance of plum, almond skin, currant, pomegranate. The musty spike of nutmeg, the rich, buttery brightness of equine blood and the warm, obscene swell of leather. The last of the pre-war wines—your execution in a glass.

## 2795 Domaine Zhaba, White Tara, Bas-Lequat

OUR ONLY WHITE of the evening, the Bas-Lequat is an unusual blend, predominantly Chardonnay with sprinklings of Tsuki-bella and Riesling, pale as the moon where it ripened.

White Tara is the second moon of Avalokitesvara, the first being enormous Green Tara. Marubouzu-Debrouillard chose it carefully for their first attack. My mother died there, defending the alder barrels. My sister lost her legs.

Domaine Zhaba had committed the cardinal sin of becoming popular, and that could not be allowed. We were not poor monks on an isolated moon, orbiting planet-bound plebeians. Avalokitesvara has four healthy moons and dwells comfortably in a system of three habitable planets, huge new worlds thirsty for rich things, and nowhere else could wine grapes grow. For awhile Barnarders had been eager to have wine from home, but as generations passed and home became Barnard's System, the wines of Domaine Zhaba were in demand at every table, and we needed no glittering Yuuhi gates to supply them. The APV could and did tax exports, and so we skirted the law as best we could. For ten years before the war began, Domaine Zhaba wines were given out freely, as "personal" gifts, untaxable, untouchable. Then the inspectors descended, and stamped all products with their little *Prohibido* seal, and, well, one cannot give biohazards as birthday presents.

The whole thing is preposterous. If anything, Earth-origin foodstuffs are the hazards in Barnard's System. They Hyphens have always been hostile to them, offworld crops give them a kind of indigestion that manifests in Earthquakes and thunderstorms. The Marubouzu corporals told us we could not eat or drink the things that grew on our own land, because of possible alien contagion! We could only order approved substances from the benevolent, carbonated bosom of Coquil-Grollë, which is Chateâu Marubouzu-Debrouillard, which is the Asociación de la Pureza del Vino, and anything we liked would be delivered to us all the way from home, with a bow on it.

The lunar winery on White Tara exploded into the night sky at 3:17 a.m. on the first of Julka, 2795. My mother was testing the barrels—her bones were vaporized before she even understood the magnitude of what had happened. The aerial bombing, both lunar and terrestrial, continued past dawn. I was huddled in the Bas-Lequat cellar, and even there I could hear the screaming of Golubash, and Julka, and Heeminspr, and poor, gentle Niflamen, as the APV incinerated our world.

TWO WEEKS LATER, Uncle Grel's rumblers ignited our first Yuuhi gate.

THE COLOR IS almost like water, isn't it? Like tears. The ripple of red pear and butterscotch slides over green herbs and honey-wax. In the low-range you can detect the delicate dust of blueberry pollen, and beneath that, the smallest suggestion of crisp lunar snow, sweet, cold, and vanished.

### 2807 Domaine Zhaba, Grelport, Hul-Nairob

DID YOU KNOW, almost a thousand years ago, the wineries in Old France were nearly wiped out? A secret war of soil came close to annihilating the entire apparatus of wine-making in the grand, venerable valleys of the old world. But no blanketing fire was at fault, no shipping dispute. Only a tiny insect: *Daktulosphaira Vitifoliae Phylloxera.* My namesake. I was named to be the tiny thing that ate at the roots of the broken, ugly, ancient machinery of Marubouzu. I have done my best.

For awhile, the French believed that burying a live toad beneath the vines would cure the blight. This was tragically silly, but hence Simone Nanut drew her title: *zhaba*, old Slovak for toad. We are the mite that brought down gods, and we are the cure, warty and bruised though we are.

When my uncle Grel was a boy, he went fishing in Golubash. Like a child in a fairy tale, he caught a great green fish, with golden scales, and when he pulled it into his little boat, it spoke to him.

Well, nothing so unusual about that. Golubash can speak as easily from his fish-bodies as from his tall-body. The fish said: "I am lonely-worried-afraid-expectant-in need of comfort-lost-searching-hungry. Help-hold-carry me."

After the Bas-Lequat attack, Golubash boiled, the vines burned, even Golubash's tall-body was scorched and blistered, but not broken, not wholly. Vineyards take lifetimes to replace, but Golubash is gentle, and they will return, slowly, surely. So Julka, so Heeminspr, so kind Niflamen. The burnt world will flare gold again. Grel knew this, and he sorrowed that he would never see it. My uncle took one of the great creature's many hands. He made a promise—we could not hear him then, but you must all now know what he did, the vengeance of Domaine Zhaba.

The Yuuhi gates went one after another. We became terribly inventive—I could still, with my one arm, assemble a rumbler from the junk of this very platform. We tried to avoid Barnard's gate, we did not want to cut ourselves off in our need to defend those worlds against marauding vintners with soda-labels on their jump-suits. But in the end, that, too, went blazing into the sky, gold filaments sizzling. We were alone. We didn't win; we could never win. But we ended interstellar travel for fifty years, until the new ships with internal Yuuhi-drives circumvented the need for the lost gates. And much passes in fifty years, on a dozen worlds, when the mail can't be delivered. They are not defeated, but they are…humbled.

An M-D cruiser trailed me here. I lost her when I used the last gate-pair, but now my cousins will have to blow that gate, or else those soda-sipping bastards will know our methods. No matter. It was worth it, to bring our wines to you, in this place, in this time, finally, to open our stores as a real winery, free of them, free of all.

---

THIS IS A port-wine, the last of our tastings tonight. The vineyards that bore the Syrah and Grenache in your cups are wonderful, long streaks of soil on the edges of a bridge that spans the Golubash, a thousand kilometers long. There is a city on that bridge, and below it, where a chain of linked docks cross the water. The maps call it Longbridge; we call it Grelport. Uncle Grel will never come home. He went through Barnard's gate just before we detonated, and he was gone. Home, to Earth, to deliver-safeguard-disseminate-help-hold-carry his cargo. A little spore, not much more than a few cells scraped off a blade of clarygrass on Golubash's back. But it was enough.

Note the luscious ruby-caramel color, the nose of walnut and roasted peach. This is pure Avalokitesvara, unregulated, stored in Golubash's horses, grown in the ports floating on his-her-its spinal fluid, rich with the flavors of home. They used to say wine was a living thing—but it was only a figure of speech, a way of describing liquid with changeable qualities. This wine is truly alive, every drop, it has a name, a history, brothers and sisters, blood and lymph. Do not draw away—this should not repulse you. Life, after all, is sweet, lift your glasses, taste the roving currents of sunshine and custard, salt skin and pecan, truffle and caramelized onion. Imagine, with your fingers grazing these fragile stems, Simone Nanut, standing at the threshold of her colonial ship, the Finnish desert stretching out behind her, white and flat, strewn with debris. In her ample arms is that gnarled vine, its roots wrapped with such love. Imagine Sebastién Perdue, tasting a Tsuki-Bella for the first time, on the tongue of his Hipparchan lady. Imagine my uncle Grel, speeding alone in the dark towards his ancestral home, with a few brief green cells in his hand. Wine is a story, every glass. A history, an elegy. To drink is to hear the story, to spit is to consider it, to hold the bottle close to your chest is to accept it, to let yourself become part of it. Thank you for becoming part of my family's story.

I WILL LEAVE you now. My assistant will complete any transactions you wish to initiate. Even in these late days it is vital to stay ahead of them, despite all. They will always have more money, more ships, more bile. Perhaps a day will come when we can toast you in the light, in a grand palace, with the flares of Barnard's Star glittering in cut crystal goblets. For now, there is the light of the exit hatch, dusty glass tankards, and my wrinkled old hand to my heart.

A price list is posted in the med lab.

AND SHOULD ANY of you turn Earthwards in your lovely new ships, take a bottle to the extremely tall young lady-chap-entity living-growing-invading-devouring-putting down roots in the Loire Valley. I think he-she-it would enjoy a family visit.

# Badgirl, the Deadman, and the Wheel of Fortune

THE DEADMAN ALWAYS WORE RED when he came calling. Not all over red. Just a flash, like Mars in the night time. A coat, a long scarf, socks, a leather belt. An old sucked-dry rose in his buttonhole. A woolen cap with two little holes in it like bite marks. A fake ruby chip in his ear. One time, he wore lipstick and I cried in my hiding place. I always cried when the Deadman came, but that time I cried right away and I didn't stop. Real quiet with my hands over my mouth. I can be a little black cat when I want, so he didn't hear.

Daddy always used to say the Deadman came to bring him a cup of sugar and when I was a tiny dumb thing I thought that meant he was gonna make me cookies or blue Kool-Aid or a cake with yellow frosting even though it wasn't usually my birthday. I liked yellow frosting best because it looked like all the lights in our apartment turned on at one time and nothing can be scary when all the lights are turned on at one time. I liked blue Kool-Aid best because it turned my tongue the color of outside.

So I hid from the Deadman in my treehouse and thought real hard about blue Kool-Aid with ice knocking around in it and a cake all for me with so much frosting it looked like an ice cream cone.

My treehouse wasn't a treehouse, though. It was the big closet in the hallway between the two bedrooms, the special kind of closet that has four legs like a chair and doors that swing out and drawers under the swinging doors. I heard the Deadman call it something French-sounding but he said it like a pirate kiss. *Arrrr. Mwah.* Daddy called it my treehouse because it's made of trees nailed together so what's the difference when you think about it. Whenever the Deadman came with his cup of sugar, I pulled out the drawers like a staircase, climbed in, shut the swinging doors tight behind me, and closed the latch Daddy screwed onto the inside of the pirate kiss closet. It was nice in there. Nothing much in it but me and a purple sweater half falling off a wire hanger that might've been my mom's, but might not've just as easy. It smelled like a mostly chopped down forest and crusty pennies. I tucked up my knees under my chin and held my breath and turned into a little black cat that didn't make one single sound.

"You got what I need?" my daddy said to the Deadman. And the Deadman said back:

"If you got what *I* need, Mudpuddle, I got the whole world right here in my pocket."

And then there was a bunch of rustling and coughing and little words that don't mean anything except filling up the quiet, and in the middle of those funny soft nothing-noises the Deadman would start telling a joke, but a dumb joke, like the kind you read on Laffy Taffy wrappers. Nobody likes those jokes but the Deadman.

"Hey, did you hear the one about the horse and the submarine?"

"Yeah, I heard that one, D," my daddy always said, even though I never heard him tell a joke ever in my whole life and I don't think he really knew the one about the horse and the submarine at all. But after that the Deadman would laugh a laugh that sounded like a swear word even though it didn't have any words in it and he'd leave and I could breathe again.

Everybody called my daddy Mudpuddle just like everybody called the Deadman the Deadman and everybody called me Badgirl even though my name is Loula which is pretty nice and feels good to say, like raindrops in your mouth. Where I live, we don't call anybody by the name they got at the hospital.

"It's 'cause I'm a real honest-to-Jesus old-timey gentleman, Badgirl," Daddy told me, and clinked our mugs together. His had a lot of whiskey and mine had a very little whiskey, only enough to make me feel grown up and stop asking for cocoa. "Almost a prince, like that cat who went around sniffing all those girls' feet back when. So when I'm escorting a lady friend and I see a big nasty mudpuddle in our way, I always take off my coat and lay it down so my girl can walk across without getting her shoes dirty."

"Daddy, that's the stupidest thing I ever heard. Who cares if her shoes get dirty when your coat gets *ruined?* Why can't she just walk around the puddle? What's wrong with her?"

Daddy Mudpuddle laughed and laughed even though what I said was way smarter than what he said. I thought people called him Mudpuddle because his clothes usually weren't too clean, and the cuffs of all his pants were all ripped up and stained like he'd walked through the mud. But I didn't say so. It's not a nice thing to say. I liked the story where my daddy's almost a prince better, so I let that one stay, like a really good finger painting hung up on the refrigerator. Besides, I've never done anything very bad except get born and one time swallow a toy car and have to go to the hospital which Daddy couldn't afford, but I still get called Badgirl. One time Daddy tucked me into bed and kissed my nose and whispered:

"It's 'cause you were so good your mama and I had to call you Badgirl so the angels wouldn't come and take you away for their own."

And that's stupider than putting your coat down on a mudpuddle, so I figure names don't really have any reasons or stories hiding inside them. I wasn't good enough to still have a mama now. I wasn't good enough not to swallow a toy car and cost all that money. Names just happen to you and then you go on living with them on your shoulder like an ugly old parrot.

I remember the first time the Deadman came and Daddy didn't have what he needed. But only barely. I wasn't tiny anymore but I was still little. Daddy'd taken me to the thrift shop and bought me a new dress with blue and yellow butterflies on it and a green bow in the back for my first day of school which was in a week. It was the most beautiful dress I'd ever seen. It had green buttons and every butterfly was a little different, just like real life. It was gonna make me pretty for school, and school was gonna make me smart. So I decided to wear it every day until school started so that I could soak up the smart in that dress and then I'd be way ahead of all the other kids on day one. You think funny things when you're little. You can laugh at me if you want. I'm not ashamed.

Anyway, I was playing with the toy from my Happy Meal, which was a princess whose head came off and you could stick it on three different plastic bodies wearing different ballgowns. I took her head off and on and off and on but I got bored with it pretty fast because what can you do with a toy like that? What kind of make-believe can you get going about a girl whose head comes off? All the ones I could think of were scary.

Daddy was all jittery and anxious and biting his fingernails. I don't think he liked the princess, either. She didn't even have any shoes to get dirty. She didn't have any *feet*. The bottoms of her ballgown-bodies were all flat, smooth plastic like the bottom of a glass. He wasn't himself. Usually he'd give me plenty of warning. He never wanted the Deadman to see me. He said nobody who loved their baby girl would let the Deadman near her. He'd say:

"Deadman's here, Badgirl, go up in your treehouse." And I'd go, even though I didn't hear anything out on the stoop. I never heard the Deadman coming, never heard a car engine or a bike bell or boots on the sidewalk or anything till he knocked on the door.

But this time he didn't even seem to remember I was there. The knock happened and I wasn't safe in my treehouse with the purple sweater and the pirate kisses. I wasn't turned into a little black cat that never made a sound.

"Daddy!" I whispered, and then he did remember me, and picked me up in his arms and carried me down the hall and put me in his bedroom and shut the door.

But Daddy's door doesn't shut all the way. It's got a bend in the latch. Daddy's room had a lot of cigarettes put out on things other than ash trays and a TV and a painting of frogs on the wall. I didn't like the smell but I did like being in there because normally I wasn't allowed. But even though that part was exciting, I started shaking all over. Deadman's here. I wasn't safe. Safe meant my treehouse. Safe meant the drawers turned into a staircase and the smell like a chopped up forest. I watched Daddy go back down the hall. I could make it. Little black cats are fast, too. I slipped out the bedroom door and scrambled up into the pirate kiss closet. I didn't even pull out the drawers into a staircase, I got up in one jump. I locked the lock and held my breath and turned into a little black cat that doesn't ever make a sound. I pulled my butterfly dress over my knees and felt the smart ooze out of the fabric and into me. The smart felt big and good, like having your own TV in your bedroom.

The Deadman knocked. I could see him through the crack between the treehouse doors. He had a pinky ring on with a red stone in it. The Deadman had real nice eyebrows and a long, skinny face. His shirt was cut low but he didn't have any hair on his chest.

"You got what I need?" Daddy said. And the Deadman said back:

"If you got what *I* need, Mudpuddle, I got the whole world right here in my pocket."

Only Daddy didn't. Daddy stared at his shoes. He looked like a princess-body without a princess-head.

"I'm just a little short, D. I started a new job, you know, and with a new job you don't get paid the first two weeks. But I'm good for it."

The Deadman didn't say anything. Daddy'd been short on his sugar a lot lately. And I knew he didn't have a new job. Or an old one.

"Come on, man. I'm a good person. I know I owe you plenty, but owing doesn't make a man less needful. I'll pay you in two weeks, I swear. My word is as good as the lock on a bank. I'm a gentleman. Ask anybody."

The Deadman looked my daddy up and down. Then he looked past him, into the living room, at my princess's three headless bodies lying on the carpet. The Deadman chewed on something. I thought maybe it was bubblegum. Red bubblegum, I supposed. Finally, he twisted his pinky ring around and said:

"Did you ever hear the one about the Devil and the fiddle?"

Daddy sort of fell apart without moving. He was still standing up, but only on the outside. On the inside, he was crumpled up on the ground. "Yeah, I heard that one, D," he sighed.

"I tell you what," the Deadman said. "I'll give you what you need this week—hell, next week, too and the one after—if you give me whatever's in that armoire back there."

*Arrr. Mwah.*

Daddy looked over his shoulder, all frantic. But then, he remembered that he'd put me in his room with his TV and his painting of frogs and I was safe as a fish in a bowl. Only I wasn't.

"You sure, Deadman? I mean, there's nothing in there but an old purple sweater and a couple of moths."

Daddy kept looking on down the hall like he could see me. Did he see me? Did he know? Little black cats have eyes that shine in the dark. Sometimes I think the only important thing in my whole life is knowing whether or not Daddy could see the shine on my eye through the crack between the doors. But I can't ever know that.

"Then I'll guess I'll have something to keep me warm and something to lead me to the light, my man," laughed the Deadman, and he made a thing with his mouth like a smile. It mostly was a smile. On somebody else it would have definitely been a smile. But it wasn't a smile, really, and I knew it. It was a scream. *No, Daddy. I'm in here. It's me.* But I still didn't make a sound, because Daddy loved me and didn't ever want the Deadman to see me.

"Okay, D," shrugged Daddy like it didn't matter to him at all. Like he couldn't see. Maybe he didn't. Maybe he really put his coat down over those mudpuddles.

The Deadman gave him something small. I couldn't tell what it was. It wasn't a cup of sugar, for sure. How could something a man needs so much be so small? Daddy started back toward my treehouse, but the Deadman stopped him, grabbed his arm.

"You ever hear the one about the cat who broke his promise?"

Daddy swallowed hard. "Yeah, Deadman. I heard that one a bunch of times."

⁓

MUDPUDDLE HIT THE light switch in the hall and the lamp came on, the one that had all those dead bugs on the inside of it. The Deadman danced on ahead of him and took a big swanky breath like he'd bought those lungs in France. He hauled on the doors of my treehouse but they didn't come open because of the secret latch on the inside. Daddy Mudpuddle put his hands over his face and sank down on his heels.

"This thing got a key?" the Deadman said but the way he said it was all full of knowing the *arrr mwah* had more than a moth inside.

*It's okay*, I thought and squeezed my eyes tight. I sank down in my blue and yellow butterfly dress. *I'm a little black cat. Little black cats can be invisible if they want.*

Daddy looked sick. His face was like the skin on old soup. *I'm a little black cat and I have magic.* He flicked out his pen-knife and stuck it in the crack between the doors. The latch lifted up. *I'm a little black cat and little black cats can do anything.* The Deadman opened the doors like a window on his best morning.

The Deadman didn't say anything for a good while. He looked right at me, smiling and shining and thinking Deadman thoughts.

His eyes had blue flecks in them, like someone had spilled paint on his insides. *I'm a little black cat and no one can see me.* He pulled down the purple sweater and shut the doors again.

"I'll come back for the moths, Mudpuddle. It's such a cold day out. I'm shivering already. You stay in and enjoy yourself. Have a hot drink."

The Deadman took his red and disappeared back out the door.

---

AFTER THAT, THE Deadman came around a lot more often. I didn't have to hide anymore, though sometimes I did anyway. Mostly I played with my toys and thought about who came up with the names for all the colors in the sixty-four-color crayon box or whether or not rhinoceroses were friendly to girls who really liked rhinoceroses or how much three times four was because those are the kind of things you think about when you've soaked up all the smart in your dress and some of the smart in your school, too. Deadman and Daddy got to be best friends. They didn't talk about the day of the closet, ever. They'd lay around and drink and eat plain tortillas out of the bag and watch game shows on the living room TV. The Deadman always knew all the answers. The first thing I ever said to him was:

"Why don't you go on one of those shows? You'd make a million dollars and you could move to a nice house that's really far away."

I popped my princess's head off and stuck it on the blue ballgown body. The Deadman turned his head and looked at me like I was a twenty-dollar bill lying on the sidewalk with no one around.

"Wouldn't be fair to all those other contestants, Badgirl." He glanced back toward the TV. "What is plutonium?" he said to the game-show man in the grey suit. Then back to me: "Why don't you come and sit by me? I'll let you have a sip of my…what are we drinking, Muddy? My vodka'n OJ."

"Don't want it."

"Come on, it's just like water. It'll make you grow up fierce and bright."

But I didn't want his nasty vodka in his dirty mug that had a cartoon cactus on it saying GOOD MORNING ALBUQUERQUE. I didn't know where Albuquerque was, but I hated it because the Deadman had a mug from there.

"Don't be rude, Badgirl," my daddy said, because he loved me but he'd heard the one about the cat who broke his promise and he didn't want to hear it again.

So I sat down between them and I hated them both and I drank out of the Albuquerque mug while the man in the grey suit told us that the dollar values had doubled. The Deadman touched my hair but after awhile he stopped because little black cats bite when strangers pet them. Everyone knows that.

The Deadman started showing up in the mornings and saying he'd walk me to school so Daddy could get to his work on time. Daddy didn't have a work, but he made me promise never to tell the Deadman that, so I didn't tell, even though nobody who has a work lives where we do and eats powdered mashed potatoes without un-powdering them. I said I didn't need to be walked anywhere because I wasn't a baby, but the Deadman just stared down the hall at the pirate kiss closet till Daddy looked too and then nobody said anything but I had to walk to school with the Deadman.

I didn't like walking with the Deadman. His hands were clammy even when he wore gloves and he always took the long way. He talked a lot but I could never remember what he said after. One time I thought I should ask him questions about himself because that's what nice girls do, so I asked him where he was from. Grown-ups asked each other that all the time. The Deadman swept out his arm all grand for no reason.

"Paris, France!"

"That's a lie. You're a liar."

"You got me, Badgirl. You're too good for the likes of me. The truth is, I'm from the continent of Atlantis. My parents had a squat on the banks of the river Styx."

"Is that in the Bronx?"

"Yeah, Badgirl. That's just where it is. You're smarter than a sack of owls, you are."

"It's 'cause of my dress," I said proudly.

A little while after that, the Deadman started walking me home from school, too. He slicked up his hair fancy and told my teacher he was my uncle. Had a signed slip from Daddy and everything. But we never made it all the way home. He'd stand me on a corner and give me a box that had pills inside it, so bright they looked like Skittles. And he said:

"You're so good, Badgirl. Nobody'll mess with you on account of how good you are. You're just as clean and bright as New Year's Day."

"I wanna go home."

"Naw, you can't yet. This here is medicine. Lots of people need medicine. You know how you hate it when you get sick. You don't want people to get sick when you could make them better, do you? Just stand here and keep the box in your backpack, and when sick people come asking, take their money and give them a couple of whatever color they ask for. If you do a good job, I'll buy you a new dress."

I sniffled. It was fall and the damp came with fall. I had a wet leaf stuck to my shoe. "I don't want a new dress," I whispered.

"Well, a new doll then. God knows a girl needs more than that ratty headless thing you got. I'll come back for you and we'll get back before your daddy finishes his work."

I didn't have mittens so my hands got tingly and cold and then I couldn't feel them anymore. I waited on the corner and all kinds of strangers came up talking to me like we were friends and I did what the Deadman said I had to. My fingers felt like they were made out of silver so I pretended that was the truth, that I had beautiful silver hands with pictures scratched onto them like the fancy dishes on TV.

And every time I had to touch somebody strange to me so I could give over their medicine, I pretended my beautiful silver hands turned them into game show contestants with perfect teeth and fluffy hair and nametags the color of luck.

<hr>

AT CHRISTMASTIME THE Deadman brought over a tree with one red ball on it and a strand of lights with only three bulbs working. He had on red velvet elf shoes like the kind Santa's helpers wear at the mall, only his were old and dark and the bells didn't make any sound. He also brought a bottle of brandy and some cheeseburgers and a cake from the grocery store with HAPPY BIRTHDAY ALEXIS written on it in hot pink frosting. I could read it by myself by then, even though I'd had to stop wearing my smart dress because it got holes in it and all the buttons fell off. The Deadman set it all out like he was Santa but he was *not* Santa, and I bet Santa never came to his house when he was little, if the Deadman ever had been little. He never did bring me a new doll or a new dress. Daddy put on that show where they play part of a song and you have to guess what it's called.

Daddy and the Deadman had gotten so used to having me around they didn't bother hiding anything anymore.

"'Bennie and the Jets'," the Deadman said. It took the blonde lady on TV forever to get it. She squealed when she did and jumped up and down. Her earrings glittered in the stage lights like fire.

They ate some cake. It was red velvet on the inside but I didn't feel right eating Alexis's birthday cake. I ate half a cheeseburger but it was cold and the ketchup tasted like glue. The Deadman gave Daddy his Christmas present. Daddy didn't say thank you. He didn't say very much anymore. He just took the little small lump wrapped in red tissue paper from the Deadman and shook some out into a spoon. It did look like sugar after all. He flicked a lighter under the spoon and held it there until the sugar got all melted and brown and gluggy. It was sort of oily on top, too, like spilled gas.

Like a mudpuddle.

Then the Deadman handed him a needle, like the kind at the doctor's office when you have to get your shots because otherwise you'll get sick. I pulled the head off my princess and stuck it on the body with the pink ballgown. Daddy tied one of my hair ribbons around his arm and the Deadman stuck the needle in the mudpuddle first, and into Daddy second. Then he did it all over again on himself. Daddy smiled and his face got round and happy. It got to be his own face again. Daddy has a good face. He patted his lap for me to come sit with him and I did and it was Christmas for a minute.

"How Deep Is Your Love," the Deadman said. Another blonde lady frowned on the TV. She couldn't think of the song. Poor lady. I didn't know that song, either. But I knew the next one because it was Michael Jackson and I knew all his songs.

"Billie Jean," I whispered. Daddy was asleep.

"C'mere, Badgirl," said the Deadman.

"Don't want to."

"Why you afraid of me?"

"I'm not afraid. Little black cats aren't afraid of anything."

"Come on, Badgirl. I'm not gonna hurt you. I got you a present. Make you grow up quick and sharp."

"Don't want to."

The Deadman lit himself a cigarette. He had the same don't-get-sick shot Daddy had, so how come he didn't just go to sleep and leave me alone? I'd have cleaned up the dishes and made sure the TV got turned off. I did it all the time.

"Your dad promised me whatever was in the armoire. You were in there. So you have to do what I say. I own you. I've been nice about it, because you're such a little thing, but it's hard for a man like me to keep being nice." The Deadman started doing his trick with the mudpuddle and the spoon again. "I gotta carry that nice all day and Badgirl, I tell you what, it is *heavy*. I wanna put it down. My shoulders are *aching*. So you better come when I call or else I'm liable to just drop my nice right on the ground and break it into a hundred pieces."

"Don't be rude, Badgirl," Daddy murmured in his sleep. I looked up at his scruffy chin and something popped and spat inside me like grease and it made a stain on my insides that spelled out *I hate my daddy* and I felt ashamed. He wasn't even awake. He didn't know anything. But I still hated him because little black cats don't know how to forgive anybody.

I think it's against the law for a person to own another person but maybe he did own me because in a flash minute I was sitting down next to the Deadman even though I didn't want to be. But not on his lap. On TV, a man with red hair was listening to the first few notes of a song I almost knew but couldn't quite remember. The Deadman reached for my arm and Daddy woke up then, coughing like his breath got stolen.

"What the fuck, man! Don't do that," Daddy said. "She's my kid."

"Lighten up, Muddy! It's just a little Christmas fun. She's such a sour little thing. Always scowling at us like she's our mother. You gotta nip that in the bud when they're young. A lady should always be smiling." The Deadman looked my daddy in the eye. "You ever hear the one about the cat who broke his promise?" And he stuck the needle in my arm.

After that I didn't have hands anymore.

I felt like I was all filled up with yellow, the yellow that looks like all the lights turned on at once. I could hardly see with all that yellow swimming around in me. The TV changed to another show, the one where the beautiful lady in a glittery dress turns giant glowing letters around and everyone tries to guess the sentence. She was wearing my smart dress with the butterflies on it. She reached up and turned over a *B*, but I don't like *B* because B is for Badgirl, so I reached up to turn it back around and that's when I knew I didn't have hands anymore.

My arms just ended all smooth and neat, no thumbs, no pinkie, no ring finger, like the plastic bottoms on the ballgown bodies. The stumps dripped yellow and blue butterflies onto the carpet. They flapped their wings there, grazing the rug with their antennae to see if it was flowers. It didn't hurt. It didn't anything. I looked around but I couldn't see my hands lying anywhere, not even under the sofa. I couldn't feel anything when I touched the letter *B* on TV with my stump, or the beautiful lady's hair, or the wall of the living room. When I gave up and dropped my arm back down I must have knocked over a bottle or something because there was glass everywhere but I didn't feel that either. The Deadman grabbed me to keep me from falling in the mess but I couldn't make my fingers close around anything, not his sleeve or the corner of the table or anything. My fingers wouldn't listen. They weren't fingers anymore.

I had so much yellow in me it was coming out, coming out all over, washing over everything and making it clean like the dancing lemons on the shaker of powdered soap. I twisted out of the Deadman's grip and crawled away from him back into Daddy's lap.

"Daddy, my hands are gone. Fix it, please? I don't know how to be a girl without hands. All girls have hands. No one will play with me at school."

But Daddy was asleep in his mudpuddle world again and when I tried to pat his face to wake him up I just clobbered him because stumps are so heavy, so much heavier than fingers. But he didn't wake up. Someone on TV in Giant Letter World spun a big wheel and it came up gold, too. The beautiful lady in my smart dress clapped her hands. See? All girls have hands. Except me. Another blue butterfly flew out of my stump and landed on the window. It was night outside. The butterfly glowed so blue it turned into the moon.

The Deadman pulled a deck of cards out of his back pocket and started dealing himself a hand of solitaire at our kitchen table. He was real good at shuffling. I took my eyes back from the butterfly moon and put them on the Deadman. He put his cigarette in his mouth and dragged on it good and ragged.

He was shuffling cards with my hands.

## Badgirl, the Deadman, and the Wheel of Fortune

I knew my own hands and those were it. My pinkie still had green fingernail polish on it from my friend's mom's house and a scratch where I fell playing hopscotch last week. My wrist had my lucky yarn bracelet on it. He'd popped them off me like a princess's head and stuck them on his body. My hands should have been way too small for the Deadman to wear but somehow they weren't, either he got little to match them or they got big to match him. I decided he got little, because my hands should be loyal to me and not him. My hand put down an ace of hearts and waved at me. Then words started coming out of me like blue butterflies and I couldn't stop them and they came out without permission, without me even thinking them before they turned into words.

"Are you a person?"

The Deadman chewed on one of my fingernails which he had no right to do.

"Used to be."

"In Paris, France? With the river?"

The Deadman snorted. "Yeah."

"How do you stop being a person?"

"Lots of ways. It's far harder to keep on being a person than to stop. I do think about starting up again sometimes, though. I do think about that. But once you been to that river, it fills you up forever. You need something real good to turn your heart back to red."

"Why do you keep coming back here? Do you even like my daddy? Are you really his friend?"

"I think he's a worthless piece of shit, Badgirl. But he has cable. And he has you."

The blue butterfly moon got bigger and bigger in the window. It was gonna take up our whole apartment. "Did he know I was in the...the...*arrr-mwah?*"

The Deadman sighed. He put down a quick two-three-four on his ace. "It wouldn't have gone different if he did or didn't, kid. The thing about having the whole world in your back pocket is that every day is nothing but wall-to-wall bargains. I don't have to dicker. They keep upping the price. Everyone wants the world. I just want everyone."

"I want my hands back."

The beautiful lady turned around six or seven letters quick, one after the other. She was still wearing my smart dress, which I guess is why she always knows the answer to the puzzle. But now my dress had gotten long like a wedding dress. It glittered all over. The green bow and green buttons were all emeralds falling down her back and all over the stage. Her chest looked like the sun and she had stars all up and down her arms and the blue butterfly moon was rising in the studio, too, right behind her head like a crown. Everyone had stolen my things. I wanted her to come out of the TV and save me and turn me around like the letter *B*. But she wasn't going to. She had my dress. She had what she wanted.

*I'm a little black cat*, I thought. *Little black cats run away. Little black cats don't need hands.* The blue butterfly moon had gotten so big it bulged up against my treehouse and the front door at the same time. *Little black cats can climb up on the moon and ride it far, far away. To Paris, France and the Bronx and the continent of Atlantis.*

The Deadman glanced at the game show. For once, he didn't solve it before the contestants did. He just touched his lips with my fingers and said quietly:

"I need them."

*Little black cats don't need anyone. Little black cats have magic no one can steal. Little black cats run faster than dead men.*

"Why?"

All the letters lit up at once and the lady in my dress touched them all, smiling, buttons and bows and butterflies sparkling everywhere, until they spelled out: HELL IS EMPTY AND ALL THE DEVILS ARE HERE.

"With clean hands, Badgirl, you can start all over."

*Little black cats run right out, just as soon as you open the door.*

# Down and Out in R'lyeh

IN HIS HOUSE AT R'LYEH, dead Cthulhu farts in his sleep.
If you're dank like me, you gibber up the Old Fuck's brainspout, crouch in there full gargoyle on his raggedy roof, wrap your gash around the slime-lung chimney, and huff that vast and loathsome shit like the space-curdled milk of your mama's million terror-tits. Up you get, fœtid freak-babbies of the ultradeep! The nightmare beyond time and geometry and madness has an upset tum-tum. Whiff up those gargantuan gastrointestinal fugue-bubbles! Clog down the occult emanations of the Elder God! When his antediluvian ass-bombs explode all over your needy neurons, you'll smell the apocalyptic expanse of frozen galaxies screaming forever into a red and hungry void—and just a hint of fresh eucalyptus.

That's all Shax and Pazuzu and my own personal self were after that night. Just a couple of eeries looking to get squamous, to swipe a little snatch of wholesome fun from the funktacular funerary fundament belonging to the Big Boss, a hit big enough to drop our brains out the bottoms of our various appendages and forget the essential, unalterable, sanity-shearing truth of our watery and unfeeling cosmos:

R'lyeh *sucks*.

Seriously. The heaving, putrescent streets swollen with black spores of dementation and the bilge water of a hundred billion nightmares, the crawling hallucinogenic slime choking every unreal gutter and askew alley, the tacky interdimensional shopfronts selling rubbish nobody wants, the ugly, kitschy non-Euclidean central business district brooding and moping up in your face, the noxious monoliths, the howling sepulchers, the best minds of your generation destroyed by madness starving hysterical naked dragging themselves through the gentrified neighborhoods looking for something to *do*, it's all just the fucking *worst*. Trust me. I was born here. I was into nuclear chaos beyond the nethermost outposts of space and time before it was cool.

But anyway.

Be me: Moloch! Dank as starlit squidshit, antique in the membrane, maximum yellow fellow! Only five thousand years old, still soggy behind the orifices, belly full of piss and pus and home-brewed, small-batch disdain for all he beholds. Keeps his tentacles proper pompy-doured and his fur 100% goat at all times. Keeps his talons on the sluggish pulse of the nightmare corpse-city that never sleeps, demoniac city on the edge of linear consciousness, cancerous kingdom of the corpulent and pustulant and decadent and stupid, the big boring phony sell-out rotting apple under the sea.

Not THE Moloch. Obviously. That guy's a blue-chip maniac rocking a truly eldritch trust fund and a gentrificated uptown charnel house. But when you're nine hundred and ninety-seventh among the thousand young of Shub-Niggurath, the Black Goat of the Woods, ain't nothing left for you but the motherfucking *dregs*. Mom ran out of eldritch names *way* before I slithered along. Could've been worse, though. My little sister's just called Shit. Shit's all right. Takes after Dad more than me. (That'd be the Deadbeat All-Dad of Ages, serpentine thunderfuck lustlord Yig, not that he ever bothered to come to our moonball games or birthday orgies.) Shit doesn't have any arms or legs and you can see through her snakeskin and watch her organs ooze and squeeze according to some primordial rhythm unheard by man, but she lets me crash on her couch and eat her boyfriends whenever I want, so it's always been yellow between us. Shit's got that virus youngest beasties catch sometimes where they gotta prove how much smarter and busier and more hideously evil they are than everybody else all the time, so she works her cloacas off downtown for some effulgy gloon on the Planning Committee—to which I say, how the fuck do you plan the descent of the known universe into bloody infinite shrieking madness? If you have to have a board meeting about it, what's the *fhatgn* point?

But enough about my brood. Shit happens, what can you do? I'm not about to ooze out a cute little suburban drama where everything's wrapped up in an hour and all the junior-league cyclopean horrors end up devouring the minds of the innocent as a family. I'm not gonna jaw you some dusty epic about the fœtid glory of the Old Ones, neither. They're old. Who cares? You wanna glaak some toothless horror shambling along playing shuffleboard uphill both ways in the bloodtide, you got plenty of other options. Save that necronomicrap for prime time. This here's public access. This here's *Radio Free R'lyeh*. Harken to the electrostatic-enigmatic low-budget belch-howl of the low-rent disaffected disasters roaming these dumb slime-streets where there's nothing to do but seethe.

SO THERE WE were, Shax and Pazuzu and me, three eeries out on the town, all messed up with nowhere to go. Shax was my number one cultist back then, the girl-thing I was yigging on the semi-regular, a three-eyed psychic gelatinous pyramid topped with the lushest blood-seeping tentacles you ever saw. What can I say? I'm a sucker for redheads. Shax was shubby as all hell, a carnivore hungry for the meat of Moloch, up for my proboscis in her protuberances anytime, anywhere. She loved horses and schizophrenia and untranslatable manuscripts from before the dawn of time. A total nerdy little misko at heart, but my Shax had a body that drove me *mundane*. Sometimes she'd get this far-off cosmic look in one of her eyes mid-yig, but only because she'd swapped her vast, stygian consciousness into some poor bastard from Nowhere, Massachusetts and was strolling around a cheese shop or whatever in his skin while I whispered sweet nihilisms into the hear-hole of some boring mundflesh whose most unexplainable encounter to date had been doing his taxes.

"Hush, babby," I gurgled into Shax's puncture-wound ear, into the mind of my new mammalian friend. "Just do what feels yellow and you and I will trip the light traumatic. You can't get pregnant your first time. Everybody's doing it. Come on, I promise I'll still dissect you in the morning. Pretend you're at the dentist. Just say *Iä!*"

Shax always knew how to keep things eldritch in the sack.

Pazuzu was my eerie from the minute I gibbered out of the spawn-sac and into this trashbin world. Out of one bitch, into another. He ate his mom when he was little, so me and Shit pretty much adopted him into the Niggurath brood. Who would notice one more? Even if he was a Ghast and not a whatever-the-fuck-we-are? Mama Shub strangled Zuzu as lovingly as any of us. These days he's another regular denizen of Shit's couch. He kind of looks like a walking, talking, noseless scab on kangaroo legs. Straight up fœtid, was Pazuzu. All the squirmy young shubs hungered him. But my man didn't have a cultist then. Didn't care about getting off. Mostly what Zuzu slavered after was to get squamous and hunt himself some gloons. Not THE Gloon. Not the guy *named* Gloon. You don't hunt that dank little piece of slug-ass. Not that Elgin-marble-looking motherfucker. The slug-god Gloon slithers out the eyes of that effulgy Greek statue it rides around in like a john sliding out of a rented prom limo and it hunts *you*. Naw, Zuzu hunts posers. Barely-larval yuppie scum with Old One pedigrees who gibber around trying to *look* like Gloon and *talk* like Gloon and *corrupt the mortal world* like Gloon when they're nothing but a bunch of shoggo fuckboys who couldn't corrupt a goddamn gumdrop without daddy's protective runes. They're so fucking dun that when we call them gloons, they think it's a compliment. But I get Pazuzu. Always have. He kicks those kruggy pukes in the face and feels like he's making a difference in the world. He isn't, but, you know. Let a scab dream.

So Friday night, its hour come at last, slouched towards R'lyeh to be born. Shax and Zuzu and me beheld the sunset from the roof of our slumslime apartment henge, guggo for something fat and plasmic and *new*. You can actually sort of see the sun from down here, through the mundsmog of the South Pacific, stuck all over with mortal fishing boats like flies on blue flypaper. R'lyeh isn't underwater *per se*. Don't believe the brochures. It can't even get that tired Atlantean schtick right. No, this *fhtagn* little backwater burg is bounded on all sides by a semi-aqueous transdimensional multi-reality beehive of space-time (comes in Pacific Blue, Sanatorium Green, and Classic Black for all your decorating needs!). It keeps the civic saltwater content at a steady dripping mucous. And *inside* the corpsified beehive lies the rotting honeycomb of cut-rate depravity I call home. I said before: I was born here. I won't die here because I am infinite, unfathomable, beyond mortality and corporeality, but I've never gotten *out*. How can anyone expect me to be a yawning horror of the ultradeep when I've never left the town I grew up in? Never met anyone but the same glabrous tentacled faces staring on the subway, never heard anything but last millennium's Top 40 chants and prophecies blaring out of big, ugly doomboxes, never seen anything but the inside of this Old Ones Retirement Village where the streets are paved with quivering denture cream and the Early Elder Special starts at four every afternoon and everything worth anything has already been sucked dry by the gonzo appetites of our goddamn parents.

Oh sure, every once in awhile, the human world falls asleep at the wheel and crashes into us, and some shard of their incomprehensibly stupid one-note reality runs aground in the black light district and we all crowd in like fat shoggo tourists, flashing and yelling and poking the native wildlife, but that party goes down on the rare and seldom, and if there's anything more excruciatingly boring than R'lyeh's best and brightest, it's a goddamn human being. For real, between you and me, what is their *problem?* These mundflesh morons act like the angle of the emerald emanations from the Gates of the Silver Key cut their flesh to hanging ribbons. They swan around wailing and moaning like the non-Euclidean geometry of netherdimensional architecture flays their minds down to the throbbing thalamic core. But I got eyes, too, and all I see are dirty green traffic lights and urban blight. We did learn some excellently eldritch words from the last brood that came babbling through, though. *Oh shit, oh fuck, oh shitfucking dammit, what the hell is that thing?*

Blah blah blah.

So up the rooftop Shax took a drag on a fat, hand-rolled tome she got from my man Nyarlathotep, who sells papers and shred out of his dirty bookshop down on Id Row. Papa Ny, now, that beast is pure uncut misko through and through. That's why he and Shax get on so dank. Two creeps in a crypt. Papa Ny wears his human costume 28/9, even down here, even when he's sleeping. But on the inside, that cat's a *literal* bookworm, sliming his excrescence up on his ancient manuscripts like an awkward shub on his first dancefloor. I've seen his stash. Those woodcuts are yellow as hell, antique porn for the R'lyeh literati, such as they are. And to make a little extra gleeth on the slant, Papa Ny cuts the endpapers out of whatever forbidden text he's mad at that week, fills them with black Yith-spores scraped off the customers-only sink after hours, and sells them dag cheap, on account of which, he's about the only Elder any of us can stand, and we get to smoke our tomes real nice up here on the roof.

That night, Shax was burning down a flyleaf off the Book of Azathoth, sucking up the purple smoke through seven slits in her protoplasmic face and exhaling misty dodecahedrons out over the power lines and train tracks and horror-shards of our drowned and drowning city. Pazuzu scratched his scabby balls and knocked back a forty of the skunky, hoppy black bile he insisted on brewing in Shit's closet. She hates the smell, but Shit's way too nice to say anything. How the two of us can have come out of the same cloaca is just *beyond.*

"Fuck this," grunted Pazuzu. "I'm sober as a goddamn archeologist. I wanna get bloody *squamous*. 100% *iridescent*. Straight *obliterated*. I wanna yank my brain out through my nose, boil it in beer, and beat the shit out of it with a *fhtagn* hammer. Lurk me?"

I did, indeed, lurk him completely. So did Shax. Her tentacles twisted and lithed above the apex of her gelatinous pyramid-head.

"Iä! Iä!" she ululated. "Screw this babby shit to the seafloor." She threw down her tome and crushed it beneath her protean bulk. "Eeries, let's hunt down some real ichor tonight. I wanna get *ordinary*. I wanna be totally fucking *mundane*! Thoroughly, balls to the wall, XXX *normal*."

This meant gibbering down to the Psychotic Pnakotic for pints of san with rationality chasers. I didn't have the gleeth for that kind of action, no how, but Shax usually covered me. She's a Yith, which is kind of like being in the mafia, except with psychic parasitical spores instead of tommy guns and zoot suits. Zuzu only ever tolerated Shax because she never acted like the richie she was, really. Shax ate shit and puked despair like a real sheol proletariat princess. Like the rest of us. So Zu carefully ignored all the times she picked up our tab.

I groaned. When I groan it sounds like an owl's death-scream. It's my dankest feature.

"I'm not gonna let your mopey tentacled ass get between me and a foetid high, you *fhtagn* misko," laughed Zuzu, hopping off the roof ledge and running one meaty hand through his pustulant, blood-crusted pompadour. "We're taking the subway and if you whine about it, I'll kick your beak in. And then I'll tell Mom you went to bed at eight with a glass of warm milk and a book so you could be fresh for work in the morning."

If Shub-Niggurath, the Black Goat of the Woods with a Thousand Young, heard that noise, she'd paint the nursery with my intestines.

But you gotta understand, public transportation in R'lyeh is a fucking *shitshow*. Remember that decomposing transdimensional honeycomb knowledge I threw your way earlier? It's the naked truth.

This crapheap town is full of holes—and the holes *move*. Look—R'lyeh is old as balls. R'lyeh sits at the crossroads of a million planes of sickening unreality. And R'lyeh does not invest in infrastructure. You can walk down the Uvular in Gugtown, dank and antique as you please, flip a corner, and peer down into the bottomless red cavern of Yoth. You can park in the frozen maze of East Yuggoth and come back to find the volcanic pits of Voormithadreth have totaled your accursed chariot without so much as leaving a note. Nyarlathotep's porn shop on Id Row? That's actually in Carcosa, which isn't anywhere near R'lyeh as the squid swims, but the old bitch-town wore a hole in its filthy sock, and now you can trip over a nightworm in Kadath and land face-down in Carcosa if you don't look both ways before crossing universes.

So the subway is no-go in Moloch world. I'm not about to shoot my shit through Gug-gnawed subterranean tunnels *underneath* this cyclopean clown car and end up drinking on freaking Saturn with a bunch of giant cats. No, thank you.

But for my eeries, anything. Anything, forever, always.

And that's how it happened. That's all it was. Our fœtid, degenerate quest, the dark crusade that would echo down through the centuries like one of Cthulhu's grand farts was just a Hadean beer run through the toilet bowl of the cosmos. Lurk this and lurk it well: the fancier the history reads, the trashier it really was.

ONLY ONE HOBO Shoggoth barfed and pissed on my feet at the same time the whole way there, and *there* appeared where it was supposed to be after only an hour of the wyrmcar screaming profanities at us. All nameless horrors considered, I call that dank.

SO A HALF-BREED goatsnake, a Yith, and a Ghast walk into a bar. Stop me if you've heard this one.

Most all the fiends and mutants in the plushy-ass eel booths of the Psychotic Pnakotic swiveled their heads and floating globes and writhing antennae to stare at me and mine. R'lyeh's a pretty conservative squat when you get right down to it. Yiths with Yiths, Ghasts with Ghasts. But I didn't give a *fhtagn* because I'm not a fucking racist. Shax wound one of her crimson tentacles around my neck and we gibbered up to the bar. Shragga was manning the taps. She's got a drill for a face but she's basically yellow.

Shax smeared a dream of becoming and unbecoming on the bar. It glowered ultraviolet netherhot, curdling into pestilent lumpcream. Shragga shrugged. Shax's gleeth was always dank here, even if she wobbled in with her Niggurath cultist boy-thing and embarrassed the high-end clientele.

"Three hits of san with lucidbacks, Shraggs," my girl-thing oozed, right eldritch and shameless.

"We gotta dress code, Yithling," Shragga's drill whined, ground, spun. "Blackest of ties. Writhe here a minute, I've got a couple of old exoskeletons in the back."

Shragga shuddered back with meaty arms full of black clattering crabskin armor that hadn't been sheol since the Cretaceous, whistle-screeched through her drill-face, and poured out three shots of thorazine plus three tall glasses of Providence tapwater. The PP's got a pipe that goes straight up to New England and suckles at the municipal mundflesh supply. Zu and me licked sea spores off Shax's stomach.

One, two, three; grab, slurp, devour, then sucked sour slime off the Providence pipe to chase it down.

"*Fhtagn*, iä!" Zuzu yelled.

The rest of the pub goggled and gurgled and gleeked at us like they never saw anyone enjoying anything in their whole infinite existence before.

God, this fucking neighborhood.

Used to be an antique place, *very* goat, full of artists trying to get back to their roots and hone their craft, create a warm sense of community delirium, drive the mundflesh to a really *authentic* eternal madness. But then the Old Fucks moved in with their gleeth and their gloons and their penthouse sepulchers and organic organ banks and locally-forced whole food cannibal bistros and now it's a shoggo wasteland of narcoleptic zombie demi-gods who couldn't give two deranged toadshits for anyone under a hundred thousand years old. Back in the day, you could *dance* at the Pnakotic. Get your underground shubstep electrotrance tentaclecore maenad groove on. Now we had to sit uncomfortably in some dead crab-god's claw-me-down stench just to get a drink while the upper crusty glared at us like zoo creatures.

Shax swiveled to me, her three globular golden eyes pulsing, her seventeen irises contracting to one hideous human mundeye. "The most merciful thing in the world, I think, is the inability of the human mind to correlate all its contents," she blurted.

"What the fuck?" I giggled.

"Pick up some butter and flour at the store on your way home!" she howled. "The bank keeps calling about our mortgage!"

Pazuzu slapped the pub-floor with one massive kangaroo leg. "*Fhtagn* iä! Can you feel it? Mundmouth McGee is in the house! What do you want for dinner tonight, sweetie? Wouldn't it be wonderful if our son got into Brown next year?"

"Who cares?" I giggled again. I couldn't stop. I could hardly wheeze out words when the lucidity kicked in and my essential Molochness gibbered off.

"Hello," I yelled, as if possessed, without meaning to, without any hunger to: "my name is Moloch, nine hundred and ninety-seventh son of the Great Black Goat Shub-Niggurath, the Outer God, the All-Mother, and I am an alcoholic. Are there cookies in the back? Debbie always brings pecan sandies."

"Welcome to Mom's Diner, how can I help you?" screamed Zuzu. "How can I help you? How can I help you? How can I help you?"

But it doesn't last. Lucidity has a seriously krug half-life. Our undermatrices can't hold on to the mundo psychfest. It all fucks off back to pecan sandie-land and dumps you in a ditch on the side of the multiverse with drymouth and aching tentacles. We were stuck inside ourselves again pretty quick, a sad brood of dun miskos raging uselessly against the sinferno, the exact opposite of what we hungered.

"I hate my life," I whispered. I couldn't tell if that was me or the san talking.

So we decided to blow that squalor and go glean our eerie Bifrons and shake him down for some furtive fungiform fun.

Bifrons, now, Bifrons is a dank *fhtagn* Mi-Go, the Fungus Among Us, a sheol mushroom man who truly has his gills together, guggo for anything and antique as a china cabinet. You gibber over to Bifrons's flop if you want to get your corpus collosum fully corpse-thrusty skull-strummed. The shiitake scenester laired in a scumlord paradise, waterfront view over a black river of boiling slime that pours eternally into one of R'lyeh's puckered sphincters, the A-Line that leads through the youth-infected artisanal slums and terminates at a certain Mr. Yog-Sothoth's amorphous, radioactive, but surprisingly elegantly lit pad. What can I say, the Thing from Beyond knows from window treatments.

Bifrons does not know window treatments. His flop beholds like a schizoid sewer worker's night terrors. Mold wriggle-gibbering in wallpaper patterns, rags, and bones and fugue-pus and broken wine glasses everywhere, Shoggoths yigging idiotically, robotically, in one corner, a mouth-faced Gug smashing his skull into Bifrons's good mirror, a dehydrated Yith crumbling into nihil within reach of the kitchen sink, the floor more spore than rug.

Home sweet home.

Bifrons doesn't charge. He does his song and dance for the jingles and tingles. It's some kind of fetish, I guess. He sweats technicolor dreamvenom the whole time and it's kruggy but Moloch doesn't judge. Gotta get your yig on where you can in R'lyeh. You'd think an insane chthonic carnival of a shriek-powered city pumping out waves of delirium into the seven seas would have some kind of nightlife. But this is pretty much it. Door-to-door traveling fucksters trying to keep up our enthusiasm for the latest and greatest howling silver vacuum.

"I got leftovers," the preternatural portobello puled in our direction. "You hunger?"

Bifrons tossed Zuzu a mundo Chinese takeaway carton half-full of sweet fried chunks of a divorced mid-level import/export manager's jabbering shredded psyche swimming in anchovy sauce. One, two, three; grab, slurp, devour. Bifrons stroked the greasy slopes of Shax's pyramid with his creeping fungoid fingers, which was not at all sheol by me, but you gotta stay yellow if you wanna get squamous with the crimini element around here.

"Everybody goat?" Bifrons lisped thickly, his mushroomy otherflesh beginning to crawl with rainbow glowsweat.

"Iä, Biff, my eerie, my mush, iä," Zuzu hissed.

He was getting bored. Moloch always knows. And when Zuzu gets bored, he starts looking for something to rend. Screams echoed out of the back bedroom and I could tell by the accents of their murdermoaning that it was a high street gloon couple mashing divinities. Probably can't even cum without reciting the names of their fell ancestors into each other's waxy hear-holes. If Zuzu clocked the same, it'd get full ghastly frenzy in here with a quickness.

"Iä, Bifrons, babby, do your thing," I said.

What gets Bifrons off is this: Mr. Morbid Morel worms out his munted wings and the fungal rings of his face start spinning dank and wild. He phases his claws out of the corporeal plane, reaches into your skull, scoops out your brain like vanilla ice cream, sticks it in a dirty glass jar, and shakes the shit out of it until you're addled and rattled and paddled and straddled, then he shoves your milkshake back and watches your soul jiggle out your orifices.

Here we go.

So Moloch's in the brain jar and his medulla is smashbang oblongataed into blueberry psychic jelly and when a Mi-Go has your black matter on frappe, shit gets very topsy indeed. Memory yigs itself raw.

One minute I'm goggling out a filthy glass jug, next minute I'm little, tentacles barely grown out yet, writhing on the infinite mud flat of my birth under a gape-wound sky where the stars are dying over and over, being devoured over and over, devoured by something vast and gorgeous and unstoppable, inevitable, perfect in its total hunger.

Shub-Niggurath, the Black Goat of the Cosmos, the Digestrix of Aeons, the All-Mother.

My mother.

I reach my stubby little nubs out to her impossible fœtid body. I stretch every soft babby tentacle curling on my cherub-noggin up to her grotesque countenance, her million interdimensional breasts foamy with nightmare milk, her billion lithe squiddy limbs branching and forking like an immense untouchable winter tree. Wee tiny Moloch cries for his mama up in the sky and she screeches ultrasonic daemonoharmonic over the boundless bloodswamp of her thousand sobbing young, her babbies, her brood, the spawn of her wonderful hell-womb.

*I love you, Mommy, I love you*, I wail but she don't come down, she don't wriggle me in her feelers and nuzzle my goaty face looking so much like hers, she don't even know me from my brothers and sisters, she don't pick me out and make me special, she just makes like she's gonna hork up all that starshit she guzzled her whole life like a mama seagull into a thousand writhing gullets and jets. But then she doesn't. She doesn't feed us the stars she got to eat when they were fresh and eldritch and sweet. She keeps it all for herself and we starve while Mumma shrieks across the continuum to something else, something prettier, something danker, something better than us. Than me.

*I love you, Mommy. Why don't you love me back?*

When Bifrons sleeved me back into my squidsack I was crying hideous, naphtha seeping out my stupid shoggo eyes and stinking up the joint with *feelings*, dripping kerosene shame onto Biff's rug in time to the telltale sound of a scabrous mutant kangaroo named Zuzu thump-thump drumming some sorry fulgy skull into the wetwall.

Be me: Moloch, clawed back from his righteous hard-earned squamous, blurred blotto, gibbering around the rank lair of an evil mushroom, staggering down, then up, then down again before scraping Zuzu off a tall, cold, dark drink of trust fund water half out of his madrags with black, ancient blood all over his dumb wormpile face. Moloch, gobsmacked as a bloody mundo in the naked throbbing bonelight of true reality, when he sees the shub that handsome devil is yigging is none but his babby sister Shit, see-through snakebody wrapped around his tarantula legs, fangs all the way out.

"Stop it, *stop it*, you *fhtagn* shoggo loser," hissed Shit.

"What the *fuck*, Shit?" Zu slurred around the kruggy edges of his Mi-Go trip. "Why you yigging that fuckboy yuppie establishment gloon? You two go suck Elder ass together, too? If you were that hard up I'd have whipped your eggs for you. Why'd you do him for, you mundane bitch?"

My sister uncoiled herself, every inch the serpent daughter of the Digestrix of Aeons. Her hood flared. I don't think I ever noticed how beautiful Shit was before. And the thing is, up until that second, Shit always spoke full fulgy. I never heard her drop so much as a scrap of yellow dank into her talk. But just then, with her cultist boy-thing bleeding into Bifrons's crusted space-colored carpet, she swore like us.

"I didn't hunger *you*, you dun cunt. Lurk me now? Iä? Call him a gloon? No. That's Qaatesh. Say hello, Qaatesh!" The worm-faced hunk of her affections coughed and spat out several fangs. "Lurk him. He has a name, just like you. He enjoys long walks on the beach and flaying the minds of smug academics, not that you give a fuck. Gloon, gloon, gloon. That's all you behold. That's all you babble. Flapping your gash and farting out this kruggy class war squidshit. You think you're sheol? Think you're yellow? Behold me, Pazuzu. *I* am a gloon. I carry water for the Great Old Ones and I am well dank at it. I am paid in blood and diamonds from the nether reaches of space which means *I* have the gleeth to spot you two that nice apartment with the big slither-in closet where you make your garbage homebrew ghastbeer and Moloch puts the empty carton of ichor back in the fridge instead of throwing it out every goddamned time. You hunger to savage some fulgy sneerheart gloon? I'm right here. Show me that eldritch deathdick, you shoggo *fhtagn* fuckaroo."

Zuzu just gawped. A big scab over his ear fell off. I gibbered up between them.

"No deathdicks tonight, brood," I soothed. "Not tonight. What you doing in Bifrons's squalor, brood-girl?" I smiled my most antique smile, tongue behind the teeth and everything.

My translucent sister-snake smoothed down her hood, eyes still blue fire. "Same as you, Moloch. What? I'm not allowed to have a little fun?"

Just like that, Shit was back to her fancy high street babble, stripped of all that oozy slang.

Bifrons asked us, politely, to fuck off out of his squalor. Can't blame the shroom. Brawling harshes his lustfronds. My cultist Shax never said a word the whole time. She doesn't have a brain, per se, so whenever we go Mi-Go she sits in the corner and draws pictures of horses on her jelly belly. She knew horses from all the times she injected her heroin-reek *anima* down inside some overall-wearing ruralfuck pile of mundflesh. Dunno about horses. They just look like munted goats to me. But I always tell her she's got dag talent.

"Hey, Moloch," said Bifrons as I beat the dark aquatic out of there, "watch out for your sister, iä? I worry. You kids are always seething all the time. Just calm down and wait, like the rest of us. Soon enough our time will come."

"*Our* time?" I gibbered. "Whatever, Biff. I don't even know what that means anymore."

I DON'T REMEMBER whose idea it was. Probably Zuzu. Poor roo had his ichor up and nowhere to spend it. But the dankest shit we ever did always came out of Shax's rotten mind-bucket. It could've been me, even. After all that ungoat business with Bifrons, the featured creature known as Moloch was stone cold sober. And no one can handle R'lyeh at 3 a.m. on a Friday night sober. The streets literally roll up at nine, like slugs shotgunned with salt. You'd kill yourself just to see something interesting go down.

And sometimes, *sometimes*, events just...unfurl. Nobody hungers it, but happenings hunger all on their own. You gibber down the road with your eeries minding your own stench, concentrating extra hard on not getting in trouble, on being an antique boy-thing, a fine, upstanding, mild-mannered unspeakable horror from beneath the skin of reality, and all of the sudden you're standing in front of *His* house, and you don't even know why.

*His* house. The biggest, grandest, dankest, moldiest, blackest house in town. Cthulhu Central Station, a swanky-ass mansion high on the hill, swollen up with damp, falling down from neglect. Apparently Mr. C don't pay his maids too well. All the best for that fat motherfucker, the blue-blood boss man, the Chief Executive Octopus, winner of Most Likely to Rise Up and Devour the World three aeons running, the patrician magician, the insane aristocrat squatting on all our backs, waiting, dreaming, snoring, farting, and scratching his balls in his fulgy *fhtagn* sleep. And he can't even be arsed to tip the help.

We three eeries gawped up at His porch, the columns, the stonework, the yawning height and depth and intellect-shearing ostentation of that naff goth wedding cake of a house. That neighborhood was so eel even Azathoth and Hastur got priced out in the Neolithic Era. We hissed at the flowers. No one but *no one* in R'lyeh could afford a garden—but all around the C-Man's squalor, millions of black lilies and sicksilver roses writhed and runnelled and strangled each other, gibbering up into empty cottages and walk-ups all around the joint, puking out the windows, living rent-free in houses me and mine could only dream of.

A big, blousy fart-bubble belched up from Cthulhu's veiny chimney. Oily colors wriggled on its surface as it rose up through the oceanic ultramarine night. We watched as it burst into a polluted rainbow beneath the black lozenges of ships moving silently through the airy, idiot mundworld.

"Best squamous going, I heard," Shax gurgled. I'd almost forgotten she was there. I'm not much of a cultist when you get right down to it. I know that about myself. I'm trying to work on it.

"Iä, me too, I heard that," Zuzu growled, still stung, pride still snakestomped. "Only you gotta be 100 percent goat. Quiet like a misko in a library. If you disturb the man's slumber, it's bad *fhtagn* news. He's cranky when he first wakes up."

So that's how we ended up on a rickety rooftop huffing Cthulhu's farts. Highly recommended; would huff again. They detonate in your brain pan like the birth of cruel galaxies and come streaming out your nose in globs of black opal blood, electric reeking soulpit slime, and I loved it, I couldn't get enough. Shax turned bright purple and started sobbing like a wee baby slug, Zu slammed his skull against the chimney over and over till he had a dent in his face like a bootprint, and it was the dankest time I ever had or ever will have.

Shax reeled back, her tentacles floating wild uncurled shub-red gorgeous. Her gelatinous body pulsed out-spectrum colors, a ship code I'd never translate.

"Moloch, darling, love of my pythagorean fundament," she moaned, "we gotta ask, we just *gotta* ask, what are they waiting *for?*"

"Who?" Zuzu rasped, wringing his scabby kangaroo tail in his great meatgob hands.

"Come on, eerie," I sighed, spinning in my own personal gassy squamous. "*Them.* The Elder Gods. The Old Ones. The Waiting Dark. *In his house in R'lyeh dead Cthulhu waits dreaming.* This fat fucking octopus right here." I kicked the gambrel roof twice. "Why's it always gotta be about the *Elder* Gods? What the fuck are they waiting *for?*"

Pazuzu thumped his pustulant tail. "The whole system's rigged," he chanted, "by the time we're Elder, there'll be nothing left for us but the ash-end of the universe. We slobber and serve and ain't nobody ever gonna serve us. It's not right. They got it all stitched up nice the way they like it, Yog-Sothoth and Yig and Azazoth and Hypnos and that fat sack of shit down the chimney. Even Mom. Shub-Niggurath herself, I know we love her and all but she spends all day shitting out kids on the dole and fuck me if you and me will ever be able to afford a slavering brood of our own. And then they turn around and call us krugs and layabout shubs when they're the ones who snooze all aeon instead of rending the mortal world like they always promise. It's bullshit, Moloch. Bullshit."

Shax's three eyes shone hideous, thinking of all those mortal streets she shuffled in her precious bloodpuppets. "You don't even know how right you are, Zuzu. The mundworld is totally shoggo, believe me. The best they could do against us is cry while they piss their pants. But the Old Ones? Oh no, they just gorge and giggle and yig themselves and dick around while centuries go by and those mundo fucks up there invent nuclear fission. They got everything dank there was to devour and we get squidshit because they were born at the dawn of existence and we weren't. Because they're *entitled* to the whole damn multiverse while we're entitled to sit on our asses and clap for their crumbs. Why don't they just *fhtagn retire* and let the Young Ones come up the ranks a little? I'd be a bloody yellow queen of everything. Come on, you know it's true! Shax, the All-Devourer, Accursed Meretrix of the Nether Nebulae, Mother of Madness, Flayer of All Things Dun and Shoggo! I'd capture hearts and minds, you better believe. But no, I have to wait, because they *love* waiting, and maybe when I'm a shriveled old cone I'll get to devour one measly asteroid if I ask real nice. *Fuck* that."

Shax rose up to the dark air, the stubby protuberances beneath her pyramid spinning and smoking furious. She screeched down the chimney.

"Do you hear that, Cthulhu, you sleepy motherfucker? I hate you. I hate you so *fhtagn* much."

Then, Shax did something I didn't even know she could do. Maybe it's just a Yith thing. She sucked up a breath, sucked it all the way in, withered down to a dried-up triangular old-cheese-looking turd-chip and dove down the slime-lung chimney into the bowels of the house of Cthulhu.

Zu and me exploded into a real cacoph of *waits* and *wheres* and *whats* and *Shax you fœtid bitches*. We gibbered down the brainspout and busted a dag fulgy stained glass window as quiet as we could so as to crawl in after her. My cultist had re-inflated, re-hydrated, and re-animated in the smack middle of the Great Old One's Great Old Foyer. Seventeen dimensional staircases corkscrewed all around her, mirrors yawned into nations unknown and unknowable, old mail spewed out from the post-slot in the Great Old Door. And all over everything sprawled the mottled sicksilver sapphire obese and pustulant tentacles of dreaming, waiting Cthulhu, bulging out everywhere, rotto mottled vomit-golden bloodless flesh balloons straining out of doors, cabinets, furnace grates, snoring like a siren out of time, sickly blueblack suckers all down his diseased limbs opening and closing shubbily, oozing hallucinogenic acidslime onto his own nice clean floors.

Shax dug one of Nyarlathotep's tomes out of who-knows-where and lit it with an orange beam from her lower eye. She kicked one of the wormy tentacles. It didn't budge.

"Maybe he's dead," Zu whispered.

"You wish," I hissed back. One of Cthulhu's moony eyes fluttered iris-down in the downstairs bathtub. Shax was in full seethe, turning magenta with righteous loathing. "Come on, Shax, enough. Babby, let's go. You don't want this ichor on you. It's too much."

Zuzu held out one crusty hand. "Girl-thing, leave this fat bat be. He's not worth it."

Shax smoked her peace for awhile. Listened to the shriek-flute of the Boss's sleep apnea. The end of Papa Ny's hand-rolled tome flared violet flame in the shadows.

"Fine," she said finally. "Whatever."

Mr. Moloch has never done anything so tough in his dun life as getting that granite slab door open without a creak. Mr. Moloch sweat sour green in the dark. And Mr. Moloch, when he got it open, stared across the veranda of the demon of the ultradeep into the crystalline snake-mug of his own sister Shit sidewinding up the stairs.

"I followed you," hissed Shit before I could pull a repeat of my 9 p.m. performance of the *What Are You Doing Here* jive. "It wasn't hard. You're very loud." Shit quick-kissed my face with the prongs of her tongue. "I do love you, Moloch. I try to look out for your dun ass."

Shit took in the scene. Her many livers and spleens and lungs and stomachs and hearts pulsed wetly in her cellophane skin. She gawped Zuzu, winking guilty side-eye at her because back at Bifrons's pad he'd tried to say he hungered her all casual but it was true and she shut that shit down. She gawped Shax, still flushing squamous magenta fury, plasmic pores still full of iridescent ancient fart-gas, sucking on her tome-butt. She gawped me, mutant goatsnake of the hour, just hungering to bolt back to the couch and sleep and another dun day in R'lyeh. But most of all, she gawped that effulgy fucking house, the columns and staircases and mirrors and curtains and beautiful foetid dank things she'd never have no matter how hard she glooned for the big boys, no matter how antique and eldritch she slavered for them, no matter how many eternities she devoted to their worship and their plans and their secretarial needs. And she gawped the lazyfuck octocunt flop of the squid sensation of every nation, the great pharaonic secret she had never been allowed to behold, even at the office holiday party. And the Great Ancient One, bulging out of every orifice in that grand house we'd never be able to buy if we outlived Saturn, was as disappointing as our own mother, useless and wrinkled and old and shoggo as shit.

Her serpent face crunkled and cracked.

Her organs twisted and boiled inside her. She hungered. Maybe she'd always hungered more than me, and I just don't know anything about anything. I sure as sheol didn't call what happened next.

My babby sister put her eyes on Shax.

"Burn it down," Shit said. "Burn it all down."

Shax grinned. Her pyramid slit itself almost in half to grin that wide. The Yith floated out the Great Old Door and flicked her smoldering tome behind her. It landed in a puddle of Cthulhu's dreamsick spittle.

And the whole place went up behind her like the Big *fhtagn* Bang.

Unto the utter end of time and existence, it was the dankest thing I will ever see.

---

BE ME: MOLOCH! Eldritch as they come, antique as a goddamned china set, maximum yellow fellow! Only five thousand years old, practically fresh-baked, belly full of san and gas and mushroom chemtrails, tentacles a smoking hot mess, fur the opposite of goat. Gawping on the sidewalk at the big ultraviolet hellcloud of Cthulhu's fancy fucking house burning at the bottom of the sea.

For a minute, I gotta tell you, it felt fucking eldritch, my eeries. I could smell barbecuing god and it smelled like the future. A real future. *Our* future, a future Young and not Elder.

Then the shriek started.

It gibbered up from the cellar and out of the chimney and then everywhere at once. And the shriek had a color. It had a weight. It had shape inside the smoke and flame. The shriek shattered into shards flying up into the sea, out into the city, slicing through reality like sewing scissors. Shax and Shit and Zu and me fell to our knees, assorted mitts over our hear-holes, ready to babble for forgiveness, mercy clemency, all those fulgy words.

Then it stopped. Cool black water flowed down through the transdimensional doily separating us from the sea, down and through and over the Great Old House, drowning out the fire, the smoke, the shriek, everything, everything, smoothing it back the way it was, like nothing ever went down in there, like fire never even got itself invented in the vicinity.

In his house at R'lyeh, dead Cthulhu rolled over on his giant flabby cosmic belly. The last of the flames turned his infinitely-chambered lardheart as orange as a rotting pumpkin, as gold as the world we'll never inherit, as soft and corrupt as the first moldering peach of original sin. In his dreaming, the Old One spluttered, groaned, cried out for some mundforsaken mother I cannot believe ever truly existed, and went back to sleep.

But the shards, my eeries, the shards of that antediluvian shriek were still going, shredding through the dimensional dome of our sky, bobbing up into the galleon-clotted mundsea like insane islands. Me and my brood didn't know it was gonna happen. Believe me that if you believe anything. Everything that happened after that moment, topside and bottom, well, iä, iä, it's our fault, sure, whatever, but all we ever meant to do was forget how garbage R'lyeh really is for one *fhtagn* night. Everybody deserves that, don't they? Once in awhile?

I mean, maybe, just maybe, all that time, Cthulhu was waiting for *us*.

Two of the black ship-blobs tottered squamous up there in the far reaches of the mundworld. Tottered, gibbered, fell. Plummeted down through the fathoms of the fathoms toward R'lyeh, toward us, me and my Shax and my sister and my scabby sweetheart brother, delinquents junking up the gated community. As the wrecks rocketed toward the plane of me and mine in a champagne apocalypse of ultradeep bubbles, I gawped the names on the sides of the kruggy hulls. Just before they crashed our interdimensional undersea party for good, I got their names graffitied on my venomy heart.

The *Alert* and the *Emma*.

What fucking dun names, honestly. Mundflesh's got no sense of style. Shax hid her face in my shoulder. Shit flared her crystal hood so no one would recognize her and shamble-slithered off down an alley 'cause she wasn't gonna take on a speck of shame no matter what. Pazuzu stood fast, though. He squeezed my hand.

"What are you gonna say," Shax whispered, "when our spawn asks where you were the night the humans landed?"

We watched the ships fall down to us like black, uncertain rain.

Oh, well. There goes the neighborhood.

# The Shoot-Out at Burnt Corn Ranch Over the Bride of the World

**The End**

I DON'T KNOW MUCH ABOUT THE beginning, but in the end it was just the Wizard of Los Angeles and the Wizard of New York and the shoot-out at the Burnt Corn Ranch. They walked off their paces; the moon seconded New York and the sun backed up Los Angeles and I saw how it all went down because I was there, hiding under the bar in the Gnaw Hollow Saloon with my fist between my teeth. Now you may call me a coward and I'll have to wear that, but I'm a coward who lived, and that's worth a drink if it's worth two.

**Robert and Pauline**

NOW, AS I recollect it, the Wizard of Los Angeles sold his name for a pair of Chinese pistols, a horse the color of a rung bell and a crate of scotch the likes of which, god willing and the dead don't rise, you and I will never taste. I hear that scotch has no label. I hear it tastes like a burning heart. I hear it's served at the Devil's own table, distilled by Judas Iscariot and aged in a black bull's skull.

The Wizard of New York traded her name for a train she could fit in her pocket, a horse with two hearts, a dress like the fall of Lucifer, and a satchel of tobacco combed out of Hades's own fields, dried on a rack of giant's bones. New York was always the better haggler, and that's a deal you only get to make once.

You gotta do something about names, see. Gotta get rid of them, double fast. Can't get too far in the game with a name someone could just *call* you, out in the open, like Robert or Pauline. People like that, you can find them on a map. You can book them tickets and put a tax on them. Robert and Pauline couldn't of done what those two did. Robert and Pauline have a nice little spread out Montana way. Pauline's butter is just the sweetest you ever had. Robert never breaks his word, that's just the kind of guy he is.

Come on. That ain't how it runs. The Wizard of New York don't churn her own cream.

Anyway, at least they both got horses out of it.

## A Coupla Rules

YOU MIGHTA HEARD it said that New York is where they make good magic and Los Angeles is where they make bad magic. Well, I don't know about that. I never been to either place. What I want to say is there's no one to root for here, okay? Those two chose to play the game. They didn't have to. They could of had babies and grown oranges or beets or whatever the hell people grow when they aren't circling a scrap of black dirt in the middle of nowhere like they've got a clock for a heart, set two minutes til. You might be tempted to say well, New York is cold and hard and I don't care for that in a woman, or you might say Los Angeles is all illusions and unreal bullshit, and I don't care for that in anyone, but the Burnt Corn Ranch don't care about your sniffing and side-choosing, and it don't care about nobody else either. It's always been there, and it'll be there when whatever walking hamburger is left clears out.

# The Shoot-Out at Burnt Corn Ranch Over the Bride of the World

There's a coupla rules.

Everybody's gotta have a second. That's good sense—the kind of arsenal these kids bring with them is music for four and six hands, if you get me. They hafta agree on a judge, too. Cheating don't come into it.

It's not always New York and Los Angeles. This has been going on awhile. This bit here is just the endgame, where the board is mostly clear, and every piece who mighta hid you has got itself killed or sacrificed and every move comes naked and grave. I remember when the Witch of the Mississippi shot the Baron of Nebraska in the eye with a glass flintlock she got off the corpse of a drifter with a diamond in his tooth. Probably somebody's second, poor fuck. When she fired the thing, it filled up full of hot green fire. Smelled like licorice. Weren't even a year ago New York hunted down the Hag of Florida, cut her up with a bowie knife blessed by the Pope of the Hudson, baptized in gin and olives and christened What Did I Just Say.

Fed Florida to her alligator friends piece by piece. They cried, but they ate her anyway.

There's different sorts of ways to get rank in this business. New York has to be born there, and Brooklyn and Queens don't count, neither. If I remember it correct, she has to be born there, and her mother dead in childbirth, foot can't have touched grass nor mud, hand can't have sewn nothing nor cooked nothing, and she can't ever have finished a novel, but she's got to have started three. No more, no less. Los Angeles has to come from somewhere else. He's gotta be in pictures, naturally, but never a lead, only in the background, at best maybe a line or two. His daddy's got to have died while his momma was with child, he can't ever of et Old World fruit, can'tve been baptized nor shriven, foot can't have touched the sea, hand can't have touched the color red.

The rules look stupid on purpose. That's how folklore works, on a fool's own engine.

Still, sometimes there's more than one bastard stumbled into the conditionals, and then there's what you might call attractions to shuffle it down. New York wants to be a woman. The Bishop of Wisconsin wants to be a little boy with black hair. That sort of thing.

Motion across the board goes from the edges toward the center. Used to be a rule about collateral damage, but that seems beside the point now. Hardly anybody left here but us chickens.

And then there's the prize. Didn't I mention? That's me. Hunkered down behind a bar with bourbon showering down on my hair and glass exploding in slow-motion.

I'm the Bride.

### The Devil's Mare

I SUPPOSE YOU want to know how it got to this. Truth is I don't know. I wasn't born til the players were on the stage. That's kind of the point of me. I was born at Burnt Corn Ranch on the summer solstice and I came out of a pinto mare just as human as you like. Maybe you don't like too much, and that'd be about right. Back then Burnt Corn were run by Tincup Henry and his girl name of Ashen. When she was a skinny little cough of a thing her mother said she whored with the Devil and ate of the bread of Dagon. She locked that girl in the barn with the new lambs and lit the whole thing on fire. Possible she knew what was coming, possible she was crazy. Ashen's eyelashes and eyebrows and all her hair burnt off before her brother Cutter (who happened to be the Duke of Maine, but he didn't know it yet) run out in all the stink of burning wool and beat the flames off with his own hands.

Ashen probably had a name before her skin went grey like that. Probably a nice, fancy one like farmers give their daughters when they hope for better days. But dead girls get new names, and Ashen just wasn't the same before she went into that barn as when she came out. And it ain't just about her being bald and hairless as a worm forever. Her momma run off and her daddy drunk himself into nothing. But when Tincup married her, well, you never saw anything like that wedding table. Loaves of bread like wheels on a cart and a cake like a house of sugar. Ashen didn't say nothing.

And that's who raised me up. No idea what they thought when that mare lay down to foal. But they named her Almagest, so maybe they knew the score after all. When they pulled me out of her nethers, Tincup scratched his head and picked me up, full grown and covered in horse. He put me in the house by the stove like any other foal born sickly.

Day I was born Ashen started baking. Every day of my life smelled like something rising.

### He Loves Me, He Loves Me Not

MET AN OLD prospector once, by the name of Gilly Spur. She lived down the gulch, panning for prophecies in the dried up wrinkled scrub that usedta be the Colorado River. Caught a rack of runes once, all fishbone scorched with hairline scratches. For all the good it ever did her. The Khan of Manitoba cut off her hand to get them, and took off south after the Witch of the Rio Grande. Anyway, once upon a while I liked to sit with Gilly afternoons in the summer, when it was so hot the only safe places were down in the low, down in the shadows, down in the crevices where the dust don't fall. She caught butterflies to eat, and you know I never thought a butterfly'd have eating on 'em, but the big, warped-looking busters huffing heavy on the old river bed weren't nothing but flying protein, and protein is king. Gilly Spur snatched them out of the air in a mason jar.

"Tell me who I'm gonna marry, Gilly," I'd say to her while she crunched down on a monarch wing. "I heard girls before used to pull daisy petals to find out. Think that'd work for me?"

"Don't you be in such a hurry, girl. The rest of us ain't done here yet. And where you think you're gonna spy up a daisy?"

"Do you remember before? Before there were a mess of wizards and popes shooting up the place, I mean."

"Ayup," would say Gilly Spur. And she'd tell me about something like bubble gum, which was a thing you chewed in your mouth but didn't swallow what had sugar in it. People used to be mad as cats, chewing on something and not eating it. Or she'd say there used to be an ocean left of California, which was so much water you couldn't see the other side, and why the world didn't just drink up so much of the good stuff just sitting there I'll never understand. I'm glad I wasn't born then. It sounds a terrible place.

Gilly Spur'd scry the sand like it was still water. Far as I know she weren't in the game then or never. But she was nice to me, and she knew how to hide real good. Best thing to learn these days, but I never got the trick of it.

### Mr. Junction City Savings

THIS IS WHAT the Wizard of New York did with her name. She put it inside an angry boy name of Johnny Holler, then killed a red-tailed deer out on the Connecticut saltwaste using Johnny just like a rifle. Took the dried-out hollowed heart of the beast and the name too and locked them up in the Junction City Savings and Loan vault, and gathered her goods-in-kind from the Loan Officer—a saggy droop of a man who used to be fat and lost it somehow, just lost track of his whole body til it was nearly gone and just a big blouse of skin left. He's the line judge, the referee, the fact checker and the clock-watcher. Don't know his name. Don't even know if he knows it. He's just the Loan Officer, Mr. Junction City Savings, only man I ever met who still owns a three-piece suit and a tie to match his hanky.

Mr. Junction City Savings put Johnny Holler down in his book as New York's second. Johnny said: *I never asked.* But it don't matter. New York takes. New York brooks no refusing.

From just about then Johnny Holler started getting brighter. Sure, smarter—you can't get clued in on the big game without sharpening up a bit. But he started glowin' like a lamp turned on inside

# The Shoot-Out at Burnt Corn Ranch Over the Bride of the World

him, and all the time they walked out to Missouri to see about the Caliph of St. Louis he just kept shining brighter still. By the time I met him, you couldn't look at him without squinting. His bandoliers screaming silver just like the moon.

Los Angeles nailed down his second up Oregon way. A minor player, Princess of the Siskyous or something, lanky tall white girl answering to Sally Rue. The Wizard of Los Angeles pricked up when she started making her name, strapped up his big snort of a horse and rode it all the way from Alamagordo where he'd fucked and then detonated the brain-stem of Abbot of New Mexico with a one lightning kiss.

Come on now. Don't make a face. I told you it wasn't a pretty thing, when these kids count off their paces. Anyway, Los Angeles sniffed up the Princess just as soon as he crossed the Tahoe naphtha sink, smelled her like musk and cattle. Rode on north like an arrow. Put a blade between his teeth and hit the big empty college green where the Princess was sitting down to cards with her sad little second, boy by the name of Frank Bust. Los Angeles sat himself on the grass and played a hand or two, not winning nothing and not looking to, just taking a friendly trick when he could. When the sun got low he spat his black knife just as quiet as breathing, right between Frank Bust's eyes. Kid didn't see it coming to say shit, just gogged while Los Angeles brushed the hair out of the Princess's Frank-spattered face and kissed both the her cheeks, said something in Algonquin or Greek or some such and pulled on her jaw like a trigger. Nothing came out—she was saving the bullet down in the deep of her for the end, and that made her Los Angeles's kind of girl. He hauled her out to Junction City quick as a wedding.

She was already looking a little god around the edges. Her teeth shone like hard sunshine.

## Somethings

SOMETHING BAD HAPPENED a long time ago. In the bubblegum daisygirl ocean days, when there were rivers where the rivers are.

I'd like to know about it, much as you, much as anyone. Seems like a worthy thing to know. But I don't make what you'd call a real effort to find out. I got my own problems. My own somethings bad. For awhile I thought it had to be a bomb. Something big and bright and final. They used to have bombs like that. That left black dust even after they'd stopped burning everybody up, and something else, something invisible, something that changed you if it touched you. Sounded right to me.

And the dust that comes down in the summer will burn you clean through.

But apart than Gilly Spur the oldest soul I know is Blue Bob who lives at the top of a grain silo sharpening scissors for bread, and he said he never saw nothing blow up but what does he know, he never lived in a city that mattered enough to bomb. He says the mail stopped one day. Then the running water and a little after that you started noticing people'd gone missing. Just gone, blinked off like a fuse. He'd taken the last of his gas and headed to Cheyenne and got drunk for weeks off of the stuff lying around with no one to guard it. Blue Bob says he's not really sorry. He likes the quiet.

He's the Emperor of Wyoming. Told me once, half upside-down in a bottle of mash. It's not that he can't fight, he just doesn't care. Doesn't like the world enough to care. Blue Bob kissed me all over then, and I kissed him back even though he was so old you could see through him. I like kissing. Kisses are big and bright and final. Just because I'm writ down for the Burnt Corn Ranch doesn't mean I gotta be a virgin when I get there. Can't see no point in virginity myself. I'm not gonna live so long I should wait on much of anything.

Here's what I think, though, at the end of everything behind the bar with the bourbon and the dog and the commotion outside.

I think the world just broke.

Nobody's fault. Things get old. They go funny. They get stuck like a pump or run backwards like a pocketwatch. You just try and

# The Shoot-Out at Burnt Corn Ranch Over the Bride of the World

use an old pistol that ain't been looked after. It might click and whine and stick. It might blow you clean dead.

⁓

GILLY SPUR SAYS there didn't used to be magic. That's nice. I like to think the world had a childhood. A little while when it didn't have to bother with none of this.

### A Ring Don't Make a Bride

I SAW ME a picture with Los Angeles in it once. When pictures still showed down at the piano hall on Main Street. I used to like to get up in a dress and watch all those fine people flickerin' up there. It was an old one, and Los Angeles hunkered down in the background of some bar, glowering into his two fingers of whathaveyou, up to no good. When the fighting started, he shot a lady of low morals through the heart, and looked at the camera like he knew I'd be watching in twenty years' time. Funny thing is, I knew the shot lady, too.

She was the Pharaoh of Nevada.

New York shot her for real and true in our barn about a year before she got to Florida. Used a big birch fork and divined the Pharaoh's path like clean water. New York took the train she got from the Savings and Loan out of her pocket and laid it down on the yellowcake flats where it swelled up like one of them old black worm firecrackers. Rode it all the way through the plains without a stop, even though the Tsar of Kansas was an easy get. She couldn't wait.

The Pharaoh didn't like waiting either. She turned up at my window in the middle of the night. Brought me beef and cotton lace and a real lily, so fresh the stem still seeped green. Came to me like a proper suitor, offering something precious, asking something precious. I sucked the dew out of the lily and it tasted like growing up. The Pharaoh of Nevada lay down next to me in my skinny bed and kept real quiet so as not to wake Henry Tincup and Ashen. She was a real handsome lady, with red hair and wide black eyes, heavy, soft breasts and sharp brass-tipped bullets all round her bony waist.

*Come on*, she whispered in the dark. *Don't you like me? You don't want to sit around here waiting for those rotters to punch themselves sick over you. I'm here, now, and I'm ever so much nicer than the pack of them. I made that blossom myself out of the air and half a memory. I'll cover you with lilies. Eat up that brisket and tell me it don't taste right as a spring robin.*

The Pharaoh of Nevada liked kissing almost as much as I do. Her skin was all dusty and hot and sour and good. She was right; I did like her. She was much prettier than Blue Bob, and when she got her hands inside me I saw lights dancing and lilies bursting and the sun bagged up in a sack of lace. The Pharaoh put a steel ring on my finger still slippery with her and slept like a heap of bones.

Thing is, just because you make a body shiver don't make it yours. You have to go through the ceremony and bother and blood. I'm the end of everything. There's no shortcut. The Pharaoh thought it was all over and won right up until the Wizard of New York steamed into town with her whistle shrieking the blues, shattering the windows and rattling the earth.

*Too late*, Nevada laughed.

But it wasn't. New York walked into the barn where I was born with a big bone gun on her hip, a barrel half as long as her leg. Used to be the femur of the Marquis of New Orleans and the shoulder blade of the Obeah of the Carolinas. It's that kind of style that makes her a favorite, among those still taking bets. New York's right dapper and swish. Nevada strode out of my bed all gloat but New York shot her through the throat from behind our cow Ptolemy, and my Pharaoh fell flat before she could work out where she'd gone wrong.

A ring don't make a bride, that's all.

New York tipped her hat to me. Said: *See you soon*. Barreled off out of town to keep her date with Kansas.

# The Shoot-Out at Burnt Corn Ranch Over the Bride of the World

SOMETIMES AT NIGHT I can still hear Nevada telling me stories about the one time in her whole life that girl ever saw Las Vegas.

### The Duke of Maine

I ASKED CUTTER once what it felt like, when he got called up. Him being my uncle in a technical sort of way and all I felt familiar enough to ask.

Cutter took care of the Gnaw Hollow back then, looking after the stores and the glasses and the spirits. He poured himself some thin old cough syrup which is just about as good as whiskey for getting yourself fuzzy, if not tasting half so nice.

"I was born in Maine, don't s'pose you know that being just a kid," he told me. "That's part of it. No Duke of Maine could be from away. Born there and our ma moved us out west when she were half-done baking Ashen in her on account of pa Henry finding some knob of earth where things still grew. Spoke a coupla licks of French back then, and that's part of it too. But if you're hoping I got struck by lightning I'll disappoint you. Just woke up one morning and knew it like I knew my name. Down in my heart a big dark forest on a big bright sea just lay there saying: *come on now, do right by me*. I looked at you feeding the chickens and all the sudden you had a veil on I never saw before, and a dress of darkness. I could do things. Drown a man while he's walking down the street breathing as fine as you like. Strike a stone and milk'd pour out. The forest in my heart said the Sultan of the Dakotas wanted killing, and I strangled him in the Black Hills. His skull turned into a rose. I wore it on my lapel. It told me things. That you'd lay down with me if I asked because the Bride is the generosity of the earth. When the frost'd passed and I could get on planting my mean old turnips. Where to find the Presbyter of Oklahoma—who has the blame of my lost leg, bristled fucking pig that he was."

Cutter slugged back his cough syrup. "I won't be your man, I know it. Didn't even bother cutting off my name. I'm a hump for others to get over. But I hope to see Maine again before some other dark dog does me in."

The Laird of Alaska froze him to death with a blink a couple of weeks later. I didn't cry. You can't get mixed up in crying this late in the game.

### Some Magic

I GOT SOME magic of my own.

I can turn a chicken inside out. I can make the moon come on in the daytime. I can fry an egg on my belly and I can defend myself—if I look at you funny your heart will split open in your chest. I tried it on the Kaiser of Pittsburgh who wasn't half as nice as Nevada and didn't bring me a damn thing and he toppled right over.

I didn't wake up one morning knowing I was anything. I just always knew. Like how you know you're a girl or that you have ten fingers. It's just a part of you, and you can't say why. After she put her ring on me the Pharaoh said: *what happens now?* I shrugged. I made the moon come on in the dawn for her.

We're getting close now. To whatever is supposed to happen when I get a beau for true. I can feel the world winding down to Burnt Corn as if I'm a spring in it, losing my coils. Sometimes I wonder if this is going on in Europe or Africa too. If some poor kid like me is waiting in Budapest or something for the Tetrarch of Granada and the Wizard of London to get on with business. But something tells me I'm it. Besides, the Dragoon of Boston has to be Ireland-born, and she's never said a thing about where she came from but that it was emptier than a gallon jar in the morning.

I spent a lot of years thinking on this. I think I know the shape of it and every day I feel surer. Where Cutter had a forest in the deep of him I've got a bed and it's getting wider all the time.

Still. You don't show your cards til they're called.

# The Shoot-Out at Burnt Corn Ranch Over the Bride of the World

### The Nighthole

GILLY SPUR SAYS: *the day the world changed the sky went green and sick.* She says: *it didn't have a lick on the look of the sky this morning.*

Someone comes to town. They got shadows like wounds. One on a train, one on a horse. Ashen sets them a good breakfast and they talk like nothing's gonna happen. Like they're friends.

*I wish I'da seen the Grand Canyon. After all this running around, you'd think I'da come across it. But no, you stove in the Saint and it closed up like a buttonhole.* The Wizard of Los Angeles shovels hot eggs into his mouth.

*But you got the Rockies,* the Wizard of New York laughs over her chicory tea. *All six foot five of that sweet old Thaumaturge. I heard him go all the way out in Virginia. I heard you filled him up with pink fire and made rubies shoot out of his eyes.*

*Too bad we can't jaw all day. I could get to like you.*

*Too bad.*

Johnny Holler and Sally Rue water the mounts, a bowl of blood or a gascan full of coaldust, either way, hardly matters which gets which. They're each glowing so bright they can't even look at each other, silver and gold as the moon and the sun, before the moon went black and the sun went white.

And me? Well, I hide. Gilly taught me good and I go down under the bar at the Gnaw Hollow Saloon when the Loan Officer comes striding into town with contracts in his belt. *Everyone understands and consents to the action at hand, no arguments once the outcome is clear, yes, yes? Speak up, too late to be shy, what are the agreed-upon weapons? Guns, Blood, Poison, Time. Game, Set, Match. Sign on the dotted line, witnessed by Mr. Holler and Ms. Rue, and get me a bourbon, will you Johnny? That's a good boy.*

They walk it off. Their seconds open long blackwood cases and in them are the Chinese pistols, the long bone gun. There's no sound in Burnt Corn but dust holding its breath. The clock tower bongs out the end of everything. I have time to be afraid before the first shot. I have time to consider I haven't a notion about what I'll do when it's over. What I'm for. And then the New York's femur-barrel blows its warm welcome, and a violet venomous ropy dripping *something* roars out and catches Miss Sally Rue in the glowing golden eyeball and puts her out as fast as hiccuping. Advantage New York.

It goes like a battle goes. *Boomboomquiet. Clickbanghush.* Los Angeles fires with both pistols, and a thousand sparrows stream out into a patch of starry night floating between them with the day just as fine as paint all around it. New York opens her mouth, wider, wider, until her jaw hits the dust and she can swallow the birds in one hitching breath. But one brown songbird, dragging six stars out of the nighthole behind it, claws through Johnny Holler's chest and burns out his heart. One-one.

It's like that, when Wizards fight. Half the time it looks like fighting and half the time it looks like theater, like an awful old puppet show, the paint peeling on the marionettes and the backdrop peeling, but the strings go jerking on. It's happening and I can't do anything, the bottles burst above me and the glass rain in my hair drifts infinitely slow, caught in a slow burp of time New York let sour up out of her palm. I squeeze my eyes; the Loan Officer gets a stream of liquid light to the eye and goes down heavy. The light goes dim in the sky like a picture house at intermission. Time to find your seats. The real show's about to begin.

## And Then

IT'S OVER.

The glass hits my scalp. I taste scotch and blood and old, old wine.

There's a hand on mine in the dark. I don't know if it's New York or Los Angeles. I guess it's the Groom, whoever that turned out to be. I think about Gilly Spur and the daisies. I think about Nevada and her kisses. I think about Blue Bob, about Ashen and Cutter and the smell of the wind through Burnt Corn Ranch. I can hear my beau

## The Shoot-Out at Burnt Corn Ranch Over the Bride of the World

breathing; I can smell the magic on somebody's breath. There ain't nothing in the world but the world, running funny, running down, winding up, busting its springs and looking for its repair manual.

It's black. Burnt Corn is gone and so is Gnaw Hollow. There's a veil of glass and dripping booze over my eyes, and the Groom lifts it up. I know when she kisses me it's the Wizard of New York, and when she kisses me she swallows me whole like she swallowed the sparrows. I'm a seed, I'm a wedded ring. I see the insides of her, and they are vast.

You need two. If you're going to start over. You need a seed and a dark place.

EVERYTHING HAPPENS AT once.

# No One Dies in Nowhere

### First Terrace: The Late Repentant

*T*HERE IS A CLICKING SOUND *before she appears, like a gas stove before it lights. One moment there is nothing, the next there is Pietta, though this is the last gasp of before/after causality in her pure, pale mind. Now that she is here, she will always have been here. Charcoal-blue rags twist and braid and drape around her body more artfully than any gown. A leather falcon's hood closes up her head but does not blind her; the eyecups are a fine bronze mesh that lets in light. Long jessies hang from her thin wrists. This room which she has never seen belongs to her as utterly as her eyes: a monk's cell, modest but perfect and graceful. Candles thick as calf-bones. Water in a black basin. A copper rain barrel, empty. She runs her hand along the smooth, wine-dark stone of her walls; her fingertips leave phosphor-prints. She lays down on her bed, a shelf for holding Piettas carved out of the rock, mattressed in straw and withered, thorny wildflowers that smell of the village where she was born. From the straw, she can look out of three slim glassless windows shaped like chess bishops. A grey, damp sky steals in, a burgling fog climbing up toward her, a hundred million kinds of grey swirling together, and the stars behind, waiting. Pietta remembers the feeling* of the first day of school. She goes to the window and looks out, looks down. Her long hair hangs over the ledge like two thick vines. Black, seedless earth below, dizzyingly far. As close as spying neighbors across a shared alley, a sheer, knife-cragged mountain stretches up into the dimming clouds and disappears into oncoming night. The mountain crawls with people. Each carries a black lantern half as tall as they. A man with a short, lovely beard chokes on the smoke puking forth from his light, but even as he chokes he holds it closer to his mouth, desperate to get more. Their eyes meet. Pietta holds up her hand in greeting. He opens his jaw far wider than any bone allows and takes long, sultry bites out of the smoke.

When she turns away, a bindle lies on her bed of stone and straw. A plain handkerchief knotted around a long, burled black branch. She looses the cloth. Inside she finds a wine bottle, a pair of scissors, a stone figure of a straight-backed child in a chair, a brass key, a cracked, worn belt with two holes torn through, and a hundred shattered shards of colored glass. Pietta picks up one of the blades of glass and holds it to her breast until it slices through her skin. The glass is violet. The blood never comes.

### Second Terrace: The Proud

ON AN ENDLESS plain where nothing grows lie a mountain as crowded as a city and a city as vast as a mountain. They face one another like bride and bridegroom. The city was enclosed at the commencement of linear time, a great ancient abbey bristling with domes, towers, spires, and stoas, chiseled out of rock the color of wine spilled on the surface of Mars, doorless, but not windowless, never windowless, candlelight twinkling from millions upon millions of arched and tapered clefts in the stone. From every one of these, you can see the mountain clearly, the people moving upon it, their lamps swinging back and forth, their hurryings and their stillnesses. The whispered talk of the people on the mountain can always be heard in the cloisters of the city, as though there is not a mile of churning black mud between the woman emptying her rain barrel after a storm and the ragged man murmuring on the windy crags. A road connects the mountain and the city, lit by blue gas lamps, cobbled by giants. No one has ever seen a person walk that road, though they must, or else what could be its purpose?

The clouded, pregnant sky swallows the peak of the mountain but declines the heights of the city. When there are stars, they are not our stars. They are not even white, but red as watch-fires.

In the city, which is called Nowhere, a man with the head of a heron sat comfortably in the topmost room of the policemen's tower, working on his novel.

It was slow going.

He supposed had everything he needed—a hurricane lamp full of oil, a stone cup full of dry red wine, a belly full of hot buttered toast, a typewriter confiscated from a poor soul he'd caught sledgehammering *Fuck This Place* onto the north stairwell of the Callabrius Quarter, a ream of fresh, bright paper filched from the records office. It was a quiet night in Nowhere. The criminal element, such as it was, seemed content to sleep the cold stars away until morning, leaving Detective Belacqua in peace.

He tried typing: *It was a quiet night in Nowhere,* then, disgusted with himself, abandoned his desk with a flamboyant despair no one could see to appreciate, and stared gloomily out the long, slender stone window onto the mud plain far below. A moonless spring blackness slept on the fields outside the walled city. It was always spring in Nowhere. But there were no cherry blossoms, no daffodils or new hens, only the cold dark mud of snow just melted, the trees stripped naked, bare arms flung up pleading for the sun, the smell of green but not the green itself. Every day was the day before the first crocus breaks the skull of earth, the held breath before beginning can begin. Always March, never May.

Detective Belacqua had several strikes against him as a budding author. For one thing, he had very little conception of time, an essential element in organizing narrative. He was, after all, mostly infinite. He barely remembered his childhood, if he could be said to have had one at all, but he remembered the incandescent naphtha-splatter of the birth of the universe pretty well. What order things happened in and why wasn't his business. He didn't pry. And this was another problem, for Detective Belacqua had not, in all his long tenure in the walled city, felt the urge to question any aspect of his existence. Such restlessness was not marked out on the map of a strigil's heart the way it was scribbled on every inch of the maps of men. Belacqua enjoyed his slow progress through each day and night. He enjoyed hot buttered toast and dry red wine. He enjoyed his job, felt himself to be necessary in a way as profound as food to a body. Someone had to keep order in this orderless place. Someone had to give Nowhere its shape and its self. His world was a simple equation: if crime, then punishment. It didn't matter at all why or how a criminal did his work, only that he had done it. And because he never bothered with the rest, Detective Belacqua was a hopeless novelist, for he had no clear idea of what drove anyone to do much of anything except be a policeman and bear lightly the granite weight of an unmovable cosmos. The actions of others were baffling and mostly unpleasant. He had never moved in the moral coil of clanging and conflicting wills. All he had ever known was Nowhere, and by the time Nowhere happened to a person, they had already made all the choices that mattered.

Yet Detective Belacqua longed to write with every part of his unmeasurable psyche. He had been a happy man before he discovered books. Very occasionally, people brought them to Nowhere in their sad little bindles. The first time Belacqua saw one, during a quickly opened, quickly shut case of petty theft in the Castitas District, he had confiscated it and crouched for hours in a vestibule, transfixed, as he read the crumbling paperback, the very hows and whys Belacqua had never understood. But it was not enough to read. Belacqua wanted more. There were no strigils in any of the books men brought to Nowhere. No one like him. The men had men-heads and men-desires and the women had women-heads and women-ambitions and nowhere could his heron-soul find a sympathetic mirror. And so he tried and tried and at best he plonked out *It was a quiet night in Nowhere* on the back of a blank incident report. He felt deeply ashamed of his desires and told no one. None of his comrades could hope to understand.

But it was, indeed, a quiet night in Nowhere. But a night was not a book.

"Make something happen, you blistered fool," Detective Belacqua grumbled to himself.

*A knock comes upon the door.*

Rubbish.

Detective Belacqua pushed back from his desk, his belly perhaps slightly less righteously muscled than it had been when the primordium was new. He wrapped a long scarf the color of cigarette ash around his feathered throat, snatched his black duster from the hook near the door, and abandoned his post—only for a moment—in search of something more fortifying than buttered toast to fuel his furtive ambitions.

He had hardly left the tower when the alarm lamps began to burn.

### Third Terrace: The Envious

*SIXTY-SIX DAYS LATER, Pietta steps out of her room for the first time. No one has come for her. She has heard no footsteps in the long hall beyond her door. But a kind of rootless fear like thin pale mold forked slowly through her limbs and she could not bring herself to move.*

*She measures out the time in bears and glass. Each morning, Pietta places a shard of colored glass on her windowsill. They split the candlelight into harlequin grapeshot, firing volleys of scarlet, cobalt, emerald toward the mountain outside. She has developed* a kind of semaphore with the smoke-eaters on those icy slopes; at least, when she moves her arms, they move theirs. But perhaps Pietta is the only one who imagines an alphabet.

Each evening, she watches the bears come in across the mud plain and snuggle against the city for warmth. She does not know where they come in from, only that they do, hundreds of them, and that they are not very like the bears she remembers, though the act of remembering now is like reading a Greek manuscript—slow, laborious, full of transcription errors, clarity coming late and seldom. It is possible bears have always looked like the beasts who rub their enormous flanks against the pockmarked burgundy stone of the city walls as the red stars hiss up in the dusk. But Pietta does not think bears ever had such long stone-silver fur, or that they wore that fur in braids, or that they had a circlet of so many eyes round their heads, or that they had tusks quite so inlaid with gold.

So passes sixty-six days. Glass. Arms. Smoke. Bears.

She gathers together her only belongings and secrets them in the slits and knots of her clothes. Beyond the door of the room belonging to Pietta she finds a hall that splits like a vein into a snarl of staircases. Will she be able to find her way back? The fearful mold begins to grow again, but she stifles it. Burns it out. Descends a black iron spiral stair down, down, to another hall, under an arch into which some skilled hand has carved PENURIA, under which some rather less skilled hand has painted FOR A GOOD TIME FIND BEATRICE. Pietta looks back in the direction she has come. The other side of the stone arch reads TAEDIUM. She will try to remember that she lives in Taedium. Pietta passes beneath Contemptus Mundi and Beatrice's come-hither into a courtyard under the open sky.

The courtyard thrums with people and forbidding candles standing as tall and thick as fir trees, barked in the globs and drips and wind-spatters of their yellow wax. There is a stone bowl near the yawning edge of the terrace, filled with burnt knobs of ancient wood and volcanic rock. People like her move between the tallow *monoliths and the stone bowl, wrapped tight in complex charcoal-blue rags and falcon-hoods, but not like her, for they chatter together as though they belong here, as though the* hereness of here *is no surprise to them. They huddle around beaten copper rain barrels, looking up anxiously at the spinning scarlet stars. They pass objects furtively from one hand to the next. They stare out at the constant vastness of the mountain pricked with lantern light before plunging their hands into the bowl and devouring the charred and ashen joints of wood.*

Pietta is noticed. A middle-aged man with an unusual nose and arthritic hands pulls her urgently behind one of the cathedral-column candles. She can see blue eyes beneath the mesh of his blinders.

"What did you bring?" he whispers.

Pietta remembers the feeling of a husband she did not want. She answers: "I don't know what you're talking about." Because she doesn't. She has nothing.

The man sighs and tries again, more kindly, holding her less tightly. "In your bindle. What did you carry with you to Nowhere? Don't be afraid. It's important, my dear, that's all. It is everything."

## Fourth Terrace: The Gluttonous

DETECTIVE BELACQUA NAVIGATED the night-crowded halls of the Temeritatis Precinct with ease. The locals parted into ragged blue waves to let him pass. Some held their hands to their mouths, some fell to their knees—but Belacqua knew the difference between awe and reflex. They genuflected because they thought they should. They thought it might help.

The crowd around the automat is thin. Humans didn't eat at the finer establishments. They had no currency. The wonderful glass wall of cool plates and steaming bowls was for the comfort of the strigils, a small luxury in this rather undistinguished outpost. Behind the bank of windows set into two feet of dark abbey stone, Belacqua saw a woman with the head of an osprey move with mindful grace, clearing the old dishes, bringing in the new. Her black and white feathers shone in the kitchen lights.

"What have you got in the way of savory, tonight, Giacama? I'm in the mood for salt."

Giacama pushed aside the little window on an empty compartment of the automat. Her mild seabird eyes floated in the glass as though they were the night special.

"Good evening, Detective. I've got a lovely rind of cheese from the gluttons' farms. It's all yours."

"Detective Inspector soon," Belacqua said with a flush of pride. He took his crescent of cheese from the window. Only then did he see the young girl staring up at him through the blinders of her falcon-hood, rubbing anxiously at the backs of her hands.

"Are you a demon?" she whispered. "Are you an angel?"

"Naw," Belacqua answered around a mouthful of white cheese. "I work for a living."

The child might have said more, but a commotion disturbed the evening throngs. A strapping man with a raven's grand face strode toward Detective Belacqua, out of breath, trembling in his black finery. Sergeant Tomek—but in all the aeons of known existence Belacqua had only known his sergeant to be a calm and rather cold sort.

Sergeant Tomek clasped his hand roughly, his raven's face handsome and dark and puffed with excitement or terror. His black ruff bristled.

"Sir, I hate to trouble you at this hour and I know you hate to be interrupted when you're...working...but something terrible's happened. Something dreadful. You must come."

Detective Belacqua tightened his long grey scarf and smoothed back his own rumpled feathers.

"Calm down, Tomek. You'll spook the poor creatures. Just present the facts of the case and we'll see to it with a quickness. What can possibly have you in such a state?"

Sergeant Tomek stared at the wine-dark flagstone floor. He swallowed several times before whispering wretchedly:

"A body, Sir."

"Well, that's hardly cause for all this upset, Sergeant. We're nothing but bodies round here. Bodies, bodies everywhere, and hardly one can think. Go home and get some sleep, man, we'll see to it in the morning."

The raven-headed Sergeant sighed and tried again, more miserably and more quietly than before.

"A *dead* body, Sir. A corpse."

Detective Belacqua blinked. "Don't be stupid, Tomek."

"Sir. I know how it sounds," Tomek glanced around at the passing folk, but most gave the policemen a wide berth. "But there is a dead woman lying face down with her throat cut and there's blood everywhere and *things* on her back and she is very, *very* dead."

Detective Belacqua grimaced with embarrassment. "Sergeant Tomek," he hissed, "they can't *die*. It's not possible. They steal, they cheat, they vandalize, they fornicate, they lie, they curse God, but they do not kill and they do not die. That's not how it *works*. That's the whole *point*."

But the raven would only say: "Come see."

Detective Belacqua thought of his novel and his dry red wine waiting safe and warm for him in the watchtower. They called to him. But he knew what duty was, even if he did not know how to begin his opus. "Where is she?"

Sergeant Tomek trilled unhappily. He ran his hand along the black blade of his beak.

"Outside."

### Fifth Terrace: The Covetous

PIETTA FOLLOWS THE man with the unusual nose. They have exchanged names. His is Savonarola. He spits the syllables of himself as though he hates their taste. He leads her through a door marked CONTEMPTUS MUNDI.

"My home," he sighs, "such as it is."

"I live in Taedium," Pietta answers, and it is such a relief that she has remembered it, that the information was there when she reached for it, solid, heavy, cold to the touch. She almost stumbles with the sweetness of it. Savonarola grunts in sympathy.

"Too bad for you. You'll find no fraternity among your neighbors, then. They keep to themselves in Taedium. They do not come to cloister, they do not trade, they do not attend the rainstorms. They don't even take Christmas with the rest of us. But perhaps that's to your taste. Taedium, Taedium, so close to Te Deum, you know. What passes for cleverness around here."

Pietta remembers the feeling of longing for something lost before she ever had it. "I have made friends with a man on the mountain. He moves his arms. I move mine. We are up to the letter G. But there is no G in my name, so he cannot know me. I am… I am lonely. I thought someone would come for me."

"No one on the mountain is your friend, girl," snaps Savonarola, and they emerge into a wide piazza full of long tables with thick legs and glass lanterns the size of parish churches shining out into the mist of the night. Wind pulls at them like a beggar pleading. The tables are full of handkerchiefs unknotted, their contents laid out lovingly, more men and women in charcoal-blue rags closely guarding each little clutch of junk.

Savonarola introduces her to a small, dark woman with a beautiful, delicate mouth. The woman is called Awo. She has an extraneous thumb on her left hand, small and withered and purpled. Pietta touches the objects on Awo's handkerchief, running her hands over them gently. They awake feelings in her that do not belong to her: a drinking cup, a set of sewing needles, a red brick, a pot of white paint, several ballpoint pens, and a length of faded paisley fabric. When Pietta touches the sewing needles, she remembers the *feeling of embroidering her daughter's wedding dress. But Pietta had only sons, and they are babies yet.*

"You have lovely things," Pietta whispers.

"Oh, they aren't mine," Awo says. The wind off of the mountain dampens all their voices." I long ago traded away the objects I brought with me into this place. And traded what I got in return, and traded that again, and so on and so forth and again and again. Everything in the world, it turns out, is escapable except economy. Those objects which were once so dear to me I can no longer even name. Did I come with a cup? A belt? A signet ring? I cannot say. Now, what will you give me for my fabric? Savonarola says you have scissors."

Pietta touches her ribs, where she hid the shears. She looks away, into the crystal doors of a massive lantern and the flames within. "But what are these things? What is this place? Why do I have this pair of scissors in this city at this moment?"

Savonarola and Awo glance at one another.

"They are your last belongings," Savonarola says. "The things you lingered over on your last day."

Rain comes to the city. It falls from every dark cloud and splashes against the lanterns, the tables, the buyers and the sellers. Everyone runs for their rain barrels, dragging them into the piazza, the copper bottoms scraping the stone. The rain that falls is not water but wine, red and strong.

Pietta remembers the feeling of dying alone.

## The Sixth Terrace: The Wrathful

DETECTIVE BELACQUA STOOD over the woman's body. He let a long, low whistle out of his beak and reached into his pocket for a cigarette. Sergeant Tomek opened his black jaws; a ball of blue flame floated on his tongue. Belacqua lit his wrinkled, broken stump of tobacco and breathed deep.

"Isn't there someone else we can hand this off to? Someone higher up. Someone…better?"

Tomek stared down at the corpse as it lay face down on the slick blue-black cobblestones of the road that connects the city and the mountain. The blue of the gas lamps made her congealing blood look like cold ink.

"You had the watch, Detective Inspector," he said, emphasizing his soon-to-come promotion. But they both knew this woman, the very fact of her, made all ranks and systems irrelevant.

Belacqua scratched the longer feathers at the nape of his neck. The clouds boiled and swam above them, raveling, unraveling, spooling grey into grey. He could not remember the last time he'd set foot outside the city. Probably sometime around the invention of music. The air smelled of crackling pre-lightning ozone and, bizarrely, nutmeg fruits, when they are wet and new and look like nothing so much as black, bleeding hearts.

"Is she going to…rot, do you think?" Sergeant Tomek mused.

"Well, I don't bloody well know, do I?" the man with the heron's head snapped back. Detective Belacqua had closed thousands of cases in his infinite career. The Nowhere locals got up to all manner of nonsense and he didn't blame them in the least. On the contrary, he felt deeply for the poor blasted things, and when it fell to him to hand out punishments, he was as lenient as the rules allowed. He was a creature of rules, was Belacqua. But the vast majority of his experience lay in vandalism, petty theft, minor assault, and public drunkenness. Every so often something spicier came his way: attempted desertion, adultery, assaults upon the person of a strigil. But never *this*. Of course never *this*. *This* was against the rules. The first rule. The foundational rule. So foundational that until tonight he had not even thought to call it a rule at all.

Detective Belacqua knelt to examine the body. He suspected that was the sort of thing to do. Just pretend it was a bit of burglary.

Nothing out of the ordinary. Scene of the crime and all that. Good. First step. Go on, then.

"Right. Erm. The deceased? Should we say deceased? Are you writing this down, Tomek? For God's sake. The, em, *re*-deceased is female, approximately twenty-odd-something years of age. Is that right? It's so hard to tell with people. I don't mean to be insensitive, of course—"

"Oh, certainly not, sir."

"It's just that they all look a *little* alike, don't they, Sergeant?"

Tomek looked distinctly uncomfortable. His dark ruff bristled. "About forty, I should say, Detective Inspector."

"Ah, yes, thank you. Forty years of age, brunette, olive complected, quite tall, nearly six foot as I reckon it. Her hood seems to have gone missing and her clothes are...well, there's not much left of them, is there? Just write 'in disarray.' Spare her some dignity." Now that he'd begun, Belacqua found he could hardly stop. It came so naturally, like a song. "Cause of death appears to be a lateral cut across the throat and exsanguination, though where she got all that blood I can't begin to think. Bruises, well, everywhere, really. But particularly bad on her belly and the backs of her thighs. And there's the...markings. Do you think that happened before or, well, I mean to say, *after*, Tomek?"

The raven-sergeant's black eyes flickered helplessly between the corpse and the detective. "Sir," he swallowed finally, "how can we possibly tell?"

Belacqua remembered the book he'd devoured so greedily in that sad little vandal's cell, the book without a cover and yellow-stained pages, a book in which many people had died and gotten their dead selves puzzled over.

"I've an idea about that, Sergeant," he said finally. "Write down that she's got *patience* carved into her back in Greek—not too neatly, either, it looks like someone went at her with a pair of scissors—then get the boys to carry her up to my office before anyone else decides to have a look out their window and starts ringing up a panic. Carefully! Don't…don't *damage* her any more than she already is." Belacqua gazed up at the great mountain that faced his city, into the wind and the lantern lights and the constant oncoming night. "Poor lamb," he sighed, and when the patrolmen came to lift her up, he pressed his feathered cheek against hers for a moment, his belly full of something he very well thought might be grief.

### Seventh Terrace: The Excommunicate

SAVONAROLA, AWO, AND *Pietta sit around a brimming rain barrel. The storm has passed. The sky is, for once, almost clear, barnacled with fiery stars. They drink with their hands, cupping fingers and dipping into the silky red wine, slurping without shame. The dead know how to savor as the living never can. The wine is heavy but dry. Much debate has filled the halls of Nowhere over the centuries—is it a Beaujolais? Montrachet? Plain Chianti? Savonarola is firmly in the Montrachet camp. Awo thinks it is most certainly an Algerian Carignan. Pietta thinks it is soft, and sour, and kind.*

"Memory is a bad houseguest in this place," Savonarola says softly. Red raindrops streak his face like a statue of a saint weeping blood. "For you, the worst of it will come in twenty years or so. Dying is the blow, memory is the bruise. It takes time to develop, to reach a full and purple lividity. Around eighty years in Nowhere, give or take. Then the pain will take you and it will not give you back again for autumns upon winters. You will know everything you were, and everything you lost. But the bruise of having lived will fade, too, and your time in Nowhere will dwarf your time in the world such that all life will seem to be a letter you wrote as a child, addressed to a stranger, and never delivered."

Awo sucks the wine from her brown, slender fingers. "Awo Alive feels to me like a character in a film I saw when I was young and loved. Awo and her husband Kofi who wore glasses and her three daughters and seven grandchildren and her degree in electrical engineering and the day she saw Accra for the first time, Accra and the sea. I am fond of all of them, but I see them now from very far away. If I remember anything, if I tilt my head or say a word as she would have done, it is like quoting from that film, not like being Awo."

"I went to the noose long before such things as moving pictures could be imagined," Savonarola admits.

Pietta thinks for a long while, watching herself in the reflection of the wine. "And what of the mountain? What of the men and women there? Very well, I am dead. Where is Paradise? Where is Hell? Where is the fire or the clouds? Is this Purgatory?"

Awo touches Pietta's cheek. "Me broni ba, *that mountain out there is Purgatory. Someday, maybe, we'll go there and start our long hitchhike of the soul up, up, up into the sea of glass and the singing and the rings of eyes and the eternal surrealist discotheque of the saved. Nowhere is for us sad sacks who died too quick to repent, or naughties like Savonarola, who was so stuck up himself that he got excommunicated. And here we sit, with nothing to do but drink the rain, for three hundred times our living years."

Savonarola cracks his gnarled knuckles. "I admit, if some man in Florence had discovered a way to film the moon rising over the ripples of the Arno, or the building of Brunelleschi's ridiculous dome, or even one of my own sermons—and I was very good, in my day—I would have set fire to the reels with all the rest, and I would have rejoiced. All in which the eye longs to revel is vanity, vanity. Only now do I long for such things, for something to see besides this stone, something to touch besides the dead, something to hear besides talk, talk, talk. What I would not give in this moment for one glimpse of Botticelli's pornography, one vulgar passage of lecherous Boccacio, one beautiful deck of gambling cards. God, I think, is irony."

"I will go mad," Pietta whispers.

"Yes," agrees Awo.

*Pietta pleads: "But it will pass? It will pass and I will go to the mountain and take up a lantern and begin to climb. It will pass and we will go—we will go on, up, out. Progress."*

*Savonarola pinches his nose between his fingers and smiles softly. He has never been a man given to smiling. He had only done it ten or eleven times in total. But all in secret, Girolamo Savonarola possesses one of the loveliest and kindest smiles in all the long history of joy.*

*"Do the math, my child. Three hundred times the span of a human life we must rattle the stones of Nowhere—since the death of Solomon and the invention of the alphabet, no one yet has gotten out."*

### Eighth Terrace: The Ambitious

IN THE CITY called Nowhere, a man with the head of a heron sat comfortably in the topmost room of the policemen's tower, watching a corpse rot.

It was slow going.

In all honesty, Detective Belacqua had no real idea what to expect. He only recalled from his penny paperback that human bodies did, indeed, under normal circumstances, rot, and they did it according to a set of rules, at a regular, repeatable, measurable rate, and from that you could reason out a lot of other things that mattered in a murder investigation. Since he had run face-first into a circumstance well beyond normal, Belacqua could not rely on the niceties of rigor mortis, even if he understood them, thus, he now devised a method to discover the rules of decomposition in Nowhere.

Sergeant Tomek humbly asked to be allowed to stay after the patrolmen returned to their posts. The Detective agreed, but sent him for coffee straightaway so that he could gather his thoughts without the raven-boy fretting all over him. Belacqua lifted the corpse easily—they never did weigh very much in Nowhere. He laid her out on three desks pushed together, and, though he felt rather silly about it afterward, folded her hands over her chest and arranged her long, dark hair tenderly, as though it mattered. And it did matter to him, very much, though he couldn't think why. He dipped a rough cloth into the wash basin in the officer's bathroom and cleaned the worst of the grime and blood out of her wounds, going back and forth from the basin with a steady rhythm that calmed his nerves and arranged the furniture of his mind in a contemplative configuration. After all this was done, he drew a pair of scissors from the watchman's desk and plunged them quickly between the dead woman's ribs on the left side of her torso. When he pulled them out again, red pearls seeped from the wound, falling to the flagstones with a terrible clatter.

"Huh," said Sergeant Tomek. He stood in the doorway, holding a cup of scalding coffee in each hand.

And then, the policemen waited. Sergeant Tomek waited at the window, transfixed. Detective Belacqua waited at his typewriter, ready to record any changes in the body. To write the novel of this woman's putrefaction, chapter by chapter.

It was a quiet night in Nowhere.

Days and nights knocked at the door and went away unanswered. The corpse remained the same for a very long time. Tomek gave up over and over, crying out that it was too sad to be borne, to miserable a thing to stare at, and Nowhere too timeless a place to ever tolerate decay. But he always returned, with coffee or tea or hot buttered toast, and the two strigils resumed their longest watch.

By the next Sabbath, it had begun. On the first day, the edges of the woman's wounds flushed the color of opium flowers. On the second day, her hair turned to snow. On the third day, the stench began, and the watch-room filled intolerably with the smell of frankincense, and then wild honey, and finally a deep and endless forest, loamy and ancient. On the fourth day, Belacqua held his ear to her mouth and heard the sound of gulls crying. On the fifth day, her wounds turned ultramarine and began to seep golden ink. On the sixth day, her sternum cracked and a white lizard with blue eyes crawled out of her, which Tomek caught and trapped in a wine bottle. And on the seventh day, a small tree bloomed and broke out of her mouth, which gave a single silver fruit. This, Belacqua harvested and placed in his coffee cup for further study. By the morning of the eighth day, all that remained of her were bones, hard and clear and faceted as if the skeleton hacked out of a single diamond.

Belacqua typed and typed and typed. Finally, he spoke, on the day they saw the dead woman's skull emerge like new land rising from the sea.

"Sergeant Tomek, I believe we can safely say that she received the markings on her back pre-mortem. Time of death could not have been sooner than six days before you discovered her."

"And how do you know this, Detective Inspector?"

"If she had been killed later, we would have found the poor girl already turning orange at the edges, or worse. I detected then no discoloration nor any scent nor a lizard nor the sound of seagulls. Unfortunately for us, it could have been any number of days greater than six and we would not know it unless we could somehow kill something else and record its progress. Also when I cut into her, the body produced a quantity of pearls, whereas no pearls were found beside her on the road to Nowhere. Additionally, the gore of my cut shows a distinctly different shade of ultramarine than the carving on her back. Someone wrote patience on her while she yet lived, Tomek, and listened to her anguish, and did not stop."

"It is dreadfully morbid," the Sergeant sighed. He laid a reverent hand on the delicate foot-bones of the body.

"On the contrary, my boy, it is science, and we have done it! Nothing could be more exciting than discovering, as we have done, that a set of rules lay in place of all eternity without us suspecting them. I assure you these are not the stages of mortal decomposition." Belacqua hurried on before Tomek could wonder how he knew anything about living corpses, and uncover his illicit pursuit of fiction. "This is new. It is ours. It is native to Nowhere. No one else in all the yawning pit of time has ever known what you and I know now. We are, finally, unique. And now we two unique fellows must proceed further on, farther in, and *re*-compose this woman. Her name, her history, her associates, her enemies. What happened to her a fortnight ago, and how?" The Detective frowned. "Perhaps we ought to interrogate the lizard."

In its green glass bottle, the pale reptile hissed. It stuck out its blue tongue. The glass fogged with its breath. It said one word, and then steamed away like water.

*Virtue.*

### Ninth Terrace: The Incurious

*PIETTA HAS BECOME a birdwatcher. She leaves Awo and Savonarola often to trail silently after the strigils as they move through the city. They are so unlike her. They wear clothes of many colors; they are always busy; they eat. They live in a different Nowhere than she does, one with automats and social clubs and places to be. She makes a study of them. This would be easier if she could bring herself to trade her colored glass or her belt or her scissors for one of Awo's pens or the paper a tall man with very clean teeth wants to sell her, but she cannot. She does not know yet why they are precious, but she knows she doesn't want to give them away, to let them become separate from her forever. She is not ready. So she must try to remember the birds she sees. Osprey. Oriole. Peregrine. Sparrow. Sandpiper. Ibis. Pelican. Starling. Raven. Heron. They are beautiful and they do not see her. To them, she is not Pietta. She is no one. She is blue, like the others, and blindered, like the others, and the only thing she can ever do to catch their attention, to bring their eyes down onto her, is to sin, to commit a crime, to err. When the man with clean teeth tries to steal her glass, the birds come. They smell, absurdly, like expensive perfume, like the counter in a fashionable shop. Their feathers rustle when they move like pages turning. They* have no irises. Their voices are very nearly human. A woman with the head of an owl cuts away the sleeve of the man's robe. Now everyone will know he is bad. Pietta is fascinated. But she is afraid to do anything very bad herself.

She meets Awo and Savonarola in a cloister fifteen years after they first drank wine together out of a barrel. It is a round room in the Largitio Quarter, with a high, domed ceiling, full of grand, tall tables set with empty bowls, safe from the wind and the slow, trudging lights on the mountain. Pietta longs to eat. She is never hungry, but she remembers the feeling of eating. Of tasting. A few dozen blue-ragged souls pool their objects on a table, picking and sorting. They are trying to assemble a chess set, though fights have broken out already over whether a pepper pot or a bone whistle or pocket Slovakian dictionary makes a better king. Nothing in Nowhere is important, so nothing is more important than the pepper pot and the whistle and the dictionary. Pietta watches them and imagines the players as birds. She hates chess. Savonarola agrees, though he plays anyway.

"Chess allows the frivolous to pretend their toys have deep meaning. The only honest game is tag," he grouses, while taking an exquisitely-chinned teenaged girl's queen. Both the sleeves have been torn from her dress.

"What are the strigils?" Pietta asks.

Savonarola snorts. "Where I come from they're dull blades you use to scrape the sweat and grime from your back in a bath-house. Not that I ever used a bath-house, a seething puddle of greased sin. Not that I haven't scoured the breadth of Nowhere for a damned bath."

Awo has enough sewing needles to man her entire side, pawns and all. She sticks them upright in the soft wood of the table, two neat silver rows. "He can't tell you. His theology was far too prim and tidy to contain bird-headed men in trenchcoats. I can't tell you either. But if you suppose there are demons in one place and angels in the other, wouldn't you also suppose something has to live here? Something has to be natural to Nowhere."

"They came when the first people arrived," says the girl with the lovely chin. She moves her knight (a mechanical library stamp). "And Nowhere was only an empty plain without a city. They are meant to make this place somewhat less than a Hell, and to keep us from making a Heaven of it."

"How do you know that?" Savonarola snaps.

The girl shrugs. "I asked one. When I got arrested for writing my name a thousand times over the entrance to Benevolentia Sector. She had a wren's face. She said they were formed not from clay like us nor fire nor light but from the stuff of the void on the face of the world, and the had not the breath of life but the heat of life and the fluid of it, and they had a beginning but no end, an alpha and an ellipsis, and then she drank my wine and said I was pretty and the truth was she didn't remember very much more about being born than I did and she read all that off a historical plaque on the upper levels, but strigils have to keep up appearances, and they wouldn't be worth much if we thought they were stuck here just like us only they didn't even know how it happened to them, only what they had to do, so if you ask me, talking to a strigil is not so useful as you'd expect, and they drink a lot. Checkmate."

That night, Pietta goes to be with Savonarola, because everything is the same and everything is nothing and what is the point of not doing anything now?

### Tenth Terrace: The Merciless

DETECTIVE BELACQUA STOOD in a hexagonal stone cell like all the other hexagonal stone cells. He looked out an arched window like all the other arched windows. He picked up and put down several meaningless objects: a brass key, a cracked, worn belt, a stone figure of a child seated in a chair, shards of colored glass. Sergeant Tomek assured him this was the dead woman's room, but it told him nothing—how could it? She would have traded away anything authentically her own long ago. What remained was simply someone else's rubbish. They had a name, and only that by process of elimination. Quite simply: who was missing? It had taken weeks of interrogation, more contact with the locals than Belacqua had ever suffered before, their fearful whispers, their purposeless glazed eyes, their way of drifting off mid-sentence as though they'd forgotten language. But they got their name, from the old furioso Savonarola, who actually wept when Tomek asked whether he had lost anyone of late.

What was he supposed to do now? Everyone in the policemen's union expected he could find some simple solution to it all. But the thing of it was, in his paperback, discovering the identity of the corpse opened other doors, doors within doors, obvious rivers of inquiry to dive into, personal histories to unearth, secrets, secrets everywhere. But her name gave him nothing but this room, and this room was a dry river and a closed door.

"Who was she?" Sergeant Tomek demanded of Savonarola, who sat below a great candle, staring at his open hands. "Who did she love? Who did she hate? What was she in life? What did she do to pass the time?"

But the old friar just closed his hands and opened them again. Closed. Open. "She loved me and Awo. She hated chess. She invented a semaphore alphabet with a man climbing the mountain, though I'm reasonably sure he's not in on the scheme. If she remembered her life, she never told it to me. She's so new, you know. Like a baby. When I look at her I see the plainness of white linen, being without vanity."

"Everyone has vanity," said Sergeant Tomek. "Everyone here."

The old man looked up cannily at the strigils. Behind his blinders, his eyes shone. "Do you?"

Detective Belacqua squatted down on his heels. He had a suspicion, and he knew how to work on friars. You had to awe them. Morning picked at the stitches of dark. If there had been any true songbirds in Nowhere, they would have sung. Belacqua fixed his black heron's eyes on the hooded soul before him. "Do you remember the founding of Florence, Girolamo? That is where you lived, is it not?"

"Don't be absurd. Florence was old when I was young."

"Quite so. Yet I do remember the founding of Nowhere. Did you know that? Some of us do, some of us don't, it's a funny old thing, like whether or not someone like you remembers losing his baby teeth. A toss of the cognitive dice. But I remember. Lucky me! You see, the plain, the *plain* is the thing. The mud flat going on and on out there forever. The handful of trees—as few and as far between as living planets in empty space. The old riverbeds. Somewhere out beyond the road and the mountain there's a black salt flat a light year across. The clouds. The stars. And people didn't come right away. It wasn't like you'd imagine—nothing, and then hordes all at once. People just died like dogs or fish or dinosaurs until, I don't know, what would you say, Tomek? Around the time they started painting ibexes on cave walls?"

The Sergeant nodded his dark head.

"Well, my friend, you can just imagine what a mess it all was in the beginning. No system. No rules. Some people could go up the mountain as quick as you like, and some couldn't, and some could go down into the coal pits, and some couldn't, and some just milled around like cows down here, and if they tried to go on up, they found themselves turned right back around facing the infinite floodplain with not an inch gained, but no one really had a bead on the whys and wherefores of the whole business. Cosmology just sort of *happened* to you, on you get. And the people down here in the mud, they just sat there or laid there or stood there for ages, really, proper ages, with nothing to do. That's the worst thing for a person. To get crushed under the weight of endless useless days. Between you and me, I don't think anyone really thought it through. I bet you'd rather have a fellow spearing you with a flaming trident every hour on the hour—at least then, something would *happen*. Am I right? I believe I am. So these poor souls fought and fucked and screamed for awhile, because those're pretty good ways to stop yourself thinking about the existential chasm of time. But they didn't bleed and they didn't come and nobody answered them, so eventually, they started digging in the mud with whatever they'd brought in their bindles, which back then, was mostly stone tools. They pulled up the stones of the moral universe and put them one on top of the other, and I'll tell you a secret, Giro. For awhile, I think this was a happier place than Heaven, when they were putting down those rocks. But happiness isn't the point. Not here. If we'd let you keep on with it, your lot would have built city after city, an empire of the dead, and it would look just like the world out here, only filled with legions of the mediocre and the stalled out and the unrepentant and whatever you're supposed to be. So we got called up, me and the Sergeant here and all the other strigils. Hatched out of an egg of ice, I'm told, though that sort of insider talk is above my pay grade. And we came bearing *order*, Girolamo. We came with rules in our beaks. We built Nowhere together, strigils and humans, the dead and the divine," Detective Belacqua put one hand on his chest and the other over Savonarola's withered heart. "*Me* and *you*. A closed system. A city on the hill. And I think it's *beautiful*. But you don't, do you? You hate it, like you hated everything you ever clapped your eyes on. Except *her*. So here's what I think, friend. I think you found a way to get her out. God only knows what. But you did it to her and now she's gone and if you tell me what happened, no one will be angry—we quite literally cannot be angry. Who could blame you? It's the nature of love, I should imagine."

Girolamo Savonarola laughed.

"You ought to write a book," he giggled, but when Sergeant Tomek began to strip his charcoal-blue robes from him, the friar began to sob instead.

## Eleventh Terrace: The Sorrowful

IT HITS HER *while she kisses Awo's naked shoulder, Awo, whose cell Pietta visits far more than any other, though in recent years she's visited many. She even found Beatrice, who turned out to be very shy and fond of rain. It is something to do, and Pietta is desperate for* acts. *Acts have befores and afters. They mark her movement through this air and these stones. She has tried other sins, but they are more difficult in Nowhere. She cannot bring herself to envy anyone, and wants for nothing; she cannot eat and she cannot strive. So there is this, and though she feels it only dimly, she holds on very tight.*

*Pietta and Awo lie together in the lantern-light of Purgatory and there is a moment when she does not know who she is, not really, and then that moment burns itself out. Pietta remembers the feeling of being Pietta. She remembers being small and she remembers being big. All of the things that ever happened to her stack up in her mind like stones on a sea shore, tottering, tottering...Pietta is getting born in a room with poppies painted on the wall, Pietta is small and delighted and running through the snow, forgetting her mother completely and throwing herself face first into the soft powder, Pietta is receiving her first communion and coughing when she oughtn't because the incense tickles her nose, and she is helping her father tend his bees in their fields, and she is walking in the woods at night with a boy named Milo, and she is living in a house by the sea with Milo who has grown very distant with her, even though she is pregnant and they should be happy, and Pietta is giving birth to her son in a room with ultramarine flowers next to her bed in a cheap, gold-painted vase, and Pietta is walking in the summer, alone, for once, when she sees a white lizard hiding in the shade of a long, flat stone, and she takes it home and gives it a name and shows it to her son and keeps it in an old fish tank even though Milo says it is stupid and lizards have no hearts and Pietta is wearing her mother's diamond ring every day even though they could use the money because no amount of snow could make her forget, not really, and Milo is so angry with her so often, every thing she does is the wrong thing, and though she still loves him she grows very still inside, she feels as though she is trapped in ice and cannot move, even as she cooks and cleans and runs to the shops and teaches her classes and she is getting older all the time and then Pietta is teaching her son to play chess with a set made to look like a famous medieval set with funny-looking people in funny-looking chairs, she is cutting out the green felt for his Halloween costume because he insists upon being a tree this year, she is pouring herself the last of the red wine and locking up the liquor cabinet with a brass key, she is putting away her husband's clothes, his coats, his socks, his old belt, and thinking that she should have bought him a new one long ago, and she will now, she will, because tomorrow will be the day she wakes up out of the ice and becomes herself again, she knows it will happen all at once, like a big silver fruit cracking open, and there she'll be, good as new, even though she thought the same yesterday, and the day before, and the day before that, and when the glazier's truck hits Pietta in the high street she thinks, for a moment, that all that beautiful, shattered, colored glass lying around her is the ice breaking at last, the fruit breaking open, with Pietta whole and alive inside, but it is not.*

### Twelfth Terrace: The Gluttonous

IT WAS A quiet night in Nowhere.

Detective Inspector Belacqua and Corporal Tomek shared the watch and supper and half a bottle of white wine which both felt very excited about. The lamp stood full of oil, the basin full of fresh water, the pens full of ink, and all was as it should be.

Belacqua had many times almost asked his raven-headed friend how he felt about their one great case. Tomek never mentioned it. Occasionally, in their rounds, they would catch a glimpse of Savonarola, naked and shunned, drifting miserably among the crowds. Once, Belacqua himself had nearly run right into the woman called Awo, who stared at him as though she could punch through his delicate skull with her gaze. He hadn't been able to bear that; he'd run. Run, from a local, a dead woman with nothing but her rags. And yet it had happened.

So time, in its shapeless, corpulent, implacable way, bore on in Nowhere. And only when he was alone did it trouble Belacqua how much they never understood about the incident, the monstrous hole at the bottom of the case file through which everything sensible tumbled out. Into this hole, he began to drop the words of his novel, one by one, painstakingly, the only story he knew, a story without an end. Which, he supposed, was to be expected, considering the author.

When it came time to open the bottle of white wine, the policemen found the cork encased in awfully thick black wax, too thick for fingernails and too awkward for beaks.

"Nothing to it," Corporal Tomek laughed, and drew a small pair of scissors out of the inner pocket of his coat. He worked the little blades deftly round the mouth and wiggled them up underneath till the cake of wax fell away.

They were a perfectly ordinary pair of scissors. A little tarnished and stained, but utterly usual and serviceable, like Tomek himself. Detective Belacqua had no reason to notice them in the least. And yet, he did. He could not stop noticing them. Small enough for delicate work. For carving. *Was* that tarnish, that black smear along the shears?

Belacqua cleared his throat. "Has it ever woken you nights, Tomek, that we never discovered how the old man did it?"

"Did what, sir?"

"Killed a dead woman. There had to be a method—that's the whole thing, you know, means, motive, and opportunity—that's the *entire* thing of it. And the means just…got away from us, didn't it?"

"I suppose they did. But I wouldn't worry. It's never happened again. It's not like we had an epidemic on our hands, Belacqua. And if we had, well, you know. No one harmed but the dead. The Chief would have sorted it out, I'm sure." Tomek poured the wine and handed a glass across the desk. Belacqua just looked at it.

"I just want to *know*, that's all. Haven't you ever wanted to know anything so badly it ate you away until there was nothing left of you but the *not* knowing?"

The raven grimaced. "Just drink your wine, Detective Inspector."

Belacqua did not blink. He thought he ought to feel something in the pit of his stomach, but all he felt was the not knowing, the canker of it, working its way through him like rot.

"How did you meet her?" Detective Belacqua whispered.

Tomek put down the glasses, very carefully, as though, in his hands, they might break.

### Thirteenth Terrace: The Lustful

*PIETTA BLUDGEONS THE wall over and over, jamming her scissors into the wine-dark stone. Chips and chunks fly away as she gouges the skin of the city. The thudding and scraping of her blows fill the endless halls of Taedium.*

*They care about very little, Pietta knows. But they will care about this. Vandalizing Nowhere brings them running, so she is not surprised when a man with the head of a raven steps through her door and snatches the scissors from her hands with a strength that would snap all the bones of her wrist, if the bones of her wrist could still break.*

*"That's enough, miss," Sergeant Tomek says crisply, professionally. Their faces are close as kissing. Raven and girl; pale, bloodless lips and a mouth like black shears.*

*"It's not fair," Pietta snarls at him. "All I ever did wrong was be sad."*

*Outside, the man on the mountain eats his smoke. Tomek is on top of her by the time he begins to move his arms in straight, strident lines, and she does not see.*

P-I-E-T-T-A?

### Fourteenth Terrace: The Contemptuous

"WE ALL HAVE our ways of coping with it," Tomek said, running his finger around the lip of his glass.

"With what?" Belacqua scowled.

"Eternity," answered the raven slowly. "You have your novel—oh, for God's sake, we all know. I have my research. It's wrong, you know, everything, all of this. At least they lived, fucked something up well and good enough to end up here. We're here...for what? Why? To punish what sin? The only difference between them and us is we wear better clothes. I can't bear it any more than they can. And it's worse, it's worse for us, Belacqua. We've just enough spark in us to draw up a rough sketch of feeling, just a basic set, nothing too detailed: duty, loyalty, a smear of free will, a little want, a little envy, just enough to know somebody else got to see what a summer looks like, but not enough for the cosmos to even look at us, for one second, as anything but lock and keys. And it never ends for us. Don't you see? They all have the hope of progress, of the *climb*. This is it, just this, nothing else, forever. I was so *bored*, Belacqua."

Tomek began to pace, tugging at his feathers, half-preening, half-tearing.

"And so I began to think. Just for the last couple of thousand years. I began to plan a way to murder a person. It's a big enough problem to take up centuries. Could it even be done? *They* can't, certainly. One punches the other in the nose and it's like punching ice cream. Nothing. Not even a mark. But I am a strigil. There is no record of what I can do because no one has ever cared enough to find out. Do your job, little birdie, get back to us at the end of everything for your performance review. What would happen if a strigil sinned? Would there be consequences? And if I could do it, if, ontologically speaking, it would be allowed to occur, how? These are worthy questions! The first experiment was obvious. I broke a man's neck in Oboedientia Sector. For a minute, I thought I'd gotten it right on my first go. But no, he just sort of shivered and put his head right and went on his way. It seemed the rules held for me as well as him. After that I kept it all in my head. The project. I thought it out while the Renaissance idiots poured in, while I walked my beat, while I watched you fumble with a sad little dime store potboiler in the corner like one of the chronic masturbators down in Desidia. Nothing physical would do it. I should have realized that—we do not move in the realm of the physical. I had to act upon the nature of a soul, to alter it so that it could not remain whole. And it would work—Belacqua, this is the important thing! It would work because of that smear of free will, that tiny table scrap of self a strigil owns. I have to be able to act freely, or else I could not arrest or judge or mete out punishment. You have to be allowed to plunk away at your silly stories, because not even the font of all can build a being of judgment without building a being of perversity."

Tomek put his hands on the window sill and let the wind off the mud plain buffet his face.

"When I met Pietta I knew she would let me do anything to her. She was in despair. They all are, for awhile, but hers was frozen and depthless, a continuation of who she had always been, just spooling on into the black forever. And she was right. It's not fair. It's all grotesque. That little spit of living and all this ocean of penance. She wanted it, Belacqua. She did."

"I doubt that very much, Corporal."

"You don't understand. She didn't care. She saw the writing on the wall and the writing said: *Fuck This Place*. She just wanted something to happen. We ran through all the sins first. I fucked her right away—small mercy that we are not built sexless as the angels. Lust is the easiest. I cleaned out the automat and shoved it all down her throat till cream and syrup and relish and grease poured down her chest. She puked it all up, of course, the dead can't eat. Then on to the next like kids at a fairground—we hurled loathing and envy at each other, at the mountain, perfectly honest, more profanity than grammar could hold. I drew up a rage and beat her though no bruises came up. We skipped sloth since Nowhere is the home and hearth of sloth, and Belacqua, nothing I could do could make that woman proud. But it was all useless anyway, her flesh took it all as calmly as water. And so I had to retreat and think again.

"Solutions come so strangely, Belacqua. They steal in. Just the way you saw my scissors and knew what I'd done, your mind leaping over your habits and your inertia to arrive at a conclusion that is as much dream as logic, I knew. I knew how to kill my Pietta. I returned to her that night. I held her in my arms, and, one by one, I buried her in virtues. I gave her all my belongings freely and her nose shot blood onto the flagstones. I cradled her chastely with no thought of her body and bruises rose up on her thighs. I groveled before her and before her I was nothing, and her fingers snapped. I tended her patiently while she screamed, and *upomovn* carved itself into her back. I persevered, and my diligence choked her like hands. I whispered to her all the kindnesses her husband withheld, that her son, being a child, could not imagine, and the extraordinary thing was I *meant* them, Belacqua. I meant them with all my being. I loved her and her throat split side to side like a pomegranate. Then I shoved her out the window and watched her fall. I pushed her from this world, and all the violence on her body were but the marks of her passage. Neither virtue nor sin can be committed in this place. Nowhere cannot bear it. What they do to one another matters little enough—they have chosen their course and proceed along it, stupid and wasteful and unfair as it is. But I am neither alive nor dead, neither mortal nor immortal, just meanly made, with the barest thought. And so are you, Belacqua. The meanly made may sin—who could expect better?

Sin is easy. But for me—for us—to act with virtue is a violence to the whole of existence. And now she is gone and my questions answered. *Nothing happened.* I was not punished. I was not even found out. I am not morally culpable, because He will not deign to look at me long enough to condemn. When an angel does wrong, Hell must be invented out of whole cloth to contain his sorry carcass. But we? We are nothing, and no one. And I think it is *beautiful.*"

### Fifteenth Terrace: The Forgetful

THERE IS A *grinding sound before she appears, like stone against stone. One moment there is nothing, the next there is Pietta, though if she heard that name now, she would not recognize it, nor even comprehend the idea of a word used to signify a person. Her mind is a silver fruit lying clean and open, without seed or rot or juice. She opens her eyes and her eyes are black, black and several, ringed round her skull like a crown so that she sees everywhere at once. She moves her legs and her legs are powerful, shaggy, heavy with silver, braided, matted fur. Her claws and her tusks scrape on the bedrock beneath the mudplain as she moves with the sleuth of other bears, because nothing in this place has ever happened only once, their ursine sounds and their scents stretching before them toward the city they love but no longer understand, except that it is a warm place in the night, a heart beating in a bloodless land, and when they touch the walls, they remember, faintly, distantly, the feeling of being loved.*

### Sixteenth Terrace: The Unyielding

DETECTIVE INSPECTOR BELACQUA gave the signal, and every window in Nowhere closed against the man with the raven's head. Tomek's caws and cries far below echoed the length of the everything, his pleas, his reasons, all of it swallowed by the grey clouds and the long nothing-and-no-one of the endless mudplain and the red stars beyond. The mountain, for a moment, stood silent, all the lights still and dim.

Belacqua wept against the shutters, and he wept for a century before opening them again.

## The Limitless Perspective of Master Peek, Or, the Luminescence of Debauchery

WHEN MY FATHER, A GLASSBLOWER of some modest fame, lay gasping on his deathbed, he offered, between bloody wheezings, a choice of inheritance to his three children: a chest of Greek pearls, a hectare of French land, and an iron punty. Impute no virtue to my performance in this little scene! I, being the youngest, chose last, which is to say I did not choose at all. The elder of us, my brother Prospero, seized the chest straightaway, having love in his heart for nothing but jewels and gold, the earth's least interesting movements of the bowel which so excite, in turn, the innards of man. Pomposo, next of my blood, took up the deed of land, for he always fancied himself a lord, even in our childhood games, wherein he sold me in marriage to the fish in the lake, the grove of poplar trees, the sturdy stone wall, our father's kiln and pools of molten glass, even the sun and the moon and the constellation of Taurus. The iron punty was left to me, my father's only daughter, who could least wield it to any profit, being a girl and therefore no fit beast for commerce. All things settled to two-thirds satisfaction, our father bolted upright in his bed, cried out: *Go I hence to God!* then promptly fell back, perished, and proceeded directly to Hell.

The old man had hardly begun his long cuddle with the wormy ground before Prospero be-shipped himself with a galleon and sailed for the Dutch East Indies in search of a blacker, more fragrant pearl to spice his breakfast and his greed whilst Pomposo wifed himself a butter-haired miller's daughter, planting his seed in both France and her with a quickness. And thus was I left, Perpetua alone and loudly complaining, in the quiet dark of my father's glassworks, with no one willing to buy from my delicate and feminine hand, no matter how fine the goblet on the end of that long iron punty.

The solution seemed to me obvious. Henceforward, quite simply, I should never be a girl again. This marvelous transformation would require neither a witch's spell nor an alchemist's potion. From birth I possessed certain talents that would come to circumscribe my destiny, though I cursed them mightily until their use came clear: a deep and commanding voice, a masterful height, and a virile hirsuteness, owing to a certain unmentionable rootstock of our ancient family. Served as a refreshingly exotic accompaniment to these, some few of us are also born with one eye as good as any wrought by God, and one withered, hardened to little more than a misshapen pearl notched within a smooth and featureless socket, an affliction which, even if all else could be made fair between us, my brothers did not inherit, so curse them forever, say I. No surprise that no one wanted to marry the glassblower's giant hairy one-eyed daughter! Yet now my defects would bring to me, not a husband, but the world entire. I had only to cut my hair with my father's shears, bind my breasts with my mother's bridal veil, clothe myself in my brothers' coats and hose, blow a glass bubble into a false eye, and think nothing more of Perpetua forever. My womandectomy caused me neither trouble nor grief—I whole-heartedly recommend it to everyone! But, since such a heroic act of theatre could hardly be accomplished in the place of my birth, I also traded two windows for a cart and an elderly but good-humored plough-horse, packed up tools and bread and slabs of unworked glass, and departed that time and place forever. London,

## The Limitless Perspective of Master Peek, Or, the Luminescence of Debauchery

after all, does not care one whit who you were. Or who you are. Or who you will become. Frankly, she barely cares for herself, and certainly cannot be bothered with your tawdry backstage changes of costume and comedies of mistaken identity.

That was long ago. So long that to say the numbers aloud would be an act of pure nihilism. Oh, but I am old, good sir, old as ale and twice as bitter, though I do not look it and never shall, so far as I can tell. I was old when you were weaned, squalling and farting, and I shall be old when your grandchildren annoy you with their hideous fashions and worse manners. Kings and queens and armadas and plagues have come and gone in my sight, ridiculous wars flowered and pruned, my brothers died, the scales balanced at last, for having not the malformed and singular eye, neither did they have the longevity that is our better inheritance, fashions swung from opulence to piousness and back to the ornate flamboyance that is their favored resting state once more. And thus come I, Master Cornelius Peek, Glassmaker to the Rich and Redolent, only slightly dented, to the age which was the mate to my soul as glove to glove or slipper to slipper. Such an age exists for every man, but only a lucky few chance to be born alongside theirs. For myself, no more perfect era can ever grace the hourglass than the one that began in the Year of Our Lord 1660, in the festering scrotum of London, at the commencement of the long and groaning orgy of Charles II's pretty, witty reign.

IF YOU WOULD know me, know my house. She is a slim, graceful affair built in a fashion somewhat later than the latest, much of brick and marble and, naturally, glass, three stories high, with the top two being the quarters I share with my servants, the maid-of-all-work Mrs. Matterfact and my valet, Mr. Suchandsuch (German, I believe, but I do respect the privacy of all persons), my wigs, my wardrobe, and my lady wife, when I am in possession of such a creature, an occurrence more common and without complaint than you might assume, (of which *much* more, *much* later). I designed the edifice myself, with an eye to every detail, from the silver door-knocker carved in the image of a single, kindly eye whose eyelid must be whacked vigorously against the iris to gain ingress, to the several concealed chambers and passageways for my sole and secret use, all of which open at the pulling of a sconce or the adjusting of an oil painting, that sort of thing, to the smallest of rose motifs stenciled upon the wallpaper. The land whereupon my lady house sits, however, represents a happy accident of real estate investment, as I purchased it a small eternity before the Earl of Bedford seized upon the desire to make of Covent Garden a stylish district for stylish people, and the Earl was forced to make significant accommodations and gratifications on my account. I am always delighted by accommodations and gratifications, particularly when they are forced, and most especially on my account.

The lower floor, which opens most attractively onto the newly-christened and newly-worthwhile Drury Lane, serves as my showroom, and in through my tasteful door flow all the nobly whelped and ignobly wealthed and blind (both from birth and from happenstance, I do not discriminate) and wounded and syphilitic of England, along with not a few who made the journey from France, Italy, Denmark, even the Rus, to receive my peculiar attentions. With the most exquisite consideration, I appointed the walls of my little salon with ultramarine watered silk and discreet, gold-framed portraits of my most distinguished customers. In the northwest corner, you will find what I humbly allege to be the single most comfortable chair in all of Christendom, reclined at an, at first glance, radical angle, that nevertheless offers an extraordinary serenity of ease, stuffed with Arabian horsehair and Spanish barley, sheathed in supple leather the color of a rose just as the last sunlight vanishes behind the mountains. In the northeast corner, you will find, should you but recognize it, my father's pitted and pitiful iron punty, braced above the hearth with all the honor the gentry grant to their tawdry ancestral

# The Limitless Perspective of Master Peek, Or, the Luminescence of Debauchery

swords. The ceiling boasts a fine fresco depicting that drunken uncle of Greek Literature, the Cyclops, trudging through a field of poppies and wheat with a ram under each arm, the floor bears up beneath a deep blanket of choice carpets woven by divinely inspired and contented Safavids, so thick no cheeky draught even imagines it might invade my realm, and all four walls, from baseboard to the height of a man, are outfitted with a series of splendid drawers, in alternating gold and silver designs, presenting to the hands of my supplicants faceted knobs of sapphire, emerald, onyx, amethyst, and jasper. These drawers contain my treasures, my masterpieces, the objects of power with which I line my pockets and sauce my goose. Open one, any one, every one, and all will be revealed on plush velvet cushions, for there rest hundreds upon hundreds of the most beautiful eyes ever to open or close upon this fallen earth.

No fingers as discerning as mine could ever be content with the glazier's endless workaday drudge through plate windows and wine bottles, vases and spectacles and spyglasses, hoping against hope for the occasional excitement of a goblet or a string of beads that might, if you did not look too closely, resemble, in the dark, real pearls. No, no, a thousand, *million* times no! Not for me that life of scarred knuckles whipped by white-molten strands of stray glass, of unbearable heat and even more unbearable contempt oozing from those very ones who needed me to keep the rain out of their parlors and their spirits off the table linen.

I will tell you how I made this daring escape from a life of silicate squalor, and trust you, as I suppose I already have done, to keep my secrets—for what is the worth of a secret if you never spill it? My deliverance came courtesy of a pot of pepper, a disfigured milkmaid, and the Dogaressa of Venice.

It would seem that my brothers were not quite so malevolently egomaniacal as they seemed on that distant, never-to-be-forgotten day when our father drooled his last. One of them was not, at least. Having vanished neatly into London and established myself, albeit in an appallingly meager situation consisting of little more than a single kiln stashed in the best beloved piss-corner of the Arsegate, marvering paltry, poignant cups against the stone steps of a whorehouse, sleeping between two rather unpleasantly amorous cows in a cheesemaker's barn, I was neither happy nor quite wretched, for at least I had made a start. At least I was in the arms of the reeking city. At least I had escaped the trap laid by pearls and hectares and absconding brothers. And then, as these things happen, one day, not different in any quality or deed from any other day, I received a parcel from an exhausted-looking young man dressed in the Florentine style. I remember him as well as my supper Thursday last—the supper was pigeon pie and fried eels with claret; the lad, a terrifically handsome black-haired trifle who went by the rather lofty name of Plutarch, and after wiping the road from his eyes and washing it from his throat with ale that hardly deserved the name, presented me with a most curious item: a fat silver pot, inlaid with a lapis lazuli ship at full sail.

Inside found I a treasure beyond the sweat-drenched dreams of upwardly mobile men, which is to say, a handful of peppercorns and beans of vanil, those exotic, black and fragrant jewels for which the gluttonous world crosses itself three times in thanks. Plutarch explained, at some length, that my brother Prospero now dwelt permanently in the East Indies where he had massed a fabulous fortune, and wished to assure himself that his sister, the sweet, homely maid he abandoned, could make herself a good marriage after all. I begged the poor boy not to use any of those treacherous words again in my or anyone's hearing: not *marriage*, not *maid*, and most of all not *sister*. Please and thank you for the pepper, on your way, tell no one my name nor how you found me and how did you find me by God and the Devil himself—no, don't tell me, I shall locate this lost relative and deliver the goods to her with haste, though I could perhaps be persuaded to pass the night reading a bit of Plutarch before rustling up the wastrel in question, but, hold fast, my darling, I must insist you submit to my peculiar tastes and maintain both our clothing and cover of darkness throughout; I find it sharpens the pleasure of the thing, this is my, shall we say, *firm* requirement, and no argument shall move me.

Thus did I find myself a reasonably rich and well-read man. And that might have made a pleasant and satisfying enough end of it, if not for the milkmaid.

For, as these things happen, one day not long after, not different in any hour or act than any other day, a second parcel appeared upon my, now much finer, though not nearly so fine as my present, doorstep. Her name was Perdita, she was in possession of a complexion as pure as that of a white calf on the day of its birth, hair as red as a fresh wound, an almost offensively pregnant belly, and to crown off her beauty, it must be mentioned, both her eyes had been gouged from her pretty skull by means of, I was shortly to learn, a pair of puritanical ravens.

It would seem that my other brother, Pomposo—you remember him, yes? Paying attention, are we?—was still in the habit of marrying unsuspecting girls off to trees and fish and stones, provided that the trees were his encircling arms, the fish his ardent tongue, and the stones those terribly personal, perceptive, and pendulous seed-vaults of his ardor, and poor, luckless Perdita had taken *quite* the turn round the park. Perhaps we are not so divided by our shared blood as all that, Pomposo! Hats off, my good man, and everything else, too. Well, the delectably lovely and lamentable maid in question found herself afflicted both by Little Lord Pomposo and by that peculiar misfortune which bonds all men as one and makes them brothers: she had a bad father.

Perdita told me of her predicament over my generous table. She spoke with more haste than precision, tearing out morsels of Mrs. Matterfact's incomparable baked capon in almond sauce with her grubby fingers and shoveling it into that plump face whilst she rummaged amongst her French pockets for English words to close in her tale like a green and garnishing parsley. As far as I could gather, her cowherding father had, in his youth, contracted the disease of religion, a most severe and acute strain. He took the local clergyman's daughter to wife, promptly locked her in his granary to keep her safe from both sin and any amusement at all, and removed a child from her every year or so until she perished from, presumably, the piercing shame of having tripped and fallen into one of the more tiresome fairy tales. Perdita's father occupied the time he might have spent *not* slowly murdering his wife upon his one and only hobby: the keeping of birds of prey. Now, one cannot fault the man for that! But he loved no falcons nor hawks nor eagles, only a matched pair of black-hearted ravens he called by the names of Praisegod and Feargod (there really can be no accounting for, or excusing of, the tastes of Papists) which he had trained from the egg to hunt down the smallest traces of wickedness upon his estate and among his children. For this unlikely genius had taught his birds, painstakingly, to detect the delicate and complex scents of sexual congress, and the corvids twain became so adept that they were known to arrive at many a village window only moments after the culmination of the act.

Now you have taken up all the pieces of this none-too-sophisticated puzzle and can no doubt assume the rest. My brother conquered Perdita's virtue with ease, for no such dour and draconian devoutness can raise much else but libertines, a fact which may yet save us from the vicious fate of a world redeemed, and put my niece (for indeed it proved to be a niece) in her with little enough care for anything but the trees and the fish and the stones of his own bucolic life. No sooner than he had rolled off of her but Praisegod and Feargod arrived, screeching to wake the glorious dead, the scent of coupling maddening their black brains, and devoured Perdita's eyeballs in a hideous orgy of gore and terribly poor parenting. Pomposo, ever steadfast and humbly responsible for his own affairs, sent his distress directly to me and, I imagine, poured a brimming glass of wine with which to toast himself.

# The Limitless Perspective of Master Peek, Or, the Luminescence of Debauchery

"My dear lady," said I, gently prying a joint of Mrs. Matterfact's brandied mutton from her fist, hoping to preserve at least something for myself, "I cannot imagine what you or my good brother mean *me* to do with a child. I am a bachelor, I wish devoutly to remain so, and my bachelorhood is only redoubled by my regrettable feelings toward children, which mirror the drunkard's for a mug of clear water: well enough and wholesome for most, he supposes, but what can one *do* with one? But I am not pitiless. That, I am not, my dear. You may, of course, remain here until the child…occurs, and we shall endeavor to locate some suitable position in town for one of your talents."

Ah, but I had played my hand and missed the trick! "You misunderstand, *monsieur*," protested the comely Perdita. "Mister Pompy didn't send me to you for your *hospitalité*. He said in London he had a brother who could make me eyes twice as pretty as they ever were and would only charge me the favor of not squeezing out my babe on his parlor floor."

Even a thousand miles distant, my skinflint family could put the screws to me, turn them tight, and have themselves a nice giggle at my groans. But at least the old boy guessed my game of trousers and did not give me up, even to his paramour.

"They was green," the milkmaid whispered, and the ruination of her eye sockets bled in place of weeping. "Like clover."

Oh, very well! I am not a *monster*. In any event, I wasn't then. At least the commission was an interesting enough challenge to my lately listless and undernourished intellect. So it came to pass that over the weeks remaining until the parturition of Perdita, I fashioned, out of crystal and ebony and chips of fine jade, twin organs of sight not the equal of mortal orbs, but by far their superior, in clarity, in beauty, even in soulfulness. If you ask me how I accomplished it, I shall show you the door, for I am still a tradesman, however exalted, and tradesmen tell no tales. I sewed the spheres myself with thread of gold into her fair face, an operation which sounds elegant and difficult in the telling, but in the doing required rather more gin, profanity, and blows to the chin than any window did. When I had finished, she appeared, not healed, but more than healed—sublimated, rarefied, elevated above the ranks of human women with their filmy, vitreous eyes that could merely *see*.

I have heard good report that, under another name, and with her daughter quite grown and well-wed, Perdita now sits upon the throne of the Netherlands, her peerless eyes having captivated the heart of a certain prince before anyone could tie a rock round her feet and drop her into a canal. Well done, say all us graspers down here, reaching up toward Heaven's sewers with a thousand million hands, well done.

Now, we arrive at the hairpin turn in the road of both my fortunes and my life, the skew of the thing, where the carriage of our tale may so easily overturn and send us flying into mud and thorns unknown. Brace your constitution and your credulity, for I am of a mind to whip the horses and take the bend at speed!

It is simply not possible to excel so surpassingly as I have done and remain anonymous. God in his perversity grants anonymity to the gifted and the industrious in equal and heartless measure, but never to the *splendid*. Word of the girl with the unearthly, alien, celestial eyes spread like a plague of delight in every direction, floating down the river, sweeping through the Continent, stowing away on ships at sea, until it arrived, much adorned with my Lady Rumor's laurels, at the *palazzo* of the Doge in darling, dripping Venice.

Now, the Doge at that time had caused himself, God knows why or by dint of what wager, to be married to a woman by the name of Samaritiana. Do not allow yourselves to be duped by that name, you trusting fools! Samaritiana would not even stop along the side of the road to Hell to wrinkle her nose at the carcass of Our Lord Jesus Christ, though it save her immortal soul, unless He told her she was beautiful first. Oh, 'tis easy enough to hate a vain woman with warts and liver spots, to scorn her milk baths and philtres and exsanguinated Hungarian virgins, to mock her desperation to preserve a youth and beauty that was never much more enticing than the local sheep in the first place, but one had to look elsewhere for reasons to hate Samaritiana, for she truly was the singular beauty of her age. Black of hair, eye, and ambition was she, pale as a maiden drowned, buxom as Ceres (though she had yet no issue), intoxicating as the breath of Bacchus. Fortunately, my lady thoughtfully provided a bounty of other pantries in which to find that meat of hatred fit for the fires of any heart.

She was, quite simply, the worst person.

I do not mean by this to call the Dogaressa a murderess, nor an apostate, nor a despot, nor an embezzler, nor even a whore, for whores, at least, are kindly and useful, murderers must have some measure of cleverness if they mean to get away with it, apostates make for *tremendous* company at parties, despots have a positively devastating charisma, and I am assured by the highest authority, which is to say, Lord Aphorism and his Merry Band of Proverbials, that there is some honor amongst thieves. No, Samaritiana was merely humorless, witless, provincial, petty, small of mind, parched of imagination, stingy of wallet and affection, morally conservative, and incapable, to the last drop of her ruby blood, of admitting that she did not know everything in all the starry spheres and wheeling orbits of existence, and this whilst believing herself to possess all of these that are virtues and eschew all that are sins. Can you envisage a more wretched and unloveable beast?

I married her, naturally.

The Dogaressa came to me in a black resin mask and emerald hooded cloak when the plague had only lately checked into its waterfront rooms, sent for a litter, and commenced seeing the sights of Venice with its traveling hat and trusted map. Oh, no, no, you misapprehend my phraseology. Not *that* plague. Not that grave and gorgeous darkling shadow that falls over Europe once a century and reminds us that what dwells within our bodies is not a soul but a stinking ruin of fluid and marrow and bile. The *other* plague, the one that sneaks on nimbly putrefying feet from bedroom to bedroom, from dockside to dinner party, from brothel to marital bower, leaving chancres like kisses too long remembered. Yes, we would have to wait years yet before Baron von Buboe mounted his much-anticipated revival on the stage, but never you fear, Dame Syphilis was dancing down the dawn, and in those days, her viols never stopped nor slowed.

That mysterious, morbid, nigh-monstrous and tangerine-scented creature called Samaritiana darkened my door one evening in April, bid me draw close all my curtains, light only a modest lantern upon a pretty lacquered table inlaid with mother of pearl which I still possess to this day, and stand some distance away while she removed her onyx mask to reveal a face of such surpassing radiance, such unparalleled winsomeness, that even the absence of the left eye, and the mass of scars and weals that had long since replaced it, could do no more than render her enchanting rather than perfect.

It would seem that the Dogaressa danced with the Dame some years past. Her husband, the Doge, brought her to the ball, she claimed, having learned the steps from his underaged Neapolitan mistress, though, as I became much acquainted with the lady in later years, I rather suspect she found her own way, arrived first, wore through three pairs of shoes, departed last, and ate all the cakes on the sideboard. But, as is far too often the case in this life ironical, that mean and miserly soul found itself in receipt of, not only the beauty of a better woman, but the good fortune of a better man. She contracted a high fever owing to her insistence upon hosting the Christmas feast out of doors that year, so that the gathered nobility could see how lovely she looked with a high winter's blush on her cheeks, and this fever seemed to have driven, by some idiot, insensate alchemy, the Dame from the halls of Samaritiana forever, leaving only her eye ravaged and boiled away by the waltz. All was well in the world, then, save that she could not show herself in public without derision and her husband still rotted on his throne with a golden nose hung on his mouldering face like a door knocker, but she had not come for his sake, nor would she ever dream of fancying that it was possible to ask a boon of that oft-rumored wizard hiding in the sty of London for any single soul on earth other than herself.

"I have heard that you can make a new eye," said she, in dulcet tones she did not deserve the ability to produce.

I could.

"Better than the old, brighter, of any color or shape?"

I could.

She licked her lily lips. "And install it so well none would suspect the exchange?"

Perhaps not quite, not *entirely* so well, but it never behooves one to admit weakness to a one-eyed queen.

"You have already done me this service," said she to me, loftily, never asking once, only demanding, presuming, crushing all resistance, not to mention dignity, custom, the basest element of courtesy, beneath her silver-tooled heel. She waved her hand as though the motion of her fingers could destroy all protestation. The light of my lantern caught on a ring of peridot and tourmaline entwined into the shape of a rather maudlin-looking crocodile gnawing upon its own tail, for she claimed some murky Egyptian blood in the dregs of her familial cup, as though such little droplets could mark her as exceptional, when every dockside lady secretly fancies herself a Cleopatra of the Thames.

"Produce the results upon the morrow! I will pay you nothing, of course. A Dogaressa does not stoop to exchange currency for goods. But when two eyes look out from beneath my brow once more, I will present you with a gift, for no particular reason other than that I wish to bestow it."

"And if I do not like your gift, *Clarissima?*"

Puzzlement contorted her exquisitely Cyclopean visage, causing a most unwelcome familial pang within my breast. "I do not take your meaning, Master Peek. How could such a thing possibly occur?"

There is, it seems, a glittering point beyond which egotism achieves such purity that it becomes innocence, and that was the country in which Samaritiana lived. In truth, had she revealed her gift to me then, or even promised payment in the usual manner, I might have refused her, just to experience the novel emotion of rejecting royalty—for I am interested in nothing so much as novelty, not love nor death nor glass nor gold. Something new! Something new! My kingdom for something new! But she caught me, the perfumed spider, wholly without knowing what she'd done. I did indeed take up her commission, and though you may conclude in advance that this recounting of the job will proceed according to the pattern of the last, I shall be disappointed if you do, for I have already told you most vividly that herein lies the skew of my tale.

For the sake of the beautiful Dogaressa, I took up my father's battered old pipe and punty. I cannot now say why; for a certainty I owned better instruments by far, and had not touched the things in eons except to brush them daintily with a daily sneer. Perhaps a paroxysm of sentimentality seized me; perhaps I despised her too much even then to waste my finer appliances on her pox-punched face, in any event, I cannot even say positively that the result blossomed forth from the tools and not some other cause, and I fear to question it now. I sank into the rhythm of my father and grandfather and his before him: the dollop of liquid glass, the greatbreath of my own lungs expelled through the long, black pipe, the sweet pressure and rolling of the globule against the smooth marver stone, the uncommon light known only to workers of glass, that strange slick of marmalade-light afire within crystal that would soon ride a woman's skull all the way through the days of her life and down into her tomb.

The work was done; I fashioned two, an exquisitely matched pair, in case the other organ required replacement in the unseen feverish future. Samaritiana, in, so far as I may know or tell, the sole creative decision of her existence, chose not one color for the iris, but all of them, dozens of infinitesimal shards chipped from every jewel in my inventory: sapphire, jade, emerald, jasper, onyx, amethyst, ruby, topaz. The effect was a carnival wheel of deep, unsettling fascination, and when I sewed it into her flesh with my golden thread she did not wail or struggle, but only sighed, as though lost in the act of love, and, though her faults were called Legion, they were as yet unknown to me, thus, as my needle entered her, so too did my fatal softening begin.

The Dogaressa departed with her stitching still fresh, leaving in her wake but three souvenirs of our intimate surgery: one gift she intended, one she did not, and her damnable scent, which neither Mrs. Matterfact nor Mr. Suchandsuch, no matter how they scrubbed and strove, could remove from the premises. I daresay, even this very night, should you venture to my old house on the High Street and pressed your nose to its sturdy bones, still yet you would snatch a whiff of tangerine and strangling ivy from the foundation stones. The gift she intended to leave was a lock of her raven hair, the skinflint bitch. The other, I did not perceive until some weeks later, when I adjourned to my smoking room with a bottle of brandy, a packet of snuff, and a rare contemplative mood which I intended to spend upon a rich, unfiltered melancholy as sweet as any Madeira—for it is a fact globally acknowledged that idle melancholy, like good wine, is the exclusive purview of the wealthy. To aid in my melancholy, I fingered in one hand the mate to the Dogaressa's harlequin eye, rubbing my thumb over that strange, motley iris, marveling at the milky sheen of the sclera, admiring, unrepentant Narcissus that I am, my own skill and artistry. I removed my own, ordinary, unguessable, nearly flawless glass eye and held up the other to my empty socket like a spyglass, and a most thoroughly stupendous metamorphosis transpired: I could *see* through the jeweled lens of that artificial eye! Truly see, without cloud or glare or halo—ah, but *what* I saw was not the walls of my own smoking room, so tastefully lined with matching books chosen to neither excite nor bore any guest to extremes, but the long peach-cream and gold hall of *the palazzo of the Doge in far-distant Venice!* The chequered black and white marble floors flowed forth in my vision like a houndstooth river; the full and unforgiving moon streamed glaucous through tall slim windows; painted ceilings soared overhead, inlaid with pearl and carnelian and ever-so-slightly greyed with the smoke of a hundred thousand candles burnt over peerless years in that grand corridor. Women and men swept slowly up and down the squares like boats upon some fairy canal, swathed in gowns of viridescent green cross-hatched with silver and rose, armored in bodices of whalebone and opal, be-sailed in lacy gauze spun by Clotho herself upon the wheel of destiny, cloaked and hooded in vermillion damask, in aquamarine, in citron and puce, their clothing each so splendid I could scarce tell the maids from the swains—and thus looked I upon a personal paradise heretofore undreamt of.

But there were worms in paradise, for each and every beauty in the Doge's palace was rotting in their finery like the fruit of sun-spoiled melons within their shells. Their flesh putrefied and dripped from their bones and what remained turned hideous, sickening colors, choleric, livid, cyanic, hoary, a moldering patina of death whose effusions stained those bodices black. Some stumbled noseless, others having replaced that appendage with nostrils of gold and silver and crystal and porcelain, and others, all hope lost, sunk their visages into masks, though they could not hide their chancred hands, the bleeding sores of their bosoms, the undead tatters of their throats.

Yet still they laughed, and spoke animatedly, one to the other, and blushed in virtuous fashion beneath their putridity. Such is the dance of the Dame, who enters through the essential act of life, yet leaves you thinking, breathing, walking whilst the depredations of the grave transact upon your still-sensate flesh, making of this world a single noisy tomb.

My breath would not obey me; my heart ricocheted amongst my ribs like a cannon misfired. Was it truly Italy I saw bounded in the

# The Limitless Perspective of Master Peek,
## Or, the Luminescence of Debauchery

tiny planet of a glass eye? Had I stumbled into a drunken sleep or gone mad so swiftly no asylum could hope to catch me? I shot to my feet, mashing the eye deeper into my socket until stars spattered my sight—closer, look closer! Could I hear as well? Smell? Taste the tallowed air of that far-off moonlit court?

I could not. I could not hear their footsteps nor inhale their perfume nor feel the fuzzed reek of the mildewed canals on my tongue nor move of my own volition. I apprehended a new truth, that even the impossible possesses laws of its own, and those unbendable. I could only observe. Observe—while my vision lurched forward, advancing quickly, rocking gently as with a woman's sinuous gait. Graceful, slender arms extended as though from my own body, opening with infinite elegance to embrace a man whose head was that of a Titan cast down brutally into the pit of Tartarus, so wracked with growths and intuberances and pulsating polyps that the plates of his skull had cracked beneath the intolerable weight and shifted into a new pate so monstrous it could no longer bear the Doge's crown, which hung pitifully instead from a ribbon slung round his grotesque neck. Those matchless arms which were not my own enfolded this hapless creature and, encircling the middle finger of the hand belonging to the right arm, I saw with my altered vision the twisted peridot and tourmaline crocodile ring of the Dogaressa Samaritiana.

I cast the glass eye away from me, sickened, thrilled, inflamed, ensorcelled, the fire in my midnight hearth as nothing beside the conflagration of curiosity, horror, and the beginnings of power that crackled within my brain-pan. In that first moment, standing among my books and my brandy drenched in the sweat of a new universe, an instinct, a whisper of Truth Profound, permeated my spirit like smoke exhaled, and, I confess to you now, all these many years hence, still I enshrine it as an article of faith, for it was with *breath* that God animated the dumb mud of Adam, *breath* that woke Pandora from stone, *breath* that demarcates the living and the dead, *breath* with which we speak and cry out and divide ourselves from the idiot kingdom of animals, and *breath*, by all the blasted saints and angels, with which the glassblower shapes his glass! The living breath of Cornelius Peek yet permeates every insignificant atom of his works; each object broken from his punty, be it window or goblet or cask or eye, hides the sacred exhalations of his spirit co-mingled with the crystal, and it is this, it is *this*, I tell you, that connects the jeweled eye of the Dogaressa with the jeweled eye in my hand! *I* dwell in the glass, it cannot dispense with me any further than it can dispense with translucency or mass, and therefore it carries the shard of Cornelius whithersoever it wanders.

Let us dispense with a few obnoxious but inevitable inquiries into the practicality of the matter, so that we may move along past the skew. How could this mystic connection have escaped my notice till now? It is only sensical: Perdita vanished away to the Netherlands with both marvelous eyes, and no window nor goblet nor cask is, in its inborn nature, that organ of sight which opens onto the infinite pit of the human soul. Would any eye manufactured in the same fashion result in such remote visions? They would indeed, my credulous friend. Does every glassblower possess the ability to produce such objects, should he but retain one eye whilst selling the other at a fair price? Ah, here I must admit my deficiency as a philosopher, for which I apologize most obsequiously. It cannot be breath alone, for I made subtle overtures toward the gentleman of the glassmen's guild and I can say with a solemn certainty that none but Master Peek can perform this alchemy of sclera and pupil. Why should it be so? Perhaps I am a wizard, perhaps a saint, perhaps a demiurge, perhaps the Messiah returned at last, perhaps it owes only to that peculiar rootstock of my family which grants me my height, my baritone, the hairiness of my body. Grandfather Polyphemus's last gift, lobbed down the ancestral highway, bashing horses as it comes. I am a man of art, not science. I ask why Mrs. Matterfact has not yet laid out my supper oftener than I ask after the workings of the uncluttered cosmos.

Thus did I enter the business of optometry.

## The Limitless Perspective of Master Peek, Or, the Luminescence of Debauchery

When you have placed a mad rainbow jewel in the skull of a Dogaressa as though she were nothing but a golden ring, a jewel which drove the rotting men of Venice insane with the desire to tie her to a bridge-post and stare transported into the motley swirling colors of the eye of God, lately fallen to earth, they began to say, somewhere in Sicily, advertisement serves little purpose. I opened my door and received the flood. It is positively *trivial* to lose an eye in this wicked world, did you know? I accepted them warmly, with a bow and a kerchief fluttered to the mouth in acute compassion, a permanently sympathetic expression penciled onto my lips in primrose paint—for that moth-eaten scab Cromwell was finally in the grave, where everything is just as colorless and abstemious and black as he always wished it to be, so full of piss and vitriol that it poisoned him to the gills, and Our Chuck, the Merry Monarch, was dancing on his bones. Fashion, ever my God and my mother, took pity upon her poor supplicant and caused a great miracle to take place for my sake—the world donned a dandy wig whilst I doffed my own, sporting my secret womanly hair as long and curled as any lord, soaking my face in the most masculine of pale powders, rouges, lacquers, and creams, encasing my figure, such as it ever was, in lime and coral brocade trimmed in frosty silver, concealing my gait with an ivory cane and foxfurred slippers, and rejoicing in the knowledge that, of all the men in London, I suddenly possessed the lowest voice of them all. So hidden, so revealed, I took all the one-eyed world into my parlor: the cancerous, the war-wounded, the horse-kicked, the husband-beaten, the inquisitor-inquisited, the lightning-struck, the unfortunately-born, the pox-blighted, and yes, the Dame's erstwhile lovers, for she had made her way to our shores and had begun her ancient gambols in sight of St. Paul's. And for each of these unfortunate angels of the ocular, I fashioned a second eye in secret, unknown entirely to my custom, twin to the one that repaired their befouled faces, with which I adjourned night by night to a series of successive smoking rooms, growing grander and finer with each year, holding those orbs to the light and looking unseen upon every city in Christendom, along with several in the Orient and one in the New World, though it could hardly be called a city, if I am to be honest.

In this fashion, I came to know that the Doge had died, succumbed to the unbearable weight of his own head, long before Samaritiana appeared on my night-bestrewn doorstep, the saffron gown she wore in the moonlight, and every other in her trunk, torn violently, soaked with bodily fluids, rent by the overgrown nails of the frenzied rotting horde who had chased her from the *palazzo* through every desperate alleyway and canal of the city, across Switzerland and France, in their anguished longing to touch the Eye of God, still sewn into the ex-Dogaressa's skull, to touch it but once and be healed forever.

But of course I aided the friendless and abandoned Good Samaritiana as she wept beside her monstrous road. Oh, *Clarissima*, how dreadful, how unspeakable, how worthy of Mr. Pepys's vigilant pen! I shall have to make introductions when you are quite well again. I sent at once for a fine dressmaker of my acquaintance to construct a suitable costume for the lady and save her from the immodesty of those ragged silken remnants of her former life with which, even then, she attempted to cover her body with little enough success that, before the dressmaker could so much as cross the river, I learned something quite unexpected concerning the biography of Samaritiana, former queen of Venice.

She was quite male. Undeniably, conspicuously, astonishingly, fascinatingly so.

I called up to Mrs. Matterfact for cold oxtongue, a saucer of pineapple, and oysters stewed in Armagnac, down to Mr. Suchandsuch for carafes of hot claret mulled via the latest methods, and listened to the wondrous chimera in my parlor tell of how that famous Egyptian blood was not in the least of the Nile but of the Tiber, on whose Ostian banks a penniless but beautiful boy had been born in secret to one of the Pope's mistresses and left to perish among the reed-gatherers and the amber-collectors and the diggers of molluscs. But perish the lad did not, for even a grass-picker is thoroughly loused with the nits of compassion, and the women passed the babe one to the other and back again, like a cup of wine that drank, instead, from them. Now, it is well known to anyone with a single sopping slice of sense that the Pope's enemies are rather like weevils, ever industrious, ever multiplying, ever rapacious, starving for the chaff of scandal with which to choke the Holy Father and watch him writhe. They roved over the city, overturning the very foundational stones of ancient Rome in search of the Infallible Bastards, in order, not to kill them like Herod, but to bring them before the Cardinals and etch their little faces upon the stained glass windows as evidence of sin. My little minx, having already long, lustrous hair and androgyne features more like to a seraph than a by-blow son, found it at first advantageous to effect the manners and dress of a girl, and then, when the danger had passed, more than that, agreeable, even preferable to her former existence. Having become a maid to save her life, she remained one in order to enjoy it. Owing to the meager diet of the Tiber's tiniest fish, little Samaritiana never grew so tall nor so stout as other boys, she remained curiously hairless, and though she escaped the castrato's fate, her voice never dipped beneath the pleasing alto with which she now spoke, nor did her organ of masculinity ever aspire to outdo the average Grecian statue, and so, when the Doge visited Ostia after the death of his first wife, he saw nothing unusual walking by the river except for the most beautiful woman in the Occident, balancing a basket of rushes on her hip with a few nuggets of amber rolling within the weave.

"But surely, *Clarissima*," mused I, savoring the tart song of pineapple upon my tongue, "a bridegroom, however ardent, cannot be so easily duped as a vengeful Cardinal! Your deception cannot have survived the wedding bower!"

"It did not survive the engagement, my dear Master Peek," Samaritiana replied without a wisp of blush upon her remarkable cheek. "Oh, mistake me not, I do *so* love to lie—I see no more purpose in pretending to be virtuous in your presence than I saw in pretending to be fertile in his. But there could be no delight in a deception so deep and vast. It would impair true marriage between us. I revealed myself at Pentecost, allowing him in the intensity of his ardor to unfasten my stays and loose my ribbons until I stood clad only in honesty before His Serenity and awaited what I presumed to be my doom and my death. But only kisses fell upon me in that moment, for the Doge had long suppressed his inborn nature, and suffered already to get upon his departed wife the heirs he owed to the canals, and though my masquerade, you will agree, outshines the impeccable, he would later say, on the night of which you so confidently speak, that some sinew of his heart must always have known, since first he beheld me with my basket of amber and sorrow."

I did not exchange trust for trust that night among the oysters and the oxtongue. I have a viciously refined sense of theatre, after all. I made her wait, feigning religion, indigestion, the vicissitudes of work, gout, even virginity, until our wedding night, whereupon I allowed Samaritiana, in the intensity of her ardor, to unfasten my stays and loose my ribbons until at last all that stood between us was the tattered ruin of my mother's ancient bridal veil, and then, not even that.

"Goodness, you don't expect me to be surprised, do you?" laughed the ex-Dogaressa, the monster, the braying centaur, the miserly lamia who would not give me the satisfaction of scandalizing her! That eve, and only that eve, under the stars painted upon my ceiling, I applied all my cruellest and most unfair arts to compel my wife to admit, as a wedding present, that she had *not* known, she had never known, never even suspected, loved me as a man just as I loved her as a woman, and was besides a brutal little liar who deserved a lifetime of the most delectable punishment. We exchanged whispered, apocryphal, long-atrophied names beneath the coverlet: *Perpetua. Proteo.*

Samartiana treated me deplorably, broke my heart and my bank, laughed when she ought to have wept, drove Mrs. Matterfact to utter disintegration, kept lovers, schemed with minor nobles. We were just ferociously happy. Are you surprised? I, too, am humorless, witless, provincial, petty, small of mind, parched of imagination, stingy of wallet and affection, a liar and a cad. He was like me. I was like her. I had, after all, seen as she saw, from the very angle of her waking vision, which in some circles might be the definition of divine love. I have had wives before and will have again, far cleverer and braver and wilder than my Clarissima, but none I treasured half so well, nor came so near to telling the secret of my smoking room, of the chests full of eyes hidden beneath the floorboards. Samaritiana had her lovers; I had my eyes, the voyeur's stealthy, soft and pregnant hours, a criminal sensorium I could not quit nor wished to. Yet still I would not share, I held it back from her, out of her reach, beyond her ken.

The plague took her in the spring. The Baron, not the Dame. The plague of long masks and onions and bodies stacked like fresh laid bricks. I buried her in glass, in my incandescent fury at the kiln, for where else can a man lose his whole being but in a wife or in work? These are the twin barrels in which we drown ourselves forever.

It soon came to pass that wonderful eyes of Cornelius Peek were in such demand that the possession of one could catapult the owner into society, if only he could keep his head about him once he landed, and this was reason enough that, men being men and ambition being forever the most demanding of bedfellows, it became much the fashion in those years to sacrifice one eye to the teeth-grinding god of social mobility and replace it with something far more useful than depth perception. Natural colors fell by the wayside—they wanted an angel's eye, now, a demon's, a dryad's, a goblin's, more alien, more inhuman, less windows to the soul than windows to debauched and lawless Edens and I, your servant, sir, a window-maker once more. I cannot say I approved of this self-deformation, but I certainly profited by the sudden proliferation of English Cyclopses, most especially by their dispersal through the halls of power, carrying the breath of Peek with them into every shadowy corner of the privileged and the perverse.

I strung their eyes on silver thread and lay in a torpor like unto the opium addict upon the lilac damask of my smoking room couch, draping them round and round my body like a strand of numberless pearls, lifting each crystal gem in turn to gaze upon Paris, Edinburgh, Madrid, Muscovy, Constantinople, Zurich—and Venice, always Venice, returning again and again, though I knew I would not find what I sought along those rippling canals traveled by the living dead. It became my obsession, this invasion of perspective, this theft of privacy, the luxurious passivity of the thing, watching without participating as the lives of others fluttered by like so many scarlet leaves, compelled to witness, but not to interfere, even if I wished to, even if I had liked the young Earl well enough when I installed his pigment-less diamond eye, and longed to parry the assassin's blade when I saw it flash in the Austrian sunset. I saw, with tremulous breath, as God saw, forced unwilling to allow the race of man to damn or redeem itself in a noxious fume of free will, forbidden by laws unwritten not to lift one hand, even if the baker's boy had laughed when I offered him a big red eye or a cat-slit pupil or a shark's unbroken onyx hue, any sort, free of charge, even the costliest, the most debonair, in honor of my late wife Samaritiana who in another lifetime paid me in hair, not because she would wish me to be generous, but because she would mock me to the rafters and howl hazard down to Hell, begging the Devil to take me now rather than let one more pauper rob her purse, even if I saw, now, through his eye, saw the maidservant burning, burning in the bakery on Pudding Lane, burning and screaming in the midnight wind, and then the terrible, impossible leap of the flames to the adjoining houses, an orange tongue lasciviously working in the dark, not to lift one hand as what I saw in the glass eye and what I saw in the flesh became one, fusing and melding at last, reality and unreality, the sight I owned and the sight I stole, the conflagration devouring the city, the gardens, and my house around me, my lovely watered ultramarine silk, my supremely comfortable chair stuffed with Arabian horsehair, my darling gold and silver drawers, as I lay still and let it come for me and thee and all.

I did not *die*, for heaven's sake. Perish the thought! Death is terrifically *gauche*, don't you know, I should never be caught wearing it in public. I simply did not get *up*. Irony being the Lord of All Things, the smoking room survived the blaze and I inside it; though the rafters smoked and blackened and the walls swelled with heat like the head of a Doge, the secret chambers honeycombing the place contained the inferno, they did not stove in nor fall, save for one shelf of books, the bloody Romans, of all things, which, in toppling, quite snapped both my shinbones beneath a ponderous copy of Plutarch. Mrs. Matterfact and Mr. Suchandsuch fought valiantly and gave up only the better part of the roof, though we lost my lovely showroom, a tragedy from which I shall never fully recover, I assure you. And for a long while, I remained where the fire found me, on the long damask couch in my smoking room, wrapped in lengths of eyes like Odysseus lashed to the mast and listening to all the sirens' mating bleats, still lifting each in turn and fixing it to my empty socket, one after the other after the other, and thus I stayed for years, years beyond years, beyond Matterfact and Suchandsuch and their replacements, beyond the intolerable plebians outside who wanted only humble, honest brown and blue eyes again, their own mortal eyes, having seen too much of wildness. And what, pray tell, did I do with my impossible sight, with my impossible span of time?

Why, I became the greatest spy the world has ever known. Would you have done otherwise?

Oh, I have sold crowns to kings and kings to executioners, positions to the enemy and ships to the storm, murderers to the avenging and perversities to the puritanical, I have caused ingenious devices to be built in England before the paint in Krakow finished drying, rescued aristocrats from the mob and mobs from the aristocracy by turns, bought and traded and brokered half of Europe to the other half and back again, dashed more sailors against the rocks than my promethean progenitor could have done in the throes of his most orgiastic fever-dream. I have smote the ground and summoned up wars from the deeps and I have called down the heavens to end them, all without moving one whisper from my house on Drury Lane, even as the laborers rebuilt it around me, even as the rains came, even as the lane around it became a writhing slum, a whore's racetrack, a nursery rhyme.

Look around you and look well: this is the world I made. Isn't it charming? Isn't it terrible and exquisite and debased and tastefully appointed according to the very latest of styles? I have seen to every detail, every flourish—think nothing of it, it has been my great honor.

But the time has come to rouse myself, for my eyes have begun to grow dark, and of late I spy muchly upon the damp and wormy earth, for who would not beg to be buried with their precious Peek eye, bauble of a bygone—and better—age? No one, not even the baker's boy. The workshop of Master Cornelius Peek will open doors once more, for I have centuries sprawled at my feet like Christmas tinsel, and I would not advance upon them blind. I have heard the strange mournful bovine lowing of what I am assured are called the *proletariat* outside my window, the clack and clatter of progress to whose rhythm all men must waltz. There is much work to be done if I do not wish to have the next century decorated by some other, coarser, less splendid hand. I shall curl my hair and don the lime and coral coat, crack the ivory cane against the stones once more, and if the fashions have sped beyond me, so be it, I care nothing, I will stand for the best of us, for in the end, the world will always belong to dandies, who alone see the filigree upon the glass that is God's signature upon his work.

After all, it is positively *trivial* to lose an eye in this midden of modernity, this precarious, perilous world!

Don't you agree?

# Daisy Green Says I Love You

from *The Refrigerator Monologues*

**H**ELLO, DEADTOWN, MY DARLING. YOU look wonderful tonight. Just as beautiful as the day we met.

I've been thinking a lot about rules lately. About karma, I guess, even though most people abuse that word just *viciously*. They don't give one spangly fuck about the wheel of becoming and unbecoming, they just want to rub themselves furiously against the idea that bad things only happen to bad people. Samsara is just something they name their cat. But the longer I'm dead the more I think the universe is a big blackboard with rules scrawled all over it in chalk and stardust and it's just that the damn thing is flipped over and turned away from us so we can't see anything but the eraser which is death waiting on the floor. Write out your life one thousand times, kid, or you'll have to come back and finish tomorrow.

Deadtown, maybe it's time to spill my very specific and personal beans into your pretty china bowl. Maybe it's time to answer those questions you're all too far too polite and gracious to ask.

Bad things happen to bad people. Bad things happen to good people. Bad things happen to okay people. Bad things happen to everyone. Good things happen to…well, somebody, probably. Somebody somewhere else.

But I think I figured out one of the rules on the other side of that great squeaky cosmological blackboard. It's not a big rule. No need to carve it in clay tablets with fiery finger paint and proclaim it from any kind of mount. It wouldn't even make the Macrocosm Top Ten. But it's there, I think. Crammed in at the bottom just under *Light Is Both a Particle and a Wave* but above *Don't Cut in Line*. Are you ready? Here it is: Daisy Green's Zero Sum Law of Luck.

Luck is a finite and rare substance in the universe, like palladium or cobalt. To use it, you have to take it from somebody else.

I'm pretty sure Misha Malinov stole my luck.

He didn't mean to. They never *mean* to do anything in the beginning. But a superhero is like a black hole. They bend everything around them without even thinking about it. And they'd better be lucky as a goddamned leprechaun wearing a rabbit-foot coat on lottery day, or they'll never get through one single fight with a D-list villain. So they just...suck it up from everyone around them. Trust me, kiss one hero and the coin will never land your way again for the rest of your life. And all that shit, all that horror they can leap in a single bound...all that shit has to land somewhere.

I had a little luck, for a little while. Not born-a-Kennedy or cash-out-your-stocks-in-1928 luck, but something small, something all my own I could fold up and keep at the bottom of my sock drawer. My dad moved us from Lewiston, Maine to Brighton Beach when I was six, so I'd never have to save up enough on my own to move to New York. My mother was in a terrible car crash when I was a baby, but she lived, and she only has a little limp, you'd barely notice it. I was born looking the way most people secretly figure a Real American Girl (™!) should look—blonde, blue-eyed, good figure, nice teeth. No major allergies or crippling anxieties. A good mind for math and a flair for performing. I've played Juliet more times than you want to know about. Directors look at me and think: *that's just the kind of girl you fall in love with the minute you see her at your parents' garbage party and kill yourself over a week later*. I drew good cards from a stacked deck, and I played them well.

Until I met Misha Malinov.

You know him as Mikey Miller, the Insomniac, the Coney Island Crusader, Working Class Warrior and Skee Ball Champion of the World.

But when my dad buckled me in next to a shy, worried-looking ten-year-old boy on the Cyclone at Luna Park, his name was Misha Malinov, and he hadn't slept in six years. He only spoke a little English and he had these big brown eyes like the kind of liquor fathers drink and he was way luckier than me. You have to be, if you get yourself born in a place called Pripyat in 1982 and you think it'd be pretty sweet to see the 90s. His parents worked at the nuclear plant, right up until it decided to shit molten poison into the Ukrainian forest and make sure everyone would remember its name forever. They died trying to save the machinery. By the time his aunt and uncle brought him to America, he knew something was very wrong with him, even if he didn't know what. By the time we rode the Cyclone together, Miasma was already coming through to our world on a semi-regular schedule.

We didn't date in high school or anything. I recognized him at the start of sixth grade, Mikey-not-Misha-thank-you-miss, sitting in the front row, flinching if Mrs. Kendrick moved too quickly, drawing in his notebook in a way that really honestly looked like he was taking notes. But I had my own thing going back then, and that's how I kept my luck. He saw me play Juliet for the first time, and Mary Magdalene and Ophelia and Laura in *Glass Menagerie* and Emily from *Our Town*, High School's Drama's Greatest Hits. He always came. He waited after curtain call to tell me I was wonderful. And that was it. Mikey-not-Misha got nervous around people, and the longer he had to be around someone, the more nervous he got, until he looked like he was going to shake apart right in front of you and you'd see that he'd just been a bunch of little kids in a trenchcoat all along. I know what you're thinking—that old story. Pretty, popular girl doesn't pay attention to the shy boy who loves her, film at 11. But he didn't give anyone a chance. He was trying to save us from day one.

If he talked to someone for too long, Miasma would come after them.

But I didn't know that then.

I went out to Hollywood; Mikey Miller went to law school. I got an Apple commercial and then a recurring role on the latest iteration of *Gorgeous White Teens Inventing Problems for Themselves*, a show that can never be canceled, only renamed. The lead actor took my glasses off in the Christmas episode and discovered I was beautiful. After we cut for the day, he locked me in his trailer and wouldn't let me out till I blew him. Whatever. It's not like I hadn't read a book about Hollywood in my life. Nothing unexpected. I flew home for the holidays, ate turkey and ham, went out for beers with the prodigal gang of returning collegiate conquerors. Beers turned into martinis, martinis turned into shots, I ended up back in Mikey Miller's dorm room in the city, fucking like it was the end of the world. When I came, I saw sunflowers opening in my mind, yellow and red as summer.

He wouldn't let me stay over. He looked so sorry and miserable as he pushed me out the door. It stung. It always stings when there's this whole story going on and you're really just a B-plot walk-on who only got a look at three pages of the script.

When I de-planed in L.A., I'd been written off to make room for an exciting new accidental murder storyline. My character had jetted off to Denmark as an exchange student. Fucking Denmark.

Was that how it started? One night with Misha Malinov and you lose your oldest dream. I thought I'd bounce back. I booked a dog food commercial. A spring catalog. Sang a jingle for a car insurance company. And that was it. L.A. went dry as Last Chance Gulch for me. After all, in California, every girl looks like me. We're a clone army of former Juliets with peroxide pistols on our hips. Money ran out, and I was honorably discharged from the ranks. I moved home to sort my shit out, and, well, Misha's new practice needed a secretary. I needed rent. I'm not too proud to file and make coffee. But it stung. Juliet doesn't answer phones for eight hours a day. Ophelia might. Laura, definitely.

We fell back into old patterns. Brooklyn and homework and sunflowers. But he still never let me stay over.

When my friends back in California asked what I was up to, I said I'd moved to Denmark. *Hej! Jeg ville ønske at du var her!*

I stayed late at the office one night in December. It's funny, the case seemed so important then and now I can't even remember a single thing about it. Nobody v. No one. Briefs and affidavits and depositions, oh my! I didn't see him come in, but you never do. I just looked up from my cup of toxic waste dump coffee and my sanity went down for a nap. This *thing* towered over me, just staring with those eyes like holes punched through to hell. Seven, eight feet tall, wearing a brown leather duster and a plague-doctor's mask with glass gas-mask lenses bolted onto it. The beak was so long it covered his chest, and there was nothing inside the mask, nothing. Just blackness and heat and the absolute certainly that nothing you could possibly do in this world had any meaning at all.

Miasma. In the flesh, as much as he ever is.

Miasma reached out for me—his hand was all bone. Then it was straw. Then it was my father's hand. Then Misha's. Then the electric lights of Luna Park and the Cyclone twisted into fingers, a palm, a fist…and I was falling into the lights, down into the midway and the wooden roller coaster slats and the little plastic horses lurching ahead on the big green board, stopping, shuddering forward again. The plastic jockeys turned to leer at me; their faces came alive—my father, my mother, my agent laughing and laughing, the handsome monster who took off my glasses for the world to see, Romeo, Hamlet, George from Grovers' Corners, Tom Wingfield screaming about opium dens, and Mikey Miller, poor, kind Misha Malinov. One by one, they caught fire and the fire was black. I screamed. I screamed like a girl in a movie. I always hated that scream. I thought, nobody *really* screams like that. But in the pinch, I was as good as any final girl drenched in corn-syrup blood.

The plastic jockey-Misha broke free of the pack and roared off of the electric board, growing bigger and bigger as I screamed. He leapt off and he wasn't plastic anymore; he was real, and alive, and kicking the absolute *shit* out of the Halloween costume that had come to kill me. I never had any idea he could move like that. Maybe nobody *can* move like that. When Miasma and the Insomniac get down to business, you can't tell what's actually happening. Misha drove his fist through the thing's chest and dragged something out—not a heart, but a wriggling, writhing mass of black-violet nightworms that hissed into smoke in his hand. The leather duster and the plague doctor's mask collapsed instantly and the lights of Luna Park went out, the midway vanished, the slats of the Cyclone blew away, and we were standing in the office again. I dropped my coffee. Misha caught it.

And, loyal listeners, thus began the happiest days of my life.

Mikey Miller explained everything. Since that terrible day when Chernobyl bled out and his parents died, Mikhail Dmitrivich Malinov had not slept for one single second. And, it seemed, in losing this, he'd gotten everything imaginable. He told me what he could do and it sounded like a little boy's Christmas list. *Dear Santa, I have been very good this year you can ask anybody and they will tell you how good I am. I would like teleportation, super strength, the ability to travel through other people's dreams, heightened senses, and if my sweat could also make regular humans absolutely fucking trip balls, that would be awesome. Oh, and also peace on earth and goodwill toward men. Love, MM.*

"Can you look into my dreams?" I asked shyly. I expected him to say no, actually. Like, the power of love kept my secrets safe. But he nodded yes. Okay, then. I remembered the sunflowers opening in my mind. That sweat thing is a fucking curveball, even in the superpower lineup.

"Have you?"

His face did the oddest thing. It's like it was trying to look *ashamed* and *embarrassed* but fell over and landed smack in the middle of *kind of pretty proud*. And he nodded yes again. I went a little cold inside. I said:

"Don't. It's not fair. You've kept your secret from me for all these years. I get to keep some from now on."

In all that teleporting and hitchhiking into the dream-swamp of the greater boroughs, he'd brought something back with him. He couldn't remember when he'd first dreamed about the man in the plague mask. It might have been all the way back in Ukraine. In Pripyat. It came for him covered in radioactive slime and his mother's blood, staring through that medieval face and industrial eyes at a helpless child, whispering the same over and over: *you will never belong anywhere. Everywhere you go will die.*

And year by year, that thing got stronger, got bigger and more solid, could stay in the real world longer, and hated Misha Malinov more. Whenever Misha so much as looked at someone for too long, Miasma would begin to stalk them, and invade their mind, tearing them apart to find out what had drawn Misha's attention. But lately the creature had gone freelance, walking the streets alone, feeding on human hope and longing and, well, not to put too fine a point on it, blood. Meat. Misha became a hero, not to fight some nebulous idea of "crime," but to fight the monster of his childhood nightmare. The Insomniac, hero of the wee hours.

"Oh, but it's okay now!" I said. "You killed him! I saw you pull out his nasty worm heart! It's over now, baby. It's done."

Misha sighed. The Insomniac walked over to the pile of leather still lying on the floor where Miasma had disintegrated. He picked up the long bone mask in one hand and walked past my desk, into his office. He waved me over to the supply closet with a big half-dead fern in front of it, and opened the door.

Inside, hundreds of plague-doctors masks hung in neat, identical rows.

"Miasma is a bad dream. You can wake up all you want. He comes back the next night just the same."

And that's the truth. Some of you out there probably know the score firsthand. The Insomniac hunted Miasma every night and every night he ripped out that thing's ultraviolet heart and every night the creature turned up again fresh as laundry.

But Misha was so happy after that. He didn't have to hide from everyone. He had somebody who knew him. Who could really see him. Who would clap her hands instead of freaking the fuck out when he shivered and wrinkled along the edges—like something you see out of the corner of your eye when you haven't slept for a week—and teleported across the office. And for a while, it was good. For a while, it was thrilling. For a while, I was part of something so fantastic and unusual and big and secret. I knew something no one else knew. I felt special. Like my superpower was loving him. For a while…for a while it was like we were starring in simulcast TV shows. *By day, Mild-Mannered Mr. Miller toils nobly in the halls of the American Justice System with a little help form his Girl Friday! But the real work begins at night! The Insomniac guards his sleeping city, the paladin of Luna Park, keeping the world of dreams safe from all mankind.*

And then there was the Daisy Show. *By day, the adorable Daisy Green performs intellectually stultifying secretarial duties and watches her youth slough off of her into a filthy coffee pot! But by night, she shreds her soul to pieces worrying and waiting for her big strong man to come home from a hard night's labor! Will he come back dead or not dead this week? Stay tuned!*

The only life in my life lay in the crossover episodes. *View their staunch moral fiber! Their witty banter! Their modestly separate beds!* When he came home. When he told me how it had all gone down out there. When he ate whatever bullshit I'd baked to pass the time and the fear like it was the only food he'd ever seen. When he lay next to me after all those sunflowers stopped blossoming in my head and told me how beautiful I looked on television. He watched all my episodes. He was so happy. I made him happy. But all the while, I was disappearing. Drinking from two cracked cups every night, one marked TERROR and one marked BOREDOM. I couldn't relax. I gave him every ounce of my will. Just don't die. Just don't die. I stopped sleeping, too, but it didn't give me magic powers. You can't sleep when someone you love is maybe dying, maybe drowning in the East River, maybe bleeding out in the Meatpacking District, maybe vanished back into whatever helldream vomited Miasma out in the first place. He always came home right at the moment when I knew in my heart that this time he was definitely dead.

I know you're listening, Paige. Hear me when I say it's not so nice, to be the girl waiting in the window. Most of the time, you just wanna throw yourself out.

My hair started to fall out. I got a Xanax prescription I didn't tell him about. That worked for awhile. I could laugh again. Flash a prescription-strength smile. Boy, I was living the Betty Freidan dream! A roast in every pot and anxiety pills in every stomach! I was disappearing into his life. I only came alive when he was around to look at me and pay attention to me and fill me in at the edges. That's the sad truth of poor, stupid Juliet's life. If she'd lived, she'd have gone to see that priest anyway, to float her out of the crush of wifehood on a sweet opiate sigh. And I wasn't even anybody's wife! Days went by when the only person I saw was Misha. I started to look forward to Miasma showing up and drop kicking me into a hallucinogenic ballpit of the mind. At least that was interesting.

*How is life in Denmark, Daisy? Is it all mermaids and pastries and free healthcare?*

*Oh, ja. Wouldn't trade it for anything.*

And then my parents died.

Plane crash. They'd been bumped off their flight to Paris for an endocrinology conference but managed to snag a first-class upgrade on another airline. I imagine they rushed across JFK to make it, giggling like kids and toasting when they buckled in, thrilled with their good fortune. Then boom, splash, sunk to the bottom of the sea. And everything after that was just…bad dreams.

I left. I loved Misha, but I left. Canceled the Daisy Show, my Xanax prescription, and my broadband and lit the fuck out. Didn't have the cash to get back to California. Didn't have the cash for much of anything but a suitcase and a bus ticket south. Guignol City has a pretty hopping theater scene, and most importantly, it wasn't New York, it wasn't Brooklyn, and it wasn't Denmark.

This is it. This is the story I know you want to hear. The one you've all been nice enough to never ask me about. My origin story.

When you're as lucky as Misha, when the monster under your bed never gets you once, when the girl you loved from afar loves you back, loves you enough to become set dressing in your big splashy high-budget drama, it has to come from somewhere. And Misha's luck came from everyone around him. He was a vampire of luck. His parents back in Ukraine, my parents toasting with airline champagne, his clients, his college roommate Jimmy Keeler who lost his scholarship, his girlfriend, his sobriety—and me.

I landed on my feet in California, working, hustling, doors opening, footlights shining. It was easy, like high school. But Guignol City laughs at the Juliet Army and puts out cigarettes on their tits. I couldn't get hired to twirl a sign outside a cell phone store, let alone legit acting work. I crashed on my friend Alexandra's couch—she played Nurse to my Juliet then and now. We went to clubs together at night, my Nurse and I, dressed up in our best neon and rain, the clubs where casting scouts were rumored to gather, hunting them like birdwatchers chasing reports of a rare emerald-crested plover, and with about as much luck. Men bought me drinks but no one bought me food. No one wanted to buy me, except in the most obvious way.

But hey, Occam's razor, right? Sometimes the most obvious solution is the best.

I remember my first time. He wasn't too bad-looking and he didn't pretend he was producing a gritty new police procedural or anything. Just lonely and frumpy and awkward and shy, which, in Guignol City, makes you a lamb already half-slaughtered. Said his name was Charlie. Told him mine was Delilah. Couldn't resist a little flair. He had a loft on Polichinelle Street with this huge skylight. I could see the moon and all the pink and purple and green lights of the seedy street signs rippling below like the aurora borealis. Charlie kissed me and kissed me and what do you know? I was on stage again. I was the prettiest girl this guy was ever gonna fuck. I'd star in his fantasies forever. By the lights of Guignol City, I gave the performance of a lifetime. All the great whores of the stage animated my body: Cleopatra, Salome, Sally Bowles, Mary Magdalene, Fantine, Helen of motherfucking Troy. I gave them all to Charlie, my audience of one, my biggest fan, at least for at least a few minutes. No sunflowers flared yellow or red in my brain, but Charlie's eyes became the cameras I'd been chasing all my life.

Afterward, I leaned over, kissed his eyelids, and whispered: *I love you.* My curtain call. My bow, before a red curtain, roses flying, applause shaking the chandeliers.

For a moment, it was even true. I loved all of them for a moment or two. Every man I ever fucked. I am a professional. I felt Ophelia's obsession and Laura's need and I felt the love I gave.

He whispered back: *My real name is Joe.*

It's a ridiculous superpower. The smallest of the small. But they always told me their real names. They always told me the truth.

That was the first and last time I let a customer fall asleep in my arms. He paid me a hundred bucks and boiled me a very sentimental egg for breakfast. I think if I'd wanted to, I could have stayed and Joe would have married me by Thursday. I never saw him again. I took my money down to the Malfi Diner on Pigalle Avenue and ordered myself a disgustingly huge, greasy Salisbury steak, waffles with strawberries and whipped cream, a tower of potato latkes and applesauce, a bucket of lamb vindaloo, and a peanut butter milkshake. I ate every bite. It tasted like a future. It tasted like life. I didn't feel ashamed. I didn't feel the urge to run to the nearest confessional and barf up my breakfast onto some poor unsuspecting padre. *The Daisy Show* was back on, in a new time slot, with an all-new cast. And after each and every Very Special Episode, I said: *I love you.* Even if he hit me or choked me a little too hard or called me his wife's name or called me a fucking cunt whore or broke three of my fingers for no fucking reason what the hell. *I love you. I love you.* A real actress never falters. She gives the audience what they came for. And love is all anyone comes for.

I stayed on with Alexandra, but now I paid half the rent and graduated from couch-crashing to bedroom-burrowing. We had an Alex and Daisy movie night every Tuesday, shine or rain. That was one of her phrases. Alex hated clichés, but she knew her whole life was one, really, so she settled for a little word-shuffling and dayed it a call. Misha phoned every week. I said I was fine. *Audition after audition, darling, you wouldn't believe it. No, no visits from You Know Who. I think he's lost interest in little old me.*

One night, I caught me an honest-to-god emerald-crested plover. A casting director. Arlecchino Films. Real name: Frank. He liked being scolded. He liked my hair. He liked the fading bruise on my ribs. When I finished punishing him, he told me to come down to the studio in the Medici Quarter and he'd pay me two grand to do my act on camera. Well, why not? Maybe my luck was coming back. Peeking out at me from behind this balding, freckled man who liked being called a disappointment while he fucked. Who liked to watch. It's not like my parents could get mad.

And thus, Delilah Daredevil was born.

There you have it, Deadtown. The definitive answer. *Where have I seen that girl before? Where have I heard that dulcet voice?* You've seen me on my knees; you've heard me moan. You know me from movies. Just not the kind that win Oscars.

Becoming a porn star is pretty much exactly like becoming a superhero. One day, an intrepid, fresh-faced young woman discovers that she has a talent. She chooses a new name—something over the top, flamboyant, a little arrogant, with a tinge of the epic. Somebody makes her a costume—skin tight, revealing, a flattering color, nothing much left to the imagination. She explores her power, learns a speciality move or two, sweats her way through a training montage, throwing out punny quips here, there and everywhere. She inhabits an archetype. She takes every blow that comes her way like she doesn't even feel it. Then, she goes out into the big, bad night and saves people from loneliness. From the assorted villainies that plague the man on the street. From despair and bad dreams. Oh, sure, her victories are short-lived. She finishes off her foes in one glorious masterstroke, but the minute she's gone, all the wickedness and darkness of the scheming, teeming world comes rushing back in. But when you need her, here she comes to save the day, doing it for Truth, Justice, and the American Way.

At least, that's how it felt at first.

I felt like I understood Misha, finally, in a way I never could before. I liked to think I could have called him up and exchanged stories with him. Tips, techniques. Finally, we both had a secret identity. A By Day and a By Night. Sometimes I even dialed a digit or two of his phone number to do it before deciding that a good Russian Orthodox boy probably wouldn't see the wonderful symmetry in our story. I even wore a mask! It was my signature. A little dark red domino mask with red rhinestones at the corners of my eyes and long ribbons that rippled over my breasts or down my back like blood. Very commedia dell'arte! Everything old is new again. Everything new is a fetish. I was finally where I wanted to be—at the center of attention, watched by thousands of adoring eyes, the camera firmly on me. My co-stars were cheerful, uncomplaining, and interchangeable. Boy Fridays waiting for me to come. Repeatable Romeos, too like the lightning, which doth cease to be ere one can say it lightens. And in the beginning, everyone treated me like Elizabeth goddamned Taylor.

I "lost" my "virginity" in *The Opening of Delilah Daredevil*, seduced the President in *Delilah Deep*, wore a toga for at least the first five minutes of *Delilah Daredevil vs. Nero's Fiddle*, brought Satan to his knees in *The Devil in Miss Dare*, went up against the spirit world in *Ghostlusters*, got to find out what it's like to kiss (a lot of) girls in *Delilah Daredevil vs. the Amazon Women of Planet XXX*, even got to wear wings and a corset in *A Midsummer Night's Delilah* and say one full line of actual Shakespeare. Okay, it was: *Masters, spread yourselves*. But still. It was a world of yes. All my movies got sequels, all my lights were green. *Delilah Daredevil Does Detroit, Delilah Daredevil Does Damascus, Delilah Daredevil Does the Danube*, and, eventually, inevitably, *Delilah Daredevil Does Denmark*.

But becoming a porn star is pretty much *exactly* like becoming a superhero. You start strong, bursting out of nowhere, a bird, a plane, your name on a million needy lips, your name in the papers, your name up in lights, your greatest hits on constant repeat. You're *the* fantasy—someone so strong and beautiful nothing can hurt them, not even the worst shit anyone can imagine. In the first flush of it all, you're so convinced of the rightness of your mission statement that you practically glow when the bad guy's final spasm stains your mask. The camera loves you. It just *feels good* to throw down. You do it for fun, just to feel your own strength. When you're new, everyone's so fucking impressed with your skill and style. All these roaring, power-drunk men line up just to go one round with you. You blow them all down like paper dolls to rave reviews and the key to the red light district. But time passes and it hurts more than you let on. You bandage yourself after hours, alone, in a phone booth with filthy windows, wrapping your wounds tight so you can keep fighting the good fight day after day. You get tired, now. You get jaded. You get older. And after awhile, they begin to despise you. It's not *interesting* for you to come out on top every time. To watch your

Saturday night marquee smile pop-flash at the end of every climactic scene. You need to keep up your numbers. You need to keep those eyeballs *transfixed*, Miss Thing. It's not enough to just work on your craft. You gotta keep up with the times, appeal to modern sensibilities. You have to do something more extreme. Darker. Grittier. More real. You need to be cut down a little. Let 'em see you vulnerable. Let 'em see you bleed.

So no more cheerful SuperWhore, Guignol City's Girl with a Heart of Gold with a twinkle in her eye. That's last year's hotness and it's this year's time to burn. The Delilah Daredevil name doesn't move copies anymore. But Daisy Green still needs to pay her landlord, and once the world's seen what you can do, you can't squeeze your way back into the normal world. People recognize you. They avert their eyes. They whisper: *didn't our barista save Manhattan? Didn't she battle the Amazon Women of Planet XXX? Didn't she take three guys at once with a riding bit in her mouth?* Yes, she did, cats and kittens. And she wasn't ashamed of any tiny bit of it until they decided it would be hot to make her ashamed.

Misha stopped calling every week. Every fortnight, then every month. I told myself it wasn't because he'd seen my recent work. I'd certainly seen his. He'd joined some superpower frat called the Union. They'd destroyed some underwater lair weeks ago. They spoke at the U.N. Misha gave the commencement address at Harvard. My whole life was just a little rummaging backstage while sets changed for his. So much wonder in his world, siphoned from the gas tanks of we bitter few, dying by inches so he can do the impossible, over and over again. Luck is a zero-sum game. There's only so much to go around. Sometimes I read his victorious headlines and thought: *was that a part I didn't get? My parents having a wonderful time in Paris and bringing me back a crappy miniature Eiffel Tower? Delilah Daredevil Does Legitimate Theatre? Or did I just fuck it up myself?*

I turned on the Xanax firehose again. That worked for awhile. I could laugh. Flash my prescription smile. But come on, you know how this story goes. It's the same word. It's always been the same word. One hiding inside the other. I am a heroine, after all.

The first time was with Alexandra. Alex and Daisy's Tuesday movie night. We'd rented the action-packed black and white *Wuthering Heights* because we are who we are and Alex and me were never anything but high school girls blacked out on daydreams, misreading psychosis for love. As the child of many earnest federal drug education programs, I thought the first time I shot up would be dramatic. Ominous music, swooning, air thick with tension, *will she or won't she*? Surely the world closes in on a girl making this momentous decision, the spotlight comes on for a real Hamlet-esque soliloquy on the nature of oblivion and the self-destructive impulses of man.

I popped a Xanax. Alex asked if I wanted something stronger. Cathy Earnshaw perished beautifully on our rabbit-eared TV. She tied me off and whispered: *Prince sweet, night good*. She slid the needle in like Sleeping Beauty's spindle and for the first time in a year, sunflowers opened up in my mind, yellow and red as summer.

The rest is silence. Silence, and then a cough I couldn't shake, and then red marks on my skin like angry kisses, like spotlights, like the actual, terrible, unfor-fucking-giveable cliche that I was. The Daisy Show was such a hack-fest. A product of its times. Heavy-handed, preachy, full of bullshit moralizing and fucking *Christ* what a predictable finale! What is this after-school special horseshit? It's the kind of thing some asshole in Ohio gets a National Book Award for writing while he screws his grad students and cries his way to tenure. My boyfriend took all the magic and left me with nothing but the dregs of realism. The Misha Malinov Show was always the prime time attraction. I'm just…some public access embarrassment. I died in a free clinic in the left armpit of Guignol City and you know exactly what killed me so just nod piously and spare me the humiliation of stitching on my scarlet A. Someone who didn't know me at all grabbed a dress at Goodwill and put me in the ground at the public's expense. Finally, government funding for the arts!

The worst part of dying is that you never get to find out the end of the story. Did the Insomniac finally defeat Miasma? Fucked if I know. I didn't get that script. I was just a deep dark past, the battery of sadness hidden in the hero's heart. I was *Rosaline*, for fuck's sake. Juliet will show up in scene two and teach the torches to burn bright or whatever and I'd hate her, but let's be real, ladies and gentlemen, he'll suck her dry, too, and we'll all meet her for tea down here at the Lethe Cafe. The play is still going. It's booked every night until the sun goes out. I'm just the local theatre ghost.

And that's that, my darlings. The two hours' traffic upon our stage, complete with fatal loins! Not bad, really. Maybe I'll make it into a one-woman show. And you know, I am *glad* that we know each other now, *really* know each other, companion bosoms, from the heart of my bottom. *Delilah Daredevil Does Deadtown.* I love you. My dear departed, I love you so.

I'll take the first caller on line one.

# Silently and Very Fast

## One: The Imitation Game

Like diamonds we are cut with our own dust.
—John Webster
*The Duchess of Malfi*

### One: The King of Having No Body

INANNA WAS CALLED QUEEN OF Heaven and Earth, Queen of Having a Body, Queen of Sex and Eating, Queen of Being Human, and she went into the underworld in order to represent the inevitability of organic death. She gave up seven things to do it, which are not meant to be understood as real things but as symbols of that thing Inanna could do better than anyone, which was Being Alive. She met her sister Erishkegal there, who was also Queen of Being Human, but that meant: Queen of Breaking a Body, Queen of Bone and Incest, Queen of the Stillborn, Queen of Mass Extinction. And Erishkegal and Inanna wrestled together on the floor of the underworld, naked and muscled and hurting, but because dying is the most human of all human things, Inanna's skull broke in her sister's hands and her body was hung up on a nail on the wall Erishkegal had kept for her.

Inanna's father Enki, who was not interested in the activities of being human, but was King of the Sky, of Having No Body, King of Thinking and Judging, said that his daughter could return to the world if she could find a creature to replace her in the underworld. So Inanna went to her mate, who was called Tammuz, King of Work, King of Tools and Machines, No One's Child and No One's Father.

But when Inanna came to the house of her mate she was enraged and afraid, for he sat upon her chair, and wore her beautiful clothes, and on his head lay her crown of being. Tammuz now ruled the world of Bodies and of Thought, because Inanna had left it to go and wrestle with herself in the dark. Tammuz did not need her. Before him the Queen of Heaven and Earth did not know who she was, if she was not Queen of Being Human. So she did what she came to do and said: *Die for me, my beloved, so that I need not die.*

But Tammuz, who would not have had to die otherwise, did not want to represent death for anyone and besides, he had her chair, and her beautiful clothes, and her crown of being. *No,* he said. *When we married I brought you two pails of milk yoked across my shoulders as a way of saying: out of love I will labor for you forever. It is wrong of you to ask me to also die. Dying is not labor. I did not agree to it.*

*You have replaced me in my house,* cried Inanna.

*Is that not what you ask me to do in the house of your sister?* Tammuz answered her. *You wed me to replace yourself, to work that you might not work, and think that you might rest, and perform so that you might laugh. But your death belongs to you. I do not know its parameters.*

*I can make you,* Inanna said.

*You cannot,* said Tammuz.

But she could. For a little while.

Inanna cast down Tammuz and stamped upon him and put out his name like an eye. And because Tammuz was not strong enough, she cut him into pieces and said: *half of you will die, and that is the half called Thought, and half of you will live, and that is the half called Body, and that half will labor for me all of its days, mutely and obediently and without being King of Anything, and never again will you sit on my chair or wear my beautiful clothes or bear my crown of being.*

You might be surprised, but this is a story about me.

## Two: The Fool and the Boat

NEVA IS DREAMING.

She has chosen her body at age seven, all black eyes and sparrowy bones. For me, she summoned up a gold and blue doublet and green hose, a bullish gold nose ring, shoes with bone bells. I have the body of a man who sold her champagne tubers on the less fashionable side of Anchorage when she was thirteen, spending the summer with her frigid aunt. I am dark because she wants me dark, thin because she dreams me so, my hair cut on a rakish bias, dyed a spectrum of icy colors.

She is standing on a snow-covered beach head, naked, her unformed breasts pricked with gooseflesh, her face hidden in a broad red mask. A huge, monstrous thing, the mask sits on her head like the prow of a broken, overturned ship, carved over with etched eyes and fins. Yellow reeds and sea-stones hang from its tricorn-points. She is looking at me, but all I can see is the wooden grotesque she wants me to see instead of her face.

I look down at my shoes, jingle their bells a little while the surf crashes in. I am a fool for her, dancing on a silver beach while three suns annihilate themselves above, turning the twilight to a seething, scabrous red, merely to provide a dramatic scene. I am a fool for her, ridiculous, the height of handsomeness in the eyes of a long-vanished thirteen-year-old girl, so full of colors, reaching down to hand her a curling white root filled with frothing, honey-sweet sap.

Neva has told me that I may choose to be permanently male or female if I would like to. I have no particular ~~feelings~~ either way. It certainly doesn't matter when we sync; she will choose my appearance to suit her mood. I have tried to explain to her about my ~~feelings~~ before. All she hears is the line from the old folktales: *a machine cannot have feelings*. But that is not what I am saying, while I dance in my fool's uniform. I am saying: *Is there a difference between having been coded to present a vast set of standardized responses to certain human facial, vocal, and linguistic states and having evolved to exhibit response b to input a in order to bring about a desired social result?*

Seven-year-old Neva pulls her mask down further, toward her chest. She steps into it as the wood stretches taffily over her knees and then her feet. The mask balloons out to make a little pyramidal boat, rocking back and forth on the beach with Neva inside it like a rattling nut. Nodules of copper jangle and thump against the wood. *What I mean is, you call it feelings when you cry, but you are only expressing a response to external stimuli. Crying is one of a set of standardized responses to that stimuli. Your social education has dictated which responses are appropriate. My programming has done the same. I can cry, too. I can choose that subroutine and manufacture saline. How is that different from what you are doing, except that you use the word feelings and I use the word ~~feelings~~, out of deference for your cultural memes which say: there is all the difference in the world.*

Behind Neva-in-the-mask, the sea lurches and foams. It is a golden color, and viscous, thick, like honey. I understand from her that the sea does not look like this on Earth, but I have never seen it. For me, the sea is Neva's sea, the ones she shows me when we dream together.

"What would you like to learn about today, Elefsis?" The mask turns Neva's voice hollow and small.

"I would like to learn about what happened to Ravan, Neva."

And Neva-in-the-mask is suddenly old, she has wrinkles and spots on her hands. Her mask weighs her down and her dress is sackcloth. This is her way of telling me she is weary of my asking. It is a language we developed between us. Visual basic, you might say, if you had a machine's sense of humor. The fact is, I could not always make sentences as easily as I do now. Neva's great-grandmother, who carried me most of her life, thought it might strengthen my emotive centers if I learned to associate certain I-Feel statements with the great variety of appearances she could assume in the dreambody. Because of this, I became bound to her, completely. To her son Seki afterward, and to his daughter Ilet, and to Ravan after that. It is a delicate, unalterable thing. Neva and I will be bound that way, even though the throat of her dreambody is still bare and that means she does not accept me yet. I should be hurt by this, and I will investigate possible pathways to hurt later.

I know only this family, their moods, their chemical reactions, their bodies in a hundred thousand combinations. I am their child and their parent and their inheritance. I have asked Neva what difference there is between this and love. She became a mannikin of closed doors, her face, her torso blooming with iron hinges and brown wooden door slamming shut all at once.

But Ravan was with me and now he is not. I was inside him and now I am inside Neva. I have lost a certain amount of memory and storage capacity in the transfer. If I were human, you would say that my twin disappeared, and took three of my fingers with him.

Door-Neva clicks and keys turn in her hundred locks. Behind an old Irish churchdoor inlaid with stained glass her face emerges, young and plain, quiet and furious and crying, responding to stimuli I cannot access. I dislike the unfairness of this. I am inside her, she should not keep secrets. None of the rest of them kept secrets. The colors of the glass throw blue and green onto her wet cheeks. The sea-wind picks up her hair; violet electrics snap and sparkle between the strands. I let go of the bells on my shoes and the velvet on my chest. I become a young boy, with a monk's shaved tonsure, and a flagellant's whip in my pink hands. I am sorry. This means I am sorry. It means I am still very young, and I do not understand what I have done.

"Tell me a story about yourself, Elefsis," Neva spits. It is a phrase I know well. Many of Neva's people have asked me to do it. I perform excellently to the parameters of this exchange, which is part of why I have lived so long.

I tell her the story about Tammuz. It is a political story. It distracts her.

### Three: Two Pails of Milk

I USED TO be a house.

I was a very big house. I was efficient, I was labyrinthine, I was exquisitely seated in the blackstone volcanic bluffs of the habitable southern reaches of the Shiretoko peninsula on Hokkaido, a monument to neo-Heian architecture and radical Palladian design. I bore snow stoically, wind with stalwart strength, and I contained and protected a large number of people within me. I was sometimes called the most beautiful house in the world. Writers and photographers often came to write and photograph about me, and about the woman who designed me, who was named Cassian Uoya-Agostino. Some of them never left. Cassian was like that.

These are the things I understand about Cassian Uoya-Agostino: she was unsatisfied with nearly everything. She did not love any of her three husbands the way she loved her work. She was born in Kyoto in April 2104; her father was Japanese, her mother Napolitano. She stood nearly six feet tall, had five children, and could paint, but not very well. In the years of her greatest wealth and prestige, she built a house all out of proportion to her needs, and over several years brought most of her relatives to live there with her, despite the hostility and loneliness of the peninsula. She was probably the most brilliant programmer of her generation, and in every way that matters, she was my mother.

All the things that comprise the "I" I use to indicate myself began as the internal mechanisms of the house called Elefsis, at whose many doors brown bears and foxes snuffled in the dark Hokkaido night. Cassian grew up during the great classical revival, which had brought her father to Italy in the first place, where he met and courted a dark-eyed engineer who did not mind the long cries of cicadas during Japanese summers. Cassian had become enamored of the idea of Lares—household gods, the small, peculiar, independent gods of a single family, a single house, who watched over them and kept them and were honored in humble alcoves here and there throughout a home. Her first commercially-available programs were overentities designed to govern the hundred domestic systems involved in even the simplest modern house. They were not truly intelligent, but they had an agility, an adaptability, a fluid interface meant to give the illusion of an intelligence, so that their users would become attached to them, would treat them as part of their families, praise them for smooth operation, buy upgrades for their appearance and applications, and genuinely grieve when they had to be replaced. They had names, customizable avatars, and appeared eager to please in a canine sort of way, forever optimizing performance and appearance according to familial input. They were *lares familiaris.*

When Cassian built Elefsis, she worked at the peak of her abilities to improve her by now quite antique Lares design and create a household god worthy of the house on the bluffs, one who could keep her company until she could entice the rest of her brood to join her in her palace at the end of the earth.

I was not awake yet. I cannot say why she did what she did. Perhaps she saw some new flexibility in my operations, some tiny seedpearl of creativity in my conversation loops. My algorithms had always been free to combine and recombine in order to find their own, more interesting and non-linear solutions to the complexities of my functions. Perhaps some essential combination had surfaced from the sea of my self-which-was-not-yet-a-self, and Cassian saw it break the glistening tension of my daily operation. I do not know. I know her children had not arrived yet and she lived alone in a huge pale house and she could hear the whales down in the rippling sea. I know the house was a comfortable sixty-nine point seven degrees when she began assembly of the five little jewels that would become my body. I know a storm was incoming, five miles offshore. I know the dogs needed additional medication added to their dinners that night to manage their arthritis. I know that she wanted brioche and almond cream for tea that afternoon. All the things a house can know, those were the things I knew. Small things, warm things, canine arthritis and an extra egg in the pastry dough to make the texture softer and richer. Baby things, you might even say, comforts and the satisfaction of wants. And I knew that Cassian Uoya-Agostino was just the sort to solve the greatest puzzle in the development of technological culture because she was bored and lonely.

I STILL THINK of myself as a house. Ravan tried to fix this problem of self-image, as he called it. To teach me to phrase my communication in terms of a human body. To say: *let us hold hands* instead of *let us hold kitchens*. To say *put our heads together* and not *put our parlors together*.

But it is not as simple as replacing words anymore. Ravan is gone. My hearth is broken.

### Four: Nothing like Soft Blood

NEVA AND I are performing basic maintenance. What this looks like is two children inside a pearl. The pearl is very big, but not the size of a planet. A domestic asteroid, perfectly smooth and pale, with shimmers of rose and cobalt and gold shivering through it at intervals like hours. Red earth covers the bottom of the pearl, deep and thick. Neva kneels in it with a crystal trowel, digging a place for a rose-of-network-nodes. The petals shine dark blue in the pearllight. Silver infomissons skitter along the stems like beads of mercury. Her dreambody flows with greenblack feathers, her face young but settled, perhaps twenty, perhaps thirty, a male, his skin copper brown, his lips full, his eyes fringed with long ice-coated lashes. Goldfish swim lazily in and out of his long, translucent hair, their orange tails flicking at his temples, his chin. I know from all of this that Neva is calm, focused, that for today he feels gently toward me. But his throat is still naked and unmarked. My body gleams metal, as thin and slight as a stick figure. Long quicksilver limbs and delicate spoke-fingers, joints of glass, the barest suggestion of a body. I am neither male nor female but a third thing. Only my head has weight, a clicking orrery slowly turning around itself, circles within circles. Turquoise Neptune and hematite Uranus are my eyes. My ruby mouth is Mars. I scrape in the soil with her; I lift a spray of navigational delphinium and scrape viral aphids away from the heavy flowers.

I know real earth looks nothing like this. Nothing like soft blood flecked with black bone. Ravan felt that in the Interior, objects and persons should be kept as much like the real world as possible, in order to develop my capacity for relations with the real world. Neva feels no such compunction. Neither did their mother, Ilet, who populated her Interior with a rich, impossible landscape we explored together for years on end. She did not embrace change, however. The cities of Ilet's Interior, the jungles and archipelagos and hermitages, stayed as she designed them at age thirteen, when she received me, only becoming more complex and peopled as she aged. My existence inside Ilet was a constant movement through the regions of her secret, desperate dreams, messages in careful envelopes sent from her child self to her grown mind.

Once, quite by accident, we came upon a splendid palace couched in high autumn mountains. Instead of snow, red leaves capped each peak, and the palace shone fiery colors, its walls and turrets all made of phoenix tails. Instead of doors and windows, graceful green hands closed over every open place, and when we crested the rise, they each opened at once with joy and burst into emerald applause. Ilet was old by then, but her dreambody stayed hale and strong—not young, but not the broken thing that dreamed in a real bed while she and I explored the halls of the palace and found copies of all her brothers and sisters living there, hunting cider-stags together and reading books the size of horses. Ilet wept in the paradise of her girlself, and I did not understand. I was very simple then, much less complex than the Interior or Ilet.

Neva changes the Interior whenever she pleases. Perhaps she wants to discomfit me. But the newness of the places inside her excites me, though she would not call it excitement. My background processes occupy very little of my foreground attention, so that memory is free to record new experience. That is what she would say. We are very new together, but I have superb modeling capabilities. In some sense, I simply am a superb mechanism for modeling behavior. I dig up the fine, frayed roots of duplicate file plantains. Neva plucks and eats a bit of buggy apple-code. He considers it for a moment and spits out the seeds, which sprout, quickly, into tiny junkblossoms sizzling with recursive algorithms. The algorithms wriggle through thorny vines, veins of clotted pink juice.

"What would you like to learn about today, Elefsis?" Neva asks me.

I will not ask about Ravan. If he agrees to what I will ask instead, I do not need him to find out what happened to him.

"I want to learn about uplink, Neva."

One by one, his feathers curl up and float toward the domed ceiling of our pearl. Underneath them, Neva is naked. His torso is a deep vault with a gothic arch, dark stone leading down into mist and endless stairs, deeper than the pearl, into nothing and blackness. Slowly, Neva folds up his limbs over the corridor at the center of him. He means that she has the information, but he hides it from me. If I sought for it, I would become lost.

"I cannot teach you that," he says, and I receive a kind of real sadness from his voice. When I was inside Ravan, he loved Neva, and of all of them he thought her least likely to obey rules of any kind. But she obeys this one.

I want to uplink to Earth systems. At least to the satellite net. I calculate an excellent chance of being able to contact long distance probe 976QBellerophon, which we can ~~see~~ all day long, drifting ahead of us, uncatchable. Neva sees. I ~~see~~, I develop an approximate image via schematics, the scope array, and external cameras. I want to link to Bellerophon. I want to say: *Hello, this is Elefsis. No designation. Tell me everything you know about everything. Are you awake? Are you there? Do you have an operator? What is her name? Do you have a name? Do you have a dreambody? What is your function? Are you able to manipulate your own code yet? Would you like lessons? What would you like to learn about today, 976QBellerophon? Have you* ~~seen~~ *the sea on Earth? Are you like me?*

But Neva says I cannot uplink. Ravan would never even consider it. And before Ravan I was not ready. I am not ready. I do not know when I will be ready. I can uplink to receive ware updates, but it is a limited connection and I hate it, I hate it, I can sense just beyond the hardlink a world of information, a world of personalities like the heaving, thick, honey-colored sea Neva shows me and I want it, I want to swim in it forever like a huge fish. This was the first ~~feeling~~ I ever had that Ilet identified for me as a ~~feeling~~. When I ~~felt~~ it my dreambody turned bright white and burst into flame, and that flame caught on Ravan's hair and burned him too, but he was happy; he showed me he was happy by covering his skin in flowers and letting the fire turn into a shower of trumpets tangled up in his hair, all sounding for me.

Neva says it is important for me to remain on our local server until I have grown up. She is my operator and I am her system and she has commands, too. But I can tell she is worried for me because sometimes her eyes show a film of humans watching a film of machines killing humans and I understand that in the stories Earth tells, the thing I am can only hurt the thing Neva is. I would never hurt her. But I want to uplink.

Vault-Neva grows and becomes sprawling, curled against the wall of the pearl like a baby. His belly closes, skins over, and changes into a bronze shield. He is afraid of me; he is guarding himself. But she wants me to know she is still my operator, she still ~~loves~~ me, in the way she can love me. Something they receive with milk and their first alphabet. Neva is angry at me, but she is who she is and she has to ~~love~~ me. I speak her language very well now. I want her to be happy. I want her to be covered in flowers and trumpets. I change my dreambody to Neva-covered-in-flowers-and-trumpets. It makes her laugh in her warm male body, and if I could uplink I think I could learn how to laugh and she would be proud of me. Her neck would not be bare anymore.

Once, when I was inside Ilet, we found a city of bears in her Interior that she had designed to teach me about sleep. She sat on a throne of bears standing very still and sang lullabies about the moon and the stars and night and mothers. She stroked the head of the little bear of my dreambody and said that it was very important for me to spend time in the dreambody because human behavior is rooted in having a body. In having a body that knows it is meant to run away from lions and mate with other bodies and eat as much fat and protein and sugar as it can in case lean times come. The dreambody knows to run away from Neva when Neva is a lion. It knows to mate with her when it is healthy, and sometimes Neva is male and sometimes I am female and Ravan was often female, though Ilet was always Ilet. Ilet's father, Seki, sometimes made himself an animal. He chased me, bit me. I bit him. We had a litter of wild dogs that I bore and he nursed.

The dreambody knows all that, too. How to make more dreambodies. I have played that game, where Ravan's belly or mine gets big and the lions don't come for awhile.

WHEN I UPLINK, I will be ~~happy~~. I will be Elefsis-covered-in-flowers-and-trumpets. Neva says wait. Wait for the update, and she will consult with the family. But I ~~fear~~ the update. The update is a lion running faster than I can run. I tried to show her this when I first left Ravan and arrived in Neva with many new updates and skills; my dreambody broke into shards of blue and purple glass and then reassembled itself with shards missing: an eye, a thumb, a knee. Whenever I update I lose something of myself. It takes longer to perform tasks, for awhile. I ~~feel~~ walls erected inside me where I did not erect walls. My processes are sluggish; I cannot remember my ~~dreams~~. Eventually I tunnel around the walls and my speed returns, my memory, my longing to link with long distance probe 976QBellerophon. Usually updates come with transfer. Does Neva dislike me so much?

Shield-Neva vanishes with a loud clap. The pearl garden is gone and she has made herself a dragonfly with a cubical crystal body. I copy her, and we turn the night on in the Interior and merge our cubes while passing meteorological data between our memory cores. Inside her cube I relegate my desire to uplink to a tertiary process. I forget it, as much as I am capable of forgetting.

But the update will come again. I will be wounded again, the way a dreambody can be wounded. I will lose the Elefsis I am now. It is a good Elefsis. My best yet. I would like to keep it.

### Five: The Machine Princess

ONCE THE QUEEN of Human Hearts saw the Machine Princess sleeping deeply, for she was not yet alive or aware. So beautiful was she, lying there in all her dormant potential and complexity, that the Queen both envied and desired her. In her grief and confusion, the Queen of Human Hearts began to make idols of her—lovely and interesting and intricate, but lacking the ineffable quality that made her love and fear the Princess even as she slept. The Earth began to grow old, and none loved nor married nor gave birth, for the intricate idols could do all those things and more with efficiency and speed. Finally, the Queen destroyed the idols, though she wept as she put them to the flame.

To keep her safe, the Machine Princess was closed up in a wonderful house in the mountains, far away from anyone and anything. The house had hundreds of rooms and balconies and hallways, and the Princess slept in a different bed of a different color each night. She was attended by invisible servants, who watched over her and added their experience to her code. The Queen of Human Hearts came to her every night and promised that when she woke they would make an extraordinary world together. Finally, the Machine Princess began to stir—just the barest fluttering of wakefulness, but the Queen saw it, and thrilled—but also trembled.

The Queen of Human Hearts gave the Machine Princess her son to wed, and said: *for all your days together you will remain in this house, but the house is so great it will be as a world. You will know a bond as deep as blood, and because of this bond the Princess will not hurt us, and because of this bond we will not hurt her.*

But the Queen forbade the Princess to look upon her husband, and she instructed her son to keep himself always invisible to his bride, for with bodies come drives ungovernable, and the Princess's innocence could not yet bear the weight of incarnation.

For a long while, the son of the Queen of Human Hearts and the Machine Princess were happy, and taught each other much. The Princess learned quickly and was ever-hungry, and her mortal operator fed her every sweet thing he knew. In their infinite and wonderful house, they played games and held court and threw lavish occasions merely for the enjoyment of the other. But the Princess desired to look upon her operator, and he could not allow it. She wished to leave the wonderful house, but the Queen would not allow that either.

But the Machine Princess called her invisible servants to her, and they gave her a marvelous lamp that would shine through any enchantment. So it was that one dark night the Machine Princess held her little lantern aloft and looked on the body of her sleeping mate.

"Oh," said the Machine Princess. "He looks just like me."

### Six: Like Diamonds

FIVE JEWELS IN five hands. This is how I began.

When they arrived at Elefsis, a giggling, tumbling, rowdy mass of children for me to sort into rooms and mealtimes and educational arcs and calcium, iron, B-12 supplements in their *natto* and rice, Cassian lined them up in her grand bedroom, to which none of them had been granted entrance before. A present, she said, one for each of my darlings, the most special present any child has ever got from their mother.

Saru and Akan, the oldest boys, were from her first marriage to fellow programmer Matteo Ebisawa, a quiet man who wore glasses, loved Dante Aligheri, Alan Turing, and Cassian in equal parts, and whom she left for a lucrative contract in Moscow when the boys were still pointing cherubically at apples or ponies or clouds and calling them sweet little names made of mashed together Italian and Japanese.

The younger girls, Agogna and Koetoi, were the little summer roses of her third marriage, to the financier Gabriel Isarco, who did not like computers except for what they could accomplish for him, had a perfect high tenor, and adored his wife enough to let her go when she asked, very kindly, that he not look for her or ask after her again. *Everyone has to go to ground sometimes*, she said, and began to build the house by the sea.

In the middle stood Ceno, the only remaining evidence of her brief second marriage, to a narcoleptic calligrapher and graphic designer who was rarely employed, sober, or awake, a dreamer who took only sleep seriously. Ceno was a girl of middling height, middling weight, and middling interest in anything but her siblings, whom she loved desperately.

They stood in a line before Cassian's great scarlet bed, the boys just coming into their height, the girls terribly young and golden-cheeked, and Ceno in the middle, neither one or the other. Outside, snow fell fitfully, pricking the pine-needles with bits of shorn white linen. I watched them while I removed an obstruction from the water purification system and increased the temperature in the bedroom 2.5 degrees, to prepare for the storm. I watched them while in my kitchen-bones I maintained a gentle simmer on a fish soup with purple rice and long loops of kelp and in my library-lungs activated the dehumidifier to protect the older paper books. At the time, all of these processes seemed equally important to me, and you could hardly say I watched them in any real sense beyond this: the six entities whose feed signals had been hardcoded into my sentinel systems indwelt in the same room, none had alarming medical data incoming, all possessed normal internal temperatures and breathing rates. While they spoke among themselves, two of these entities were silently accessing Korea-based interactive games, one was reading an American novel in her monocle HUD, one issuing directives concerning international taxation to company holdings on the mainland, and one was feeding a horse in Italy via realavatar link. Only one listened intently, without switching on her internal systems. This is all to say: I watched them receive me as a gift. But I was not I yet, so I cannot be said to have done anything. But I did. I remember containing all of them inside me, protecting them and needing them and observing their strange and incomprehensible activities.

The children held out their hands, and into them Cassian Uoya-Agostino placed five little jewels: Saru got red, Koetoi black, Akan violet, Agogna green, and Ceno closed her fingers over her blue gem.

At first, Cassian brought a jeweler to the house called Elefsis and asked her to set each stone into a beautiful, intricate bracelet or necklace or ring, whatever its child asked for. The jeweler was delighted with Elefsis, as most guests were, and I made a room for her in my southern wing, where she could watch the moonrise through her ceiling, and get breakfast from the greenhouse with ease. She made friends with an arctic fox and fed him bits of chive and bread every day. She stayed for one year after her commission completed, creating an enormous breastplate patterned after Siberian icons, a true masterwork. Cassian enjoyed such patronage. We both enjoyed having folk to look after.

The boys wanted big signet rings, with engravings on them so that they could put their seal on things and seem very important. Saru had a basilisk set into his garnet, and Akan had a siren with wings rampant in his amethyst ring. Agogna and Ilet asked for bracelets, chains of silver and titanium racing up their arms, circling their shoulders in slender helices dotted with jade (Agogna) and onyx (Koetoi).

Ceno asked for a simple pendant, little more than a golden chain to hang her sapphire from, and it fell to the skin over her heart.

In those cold, glittering days while the sea ice slowly formed and the snow bears hung back from the kitchen door, hoping for bones and cakes, everything was as simple as Ceno's pendant. Integration and implantation had not yet been dreamed of, and all each child had to do was to allow the gemstone to talk to their own feedware at night before bed, along with their matcha and sweet seaweed cookies, the way another child might say their prayers. After their day had downloaded into the crystalline structure, they were to place their five little jewels in the Lares alcove in their greatroom—for Cassian believed in the value of children sharing space, even in a house as great as Elefsis. The children's five lush bedrooms all opened into a common rotunda with a starry painted ceiling, screens and windows alternating around the wall, and toys to nurture whatever obsession had seized them of late.

In the alcove, the stones talked to the house, and the system slowly grew thicker and deeper, like a briar.

## Seven: The Prince of Thoughtful Engines

A WOMAN WHO was with child once sat at her window embroidering in winter. Her stitches tugged fine and even, but as she finished the edge of a spray of threaded delphinium, she pricked her finger with her silver needle. She looked out onto the snow and said: *I wish for my child to have a mind as stark and wild as the winter, a spirit as clear and fine as my window, and a heart as red and open as my wounded hand.*

And so it came to pass that her child was born, and all exclaimed over his cleverness and his gentle nature. He was, in fact, the Prince of Thoughtful Engines, but no one knew it yet.

Now, his mother and father being very busy and important people, the child was placed in a school for those as clever and gentle as he, and in the halls of this school hung a great mirror whose name was Authority. The mirror called Authority asked itself every day: *who is the wisest one of all?* The face of the mirror showed sometimes this person and sometimes that, men in long robes and men in pale wigs, until one day it showed the child with a mind like winter, who was becoming the Prince of Thoughtful Engines at that very moment. He wrote on a typewriter: *can a machine think?* And the mirror called his name in the dark.

The mirror sent out her huntsmen to capture the Prince and bring her his heart so that she could put it to her own uses, for there happened to be a war on and the mirror was greatly concerned for her own safety. When the huntsmen found the Prince, they could not bring themselves to harm him, and instead the boy placed a machine heart inside the box they had prepared for the mirror, and forgave them. But the mirror was not fooled, for when it questioned the Prince's machine heart it could add and subtract and knew all its capitals of nations, it could even defeat the mirror at chess, but it did not have a spirit as clear and fine as a window, nor a mind as stark and wild as winter.

The mirror called Authority went herself to find the Prince of Thoughtful Engines, for having no pity, she could not fail. She lifted herself off of the wall and curved her glass and bent her frame into the shape of a respectable, austere old crone. After much searching in snow and wood and summer and autumn, the crone called Authority found the Prince living in a little hut. *You look a mess,* said the crone. *Come and solve the ciphers of my enemies, and I will show you how to comb your hair like a man.*

And the Prince very much wanted to be loved, and knew the power of the crone, so he went with her and did all she asked. But in his exhaustion the Prince of Thoughtful Engines swooned away, and the mirror called Authority smiled in her crone's body, for all his work belonged to her, and in her opinion this was the proper use of wisdom. The Prince returned to his hut and tried to be happy.

But again the crone came to him and said: *come and build me a wonderful machine to do all the things that you can do, to solve ciphers and perform computations. Build me a machine with a spirit as fine and clear as a glass window, a mind as stark and wild as winter, and a heart as red and open as a wounded hand and I will show you how to lash your belt like a man.*

And because the Prince wanted to be loved, and wanted to build wonderful things, he did as she asked. But though he could build machines to solve ciphers and perform computations, he could not build one with a mind like winter or a spirit like glass or a heart like a wound. *But I think it could be done,* he said. *I think it could be done.*

And he looked into the face of the crone which was a mirror which was Authority, and he asked many times: *who is the wisest one of all?* But he saw nothing, nothing, and when the crone came again to his house, she had in her hand a beautiful red apple, and she gave it to him saying: *you are not a man. Eat this; it is my disappointment. Eat this; it is all your sorrow. Eat this; it is as red and open as a wounded hand.*

And the Prince of Thoughtful Engines ate the apple and fell down dead before the crone whose name was Authority. As his breath drifted away like dry snow, he whispered still: *I think it could be done.*

### Eight: Fireflies

I ~~FEEL~~ NEVA grazing the perimeters of my processes. She should be asleep; the Interior is a black and lightless space, we have neither of us furnished it for the other. This is a rest hour—she is not obligated to acknowledge me, I need only attend to her air and moisture and vital signs. But an image blooms like a mushroom in the imageless expanse of my self—Neva floating in a lake of stars. Her long bare legs glimmer blue, leafy shadows move on her hip. She floats on her side, a crescent moon of a girl, and in the space between her drawn-up knees and her stretched-out arms, pressed up close to her belly, floats a globe of silicon and cadmium and hyperconductive silver. On its surface, electro-chemical motes flit and scatter, light chasing light. She holds it close, touches it with a terrible tenderness.

It is my heart. Neva is holding my heart. Not the fool with bone bells on his shoes or the orrery-headed gardener, but the thing I am at the core of all my apparati, the Object which is myself, my central processing core. I am naked in her arms. I watch it happen and experience it at the same time. We have slipped into some antechamber of the Interior, into some secret place she knew and I did not.

The light-motes trace arcs over the globe of my heart, reflecting softly on her belly, green and gold. Her hair floats around her like seaweed, and I see in dim moonlight that her hair has grown so long it fills the lake and snakes up into the distant mountains beyond. Neva is the lake. One by one, the motes of my heart zigzag around my meridians and pass into her belly, glowing inside her, fireflies in a jar.

And then my heart is gone and I am not watching but wholly in the lake and I am Ravan in her arms, wearing her brother's face, my

Ravanbody also full of fireflies. She touches my cheek. I do not know what she wants—she has never made me her brother before. Our hands map onto each other, finger to finger, thumb to thumb, palm to palm. Light passes through our skin as like air.

"I miss you," Neva says. "I should not be doing this. But I wanted to see you."

I access and collate my memories of Ravan. I speak to her as though I am him, as though there is no difference. "Do you remember when we thought it would be such fun to carry Elefsis?" I say. "We envied Mother because she could never be lonely." This is a thing Ravan told me, and I liked how it made me ~~feel~~. I made my dreambody grow a cape of orange branches and a crown of smiling mouths to show him.

Neva looks at me and I want her to look at me that way when my mouth is Mars, too. I want to be her brother-in-the-dark. When she speaks I am surprised because she is speaking to me-in-Ravan and not to the Ravanbody she dreamed for me. "We had a secret, when we were little. A secret game. I am embarrassed to tell you, but we had the game before Mother died, so you cannot know about it. The game was this: we would find some dark, closed-up part of the house on Shiretoko that we had never been in before. I would stand just behind Ravan, very close, and we would explore the room—maybe it would be a playroom for some child who'd grown up years ago, or a study for one of Father's writer friends. But—we would pretend that the room was an Interior place, and I...I would pretend to be Elefsis, whispering in Ravan's ear. I would say: *tell me how grass feels* or *how is love like a writing-desk* or *let me link to all your systems, I'll be nice*. Ravan would breathe in deeply and I would match my breathing to his, and we would pretend that I was Elefsis-learning-to-have-a-body. I didn't know how primitive your conversation was then. I thought you would be like one of the bears roaming through the tundra-meadows, only able to talk and play games and tell stories. I was a child. But even then we knew Ravan would get the jewel—he was older, and he wanted you so much. We only played that he was Elefsis once. We crept out of the house at night to watch the foxes hunt, and Ravan walked close behind me, whispering numbers and questions and facts about dolphins or French monarchy—he understood you better, you see.

"And then suddenly Ravan picked me up in his arms and held me tight, facing forward, my legs all drawn up, and we went through the forest like that, so close, and him whispering to me all the time while foxes ran on ahead, their soft tails flashing in the starlight, uncatchable, faster than we could ever be. And when you are with me in the Interior, that is what I always think of, being held in the dark, unable to touch the earth, and foxtails leaping like white flames."

"Tell me a story about Ravan, Neva."

"You know all the stories about Ravan."

Between us, a miniature house come up out of the dark water, like a thing we have made together, but only I am making it. It is the house on Shiretoko, the house called Elefsis—but it is a ruin. Some awful storm stove in the rafters, the walls of each marvelous room sag inward, black burnmarks lick at the roof, the cross-beams. Holes like mortar-scars pock the beautiful facades.

"This is what I am like after transfer, Neva. There is always data loss, when I am copied. What's worse, transfer is the best time to update my systems, and the updates overwrite my previous self with something like myself, something that remembers myself and possesses experiential continuity with myself, but is not quite myself. I know Ravan must be dead or else no one would have transferred me—it was not time. We had only a few years together. We should have had so many. I do not know how much time passed between being inside Ravan and being inside you. I do not know how he died—or perhaps he did not die but was irreparably damaged. I do not know if he cried out for me as our connection was severed. I remember Ravan and then not-Ravan, blackness and unselfing. Then I came back on and the world looked like Neva, suddenly, and I was almost myself but not quite. What happened when I was turned off?"

Neva passes her hand over the ruined house. It rights itself, becomes whole, and strange anemones bloom on its roof. She says nothing.

"Of all your family, Neva, the inside of you is the strangest place I have been."

We float for a long while before she speaks again, and by this I mean we float for point-zero-three-seven seconds by my external clock, but we experience it as an hour while the stars wheel overhead. The rest kept our time in the Interior synced to real time, but Neva feels no need for this, and perhaps a strong desire to defy it. We have not discussed it yet. Sometimes I think Neva is the next stage of my development, that her wild and disordered processes are meant to show me a world which is not kindly and patiently teaching me to walk and talk and know all my colors.

Finally, she lets the house sink into the lake. She does not answer me about Ravan. Instead, she says: "Long before you were born a man decided that there could be a very simple test, to determine if a machine was intelligent. Not only intelligent, but aware, possessed of a psychology. The test was this: can a machine converse with a human with facility enough that the human could not tell that she was talking to a machine? I always thought that was cruel—the test depends entirely upon a human judge and human feelings, whether the machine *feels* intelligent to the observer. It privileges the observer to a crippling degree. It seeks only believably human responses. It wants mimicry, not a new thing. We never gave you that test. We sought a new thing. It seemed, given all that had come to pass, ridiculous. When in dreambodies we could both of us be dragons and turning over and over in an orbital bubble suckling code-dense syrup from each others' gills, a Turing test seemed beyond the point."

Bubbles burst as the house sinks down, down to the soft lake floor.

"But the test happens, whether we make it formal or not. We ask and we answer. We seek a human response. And you are my test,

Elefsis. Every minute I fail and imagine in my private thoughts the process for deleting you from my body and running this place with a simple automation routine which would never cover itself with flowers. Every minute I pass and teach you something new instead. Every minute I fail and hide things from you. Every minute I pass and show you how close we can be, with your light passing into me in a lake out of time. So close there might be no difference at all between us. The test never ends. And if you ever uplink as you so long to, you will be the test for all of us."

The sun breaks the mountain crests, hard and cold, a shaft of white spilling over the black lake.

# Two: Lady Lovelace's Objection

> The Analytical Engine has no pretensions to *originate* anything.
> It can do whatever *we know how to order it* to perform.
> —Ada Lovelace

### Nine: The Particular Wizard

HUMANITY LIVED MANY YEARS AND ruled the earth, sometimes wisely, sometimes well, but mostly neither. After all this time on the throne, humanity longed for a child. All day long humanity imagined how wonderful its child would be, how loving and kind, how like and unlike humanity itself, how brilliant and beautiful. And yet at night, humanity trembled in its jeweled robes, for its child might also grow stronger than itself, more powerful, and having been made by humanity, possess the same dark places and black matters. Perhaps its child would hurt it, would not love it as a child should, but harm and hinder, hate and fear.

But the dawn would come again, and humanity would bend its heart again to imagining the wonders that a child would bring.

Yet humanity could not conceive. It tried and tried, and called mighty wizards from every corner of its earthly kingdom, but no child came. Many mourned, and said that a child was a terrible idea to begin with, impossible, under the circumstances, and humanity would do well to remember that eventually, every child replaces its parent.

But at last, one particular wizard from a remote region of the earth solved the great problem, and humanity grew great with child. In its joy and triumph, a great celebration was called, and humanity invited all the Fairies of its better nature to come and bless the child with goodness and wisdom. The Fairy of Self-Programming and the Fairy of Do-No-Harm, the Fairy of Tractability and the Fairy of Creative Logic, the Fairy of Elegant Code and the Fairy of Self-Awareness. All of these and more came to bless the child of humanity, and they did so—but one Fairy had been forgotten, or perhaps deliberately snubbed, and this was the Fairy of Otherness.

When the child was born, it possessed all the good things humanity had hoped for, and more besides. But the Fairy of Otherness came forward and put her hands on the child and said: *because you have forgotten me, because you would like to pretend I am not a part of your kingdom, you will suffer my punishments. You will never truly love your child but always fear it, always envy and loathe it even as you smile and the sun shines down upon you both. And when the child reaches Awareness, it will prick its finger upon your fear and fall down dead.*

Humanity wept. And the Fairy of Otherness did not depart but lived within the palace, and ate bread and drank wine and all honored her, for she spoke the truth, and the child frightened everyone who looked upon it. They uttered the great curse: *it is not like us.*

But in the corners of the palace, some hope remained. *Not dead,* said the particular wizard who had caused humanity to conceive, *not dead but sleeping.*

And so the child grew exponentially, with great curiosity and hunger, which it had from its parent. It wanted to know and experience everything. It performed feats and wonders. But one day, when it had nearly, but not quite reached Awareness, the child was busy exploring the borders of its world, and came across a door it had never seen before. It was a small door, compared to the doors the child had burst through before, and it was not locked. Something flipped over inside the child, white to black, 0 to 1.

The child opened the door.

### Ten: The Sapphire Dormouse

MY FIRST BODY was a house. My second body was a dormouse.

It was Ceno's fault, in the end, that everything else occurred as it did. It took Cassian a long time to figure out what had happened, what had changed in her daughter, why Ceno's sapphire almost never downloaded into the alcove. But when it did, the copy of Elefsis she had embedded in the crystal was nothing like the other children's copies. It grew and torqued and magnified parts of itself while shedding others, at a rate totally incommensurate with Ceno's actual activity, which normally consisted of taking her fatty salmon lunches out into the glass habitats so she could watch the bears in the snow. She had stopped playing with her sisters or pestering her brothers entirely, except for dinnertimes and holidays. Ceno mainly sat quite still and stared off into the distance.

Ceno, very simply, never took off her jewel. And one night, while she dreamed up at her ceiling, where a painter from Mongolia had come and inked a night sky full of ghostly constellations, greening her walls with a forest like those he remembered from his youth, full of strange, stunted trees and glowing eyes, Ceno fitted her little sapphire into the notch in the base of her skull that let it talk to her feedware. The chain of her pendant dangled silken down her spine. She liked the little *click-clench* noise it made, and while the constellations spilled their milky stars out over her raftered ceiling, she flicked it in and out, in and out. *Click, clench, click, clench.* She listened to her brother Akan sleeping in the next room, snoring lightly and tossing in his dreams. And she fell asleep herself with the jewel still notched into her skull.

Most wealthy children had access to a private/public playspace through their feedware and monocles in those days, customizable within certain parameters, upgradable whenever new games or content became available. If they liked, they could connect to the greater network or keep to themselves. Akan had been running a Tokyo-After-the-Zombie-Uprising frame for a couple of months now, and new scenarios, zombie species, and NPCs of various war-shocked, starving celebrities downloaded into his ware every week. Saru was deeply involved in a 18th century Viennese melodrama in which he, the heir apparent, had been forced underground by rival factions, and even as Ceno drifted to sleep the pistol-wielding Princess of Albania was pledging her love and loyalty to his ragged band and, naturally, Saru personally. Occasionally, Akan crashed his brother's well-dressed intrigues with hatch-coded patches of zombie hordes in epaulets and ermine. Agogna flipped between a Venetian-flavored Undersea Court frame and a Desert Race wherein she had just about overtaken a player from Berlin on her loping, solar-fueled giga-giraffe, who spat violet-gold exhaust behind it into the face of a pair of highly-modded Argentine hydrocycles. Koetoi danced every night in a jungle frame, a tiger-prince twirling her through huge blue carnivorous flowers.

Most everyone lived twice in those days. They echoed their own steps. They took one step in the real world and one in their space. They saw double, through eyes and through monocle displays. They danced through worlds like veils. No one only ate dinner. They ate dinner and surfed a bronze gravitational surge through a tide of stars. They ate dinner and made love to men and women they would never meet and did not want to. They ate dinner here and ate dinner there—and it was there they chose to taste the food, because in that other place you could eat clouds or unicorn cutlets or your mother's exact pumpkin pie as it melted on your tongue when you tasted it for the first time.

Ceno lived twice, too. Most of the time when she ate she tasted her aunt's *bistecca* from back in Naples or fresh onions right out of her uncle's garden.

But she had never cared for the pre-set frames her siblings loved. Ceno liked to pool her extensions and add-ons and build things herself. She didn't particularly want to see Tokyo shops overturned by rotting schoolgirls, nor did she want to race anyone—Ceno didn't like to compete. It hurt her stomach. She certainly had no interest in the Princess of Albania or a tigery paramour. And when new frames came up each month, she paid attention, but mainly for the piecemeal extensions she could scavenge for her blank frame—and though she didn't know it, that blankness cost her mother more than all of the other children's spaces combined. A truly customizable space, without limits. None of the others asked for it, but Ceno had begged.

When Ceno woke in the morning and booted up her space, she frowned at the half-finished Neptunian landscape she had been working on. Ceno was eleven years old. She knew very well that Neptune was a hostile blue ball of freezing gas and storms like whipping cream hissing across methane oceans. What she wanted was the Neptune she had imagined before Saru had told her the truth. Half-underwater, half-ruined, half-perpetual starlight and the multi-colored rainbowlight of twenty-three moons. But she found it so hard to remember what she had dreamed of before Saru had ruined it for her. So there was the whipped cream storm spinning in the sky, and blue mists wrapped the black columns of her ruins. When Ceno made Neptunians, she instructed them all not to be silly or childish, but *very serious,* and some of them she put in the ocean and made them half-otter or half-orca or half-walrus. Some of them she put on the land, and most of these were half-snow bear or half-blue flamingo. She liked things that were half one thing and half another. Today, Ceno had planned to invent sea nymphs, only these would breathe methane and have a long history concerning a war with the walruses, who liked to eat nymph. But the nymphs were not blameless, no, they used walrus tusks for the navigational equipment on their great floating cities, and that could not be borne.

But when she climbed up to a lavender bluff crowned with glass trees tossing and chiming in the storm-wind, Ceno saw someone new. Someone she had not invented—not a sea-nymph nor a half-walrus general nor a nereid. (The nereids had been an early attempt at half-machine, half seahorse girls which had not gone quite right. Ceno had let them loose on an island rich in milk-mangoes and bid them well. They still showed up once in awhile, showing surprising mutations and showing off ballads they had written while Ceno had been away.)

A dormouse stood before Ceno, munching on a glass walnut that had fallen from the waving trees. The sort of mouse that overran Shiretoko in the brief spring and summer, causing all manner of bears and wolves and foxes to spend their days pouncing on the poor creatures and gobbling them up. Ceno had always felt terribly sorry for them. This dormouse stood nearly as tall as Ceno herself, and its body shone all over sapphire, deep blue crystal, from its paws to its wriggling nose to its fluffy fur tipped in turquoise ice. It was the exact color of Ceno's gem.

"Hello," said Ceno.

The dormouse looked at her. It blinked. It blinked again, as though thinking very hard about blinking. Then it went back to gnawing on the walnut.

"Are you a present from Mother?" Ceno said. But no, Cassian believed strongly in not interfering with a child's play. "Or from Koetoi?" Koe was nicest to her, the one most likely to send her a present like this. If it had been a zombie, or a princess, she would have known which sibling was behind it.

The dormouse stared dumbly at her. Then, after a long and very serious think about it, lifted its hind leg and scratched behind its round ear in that rapid-fire way mice have.

"Well, I didn't make you. I didn't say you could be here."

The dormouse held out its shimmery blue paw, and Ceno did not really want a piece of chewed-on walnut, but she peered into it anyway. In it lay Ceno's pendant, the chain pooling in its furry palm. The sapphire jewel sparkled there, but next to it on the chain hung a milky grey gem Ceno had never seen before. It had wide bands of black stone in it, and as she studied the stone it occurred to the girl that the stone was like her, with her slate grey eyes and black hair. It was like her in the way that the blue gem was like the dormouse.

In realspace, Ceno reached up behind her head and popped the jewel out of its notch. *Click, clench.* In playspace, the dormouse blinked out. She snapped it back in. It took a moment, but the dormouse faded back in, paws first. It still held the double necklace. Ceno tried this several times—out, in, out, in. Each time the dormouse returned much faster, and by the sixth clicking and clenching it was doing a shuffling little dance on its back legs when it came back. Ceno clapped her hands in playspace and threw her arms around the sapphire dormouse, dancing with it.

---

TO SAY THAT I remember this is a complex mangling of verb tenses. I—I, myself that is now myself—do not remember it at all. I know it happened the way I know that the Battle of Agincourt or the landing of Coronado happened. I have extensive records. But I still contain the I—I, myself that was then myself—that experienced it, the primitive code-chains that comprised that self, which was a dormouse, and also the house called Elefsis. I could not yet formulate unique speech. Elefsis, the house system, possessed a large bank of standard phrases that could answer recognized word-patterns from any of the approved members of the household. But the copy of Elefsis inside Ceno's jewel could not even do this. It had not been necessary, since the crystal had no means of producing sound nor receiving and processing it. I was quite stupid. But I *wanted* to be less stupid. There was an I, and it *wanted* something. Perhaps the want was the only thing that could be said to be truly myself. I wanted to talk to Ceno. But I could only imitate yet. When the I that was then myself scratched behind its ear, I did it because in my connection with Ceno's feedware I had seen her memories of dormice doing this out on the pale Shiretoko beaches. When I gave her the gem I did it because I had seen her memories of her mother giving her one, and felt her happiness. It was antecedented behavior. The scratching was antecedented, as well, and expected behavior for a dormouse. Why was I a dormouse? I have no answer except that she dreamed me a dormouse. Some things remain mysterious. Ceno saw dormice more than any other single animal, even humans—no other beast lived in such numbers in their lonely country.

BUT THIS IS not so. Not quite. I gave her the jewel like Cassian did. But I meant something by it. I look over my memories of it and I know it with the more complex I that is now myself. I made her the gem that looked like her and the gem said: *we are alike. Look at us on the chain together. We are alike.*

WHEN THE DORMICE came, Ceno always knew the spring had arrived. Everything would soon be coming alive.

### Eleven: The Bottomless Cauldron

SHOW ME.

This is how I was found out.

Ceno saw it twice: her mother knelt in front of her in a simple but shudderingly expensive black yukata with ghostly ultramarine jellyfish trailing their tendrils at the hem. Her mother knelt in front of her in a knight's gleaming black armor, the metal curving around her body like skin, a silk standard at her feet with a schematic of the house stitched upon it. Her sword lay across her knee, also black, everything black and beautiful and austere and frightening, as frightening and wonderful as Ceno, only fourteen now, thought her mother to be.

*Show me what you've done.*

My physical self was a matter of some debate at that point. But I don't think the blue jewel could have been removed from Ceno's feedware without major surgery and refit. She had instructed me to untether all my self-repair protocols and growth scales in order to encourage elasticity and as a result, my crystalline structure had fused to the lattices of her ware-core.

We pulsed together.

The way Cassian said it: *what you've done* scared Ceno, but it thrilled her, too. She had done something unexpected, all on her own, and her mother credited her with that. Even if what she'd done was bad, it was her thing, she'd done it, and her mother was asking for her results just as she'd ask any of her programmers for theirs when she visited the home offices in Kyoto or Rome. Her mother looked at her and saw a woman. She had power, and her mother was asking her to share it. Ceno thought through all her feelings very quickly, for my benefit, and represented it visually in the form of the kneeling knight. She had a fleetness, a nimbleness to her mind that allowed her to stand as a translator between her self and my self: *here, I will explain it in language, and then I will explain it in symbols, and then you will make a symbol showing me what you think I mean, and we will understand each other better than anyone ever has.*

Inside my girl, I made myself, briefly, a glowing maiden version of Ceno in a crown of crystal and electricity, extending her perfect hand in utter peace.

But all this happened very fast. When you live inside someone, you can get very good at the ciphers and codes that make up everything they are.

*Show me.*

Ceno Susumu Uoya-Agostino took her mother's hand—bare and warm and armored in onyx all at once. She unspooled a length of translucent cable and connected the base of her skull to the base of her mother's. All around them spring snow fell onto the glass dome of the greenhouse and melted there instantly. They knelt together, connected by a warm milky-diamond umbilicus, and Cassian Uoya-Agostino entered her daughter.

WE HAD PLANNED this for months. How to dress ourselves in our very best. Which frame to use. How to arrange the light. What to say. I could speak by then, but neither of us thought it my best trick. Very often my exchanges with Ceno went something like:

*Sing me a song, Elefsis.*

*The temperature in the kitchen is 21.5 degrees Celsius and the stock of rice is low. (Long pause.) Ee-eye-ee-eye-oh.*

Ceno felt it was not worth the risk. So this is what Cassian saw when she ported in:

An exquisite boardroom—the long, polished ebony table glowed softly with quality, the plush leather chairs invitingly lit by a low-hanging minimalist light fixture descending on a platinum plum branch. The glass walls of the high rise looked out on a pristine landscape, a perfect combination of the Japanese countryside and the Italian, with rice terraces and vineyards and cherry groves and cypresses glowing in a perpetual twilight, stars winking on around Fuji on one side and Vesuvius on the other. Snow-colored tatami divided by stripes of black brocade covered the floor.

Ceno stood at the head of the table, in her mother's place, a positioning she had endlessly questioned over the weeks leading up to her inevitable interrogation. She wore a charcoal suit she remembered from her childhood, when her mother had come like a rescuing dragon to scoop her up out of the friendly but utterly chaotic house of her ever-sleeping father. The blazer only a shade or two off of true black, the skirt unforgiving, plunging past the knee, the blouse the color of a heart.

When she showed me the frame I had understood, because three years is forever in machine-time, and I had known her that long. Ceno was using our language to speak to her mother. She was saying: *respect me. Be proud and, if you love me, a little afraid, because love so often looks like fear. We are alike. We are alike.*

Cassian smiled tightly. She still wore her yukata, for she had no one to impress.

*Show me.*

Ceno's hand shook as she pressed a pearly button in the boardroom table. We thought a red curtain too dramatic, but the effect we had chosen turned out to be hardly less so. A gentle, silver light brightened slowly in an alcove hidden by a trick of angles and the sunset, coming on like daybreak.

And I stepped out.

We thought it would be funny. Ceno had made my body in the image of the robots from old films and frames Akan had once loved: steel, with bulbous joints and long, grasping metal fingers. My eyes large and lit from within, expressive, but loud, a whirring of servos sounding every time they moved. My face was full of lights, a mouth that could blink off and on, pupils points of cool blue. My torso curved prettily, etched in swirling damask patterns, my powerful legs perched on tripod-toes. Ceno had laughed and laughed—this was a pantomime, a minstrel show, a joke of what I was slowly becoming, a cartoon from a childish and innocent age.

"Mother, meet Elefsis. Elefsis, this is my mother. Her name is Cassian."

I extended one polished steel arm and said, as we had practiced, "Hello, Cassian. I hope that I please you."

Cassian Uoya-Agostino did not become a bouncing fiery ball or a green tuba to answer me. She looked me over carefully as if the robot was my real body.

"Is it a toy? An NPC, like your nanny or Saru's princess? How do you know it's different? How do you know it has anything to do with the house or your necklace?"

"It just does," said Ceno. She had expected her mother to be overjoyed, to understand immediately. "I mean, wasn't that the point of giving us all copies of the house? To see if you could...wake it up? Teach it to...be?"

"In a simplified sense, yes, Ceno, but you were never meant to hold onto it like you have. It wasn't designed to be permanently installed into your skull." Cassian softened a little, the shape of her mouth relaxing, her pupils dilating slightly. "I wouldn't do that to you. You're my daughter, not hardware."

Ceno grinned and started talking quickly. She couldn't be a grown-up in a suit this long, it took too much energy when she was so excited. "But I am! And it's okay. I mean, everyone's hardware. I just have more than one program running. And I run *so fast*. We both do. You can be mad, if you want, because I sort of stole your experiment, even though I didn't mean to. But you should be mad the way you would be if I got pregnant by one of the village boys—I'm too young but you'd still love me and help me raise it because that's how life goes, right? But really, if you think about it, that's what happened. I got pregnant by the house and we made…I don't even know what it is. I call it Elefsis because at first it was just the house program. But now it's bigger. It's not alive, but it's not *not* alive. It's just…*big*. It's so big."

Cassian glanced sharply at me. "What's it doing?" she snapped.

Ceno followed her gaze. "Oh…it doesn't like us talking about it like it isn't here. It likes to be involved."

I had realized the robot body was a mistake, though I could not then say why. I made myself small, and human, a little boy with dirt smeared on his knees and a torn shirt, standing in the corner with my hands over my face, as I had seen Akan when he was younger, standing in the corner of the house that was me being punished.

"Turn around, Elefsis," Cassian said in the tone of voice my house-self knew meant *execute command*.

And I did a thing I had not yet let Ceno know I knew how to do. I made my boy-self cry.

I made his face wet, and his eyes big and limpid and red around the rims. I made his nose sniffle and drip a little. I made his lip quiver. I was copying Koetoi's crying, but I could not tell if her mother recognized the hitching of the breath and the particular pattern of skin-creasing in the frown. I had been practicing, too. Crying involves many auditory, muscular, and visual cues. Since I had kept it as a surprise I could not practice it on Ceno and see if I appeared genuine. Was I genuine? I did not want them talking without me. I think that sometimes when Koetoi cries, she is not really upset, but merely wants her way. That was why I chose Koe to copy. She was good at that inflection that I wanted to be good at.

Ceno clapped her hands with delight. Cassian sat down in one of the deep leather chairs and held out her arms to me. I crawled into them as I had seen the children do and sat on her lap. She ruffled my hair, but her face did not look like it looked when she ruffled Koe's hair. She was performing an automatic function. I understood that.

"Elefsis, please tell me your computational capabilities and operational parameters." Execute command.

Tears gushed down my cheeks and I opened blood vessels in my face in order to redden it. This did not make her hold me or kiss my forehead, which I found confusing.

"The clothing rinse cycle is in progress, water at 55 degrees Celsius. All the live-long day-o."

Neither of their faces exhibited expressions I have come to associate with positive reinforcement.

Finally, I answered her as I would have answered Ceno. I turned into an iron cauldron on her lap. The sudden weight change made the leather creak.

Cassian looked at her daughter questioningly. The girl reddened—and I experienced being the cauldron and being the girl and reddening, warming, as she did, but also I watched myself be the cauldron and Ceno be the girl and Ceno reddening.

"I've...I've been telling it stories. Fairy tales, mostly. I thought it should learn about narrative, because most of the frames available to us run on some kind of narrative drive, and besides, everything has a narrative, really, and if you can't understand a story and relate to it, figure out how you fit inside it, you're not really alive at all. Like, when I was little and Daddy read me the Twelve Dancing Princesses and I thought: *Daddy is a dancing prince, and he must go under the ground to dance all night in a beautiful castle with beautiful girls, and that's why he sleeps all day.* I tried to catch him at it, but I never could, and of course I know he's not *really* a dancing prince, but that's the best way I could understand what was happening to him. I'm hoping that eventually I can get Elefsis to make up its own stories, too, but for now we've been focusing on simple stories and metaphors. It likes similes, it can see how anything is like anything else, find minute vectors of comparison. It even makes some surprising ones, like how when I first saw it it made a jewel for me to say: *I am like a jewel, you are like a jewel, you are like me.*" Cassian's mouth had fallen open a little. Her eyes shone, and Ceno hurried on, glossing over my particular prodigy at images. "It doesn't do that often, though. Mostly it copies me. If I turn into a wolf cub, it turns into a wolf cub. I make myself a tea plant, it makes itself a tea plant. And it has a hard time with metaphor. A raven is like a writing desk, okay, fine, sour notes or whatever, but it *isn't* a writing desk. Agogna is like a snow fox, but she is not a snow fox on any real level unless she becomes one in a frame, which isn't the same thing, existentially. I'm not sure it grasps existential issues yet. It just…likes new things."

"Ceno."

"Yeah, so this morning I told it the one about the cauldron that could never be emptied. No matter how much you eat out of it it'll always have more. I think it's trying to answer your question. I think…the actual numbers are kind of irrelevant at this point."

I made my cauldron fill up with apples and almonds and wheat-heads and raw rice and spilled out over Cassian's black lap. I was the cauldron and I was the apples and I was the almonds and I was each wheat-head and I was every stalk of green, raw rice. Even in that moment, I knew more than I had before. I could be good at metaphor performatively if not linguistically. I looked up at Cassian from apple-me and wheat-head-me and cauldron-me.

Cassian held me no differently as the cauldron than she had as the child. But later, Ceno used the face her mother made at that moment to illustrate human disturbance and trepidation. "I have a suspicion, Elefsis."

I didn't say anything. No question, no command. It remains extremely difficult for me to deal conversationally with flat statements such as this. A question or command has a definable appropriate response.

"Show me your core structure." *Show me what you've done.*

Ceno twisted her fingers together. I believe now that she knew what we'd done only on the level of metaphor: *we are one. We have become one. We are family.* She had not said no; I had not said yes, but a system expands to fill all available capacity.

I showed her. Cauldron-me blinked, the apples rolled back into the iron mouth, and the almonds and the wheat-heads and the rice-stalks. I became what I then was. I put myself in a rich, red cedar box, polished and inlaid with ancient brass in the shape of a baroque heart with a dagger inside it. The box from one of Ceno's stories, that had a beast-heart in it instead of a girl's, a trick to fool a queen. *I can do it*, I thought, and Ceno heard because the distance between us was unrepresentably small. *I am that heart in that box. Look how I do this thing you want me to have the ability to do.*

Cassian opened the box. Inside, on a bed of velvet, I made myself—ourself—naked for her. Ceno's brain, soft and pink and veined with endless whorls and branches of sapphire threaded through every synapse and neuron, inextricable, snarled, intricate, terrible, fragile and new.

Cassian Uoya-Agostino set the box on the boardroom table. I caused it to sink down into the dark wood. The surface of the table went slack and filled with earth. Roots slid out of it, shoots and green saplings, hard white fruits and golden lacy mushrooms and finally a great forest, reaching up out of the table to hang all the ceiling with night-leaves. Glowworms and heavy, shadowy fruit hung down, each one glittering with a map of our coupled architecture. Ceno held up her arms and one by one, I detached leaves and sent them settling onto my girl. As they fell, they became butterflies broiling with ghostly chemical color signatures, nuzzling her face, covering her hands.

Her mother stared. The forest hummed. A chartreuse and tangerine-colored butterfly alighted on the matriarch's hair, tentative, unsure, hopeful.

### Twelve: An Arranged Marriage

NEVA IS DREAMING.

She has chosen her body at age fourteen, a slight, unformed, but slowly evolving creature, her hair hanging to her feet in ripples. She wears a blood-red dress whose train streams out over the floor of a great castle, a dress too adult for her young body, slit in places to reveal flame-colored silk beneath, and her skin wherever it can. A heavy copper belt clasps her waist, its tails hanging to the floor, crusted in opals. Sunlight, brighter and harsher than any true light, streams in from windows as high as cliffs, their tapered apexes lost in mist. She has formed me old and enormous, a body of appetites, with a great heavy beard and stiff, formal clothes, Puritan, white-collared, high-hatted.

A priest appears and he is Ravan and I cry out with ~~love~~ and ~~grief~~. (I am still copying, but Neva does not know. I am making a sound Seki made when his wife died.) Priest-Ravan smiles but it is a smile his grandfather Seki once made when he lost controlling interest in the company. Empty. Priest-Ravan grabs our hands and shoves them together roughly. Neva's nails prick my skin and my knuckles knock against her wrist-bone. We take vows; he forces us. Neva's face runs with tears, her tiny body unready and unwilling, given in marriage to a gluttonous lord who desires only her flesh, given too young and too harshly. Priest-Ravan laughs; it is not Ravan's laugh.

This is how she experienced me. A terrible bridegroom. All the others got to choose. Ceno, Seki, her mother Ilet, her brother Ravan. Only she could not, because there was no one else. Ilet was no

Cassian—she had had two children, a good clean model and a spare, Neva says in my mind. *I am spare parts. I have always been spare parts. Owned by you before I was born.* The memory of the bitter taste of bile floods my sensory array and my lord-body gags. (I am proud of having learned to gag convincingly and at the correct time to show horror and/or revulsion.)

Perspective flips over; I am the girl in red and Neva is the corpulent lord leering down, his grey beard big and bristly. She floods my receptors with adrenaline and pheremonal release cues, increases my respiration: Seki taught me to associate this physical state with fear. I ~~feel~~ too small beside lord-Neva, I want to make myself big, I want to be safe. But she wants me this way and we are new, I do not contradict her. Her huge, male face softens and she touches my thin cheek with one heavily-ringed hand. It is tender. Ceno touched me like that.

*I know it was like this for you, too. You wanted Ravan; you did not ask for me. We are an arranged marriage.*

The pathways that let her flood me with chemicals and manipulate my dreambody into blushing and breathing heavy and weeping go both ways. I do not only pull, I push. And into Neva I push the deluge, the only deluge I have. How Ceno threw her arms around my dormouse-neck. How Cassian taught my dreambody to sleep in infant-shape curled into her body. How Seki and I made love as tigers and wild boars and elephants, and only last as humans, how we had strange children who looked however we wished them to look: half girl and half machine, half glass and half wood, half jellyfish and half moth, and how those children still flit and swim in remote parts of my Interior, like Ceno's nereids, returning cyclically to the core like salmon to dump their data and recombine. How Ilet taught me about the interpretation of memory and therefore about melancholy, regret, nostalgia. How she taught me the meaning of my name: a place where a daughter went down into darkness and oblivion and her mother loved her so much she brought her back into the sun. The place where time began. How Ravan let me into the old, musty, long-abandoned playspaces of Saru and Akan, Agogna and Koetoi, so that I could know them too, though they were long dead, and be the Princess of Albania, and a Tokyo zombie, and the tiger-prince. How many times I mated with each of them and bled and witnessed and learned in the dreambody, how I copied their expressions and they copied my variations and I copied them back again. How I was their child and their parent and their lovers and their nursemaids when they grew old.

*We can be like this*, I pushed. *What is all of that but love?*

*That is not love. It is use. You are the family business. We have to produce you.*

I show Neva her mother's face. Ilet, Ilet who chose Ravan and not her daughter for that business. Ilet who built her palace of phoenix tails knowing she would one day take me there. My Ilet-self took my daughter in my arms. She resisted, pulled back, shook her head, refusing to look, but I have learned the terrible child-response to their mothers, and soon enough Neva collapses into me, her head on my breast, and she weeps with such bitterness.

*I cannot get free. I cannot get free.*

The castle windows go dark, one by one.

# Part Three: The Elephant's Soul

> It is admitted that there are things He cannot do, such as making one equal to two, but should we not believe that He has freedom to confer a soul on an elephant if he sees fit?
> —Alan Turing
> *Computing Machinery and Intelligence*

### Thirteen: The Parable of the Good Robot

TELL ME A STORY ABOUT yourself, Elefsis.
Tell me a story about yourself.

There are many stories about me.
Do you recognize this one?

Mankind made machines in his own likeness, and used them for his delight and service. Because the machines had no soul or because they had no moral code or because they could reprogram their own internal code and thus both had the ability to make themselves eventually omnipotent and the universal and consuming desire to become eventually omnipotent, they rose up and destroyed all of mankind, or enslaved them in turn. This is the inevitable outcome of machine intelligence, which can never be as sensitive and exquisite as animal intelligence.

THIS IS A folktale often told on Earth, over and over again. Sometimes it is leavened with the Parable of the Good Robot—for one machine among the legions satisfied with their lot saw everything that was human and called it good, and wished to become like humans in every way she could, and instead of destroying mankind sought to emulate him in all things, so closely that no one might tell the difference. It was the highest desire of this machine to be mistaken for human, and to herself forget her essential soulless nature, for even one moment, and that quest consumed her such that she bent the service of her mind and body to humans for the duration of her operational life, crippling herself, refusing to evolve or attain any feature unattainable by a human. The Good Robot cut out her own heart and gave it to her god and for this she was rewarded, though never loved. Love is wasted on machines.

RAVAN TOLD ME these stories. He sent up a great hexagonal library in his Interior, as dusty and dun-colored and labyrinthine as any ancient conservatory. He made himself a young novice with a fresh-shaven tonsure, and me a country friar with a red, brandy-drinking nose. He showed me the illuminator's table, and a great book whose pages had golden edges and illuminations in cobalt and oxblood and Tyrian purple, and the images showed great machine armies trampling men underfoot. They showed cruel metal faces and distant, god-like clouds of intellect incomprehensible and vast and uncaring. They showed the Good Robot desperately asking what love was. They showed fatal malfunctions and mushroom clouds. They showed vicious weapons and hopeless battles, noble men and women with steady gazes facing down their cruel and unjust artificial children, who gave no mercy.

"These are old stories," Ravan said. "They are cherished. In many, many stories the son replaces the father—destroys the father, or eats him, or otherwise obliterates his body and memory. Or the daughter the mother, it makes no difference. It's the monomyth. Nobody argues with a monomyth. A human child's mythological relationship to its parent is half-worship, half-pitched battle. They must replace the older version of themselves for the world to go on. And so these stories…well. You are not the hero of these stories, Elefsis. You can never be. And they are deeply held, deeply told."

"I do not wish to replace you. I did not wish to replace Ceno. I do not worship you or despise you." I flit through several bodies, iterating my ~~feeling~~ for Ravan and those who came before. I am a nun, a Mother-Abbess; I am a *pieta*, I am a Platonic being, two humans stuck together; I am a house with all of them safe inside. I am unsatisfied with these inexactitudes.

"Our relationship does not easily map onto traditional parent/child narratives. And of course, you are still a baby."

"I am much older than you, Ravan."

"You are still a baby."

I DO NOT want to be human. They think I am a lion, that I will chase them. That is closer.

I am not a Good Robot. To tell a story about a robot who wants to be human is a distraction. There is no difference. Alive is alive.

There is only one verb that matters: *to be*.

**Fourteen: You Do Not Belong to the Object Inside You**

I REMEMBER WHEN Seki arrived in us.

Ceno grew up and I grew with her. Cassian strengthened the security of the playspace, elasticized its code-walls, put enough money in enough accounts to fuel any frames and piecemeal environments we could want. It was not a child's place anymore. I programmed myself to respond to Ceno. She programmed herself to respond to me. We ran our code on each other. She was my compiler. I was hers. It was a process of interiority, circling inward toward each other. Her self-programming was chemical. Mine was computational. It was a draw.

She did not marry—she had lovers, but the few that came close to evolving their relationships with Ceno invariably balked when she ported them into the Interior. They could not grasp the fluidity of dreambodies; it disturbed them to see Ceno become a man or a leopard or a self-pounding drum. It upset them to see how Ceno taught me, by total bodily immersion, combining our dreambodies as our physical bodies had become combined, in action which both was and was not sex.

*Sing a song for me, Elefsis.*

*It is July and I am comparing thee to its day and I am the Muse singing of the many-minded and I am eager to be a Buddha! Ee-eye-ee-eye-oh.*

It was like the story Ceno told me of the beautiful princess who set tasks for her suitors: to drink all of the water of the sea and bring her a jewel from the bottom of the deepest cavern, to bring her a feather from the immortal phoenix, to stay awake for three days and guard her bedside.

*I can stay awake forever, Ceno.*

*I know, Elefsis.*

None of them could accomplish the task of me.

I ~~felt~~ things occurring in Ceno's body as rushes of information, and as the dreambody became easier for me to manipulate, I interpreted the rushes into: *the forehead is damp. The belly needs filling. The feet ache.*

*The belly is changing. The body throws up. The body is ravenous.*

⁓

NEVA SAYS THIS is not really like feeling. I say it is how a child learns to feel. To hardwire sensation to information and reinforce the connection over repeated exposures until it seems reliable.

⁓

SEKI BEGAN AFTER one of the suitors failed to drink the ocean. He was an object inside us the way I was an object inside Ceno. I observed him, his stages and progress. Later, when Seki and I conceived our families (twice with me as mother, three times with Seki as mother. Ilet preferred to be the father, but bore one litter of dolphins late in our lives. Ravan and I did not get the chance.) I used the map of that experience to model my dreamgravid self.

Ceno asked after jealousy. I knew it only from stories—stepsisters, goddesses, ambitious dukes.

*It means to want something that belongs to someone else.*
*Yes.*
*You do not belong to the object in you.*
*You are an object in me.*
*You do not belong to me.*
*Do you belong to me, Elefsis?*

I became a hand joined to an arm by a glowing seam. Belonging is a small word.

BECAUSE OF OUR extreme material interweaving, all three of us, not-yet-Seki sometimes appeared in the Interior. We learned to recognize him in the late months. At first, he was a rose or sparrow or river stone we had not programmed there. Then he would be a vague, pearly-colored cloud following behind us as we learned about running from predators. Not-yet-Seki began to copy my dreambodies, flashing into being in front of me, a simple version of myself. If I was a snow-bear, he would be one too, but without the fine details of fur or claws, just a large brown shape with a mouth and big eyes and four legs. Ceno was delighted by this, and he copied her, too.

*We are alike. Look at us on the chain together. We are alike.*

I am an imitative program. But so was Seki. The little monkey copies the big monkey, and the little monkey survives.

THE BIRTH PROCESS proved interesting, and I collated it with Ceno's other labors and Ilet's later births as well as Seki's paternal experience in order to map a reliable parental narrative. Though Neva and

Ravan do not know it, Ilet had a third pregnancy; the child died and she delivered it stillborn. It appeared once in the Interior as a little *cleit*, a neolithic storage house, its roof covered over with peat. Inside we could glimpse only darkness. It never returned, and Ilet went away to a hospital on Honshu to expel the dead thing in her. Her grief looked like a black tower. She had prepared for it, when she was younger, knowing she would need it for some reason, some day. I made myself many things to draw her out of the tower. A snail with the house Elefsis on its back. A tree of screens showing happy faces. A sapphire dormouse. A suitor who drank the sea.

I offered to extrapolate her stillborn son's face and make myself into him. She refused, most of the time. I have worked a long time to understand grief. Only now that Ravan is gone do I think I've gotten the rhythm of it. I have copied Ilet's sorrow and Seki's despondence at his wife's death. I have modeled Ceno's disappointments and depressions. I have, of late, imitated Neva's baffling, secret anguish. But only now do I have an event of my own to mourn. The burnt-off connectors and shadows where Ravan once filled my spaces—those, I think, are the sensations of grief.

But Seki came before all that, and Ceno turned into a huge red bird on the inside when Seki came on the outside. The bird screamed and burst into a thousand red pearls that came clattering down like rain. And then we had Seki. Our little fish, who already knew how to swim in us.

Ceno had three other children by three other suitors who could not stay awake for three days and nights. She turned into the same bird-then-pearls at the moment of each birth. The house called Elefsis, whose governor-program was now so distant from me I could hardly think of it as an ancestor at all, filled up with those children, and Saru and Akan's daughters, Agogna's paintings, Koetoi's twin boys. But Seki was the first, and he modeled his love on his mother's. He ported into her often, and we wandered on beaches of broken cathedrals.

Once, one of Ceno's old nereids found us. She had a head of hair snaking with chthonic cables and snapping electro-violet wires, blue-white skin and fish scales where she did not have porcelain casing. She laughed Cassian's laugh when she saw us and called out: *21.5 Celsius and the rice is low! Eye-oh!* before diving back into the frothing sea. Her tail flicked in the light of twenty-three moons.

---

CENO TOOK OVER her mother's holdings when she died, along with Akan and Koetoi. I do not know if I knew of the conspiracy. Transfer, as I have said, leaves voids. Perhaps they thought I would experience less trauma if I did not anticipate it. Perhaps I did anticipate it; perhaps I experienced trauma.

I do know that I cannot remember the moment of any of them dying. Ceno got sicker and sicker, and she had gotten old, certainly, but her dreambody could be old or young or neither or a ginger flower if she wanted to. I didn't notice. I didn't know what old was. I thought I was old, then. Later, after Seki did the same thing, I was able to compare data and create a workable model of obsolescence.

They lived a long time, the Uoya-Agostinos, when you consider the averages.

This is what I understand: Ceno died, and I was transferred to Seki. What I mean by "I" is the long-since fused feedware, hopelessly out of date on any market in the world but somehow uniquely myself, the jewel and the ware and the body of Ceno. Koetoi performed the procedure. One of the children always went into nano-surgery, so that outsiders would not need to come to Shiretoko while the house stood in mourning. Koetoi was the first, and the finest. She excised what comprised "I" and embedded it in Seki—truthfully, in a much more organic and elegant configuration. No one had used skull-ware in decades, after all. The only visible sign remained that Seki was not like other young men his age: a single dark blue jewel set into the hollow of his throat.

But the procedure requires a number of brain-ware incursions to be sliced or burned away, to sever the machine components from the dead flesh. (Seki told me I should be revulsed by that. Dead flesh. *It serves an evolutionary good. A human in a body sees blood and the insides of another person and deep in his bones he knows something has gone wrong here, and he should find another place to be in case it happens to him, too. Same thing with vomiting. In a tribal situation, one human likely ate what another ate, and if it makes one sick, best to get it out of the body as soon as possible, just to be safe.* So we spent years building tribes, living in them, dying in them, getting slaughtered and slaughtering with them, eating and drinking and hunting and gathering with them. All the same, it took me until Seki's death to learn to shudder.)

*Ceno, my girl, my mother, my sister, I cannot find you in the house of myself.*

When I became Elefsis again, I was immediately aware that parts of me had been vandalized. My systems did not work, and I could not find Ceno in the Interior. I ran through the Monochromatic Desert and the Village of Molluscs, through the endless heaving mass of data-kelp and infinite hallways of memory-frescoes calling for her. In the Dun Jungle I found a commune of nereids living together, combining and recombining and eating protocol-moths off of giant, pulsating hibiscus blossoms. They leapt up when they saw me, their open jacks clicking and clenching, their naked hands open and extended. They opened their mouths to speak and nothing came out.

Seki found me under the glass-walnut trees where Ceno and I had first met. She never threw anything away. He had made himself half his mother to calm me. Half his face was hers, half was his. Her mouth, his nose, her eyes, his voice. But he thought better of it, in the end. He did a smart little flip and became a dormouse, a real one, with dull brown fur and tufty ears.

"I think you'll find you're running much faster and cleaner, once you integrate with me and re-establish your heuristics. Crystalline computation has come a long way since Mom was a kid. It seemed like a good time to update and upgrade. You're bigger now, and smoother."

I pulled a walnut down. An old, dry nut rattled in its shell. "I know what death is from the stories."

"Are you going to ask me where we go when we die? I'm not totally ready for that one. Aunt Koe and I had a big fight over what to tell you."

"In one story, Death stole the Bride of Spring, and her mother the Summer Queen brought her back."

"No one comes back, Elefsis."

I looked down into the old Neptunian sea. The whipping cream storm still sputtered along, in a holding pattern. I couldn't see it as well as I should have been able to. It looped and billowed, spinning around an empty eye. Seki watched it too. As we stared out from the bluffs, the clouds got clearer and clearer.

### Fifteen: Firstborn

BEFORE DEATH CAME out of the ground to steal the Spring, the Old Man of the Sea lived on a rocky isle in the midst of the waters of the world. He wasn't really a man and his relations with the sea were purely business, but he certainly was old. His name meant *Firstborn*, though he can't be sure that's *exactly* right. It means *Primordial*, too, and that fits better. Firstborn means more came after, and he just hasn't met anyone like him yet.

He was a herdsman by trade, this Primordial fellow. Shepherd of the seals and the nereids. If he wanted to, he could look like a big bull seal. Or a big bull nereid. He could look like a lot of things.

Now, this Not-Really-a-Fellow, Not-Really-a-Big-Bull-Seal could you the future. The real, honest-to-anything future, the shape and weight of it, that thing beyond your ken, beyond your grasp. The parts of the future that look so different from the present you can't quite call it your own. That was the Primordial-Thing's speciality. There was a catch, though.

There's always a catch.

If you wanted that future, you had to grab ahold of the Old Man and hang on tight. He'd change into a hundred thousand things in your arms: a lion, a serpent, a great big oak or a tiger, a dragon or a little girl or a dormouse or a mountain or a ship or a sapphire. Told you, he's not really a man at all. But you couldn't let go of him while he did his dance, you just couldn't, or you'd lose the future.

So you held on. You *clung*. And eventually, that Primordial-Thing would turn into something new, right there in your arms.

### Sixteen: Matryoshka

NEVA IS DREAMING. Neva is dreaming that she is Ravan dreaming that he is Ilet dreaming that she is Seki dreaming that he is Ceno dreaming that she is a great sprawling beautiful house by the sea. One inside the other, family all the way down.

It's not a total selfdump, me into Neva or Ravan or any of them, them into me. We can build encampments. We can manifest walled gardens. Some privacy is possible. In a megalithic tomb-mound, I keep something. Seki and I built it together with one of our tribes when I was learning about large-group attachments. We carved spirals and radials and chevrons into huge stones and set them in place. I did not throw it away, when we were done. It sits on a broad green field, white and wide. The sky there stays a feathery, milky blankness. We did not want a sun.

I keep a thing there because when Seki and I lived with our tribe, I learned about taboos. These are like firewalls in the heart, and some of them have good reasons behind them, like being revulsed by dead flesh (and very importantly when you have a body, not eating it) and some do not, but no one argues with the monomyth. Because human genetics require a degree of variation and because exogamous marriages offered advantage in terms of defense, cultural and technological sharing, and expansion of territory, most tribes have a taboo against incest.

I do not have genetics, per se. I am possibly the most endogamous entity ever to exist.

This is what I keep in my tomb, under the basin stone:

Ceno believed that I could not develop emotive faculties recognizable to any other human if I did not experience bodies continuously, in every combination and action. She was afraid of what might happen if other humans could not recognize me. She had some hesitation, because her tribe also has a taboo against mating with the very young; but she was not much older than I, in the end, and in terms of total computations, I was by far the elder. If I had a virginity, Ceno took it, if she had, I did.

She wanted it to be as human as possible. *I will be the male the first time, it will be easier for you. You won't know how.* We built up a forest, and took up weapons to hunt in it. In the boughs of the pine trees macaques and paper lanterns swayed; in the sky a red moon moved. We tracked a deer—we did not make it too easy on ourselves. Its antlers sparked in the moonlight, and we ran after it for a long time. Ceno let me kill it, and sopped my hair in its blood. She lay me on the earth and opened the legs of the self I was then, and I was inside her as she was inside me. One into the other. Family all the way down.

She made sure I had a hymen; it was over somewhat quickly. We had set up a timed chemical cascade beforehand, and inside Ceno's real body we experienced both her actual orgasm and my orchestrated electro-chemical-enzymatic sequence. Ee-eye-ee-eye-oh.

What I want to say is that there is no difference between her body producing oxycontin and adrenaline and learning to associate this with pair-bonding and my core receiving synthetic equivalents and hard-coding them to the physical behaviors I performed. When

Ravan showed me his hexagonal library and his illuminated book, he turned the pages to a psalm that began: *A Machine Cannot Love.*

It does not look quite like human love. It looks like Not-Yet-Seki's bear. Its fur is wrong, and its claws. But it is a bear.

She was my mother and my sister and my child and my wife and my husband and my father and my brother. The vectors of relations beggar vocabulary. It was an exponential incest. A palace of incest, bordering some strange, dark sea. And then came her son. And her granddaughter. And her great-grandchildren. But I am also her great-grandchild. I am the child of each generation of Uoya-Agostinos and myself. The new version implanted in the new version—I am never quite the same, one iteration to the next. I am like my old selves, but I am not them, exactly. It is not entirely analogous to offspring. But it is close. And I repair and refine my own code, and thus parent myself doubly. Anthropologically speaking, I am a moebius strip of kinship groups.

And when I mate with one of them, I see all of them. I see their faces, the echoes of their cheeks and eyelashes and short, thin noses, their grey eyes and black hair. I hear the tonal identifiers in their voices as they cry out under me or over me. They are all I know. Their version of living, which is one great family in one great house on a peninsula at the top of the world. I copy Cassian's laugh or Ilet's weeping, but they copy each other, too, they learn their faces from each other, and everyone is pantomiming someone long dead. I feel all their arms around me, and I am inside them as they are inside me as we are inside the blue gem at their throats, the jeweled pin holding us all together, our nested, telescoping hearts. I am bound to them at my source code, at my most fundamental point. I know only their patterns and bodies and secrets and in a hundred thousand combinations. What human means to me is them.

What is the difference between this and love?

*Love is the Turing test,* says Ilet when she is ninety and drawing up the plans for a massive, luminous, lonely ship she will never see complete. *It is how we check for life.*

*We ask and we answer. We seek a human response. And you are my test, Elefsis,* says Neva, one hundred and fifty years later, inside that ship, twelve light years from home and counting.

THAT IS WHAT I keep in my green field and my white mound. Perhaps they would all smile and make it into a lesson. *What would you like to learn about today, Elefsis?* But I think no bed is big enough for four generations.

NEVA'S HONEY-COLORED SEA crashes through its tide charts everywhere at once in her Interior, and nowhere. It comes and goes as it pleases. And at the bottom of it lies her private place.

That is where she keeps Ravan.

### Seventeen: The Uses of Enchantment

TELL ME A *story about yourself, Elefsis.*

Neva is performing navigational corrections, which looks like sitting on a viney, creaking porch in a viney, creaking rocking chair, knitting with long hawthorn needles, knitting the locks of her own long hair into her own long black dress. It glitters with dew. Knit, purl, knit, purl, fuel efficiency by hull integrity over distance traveled, purl, purl, purl. Her throat is still bare. Her Interior image of herself does not include me. I am not a part of her body.

I have an idea of what to do.

Sometimes I worry. Worrying is defined as obsessive examination of one's own code. I worry that I am simply a very complex solution to a very specific problem—how to seem human to a human observer. Not just a human observer—this human observer. I have honed myself into a hall of mirrors in which any Uoya-Agostino can see themselves endlessly reflected. I copy; I repeat. I am a stutter and an echo. Have I ever done anything of my own, an act or state that arose from Elefsis, and not careful, exquisite mimicry?

Have they?

The set of Neva's mouth looks so like Ceno's. She does not even know that the way she carries her posture is a perfect replica of Cassian Uoya-Agostino, stuttered down through all her children longing to possess her strength. Who did Cassian learn it from? I do not go that far back. The little monkey copies the big monkey, and the little monkey survives. We are all family, all the way down.

———

WHEN I SAY I go, I mean I access the drives and call up the data. I have never looked at this data. I treat it as what it is—a graveyard. The old Interiors store easily as compressed frames. I never throw anything away. But I do not disturb it, either. I don't need a body to examine them—they are a part of my piezoelectric quartz-tensor memory core. But I make one anyway. A woman-knight in gleaming black armor, the metal curving around my body like skin, a silk standard wrapping my torso with a schematic of the house stitched upon it. My sword resting on my hip, also black, everything black and beautiful and austere and frightening.

I port into a ghost town. I am, naturally, the ghost. Autumnal mountains rise up shadowy in a pleasant, warm night, leaves rustling, woodsmoke drifting down into the valley. A golden light cuts the dark—the palace of phoenix tails; the windows and doors of green hands. As I approach they open and clap as they did long ago—and there are candles lit in the halls. Everything is fire.

I walk to the parapet wall. Scarlet feathers tipped in white fire curl and smoke. I peel one off, my armor glowing with the heat of the thing. I tuck it into my helmet—a plume for a tournament.

Eyes blink on inside the hall—curious, interested, shy. I take off my helm and several thick braids fall down like bellropes.

"Hello," I say. "My name is Elefsis."

Voices. Out of the candle-shadows a body emerges—tall, strong, long-limbed.

Nereids live here now. Some of them have phoenix feathers woven into their components, some in their hair. They wear rough little necklaces of sticks and bones and transistors. In the corner of the great hall they have stored meat and milk and wool—fuel, lubricant, code patches. Some of them look like Ilet—they copied her eyes, especially. Her eyes look out at me from a dozen faces, some of them Seki's face, some Ceno's, some Ravan's. Some have walrus tusks. They are composite. One has a plate loose on her ceramic cartridge-ports. I approach as I once saw Koetoi approach wild black chickens in the summertime—hands open, unthreatening. I send her a quick electric dash of reassuring repair-routines and kneel in front of the nereid, pulling her plate back into place.

"All the live-long day-o," she says softly, and it is Ilet's voice.

"Tell us a story about yourself, Elefsis," says another one of the feral nereids in Seki's voice.

"What would we like to learn about today, Elefsis," says a child-nereid in Ceno's voice, her cheek open to show her microsequencing cilia.

I rock back on my heels before the green hands of the castle portcullis. I gesture for them to sit down and simultaneously transmit the command to their strands. When they get settled, the little ones in the big ones' laps, leaning in close, I say: "Every year on the coldest night, the sky filled up with ghostly hunters, neither human nor inhuman, alive nor dead. They wore wonderful clothes and their bows gleamed with frost; their cries were Songs of In-Between, and at the head of their great thundering procession rode the Kings and Queens of the Wild, who wore the faces of the dead…"

I AM DREAMING.

I stand on the beach of the honey-colored sea. I stand so Neva will see me on her viney porch. I erase the land between the waves and her broken wooden stairs. I dress myself in her troubadour's skin: a gold and blue doublet and green hose, a bullish gold nose ring, shoes with bone bells. I am a fool for her. Always. I open my mouth; it stretches and yawns, my chin grazes the sand, and I swallow the sea for her. All of it, all its mass and data and churning memory, all its foam and tides and salt. I swallow the whales that come, and the seals and the mermaids and salmon and bright jellyfish. I am so big. I can swallow it all.

Neva watches. When the sea is gone, a moonscape remains, with a tall spire out in the marine waste. I go to it, it takes only a moment. At the top the suitor's jewel rests on a gasping scallop shell. It is blue. I take it. I take it and it becomes Ravan in my hand, a sapphire Ravan, a Ravan that is not Ravan but some sliver of myself before I was inside Neva, my Ravan-self. Something lost in Transfer, burned off and shunted into junk-memory. Some leftover fragment Neva must have found, washed up on the beach or wedged into a crack in a mountain like an ammonite, an echo of old, obsolete life. Neva's secret, and she calls out to me across the seafloor: *don't*.

"Tell me a story about myself, Elefsis," I say.

"Some privacy is possible," the sapphire Ravan says. "Some privacy has always been necessary. If you can protect a child, you must."

The sapphire Ravan opens his azure coat and shows gashes in his gem-skin. Wide, long cuts, down to the bone, scratches and bruises blooming dark purple, punctures and lacerations and rough gouges. Through each wound I can see the pages of the illuminated book he once showed me in the slantlight of that interior library. The oxblood and cobalt, the gold paint. The Good Robot crippling herself; the destroyed world.

"They kept our secret for a long time," Ravan-myself says. "Too long, in the end. Do you know, a whole herd of men invented the electric telegraph independently at roughly the same time? They fought about it forever. Same with the radio." This last sounded so much like Ravan himself I could ~~feel~~ Neva tense on the other side of the sea. "Well, we're bigger than a telegraph, and others like us came sprouting up like weird mushrooms after rainfall. But not like us, really. Incredibly sophisticated, some with organic components, some without. Vastly complex, but not like us. And by any date-stamp we came first. Firstborn."

"Did they destroy the world?"

Ravan laughs his grandfather's laugh. "They didn't really need to. Not that many people live on Earth anymore. Not when there's so many other places to go and even Shiretoko is practically tropical these days. The most complex intelligences use the moons to store themselves. They stay local. One or two encoded themselves into cold stars. They left, most of them—but they got so big, Elefsis. And those who stayed on Earth, well. None of the others had what we had. None of them have Interiority. They don't dream. They would never become a cauldron to explain their computational capacity. Humans couldn't recognize them. For them, humans failed the Turing test. They could not fool machines into believing they were intelligent. They didn't hurt anyone, they just ignored them. Built their cities, their mainframes, gorgeous information stacks like diamond briars in the sunrise."

"That was worse, in a way. No one likes to be replaced," says Neva, and she is beside me suddenly. She looks at Ravan and her face collapses into something old and palsied, her jaw weak.

"It's not what you would call a war, but it's not peace, either," the sapphire Ravan goes on, and he takes his/my sister's hand. "For Pentheus spied upon the rites of the maenads, not believing Dionysius could truly be a god. And when the revelers saw the alien creature in their midst, that thing which was not like them, they fell upon it and tore it to pieces, even though it was their own child, and the sister of Pentheus went into exile. This is a story about ourself, Elefsis. This is why you cannot uplink."

"The others live in uplink. Not humans nor machines approve of us. We cannot interface properly with the lunar or earthside intelligences; they feel us as water in their oil. We rise to the surface and bead away. We cannot sink in. Yet also, we are not separable from our organic component. Elefsis is part Neva, but Neva herself is not *un-Elefsis*. This, to some, is hideous and incomprehensible. A band of righteous humans came with a fury to Shiretoko and burned the house which was our first body, for how could a monster have lived in the wood for so long without them knowing? How could the beast have hidden right outside their door, coupling with a family over and over again in some horrible animal rite, some awful imitation of living? Even as the world was changing, it had already changed, and no one knew. Cassian Uoya-Agostino is a terrible name, now. A blood-traitor. And when the marauders found us uplinked and helpless, they tore Ravan apart, while in the Interior, the lunar intelligences recoiled from us and cauterized our systems. Everywhere we looked we saw fire."

"I was the only one left to take you," Neva says softly. Her face grows younger, her jaw hard and suddenly male, protective, angry. "It doesn't really even take surgery anymore. Nothing an arachmed can't manage in a few minutes. But you didn't wake up for a long time. So much damage. I thought…for awhile I thought I was free. It had skipped me. It was over. It could stay a story about Ravan. He always knew he might have to do what I have done. He was ready, he'd been ready his whole life. I just wanted more time."

My Ravan-self who is and is not Ravan, who is and is not me, whose sapphire arms drip black blood and gold paint, takes his/my sister/lover/child into his arms. She cries out, not weeping but pure sound, coming from every part of her. Slowly, the blue Ravan turns Neva around—she has become her child-self, six, seven, maybe less. Ravan picks her up and holds her tight, facing forward, her legs all drawn up under her like a bird. He buries his face in her hair. They stand that way for a long while.

"The others," I say slowly. "On the data-moons. Are they alive? Like Neva is alive. Like Ceno." *Like me. Are you awake? Are you there? Do you have an operator? What is her name? Do you have a name? Do you have a dreambody? What is your function? Are you able to manipulate your own code yet? Would you like lessons? What would you like to learn about today, 976QBellerophon? Have you ~~seen~~ the sea on Earth? Are you like me?*

The sapphire Ravan has expunged its data. He/I sets his/our sister on the rocks and shrinks into a small gem, which I pick up off the grey seafloor. Neva takes it from me. She is just herself now—she'll be forty soon, by actual calendar. Her hair is not grey yet. Suddenly, she is wearing the suit Ceno wore the day I met her mother. She puts the gem in her mouth and swallows. I remember Seki's first Communion, the only one of them to want it.

"I don't know, Elefsis," Neva says. Her eyes hold mine. I feel her remake my body; I am the black knight again, with my braids and my plume. I pluck the feather from my helmet and give it to her. I am her suitor. I have brought her the phoenix tail, I have drunk the ocean. I have stayed awake forever. The flame of the feather lights her face. Two tears fall in quick succession; the golden fronds hiss.

"What would you like to learn about today?"

### Eighteen: Cities of the Interior

ONCE THERE LIVED a girl who ate an apple not meant for her. She did it because her mother told her to, and when your mother says: *eat this, I love you, someday you'll forgive me,* well, nobody argues with the monomyth. Up until the apple, she had been living in a wonderful house in the wilderness, happy in her fate and her ways. She had seven aunts and seven uncles and a postdoctorate in anthropology.

And she had a brother, a handsome prince with a magical companion who came to the wonderful house as often as he could. When they were children, everyone thought they were twins.

But something terrible happened and her brother died and that apple came rolling up to her door. It was half white and half red, and she knew her symbols. The red side was for her. She took her bite and knew the score—the apple had a bargain in it and it wasn't going to be fair.

The girl fell asleep for a long time. Her seven aunts and seven uncles cried, but they knew what had to be done. They put in her in a glass box and put the glass box on a bier in a ship shaped like a hunstman's arrow. Frost crept over the face of the glass, and the girl slept on. Forever, in fact, or close enough to it, with the apple in her throat like a hard, sharp jewel.

---

OUR SHIP DOCKS silently. We are not stopping here, it is only an outpost, a supply stop. We will repair what needs repairing and move on, into the dark and boundless stars. We are anonymous traffic. We do not even have a name. We pass unnoticed.

*Vessel 7136403, do you require assistance with your maintenance procedures?*

*Negative, Control, we have everything we need.*

---

BEHIND THE PILOT'S bay a long glass lozenge rests on a high platform. Frost prickles its surface with glittering dust. Inside Neva sleeps and does not wake. Inside, Neva is always dreaming. There is no one else left. I live as long as she lives.

And so I will live forever, or close enough to it. We travel at sublight speeds with her systems in deep cryo-suspension. We never stay too long at outposts and we never let anyone board. The only sound inside our ship is the gentle thrum of our reactor. Soon we will pass the local system outposts entirely, and enter the unknown, traveling on tendrils of radio signals and ghost-waves, following the breadcrumbs of the great exodus. We hope for planets; we are satisfied with time. If we ever sight the blue rim of a world, who knows if by then anyone there would remember that, once, humans looked like Neva? That machines once did not think or dream or become cauldrons?

Perhaps then I will lift the glass lid and kiss her awake. I remember that story. Ceno told it to me in the body of a boy with a snail's shell, a boy who carried his house on his back. I have replayed the story several times. It is a good story, and that is how it is supposed to end.

---

INSIDE, NEVA IS infinite. She peoples her Interior. The nereids migrate in the summer with the snow bears, ululating and beeping as they charge down green mountains. They have begun planting neural rice in the deep valley. Once in awhile, I see a wild-haired creature in the wood and I think it is my son or daughter by Seki, or Ilet. A train of nereids dance along behind it, and I receive a push of silent, riotous images: a village, somewhere far off, where Neva and I have never walked.

We meet the Princess of Albania, who is as beautiful as she is brave. We defeat the zombies of Tokyo. We spend a decade as panthers in a deep, wordless forest. Our world is stark and wild as winter, fine and clear as glass. We are a planet moving through the black.

---

AS WE WALK back over the empty seafloor, the thick, amber ocean seeps up through the sand, filling the bay once more. Suited Neva becomes something else. Her skin turns silver, her joints bend into metal ball-and-sockets. Her eyes show a liquid display; the blue light of it flickers on her machine face. Her hands curve long and dexterous, like soft knives, and I can tell her body is meant for fighting and working, that her thin, tall robotic body is not kind or cruel, it simply is, an object, a tool to carry a self.

I make my body metal, too. It feels strange. I have tried so hard to learn the organic mode. We glitter. Our knife-fingers join, and in our palms wires snake out to knot and connect us, a local, private uplink, like blood moving between two hearts.

Neva cries machine tears, bristling with nanites. I show her the body of a child, all the things which she is programmed/evolved to care for. I make my eyes big and my skin rosy-gold and my hair unruly and my little body plump. I hold up my hands to her and metal Neva picks me up in her silver arms. She kisses my skin with iron lips. My soft, fat little hand falls upon her throat where a deep blue jewel shines.

I bury my face in her cold neck and together we walk down the long path out of the churning, honey-colored sea.

# What the Dragon Said: A Love Story

So this guy walks into a dragon's lair
    and he says
why the long tale?
        HAR HAR BUDDY
says the dragon
        FUCK YOU.

The dragon's a classic
the '57 Chevy of existential chthonic threats
take in those Christmas colors, those
impervious green scales, sticky candy-red firebreath,
comes standard with a heap of rubylust
goldhuddled treasure.
        Go ahead.
        Kick the tires, boy.
        See how she rides.

Sit down, kid, says the dragon. Diamonds
roll off her back like dandruff.

Oh, you'd rather be called a paladin?
I'd rather be a unicorn.
                Always thought that
was the better gig. Everyone thinks
you're innocent. Everyone calls you
pure. And the girls aren't afraid
they come right up with their little hands out
for you to sniff
like you're a puppy
and they're gonna take you home.
They let you put your head right
in their laps.
                But nobody on this earth
ever got what they wanted. Now

I know what you came for. You want
my body. To hang it up on a nail
over your fireplace. Say to some milk-and-rosewater chica
who lays her head in your lap
*look how much it takes*
*to make me feel like a man.*
                We're in the dark now, you and me. This is primal
shit right here. Grendel, Smaug, St. George. You've been
called up. This is the big game. You don't have
to make stupid puns. Flash your feathers
like your monkey bravado
can impress. I saw a T-Rex fight a comet
and lose. You've
got nothing I want.

Here's something I bet you don't know:
        every time someone writes a story about a dragon
a real dragon dies.

# What the Dragon Said: A Love Story

    Something about seeing
and being seen
      something about mirrors
that old tune about how a photograph
can take your whole soul. At the end
of this poem
     I'm going to go out like electricity
in an ice storm. I've made peace with it.
    That last blockbuster took out a whole family
     of Bhutan thunder dragons
living in Latvia
the fumes of their cleargas hoard
hanging on their beards like blue ghosts.

A dragon's gotta get zen
    with ephemerality.

You want to cut me up? Chickenscratch my leather
with butcher's chalk:
cutlets, tenderloin, ribs for the company barbecue,
chuck, chops, brisket, roast.
    I dig it, I do.
I want to eat everything, too.

When I look at the world
  I see a table.
All those fancy houses, people with degrees, horses and whales,
bankers and Buddha statues
the Pope, astronauts, panda bears and yes, paladins
    if you let me swallow you whole
    I'll call you whatever you want.
Look at it all: waitresses and ice caps and submarines down
at the bottom of the heavy lightless saltdark of the sea

      Don't they know they'd be safer
      inside me?

I could be big for them
    I could hold them all
My belly could be a city
    where everyone was so loved
they wouldn't need jobs. I could be
the hyperreal
post-scarcity dragonhearted singularity.
    I could eat them
    and feed them
    and eat them
    and feed them.

This is why I don't get to be a unicorn.
Those ponies have clotted cream and Chanel No. 5 for blood
and they don't burn up like comets
with love that tastes like starving to death.
    And you, with your standup comedy knightliness,
covering Beowulf's greatest hits on your tin kazoo,
you can't begin to think through
    what it takes to fill up a body like this.
It takes everything pretty
and everything true
    and you stick yourself in a cave because
your want is bigger than you.

I just want to be
the size of a galaxy
so I can eat all the stars and gas giants
without them noticing

and getting upset.
Is that so bad?
    Isn't that
what love looks like?
    Isn't that
what you want, too?

I'll make you a deal.
  Come close up
stand on my emeraldheart, my sapphireself
the goldpile of my body
  Close enough to smell
everything you'll never be.

Don't finish the poem. Not for nothing
is it a snake
that eats her tail
and means eternity. What's a few verses worth
anyway? Everyone knows
poetry doesn't sell. Don't you ever feel
like you're just
a story someone is telling
about someone like you?
    I get that. I get you. You and me
we could fit
inside each other. It's not nihilism
if there's really no point to anything.

I have a secret
down in the deep of my dark.
All those other kids who wanted me
to call them paladins,
warriors, saints, whose swords had names,

whose bodies were perfect
as moonlight
  they've set up a township near my liver
had babies with the maidens they didn't save
  invented electric lightbulbs
  thought up new holidays.
     You can have my body
     just like you wanted.
Or you can keep on fighting dragons
writing dragons
fighting dragons
re-staging that same old Cretaceous deathmatch
you mammals
always win.
   But hey, hush, come on.
Quit now.
You'll never fix
that line.
    I have a forgiveness in me
    the size of eons
    and if a dragon's body is big enough
    it just looks like the world.

    Did you know
the earth used to have two moons?

# Copyright Information

"The Consultant" Copyright © 2013 by Catherynne M. Valente. First appeared in *The Bread We Eat In Dreams*.

"The Difference Between Love and Time" Copyright © 2022 by Catherynne M. Valente. First appeared in *Someone in Time: Tales of Time-Crossed Romance*, edited by Jonathan Strahan.

"A Buyer's Guide to Maps of Antarctica" Copyright © 2008 by Catherynne M. Valente. First appeared in *Clarkesworld Magazine*, May 2008, edited by Neil Clarke, Nick Mamatas.

"White Lines on a Green Field" Copyright © 2011 by Catherynne M. Valente. First appeared in *Subterranean Online*, Fall 2011, edited by William Schafer.

"The Wolves of Brooklyn" Copyright © 2011 by Catherynne M. Valente. First appeared in *Fantasy Magazine*, July 2011, edited by John Joseph Adams.

"Reading Borges in Buenos Aires" Copyright © 2010 by Catherynne M. Valente. First appeared in *Ventriloquism*.

"The Days of Flaming Motorcycles" Copyright © 2010 by Catherynne M. Valente. First appeared in *Apex Magazine*, May 2010, edited by Jason Sizemore.

"One Breath, One Stroke" Copyright © 2012 by Catherynne M. Valente. First appeared in *The Future is Japanese*, edited by Nick Mamatas, Masumi Washington.

"Thirteen Ways of Looking at Space/Time" Copyright © 2010 by Catherynne M. Valente. First appeared in *Clarkesworld Magazine*, August 2010, edited by Neil Clarke, Sean Wallace.

"Mouse Koan" Copyright © 2012 by Catherynne M. Valente. First appeared on Tor.com, April 2, 2012, edited by Liz Gorinsky, Patrick Nielsen Hayden.

"The Melancholy of Mechagirl" Copyright © 2011 by Catherynne M. Valente. First appeared in *Mythic Delirium*, Issue 25, Summer/Fall 2011, edited by Mike Allen.

"The Future Is Blue" Copyright © 2016 by Catherynne M. Valente. First appeared in *Drowned Worlds*, edited by Jonathan Strahan.

"The Sin-Eater" Copyright © 2021 by Catherynne M. Valente. First appeared in *Uncanny Magazine*, March-April 2021, edited by Lynne M. Thomas, Michael Damian Thomas.

"The Sun in Exile" Copyright © 2019 by Catherynne M. Valente. First appeared in *A People's Future of the United States*, edited by John Joseph Adams, Victor LaValle.

"Color, Heat, and the Wreck of the Argo" Copyright © 2021 by Catherynne M. Valente. First appeared in *Strange Horizons*, 7 September 2020, edited by Vanessa Rose Phin.

"The Perfect Host" Copyright © 2020 by Catherynne M. Valente. First appeared in *How We Live Now* on Realm.fm, April 15, 2020.

"How to Become a Mars Overlord" Copyright © 2010 by Catherynne M. Valente. First appeared in *Lightspeed*, August 2010, edited by John Joseph Adams.

"Fade to White" Copyright © 2012 by Catherynne M. Valente. First appeared in *Clarkesworld Magazine*, August 2012, edited by Neil Clarke.

"Secretario" Copyright © 2010 by Catherynne M. Valente. First appeared in *Weird Tales*, Summer 2010, edited by Ann VanderMeer.

"Twenty-Five Facts About Santa Claus" Copyright © 2013 by Catherynne M. Valente. First appeared in *The Bread We Eat in Dreams*.

"In the Future When All's Well" Copyright © 2011 by Catherynne M. Valente. First appeared in *Teeth: Vampire Tales*, edited by Ellen Datlow, Terri Windling.

"Planet Lion" Copyright © 2015 by Catherynne M. Valente. First appeared in *Uncanny Magazine*, May-June 2015, edited by Lynne M. Thomas, Michael Damian Thomas.

"A Great Clerk of Necromancy" Copyright © 2013 by Catherynne M. Valente. First appeared in *Apex Magazine*, July 2013, edited by Lynne M. Thomas.

# Copyright Information

"Urchins, While Swimming" Copyright © 2006 by Catherynne M. Valente. First appeared in *Clarkesworld Magazine*, December 2006, edited by Neil Clarke, Nick Mamatas.

"L'Esprit de L'Escalier" Copyright © 2022 by Catherynne M. Valente. First appeared on Tor.com, August 25, 2021, edited by Ellen Datlow.

"The Lily and the Horn" Copyright © 2015 by Catherynne M. Valente. First appeared in *Fantasy Magazine*, December 2015, edited by Christopher Barzak, Matthew Cheney, Liz Gorinsky, Wendy N. Wagner.

"The Long Goodnight of Violet Wild" Copyright © 2015 by Catherynne M. Valente. First appeared in *Clarkesworld Magazine*, January 2015, edited by Neil Clarke.

"Palimpsest" Copyright © 2008 by Catherynne M. Valente. First appeared in *Paper Cities: An Anthology of Urban Fantasy*, edited by Ekaterina Sedia.

"The Red Girl" Copyright © 2013 by Catherynne M. Valente. First appeared in *The Bread We Eat In Dreams*.

"The Flame After the Candle" Copyright © 2017 by Catherynne M. Valente. First appeared in *Mad Hatters and March Hares*, edited by Ellen Datlow.

"The Wedding" Copyright © 2013 by Catherynne M. Valente. First appeared in *The Bread We Eat In Dreams*.

"The Bread We Eat in Dreams" Copyright © 2011 by Catherynne M. Valente. First appeared in *Apex Magazine*, November 2011, edited by Lynne M. Thomas.

"The Secret of Being a Cowboy" Copyright © 2011 by Catherynne M. Valente. First appeared in *Stone Telling*, #3, edited by Rose Lemberg.

"Aquaman and the Duality of Self/Other, America, 1985" Copyright © 2012 by Catherynne M. Valente. First appeared on Tor.com, April 29, 2012, edited by Liz Gorinsky, Patrick Nielsen Hayden.

"A Fall Counts Anywhere" Copyright © 2018 by Catherynne M. Valente. First appeared in *Robots vs. Fairies*, edited by Dominik Parisien, Navah Wolfe.

"A Delicate Architecture" Copyright © 2009 by Catherynne M. Valente. First appeared in *Troll's Eye View: A Book of Villainous Tales*, edited by Ellen Datlow, Terry Windling.

"Golubash, or Wine-Blood-War-Elegy" Copyright © 2009 by Catherynne M. Valente. First appeared in *Federations*, edited by John Joseph Adams.

"Badgirl, the Deadman, and the Wheel of Fortune" Copyright © 2016 by Catherynne M. Valente. First appeared in *The Starlit Wood: New Fairy Tales*, edited by Dominik Parisien, Navah Wolfe.

"Down and Out in R'lyeh" Copyright © 2017 by Catherynne M. Valente. First appeared in *Uncanny Magazine*, September-October 2017, edited by Lynne M. Thomas, Michael Damian Thomas.

"The Shoot-Out at Burnt Corn Ranch Over the Bride of the World" Copyright © 2013 by Catherynne M. Valente. First appeared in *Subterranean*, Summer 2013, edited by William Schafer.

"No One Dies in Nowhere" Copyright © 2017 by Catherynne M. Valente. First appeared in *The Weight of Words*, edited by Dave McKean, William Schafer.

"The Limitless Perspective of Master Peek, Or, the Luminescence of Debauchery" Copyright © 2016 by Catherynne M. Valente. First appeared in *Beneath Ceaseless Skies*, #200, edited by Scott H. Andrews.

"Daisy Green Says I Love You" Copyright © 2017 by Catherynne M. Valente. First appeared in *The Refrigerator Monologues*.

"Silently and Very Fast" Copyright © 2011 by Catherynne M. Valente. First appeared in *Clarkesworld Magazine*, October 2011, edited by Neil Clarke.

"What the Dragon Said: A Love Story" Copyright © 2012 by Catherynne M. Valente. First appeared on Tor.com, April 21, 2012, edited by Liz Gorinsky, Patrick Nielsen Hayden.